Dragon Swan

Written by

Adrianna M. Scovill

Dragon Swan

(Dragon Hearts novel #4)

This book is a work of fiction. All names, characters, places,
and incidents are a product of the author's imagination,
or are used fictitiously. Any resemblance to real
people or events is entirely coincidental.

First printing August 2014

savageimagination.com
facebook.com/AdriannaMScovill

Cover artwork by Mary Clare
maryclaresartwork.com

ISBN-13: 978-1500724771
ISBN-10: 1500724777

Chapter One

In a life full of difficult and frightening decisions, this was the most difficult, the most frightening and, without a doubt, the most foolish. The chances of making it off alive were next to none, and she tried to fight the terror beginning to claw its way through her. She knew that panicking would not help; what was done was done, and for better or worse, there was no turning back.

And what about Luca? Even with his help, she would almost certainly die—either on the ship, or shortly after being thrown overboard to perish in the sea. If, by some miracle, she made it to her destination alive, she would surely not be in the same condition as when she'd left, and Luca was bound to suffer for her rashness, as well.

Ella would not risk Luca's safety for anything in the world. Unless it was to protect Travis.

At the thought of Travis and Luca, the fear surged again. In many ways, her life was currently in Luca's hands. Luca's life, however, was in hers, too, and Travis—

She shook her head, trying to swallow the lump in her throat. It was impossible for her to help Travis at the moment, but she had every intention of getting to him—or dying trying. She felt tears sting her eyes and blinked them back, angry with herself for the weakness. She had a long road—well, not road, exactly—ahead of her, and her time would best be spent coming up with a plan and keeping out of sight. The plan was for when she got off the ship, and the hiding was so she'd be alive to execute the plan.

They'd been underway for only an hour, and the uncertain future loomed impossibly large before her. Months...How could she possibly hope to remain undiscovered for *months?* It was ridiculous. What had she been thinking? Well, she hadn't been thinking, had she? The sight of her brother, in chains, being loaded onto the slave ship, her inability to get to him, her failure to protect him, had served to rob her of her rationality.

Luca was set to bring her food and drink whenever it was safe, and who knew how long that would be? Although he had minimal experience running sails, he was new to the crew of *Voyage*, and she had made him promise not to put himself at unnecessary risk. Captain Swan had quite a reputation for ruthlessness, and she shuddered to think of what would befall poor, sweet, chivalrous Luca if the pirate got wise to Luca's assistance to the stowaway.

Of all the ships setting sail, why were there only two heading for Bohannon? The illegal slave ship, *Enterprise*, and Captain Swan's *Voyage*? It seemed like another stroke of bad luck in a life painted by them. *Voyage* was her only way to reach the port where her brother was being taken.

Regardless of all the other fears she had to deal with, and the uncertainty of her brother's fate, the gentle rocking of the ship brought its own overwhelming apprehension. The thought of spending months, alone, tucked away like a rat, without so much as a change of clothes or a glimpse of sunlight...She shivered, hugging herself. She might not have to be discovered in order to pay for her impulsiveness. She could succumb to illness long before reaching Bohannon.

There were so many dangers to consider, her head reeled with the magnitude of her decision. She pulled a deep, slow breath in through her nostrils, closing her eyes. She had to remain calm. What was done was done, and she had to keep reminding herself of that. A good decision or bad, she'd made her choice; she was on the ship, and that was that. Luca was going to be bringing her food and water, and emptying her chamber pot. She would learn to live with the embarrassment surrounding that, and she would have to get used to relying on someone else, for a change. She'd known Luca for...Well, practically her whole life, and he was the only friend she had at the moment.

She took another deep breath, and it helped to calm her a bit. The lack of fresh air and sunlight would surely take its toll on her, but she was generally healthy, with a strong constitution, and as long as she had food and water, she should be able to make it a couple of months without getting too ill. If she stayed near the dungeon, she should be able to remain undiscovered—so long as no one was imprisoned there, anyway, and she would have to cross that bridge if and when it arose. Everything else would come in time.

Time was something she was going to have plenty of.

*   *   *

"El?"

The voice, little more than a whisper, woke her with a jolt, and her heart jumped in her chest. She held her breath, waiting, listening, trying to get her bearings. The room seemed to be swaying around her, and she blinked into the darkness, finally remembering where she was.

"El?" he whispered again.

It was painfully dark in the dungeon of the ship, and the glow of his lantern shone like the sun as he crept around the barrels. Squinting her eyes against the sudden brightness, Ella could just make out Luca's familiar and welcome face, lined with concern, cast in the orange glow. "Here," she answered in a low voice. She struggled to push to her feet; the swaying of the floor seemed to work against her, and her legs were cramped from her awkward sleeping position. She was going to have to remind herself to stay limber and exercised, or all of her muscles would melt away during the coming journey of seclusion.

"There you are," Luca said, heading toward her, the relief in his voice unmistakable. "Are you alright?"

"Yes," she answered, glancing past him at the stairs. "Did anyone see you leave?"

He shook his head. "It's late. I'm sorry."

"That's alright," she said, reaching for the canvas sack. He handed it over, and her stomach rumbled at the thought of food. How long had it been since she'd eaten? She tried to remember, frowning. She supposed it didn't matter, but she thought it had been more than twenty-four hours. Since before Travis was loaded up in chains, for sure. She'd grown accustomed to irregular meals, sometimes going two or three days without any real food, and she found her thoughts turning once more to her brother.

She'd done her best to shelter him, and he had never gone a day without food. Was he being fed, now? Was his stomach empty and achy, adding to his fear and misery? She swallowed the lump in her throat, suddenly dangerously close to losing the battle with her emotions.

"Hey," Luca said, putting his hand on her arm. "We're going to get him back, El. You'll see. Don't worry, please?"

"You should get back before someone misses you," she answered after a moment spent fighting back her tears.

He hesitated, regarding her in the lantern's glow, and it was clear he wanted to say more. In the end, he simply nodded and started to turn away.

"Luca," she said, and he looked back—perhaps too eagerly. "Be safe. Please."

He smiled, a flash of white teeth and a hint of the old, carefree boy he'd once been. "No one will be patrolling in a couple of hours. Don't go too far, but you can stretch your legs. I'll be back tomorrow."

"Thank you," she said, well aware that a simple thanks did nothing to cover the debt she owed him. No matter what happened during or after this trip, Luca had willingly put his life on the line for her. There were only two people who would do that, and she was on her way to rescue the other. "Goodnight."

When Luca was gone, the darkness pressed in on her, and she blinked, trying desperately to reclaim some semblance of vision. She felt inside the bag, and found a piece of bread, and an apple, and a chunk of cheese, as well as a skin of water. She was surprised, most of all by the fruit. Was it bruised and wormy? She didn't know. It didn't feel squishy, and she wondered if it was a blessing that she couldn't see it. She ate it quickly, core and all, and the juicy sweetness was a shock to her mouth and stomach.

She knew she should ration herself, because there was no way of knowing if Luca would be able to safely bring her any provisions the next evening as planned. Her stomach rumbled, however, and she knew that she didn't have the strength to deny herself. She made a silent vow that she would do better with the next meal, that she would make it last. For now, however, her hunger would not be denied, and the bread and cheese followed the apple.

Ella had a candle, and a meager supply of matches. She sat in the dark, not just to conserve them, and not even out of fear of discovery. It was a fear of fire, more than being found, that kept her from lighting the small fire through most of the following days. At night—at least, when Luca said it was night—she would venture from her hiding place behind the crates near the dungeon, and she would pace to stretch her legs and give her body some activity.

The constant swaying and creaking of the ship began to take their toll, and after several days she always felt ill. Walking helped, a bit, but being unable to breathe fresh air, unable to see the sun or even determine day from night, and the unfamiliar, unending motion around her made her queasy and miserable.

Luca came every evening with a meager supply of food.

Until he didn't.

Ella had thought she was judging the passage of time as accurately as could be expected, but she also knew that the darkness and nausea and loneliness and oppressing boredom were all conspiring to drive her mad, and she knew that time, of all things, was a slippery and tricky beast. She waited, thinking she must have misjudged. She waited longer, her unease growing.

She knew it was possible that he'd simply been unable to get away unseen. They'd discussed the possibility. She'd, of course, made him promise that he wouldn't unnecessarily endanger himself, so if it was unsafe for him to sneak away, he wasn't supposed to do it. The nausea took some of the edge from her hunger, and it wouldn't be the first night she'd gone without a meal, anyway. He would surely come as soon as he could.

If only she knew he was alright. If only she could be sure, she thought it would be far easier to bear the hunger and loneliness. She moved about a bit, cautiously, in the dark, afraid to strike a match. She didn't dare venture away from the dungeon. There was no way of knowing why Luca hadn't come, or what was going on above her, or who might be patrolling the ship.

She sat back down, wishing she had something more comfortable than a burlap sack and knowing she should be grateful for even that much. Her mind immediately began the tiresome task of identifying and considering every little thing that could have gone wrong for Luca.

She hadn't gotten very far, however, when she heard footsteps on the stairs. She caught her breath, her heart suddenly slamming in her ribcage. She waited for the sound of Luca's voice, desperately hoping for it.

They weren't Luca's boots on the stairs, however, and she knew it. The steps were far too heavy. Luca, even when he wasn't trying to be stealthy, had always had a light, quiet, graceful step, something she'd often tried to emulate. Whoever was coming into the dungeon was making no attempt to conceal his passage, and she hunkered further down, hugging her knees to her chest.

Was she concealed? She was alarmed to realize she had no real idea. She thought she was hidden behind the crates. She was almost certain. If she stretched her fingers, she could feel the wooden boxes before her. Once the glow of the coming lantern swelled into the room, however, would she be easily seen? Was her whole side exposed? Or, had she forgotten to tuck away her chamber pot? Her brain, left underused for days, insisted that she'd done something wrong, that she would be discovered, and that Luca, if he hadn't already been killed, would be.

She watched the light grow, squinting against it. Would he smell her? She imagined she could smell her own stench, and wondered, briefly, strangely, how much worse it would be if she made it to Bohannon.

She couldn't see the man's face, just a shine of light against his eyes, and she held her breath as he reached the bottom of the stairs and hesitated. Was he

6

trying to sort out her location, based on the reek of her clothes and the thump of her heart? Or, was he simply waiting for his eyes to adjust to the dimness?

After a couple of moments, the man walked into the room, holding his lantern aloft so that the glow fell back onto his face. She could see his beard, and a light, puckered scar along the side of his face, and she could see that his eyes were not directed toward her. Still, she waited, sure that she would be discovered at any moment. He walked around the room, his boots echoing on the boards. He held the lantern out, a few times, to examine crates, and she finally realized that he was simply making a routine check.

She didn't relax, or allow herself a moment of relief, however. There was still a very real danger of discovery. And, even if she escaped his notice this time, she had no idea if or when the next check was scheduled. This was the first time she'd seen anyone but Luca in days. Would they check the inventory every day, now? Every week? After a month? Luca had not mentioned any sort of plan, and routine checks might very well end up being the death of her.

When his lantern light swung across the boxes she was hiding behind, the pale light reaching around and over the crates to briefly embrace her, she closed her eyes and waited, knowing there was nothing more she could do. He would leave, or he wouldn't.

After a few seconds, he did, his footsteps and light retreating, leaving her once again alone, hugging her knees, filled with a strange mixture of relief and despair.

She waited for a long time, staring into the darkness, slowly letting her heart rate return to normal. Her ears strained for some sound above the creaking of the ship and the rush of the water below her. There was nothing. She was alone, and she suddenly struggled under the crushing weight of that knowledge. In a way, she had always been alone. She'd had her brother, and Travis loved her, and she loved him. And, they'd had Luca, their best friend. The burden had always been on her, however, to make things alright, to keep them all safe, to put food in Travis's belly.

She was tired. She was tired of being hungry and scared and lonely, tired of having sore muscles and blisters on her hands and feet from working until she was ready to drop. She was tired of the uncaring stares of people passing by. She was tired of carrying the weight of the world.

She put her hands over her face and pulled in a deep, shaky breath, choking back a sob. She was not going to give in to this. She took another breath. She would not cry for herself and lament her own exhaustion when Travis was surely suffering for her negligence. So, she was tired. Big deal. She'd fight through it, just like she always had. If she were on her own, she might give up, but she wasn't. She had a reason to keep going, a reason to put up with the achy muscles and tight, empty belly, a reason to endure the blisters and blank looks.

Travis was her reason, and she would not abandon him. No matter what it took, she would get him back, and she would keep him safe. She wouldn't fail him again. If she had to sit in the dark, hungry and cold and lonely, marinated in her own stench, she would, for two months, three, or six, as long as necessary.

She took another deep breath, this one far steadier. Crying about it would help nothing.

With the threatening tears banished, Ella curled up onto her burlap, ignoring the stab of hunger, and closed her dry eyes. After a while, she finally found sleep.

* * *

She opened her eyes and blinked several times, trying to convince her brain that her unseeing eyes actually *were* opened as she stared blindly into the darkness, her heart racing. She listened, unmoving, knowing that there was a reason for her abrupt awakening.

There it was.

The sound of voices, something she hadn't heard in...how long, exactly? She wasn't sure. Too long and, at the same time, not long enough. It was difficult to place them, but they were moving closer, and she drew herself up as tightly as she could, tucking her face into her arms so that the coming lanterns wouldn't reflect off her eyes and give her away.

They were coming down the stairs, now. How many? Three or four, she thought.

"Thought you could get away with it, eh?" one of them was saying, and her stomach suddenly clenched in real fear. Were they locking someone in the dungeon? She had always known that danger was possible, but all she'd been able to do was pray the day wouldn't come. If they left the prisoner in the dark, she could probably sneak away without the person being aware. She wasn't sure where she would go, but she would find another hiding place, somewhere, because she had no choice.

What if they left a lantern lit for the prisoner, though? She would have far more difficulty sneaking away, then, and if the prisoner saw her, he would almost certainly raise an alarm to alert the captain to her presence. What better way to ingratiate himself, after all, than discovering a stowaway? Her hollow stomach churned, and she waited, hoping her stomach wouldn't make some noise that would give away her location.

"We tol' you from the beginnin' kid," one of the men was saying.

"I didn't steal. I was just saving it."

She felt a sudden coldness slide through her body, and she wanted to shake her head to negate what her brain was telling her.

Luca.

No.

"Get in."

"Please. Listen. I swear, I wasn't stealing anything. Let me talk to the captain."

There were sounds of a brief scuffle, and a few muffled curses, and then

8

the iron door slammed closed with a clang that made Ella jump. She silently cursed herself, immediately stilling, her heart in her throat. The sound of the door seemed to reverberate through the room forever, and then she heard the bootheels clomping up the stairs. She swallowed, lifting her head cautiously, slowly, to find that the room was filled with a soft, flickering light.

Where a few moments ago she'd been praying for darkness, she was now grateful for the light. She no longer had to worry about the prisoner learning of her presence, because he already knew. She waited for as long as she could, listening until she could no longer hear the footsteps or voices, waited until she was sure they were alone.

Then, she slowly uncurled herself, stretching her legs with a wince, and crawled from behind the crates.

Luca was sitting on the floor in the middle of the cell, his arms wrapped around his knees, staring at her with the pale orange light in his eyes. The lantern was hung on a rod, hanging a few inches out from the wall, just out of his reach on the freedom side of the bars. "I'm sorry, Ella," he said, and his voice cracked.

She shook her head, brushing her filthy hair from her face. She felt tears stinging her eyes, not tears for herself but for him, and she hurried to the bars. "No, Luca, I'm sorry," she said. "This is all my fault. I'm so sorry. You shouldn't be in here."

"It's alright, Ella. Listen. They'll bring me food. All you have to do is stay hidden, and we can share whatever they bring me."

She pressed her forehead against one of the cold, metal bars, and closed her eyes. "I'll get you out of this, Luca. I don't know how, but...I will. I promise."

"Don't worry about me," he said, and although he was still speaking quietly, his voice was surprisingly sharp. "This is about Travis, and you need to get him back. That's all that matters. I can take care of myself."

Can you? she thought. In the shadows of the cell, his knees drawn up, he looked impossibly young, and she suddenly had an image of him as a little boy—How old had he been? Nine? Travis was seven, then. Luca had just discovered that his grandmother, who'd been the only guardian he'd ever known, was dead. Travis and Ella, then thirteen herself, had found him, huddled up much like he was now, with tears cutting tracks through the filth on his cheeks.

That was ten years ago, however, and now his eyes were dry. He might be scared, but he was harder than he'd been; they all were. Even Travis, although she'd done her best to shelter him from so much.

They'd all grown up fast and hard, and if the captain's men thought they were going to be able to break Luca, they were in for a surprise. Behind that thin, young face was a witty, intelligent, kind mind, and inside that narrow, bony body was the heart of a knight.

"I'll get you both out of this," she said, finally. Travis and Luca were the only family she had, and she would not lose them. She couldn't. If she lost them, there would be nothing left of herself.

9

As sorry as she was that Luca was being held prisoner, because of her, she was also grateful for the company. The following days passed far more quickly and easily, as they sat on each side of the bars, speaking in hushed voices about funny memories—and, salted through the years of hardship, there were a surprisingly high number of funny memories—and dreams of the future.

Someone came to feed Luca twice a day, and empty his chamber pot. The pot fit through the slot in the bars, and Ella had begun emptying her own into Luca's each evening before the man with the scar would come to remove the waste. The scarred man, whom Luca said was named Ivan, would replace the dirty pot with a clean one, never commenting if he thought there was more waste than there should be.

In fact, Ivan never said anything during his short visits. Morning and evening, he brought food and water, exchanged the pots, and filled the lantern. Luca always thanked him, and Ivan always nodded before leaving. When he was gone, Ella would venture out of hiding, and she and Luca would share his meals. Sometimes there was stew—it was usually less than hot by the time they got it, but it was still the best thing she'd had to eat in a very long time, and she and Luca would take turns with the spoon until the bowl was empty.

The following morning, Ivan would collect the bowl and spoon when he brought breakfast, and the routine continued for several days. In spite of the circumstances, the schedule was comforting, almost as comforting as Luca's presence to break up the lonely monotony of her days.

And, then, everything changed, again.

She and Luca had just finished their respective halves of a slice of crusty bread, and were laughing quietly about the time Travis had brought home a toad that he'd fully intended to name Hoppy, a toad that he'd planned to carry around in his pocket and keep forever.

"Remember the look on his face when that little girl—what was her name?"

"Maisy."

"Right. When Maisy said that she wouldn't ever go near—" Luca broke off abruptly, and she saw the alarm on his face. She scrambled for cover without stopping to think, but it was too late. She'd known immediately, by the look in Luca's glowing eyes, that it was too late.

Still, the steps on the stairs were unhurried, and she allowed herself a few moments to hope, as she crouched behind the crates with her heart galloping in her chest. Luca was silent, and the bootsteps thumping down the stairs were the only sound filling the dungeon. They reached the floor and crossed, still at a casual pace, toward her. As the sound grew closer, and closer, she clenched her fists, cursing his slowness. Why couldn't he just get it over with?

His large, bearded, scarred face appeared above the crates, and she was instantly sorry for the thought. She held still, even though she knew he could see her. He was staring right at her.

"Come on," he said, his voice low and gruff. It was the first time she'd heard him speak, even though she'd seen him twice a day for the better part of a week, and yet his voice was exactly how she would've imagined it. He reached a large hand toward her, and she shrank away.

She wanted to run, but where would she go? Luca was standing, hands fisted around the bars of his cell, his knuckles pale in the lantern's glow. "Leave her alone, Ivan," he said. "She's not hurting anything."

Ivan ignored him. "Come on," he repeated, reaching for her arm again. There was nowhere to go, and his large fingers fastened around her thin upper arm. He could've hauled her out easily, but he gave her a moment to come on her own. After only the briefest weighing of pros and cons, she raised herself out of hiding, trying to tamp down her fear. She stood before him, held loosely by one arm, staring up into his large face.

"Get your hand off her," Luca said, sounding desperate.

"It's alright, Luca," she said. She wanted to ask Ivan for mercy, too, wanted to implore him to go back up and pretend he'd never seen her. She couldn't bring herself to beg, however.

"What's your name?" Ivan asked, gruffly.

She stared at him, mutinously silent, fighting the urge to yank her arm from his so-far-gentle grasp.

"Fine. Let's go."

"Ivan," Luca said, rattling the bars, slightly. "Come on. Please. Just—"

"Stealing food is nothing compared to harboring a stowaway," Ivan said, shooting him a quick look. It was difficult to tell in the lantern light, but Ella thought that Luca paled. What was the punishment for harboring a stowaway? She couldn't let him be killed.

"He didn't know I was here," she said, and Ivan's gaze swung back to her.

"Right. Let's go," he repeated.

She took a deep breath. "No," she said. "Get your hand off me."

There was no mistaking his surprise, as his eyebrows reached toward his hairline. "Are you sure you don't want to come easily?"

Swallowing her fear, she opened her mouth to speak. She wasn't even sure what she intended to say, but Ivan must have seen the stubborn pride in her face, because before she'd uttered another word, he moved with surprising speed.

Luca shouted, banging on the bars, and Ella let out a little sound—more of surprise than actual fear—as Ivan bent, scooped her up, and threw her over his shoulder. She kicked her legs, and he almost dropped her headfirst over his back. He clamped an arm across the backs of her legs, turned, and started toward the stairs.

Luca was hollering, but she could scarcely hear him over the roaring in her ears. Her cheeks flamed with anger and humiliation, and she beat at Ivan's back with her fists, cursing him. Under the anger and humiliation, however, the fear was surging. He paid no attention to her blows, or her words, and he

11

carried her easily, his steps echoing up the stairs. The higher they went, the more her stomach burned with fear, because she did not know what punishment was coming.

Would they simply throw her overboard to drown or be eaten by sea creatures? It seemed far too much to hope for that she would be imprisoned with Luca.

Finally, after it seemed as though she'd been over Ivan's shoulder for a hellish length of time, up stairs and through rooms and up more stairs, she finally blinked against the sudden daylight. She squinted, because the brightness hurt her unaccustomed eyes. She had long since given up pounding on Ivan's back, afraid that they would both tumble down the stairs with broken necks.

The sun was heavy and low, burning red above the unbroken horizon. As Ivan stepped onto the deck, and turned, Ella's squinted gaze swung across several men, all of them staring at her. She swallowed the lump of fear, painfully aware of the fact that she was wearing a filthy dress and that the only reason she wasn't completely exposed up to the waist was because of Ivan's tight arm, holding her against his shoulder and her skirt against her thighs.

She counted five men, ten, and then she stopped counting, because the numbers didn't matter. Intent was what mattered, and soon their looks of surprise would change to something else. Her eyes were watering, and she told herself that it was simply from the sting of salty air and the glare of the fat sun. The wind swirled her hair around her face, obscuring the men from view, and she was bitterly glad.

Ivan pulled her forward without warning, spinning her and lowering her to her feet so quickly that she stumbled, disoriented and dizzy. He grabbed her arm to steady her and she resisted the urge to pull away and run. Where would she go? She could fling herself into the ocean, or she could face judgement on the ship, and she wasn't sure which would give her better odds.

"Captain," Ivan said, and then Ella's watery eyes found him. Captain Swan. He was standing on the rail, near the front of the ship, one hand holding the rope angled past his head. He was staring out at the sea, east, toward the coming night, his dark hair blown back from his face.

In spite of the rush of wind, he turned his head at the sound of Ivan's voice. His dark gaze raked over Ella's body, quickly, and her mouth went dry. She tried to swallow and couldn't. She wanted to hug herself, to go into a defensive posture, but her pride wouldn't let her. Instead, she raised her chin, blinking away the moisture in her eyes, and squared her shoulders.

Captain Swan's dark eyebrows were drawn together, his jaw clenched. "Hell," he said, the sound carried to her on the wind. He stepped casually from the railing, dropping to the deck three feet below with surprising grace and ease. He glanced down the length of her body again, and she clenched her teeth and fists, refusing to squirm. "What's going on, here?" the captain asked, looking past her toward Ivan.

"Stowaway, Cap," Ivan said, pushing her forward a step. "Found her hiding out in the dungeon when I went to feed the prisoner."

Hearing Luca referred to as *the prisoner* made her choke back angry words of defense. She wouldn't do herself, or Luca, any favors by antagonizing these men.

"How'd you get on board?" the captain asked. His eyebrows were still dipped in a scowl, and his expression was forbidding. She could feel the butterflies swarming in her stomach, and swallowed, holding her silence. A muscle in his jaw clenched, and she knew that he was unused to being denied answers. He clasped his hands behind his back. He was dressed in black, from shoulder to foot, the clothes as dark as his glossy black hair. Even his sword was sheathed in black. "What's your name?" he asked.

She considered her options, and knew that she was at his mercy. While her pride wanted her to hold her ground and her tongue, she knew that it would be foolish. There was no friendliness in his face, no gentleness, and she knew she had little hope of being shown leniency. That was no reason to ask for the worst, however. "Ella," she answered, in the nick of time. She'd seen his impatience swelling with each heartbeat.

"And what, pray tell, are you doing on my ship?"

"Staying out of the way," she said, before she could stop herself.

His dark eyebrows lifted for a moment, then lowered. "Who's been helping you?"

"No one," she said, mentally preparing herself for Ivan's contradiction. She didn't think that they could prove Luca had anything to do with her, but she knew that they wouldn't need proof to condemn him. She silently cursed herself, again, for being so stupid. How could she not have heard Ivan's approach? He had known he would find someone, or something, and that was why he'd softened his footsteps. That was no excuse for her carelessness, though.

"Why are you on my ship?"

"I needed a ride."

What's wrong with you? Stop being a smartass. Apologize, ask for mercy. The captain strode toward her, suddenly, and her breath caught. He drew his hands from behind his back, and she flinched—it was instinctive, and she hated herself for it. It was only a small wince, and she immediately raised her chin again, but she felt her cheeks flame at the show of weakness.

The captain stared at her for a moment from under his black brows. The low sun glowed in his dark eyes. "What's to keep me from tossing you to the sharks?" he asked.

"Basic human decency?" she blurted. She wanted to clap a hand over her own mouth to shut herself up. She heard Ivan snort behind her, and saw the surprise momentarily soften the captain's expression.

Then, with a flash of white teeth, the captain bowed with a flourish. She managed to keep from flinching, this time, at the sudden movement, but her heart stuttered in her ribcage. "Perhaps you're unaware of who I am," he said, and under the rush of wind, she heard several of the men behind her laughing.

13

"Allow me to introduce myself. I'm—"

"Captain Swan," she interrupted, unable to stomach being mocked. "I know who you are. Why do you think I was hiding below?"

"Hold your tongue, lass," Ivan said, but the captain held up a hand.

"Unauthorized passage is punishable by death," Captain Swan said. "Have you nothing to say in your own defense?"

She struggled for a moment, trying to force her tongue to form an apology. "I was desperate," she finally admitted, the closest she could manage. She waited for further ridicule, and the captain was silent. His eyes traveled down the length of her body for a third time, and she tried to imagine what he was seeing: Oily hair, tangled and matted; grimy face, and eyes circled by dark smudges; filthy, wrinkled dress; dirty, bare feet. Could he smell her, too?

"Take her to the bunks," he said, finally.

She felt a surge of alarm at the thought of all the men that might be waiting there. She knew she should beg; she should drop to her knees and apologize. She clenched her jaw and held her silence. She would endure anything she had to in order to get to Travis, and to protect Luca, and she would not let them see her weakness again.

"She can sleep in the thief's bed," the captain said.

"He's not a—" She broke off. She'd been distracted, and she wanted to punch herself in the face. She closed her eyes, briefly, to avoid the smug look on the captain's face. Finally, taking a deep breath through her nose, she opened her eyes and met his dark gaze.

"Stealing food is the least forgivable offense on this ship," he said, quietly. "Aside from harboring a stowaway."

"He didn't steal food," she said. There was no sense continuing to claim she didn't know Luca. She'd already stepped into the trap, and she couldn't unspring it from her stupid foot. She would defend him to her last breath, though.

"He was caught red-handed, yes?" Captain Swan asked, looking at Ivan.

"Yes, sir," Ivan answered. "He was stashing food in a sack."

"He wasn't stealing. He was—"

"Oh, I see now very well what he was doing, Ella," the captain said, his voice silky and low, barely audible above the wind. "Go. I'll decide what to do with you tomorrow."

After the men have all had their fill of me? she thought, still struggling to hold on to some semblance of courage. The captain had already begun to turn away, clearly dismissing her, and Ivan once more had a hold on her arm. He started to tug her backward. "Wait. Wait!" Ella cried. "Please." There, she'd finally said it.

Captain Swan turned back. "Yes?" he said, sounding bored.

"Please," she said again, ignoring the bitter taste it left on her tongue. "Let Luca go."

The captain tipped his head to regard her, and asked, softly, "And where would you sleep, then?"

14

His voice and steady stare sent a small shiver through her, and she clenched her fists again. "I'll take his place in the dungeon," she suggested.

"Oh, I don't think so. Ivan," Swan answered, with a small gesture.

"Yes, Cap," Ivan said, pulling on her arm.

"Wait," she said, again, but the captain was walking away, and he didn't look back again.

"Come, lass," Ivan told her. He pulled, gently. For a moment, she held her ground. Until he said, "Don't make me carry you again."

With a curse, and a wave of anger and frustration and fear that almost swallowed her, she allowed herself to be led back toward the stairs.

Think about Travis, she thought. *You can endure anything, because all that matters is getting to him.*

* * *

"Here you are."

Ella stood beside the neatly-made bunk, avoiding eye contact with the men staring at her. Some of them were sitting at a wooden table attached to the floor, some were sitting on their own beds, some were standing, all were gaping. Her heart was thudding and her palms were sweating, but she was trying her best not to let them see just how frightened she was.

"No one's slept here since Luca," Ivan added.

She glanced at the bed, imagining Luca making the bed just hours before being led to the dungeon.

"Lights out at ten."

She blinked at Ivan, thinking, *Is that when it will start, then? Who will be first? You?*

"Supper is in an hour."

At the very mention of food, her stomach clenched. She was hungry, of course. She'd had only half a piece of bread before being captured. She could deal with the hunger, though. What she couldn't handle was the thought of Luca, alone in the dungeon, because of her.

"You won't eat with us," Ivan continued. She would have told him that she had no desire to eat, but he didn't give her the chance. "You smell. You'd ruin the meal for everyone."

At that, almost all of the men laughed, and she felt her cheeks heat.

"Someone will bring you your supper," Ivan said, and at that, she looked up, surprised. "You may eat at your bunk."

"I'm not hungry," she heard herself say.

Ivan frowned. "Whether you eat or not is your business. Do not leave this room without permission. Is that clear?"

"Or what? You'll lock me in the dungeon?" she asked, wondering again at her inability to keep from antagonizing.

"What sort of punishment would that be?" he returned, with the hint of a smile. She felt her skin crawl, and crossed her arms over her chest. Without

15

another word, Ivan turned and strode from the room, leaving her with half a dozen men watching her.

Ella sat on the bottom bunk she'd been ascribed, and drew her legs up. None of the men made any move toward her, and none of them spoke to her. After a few moments, some of them went back to their own conversations, throwing her occasional glances. Ella curled up, as tightly as she could, with her back pressed against the wooden wall, her head on the pillow that had last been used by Luca.

She stayed like that, afraid to close her eyes, until the men filed out— presumably for supper. Ivan came in, and set a bowl on the table. Stew, or soup, it seemed, with a piece of bread sticking up from the side. He set a tin cup beside it, sloshing the tiniest bit of liquid onto the table. He turned to leave without a word.

Ella, who hadn't spoken in over an hour, asked, "Did you take Luca his supper?"

Or, like his bed, was she supposed to take that from him, as well?

Ivan looked back, peering into the shadows of the bunk where she was curled. "Yes," he answered after a moment, and she felt a small flush of relief.

"Thank you," she heard herself say, and Ivan appeared surprised.

"You should eat," he said. Before she could respond, he was gone.

Ella stared at the steam rising from the bowl. Hot food. Not cold, not lukewarm, but hot. How long had it been?

Her stomach gurgled at the smell. She closed her eyes, struggling with her resolve. What would happen when the men returned? No, she wouldn't be lulled by the kindness of food, would not be fooled by the fact that she'd so far been left alone. She stayed on the bed, with her eyes closed, waiting for the men to file in.

* * *

"The Cap ain't gonna be happy about this," someone said. Ella kept her eyes squinted almost closed, watching through the curtain of her lashes. "Waste o' food."

"Take the bowl to Timón. Have him dump it back in the pot." That was Ivan.

Ella remained in a ball, tensed, waiting, and she heard chairs scrape back and saw men sitting at the table. Under her lids, she saw them dealing cards. After a while, one of the men walked toward her, and she held her breath, waiting. He stepped onto her mattress, and pulled himself up onto the bunk above hers. She heard the frame creak as he shifted, making himself comfortable.

Many of the men were drinking, and as time passed, they got louder, and the jokes got dirtier, and still Ella waited. How many men were in the room, now? A dozen? She could see Ivan, drinking with the rest of them. Every once in a while, he would look in her direction, and she prayed he couldn't see the shine of her eyes through her lashes.

Her muscles ached from holding herself so tightly, from being tensed for so long. She wanted so badly to relax, but she refused to let her guard down. She would not be caught unaware. She might be determined to survive whatever she needed to survive, but that didn't mean she would succumb easily.

"Lights out," Ivan announced, suddenly, and the sound of his voice ringing over all the other sounds of merry men made her jump. Men pushed back their chairs, stubbed out cigars, and headed—some stumbling—toward their beds. She was surprised, not just by their ready acquiescence, but by the lateness of hour. Was it really ten, then? In spite of her body's ache and exhaustion, she found it difficult to believe she'd been in bed for so long.

Ivan strode toward her, and she curled her fingers into her dirty dress. He bent over and his large face filled her sight.

"Do you need to use the pot?" he asked. She didn't answer, but her cheeks darkened, and even as shrouded as she was in shadows, she knew that her attempt at feigning sleep was not fooling him. He leaned his face closer, and she expected to smell liquor on his breath. She didn't. He smelled of cigar smoke. "Through the door to the right. If you go, I'll be timing you, and if you're not back in five minutes, I'll come to get you."

She swallowed. She did need to go. How long had it been? It seemed like a lifetime. Before she could make up her mind, Ivan spoke again.

"No one is going to touch you, girl," he said. "Go use the pot, then go to sleep." He disappeared from her vision, and she blinked in surprise. She heard his voice from somewhere to the left. "Five minutes."

Chapter Two

At some point a couple of hours before dawn, Ella finally fell asleep to the sounds of the creaking ship and snoring men. She awoke with a jolt, a short time later, as those same men began to rise from their beds to ready themselves for the day. She couldn't see outside, so she had no idea if the sun was up or not. All she knew for sure was that she'd been left alone all night, and that the men were speaking in hushed tones that seemed out of character. Were they using low voices because they'd enjoyed too much drink the night before? Or, because they were trying not to wake her?

Steeling her courage, she pushed herself up into a sitting position, and every eye in the room turned toward her. Conversations trailed off, and an unnatural silence descended, making her wish she'd pretended to sleep longer. She felt like she should say something, and had no idea what that something should be. She did not know how to be charming, or how to bat her eyelashes at men, and it wouldn't matter if she did. Her clothes smelled atrocious, as did she, and she knew she must look awful.

Plus, what would be the point of trying to ingratiate herself? It was her day of judgement, and although she'd been left unharmed for a single night, she knew it wouldn't and couldn't last. Trying to convince any of these men to protect her would only be putting them in harm's way, and she had enough lives in her hands.

Someone cleared his throat, and the men jumped back into whatever they were doing, picking up conversations in mid-stream and buttoning shirts and filing out for breakfast. Her stomach rumbled at the thought of breakfast, and she closed her eyes, taking a deep breath. Even though she'd only slept a couple of uneasy hours, she felt marginally better—calmer, more in control of her emotions.

When she opened her eyes, she was surprised to find that there was only one other person in the room.

Ivan.

He was holding a bowl of oatmeal, and he held it up briefly before setting it on the table. There was some sort of fruit on top. Peaches? Her stomach gurgled, again. She'd had peaches a couple of times in her life, and could almost taste the sweetness in her mouth.

"You should eat," Ivan said. He stood for a moment, regarding her. She'd made no move to leave the bed. "Once the men have gone above, you can get cleaned up a bit before the night shift comes down. We're to see the captain in an hour."

She cleared her throat. "How's Luca?" she asked, ignoring her eyes' desire to return to the bowl on the table.

"He won't eat," Ivan answered after a brief hesitation. "He threw his bowl at me, this morning." He sounded impassive, unconcerned, and Ella wondered if that was an act. Would Luca be flogged, or worse, if he kept up such defiance?

"Please don't hurt him," she said. "This isn't his fault. He's just—"

"Eat, and clean up, and I'll return for you in an hour."

She bit back her angry retort, but it didn't matter; he'd already turned away, and in a moment she was alone with the taunting food. She thought of Luca, alone in the shadowy dungeon, afraid and hungry and worried most of all about her, and she crossed her arms over her stomach. She closed her eyes to keep them from staring at the sliced peaches, and tried to think of something she could say to Captain Swan to convince him to free Luca and allow her passage the rest of the way to Bohannon.

She considered trying to sneak down to the dungeon, to reassure herself that Luca was alive and relatively well, and to assure him that the same was true of her. She was pretty sure she could find her way, as the layout of the ship's levels hadn't seemed particularly complicated, but she dismissed the idea. Ivan would find her, and haul her back up, and he and the captain would both be even angrier. So far, she hadn't been given such a bad go of things, and there was no reason to make things worse before she knew what punishment was planned for her.

She was still sitting on the bed when Ivan returned. After the voices of the men had all faded away, she had sneaked out of the room to use the chamber pot, quickly and nervously, afraid that someone would burst in on her at any moment. She'd returned in a hurry to her bunk, and had not moved since. She'd resisted the temptation of the food, and the lure of being able to clean up a bit, even though she had to question whether she was really hurting anyone but herself with her defiance.

Her eyes were closed when Ivan returned, but she heard his heavy approach and heard his exasperated sigh, and she opened her eyes. She expected some sort of reprimand, especially when she saw the dark frown creasing his forehead. No angry words came, however, and he gestured with a quick flick of his wrist. "Come," he said.

She got off the bed without argument. He stepped aside so she could precede him from the room, and she did, trying to calm her racing heart. This was it. The moment of truth. She went up the stairs, painfully aware of his large frame blocking her retreat, following her up to her judgement.

The sun had barely broken free of the sea, and the ship was cast in pale, early light. She paused for a moment at the top of the stairs, caught off guard by the beauty of the morning sky. She stepped toward the railing, automatically, her face turned toward the sun. The sky was painted in red and orange and pink, and the ocean stretched out to meet it. There was no land in sight, there were no other ships, there was nothing but sea and sky. She swallowed, overwhelmed by the magnitude.

Ivan cleared his throat, and she started, drawn from her reverie. She looked around, and felt her cheeks begin to warm. There were only a few men on this side of the ship, working, and they were doing their best to ignore her. The captain was several yards away, however, one hip leaned against the rail, his arms and ankles crossed, regarding her. He was dressed in black again—or still, perhaps—and the morning light glistened in the dark waves of his hair. Her heart stuttered in surprise at her body's instant reaction to his masculinity. Her mouth had once again gone dry, and she was alarmed to find that it was not merely from fear.

"I trust you slept well?" he asked. His eyes skated down the length of her body, then back to her face.

She somehow managed to suppress a shiver. She tried to swallow. "Uh. Yes. Thank you." It seemed an absurd thing to say, and his face showed a moment's surprise, too. He gave a small nod in acknowledgment, and she fidgeted, feeling self-conscious and indecent and more than a little confused.

"Are you ready to tell me why you're on my ship?"

She hesitated. Then, biting her lip, she shook her head. A part of her wanted to swallow her pride, drop to her knees, and tell him her story, begging him for his help. For all she knew, he was a member of the slave traders himself, though, and the men taking Travis to Bohannon could be his friends. Hell, they could be his family. She knew nothing substantial about Captain Swan, and she could not expect any help from him. She could not expect any help from anyone. She and Luca and Travis had learned long ago that they had themselves to depend upon and no one else.

"How did you get on board?"

She pressed her lips together. "I...just sneaked on," she mumbled, knowing that he wouldn't buy it and knowing that she couldn't tell the truth. Luca's complicity was already clear, but its extent was not.

"Impossible," he answered, his voice surprisingly soft, almost lost in the breeze. Then, before she could answer, he straightened, uncrossing his arms. "I hear you didn't eat your stew, last night."

She shook her head. Ivan said, "Or breakfast." She winced at the accusation in his voice, and saw the captain's dark eyebrows drop into a scowl. She tried to remember why she'd refused the food, when it seemed now that it had been a kindness that they had not needed to extend.

"I will not abide food being wasted on my ship," Captain Swan said.

"Luca's locked up for stealing food," she shot back, her temper flaring—it was a defense mechanism that she embraced gladly. "I was trying to pay his debt."

"He's not eating, either," Ivan supplied, and she silently cursed him. The captain's lips pressed together into a tight line.

"He just wants to make sure I'm alright," she said, fighting her rising desperation. "Please, don't hurt him. Just...lock me up. Let me—"

"You want to share a cell with him?" the captain asked.

"He doesn't belong there," she answered, squaring her shoulders. "If you won't let him out, at least...let us be together. If we each know the other's alright, we won't cause you any trouble. I...promise."

"Tell me how you got on board."

She clenched her fists and shook her head.

"It's a beautiful morning, isn't it?" Captain Swan asked, gesturing toward the rising sun. He looked at Ivan and sighed. "Take her back to the bunks."

He was right, it was a beautiful morning, and the ocean breeze on her face made her feel almost human again. The thought of returning to the closed room below filled her with dread. "Wait," she said, but when the captain looked at her, she stopped, unsure what to say. She couldn't give him what he wanted, and she wouldn't beg for fresh air.

The captain nodded. "Ivan," he said, and Ivan grabbed her arm. *Here we are again*, she thought. *The sun's in the opposite side of the sky, and we're in the same place.* She turned her back on the captain, heading for the stairs with her back as straight as she could manage. She shot one last glance toward the colorful sky, wondering if she would live to see another sunrise. Before stepping down the first step, she pulled in a deep breath of salty air, preparing herself for the staleness of the bunks.

"Get her some clean clothes, Ivan," the captain called, and she bit her lip, once again made painfully aware of how filthy and smelly she was.

She expected Ivan to tell the captain that she'd refused the opportunity to get cleaned up, as well. Instead, he only answered, "Yes, Cap."

"Something in all black, preferably," she muttered. To her surprise, she heard Ivan snort behind her. She didn't look around, although she was fairly confident that she'd spoken too quietly for the captain to hear her.

She and Ivan descended in silence, and she led the way to the bunks, taking in as many details as she could about the passageways. She passed three men along the way, and each of them stepped aside, pausing until she and Ivan had gone by. Once she was back in the room she'd slept in, she let out a slow breath, knowing that, for as long as the captain's current mood held, this was to be her cell. It was more comfortable than Luca's, and for that, she felt guilty. She was no less a prisoner, though.

Her oatmeal was still sitting on the table, and she passed it, making her way toward her bed.

"You should eat," Ivan said, again, as she lowered herself to the edge of the bottom bunk. When she met his eyes, he shook his head, pursing his lips. "Suit yourself. I'll bring you clean clothes."

She held her silence. In spite of the hollow ache in her stomach, the thought of washing up, brushing her hair and teeth, and putting on clean clothes, was far more alluring than the food. She hated the grime on her skin and the stench on her clothes. They weren't even halfway to Bohannon, yet. She'd expected the journey to be difficult, and she wasn't going to break, now. If she'd remained undiscovered, she would not have had a chance to clean up. It wasn't her comfort they were concerned about, anyway, but their own.

If they didn't want to smell her, they could put her below with Luca.

And you'll have another month and a half without a glimpse of the sky or a scent of wind, she thought.

Yes, but she'd been prepared for that, hadn't she?

Maybe. It would've been easier, if she'd never stepped on deck. Now she knew what the world was like just a short climb away, and it made the thought of the dungeon seem more torturous.

Ivan returned in a few minutes and tossed clothes onto the bed beside her. She glanced down at them. They were men's, of course, but almost small enough to fit her. If she wanted to put them on. "Can you read?" Ivan asked.

Her pride drew angry words to her lips, and she bit them back. "Yes," she answered instead. He set a book on the table beside the oatmeal.

"You'll have the room to yourself, for the most part. Most of the men won't return until evening. The night shift sleeps in the next room. Don't get any ideas, though. I'll be checking on you, and if you're not here—"

"I get it," she snapped, hiding her surprise. She was going to be left alone? All day?

And what will tonight bring? she wondered.

"I don't think you do," he shot back. "Eat something, for God's sake."

He was gone in a few clumping bootsteps, and she stared after him. She looked down at her filthy hands, and felt tears sting her eyes. Her nerves felt raw, her emotions unpredictable, and she knew that hunger and lack of sleep were the main reasons. She got up and walked to the table, reaching for the tin cup. She drained the lukewarm water from it in two long swallows, wincing as the liquid hit her empty stomach. She picked up the book and turned it over in her hands, examining the cover.

She carried it back to the bed and sat down, setting it on the blanket beside her. Her eyes drifted back to the bowl on the table and she forced them away, making a sound of irritation. The water was gurgling in her stomach, and she lay down, pulling her knees up. A vague plan had begun to form in her tired mind. If she waited until Ivan came to check on her, then perhaps she could make her move. She had no idea how often he planned to show up, but he couldn't possibly come in every couple of minutes. If, after his first check, she waited until he was gone, could she sneak into the dungeon to see Luca and get back to the bunks before Ivan knew she was gone? As long as she didn't run into anyone, she thought it was likely.

If she could see Luca, she would feel better, and she knew that if he saw her, he would relax a bit, too.

She pushed the book aside. She had a dull headache, and the rocking of the ship was beginning to get to her, again. It was so much better when she was up on her feet, moving around. She considered getting up to pace, and decided to rest a bit, instead. As soon as Ivan came to check on her, she would make her move and prove to herself that Luca was alright.

She closed her eyes, thinking of the day Travis had brought the toad to them, excitement stamped on his young face. He had always been such a happy boy. It was a miracle, really. His contagious laugh had always brought a smile to all the faces around him. No matter how tired Ella was, that laugh had always made her happy.

She fell asleep that way, curled around the unopened book, the image of Travis and Luca laughing in her mind.

She didn't wake when Ivan came to check on her, not the first time, or the second, or the third.

* * *

"You think she's dead?"

"Smells like it."

The quiet voices were followed by a few laughs, and Ella frowned, trying to struggle out of her grogginess.

"Shit. I think she's waking up."

"What are you doing in here?"

There was a quick rustle of movement. "Nothing, Ive," one of the voices said, sounding defensive. "Just came to get something."

"It's almost supper time. Go wash the slime from your hands."

And still Ella was having difficulty making sense of her surroundings. It couldn't possibly be supper time. They'd eaten breakfast just...what? A couple of hours ago?

"We weren't gonna touch her," someone muttered as they left the room, and she felt her skin crawl. How long had they been in the room with her, while she was unaware? She forced her eyes all the way open, horrified to find that she'd slept through the comings and goings of who knew how many men. Had she really slept the entire day away? She sat up quickly, and the world swam around her. Her head thumped, and her empty stomach churned.

She wasn't stupid. She knew that the headache and lightheadedness were symptoms of her hunger. It wasn't the first time she'd endured such side effects. If she made it off *Voyage* alive, it probably wouldn't be the last time, either. Ivan was standing in the middle of the room, staring at her. She must have slept restlessly, because the book and clean clothes had been knocked to the floor. She bent to retrieve them, gritting her teeth against the dizziness.

"Are you alright?" Ivan asked.

"Fine," she said. "I guess I fell asleep." She set the clothes and book on the bed. Her mouth felt cottony, and she rubbed her tongue on the roof of her mouth, trying to work up enough spit to swallow.

"The captain wants to see you again."

"Of course," she said, frowning. He was going to ask her the same questions, and she was going to give him the same answers—or lack of answers—and she would once more be banished to the bunks. What was the point?

"Would you like to eat, first?"

"No," she snapped, rubbing a hand over her face. She steeled herself for the lightheadedness and pushed herself to her feet. She swayed slightly, holding the bunk above her head to steady herself. She hoped he would attribute her unsteadiness to a lack of experience in sailing. "Have you seen Luca?"

"Not yet," Ivan said, stepping aside for her to pass. "I'll take him his supper shortly."

Ella's legs felt heavy and weak, and by the time she'd made it halfway up to the main deck, she was breathing heavily. Her head pounded, the constant thudding making it difficult to think of anything else. She felt bile at the back of her throat and knew there was nothing in her stomach to throw up. She paused near the top, and Ivan stopped behind her. She closed her eyes, trying to catch her breath and gather some strength.

"Alright?" Ivan asked.

"Fine," she said. "Just tired."

He didn't answer, and after a few moments, she stepped out into the orange glow of evening. Sunset to sunrise to sunset. It was a cruelly beautiful loop.

"Were you given clean clothes?" a voice asked from her left, and she started to turn, stumbling. Ivan grabbed her arm to steady her. The captain was scowling at her.

She frowned in return, trying to remember the question. "Yes," she answered.

"And you chose to remain smelling like a garbage bin?"

She crossed her arms. "That's right."

"With no concern for those who have to endure it?"

"You could send me to the dungeon," she retorted.

"So you'd sentence your beloved to the smell?"

Beloved? Who was he talking about? She was having difficulty concentrating through the thumping in her skull, and she simply stared at him, unable to hide her confusion.

"God damn it," the captain said, suddenly, his voice full of anger. Not irritation, but real anger, and the dark look on his face was truly alarming. "Have you eaten anything?"

When she didn't answer, Ivan did: "No, Cap. Neither has Luca."

Ella opened her mouth to say something—she wasn't sure what—in Luca's defense, but the world was swimming around her, and she couldn't think of any words that made sense. The colors of the sunset were blurring and swirling, and the deck seemed to be tilting beneath her.

"Damn it," Captain Swan said again, and his voice seemed impossibly distant. She suddenly realized she was falling, and she tried to brace herself for impact. She never hit the deck, though, and after a few moments of confusion, she realized that she was being carried. She tried to open her eyes, but her lids felt heavy and the pain in her head made it impossible to focus.

She wasn't sure where she was being taken, and couldn't quite muster the energy to care. She was completely and utterly at their mercy, now, even more than before, and it was almost a relief. She couldn't fight now if she wanted to.

She was lowered onto a bed, and she finally managed to open her eyes. She was dully surprised to find the captain looking down at her. She'd assumed it was Ivan carrying her. She realized that she could smell him, Captain Swan. He smelled like soap and seawater, and the combination was strangely appealing. And what did she smell like? A garbage bin, according to him.

"Open your mouth."

She blinked at him, surprised and confused.

"Now."

She saw that he was holding a spoonful of something toward her mouth, and her stomach immediately clenched. She was half-sitting, propped against a pillow, and realized belatedly that there was no bunk above her head. Where was she? She tried in vain to blink the room into focus. Where had he gotten food? Had she blacked out? She couldn't make sense of anything.

"Eat, or I'll stop feeding your boyfriend."

*Boyfriend? Beloved...*Somehow, her laboring brain finally managed to figure out that he meant Luca.

Eat, or I'll stop feeding Luca.

He's not eating, anyway, she thought, and immediately knew that wasn't the point. She couldn't let her own foolish stubbornness further endanger Luca. She looked into the captain's dark eyes, and saw a steely stubbornness that matched her own.

She closed her eyes against the threatening tears and opened her mouth, like a dutiful child, and her tongue was flooded with salty broth. She swallowed it eagerly, horrified to feel her chin quivering. *You will not cry,* she told herself. *You will not cry.*

She allowed herself to be fed because she was too weak to feed herself, and she had no one except herself to blame for that. What was her pride worth, anyway?

"Lie down."

The soup was warm in her belly, and she allowed herself to be shifted until she was laying on her side. He could do anything he wanted, and she waited to see if his mercy would continue.

"Sleep. I'll wake you in a couple of hours to eat again."

"Why?" she mumbled. Her eyes were closed. She didn't want to see him. She was suffocating under her humiliation, and she was too tired to fight her emotions.

"Basic human decency?" came his soft reply, and she tucked her chin against her chest, hoping he couldn't see the tears slipping from the corners of her eyes.

"You should toss me overboard," she whispered. *I've made such a mess of everything. I'm going to rescue Travis? That's a joke. He wouldn't be in trouble if it wasn't for me. Some protector I turned out to be.* "I'm tired," she said.

"Well, no wonder," he muttered.

"That's not what I meant," she mumbled. Her words sounded slurred, and she could feel herself succumbing to the pull of unconsciousness.

"I know," he answered, and then she was out.

* * *

"Sit up. Open your eyes."

She struggled to comply without quite knowing why. A hand on her arm helped her upright, and she blinked her bleary eyes, trying to focus. Her head felt better, and she wondered how many hours she'd been asleep. When she thought of the things she'd said, after he'd fed her the soup, she felt a flush of embarrassment.

"Open your mouth," he said.

"Do you carry soup in your pocket?" she asked.

To her surprise, she heard a chuckle, and she squinted, trying to bring his face into focus. The room was shadowy, dim, and she couldn't quite make out his features. She felt a stab of disappointment. She would like to see what he looked like when he was laughing.

"Open," he commanded again.

"I can do it," she said, reaching for the bowl.

"Look at your hands," he said. His voice was soft and undeniable. She blinked down at her hands, and they were trembling. She stared at her dirty, shaking hands as though they belonged to someone else, and for a moment, it was almost as if they did. How had the series of choices she'd made in her life led her to this point? "Open," he said again, and she did, closing her eyes as she did so. "You know," he said, after a few moments of spooning soup into her mouth, "pride is a dangerous thing."

"It's all I have," she blurted before she knew the words were going to leave her mouth.

He didn't answer, and she peeked under her lashes, trying to make out his expression. "There's water beside the bed, here, and a pot if you need it," he finally said, straightening with a rustle of clothing.

"Where am I?"

"In my room."

Her stomach fluttered nervously. She tried not to think about what sort of payment he would be expecting for his hospitality. "Captain Swan," she said, when he started to turn away.

"Yes, Ella?" he answered, pausing with his back to her.

"Did Ivan feed Luca?"

He was silent for long moments, before finally answering, "Yes." He headed toward the door.

"Did he eat?" she asked, afraid of the answer.

"No," he said, without looking back. "But I'll see to that. Sleep."

I'll see to that, she thought. *What does that mean?*

She was still trying to puzzle it through when she fell asleep again.

* * *

The next time she opened her eyes, the room was filled with soft strands of sunlight. She felt remarkably better, and she marveled at what two bowls of watery soup and an abundance of sleep could do. She lay still for a few minutes, getting her thoughts in order. She needed to pee, and she was thirsty.

More importantly, she needed to check to see if Luca was alright.

She also had to figure out why Captain Swan had taken care of her, and brought her to his private cabin. If she knew what he expected from her, she could prepare herself for it.

She heard a rustle of papers, and shifted her gaze toward the right side of the room. A desk sat in a bar of sunlight, and the captain was seated behind it. He had several papers in his hands, but he wasn't looking at them. He was watching her, and she felt another nervous flutter. She cleared her throat and pushed herself up.

"Morning," she muttered, feeling stupid and embarrassed.

"Morning," he drawled, sounding strangely amused. She glanced at him, then away. She knew she was indebted to him, and it was a feeling she didn't relish. "Feel better?"

"Yes." Then, because it was the right thing to do, she added, "Thank you."

"That must have hurt," he remarked, and her fists clenched.

"What do you want?" she asked. There was no sense in beating around the bush. Best to lay the situation bare.

"For the soup? Or for letting you dirty my sheets?"

She blanched, looking down at the bed. He was right; she was filthy, and there was no way he would be able to sleep there without smelling her stench. "Both," she muttered.

He didn't answer for long moments. Then he set the papers down and leaned back in his chair with a small sigh. "I spoke to Timón. Have you met him?"

"I haven't 'met' anyone," she said, frowning. "I only know Ivan's name because Luca told me."

"Hm," he answered. "Timón is the cook. He prepares all our meals, keeps track of the food supply."

He waited for her to say something, but she wasn't sure what his point was. "Oh," she finally answered, lamely.

"I can only assume that you've been on the ship since we left Baytown. That a fairy didn't drop you in on us a week out to sea."

She remained silent.

"We have exactly the amount of stores we should, according to Timón. And believe me, he checked carefully. Timón takes his job very seriously."

"I'm not following," she said, spreading her hands. She needed to pee, and she wanted an answer to her question—what did he want from her? Why did he seem so obsessed with food? They had plenty on the ship.

"We're two weeks from shore," he said, and his voice held an edge that wasn't there before. "What did you eat?"

She pressed her lips together. Was he trying to trick her into condemning Luca?

"Just answer the question," he said, and she struggled not to quail under his heavy glare.

"I ate half of Luca's food," she answered, quietly.

"My crew is on a very strict diet. The proper nutrition is key to surviving a trip like this. If Luca was only eating half of his food, he was putting everyone at risk. If he'd passed out—"

"Would you make up your mind?" she snapped.

In a low voice, he said, "Pardon me?"

"Would you decide what you're really upset about? Luca was locked up because he stole food. Well, I *told* you, he didn't. Even if I'd wanted him to—which I didn't—he never would've agreed to it. We didn't set out to hurt anyone else. You never would've known I was here! First, you're angry because you thought he stole food. Then, you're angry because I'm not eating, which is saving you food. Now, you're pissed to find out that I told you the truth, that we didn't steal anything."

"No. Nothing except passage across the ocean," he said.

She spread her hands. "What do you want?" she repeated.

"I want you to clean yourself up, and change your clothes. I want you to eat breakfast. Then, when you can stand up without falling over, I want you to go down and find Timón and Rashad. They'll give you work to do. I assume you're willing to work?"

"Yes," she said, through clenched teeth. It was a far more generous offer than she deserved, and the knowledge galled her. She waited to see if there was more. When he simply sat there, his dark eyes unreadable, she asked, "What about Luca?"

"He's eating, now."

"But he—"

"Is still a prisoner for his crime."

"So, I'll work with the cook and...whoever Rashad is," she said, hoping they were men with some sense of honor. "What do I have to do to earn Luca's freedom?"

"That's not open for discussion at the moment."

"I'll do anything," she said.

"Including whoring yourself out?"

She swallowed, thinking once more, *What's my pride worth, anyway? Not Luca's life.* "Yes," she said. The word tasted dirty on her tongue, and she wasn't even certain she could back it up. Would she be able to suffer so much pain and degradation in silence? Would she allow herself to be violated in the worst way imaginable to save Luca?

Yes, she said, praying it was true. She wanted to believe she was strong enough, she was determined to *be* strong enough.

Captain Swan pushed his chair back and stood, and her mouth was alarmingly dry. As he walked toward her, she tried to tell herself that he wouldn't try anything now—not before she'd cleaned up and changed clothes. If nothing else, the smell should deter him, right? Nevertheless, when he neared the bed, she tensed, doing her best to prepare herself. Perhaps it wouldn't be so horrible. She couldn't deny to herself that she found him attractive. If he wasn't too rough, if he didn't hurt her too badly, maybe she could pretend it was something else.

"Once you've cleaned yourself up, strip the sheets off the bed and take them to Rashad. He'll show you how to wash them. Eat first, though. Remember that every meal you skip is a meal that Luca will miss, as well."

She opened her mouth, but he didn't wait for her response. He opened the door and disappeared, pulling it firmly shut behind himself. She stared at the closed door, with her heart pounding in her chest. Had he rejected her offer, or given her a temporary reprieve? She didn't know, and the uncertainty made her feel jittery.

She looked at the small table beside the head of the bed. Oatmeal and peaches, again, and her mouth watered at the sight. It must be cold, but what did that matter? The captain's final words echoed in her ears, and she reached for the bowl. He'd said that Luca was eating. Could she take his word for that? Perhaps, once she found Timón and Rashad, she could think of an excuse to get into the dungeon.

She tasted a spoonful of cold oatmeal, and her stomach gurgled eagerly. She still needed to pee, but she finished her food, first. Then she crept to the door and peeked through the window, looking for some sign of the captain. The cabin was ringed with windows, and she could see the sea in three directions. Through the door's window, she could see down to the deck, and partway along that side of the ship, and there was no sign of Captain Swan or anyone else. She frowned. There must be a dozen men on deck, somewhere, and yet none of them were in sight. She looked down and saw that the door had a lock. She flipped the metal latch down, a bit apprehensively. If he returned to find himself locked out of his cabin, how would he react? Would he break down his own door? Well, he wouldn't need to if he had the key, and he likely wouldn't be stupid enough to leave her inside without taking it with him.

Resolved to finish her tasks as quickly as possible, and in privacy, she started by using the chamber pot to empty her bladder. She found the clothes he'd left, neatly folded, beside a barrel of cool water and beneath a mirror. There was a rag and a bar of soap, and a razor. She reached toward them, disturbed by her own eagerness. It wasn't a matter of vanity, exactly. She knew she was no beauty, no matter how clean she was. What she wanted was to feel like a real person, instead of a gutter rat.

She looked at herself in the mirror, and felt a shock run all the way through her. When was the last time she'd looked at herself? Months? A year? What did her appearance matter?

Her cheeks were sunken, though, and her eyes ringed by purple smudges that sleeping most of a day and night had not been able to banish. Her hair was awful, but she'd expected that. She'd expected the paleness, too. She'd been out of the sun for weeks. She'd even expected thinness. Her meals had been far from regular, long before boarding *Voyage*.

What she hadn't expected was...everything. She looked half-starved. No, more than half. Her skin was tight and pale and almost translucent, and her eyes seemed alarmingly large in her shrunken face. Suddenly forgetting that the room was surrounded by windows, she pulled her nasty dress off and dropped it to the floor. She held her arms out before herself, staring. Bones with skin, that's all she was. She stood in her underwear, looking down at her body. She poked at her stomach, her hipbones, her ribcage. No wonder the captain had rejected her offer. No wonder the men had left her alone. After only two weeks abroad, none of them could possibly be so desperate.

She met her eyes in the mirror. *You're going to rescue Travis? You passed out after climbing a few stairs, and no wonder.* Her lips were dry, chapped, but there were no cold sores. She had Luca to thank for that. He'd given her as much of his food as he could sneak away from the table, and without it, she would be even worse off. She thought again of Travis, who'd never known, the way she did, what it was like to be really and truly hungry. Did he know, now? Was he suffering the pangs of an empty stomach and the effects of malnutrition? Were there bags under his eyes and hollows in his cheeks?

She dipped the washrag into the barrel and scrubbed at her face with it. She felt a sob, lodged in her throat, trying to choke her, and she fought it back, refusing to give in. She soaped the rag and scrubbed her arms until they felt raw. She caught sight of herself in the mirror, again, and she looked insane. Tears were streaming down her face, and she was biting her lip hard enough to draw blood. She turned her face away from her reflection and concentrated on getting the weeks of dirt and sweat from her body.

You need to do better, Ella, she thought. She remembered, vaguely, telling Captain Swan to throw her overboard the night before. She'd been so ready to give up, hadn't she? She was tired, she'd said. She shook her head. *A new day is starting,* she thought, scrubbing, scrubbing. *You need to do better. You WILL do better.*

* * *

At some point, she came to her senses and realized that she hadn't even closed the curtains over the windows. She'd locked the door so no one would burst in on her, ignoring the fact, in her alarm over her appearance, that anyone could be watching her through any of the windows. She glanced around, and still didn't see anyone. It didn't really matter. What was done was done. She'd shaved her legs and armpits, a task that hadn't been done more than a couple of times a year in her adult life. Her skin felt shiny and raw from head to toe, shiny and raw and *clean.*

She washed her hair four times, working the bar of soap until it was just a sliver, lathering from root to tip repeatedly until she could run his comb through the tangles. She looked into the murky water of the barrel, disgusted by the knowledge that all of that muck had come from her hair and skin. The water would have to be changed. She wondered if she would be expected to do that. She would certainly try, although she wasn't sure her scrawny arms would carry many buckets before giving out.

She spotted his toothbrush and hesitated. After a moment, she conducted a quick search and discovered that there were no others. She looked at it again, wondering if it would be worth incurring his possible wrath. There must be more, somewhere on the ship. Maybe Luca had one. It wouldn't be the first time they'd shared one.

Her hand reached for Captain Swan's toothbrush before she could stop it. She ran her thumb across the bristles. They were still damp from his use. She met her own eyes for a moment, and thought she saw a challenge there. Her body felt clean for the first time in...she couldn't remember how long. From her tingly scalp to her tingly toes. Everything except her mouth.

She'd already begun scrubbing at her teeth before she could give it too much thought, and then there was no turning back. She scoured her tongue, and then her teeth again, until she was afraid her gums would bleed. The water in the barrel was too dirty to rinse the brush, so she poured some clean drinking water from the skin by the bed, rinsing the bristles thoroughly. Then she rinsed her mouth, spitting into the barrel, before drinking the rest of the water in the canteen.

She had no clean undergarments, but she supposed she could clean them after Rashad had shown her where to wash the sheets. She wasn't sure they were salvageable, but they were all she had. In the meantime, she pulled on the pants and shirt the captain had left her. They were baggy, but she'd been provided a belt, and she cinched it tightly around her waist. She looked down at herself. Her breasts were small, anyway, and made even more so by starvation, barely noticeable under the loose shirt. She sighed.

She glanced at the clock hung on the wall. How long had she taken? She should've kept track. He hadn't come pounding on the door, but he was probably growing more impatient by the minute. She hurried to strip the sheets and blankets from the bed, and gathered them into a pile, along with her dress. She tucked her undergarments in between and threw the washrag on top. She unlocked the door, pulled it open, and stuck her head out. Still no sign of anyone. Was that normal? She didn't know. She knew nothing about sailing.

Bucking up her courage, she curled the bundle of dirty laundry and scooped it into her arms. She was still barefoot, and when she stepped out of the cabin, the sun-warmed wood heated the bottoms of her feet. There were a few steps to go down to the deck, and she made her way carefully, holding the sheets to the side so she could see her feet. When she was at the bottom, she paused to look out at the expanse of sparkling water. She scanned the horizon, once again seeing nothing to break the even line between water and sky.

She had never in her life been more aware of her smallness. As she stared out over the water, it was difficult to imagine that it could ever end. Was there really land, out there? Were there really other ships? Where was the slave ship carrying Travis and the other unfortunate prisoners? Captain Swan's ship had left less than two days after them, and she didn't know if she should be able to see them off the front bow or not.

"Have you ever been to sea?"

31

His voice startled her, and she turned, almost dropping the laundry. She bit her sore lip, then immediately released it, not wanting to draw blood again. The captain's eyes slid to her mouth, and his eyebrows dipped into a small frown.

"No," she answered, and his eyes returned to hers. "It's crazy how...big it is." As soon as she'd said it, she felt like an idiot. She braced herself for ridicule, but Captain Swan stepped over to the rail and surveyed the water.

"Crazy," he agreed, and he sounded musing rather than mocking. Still, she couldn't be sure. His moods seemed to shift so suddenly. "Do you need help with those?" he asked, still looking out at the ocean.

It took her a moment to follow his change in conversation. "No," she said. "Thank you," she added, starting past him.

"Do you remember who you're supposed to find?"

"Sure. Timón and Rashad."

"Did you find everything you needed?" he asked, finally turning toward her.

"Uh. Yes. Thank you," she said, her heart slamming in her chest. Why did his nearness make her so nervous? Yes, she'd offered him a proposition that she wasn't sure she was even remotely prepared to keep, but he'd so far done nothing to harm her. He'd been far kinder than she had any right to expect, in fact. *Who are you kidding? It's not fear you're feeling*, she thought, and she felt a telltale blush creeping up her throat. *Don't be ridiculous*, she immediately scolded herself. *Just because you're cleaner doesn't mean you're any less of a pale, scrawny, plain-faced girl.*

"Good," he said after a few beats.

She nodded and turned away once again, heading for the doorway that would lead her down below. As she stepped carefully into the shadows, she paused again and looked back. Captain Swan was watching her, and she felt a small jolt when she met his eyes. He seemed suddenly uncomfortable; she'd never seen him looking ill-at-ease.

"I used your toothbrush," she heard herself admit. She was blushing, and her heart was racing. Would he be angry?

His dark eyebrows went up in surprise and, after a moment, one corner of his mouth quirked upward. She felt a wave of relief. "Thank you for telling me," he said, and he sounded amused.

"And...I'll change the water, when I'm done with the laundry."

He waved a hand. "Don't worry about it."

"I...I don't mind doing it," she said, wondering if he cared whether she minded or not.

She was standing sideways in the doorway, the sheets held in a large bundle before her. His gaze skated down the length of her body, again. This time, however, after having seen herself clearly, she had a far better idea of what he was seeing. "I don't think you're ready for the heavy work, yet," he murmured, and she suppressed a shiver. Her brain was telling her that he couldn't possibly find her attractive, and her body was telling her that she wasn't imagining the double meaning in his words.

She could think of nothing to say. She was way out of her element, and was painfully aware of the fact.

"Watch your step," he said, and she knew that she'd been dismissed. Her relief battled briefly with an unexpected stab of disappointment, and she gave herself a mental shake. What was wrong with her, anyway? It should take more than peaches and soap to turn her into a silly girl.

Her arms were already feeling weak and achy. She readjusted her grip and made her way, slowly and carefully, down the steps. The dimness swallowed her, and she smelled the familiar stale air. It wasn't so bad, now that she'd had more than a lungful of fresh air. She hoped that Luca was doing alright with his confinement.

She had just reached the bottom of the stairs when she heard the heavy thud of boots on the stairs behind her. She paused to catch her breath and again readjust the bundle in her tired arms, and by the time she'd started down the corridor, Ivan had reached her side.

"Here, let me get that," he said, reaching for the sheets.

"I'm fine," she answered.

"The captain sent me to help you."

"He did?" she asked after a moment, once more surprised.

"You can imagine why he might not have confidence in your strength?" he said, pulling the wad of laundry from her skinny arms.

"Thank you," she muttered, scowling.

"Follow me," he said. "I'll take you to the galley."

*　*　*

Rashad was the darkest man she'd ever seen in her life. In the dim lantern-light, only his eyes and teeth were visible. He was in charge of cleaning, everything from laundry to chamber pots to dishes to mopping the decks. He'd helped her clean her bundle of linen and carry it upstairs, and they'd hung the articles to dry. Everything except her undergarments, which she'd hung over a rack in the small room where he kept his cleaning supplies. It was embarrassing enough that he should see them, without exposing them to the entire crew. And the captain.

After the laundry lesson, she helped Rashad clean the breakfast dishes. He refused to let her help scrub the chamber pots, in spite of her insistence that she was meant to assist him with everything. Instead, he sent her to see if Timón needed any help, and there she got into a brief argument with the cook when she suggested there might be more creative ways to prepare the potatoes he was planning to boil for dinner.

*　*　*

"The crew is on a very strict diet."

Ella tried to hide her irritation. "I know. Captain Swan told me. I'm not suggesting you change the food, or rations. Just the way it's prepared."

"I've been cooking for Captain Swan and his men for ten years," Timón said, raising his chin.

Ella was surprised. Ten years was a long time. The image of Luca, after his grandmother's death, once again rose, unbidden, to her mind. Ten years ago, Luca had been just a heartbroken child. Now, he was in prison in the dungeon of a ship set for Bohannon, a city on the far side of the ocean in a country she'd never thought she'd see.

"I've tasted your cooking," she said. "And it's good, don't get me wrong. I'm just saying...I know how to improvise. I didn't mean to overstep," she added at the sight of the chef's scowl. "I'm here to help. I...Forget I said anything."

He was silent for long moments. Finally, he said, "Give me an example."

* * *

About half of the crew made their way into the room off the galley for a midday meal, beans and rice that Ella had helped prepare. There were ten men—Timón had told her that there were twenty-one men working on the ship, including himself and Rashad but excluding the captain, Ivan, and Luca. She didn't ask why Ivan was excluded from the count. He seemed to be the captain's right-hand man.

As the crewmen came into the room, she and Timón were putting the food on the table. Several of the men paused when they saw her, and she tried her best to ignore her self-consciousness. Ivan was the last to enter, and he sat at the head of the table. Timón told her to serve the men, and she hurried to obey, spooning the mixture into their bowls as she made her way around the table. Most of them thanked her, but a few simply gaped at her as though they'd never seen a girl in their lives.

"Thank you," Ivan said, when she'd served him.

"The captain said that Luca started eating?" she asked. She kept her voice low, and still knew that many of the other men were straining to hear their conversation.

"That's right."

"Do you think...maybe I could help take him his supper?"

Ivan frowned, and said, "You'd have to talk to Cap about that."

She considered pushing the idea, and resisted. Captain Swan and Ivan had both told her that Luca was eating. Perhaps that would have to be enough for the time being. She continued around the table until everyone had food. Then she returned to Timón's side. "How long until the rest of the men come in?" she asked. For the midday meal, they came in two shifts, she'd been told. Only a handful of men worked the decks at night, and so supper was a larger affair.

"Half an hour or so," he answered.

"Do you mind if I go see if Rashad needs any help until then?"

Timón looked at her. "You should eat," he said. "You've been working all morning."

It was true that she was tired and a bit hungry, but she also felt good. Working, and knowing she was making herself useful, felt good. "I will, later," she said. She thought of the captain's warning: *Every meal you skip will be one that Luca goes without, as well.* Well, Luca didn't get lunch, anyway, she reasoned. Nevertheless, she shot an uneasy glance toward Ivan. He didn't seem to be paying her any attention.

"I'll be back for the next serving," she told Timón. "I promise."

"Very well."

*   *   *

The ship was sailing at a good clip, and the steady wind had dried the laundry in no time. She and Rashad stripped them off the line, folded them, and carried them down the stairs. There wasn't enough time to remake Captain Swan's bed, yet. She would have to wait until after the second half of crewmen had been served.

Would the captain himself join that group, sitting at the head of the table instead of Ivan? She felt a thrill of anticipation at the idea, but he never showed up. She didn't have the nerve to ask Timón if that was usual, or not. She served the men their rice and beans, and poured their coffee, and then helped Rashad clean the bowls and pans and spoons.

Then she gathered the clean sheets and blankets and headed up the stairs to make the captain's bed.

She'd completely forgotten about getting herself lunch. It hadn't been that long since breakfast, not for a girl who couldn't remember the last time she'd had three meals in a day. It seemed unimportant.

Until she walked into the captain's cabin.

Chapter Three

She stopped, startled to find the captain in his room. She realized belatedly that she should have knocked. She'd assumed that he would be working somewhere on the deck, and she'd been so distracted by the blue sky that she'd already walked into the cabin before she realized what she was doing.

While she was caught off guard, and embarrassed, he seemed to have been waiting for her.

"I should've knocked," she muttered, resisting the urge to back out of the room.

He waved away her concern. "If I hadn't wanted you in here, I would've locked the door," he said. His voice sounded mild, but there was something underneath that caught her attention, and she looked more closely at his face. Was he upset with her? She tried to think of what else she might have done wrong.

Then she saw it. On the table, a bowl of rice and beans. It wasn't his, she knew that in an instant. It was there for her, and she felt her heart skip. *Uh-oh*, she thought.

"Lunch was good," he said. "Did you try it?"

She hesitated, seeing the trap plainly and still unsure how to avoid it. "I forgot," she admitted, finally deciding on honesty.

"You forgot to eat?" he asked, lifting his dark brows.

"I'm not used to...eating," she finished lamely.

His eyebrows dropped into a scowl. "Obviously," he said. "We did have a deal, did we not? I made myself understood?"

She swallowed. "Yes," she said, "Please, don't punish Luca for my stupidity. It won't happen again, I promise."

It was his turn to hesitate. She thought he was caught off guard by her sincerity. "Do you think it's odd I should have to blackmail you to eat?"

She sighed and ran a hand over her face, then turned and set the sheets and blankets on the edge of the bare mattress. "I'll do better," she said.

He regarded her for a few moments. "Very well," he answered, and she was relieved. "Eat before you make the bed, yes?"

"Sure. Alright," she said, moving toward the table. She reached for the bowl, then looked up at him, feeling a little shy. "Did you already eat?"

"Yes," he said, and was she imagining the regret in his expression? He cleared his throat. "I'll see you later," he added, heading for the door. He paused on his way out. "Ivan said you asked to take Luca his supper."

Crap, she thought. She hadn't planned on asking him, at least not yet. "Yes," she answered. "I just thought—"

"I'll allow it."

She stopped, surprised, and hesitated, waiting for the catch.

"Supper only. And if you try to free him—"

"I won't," she promised, quickly. While she desperately wanted Luca out of his cell, she knew it would be a mistake to press her luck.

Captain Swan turned toward her, and his expression was unreadable. "How long have you known Luca?" he asked.

She had no idea why he was asking, and yet she took only a heartbeat to decide to answer. How and why she'd stowed away on his ship were things he wanted to know that she was unwilling to tell him. This was something she could concede. "Since we were kids," she said. "He was...nine, I was around thirteen."

"You were friends?"

"We've always been friends. My—" she broke off. She'd been about to tell him that her brother had met Luca before her, and had told her about the older boy. Swan was staring at her, his expression still impassive. She cleared her throat. "We've always been friends," she repeated, wondering if he was going to let her get away with the slip.

He seemed about to say something, and she pressed her lips together. A part of her wanted to tell him about Travis, and beg him for his help. He would certainly have a better chance of negotiating Travis's freedom than she would. Why would he help her, though? She had nothing to offer; her pride and virtue were not even enough to bargain for Luca's freedom.

She could beg and plead and cry. She could tell him of their struggles, and how they only had each other. Would he sympathize? She wanted to believe he would, and couldn't risk it. She still didn't know how the captain felt about the slave trade, or what his intentions toward her were after landing. Yes, he'd allowed her to begin working, rather than locking her up. Did he expect that to pay for her passage, though? Or was he expecting her indebtedness to go beyond that?

She might need to make a break for it, when they reached land, if it looked as though he didn't plan to let her go free and clear. If that happened, and she could escape, she would have to get to Travis without anyone—except Luca—knowing where she was going. If she could even find Travis. How far ahead of them would that ship land?

She suddenly realized that the silence was stretching out, and she forced herself to meet the captain's eyes. She had to remember that, in spite of his relative kindness, they were not friends. They would never be friends, and she could not depend on his mercy to save her brother.

"I trust you're feeling well enough to return to the bunks, tonight?" he said, finally.

Whatever she'd been expecting him to say, that wasn't it. She knew she should be relieved that he didn't expect her to stay in his cabin with him. She *was* relieved. She felt an unexpected twinge of hurt, too, and she couldn't justify that to herself. She didn't want to whore herself out, but the fact that he didn't even seem interested in her willingness to do so was not a boost to her self-esteem. She crossed her arms over her chest. "Of course," she said. "If that's what you want." As soon as the words left her mouth, she regretted them. Why had she said that? It made it sound like it wasn't what *she* wanted, and he already thought she was a whore.

He frowned at her. He seemed to do that a lot. "Make sure you eat before you take Luca his food."

She nodded, and he left without another word. She looked down at her bowl, and let out a deep breath. So, she was going back to the bunks. She wasn't as afraid of the men as she'd been the first night. She'd only met a few of them, officially, but none of the others had given her any reason to fear them. They'd all stared, of course. None of them had stared in a way that frightened her, however, and now that she'd seen herself, she knew that they would have very little reason to desire her. Even if she was the only girl they'd seen in weeks.

Plus, she was going to see Luca. Aside from knowing Travis was alive and well, there was nothing that could make her feel better.

*   *   *

Ella barely tasted her food. She was more excited about seeing Luca than getting much-needed nutrition into her body, and she had just enough presence of mind to realize how strange that was. When she finished, eating her supper in the galley, she hurried into the dining room to find Ivan. He was sitting at the table, and looked up at her entrance. There were a few others there, still finishing their supper, but Timón had already cleared Ivan's bowl away. He seemed to be waiting for her.

Ella had Luca's food, and Ivan pushed to his feet, coming around the table to reach for the tray. Ella shook her head, pulling it back, and he relented with a scowl, gesturing for her to precede him toward the stairs leading down. She had to force herself not to rush, because she was afraid she would tumble down the steps, spilling the food and possibly breaking her neck. When she reached the bottom, she hurried toward the dungeon, not even giving her eyes a chance to adjust to the dimmer lighting.

Luca scrambled to his feet at the sight of her, her name tumbling from his lips in surprise and relief. She felt tears sting her eyes as she crossed to him. She handed him the tray through the slot in the bars, and he immediately set it on the floor, reaching for her hand through the bars. She leaned forward, pressing her forehead against his, biting her lip to keep from crying.

She could see him—really see him, as she'd finally seen herself—and what she saw was disturbing. He was pale, and frighteningly thin, although not so much as her. He had bags under his eyes. What a pair they must make.

"Are you alright?" he asked, pulling back to look at her. "They haven't hurt you?"

She shook her head. "I'm fine. I'm...working with Timón and Rashad."

He nodded. "Ivan said so," he said, glancing past her toward where Ivan, she assumed, was lurking in the doorway. She didn't look around. "Are they letting you eat?"

Letting me? More like forcing me, she thought. "Yes," she answered.

38

"I refused to eat, but...they told me if I didn't eat, they wouldn't feed you, either."

So, that was how Captain Swan had gotten him to eat. Interesting. He'd blackmailed each of them with the other. It was a smart, and effective, play, and she couldn't help wondering again what the captain stood to gain. "I want you to eat, Luca," she said. "You're too thin." Well, if that wasn't the pot calling the kettle black.

"You should talk," he said. He squeezed her hand. "It's good to see you, though."

"I'm trying to get you out of here, Luca. This is all my fault."

He shook his head. "Don't worry about me," he answered. "All that matters is getting to—"

"We'll figure it out," she interrupted, before he could mention her brother's name. Or, perhaps he'd been about to say 'Bohannon.' Either way, it was none of Ivan's business, and she knew he'd be reporting their conversation to the captain the first chance he got.

Luca pressed his lips together and nodded. "It's good to see you," he repeated, smiling. The girls had always loved Luca's smile, but the way he was looking at her made Ella a little uneasy. There had never been, and would never be, anything romantic between them. She'd known for a long time that he had a crush on her, and she also knew that he would make someone a wonderful husband. He would work harder than anyone to provide for his family, and there were few people in the world with kinder hearts than his. She couldn't say she'd never considered pursuing something more than friendship. She had. It wasn't as though she was getting any other offers.

The truth was, he was like a brother to her, and she would never see him as anything else. She loved him. She would die for him. She would kill for him. That was all she could offer him.

For some reason her thoughts turned, unwanted, to Captain Swan and the offer she'd made him. She would do anything to protect her family, and Luca and Travis were her family. She brushed Luca's dirty hair from his forehead, and the thought of letting him out of her sight again made her gut clench.

"I have to go, Luca, I'm sorry," she said. "I'll try to come back tomorrow night, and I'll figure out a way to get you out of here."

"Don't worry about me," he said, again. "Just take care of yourself."

She pulled his head forward and kissed his forehead between the bars. "Be well, Luca. Please."

"I love you, you know, El?" he said, his eyes shining in the lantern light. He looked so young, and underfed, and earnest, and that earnestness made her heart hurt.

"I love you, too," she said, knowing that it wasn't the same and knowing that her love was no less pure because of that. "I'll see you as soon as I can."

* * *

39

Ella had actually worked for the first time in about two weeks, and her body was still painfully weak from malnourishment. She lay in her bunk, listening to the cacophony of snores, exhausted and unable to sleep. Her mind was restless, keeping her awake with a constant stream of topics. She knew morning would come soon, and she knew that she would work even harder than the day before. She would prove herself to be an asset, and she would try her best to earn Luca's freedom.

Walking away from him had felt like abandonment, and a part of her believed she should have planted herself on the floor beside his cell and refused to leave. What would the captain have done, then? Would he have had her forcibly removed? She knew that he had been kind and gentle when he'd tended to her after her fainting spell, but aside from that, she still had no idea what he was capable of or what motivated him.

Her worry about Luca was minimal compared to her fear about Travis. She'd never gone more than a day without seeing him since he was born, and the uncertainty about his well-being now, after weeks of being away from him, was a constant burn in her stomach and mind.

Why, then, in spite of her worry about Travis, did her mind keep turning to Captain Swan, too?

And, why did her belly give a little flutter each time his face rose into her mind?

She rolled over onto her side, staring at the wall. She was terrified that he would take her up on her offer, and yet there was a part of her that was curious. No, more than curious. There was a part of her that wanted to know what it would be like. She'd often dreamed that some handsome, chivalrous man would swoop in and rescue her and Travis and Luca from their life of work and filth and hunger, and she'd always known that it was a foolish daydream. She was not stupid, or unrealistic.

While other girls her age had been batting their lashes at boys and stocking their hope chests and writing in diaries, she'd been working her fingers raw to provide food for her small family of three. She couldn't allow herself to sit around and feel sorry for herself. She'd done what she had to do, and she wouldn't trade Travis and Luca for anything. There had been no time for courting, and no one asking, anyway. There had been a few tentative attempts, over the years, by young men to strike up conversations. She'd shut them down before they could start, knowing it would be unfair to all of them to entertain the idea.

She'd long ago accepted that she might never fall in love and get married, and if she did, it would be later than usual—after Travis and Luca no longer needed her so much. A few nights, if she was being honest, she'd lain awake thinking about what it might be like. To be looked at like she was beautiful, and special. To walk at sunset, hand in hand with someone who cared about nothing more than being beside her. To be kissed. To be loved, both emotionally and physically. About the latter of which, she knew embarrassingly little.

40

Captain Swan was no knight in shining armor, so why had he managed to awaken a yearning in her that no one before him ever had? She couldn't answer that for herself, and she was annoyed that she was allowing him to take over so much of her thoughts. It was true that there was currently nothing she could do to help Travis, but there was nothing she could do about a stupid attraction to the captain of *Voyage*, either. If he accepted her offer, she might have her curiosity sated, but she certainly couldn't afford to delude herself into thinking that there would be any emotions involved. Even if he was kind, and gentle, and took care not to hurt her, it would still be nothing more than a business deal to him.

She couldn't bear having her back to the room of sleeping sailors any longer, and she rolled over, suppressing a sigh of irritation. She was the only one awake, and she wondered briefly if she would be able to sneak from the room without waking anyone. She knew she couldn't go see Luca; he was probably asleep, and even if he wasn't, there was no sense in bothering him with her own sleeplessness. Besides, Ivan would probably catch her, one way or another, and report directly to Captain Swan. That certainly wouldn't help her cause, or Luca's.

The thought of stretching her legs was too tempting to dismiss, however, and she lay there for long moments, undecided, listening to the sounds of slumber. If she got up, and drew someone's attention, she could always claim to be heading to use the chamber pot—an embarrassing but plausible lie.

Before her brain had fully decided, her feet were on the wood, and she pushed herself up, wincing at the creak of her bed. No one spoke, or even shifted. It was dark. The only light in the room was the faint glow of the lantern in the corridor, but she'd had a long time for her eyes to adjust while she lay out of sleep's reach, and she could make out Ivan's bulk in his bunk. She was pretty sure his back was to her, and she crept toward the door, telling herself that she wasn't doing anything wrong, anyway. If she was supposed to be a prisoner, she should be locked in the dungeon with Luca. If she was expected to work alongside the men, she should be allowed a little nighttime pacing, right?

She knew she was kidding herself and didn't care. She was up, and she wasn't going to turn back, now. What was the worst they could do to her?

That was a dangerous question, and she shoved it away before her overactive mind could think of a dozen horrible answers. She walked quietly from the room, her bare feet silent on the wooden floor. She was wearing the baggy clothes she'd been given. She'd learned that most of the men slept in the same clothes they wore during the day. She imagined that, were it not for her unexpected presence in their midst, many, if not all of them, would sleep in their underwear, instead. She was grateful for their deference.

Her dress, washed but still stained and thin, was the only article of clothing she owned that she wasn't wearing. Once dry, she'd put her undergarments on under her borrowed clothes. After a few days of working, cooking and cleaning, she would have to wash them again.

She had every intention of simply pacing for a while, expending some energy in the hallway, and she scarcely realized that she'd changed her plan until her hand was on the door at the top of the stairs. She hesitated there, wondering how serious a transgression it might be considered to wander on deck in the middle of the night. There was a night crew, a few men watching the black ocean and adjusting the rigging as the winds required. She didn't really know any of them, and she had no idea how they would react to seeing her appear from below. Would they run to the captain's cabin to alert him to her presence?

She squared her shoulders. It wasn't as though she meant to sabotage the ship, or disrupt anyone's work. All she wanted was a glimpse of the moon and some fresh air. Was that really so much to ask for? She let out a breath and opened the door, stepping out onto the night-cooled planks.

The moon was huge in the sky, and bright, shimmering on the dark, lapping water. Lanterns kept the deck fairly well-lit, but the men, wherever they were, were silent. Even the rush of wind seemed hushed, and Ella turned her face into that cool breeze and tipped her head back to look at the stars. It was strange to think that they were the same stars she and her brother had gazed upon with their father, when Travis was barely more than a baby and Ella had not yet learned just how cruel life could be.

She felt the sting of tears in her eyes and couldn't fool herself into believing it was simply the sting of salty wind. Sometimes, her parents' faces seemed so large and close that she ached to reach out and touch their cheeks. Other times, they were impossibly distant, and she feared they would disappear from her memory. Travis looked like their father, although he had their mother's green eyes.

Ella didn't think she looked like either of her parents. If they suddenly appeared, alive and well, would they know her? Would they recognize her gaunt features as those of the laughing little girl they'd known?

She took a deep breath, taking comfort from the familiar smell of brine and night air. She'd never been out to sea, but she'd grown up near the ocean. She walked over to the railing, beneath the soft flapping of sails, and stared out at the dark, shimmery water. A person lost in that expanse would surely be lost forever. She braced her hands on the cool rail and leaned forward to look down at the rush of water as the ship sliced its way through the night. She closed her eyes, letting the wind brush her hair across her face and the motion of the waves soothe her.

The ship seemed deserted, and she could almost believe that she was all alone, transported to a ghost ship in some dark and mysterious sea, destined to sail forever in unending night and solitude. Rather than disturbing, the idea was strangely comforting, and relaxing.

"Trouble sleeping?"

His voice was low, almost a part of the wind, and she turned, startled. She felt absurdly guilty, as though she'd been caught doing something illicit, and a part of her prepared to go on defense. As soon as she caught sight of him, all words deserted her. The moonlight shone on his hair as it blew across his forehead. He was leaning against a post, his arms and ankles crossed, his expression unreadable in the shadows. When their eyes met, she felt a jolt of awareness that tightened her lower belly and made her heart stumble in her chest. She swallowed, resisting the urge to race for the stairs before she could make a complete fool of herself.

She tried to remember what his question was, and couldn't. An apology rose to her lips—an apology for venturing from bed and trespassing onto the deck without permission—but her pride kept it unspoken. "I just..." She gestured toward the water, feeling like an idiot. She was glad he couldn't see her reddening face. Had she ever been in his presence without blushing?

He straightened and walked over to stand beside her, looking out over the water. "It's late," he said.

"Don't worry. I'll be ready to work," she said, and it sounded accusatory and rude even to her own ears.

"Don't misunderstand me," he answered, quietly, without looking at her. "I was only making an observation."

"Why aren't you sleeping?" she asked. She managed to make it sound slightly less accusatory.

"I rarely sleep," he answered, and his somber honesty surprised her and made her feel even more guilty for her rudeness.

She turned to survey the water, feeling nervous and awkward in her awareness of his nearness. If she took half a step to her right, they would be almost hip to hip. She swallowed. Her mouth was dry. She tried to think of something else to say, something friendlier.

"How long have you had this ship?" she heard herself ask.

He cleared his throat. "Eleven years," he answered.

In spite of the fact that Timón had said he'd worked for Captain Swan for ten years, she was surprised. "You must have been young...?"

"A bit younger than you are now," he murmured. He took a deep breath and let it out slowly. "Why can't you sleep?"

She chewed on her lip as she considered how she could possibly answer that question. She saw him, from the corner of her eye, turn his head to regard her in the moonlight. "When you were a little boy, is this where you saw yourself?" she finally asked, thinking of all the dreams she'd had as a small child. In the middle of the ocean, under a bright moon and sparkling stars, beside a handsome man, bound for exotic locations...It sounded romantic, and if not for the cruel reality of why she was on the ship, it might have come from one of the those young fantasies.

"More or less," he said, and something in his tone made her turn her head to look at him. When their eyes caught, so did her breath. "You?"

"Me?" she answered, confused and flustered.

"What did you dream of as a girl?"

"Before my parents died—" She stopped, frowning.

"Please, continue," he said, quietly.

Maybe it was the moonlight, and the cool brush of wind, and the murmur of water, or maybe it was the softness of his voice, or her powerful and unexpected attraction to him...Or, maybe it was just because he said 'please.' Whatever the reason, she found herself answering honestly. "Before my parents died," she repeated, "I suppose I dreamed of things like this." She looked out at the water. "Traveling, adventure, romance..." She cleared her throat, suddenly embarrassed. She fought the urge to explain what she meant, waiting instead to see how he would react.

After a few moments of silence, he asked, "What did you dream of after your parents...died?"

"Hope," she said, without thinking. She pressed her lips together.

"And now?"

"Rest," she said, looking down at the water.

"Hope, and rest," he said, quietly, and she looked sideways at him. He was staring out at the ocean, again. "Are you hoping to...start over?"

"Start over," she repeated, sighing.

"In Bohannon?"

"I haven't thought that far ahead," she admitted.

"You do know what type of place Bohannon is?"

"I've heard."

"There are good people and good opportunities, but there are also dangers. More than in most places, because Bohannon's population is always changing."

"Perhaps not so different than Baytown," she suggested.

"They are cut from the same cloth," he allowed. "You expect that Luca will protect you?"

She scowled. "I don't expect anyone to protect me," she said.

"No, I suppose not," he murmured after a moment. He turned toward her, and her heart stuttered again. "You should sleep."

"Is that an order?" she asked, before she could stop herself. She was still bristling from his question about Luca, and warning about Bohannon. The truth was, his words had made her realize that she had no idea what would happen after (*if*) she got Travis back. She'd been actively avoiding that topic in her own mind, afraid that examining the idea too closely would drown her in panic. They would never be able to afford transportation back to Baytown, even if she somehow managed to find work in Bohannon. In reality, they had nothing to return to Baytown for, but the thought of starting over, in a strange country, with no money and nowhere to live, was terrifying.

He regarded her for a few heartbeats. Suddenly, he grinned, his teeth a white flash in the moonlight, and her belly contracted in response. "Do I strike you as particularly foolish?" he asked, the amusement in his voice evident.

"I—What?"

He leaned toward her, and she thought he was going to kiss her. She was incapable of sorting out how she felt about that. He held her gaze and stopped, his mouth several inches from hers, to say, "I would assume that commanding you to sleep would result in you staying awake for a week simply to spite me."

She licked her lips nervously, and his eyes slid to her mouth. She again held her breath, waiting to see if he would lower his head the rest of the way. A part of her wanted to take matters into her own hands and kiss him. She felt a thrill of expectation at the thought, as well as a rush of fear. The idea was bold, but she was not. She was terrified that he would shove her away in disgust, or ridicule her for childish fantasies. So she waited instead, fidgeting nervously.

Captain Swan let out a slow breath, indistinguishable from the wind against her face. "It's a...request," he finally said. He pulled back, and the wind seemed to swirl in his sudden absence. "Goodnight, Ella," he said, and then he was gone, striding away from her, leaving her to hug her arms around herself and glance around for witnesses to her embarrassment. She didn't see anyone, and she hurried toward the stairs.

* * *

She awoke with the rising of the crewmen, after a few hours of sleep, and sighed. She pushed herself up, ignoring the looks the men shot her as they yawned and scrubbed their hands over their faces and filed out of the room. She ran her fingers through the tangles of her hair and sighed again. She didn't have time to worry about her appearance, and didn't really expect anyone to care. She should've been up earlier, to help Timón prepare breakfast, and she was annoyed that no one had come to wake her.

She met Ivan's eyes across the room and frowned. He lifted his eyebrows and left the room without comment.

Ella got up, stretched her lower back, and sighed again. She made her way toward the exit, and the men still in the room stepped aside to let her pass. She didn't dare try to get to the chamber pot with so many sailors milling about, and she was glad that she'd gone after leaving the deck, before returning to bed. She would be good for a couple of hours, at least, and by then she would hopefully be able to grab a few moments of privacy.

She found Timón. He glanced up from the pot of oatmeal, and said, "Good morning."

An accusation rose to her tongue: *Why didn't you wake me?* With effort, she choked it off and forced herself, instead, to say, "I'm sorry I overslept."

"No worries," Timón answered. "Breakfast is the easiest meal. You're in time to help serve."

"Alright," she said. "You want me to take this out?"

"Thanks."

She reached for it, then hesitated. "Timón," she said. "If I'm late again, would you wake me?"

He frowned. "Didn't seem worth disturbing your sleep, lass."

She was strangely touched by his consideration, and knew she couldn't afford to accept any special treatment. She had much to prove, to him, to herself, to the captain...To the whole crew. "Thank you, but I need to work," she answered.

"Sure thing," he said.

After she'd served breakfast to all of the crew, she ate her own meal in the galley, standing near the dirty dishes she would soon begin washing. She would have put her own breakfast off a while longer, as she didn't have much appetite, but she knew that Ivan was waiting to take Luca his meal until after she'd finished her own.

Ella washed the dishes before Rashad returned from cleaning the chamber pots, and together they stripped the sheets off a few of the bunks, washed them, and hung them out to dry. Before she knew it, it was time to help prepare the midday meal. Halfway through, she burned her wrist and cursed, jumping, spilling most of a pot of boiling water onto the floor and splattering her bare feet and calves.

"Here, let me see," Timón said, reaching for her wrist. She pulled away, swearing again, her annoyance with herself outweighing the pain in her wrist and sting in her feet.

"It's fine," she said. "That was stupid." She grabbed for a rag to begin mopping the floor. Before she could bend down, Timón stepped in front of her.

"You need some salve. It's going to start blistering."

"It's fine," she repeated. She wasn't so sure, though. She reached for a cool, damp cloth and pressed it against her hot skin.

"Cap'll kill me," Timón said, and that got her attention. She bit her lip. She didn't want to get Timón, or anyone else, in trouble with her own stupid stubbornness. She sighed.

"Alright," she said. "What should I put on it?"

A few minutes later, she had a strip of gauze wrapped around her wrist to keep the cooling salve against her injured skin, and she was back at work preparing chili and hard biscuits. The crew came in shifts to eat, and several of them commended Timón on a superior midday meal. Timón, in turn, informed them that Ella deserved all of the credit, and she tried not to show her discomfort when they murmured awkward words of appreciation in her general direction.

After lunch, she and Rashad remade the beds they'd stripped with freshly laundered sheets, and he told her that she should take a break. She insisted that she wanted to keep working, even offering to do the next round of bedding—scheduled for the following day, according to Rashad's plans—and Rashad in turn insisted that there was nothing to be done at the moment.

She knew that she would only stew in her own irritation if her hands were left idle, so she returned to Timón. She asked what the plans for supper entailed, suggesting there might be something she could begin to prepare in advance.

"If you want, you could fetch some potatoes," he answered.

She frowned, glancing toward the box they were normally stored in. There were three left. Not nearly enough for a meal for so many men. "From where?" she asked, uncertainly.

Following her gaze, Timón said, "They're on the port deck. You can take a sack, bring a dozen or so. You can grab some carrots, too."

"Sure. Alright. On the port deck," she repeated, reaching for the burlap bag.

"You want me to show you?"

She shook her head. "No. I'll find it. I'll be right back."

A few minutes later, she was standing on the deck with her sack in her hand, feeling like a complete moron. A young man, around her own age, was walking past with a coil of rope.

Steeling herself, she said, "Excuse me. Uh—"

"Marty," he supplied, glancing around as he stopped beside her.

"Right. Marty. Um...could you tell me...where the port deck is?" she asked.

He looked puzzled. "Other side, miss," he answered.

"Oh. Right. Thanks," she said, and with a polite nod, he started away. Ella walked around the ship, without speaking to anyone else. She didn't see the captain and wondered if he was in his cabin. Did he sleep in the afternoons to make up for his long nights? She somehow doubted it. He was probably counting his gold doubloons, somewhere.

When she got to the other side of the ship, she wandered back and forth, trying to look like she wasn't completely lost and confused. She had no idea what she was looking for, and she cursed herself for refusing Timón's offer to show her to the bins. Why would they keep vegetables on the deck, anyway? Wouldn't they be safer, and drier, in the stores below with the dry goods? She felt her frustration mounting, and she knew she should ask someone else for further help. She thought of the captain's admonishment: *Pride can be a dangerous thing.*

As though her thoughts had summoned him, she heard his voice and closed her eyes, briefly, wishing she'd taken the time to freshen up and comb her hair.

"May I help you find something?" he asked.

She turned toward him, and her lips parted in surprise. It was the first time she'd seen him in anything other than all black. He was wearing black pants and a white shirt, unbuttoned at the collar, revealing a few curls of dark hair. She realized she was staring, and jerked her eyes up to his, heat immediately staining her cheeks.

"What happened to your wrist?" he asked, his eyebrows drawn together.

She looked down, startled. She'd mostly forgotten the injury. The pain was almost gone, thanks to Timón's ministrations. "Oh. Nothing. I just burned myself."

"How badly?"

She shook her head. "It's fine. Timón put some salve on it."

"He shouldn't have you doing things you aren't—"

"It was my fault," she snapped.

"—trained for," he finished, his scowl darkening.

"I'm qualified to boil water," she said, her own frown matching his. "I just wasn't paying attention."

47

"Perhaps you didn't get enough sleep," he suggested. The hint of a smile played at his lips, and she felt her anger dissolve. She gave her head a small shake, exasperated and amused at the same time. "May I help you find something?" he asked, again.

"Yeah. The goddamned potatoes and carrots," she said.

His frown disappeared, and after a moment, his look of surprise did, as well, and he laughed. A real, genuine laugh, and the sparkle in his eyes was contagious. She laughed, too, shaking her head again. "I can see where that would be a problem," he said, with a grin. He stepped past her, and she suppressed a shiver when his arm brushed against hers. "Here," he said, reaching toward a handle set into a section of deck two feet higher than the rest. As she watched, he pulled, swinging up a section of planks to reveal an expanse of earth below.

She stepped forward, stunned. "You have a garden?" she asked. "How—Is that normal?"

"Normal? Not all ships have them, if that's what you're asking."

"Not all captains care about their crew's diet, you mean," she said, her thoughts inevitably turning toward Travis.

"Hm," he answered. "Does it hurt?"

"Does what hurt?" she asked, reaching for a trowel laying at the edge of the dirt. She glanced at him, flustered—as usual—by his nearness.

"Your wrist."

"Oh. No."

"You're really not concerned about yourself at all, are you?" His words could have been accusatory, but his tone was not, and she met his eyes.

"There are more important things to worry about," she muttered, frowning.

"Hm," he said, again. Then, after a moment, "I'll get someone to help you carry the sack downstairs."

"Thank you. That's not necessary."

His amusement seemed to be long gone, and his scowl returned. "I insist," he said.

"I can carry a dozen potatoes, for crying out loud," she shot back.

His jaw clenched, and she was sure he was going to push the issue. Instead, he answered, "Fine. Have it your way."

It wasn't until after he'd walked away that she realized she'd thrown his consideration back in his face. No wonder he was angry. She wondered, not for the first time, if there was something fundamentally wrong with her. She had such difficulty relating to people—accepting their kindness, in particular. Surely that wasn't normal. Wouldn't any other woman have been grateful for his offer of assistance, instead of starting an argument?

She shoved the trowel into the dirt, angrily, digging up several potatoes at once.

* * *

Captain Swan was right. Pride was a dangerous thing, a thing that had often gotten her into trouble. She knew that she should apologize and wondered why it was so hard for her tongue to form the words. She looked at herself in the mirror that the crewmen used to shave—at least, the handful of them who actually *did* shave. She combed her hair out with her fingers, smoothing it down. There was nothing else she could do to improve her appearance. The dark circles around her eyes weren't going anywhere, and neither were the sunken cheeks, at least not without a couple of weeks of regular meals. Maybe more than a couple of weeks, she thought, examining herself critically.

She'd asked Timón who delivered the captain's meals, and he'd told her that he usually did it himself. The rest of the time, it was Ivan. She'd considered asking if she could deliver supper to the cabin, thinking it would be a good way to apologize in person. She'd rejected the idea, however. She'd feel like she was imposing, forcing her presence onto him, and he might just slam the door in her face or order her back to the galley, anyway.

The men had all been fed. She'd eaten, too. Now, it was time to take Luca his meal, and she and Ivan ventured down the stairs together, into the dimness. Luca smiled when he saw her, and that made her day a little bit better. They talked for a few minutes, and then she had to leave him again.

That night, she lay awake until a few hours before dawn, again. A part of her longed to crawl from her bunk, and climb the stairs to the moonlit deck, once more. She thought that, just maybe, it would be possible to reclaim some of the honest camaraderie they'd so briefly shared. In the daytime, it seemed harder. She always felt defensive, which made her go on offense.

She didn't leave her bed that night. She woke early, when Timón rose, and joined him in the galley to prepare breakfast. She was tired and cranky, but threw herself into another hard day's work with gusto. Aside from hanging the next round of sheets, and later hauling them down, she didn't venture onto the deck, and during her ministrations with the laundry, she didn't see the captain.

In fact, she didn't see him for three days or long, mostly-sleepless nights.

She wasn't sure which she missed the most—the fresh air, the smell of the ocean, the sun, the moon...or the nervous flutter in her stomach she felt whenever she was near Captain Swan. She wondered if he'd noticed her absence at all, or if he was glad to have a break from her awkward rudeness. Perhaps he'd been intentionally avoiding her.

Then, as she was serving supper on the fourth night, Ivan informed her that the captain wanted to see her in his cabin. She immediately felt a shiver of unease as she tried to imagine what she might have done to draw his scorn; at the same time, she felt a thrill of anticipation, and was disgusted with herself for it. Ivan told her that she was to take the captain his meal, and so she prepared a tray and made her way carefully up the dimly-lit stairs. She almost dropped it, fumbling to open the door at the top, and managed to make her way onto the deck without mishap.

Several men were about, and a couple of them smiled—encouragingly, she thought—at her as she walked the deck toward the captain's quarters. With each step, her apprehension mounted. She was pretty sure she'd been doing a good job. She'd done everything Timón, Rashad, and Ivan had told her to do, in spite of her natural tendency to buck authority. She wasn't sleeping much, but she was eating three meals a day, and her cheeks were already filling out a little. The bruises around her eyes were more related to her insomnia than her lack of nutrition, now, and she could do nothing about them.

She'd also begun her menstruation, something she'd been dreading. When she'd planned on being a stowaway, in the dark and lonely recesses of the ship, she'd known her cycle would cause problems. It was one of the things she'd most worried about, because she was to have no access to water aside from what Luca could bring her, and no way to launder her clothes or cloths, and no way to clean herself. Living in the bunks was, in some regards, a great relief. In other ways, it was even more stressful, because her lack of privacy— normally bearable—was much more difficult to deal with.

There was the pain, as well. Ella had always suffered severe menstrual cramps for up to three days, beginning the day before the actual start of flow. It was something she'd always had to deal with, and she did her best to keep herself busy when all she wanted to do was drink half a bottle of liquor, curl up in bed, and sleep for two days until the worst was over. She had never had that option, and never less so than now.

She knocked on the cabin door, trying to calm her jittery nerves. She had a dull headache, another symptom of her cycle that should be gone in a day or so. She knew she looked paler even than usual, because Timón and Rashad had both commented on the fact. There was nothing she could do about that, either.

The door opened, and the captain—gorgeous enough to steal her breath— reached for the tray. He pulled it from her suddenly-loose fingers and stepped aside, gesturing for her to enter. Her legs felt shaky, and she concentrated on walking into the room without stumbling.

"You look ill," he said, without preamble. He closed the door and moved to set the tray on the edge of his desk.

"Oh, flattery," she heard herself quip, and she groaned inwardly. *Let's not start already*, she thought. *Can't you just behave like a lady for once in your life?*

"Are you still suffering seasickness?" he asked, choosing to ignore her sarcasm.

She bit her lip and shook her head. "I'm fine," she said. "Uh, Ivan said you wanted to see me?"

He frowned. "Still not sleeping?" he asked. She noted that he looked more tired than usual, as well, and refrained from pointing it out. Instead, she shrugged, not quite trusting herself to speak civilly. "You are eating," he said, and that wasn't a question. Why would it be? He would have been told, likely by several different men, if she weren't.

She made a sound of exasperation. Her headache, exhaustion, and cramps were not helping her patience. "Is this what you wanted to see me about? To tell me I look tired and sick and underfed?" she asked, and she could only assume that it was the hormones in her body that were making her feel overly emotional.

He regarded her from beneath dark, knitted brows for several moments. "I didn't intend to hurt your feelings," he said, and he sounded genuinely perplexed. "Please, sit down."

She sat carefully in the wooden chair facing his desk, and after a moment's hesitation, he took his seat behind the desk.

"Ivan tells me you should be allowed to tend to Luca on your own."

It took a moment for the words to sink in, and they came as a pleasant surprise. She would, of course, prefer to have Luca released, but having a few minutes of privacy each day would be the next best thing. Instead of simply thanking the captain, as her tired brain knew she should, she heard herself ask, "Do you take Ivan's word for everything?"

"I trust him more than anyone," he answered.

"Oh," she said, rubbing her eye with the heel of her hand. She sighed. "I'm sorry." *There. You said it.*

"No, *I'm* sorry," he countered, and she was surprised again. "I've been...out of sorts. And negligent."

"Negligent?" she repeated, cautiously.

"It's been brought to my attention that you're working yourself exceptionally hard."

She frowned. "I thought I was supposed to be working. If I'm doing something wrong—"

"As much as I appreciate Timón, your presence has vastly improved the food. Rashad complains you leave nothing for him to do. And Ivan says that you have not balked at a single task."

Still frowning, she asked, "So what's the problem?"

"The problem is the welt that's still on your wrist after three days, the cuts and blisters on your hands, the circles around your eyes, the fact that you're as white as a ghost and haven't had more than five minutes of fresh air a day."

So, he had noticed her absence from the deck. In spite of everything, she felt a rush of pleasure at the thought. "I don't understand what you want from me," she said, spreading her hands.

"Is it your time of the month?"

She stared at him, completely shocked. "I—That's—none of—" She broke off, her face aflame with embarrassment and indignation.

"I've seen women laid out in bed for days during their cycle," he said, and was it her imagination, or were there small blossoms of color in his cheeks, as well?

"I'm not in bed," she snapped, crossing her arms over her stomach. "I've worked through it, just like always, so you have no reason to worry."

He reached into a desk drawer and brought out a small glass bottle. "I want you to drink a bit of this."

51

"What? Why? What is it?"

"It will help with the pain. And, help you sleep."

"I don't need help with either," she said, placing her hands on the desk. "May I leave?"

"No," he snapped, and she clenched her jaw. He let out a breath. "Ella," he said, clearly striving for a tone of patience, "It will make you feel better. Would you just do something without fighting, for once?"

She didn't want to admit to herself how tempting it was. To be free of the clenching pain in her belly, of the dull thudding in her head, to be able to sleep through the night...She shook her head. She couldn't give in to that weakness, because it would make the pain that much harder to bear the next time.

"I can force you," he said, quietly.

She swallowed nervously, and raised her chin a bit to cover. "Then pour it down my throat. But don't expect it to be easy."

He glared at her for a moment. Then, to her surprise, he laughed. Shaking his head, he ran a hand over his face. "I'll make a deal with you," he said. "If you eat this bowl—"

"That's yours," she objected. Of course, he must know that she hadn't yet had her own.

He held up a hand. "If you eat it, and drink some of this, I will consider letting Luca out."

She was afraid to get her hopes up. "Consider?" she asked, suspiciously.

"I'll speak to him. I need to make sure he's willing to return to work, and that he poses no threat to anyone in my crew."

"Luca isn't a threat," she said.

"Then there shouldn't be a problem," he answered, raising his eyebrows.

She hesitated. "How do I know I can trust you?" she asked.

His humor, as quickly as it had come, was gone. "First of all, I'm a man of my word," he said, and she felt a shiver at the cold steel in his voice. "Secondly, I have nothing to gain. So, make up your mind. I have things to do."

You hurt his feelings, she thought, sure that it was true even though she found it difficult to believe her opinion would matter to him. She realized that he was right: If he was telling the truth about the vial containing something that would make her feel better, then he was trying to help her—And, in order to help her, he was willing to give her something that she desperately wanted. It didn't make sense. Short of an insidious plan to force himself on her while she was incapacitated, he *would* gain nothing, and she didn't understand why he would strike such a bargain.

There had to be an ulterior motive, something she hadn't caught on to.

If it was worth a shot at getting Luca out, though, didn't she have to do it?

"Alright," she heard herself agree. "I'll go take Luca his supper, and—"

"Ivan will do it."

"Luca will be upset if I don't show up."

Frowning: "He's an adult. He'll deal with the disappointment."

"That's not what I meant," she shot back.

"You'll explain tomorrow. Or don't. Doesn't matter to me."

"Doesn't it? You seem to like controlling things," she said, glaring at him.

"It's within my rights to kill him, you know. Both of you, actually. The fact that I've refrained, in spite of provocation, should say something about my control. Make a decision."

For a moment, she was unable to speak. She wanted to argue, and she didn't even know why. Who was she hurting, except herself, and Luca? Certainly not the captain. She licked her lips, wrestling with her own stupid pride. After a moment of silence, she cleared her throat and, feeling as though she'd lost a war she didn't even understand why she was fighting, said, "Alright. You win."

"Have I?" he muttered.

Chapter Four

They were fed twice a day, stale and moldy bread and runny, fishy soup. They had some light, a few flickering lanterns, although it seemed likely that they would fall permanently dark before land was reached. They had no fresh air or sunlight, and the only exercise they got was pacing back and forth in the dimness, and shuffling to the filthy chamber pots and back. They were kept in two separate rooms, each group only vaguely aware of who was in the other.

One room was for the women and children, and the other for the men.

Travis was the oldest male in the room designated for women and children. He and Kyra were the only teenagers in the room. Kyra was sixteen, Travis was seventeen, and they were strangely suspended in an age group of their own. There were two older women—Tabitha, who was in her thirties, and Portia, who was close to sixty. There were seven children younger than Travis and Kyra, the oldest of whom was a boy named Garrett who was twelve. Of those seven children, only one was a girl, an eight-year-old named Angel.

Most of the children were white, with the exception of Angel and her twin brother, Anthony. Tabitha and Portia were both dark-skinned, Portia darker than Tabitha, and from the few glimpses Travis had gotten, it seemed that the men in the other room covered a wide range of skin colors. He had estimated that there was somewhere between a dozen and a score of men, but it was difficult to say for certain.

Travis was smelly, dirty, hungry, and scared. They'd been on the ship for weeks, it was impossible to say how many, and he didn't know if they'd reached the halfway mark in the journey or not. He didn't think so. It seemed as though the trip would never end. Sometimes he thought that would be for the best—after all, he had no idea what would happen when they reached land, but knew that his life was not likely to be pleasant. Other times, when the monotonous misery was threatening to crush him, he thought that anything would be an improvement over the ship.

Travis wanted to see his sister. He missed her terribly, and when he was struggling not to cry himself to sleep each night, it was her face that he pictured to help himself through. He wanted to tell her how much he loved her, but he also wanted to tell her that he was sorry. He'd been stupid, and by getting himself captured, he'd left her and Luca alone. His sister had always worked herself to exhaustion to keep him fed and clothed and sheltered, and there was a part of him that couldn't help thinking she'd be better off without him. She and Luca would have only each other to worry about, and Luca had always been more of a help, anyway. It didn't really matter that Ella had refused to let Travis work while he was in school—It didn't matter that he'd begged her to let him quit school to start working, to ease the load. It didn't even matter that quitting school would have been a sacrifice for him, because he loved school more than almost anything, or that it was a sacrifice he would have willingly made to lighten the dark circles around his sister's eyes.

None of that mattered, because in the end he'd failed her—and himself—by getting his stupid ass locked in the belly of a slave ship.

They were brought a tray of bitter bread and a pot of soup each morning and evening. They were given spoons but no bowls, and they were left to share the pot as they saw fit. Travis had had a lot of time to ponder this method. He wondered why their keepers were not more concerned with making sure the children had enough to eat, and had decided that it was, perhaps, a way to weed the weak from the survivors.

The children were at the mercy of Travis and the three women.

They made sure that the children ate in order, from the youngest first. Kyra had actually suggested it, the first day, when they'd all been hungry and terrified and looking for some way to figure out how to deal with the lot they'd been given. The system had served them well for their time on the ship, and the children all sat, patiently, clutching their spoons and waiting for their turns. They ate in groups, Robbie and the twins in the first group and the other four boys in the second, and although the children tried to limit themselves, they were just children who didn't understand rations and didn't have willpower to ignore their hunger when they had food dripping from their spoons.

There had been several times when there was no more than a mouthful left for Tabitha and Portia, each. On those occasions, Travis got no more than a spoonful himself, because taking more would leave them with nothing. He had tried repeatedly to refuse his share, and the women had sworn that they wouldn't touch the remaining soup if he didn't eat first. They reminded him of his sister, which made him feel guilty and frustrated and homesick. The two women were wasting away before his eyes, and he wondered if they would make it off the ship alive.

If they died, would the guards even notice? Would they care? Would they leave the bodies to rot with Travis and Kyra and the kids? He tried not to think such horrible things and found himself unable to keep his mind from imagining the worst. He wondered how the men were faring, and he also wondered—not for the first time—why he'd been placed with the children rather than the men. Yes, he was technically a child at the age of seventeen, but it was close enough that he supposed it could have been called either way. He figured his time as a prisoner would have been very different if he'd been put in the other room.

The men were in chains, fastened to the walls and floor, while the women and children—and Travis—were not. During a brief glimpse into the other room, Travis had seen one of the guards hit a prisoner in the head with the handle of a sword, and the next time the door was opened, that prisoner was nowhere in sight. Was he dead? Travis didn't know.

None of the children or women had been touched, so far. They'd been left alone, fed and watered twice a day like livestock, their chamber pots emptied once a day. Even though they were all scared and miserable, they had become almost complacent in their state of neglect. For weeks, none of them had been harmed. None of them had been separated from the rest.

Then everything changed.

No one ever came to check on them during the day. They only saw guards in the morning and evening. When the door opened in what had to be either the middle of the day or the middle of the night—they were fed the same disgusting food for both meals, and it had become impossible to tell one from the other—they all knew, instantly, that something bad was coming. Even the youngest children seemed to realize it, and they huddled together in the shadowy corner.

"You," the man in the doorway said, pointing at Tabitha. "Come here."

Travis looked at her. And he knew. He knew that she'd been expecting it, and the look on Portia's face said that she had, as well. The older woman met his eyes and gave her head the tiniest shake, telling him not to speak up. He saw Tabitha, her face composed as she tried desperately to appear brave for the sake of the children, getting slowly to her feet. He could feel the frustration and helplessness boiling up within him, could feel the anger building as he looked at the face of the guard—a man who wouldn't blink if he walked into the room to find all of the children dead at his feet.

Kyra might be safe. If they left her unspoiled, and cleaned her up, she would likely fetch them a hefty price. A young, pretty virgin, delivered up to some ugly, eager, cruel rich man, and every hope and dream she'd ever entertained would be smashed at her feet. Until then, she might be safe. Or, maybe not. Perhaps profit was not enough to sway some of these men.

Tabitha and Portia were a different matter entirely. There was no reason to leave them unmolested, as they were to be sold as workers and were almost certainly not virgins, anymore. The crew had been at sea for a few weeks, and they'd become antsy. They were ready for some fun.

Travis pushed himself to his feet, and he saw the alarm on the faces of the three women. Portia shook her head, and Kyra reached for his arm. He stepped aside, keeping his eyes on the guard. People had always sacrificed for him, his whole life. Ella, more than anyone else. Tabitha and Portia had insisted he eat before them, as Ella had always done, and he'd let them talk him into it. In spite of his own guilt, he'd always given in.

He was done giving in. Someone had always been there to protect him. Yes, he'd gotten snatched by the docks, but even then, Tabitha and Portia had come into his life, determined to look after him and everyone else. And who would protect them? If not him, then who? Nobody.

"Sit down, boy," the guard said, pointing at him while motioning for Tabitha with the other hand.

"No," Travis said. He clenched his hands to keep them from shaking. "You're not taking her."

"Travis, don't," Tabitha said, holding up a hand. Her voice was trembling; she was trying so hard to be brave. Her eyes were wide and bright in her dark face. "It's alright, really."

She was moving forward, and Travis stepped in front of her, moving before he could think about it. The guard pulled a narrow club from his belt, and said,

"You'd better sit the fuck down."

"Travis," Tabitha said, pulling on his arm. To the guard: "Please, don't hurt him, I'm coming."

Travis shook off her hand. He opened his mouth to speak, but the guard brought his club down so quickly that Travis had only begun to raise his arm in defense when it struck the side of his head. Pain exploded in his skull, and he staggered into Tabitha. She tried to hold him up, yelling his name, but he felt the wooden floor slam into his side. The world was a white-hot blur, filled with the sounds of people calling his name.

It was Angel's voice that he heard the most clearly, and he knew that she and many of the other children were crying. He blinked, pulling in a slow breath. He could see the guard, a smirk on his face, pulling Tabitha by the arm. For Travis, his whole life turned on that single moment, and he knew that if he stayed on the floor and let her leave, his life would continue to be that of a coward, willing to let others fight his battles for him. He would deserve the chains of slavery he would be sold into. Ella would be better off never knowing how her sacrifices for him had been in vain. He would be a disappointment to her, the one thing he'd always feared more than anything else.

He planted his palms on the floor and pushed himself up. The man wasn't even looking at him, anymore. Why would he? He'd pegged Travis as a scared boy from the beginning, and a scared boy was not going to attack the man who'd nearly brained him seconds before. It was the sudden and unnatural silence in the room that drew the guard's attention, but by then it was too late. He had already pushed Tabitha through the doorway, into the room with the chained prisoners, and was reaching for the doorknob when he started to turn, alarmed by the hush.

His eyes widened and his hand started for his belt—reaching for the sword, this time, not the club—but Travis's shoulder was already plowing into his gut. The pain in Travis's head was making it difficult for him to see clearly, and as he drove the guard backward, and they both crashed to the floor, he had just enough presence of mind to twist his body into a roll to keep from hitting his head on the planks. That twist probably saved his life, because the guard was fast. As Travis rolled onto his knees, the sword's blade whizzed past his head, and Travis didn't even have time to wonder how the other man had drawn so quickly. As the blade stuck—and, oh, it must be sharp—into the floor, Travis got his bare feet planted and shoved off.

The guard was tugging on his sword, cursing, and he threw up an elbow, catching Travis in the chin. Travis reeled sideways but kept his forward momentum, again crashing into the guard and knocking him to the floor. The sword came out of the floor with a small screech, lost in the pounding of blood in Travis's head. Travis landed on top of the other man and slammed his fist into the guard's face before he could think about a course of action. The shock ran up his arm, and blood sprayed from the man's mouth. Travis's stomach churned, and he hesitated—He'd never punched anyone in the face in his life.

"Kid!" someone shouted, and he flinched, catching movement from the corner of his eye as the guard brought the handle of his sword down toward Travis's head. Travis had enough time to deflect the blow, and he wrapped a hand around the guard's wrist, slamming his knuckles down against the floor. The guard used Travis's shift in weight against him, and threw him to the side.

Travis rolled again, this time coming up with the sword in his hands. He'd never wielded a sword in his life, and it felt heavy and foreign and comforting in his hands. As he stood, breathing heavily and bleeding, staring at the guard—also breathing heavily and bleeding—Travis finally became aware of the prisoners chained all around the perimeter of the room. It was one of them who'd called out a warning, although he didn't know which.

"You're dead, you little fuck," the guard said, probing his bloody lip with his tongue. He was holding his club loosely, although there was nothing relaxed about his posture.

Tabitha and Kyra were in the doorway between the two rooms. There were no other guards in sight. How long could that last, though? The moment this asshole in front of Travis raised a shout, more would surely come down at a run.

There was, of course, no way to undo what had been done. For Travis, there was no going back. He would be killed, sooner or later, for his defiance. He meant to take as many of them with him as he could. He raised the sword, testing its weight in his hand. The guard grinned, showing his bloody teeth. "I'm going to enjoy killing you," he said, and Travis absolutely believed him.

At the sound of boots at the top of the stairs, the man's grin widened, and Travis's stomach clenched in fear. He knew he was running out of time, and his hesitation was going to cost him his life before he could even begin to really fight. What was wrong with him? It wasn't like killing just any man on the street. This man was a monster, willing to steal children and rape women. What would Travis do if, instead of Tabitha, it were Ella that the man had come for?

Travis gritted his teeth and stepped forward.

"Kid. Here."

As the prisoner spoke, the guard started to turn his head, startled. He caught himself in time, quickly turning his attention back to Travis, but that was alright. In a moment of perfect clarity, sharp comprehension sliced through the pain in his head, and Travis saw the plan unfold in a heartbeat. He moved without another second of hesitation. He swung the sword from his right, with no intention of hitting the guard.

The guard didn't know that, and he threw his club up and dodged to Travis's left. Travis pulled up short and grabbed the club, yanking the startled and confused guard further off-balance. As the man stumbled, Travis smashed the handle of the sword into the guard's face and kicked his feet out from under him, letting go of the club.

"Go, kid," someone said. Travis had just enough time to see the guard tumble to the floor, and one of the prisoner's legs wrap around his neck, and then Travis was in the other room, shoving the door shut. Tabitha and Kyra had already moved out of his way, but Travis motioned them back. He knew what was going to happen, and he knew that he'd already made his choice. Letting the prisoner take the blame for what Travis had done was not something that Travis wanted to do, and yet he knew—as that prisoner did—that it was far more important to protect the women and children.

"Sit down," Travis said, keeping his voice low. The other guard must be almost to the bottom of the stairs. "Hurry." Kyra ran into the corner, and sat down with Anthony and two other boys. Tabitha lowered herself beside Angel as Travis ran across the room and shoved the sword under a blanket. He dropped on top of the blanket and motioned for Garrett to join him. Garrett, the second-oldest boy at twelve, scrambled over to sit beside him.

The other room was suddenly filled with shouts and the rattle of chains, and Travis could see the scene playing out as clearly as if the door were still open. He closed his eyes, but that did nothing to rid him of the image. The pounding of boots down the stairs signaled the arrival of more men—three, Travis thought, although it was difficult to tell for sure. In a few moments, the door opened, and two men appeared in the space. Both had their swords drawn. Their gazes slid across the huddled children, Travis, the women...

Travis hoped that the blood on the side of his head was masked by his dark hair and the shadows of the room. He kept his features as blank as possible.

"What's going on?" Kyra asked. Travis was impressed. While the fear in her voice was real, she'd managed the perfect combination of innocence and uncertainty.

"Someone come in here?" one of the guards asked, scowling.

"In here?" Portia asked, frowning in apparent confusion.

"It ain't feedin' time," Garrett said, momentarily drawing the gazes of the guards. Then their eyes slid back to Tabitha, and Travis tensed. In the other room, he could see the prisoner being beaten, and Travis wanted to scream and cry and throw up at the same time. His fists were clenched by his sides, and he waited to see what the guards' next move would be. Did they care more about playing with Tabitha than they did about their friend in the other room with a broken neck?

"Where's his sword?" someone—one of the guards—asked. The moment of truth was approaching.

"He didn't have a fucking sword or you'd be dead." That was one of the prisoners, although not the one that had killed the guard. Travis was pretty sure that prisoner was dead already.

There was a whoosh and a thud as a club connected with the mouthy prisoner's head, and several other men shouted and yanked on their chains, cursing the guards and calling them cowards and a colorful collection of other insults. "Search them all," one of the guards said.

"He probably forgot to put it on," one of the men in the doorway said, over his shoulder, and Travis felt a sliver of hope. He knew that no reprieve would last forever, but if he could just be left alone long enough to come up with a plan, he thought he might be able to figure out a way to do more damage to the slave traders' ranks.

"He's wearing his sheath."

"Then he probably didn't notice it was empty."

"Search them all," someone repeated, and there were curses and sounds of struggle and clanks of chains as the guards—not without difficulty, by the sounds of it—searched through the foul clothing of the prisoners, checking under and around each man to make sure they weren't hiding a sword. Those prisoners did not have access to chamber pots the way the women and children did, and Travis felt a bitter satisfaction in the knowledge that the guards were likely smeared in shit by the time they'd completed their search.

Would they search in the other room, as well? Would they give up the search but try to take Tabitha again?

"It's not here."

"It's probably by his bunk."

"Get him upstairs, let Hunt know what happened."

"What about the woman?" The question was whiny, laced with disappointment, and Travis met Tabitha's eyes.

"Now? You don't think Hunt's going to be a little upset about Saurel getting his stupid ass killed? Get the body upstairs."

The door between the two rooms was pulled shut and locked, and Travis stayed frozen, listening to the sounds of the guards retreating up the stairs with their deceased Saurel. A part of him expected it to be a trick. Any moment, the door could burst open, and the men could barge in, demanding to search the blanket beneath him. He waited, until the silence on the other side of the door had stretched out for a minute.

"What do we do now?" Garrett asked him, with a slight tremor in his voice.

"That was downright *foolish*, boy," Portia said, as Travis ran a shaky hand over his face.

"She's right. You never shoulda done it," Tabitha said. "But...thank you."

Travis took a deep breath and let it out slowly, finally convinced that he had a brief respite. "They're going to be back," he said. "Maybe later, maybe in a minute. Listen to me. When that door opens, you all need to stay as far away from it as possible." He stood up on shaky legs. His head was throbbing, and he took another deep breath, trying to calm his racing heart. He walked to the door and checked to make sure it was really locked. It was.

Pressing his mouth close to the wood, he called, cautiously, "Hello?"

"They're gone, boy," one of the prisoners answered. The voice was muffled, hard to hear.

"How many people are hurt?" Travis asked.

"Ricksy's dead, but don't worry none on him. He killed that sumbitch, and that'd be a good enough reason for Ricksy to die happy."

Yeah. To die happy, having your head smashed in, Travis thought, swallowing his rising bile. "I'm sorry," he said. He wasn't even sure they would hear him.

"No time for sorry, kid," one of the other men answered. "Question is, when the time comes, you gonna be able to use that sword?"

Travis closed his eyes and leaned his forehead against the door, remembering what it had felt like to lay on the grass as a little boy, clutching his sister's hand as they stared up at the stars, with the salty breeze brushing the hair from their foreheads. He would almost certainly never see the stars again. He would almost certainly never see his sister again.

"I'll use it," he answered.

*   *   *

Captain Swan stood on the railing of his ship, staring out at the dark water, holding the taut rope angled past his head. It was the same position he'd been in when he'd first learned of Ella's presence on his ship.

The rail was curved beneath his feet, and as the ship rocked along, he looked down at the rush of water, wondering what would happen if he slipped from the edge and disappeared beneath the dark waves. Someone would probably see him. There weren't many men on deck at night, but they were vigilant and alert, and they were loyal. If they saw their captain plunge into the ocean, they would rush to drop the sails and one or more of the dinghies. They would search for him, perhaps for far longer than they should. And then, eventually it would fall on Ivan to declare his friend and captain lost, and to take over command of the ship. Most men would probably accept such a transition, and if there were any who questioned it, Captain Swan was confident that Ivan could deal with the situation.

He sighed, giving himself a mental shake. He wasn't usually prone to such melancholy musings, although his sleeplessness had gotten worse in the last year or so. That surely had something to do with his somber mood. The girl currently asleep in his bed probably contributed, as well. Captain Swan was not proud of the way he allowed her to get under his skin. He was usually in far better control of his temper.

He wanted to despise her for sneaking onto his ship, and for getting Luca to help her do it. He was angry because he still didn't know how they'd managed it, or how long it had been planned. Had Luca gotten the job solely to help Ella hide away on board? Luca had been an impulse hire on the captain's part, the day before setting sail, and that was partly what galled Swan. He'd needed someone to fill the position when one of his crew members quit without warning, but there were plenty of men—bigger, stronger, and more experienced than Luca—willing to take the job. Luca had shown up out of nowhere, with dirty hair and torn clothes and a sullen expression, asking for a job with surprising earnestness.

And Swan had seen himself in the young man's face, that was the truth. Had that all been a lie? Were his instincts really so far off?

So, yes, he wanted to hate the pair of them, and he was perhaps angriest of all with himself for his sudden sentimentality. Every time he looked into Ella's large, frightened, determined eyes, all he wanted was to protect her. He wanted to beg her to trust him, to confide in him and let him help her ward off whatever demons she was running from. He wanted to offer her a life of wealth and comfort, because he knew that she did not even dare to hope for such things.

He wanted her to look at him, not with fear or anger or distrust, but with love and understanding. He wanted her to forgive him for being an ass. She was the one who'd broken the law and the rules of his ship, and yet he wanted her forgiveness. He wondered if he was going insane.

She had no idea that she was beautiful, beneath the pale and tired and malnourished exterior, and he wanted to blame Luca for that. He had to give the kid credit, however, for trying to protect her, and for almost pulling off whatever plan they'd concocted to get across the sea. Swan was not proud of himself for keeping Luca in the dungeon for so long. It was well within his rights—Most captains would have killed the boy, in fact. Still, he had to admit to himself that Luca's imprisonment was not about his crime, anymore. How could he blame the kid for helping Ella, with anything she asked for? Swan wasn't sure he wouldn't do the same thing.

No, he'd kept Luca locked up for other reasons, reasons that he didn't want to examine too closely—not even in his pensive mood, between the bright moon and the dark sea.

Now he was forced to consider letting the young man out, because he'd given his word.

In five days, weather-permitting, they would be anchoring off the coast of Tarot, and he wasn't sure what would happen then. Would Luca and Ella decide they wanted to stay on the island, instead of continuing to Bohannon? In many ways, life would be more difficult on Tarot. In other ways, it might be safer for them. They really seemed to have no idea what kind of place they were bound for, and their naiveté would end up getting them killed in spite of their best intentions.

It would be their decision whether they stayed or not. He wouldn't force them to return to the ship. He had no intention of locking them up when they reached the mainland, or charging them with any crime, even though he knew that they were both under the impression he would.

In two days, he would be seeing Meena. He hadn't seen her in half a year, because he hadn't detoured to Tarot on his last trip. Perhaps seeing her would help him. She had always been able to relieve at least some of his tension, and if he could get some sleep, maybe he could get a better handle on his temper and traitorous mind. Meena would be happy to see him; she always was. He'd known her for a decade, and she was one of the few people who'd remained a constant in his life.

His attraction to Ella was an unwelcome surprise. She did not, and would not, wish for his advances. Besides, half of the time she looked like she was about to fall over. How could he possibly imagine kissing her when she looked like that? He couldn't see her *without* imagining what her lips would feel like beneath his, though. She was far too thin, and he wanted to force-feed her until the hollows left her cheeks. In spite of the thinness, he couldn't stop imagining the feel of her warm body pressed against his, couldn't stop imagining her smooth skin beneath his hands.

She would be horrified if she knew the things he thought of when he looked at her. She'd offered herself to him, in exchange for Luca's freedom. She seemed to believe that Swan had rejected the offer because he didn't desire her. She was wrong.

Frowning, he tried to turn his inappropriate thoughts. In Tarot, there would be willing women to greet his crew, and Meena would be there. She might be married. It had been a long time, after all. If that was the case, there would be someone else willing to enjoy his company for a spell. He tried to hold Meena's image in his mind—her dark skin, wide-set eyes, her glossy and muscular body, naked beneath him...

Her body, so unlike Ella's, had always given him pleasure. Meena's beauty had drawn his eye from the moment he'd first set foot on Tarot when he was barely older than Luca. Her skin was warm and inviting, her breasts plump, her stomach tight from years of work, her touch experienced. He hadn't been with a woman since the last time he'd visited Meena, and he didn't know why. No wonder he was antsy and out of sorts. He'd spent far too much time on his ship in the past year, and the brief times he'd gone ashore, he'd made no effort to seek out female companionship.

Seeing Meena would be a welcome, and long-overdue, diversion. His body was tightening already at the thought, and he shifted his weight. He would feel better after they reached Tarot.

He tried to ignore the fact that it was not Meena's face that kept filling his thoughts. He tried to deny to himself that it was not Meena's body that he was imagining, writhing beneath him, coated in sweat. It was a thinner, and far paler, stomach that his mind's hands were roaming. It was not Meena's voice, calling his name.

He looked down at the glimmering sea. Perhaps he should step off the rail, after all.

*   *   *

Ella opened her eyes and lay still, staring at the ceiling, trying to figure out what was wrong. It took her a moment to realize where she was, and then the pieces began falling into place. She was in Captain Swan's bed, again. A quick glance around the room assured her that he was not there. The morning sun was creeping past the edges of the drawn curtains, filling the room with a muffled, yet cheerful, light.

The pain was gone. All of it. That's what was wrong. The headache, the menstrual cramps, the muscle aches, the sore feet, everything. Gone. When was the last time she'd slept an entire night away? She couldn't remember.

When was the last time she'd opened her eyes in the morning feeling relaxed and rested and pain-free? Although she knew there'd been a time when every morning greeted her that way, it was long past, and not since her childhood had she known such an awakening.

She wasn't sure she wanted to get up, or return to the real world, but thoughts of her brother and Luca had already crept into her mind, and she swung her legs off the bed. On the desk, there was a bowl of oatmeal. She got up and stretched, wondering if the captain had been out all night. She felt a little guilty for sleeping, and so well, in his bed when he was clearly in need of a good night's sleep himself. She wondered why she should care. He was the man who'd kept Luca locked in a dungeon.

He was also the man who'd promised to let Luca go. No, he was the man who'd promised to *think about* letting Luca go. She wanted to believe that the captain would do the right thing. He'd shown kindness, repeatedly. He'd also shown anger and impulsiveness, and had proven himself to be irritable and domineering. She was still trying to figure him out. More importantly, she was still trying to figure out what he wanted from her. He told her to work, then complained that she was working too hard. He spoke of diet and food supplies, and yet he insisted that she eat more than her fair share. He blackmailed her with threats against Luca, and yet he bargained for nothing that would benefit himself.

Tucked under the bowl on the desk was a note, written in slanted, decorative script. *Ella. Please take advantage of this opportunity to freshen up. Do not unlock the door or open the curtains until it's safe for me to enter. There are clean clothes. Eat first.*

It was signed simply, *Swan*. Then, below that, *P.S. You'll find a new toothbrush beside the basin.*

Ella grinned. She'd been given one to use while back in the bunks, but this one was symbolic.

She was surprised that he hadn't signed his name with his title, and she found herself wondering what his first name was. Maybe it was the medicine he'd had her drink, or the simple fact that she was rested and pain-free, but whatever the reason, his note made her unaccountably happy. The idea of availing herself of clean water, and soap, was something she'd been afraid to hope for and too proud to ask for.

She ate her breakfast quickly, so she could get freshened up as soon as possible. The note offered privacy, but the captain, of course, would have a key to his cabin. If he chose to come in while she was in a delicate and embarrassing position, well...there was nothing she could do about that. He knew she was menstruating, so it seemed unlikely that he would try anything.

She read his note again, marveling at the fancy and even cursive, and again wondering about his name.

* * *

It was nearly an hour later when she opened the door. Captain Swan was standing a short distance away, his hands clasped behind his back, surveying the ocean. She was startled to find him so near, and she raised a nervous hand to her damp hair.

He turned at the quiet sound of the door opening, lowering his hands to his sides. His gaze quickly slid down her body before returning to her face. He looked grim. "Good morning," he said, without inflection.

"Morning," she muttered, fighting the urge to look away. "Sorry if I kept you waiting." She scarcely noticed the apology, that time. The mere sight of him had struck her almost dumb with an alarming flare of desire. She hoped he couldn't read it on her face, or in the tremble of her hands.

"Are you feeling better?" he asked, frowning slightly.

She cleared her throat. "Uh. Yes, thank you."

"You need to eat more."

She was surprised, and swallowed. "Sir?" she asked.

"You're far too thin," he muttered, his scowl deepening, and she tried not to be hurt by the observation. Her examination of herself in the mirror had told her the same thing, although it had also shown her the progress that her body had made in a relatively short time. Would it kill him to say something nice?

"I'm eating the same thing as the men," she said, struggling to keep the emotion from her face. She was confused by her own reaction. What had she expected? To walk outside and sweep him off his feet with her beauty? Of course not. Even if she could somehow become someone he found attractive, there would never be anything romantic between them. Fantasizing anything else would only lead to heartache.

"Maybe you need to eat more than us," he returned. Well, he certainly seemed cranky. More so than usual. Was it because he'd had another long, sleepless night while she'd slumbered peacefully in his bed? "Or work less," he added, quietly.

She opened her mouth, then closed it. Every word rising to her lips was angry and defensive and full of a hurt that she didn't understand and didn't want to reveal. She remained silent, because that seemed the safest course of action. Her good mood was rapidly draining away.

"We have no extra bunks," he said, and she blinked at the non sequitur. It took her a moment to follow his change of direction, and she felt her alarm begin to rise. There would be no bunk for Luca, an excuse to keep him locked up.

"Wait," she said, stepping forward. "You said—I'll sleep on the floor. I'll sleep on the deck."

"You will *not* sleep on the floor. Or on the deck," he said, sounding angry.

"Then put me in his place," she said slowly, her cheeks flaming with anger of her own. "We had a deal."

"I keep my word," he snapped. He took a deep breath, and said, in a calmer voice, "You'll sleep in my room."

She stared at him, completely stunned, as his words slowly settled over her.

She opened her mouth, and closed it again. She'd been the one to offer, hadn't she? To do anything to save Luca?

His jaw was set. He was clearly expecting an argument. "Is that going to be a problem?" he asked.

She shook her head, then licked her lips nervously. "Then you'll...let Luca out and...let him go back to work. You won't try to...have him locked up when we get to port?"

"Luca will have his freedom, and when we reach land, so will you," he answered tightly.

She crossed her arms over her chest, then dropped them to her sides. "Alright," she said. Her lips felt numb. Her mind and body were a swirl of confused feelings. The desire was there, now fueled by a thrill of anticipation. At war with those were the fear and insecurity and humiliation. She swallowed again.

"Fine," he answered. Why in God's name did he sound so cross? It was his negotiation, and he should be happy that she'd given in so easily. She fidgeted with the edge of her shirt, trying to keep her shoulders squared and—most importantly—trying to keep the fear and hurt from her eyes. He let out a slow breath through his nose. "Let's go."

"Go?" she repeated, her heart stammering. *He doesn't want you now*, she thought, reminding herself that it was her time of the month.

"Let's go see your boyfriend," he said, flashing his teeth in a smile that didn't touch his eyes.

*   *   *

Luca jumped up when he saw her at the bottom of the stairs. "El," he said. "Are you alright? Ivan said you weren't feeling well last night."

"I'm fine," she said, forcing a smile. "How are you?"

As she walked across the room, the captain stepped into sight, and she saw Luca frown in confusion. And concern. "What's going on?" he asked.

"Don't worry, Luca," Ella said, trying to reassure him.

"Your beloved Ella has convinced me to consider letting you out," Captain Swan said.

Ella glanced at the captain, unsure which part of his statement was the most disturbing.

"Consider?" Luca repeated, although when he met Ella's eyes, she knew it was the other word—*beloved*—that he was truly stuck on.

"That's right," the captain said, clasping his hands behind his back. "I have just a couple of questions for you."

Uh-oh, Ella thought with an inward groan. This was not going well at all.

"First of all. Did you ask for a job only to sneak your girlfriend onto my ship?"

"I—what?" Luca looked at Ella, and she nodded. There was no point in lying. "Alright. Yes. But I liked working for you. Sir."

"Why did you choose my ship?"

Luca and Ella looked at each other. "You were the first one heading to Bohannon, sir," Luca muttered.

"What's in Bohannon?"

"I've never been."

"Funny. Well, I'll tell you. Murderers, rapists, thieves, that's what's in Bohannon."

Ella and Luca both remained silent. Ella didn't know why the captain was acting like such an ass when they already had an agreement in place. Was he sorry he'd made the deal?

"You two will not be sharing a bunk," the captain said.

The words fell into the silence and hung there. Ella felt her face heat.

"I'll sleep on the floor," Luca finally managed.

The captain looked at Ella, and she swallowed the apprehension climbing her throat. This was a test, she realized. She hadn't seen it coming, and she cursed herself. There was no easy way out. She met Luca's eyes, and she saw the beginning of understanding creeping into his. She didn't want to hurt him, but she had to think about the long-term. Their time on *Voyage* would not be infinite.

"I'm moving into the captain's cabin," she said. Her lips felt cold in her hot face, and she somehow managed to keep her eyes from dropping to the floor. "You'll have your bunk back."

"What?" Luca asked, staring at her. "No. *Hell* no."

In spite of everything—her love for Luca, and the knowledge that he wanted to protect her, and her own apprehension—she felt a twinge of indignant anger. She had always, and would always, respect Luca's opinion, but that didn't mean he could tell her what to do.

The captain was silent, watching the scene play out, and she silently cursed him. "It's not up to you, Luca," she said.

Luca's jaw clenched. His eyes were shining with anger. "No? Who's it up to? You?"

"That's right," she said.

"Right," he sneered, glaring at the captain.

"Luca, look at me," she said, stepping up to the bars. He did, finally, grudgingly, and she said, "Whatever it takes. *Whatever it takes*, Luca."

"No," Luca shot back. "Not this," he said, gesturing toward Captain Swan.

Ella reached through the bars and grabbed Luca's shoulders. "Trust me, Luca," she said.

He shook his head, and she saw with horror that he was struggling not to cry. "Don't do this, El," he said, and his voice cracked. For a moment, she saw him again, as that little boy, afraid and alone and brokenhearted. She felt tears sting her own eyes in response to his pain.

She couldn't let herself be swayed by emotion. "Luca," she said, sharply, giving his shoulders a shake. "Enough. The deal's been made. We said whatever it takes. I meant those words. Did you?"

He stared at her, his young face full of anger and hurt and confusion. "Yes," he finally answered.

"Then you need to trust me. And you need to stop acting like a child." She saw that her words had wounded him, and she wanted to call them back. She couldn't. They needed to be said, because she couldn't let Luca's pride—or her own—keep them from Travis. She prayed that, at the end of it all, Luca would understand and forgive her. "We're going to work on this ship until it reaches Bohannon. We're going to show the entire crew that you and I, we know how to work hard. Don't we, Luca?"

"Yes," he muttered.

"The captain has been generous to offer our freedom," she added.

Luca clenched his jaw.

"I need you to be with me, Luca," she said, momentarily losing the tight hold she had on her emotions. She cleared her throat. "Are you with me?"

Luca took a deep breath and let it out slowly, making a valiant effort to get control of himself. He met Ella's eyes, and his face almost crumpled. He managed to compose himself, and took another breath. "Always," he vowed. "Whatever it takes."

Her love and gratitude swelled, and she squeezed his shoulders. "We'll get through," she whispered.

For several moments, the room was again plunged into silence. The quiet was broken by the jangle of keys, and she drew back, turning toward the captain. He didn't look at her as he stepped forward to unlock the door. His face was unreadable, and she wondered if she'd made him angrier.

As soon as the door was opened, Luca walked out and raised his arms, and Ella stepped gratefully into his embrace.

* * *

What do we do, Travis?

Kyra's question rang in his ears, long after everyone else had fallen into uneasy sleep. Travis and Kyra were sitting side by side, their knees drawn to their chests. The sword was under the blanket beside Travis. At the sound of men approaching a few hours earlier, he'd tensed, ready to grab it, but they'd brought food and water, as normal.

From the shouting and clanging raised in the other room, however, it was clear that the chained men had not been given their regular provisions. It was Travis's fault they were being deprived, and he wondered how long the prisoners would suffer thirst before ratting him out to the guards.

It didn't really matter, he supposed, because he could not just sit around while they were denied their needs.

What do we do, Travis?

Something, but what? He was going to have to make a move, and soon. Maybe the children would be given their next stew, maybe not. Maybe the men in the other room would remain silent, maybe not. Maybe the guards would continue to believe the dead guard had left his sword somewhere.

Maybe not.

Had they searched for it? Was its absence bothering them, or had it already slipped their minds? He didn't know, but he did know that his possession of the weapon was going to have to come to their attention, and likely soon. He looked at the huddled children, sleeping all around him, some of them sucking their thumbs even though they were too old to do so. Tabitha and Portia were sleeping, too. They'd lost so much weight, already. He was reminded again, unpleasantly, of his sister.

"I'm going to fight," he said, quietly. He looked at the flickering lantern and knew that they likely wouldn't get another refill. He got to his feet. His head still hurt, although the ache was dull. He walked over and turned the flame as low as he dared without extinguishing it. If he had access to matches, he would gladly put the light out completely until morning to conserve fuel. He had no way to relight it, however.

"We'll fight," she answered. She sounded terrified by the idea.

"No. Me. You need to keep the kids out of the way. I'm going to take out as many as I can, but I can't let—"

"I won't sit by and let them kill you," she interrupted.

"Kyra," he said, turning toward her. "Listen to me. This is fucked up, alright? But you guys have to make it off this damn boat. There has to be someone who will help. In Bohannon, or...There has to be someone. When you get free, I need you to somehow get a message to my sister. I don't...Just write a letter to Ella Fisher in Baytown, I have to hope it'll get to her eventually. Tell her what happened and that I said I love her."

"You can tell her yourself. We're getting out of here," she said.

In spite of himself, he smiled. She had spunk, this girl, and he found himself wishing they'd met before getting stuck together on the ship. She was from the orphanage; he knew because she'd told him, not because he'd ever seen her. Unlike most of the other kids, Travis had never been in an orphanage. He owed that to his sister—and, Luca, too, because he'd helped. Travis had someone—two people—who would miss him, who already *did* miss him. Did any of these other kids have that? Angel and Anthony had each other, but would they be split up once they reached Bohannon?

Kyra had no family, Travis knew that. She'd been in the orphanage since she was eight.

Without Ella, Travis and Luca would have been there, also. Would he and Kyra have been friends?

Even under the grime and smell, he knew she was pretty. Maybe more than pretty. Would she have noticed him at all, if they hadn't been forced into each other's company? Some of the girls in school thought he was cute, he could tell by the way they giggled and whispered behind their hands whenever he said hello to them. They'd always been intimidating, traveling in groups. He'd never had the courage to try singling one away from the pack to ask her out, and wouldn't have been able to take her anywhere, anyway.

69

He thought it might have been different with Kyra, though. Maybe it was just because she'd grown up in an orphanage, and knew what it was like to have little to call her own, but he knew instinctively that she would not care whether he could pay for a fancy dinner or buy her jewelry. He could imagine them walking along the beach at sunset, hand in hand, and he knew it would be easy and relaxed. What would Luca say if he knew that Travis had suddenly become such a romantic?

Travis smiled, but it was filled with sadness. He wished more than anything that he could tell Luca about Kyra, and introduce her to Ella. He knew he would never get that chance, and he struggled to wrap his head around the fact. He couldn't get bogged down by regrets, because he'd made his choice. He couldn't, and wouldn't, back away from it now. Did he regret not having a chance to explore the feelings that he might have for Kyra? Yes. Did he regret that he would never be able to see Luca again? Absolutely. Did he regret that he would never be able to hug his sister again?

More than anything.

He was scared. No, he was terrified. He didn't want to die. He didn't want to kill, either. He would do both, however, in spite of his fear, because of Kyra, and Garrett, and Angel, Anthony, and all the others. Maybe his death wouldn't save them, in the end, but it would give them a better chance. He would do his very best to give them a chance at a life, because at seventeen, he'd already lived twice as long as some of them.

Kyra was looking at him, and he met her eyes, and he knew that she could see the fear shining in his. He could see it reflected in hers, and he knew that he would have to get control of his emotions before the other kids woke up. He couldn't let them see how frightened he was. He also had to think of a way to convince Portia and Tabitha, like Kyra, to keep the children out of the way when the fighting began.

He wondered if there was any chance of getting some or all of the prisoners in the other room free. If he could kill the right guard, he might be able to get a set of keys, but the men that normally came down to feed and water them did not appear to have any. Could he hack away the wood around their chains with the sword? They would still be shackled with heavy metal chains, but they would be free from the walls, at least. Then they could fight, too. Those who were willing. He supposed it was possible that some of them would join the pirates, in an attempt to save their own hides, but he thought that most would want to protect the children. It might be a fantasy, anyway. He would likely not get a chance to free them. It was something to consider, however.

And, then, all thoughts of the prisoners and guards fled his mind, because Kyra leaned forward—quickly, before she could chicken out—and kissed him. They were dirty, both of them, smelling of unwashed bodies, with greasy hair and bad breath, and in that moment, it didn't matter. Their lips were dry and chapped, and inexperienced, and that didn't matter, either. Travis raised his hand to her face, momentarily lost in the feel of her mouth against his, and he had just enough presence of mind to lament the knowledge that his first kiss might also be his last.

When she pulled away, she laid her head on his shoulder, and he wrapped his arm around her. He blinked to shed the tears from his eyes. It was going to be a long night, but he had to come up with a plan.

Is it night? he wondered. He honestly had no idea. It seemed like nighttime, with the soft sounds of slumber around him. He also realized that he would probably never know for sure.

*   *   *

Luca was sent to eat, wash up, and change his clothes before joining the deckhands. Ella went to join Rashad, who was scrubbing floors. She didn't see Luca again until supper, when he'd taken his place with the other men at the table. She hadn't seen Captain Swan at all since he'd left them near the bunks to return to the deck. She was apprehensive about facing him, because she had no idea what kind of mood he was in or what she should say to him. She was angry with him for putting her on the spot with Luca. She was worried about the deal she'd struck with him, and what he would expect from her. She was nervous about her body's reaction to his presence, and that she might really embarrass herself if he actually touched her.

And, in spite of her anger and worry, she was grateful. No matter what the cost to her, he'd let Luca out. He'd also, apparently, spread some sort of instruction amongst the crew not to give Luca a hard time. She'd been a bit worried that, freshly released from the dungeon, Luca would be given a cold shoulder. Or worse. From what she could see, the crewmen seemed to be ignoring the fact that he'd been absent from their presence for a while. It was Luca who seemed reserved, almost aloof, rather than his crew mates.

He could barely meet her eyes when she served the evening meal. He looked exhausted. She knew from experience how hard the first day back to work could be after languishing in a dungeon. Although she hadn't actually been in the cell, she might as well have been.

After she'd finished the dishes, she went to find him, to say goodnight. Several of the men were playing cards in the bunk room, although Luca wasn't one of them. He was lying on his bunk—her bunk, for a while—with his hands laced behind his head, staring at the bed above him. Ella hesitated, but her hesitation made her angry. She didn't have to justify herself to him. He had no right to judge her; he'd known her long enough to know that she would do anything for her family. Anything. Since she'd long considered him to be one-third of her family, he should appreciate her sacrifices rather than condemn them.

With her anger came guilt. She knew that she'd hurt him. She also knew that, since she'd never encouraged any feelings from him other than those of a brother, his expectations were unfair. It didn't matter. She still felt responsible for his pain.

71

She walked over to him and said, "I just came to say goodnight, Luca."

"Goodnight," he answered, without looking at her.

She hesitated again. "I don't want you to be hurt, Luca, and I don't want you to be angry with me."

"I'm not angry," he said. "I'm...disappointed."

That was worse. "That's not fair," she said. "You know why—"

"I understand, El." He finally turned his head to look at her. "I just need time to...adjust. I'll talk to you tomorrow."

The anger bubbled up again. "You need time to adjust? You're disappointed? You know what, Luca? I'm disappointed. The one time I really—" She stopped, compressing her lips. She was suddenly aware of how many men were pretending not to listen. "Forget it," she said, instead. "You just lay here and sulk until you've adjusted. Let me know when I'm worthy of your friendship."

She turned and strode from the room before she could give in to the threatening tears. She went up the stairs and stepped into the cool evening air, pulling in a deep and calming breath. Her cheeks felt hot, and her hands were trembling. She still didn't think she had anything to worry about from the captain, not physically, for a couple of days at least. She was worried about a confrontation with him, however, and she knew she had to put Luca and her hurt feelings aside.

She glanced around the deck, and didn't see Captain Swan. She chewed her lip for a moment, undecided. Should she go looking for him? He could be on the other side of the ship, or he could be in his cabin. She supposed the smartest course of action would be to go to his room, as she'd be expected to end up there, anyway. If he wasn't already there, he could find her easily enough. She took another deep breath, releasing it slowly. The sea breeze was remarkably calming. The sun was just below the edge of the water, and the sky was red and purple and dark blue. Stars sparkled in the east. She wondered if the clear skies and calm water would last.

She turned into the wind and made her way toward the cabin, trying to ignore the feeling that all of the crewmen were watching her. It wasn't just going to be Luca judging her for her sleeping arrangements, and she knew that. By striking her bargain, she'd already become a whore.

She hesitated at the door to the cabin, biting her lip. The curtains were all drawn. She raised her hand and knocked on the door.

"It's open," Captain Swan's voice said from inside.

When she walked in, he was sitting on the edge of the bed with his elbows on his knees and his hands dangling between. His hair was slightly mussed, and he looked like he'd been sleeping—and, like he needed about ten hours more sleep. His dark gaze met hers, and her skin felt tingly. Just the sight of him, on his bed, made her belly tighten, and she wondered how a single look could make her feel antsy with desire.

"I didn't mean to disturb you," she heard herself mutter as she fidgeted in the doorway.

He motioned with a hand for her to enter, and she hesitated only a moment before stepping inside and shutting the door. He scrubbed his hand over his face. "I was just leaving," he said. "Make yourself at home."

She felt a swirl of doubt, and asked, haltingly, "You're not...staying?"

He stood slowly, and the room suddenly seemed half the size. She swallowed, not quite sure if she wanted to run toward him or away from him. "No," he said, with a slight frown. He walked toward the door, and she stepped aside awkwardly, her face flaming. She didn't know what was expected of her. She hated the feeling. He stopped with his hand on the doorknob and turned his head toward her. "I behaved very badly, earlier," he said, further surprising, and confusing, her. "For what it's worth, I'm sorry."

She opened her mouth, closed it, and nodded. What should she say? That because of him, Luca was barely speaking to her? Because of him, the crew all thought she was a whore? Were those things really his fault? Luca was responsible for his own behavior, and she was hurt by his disappointment. She'd made the bargain, though.

He pulled the door open. "Wait," she said, surprising both of them. He looked at her again, his expression suddenly wary. "You need more sleep. You should stay." She refused to give in to her embarrassment, and managed to hold his gaze.

He regarded her for long moments, then sighed. "No," he said, softly. "I shouldn't. Goodnight, Ella."

Before she could say anything else—or think of anything else—he'd stepped from the cabin and pulled the door shut. She stared at it, her heart thudding, wondering if she should follow him. The idea was crazy, and she wasn't sure why she was even considering it. They weren't friends. He didn't seem to like her much at all. Why would she force her company onto him when he was clearly anxious to be away from her?

Because he seemed...sad. Tired, yes, and regretful for his earlier behavior, but there was something else, something that she thought she could almost recognize. The look in his eyes was the look of a captain who would stand on the rail of his ship, staring out at the unending ocean, silent and somber. The look of a man who would eat supper, alone in his room, completely separated from the crew laughing and sharing a meal one level below.

Instead of following him, she went to sit on the bed. She knew that if he made an advance—after her cycle had ended—that she would have no choice but to acquiesce. More frightening was the knowledge that a large part of her would not want to refuse him, anyway. She was on a slippery slope, and she knew it. In spite of his temper, and his ability to incite hers, she thought that she could be in real danger of developing feelings for him that she had no business having, or even considering. She knew nothing about him or his past except for rumors of his ruthless piracy—something she'd yet to witness. Her life was in his hands, and had been since she'd first set foot on his ship. Luca's life was in his hands. And, although Captain Swan didn't know it, Travis's life was in his hands, as well.

* * *

She only slept a few hours and woke when the dawn's early light was creeping past the edges of the curtains. She hadn't locked the door, and a part of her had expected him to return at some point. He had apparently remained on deck all night, however, and she felt a surge of guilt for stealing his bed. She knew it was ridiculous, and she felt it anyway. She got up and peeked through the curtain beside the door, before flicking the lock. She got freshened up as quickly as possible, and made the bed. Then, on second thought, she turned the blanket down, just in case he was planning on catching some sleep before the morning passed.

When she unlocked and opened the door, he was standing there, and her heart jumped. She stared out at him, surprised to so abruptly find herself face to face with the subject of her thoughts. He was dressed in the same clothes from the day before, of course, as he hadn't returned to his room. His dark hair was windblown, his cheeks just a little reddened by the cool sea air, and the weariness around his eyes added to the grimness of his expression.

He was holding two bowls of oatmeal. Had he been waiting for her to open the door?

"Hello," he said.

She swallowed, fidgeting with her shirt. "Hi," she answered. He seemed unnaturally subdued, and she had an unexpected urge to brush his hair from his forehead. It was so tempting, in fact, that for a moment she thought she was going to throw caution to the wind and do it, and she wondered how he would react. She could almost feel the silky smoothness of his hair on her fingers.

"May I come in?" he asked.

"Oh. Shit," she blurted, moving back quickly.

As he stepped into his cabin, he grinned, suddenly and unexpectedly, and it completely transformed his face. His eyes, full of sober weariness a moment before, sparkled with humor, and she wondered if he knew what she'd been thinking. "I think perhaps you've spent too much time with my crew," he said.

"No, I've always talked like this," she muttered. "I was never accused of being a lady."

"I find the company of ladies to be...tiresome," he said. He was still smiling, in spite of the faint frown creasing his forehead. She wasn't sure what she was supposed to say. She was almost certain he'd paid her a compliment. "Here," he said after a moment, extending one of the breakfast bowls toward her.

Looking down, she noted that the bowl he was handing her was suspiciously fuller than his own. "You really are trying to fatten me up, aren't you?" she said.

"You're far too thin," he repeated, moving past her to sit at the desk. She hesitated in the middle of the room. He'd left the door open. Was she supposed to sit down? Eat with him? Leave? She wasn't sure. Everything about him filled her with constant uncertainty.

"For what?" she heard herself ask.

Taking his seat, he regarded her with raised eyebrows. "Your health?" he suggested.

"Oh," she said. She looked at her bowl. She chewed her lip. The curtains were still drawn, but the open door was allowing the morning glow to fill the cabin, and the breeze was cool and refreshing.

"I don't mean to insult you," he said, quietly. She glanced up. It occurred to her for the first time that he might be just as confused by her as she was by him. The almost ever-present frown was there on his forehead.

"I'm not insulted," she muttered. "Just...confused."

He mulled that over in silence for a few moments. "You're welcome to sit, if you'd like," he said.

She debated, fidgeting, before moving forward to sit in the chair opposite his desk. "Thanks," she said. She glanced up again and caught his gaze, and suddenly found herself unable to look away.

"Would you tell me something?" he asked. "Now that Luca's freedom is guaranteed, no matter what your answer?"

She shifted in her seat, setting her bowl on the edge of the desk. He scowled at it but didn't comment. "Is it?" she asked. "Guaranteed?"

"It is," he said, his features once more set in grim lines.

"You want to know how I got on the ship?" When he nodded, she hesitated, again chewing her lip, trying to judge whether or not she should trust his word. "He carried me on in his duffel," she finally said. "Over his shoulder."

Captain Swan stared at her, his expression unreadable. After a few moments, he leaned back in his chair. "You allowed yourself to be put into a sack?" he asked, quietly.

Tamping down her flare of annoyance, she frowned and answered, "I wasn't *put into* a sack, I got into it myself."

"And that little whelp carried you over his shoulder? Further proof you need to eat more."

"He's not—" She stopped, pressing her lips together. She took a deep breath and let it out slowly. "Well, once you've fattened me up, I guess he won't be carrying me off the ship," she said instead. "May I ask *you* a question?"

He answered with a small nod.

"Why did you hire him? I'm sure you had a dozen men vying for the opening."

He was still leaning back in his chair, and he tipped his head as he considered the question. "He reminded me of myself, I suppose," he said. She was surprised by his honesty, as much as by the idea of Luca and Captain Swan being similar.

"It's hard to imagine you being like him," she admitted.

"Is it?" he asked, and she got the distinct impression that his question meant something that she couldn't quite catch hold of. "Well, perhaps. It was a long time ago."

"It can't have been that long...How old are you?"

He smiled. "Thirty-one. Trust me, it's been a long time. Would you please eat your breakfast?"

"It's rude to eat while you're talking," she retorted.

"I take more offense to you starving yourself."

She scowled. "I'm not starving myself," she muttered, reaching for her bowl. "Besides, I don't understand why you care."

"No? Well, let's just say, while you're on my ship, you're my responsibility."

"Oh."

"Speaking of which, you seem to be feeling better today, yes?"

"Wish I had some of that every month," she said. Then, realizing how easily she'd tossed out a reference to a very personal thing, she dropped her eyes to her oatmeal.

"Hopefully you'll come to me next time instead of suffering in silence."

"Next time?"

"I assume you'll still be on the ship in a month," he said, frowning.

"Unless you toss me off," she answered.

"Or unless you decide you don't want to go to Bohannon," he said, quietly.

She knew her expression must show her confusion. She gestured toward the windows. "It's a little damp here, I was thinking of someplace drier."

He smiled dutifully. "I was thinking of an island. Tarot, to be exact. We'll be there in less than a week."

She felt a flare of sudden panic. "We're stopping? For how long?"

He studied her with a hint of concern. "Less than a day. As long as it takes to load and unload supplies. Is there a problem?"

Problem? Like the slower we go and the longer we stop, the further away my brother gets, and once he's on land I have no idea how I'm even supposed to find him? She shook her head, trying to calm her racing heart. There was nothing she could do to get to him any faster. She certainly couldn't expect Captain Swan to change his itinerary. Until she was off the ship, she had to accept the fact that she was not in control. Once she got to Bohannon, she would be able to decide her best course of action, and until then there was no sense in torturing herself with the knowledge of what she couldn't change.

"You're in a hurry to get to Bohannon?" he asked.

"Not exactly," she muttered, biting her lip. "Just..."

"In a hurry to get off the ship?" he suggested. His expression was once more unreadable.

"Not exactly that, either," she admitted. She started eating her oatmeal before she could tell him anything more. He was watching her, and she felt self-conscious, but she tried not to fidget.

After a few moments, he cleared his throat and picked up his own bowl.

"You might find you like Tarot," he said. "At the very least, Meena might be able to find you some more...comfortable clothing."

"I like these," she said. "I mean, they're a little big, but...I've never been much for dresses."

"You were wearing a dress when you, uh...climbed into the sack," he pointed out.

She laughed. "Yeah, well...I wasn't thinking long-term, really."

"You didn't bring a change of clothes. Ivan found your shoes, and not much else."

She shook her head. How was she supposed to admit that she had next to no clothing, or explain that she would have left without it even if she'd had a gigantic closet full of beautiful outfits? She put more food into her mouth, and the captain followed her lead, eating to let the silence stretch out. After a while, she glanced up at him and asked, "Who's Meena?"

He remained silent for a few moments longer, and she realized that he was now the one who looked uncomfortable. That was a nice change, although she couldn't help wondering why. "A friend who lives on the island," he finally answered.

"A friend?" she repeated. He must hear her skepticism, brought on by his discomfort.

"I've known her for ten years, now," he said. Meeting her eyes, he added, "How long did you say you've known Luca?"

She felt heat staining her cheeks and wasn't even sure why. She turned her attention back to her food. "About that long," she mumbled. She wanted to tell him that there was nothing romantic between herself and Luca, and couldn't find the words. It wasn't just because she'd lied—or at least let him assume without correcting him. She was afraid that he wouldn't care, one way or the other, and that was what really stayed her tongue.

"I thought you might want to find something to do on the deck, today," he said, unexpectedly.

She swallowed her oatmeal. "What do you mean?"

"Fresh air. Sun," he said, gesturing with his spoon. "We're going to come into a storm or two after Tarot. Rough waters, rain, wind...You should get as much time on the deck as possible."

"Storms?" she asked. Hadn't she been worrying about the weather just that morning? "How do you know?"

He smiled. "Besides," he said, ignoring her question. "It's Rashad's day off."

"Oh. Well..."

"You could sit on the deck and read a book, or something," he suggested.

The concept was so completely unexpected and foreign that for a moment she simply stared at him. Part of her rebelled at the very idea of relaxing in the sun with a book when her brother was being held prisoner in the bowels of a slave ship and Luca was working as a deckhand. The other part of her longed for such normalcy and ease. When was the last time she'd read a book? She couldn't even remember for sure. She had little time for leisure.

"You do...read?" he asked, looking even more uncomfortable—and a little concerned.

She scowled. "Of course I read," she said, struggling to keep from lashing out. There was no sense letting her pride get the best of her—How would he know, after all? "I just haven't had much time for it, lately."

He pointed toward a cabinet fastened to the wall. "Inside there, you'll find a wide range of books. Whether or not any of them will interest you, I can't say, but you're welcome to help yourself. You can stay in here, or find someplace out of the way outside. I'm going to lie down for an hour or so."

The thought of hanging around and watching him sleep was disturbingly tempting. What was the matter with her, anyway? Had she completely lost her mind? "Thanks," she heard herself say. "I appreciate the offer. I really do. I just...prefer to find something to make myself useful. Keep busy, you know."

He spread his hands. He seemed disappointed. "Suit yourself," he answered. He stood, and she was once again mesmerized by his easy grace. It made her feel awkward and clumsy, and she was sitting down. "Could you close the door, please, on your way out?"

"Of course," she said. When he'd walked past her and sat on the edge of his bed, she hurried to finish the last of her breakfast. He had already laid down, and had his hands clasped behind his head and his eyes closed, when she gathered their two bowls and got to her feet. She found herself staring at his relaxed profile and gave herself a mental shake, heading toward the door.

"Ella," he said when she'd reached the doorway.

She stopped, startled, and looked back. His eyes were still closed. "Yes, Captain Swan?" she asked, shifting her weight nervously.

"Thanks for having breakfast with me," he said.

She hesitated. She didn't know how to respond. "Thank you," she finally answered, before quickly escaping the cabin. She pulled the door shut, and turned, bowls stacked in one hand, to find Ivan regarding her from several yards away. He nodded once, slowly, in greeting. She raised her empty hand in acknowledgment and hurried on her way.

She felt a little relieved when she reached the stairs. As stifling as the air was, compared to the open deck, it was also strangely comforting. She'd spent so much time working below, the dimness and closeness were familiar. So were the men, although she felt that they were all judging her now. That was the real reason she needed to get back to work, the reason she'd been unable to voice to the captain. If the men all believed, as she would expect them to, that she'd become the captain's whore, then she couldn't very well lounge around in the sun reading a book. If she wanted to maintain any modicum of respect, after working so hard to earn a place, she would have to continue working as hard as she could.

Rounding the corner toward the galley, she ran into Luca—literally. She cursed, frantically trying to keep hold of the clanking bowls, and Luca grabbed her arm to steady her.

"El, I'm sorry," he said. He took the bowls from her.

She pushed her hair from her forehead. "Don't worry about it, it's fine," she said.

"No, I mean about last night. I'm sorry."

She studied his familiar face and knew that he'd spent a mostly-sleepless night. There seemed to be a lot of that going around. "Me, too," she said.

He shook his head. His expression was pained. "I had no right to...Look, El, I won't say I'm not upset by...you know. But...I understand why you're doing it, and..."

Ella knew she could set his mind at ease a bit, but what would be the point? Nothing had happened, yet, but there was plenty of time for the captain to call in the payment on their bargain. If they got to Bohannon, and Captain Swan had still not touched her, then she could put Luca's worries to rest. Until then, he might as well believe the worst.

"I told you I was with you, no matter what. Always. Then I acted like a...jealous little kid. Sorry. It won't happen again."

Ella put a hand against his chest. "Thank you, Luca," she said. "I never meant for you to get hurt."

"We'll get through this, and we'll get him back. You'll see."

She nodded, then reached for the bowls. "I'm going to get to the kitchen," she said. "You'd better go...wherever you're supposed to be working. I'll see you later, alright?"

"Sure. You know...I love you, right?"

She swallowed. "Yeah," she said. "I love you, too," she said, knowing by the look in his eyes that he recognized the difference.

* * *

The time to eat had long come and passed, and no one had appeared. The door was still locked. From the other room, the calls of men could be heard, as they shouted toward the stairs that they needed water, that the children needed food, and from the stairs came no response.

They still had some water left, although Travis knew the men in the other room did not. The children were hungry, but they were not yet starving. They could last longer than Portia and Tabitha, who'd had far less to eat over the weeks and would suffer greatly without the few mouthfuls of stew a day they'd been subsisting on.

Travis pulled on the door handle, testing the strength of the door. There was no give; the door was thick, heavy, and sturdy. He didn't think there was any chance he'd be able to break it down. He might be able to remove the hinges, if he used the sword as a lever. He would have to wait a little longer, however, to see if someone would come before things reached that desperate a point. He didn't want to risk damaging the sword, as it was the only weapon he had.

Portia was telling the children a story, a tale that Travis knew. It was a story his own mother had told him, long ago. After his parents' deaths, he'd asked Ella to tell him that story, and she had, every night for over a week. He'd never thanked her for that. He had no doubt that she knew he loved her. Did she know how much he appreciated everything she'd done for him, though?

Chapter Five

"Hey there beautiful."

Ella turned, startled. She'd been concentrating on digging up potatoes, and thinking about how she'd scarcely seen Captain Swan the evening before. When she went to the cabin, he'd already eaten his supper and was out on the front of the ship, surveying the water through a spyglass. He hadn't come in all night, at least not that she'd heard, and she'd left early to go help Timón with breakfast.

She looked up at the young man casting a shadow across her. She knew his name—Bart. Bartholomew, she thought. Aside from excusing himself when they passed in the hall, or thanking her for a meal, he'd never spoken to her before. Now, his words were slurred, and he was smiling down at her like an idiot. A drunken idiot.

For weeks, Ella had managed to avoid trouble with the men, and she was grateful for the wide berth they generally gave her. They seemed almost frightened of her, in fact. Now, looking at Bart's lopsided grin, she felt her stomach sink. None of the men were typically drunk during the day. She was sure that Captain Swan would not tolerate the consumption of liquor by the men on duty.

"Hello," she said. She tried to sound as polite, and dismissive, as possible. She didn't want to offend him, and she didn't want to encourage him.

"Whatchoo doin here?"

"Digging potatoes," she said. She turned her attention back to her task, but she was tense.

He tapped her on the shoulder, and she clenched her jaw. Well, that answered the question about whether or not he would touch her. She glanced to the left and right, and no one else was in sight. She had to defuse the situation before things got out of hand. She didn't want Bart to be in trouble, but she also didn't want any trouble from him. "Hey. Hey you," he said.

She turned and stood, because she couldn't stand being below him, with her back to him, any longer. "I'm a little busy here, Bart," she said. She still strove to keep her tone polite.

His face showed delayed surprise. "You know my name," he said, grinning.

"Sure. You're Bart, and I'm Ella. I have work to do, though, Bart. How about you? Do you have work to do?"

He looked confused. His face screwed up in concentration. "I wanna talk to you."

"You should probably go see if Timón has any coffee." He was young. Probably closer to Luca's age than her own. His hair was shaggy, his chin smooth, and she knew from his eyes that he wasn't going away so easily. He was drunk, and he was looking at her like he'd just discovered a shiny new toy. She had no interest in being anyone's toy, and she tried to think of something she could say to distract him.

"You're real pretty," he said, and she suppressed a groan. She wasn't afraid, exactly. If she yelled for help, she was sure someone would come to her assistance. She didn't want to do that, and didn't think it would get to that point. Bart was so drunk, it would probably be easy to confuse him, knock him down. He might be stronger than she was, but she was pretty confident she could fight him off if she had to.

"I'm busy," she answered, raising her chin. She was obviously going to have to be less subtle.

He reached out and ran a finger along her arm. She pulled away, and he grabbed her wrist. "Don't be like that," he said, sounding plaintive. "Cap don't gotta know."

We're standing on the open deck, you idiot, she thought. *Anyone could see or hear you.* She tried to pull away again and he tightened his grip on her wrist.

"Let go of me," she said, through her teeth, keeping her voice low. "Now."

He leaned forward. "I'm younger than—" *the captain,* she assumed he was going to say, but he didn't finish. There was a flash of movement beside her, startling her, and as she flinched and turned, a fist slammed into Bart's face. He reeled backward, and Luca followed, tackling him to the deck.

"Luca!" she cried, trying belatedly to grab his arm. Her heart was slamming in her chest. This had gotten way out of hand, and she had to put an end to it before things got worse. Luca had just gotten out of the dungeon. What was the punishment for fighting on deck? "Luca," she said again, hurrying forward. She grabbed his arm, and he shook her off, punching Bart again.

Bart was drunk, and a little slow to react, but his natural fighting instincts had finally kicked in, and he managed to throw Luca—who weighed considerably less than him and was scrawny—to the side. Even as Luca scrambled to right himself, Bart rolled and knocked him down, and now it was Bart punching Luca.

Ella grabbed the back of Bart's shirt and tried to pull him off. He threw an elbow into her stomach, and she clamped her mouth shut to keep from crying out at the sudden pain. Even as she fought to catch her breath, she pulled again, almost dislodging Bart from Luca. Luca was pushing the other man's chin up from below, swearing as Bart hit him in the head twice.

As suddenly as Luca had appeared, Captain Swan was beside her. He grabbed the back of Bart's belt and yanked him off Luca. Bart tried to turn in his drunken confusion, swinging out, and his hand caught Ella in the mouth. She flinched and cursed, and the captain turned and slammed Bart against the railing. Bart finally realized who had hold of him, and he paled considerably.

Ivan was hauling Luca to his feet—no easy task, since Luca was still swinging and trying to get to Bart. "Knock it off," Ivan said, tugging on the collar of Luca's shirt.

"Do not move," the captain told Bart, pointing a finger at his chest.

Turning toward Luca, the captain said, "What the hell is going on here?"

"He come outta nowhere'n hit me," Bart said.

"Fuck you," Luca spat, struggling against Ivan's hold.

"Stop, Luca," Ella said. She was trying not to cry. The combination of frustration and pain were making it difficult to control her emotions. "Please."

Luca finally looked at her, and to her relief, he stopped struggling.

"Who started this?" the captain asked.

"He did," Bart and Luca answered in unison.

"Fighting will not be tolerated on my ship," the captain said, in a dangerously low voice. "As you both know. So, I will ask only once more. Who threw the first punch?"

Ella met Luca's eyes, and the pain in her stomach wasn't the main reason for her nausea. "I did," Luca answered. He raised his chin defiantly. He looked angry, but also frightened. He was surely envisioning the next month or so in the dungeon.

"It's my fault," she said, quickly. "Please. It's my fault. It was a misunderstanding."

"Misunderstanding, how?" the captain asked, turning his head toward her.

"Yeah. Misunderstanding how?" Luca repeated. Looking at Bart, he said, "If you touch her again, I'll fucking kill you."

Bart seemed to be sobering up quite quickly, now, and looked ill.

Captain Swan looked from Luca, to Bart, and finally turned all the way toward Ella. Once again, his expression was unreadable. His jaw was clenched, and she found herself wondering what he was thinking. She seemed to spend so much of her time trying to figure out what he was thinking. "Did he touch you?" he asked.

She hesitated. His dark gaze was holding hers, and she found herself completely incapable of looking away. "It was a misunderstanding," she repeated.

"Really," he said. "So, Luca started a fight for no reason?"

"Of course not," she said, scowling, knowing that there was no way he was going to let this become a non-issue.

He turned away from her, and she crossed her arms. "Bart. Go below. Get sober and don't let me see you until I send for you. Now."

Bart didn't have to be told twice. He scurried past, heading for the stairs, and she couldn't help it—she felt sorry for him. If things had gone any further, if he'd actually hurt her or tried to, she might feel differently. She did not think he was a bad guy, though, and that was the problem. He was drunk and making poor decisions, and he would surely regret his behavior. Luca had come to her defense, and she couldn't fault him for that. They were protective of each other, and always had been.

"Luca," Captain Swan said, and he took a step toward the younger man. At the captain's nod, Ivan released his hold on Luca, who adjusted his shoulders sullenly. "I will say this very carefully. Fighting will not be tolerated. Go back to work, and stay away from Bart. If it happens again, I will put you back in your cell."

"If he touches her again—"

"He won't," the captain said, and Luca blinked in surprise at the steel in Swan's voice. "See to the blood on your face, and get back to work."

Luca hesitated, looking at Ella. "I'm sorry," she told him, because she truly was. For once, she didn't have to fight to utter the apology.

Luca shook his head, then sighed. "You apologize too much," he muttered. He turned and strode away, apparently deciding he had no interest in cleaning the blood off his face before returning to work.

"I apologize too much?" she mumbled, with a small snort. She usually choked on the words, if she even managed to form them. She glanced at Swan. "You'd probably disagree with that."

The captain turned toward her, but there was no trace of humor on his face. "Wait for me in the cabin."

She pressed her lips together in spite of the pain it caused. What had she done to warrant punishment? She'd been digging potatoes, for crying out loud, minding her own business. She wanted to refuse, because she did not relish the idea of being ordered about. She also wanted to refuse because she didn't like the idea of being in the cabin alone with him if he was in a foul mood.

He reached a hand toward her face, and she flinched. It was instinctive, and she cursed herself for the show of weakness. She saw the muscle in his jaw twitch. He took her chin, gently, between his thumb and forefinger, turning her face toward the sun. She assumed there must be a red mark where Bart had accidentally hit her, in addition to the bloody lip, but she was more concerned about the elbow she'd taken to her stomach. There would be a pretty big bruise by the next day, she would bet.

Captain Swan put his forefinger under her chin and gently ran his thumb across the side of her lip, wiping away the smear of blood. She suddenly couldn't breathe. His eyes slid from her mouth, up to her own startled gaze. His dark hair was blown across his forehead. She wanted to brush it back.

"Wait for me in the cabin," he repeated, his voice low and commanding and undeniable. "Please," he added. At the last word, she thought there was just a trace of humor in his eyes.

"Fine," she said, turning away. She was annoyed with herself for once again letting him have such an overwhelming effect on her. Had she no control of herself when he was nearby? Was she so powerless to resist a handsome face? Ivan stepped out of her way, and she stalked toward the cabin, feeling as though a dozen pairs of eyes were watching her.

Were the crewmen watching her? She didn't know, because she didn't look around. Was Luca watching her? If so, what did he think of her going to the captain's cabin? Did it strike him as yet another betrayal? Would she ever be able to repair their relationship? Or would Luca hate her after this trip? They had to get Travis back, and she knew that Luca felt that as strongly as she did. After that, however, would they be able to go back to the easy friendship they'd shared? Could they be a family again?

She blinked back her tears, because they would help nothing. She went into the cabin and—barely—resisted the urge to slam the door behind herself. She went to the mirror and looked at herself. Her lip was split. She carefully wiped the new blood from the small cut. She could see that her chin was a little red. It might even bruise, but that was no big deal. She was pale, and her skin would bruise easily. She raised her shirt to look at her stomach, and there was a red mark there, as well. She prodded at it with her finger, gently, and winced.

The door opened and she looked up, startled. She dropped her shirt over her stomach.

The captain was standing in the doorway, and he seemed startled, as well. Actually, for a moment, he looked frozen. Then, he closed his mouth, shut the door with a click, and cleared his throat. "Are you alright?" he asked.

"I'm fine." She crossed her arms again.

"Yes?"

She lifted her chin. "Yes," she said.

"Tell me what happened."

She raised her eyebrows to keep from scowling at him. "Nothing," she answered.

"Obviously not true."

"I told you, it was a misunderstanding," she repeated, fighting her exasperation. "He's drunk."

"That's no excuse. What did he do?"

"He grabbed my arm. That's it."

"What did you do?"

"I told him to get his hands off me. Then Luca came out of nowhere..."

"What happened to your stomach?"

She bit her lip and winced, releasing it immediately. "That was an accident," she mumbled, dropping her gaze to the floor.

"Who was it?"

"It was an accident," she repeated.

"Who?"

She clenched her teeth, glaring at the floor. "Bart," she finally answered. "Elbowed me when I was trying to pull him off Luca. I don't even think he knew he did it, though."

The captain crossed the room in three strides, and she looked up, trying not to cower. "Let's get a few things straight, alright? First of all, I place high value on honesty. I will not tolerate being lied to by my crew, and that includes you while you're on my ship. I appreciate the fact that Luca admitted to throwing the first punch, but fighting will also not be tolerated. Secondly, the men are not to touch you, and they know that. If any one of them lays a single finger on you, I expect to hear about it. Is that clear?"

She was too stunned to do anything except nod. He'd told the men to keep their hands off of her? When? And, what had he told them? That he was the only one allowed to touch her? Or had he left that to their imaginations?

"Third—when Luca said you apologize too much, I'm pretty sure he meant that you apologize for the wrong things."

"What should I apologize for?" she said, before she could stop herself.

He raised his hand, quickly, and she flinched again. She cursed herself.

"And that," he said, quietly, pointing at her face. "Brings us to number four. Have I hurt you?"

Not yet, she thought. She shook her head.

"Am I angry? Yes. I imagine not for the reasons you believe. I have not hit you, will not *ever* hit you, and—"

"I'm sorry," she blurted, and she actually meant it, surprising herself. In a matter of minutes, she'd flinched from him twice, instinctively, and he was right—he'd never hit her, and she suddenly realized that her instincts had hurt his feelings.

He stared at her, a slight frown on his forehead. He seemed puzzled, and it again occurred to her that perhaps he didn't understand her any better than she understood him. His gaze slid to her lip and his frown darkened. "You should put a cold rag on that. It's going to swell."

"You've been kinder than I have a right to expect. I didn't mean to offend you," she said.

"Kinder than you have a right to expect," he muttered, with a small shake of his head. He sighed and ran a hand through his hair. "You tell me, what sort of treatment do you deserve?"

"I just meant...I know I can be...contrary."

His eyebrows went up, and he laughed. A genuine, surprised laugh, and she felt her stomach flutter in response. "Contrary?" he repeated, and there was a sudden twinkle of humor in his eyes. "Antagonistic, you mean?"

She scowled. "Alright. Fine," she said. He laughed again, and she found herself smiling in response. She was even more surprised than he was. "I guess I can admit that," she said, and the atmosphere of the cabin was suddenly far less tense. She felt an unexpected rush of relief. She didn't like the feeling of having him upset with her. She did like to see him smile. Why did she spend so much of her time making him frown? She decided that she was going to try exceptionally hard to be less contrary—or antagonistic. She was going to try to make him laugh, or at least smile, more than she made him scowl. They were going to be stuck on the ship together for another month, at least. She didn't want that whole time to be spent with them glaring at each other.

"Shall we go over the points we've covered, then?" he asked, still smiling.

"Honesty. No touching. Apologize for the right things. No flinching."

He laughed again, and she felt a sense of satisfaction. And a pull of desire. "Close enough, I suppose," he said.

It occurred to her that she couldn't really promise any of those things. Honesty? She couldn't tell him the truth about herself and Luca. Not now, at least. No touching? Well, she didn't exactly have control over that, did she? It wasn't as though she was going to invite anyone on the ship to touch her. *Even him?* her mind whispered, and she ignored it. Apologize when she was wrong? She could make an effort, but she knew she had issues with pride. No flinching? How did a person control instinctual reactions?

And, yet, they were not unreasonable requests. She wanted to give him what he'd asked for. She wanted him to be pleased with her, and the realization frightened her far more than her attraction to him. She was not used to needing someone's approval. She was not used to caring whether or not someone thought she was pretty. She was not used to relying on someone to tell her what she could or could not do. She was not used to any of the feelings that the captain of *Voyage* stirred within her.

He was staring at her, and she realized that she was just standing there, like an idiot. Was he waiting for her to say something? Do something? "Why is your ship called *Voyage*?" she asked. It was the first thing she could think of. She'd been wondering about his name lately, which led her to ponder the name of his vessel. The more she considered it, the more she thought it was an odd choice of names.

"You don't like the name of my ship?" he asked. He didn't seem offended, simply a little bemused.

"Oh, no, it's fine," she hurried to say. "It just seems sort of...like...shouldn't it be called *Voyager*, instead? Or...I don't know," she finished lamely, blushing. She regretted the question, because she felt stupid.

"Because the voyager is going somewhere, in search of adventure," he said, quietly. "But, if you have no destination, then the ship itself is the adventure, yes?"

"Oh," she said, after a moment. She hesitated, gathered her courage, and said, "You...have a destination, though...?" She couldn't hide her confusion.

He seemed to consider her words for a moment. "I suppose it would seem strange," he allowed, finally. "Do you believe that names say a great deal about a person or thing, or place?"

She hesitated again. "How do you mean?"

"Do you think a person's name reflects who or what they are in life?"

"You mean like Swan?" she asked, with a small smile.

He shrugged. "I suppose Swan would seem apropos, in a way, although that's not what I meant."

"Some names mean something, I guess. But my name, for example...What would that mean?"

"Ella is a beautiful name," he answered, quietly, and she felt a shiver of pleasure ripple through her. She had an insane urge to reach out and put her hand against his chest. She wanted to feel his heartbeat. "It suits you."

"I always thought it was...too feminine for me," she heard herself admit, flushing in embarrassment at the unexpected compliment.

"You don't think you're feminine?" he asked with a small smile.

"I'm built like a boy," she mumbled, blushing darker still.

To her surprise, he laughed, a quiet sound. "I assure you, you're not," he murmured.

"Thanks," she finally managed. She had no idea what else to say.

"What's your last name?"

She considered, briefly, whether or not to answer. What could it hurt, though? When they reached Bohannon, she was going after Travis. She would never see Captain Swan again. It wasn't as though he would come after her, whether he knew her last name or not. "Fisher," she said. Before he could comment, she asked, quickly, "What's your first name?"

He was silent for several seconds, and she didn't think he was going to answer. "Colin," he finally said. "When I was a boy, the kids called me Dusty."

"Why?" she asked, frowning.

"I was always dirty. Did you know that you can clean a ship from top to bottom, and spend months in the middle of nothing but water, and still have a layer of dust settled by the time you reach land again? Still, it's cleaner out here." He paused. "I've often felt like dust in the wind," he added, quietly. It was apparent that he hadn't meant to admit so much, and he suddenly looked uncomfortable. He cleared his throat. He forced a smile that didn't quite reach his eyes. "Dusty Swan. I suppose names might mean something."

"I think Colin's a pretty name," she said. "Colin Swan." She smiled, because it really did have a nice ring to it. Maybe he was right about the importance of names, because his did seem to suit him. "You don't seem dirty anymore. You always smell like soap."

To her relief, he laughed, and some of his unease seemed to slide away. "Clean Colin, now. That's me, I guess. On my voyage to nowhere. I wasn't born with the last name Swan."

"No?" She was surprised, but before she could ask when, where, or how he'd gotten the name, he spoke again.

"When you marry Luca, your last name will be Bella?"

"That's right," she answered. She fidgeted. The mention of Luca made her uncomfortable, because he represented one major lie that she was perpetuating.

"Ella Bella?" he said, raising his eyebrows. She had never given it much thought, because marrying Luca had never been a real possibility for her. Hearing it aloud, however, was strange. "I don't think it works." Before she could respond, he grimaced. "Sorry. That was inappropriate."

"It's alright," she muttered, thinking that *Ella Swan* was a much more appealing name. "I never thought about it much."

"No?" he asked, sounding surprised. Why wouldn't he be? She'd asked about the name of his ship, starting this whole conversation and proving that she placed some importance on monikers. Then she told him she'd given very little thought to what her name would be when she married the man she was supposedly going to marry? It would seem strange. She couldn't explain to him that Luca's last name would never be hers.

She shrugged. She searched for something to say. "So they didn't call you Colin as a kid?" she asked. She wanted to ask about his last name and refrained. In light of her lies, it seemed inappropriate to ask such personal details.

"Sometimes. People have called me Swan since...I was a boy. Since I took the name. The adults. The kids called me Dusty. I don't think, in hindsight, they meant it to be mean. I'm mostly called Swan, or on this ship, Captain or Cap." It was his turn to shrug.

"What should I call you?" she asked. It was an odd question, considering the fact that they'd known each other for a while already. If she was going to make an effort to be more civil, however, she should at least know what he expected of her. She wanted him to say she could call him by his given name. She wanted to be invited to share a familiarity that even Ivan didn't seem a part of.

"That's entirely up to you," he answered after a few moments of silence. He was studying her so intensely, she was afraid he could read her mind. What would he think of all the inappropriate thoughts running through her head?

She nodded, because she wasn't sure what to say.

"Well, I'll leave you to get cleaned up," he said abruptly. "You need to put a cool rag on your lip. Let me know if you need anything."

"I will. Thanks," she answered. She was disappointed that he was leaving.

He regarded her for another moment, then turned and crossed to the door. He opened it, then hesitated with his back to her. She waited, wondering if she should say something. "It would be nice to hear my name once in a while," he said. Then, as she stood, stunned and inexplicably happy, he went out and shut the door.

She hugged herself, barely aware of the pain in her stomach, and grinned.

*   *   *

"Everyone stay back against the wall. No matter what happens." *If I get killed in front of you? I'm sorry about that. I really am.* Travis had never been more afraid in his life, and he struggled to keep his hands steady. He stood beside the door, waiting, the sword raised so it was parallel to the floor. He prayed he was making the right decision. No one had come to feed the children for almost two days and nights. No one had come at all. They were out of water. The light was almost out.

The person on the other side of the door either had food and water, or didn't. Either way, the situation was desperate. Travis had been devising a plan to pry the hinges off the door when he'd finally heard the sounds of someone approaching. He heard the men rattling their chains and shouting, some cursing and some pleading, and he knew that they had gone even longer without food and water. How long before they would start succumbing to starvation or, more likely, dehydration?

One of two things was about to happen. The door would open, and either the man outside would kill Travis, or Travis would kill him. There was no way of knowing whether the guard had food and water for the kids. If he did, and Travis succeeded in surviving, he planned on divvying up the sustenance and waiting until the next person came to check on the first. It would be far easier to deal with as many of them as possible on a one-on-one basis. For as long as that could last.

If the guard did not have food, however, then Travis would have to go in search of some, and that would mean fighting on the fly—something he had no experience with. He knew he would likely not live to return to the children, and Kyra and the others, with food or water, and knew that he had to try. He was not going to give up, no matter what.

"Stay back," he repeated, again, keeping his voice low as he heard the lock rattle. He met Kyra's eyes. They'd discussed it, and as much as she disliked the idea, she agreed with him that the most important thing was keeping the kids as safe as possible. It was her job to keep them back. He had to trust that she would do it. He wanted to believe that Tabitha and Portia would follow suit, but they seemed more unpredictable.

The door swung open slowly, and Travis waited, breath held, his shoulder pressed against the wall. The pot of food appeared first, and Travis felt a moment's hesitation. Had he made a mistake? Perhaps he could have kept the sword under the blanket, and if the food and water started coming again, they could have gone on—

But, no. One way or another, the time of sitting around praying for a drink of dirty, tepid water was over.

There was no time for second-guessing. There was no time for hesitation. The man started to turn his head toward Travis, finally sensing his presence as he stepped into the room, and Travis swung the sword. He squinted his eyes almost closed, and his stomach clenched into a painful fist of fear and horror, and his stolen blade caught the startled guard in the throat and blood sprayed.

One of the kids screamed, and almost all of them were crying.

The guard dropped the pot of stew and staggered back several steps, his hands going to his throat as his mouth opened and closed like that of a fish out of water. His head, nearly severed, tipped backward, and his wound gaped, and blood continued to pulse, and his knees buckled. Desperately trying not to vomit, barely aware of the tears coursing down his filthy cheeks, Travis shoved the man backward as he fell, so that he crumpled into the other room. As the man lay on the floor, twitching, his feet kicking weakly as his life pumped out of him, Travis stood in the doorway with the bloody sword hanging loosely by his side.

He felt scared and sick and stunned.

The guard had two canteens of water slung over his shoulder. They were on the floor in the pooling blood. Travis swallowed convulsively, knowing he would have to fish them out of that warm, sticky pool. Would the man grab him? Would he have a little fight left in him?

"Kid," one of the prisoners said, and Travis blinked, tearing his gaze away from the body. The lantern in their room was almost extinguished, too, and he squinted, trying to focus on the man who'd spoken. "Wake up, kid. Get the water and get back in the room before someone else comes."

Travis stared. He felt slow and dazed. He tried to remember his plan. The prisoner was right; he was supposed to go back into the other room. It seemed almost ridiculous now, though. He wouldn't be able to deal with the guards one at a time. The moment someone reached the bottom of the stairs and saw the flood of blood and the dead guard, he would either yell for more men or retreat up the stairs. He certainly would not simply walk into an ambush.

"Kid," the man repeated.

Travis shook his head and closed his mouth, taking a deep breath through his nose. He swallowed again. His hands were trembling so badly he could scarcely hold the sword. He knew that there was still no time for such cowardice, however. He was fully committed and couldn't change his mind now if he wanted to. He'd taken a life, and there was no going back. He moved quickly, before his mind could shut down. He bent and grabbed the straps of the water skins, pulling them off the length of the guard's limp and bloody arm. There was no reason to worry about him grabbing Travis, or putting up a fight; the man was dead.

Travis turned to find Tabitha behind him. He thrust one of the bloody canteens at her and pointed at the stew. "Divide this up. Make sure everyone gets some. Keep this door shut. Go."

"Travis—"

He pulled the door shut, and she had to step out of the way. He couldn't afford to let her try to talk him out of it. "Go," he repeated. He knew that he should eat something, and didn't know if there was time. The smell of blood was making him nauseous, but the fishy smell of stew made him acutely aware of his hunger, too. It was an unsettling combination. The guard's key was still dangling from the lock. Travis pulled it out and shoved it in his pocket. There were no keys for the prisoners' chains.

Clamping the sword beneath his arm, Travis used his shirt to wipe away the wet blood near the mouth of the water skin. He unscrewed the lid and took a quick swallow, enough to wet his dry mouth and soothe his scratchy throat. Then he crossed to the nearest man, and handed him the canteen. While the prisoner took a drink, then passed it to the next man, Travis returned to the dead guard.

Glancing toward the stairs, he bent and unbuckled the man's belt. He pulled it out from beneath the man's body, grimacing at the slime of blood, and put it around his own waist before he could let his disgust dissuade him.

The guard's sheathed sword now hung, streaked with redness, along Travis's leg. It was not comforting. He went to the bottom of the stairs and cautiously peeked up the dim well. There was no sign of anyone, yet. He stepped out of sight and leaned his back against the wall, closing his eyes as he tried to come to terms with what he'd done, and what he was planning to do. He wished it would happen quicker, so he didn't have so much time to think.

"Be strong, kid," one of the men said, and that helped, a bit. They couldn't help him fight, not unless he could find some keys to free them, but they'd already proven that they were capable of killing if he could get the guards into their reach. They were still passing the water, and Travis surveyed them in the dimness, counting. Fifteen men that were alive. Two that were dead, still chained to the wall. One of them was the man that had broken the other guard's neck.

Travis looked away, quickly. Only half of the chains were occupied. Had the others been empty from the start? Or had the guards killed other men and removed the bodies? He didn't know, and was afraid to ask. It wasn't just because he didn't know if he wanted the answer; he didn't want to risk someone at the top of the stairs hearing his voice. He waited in silence, until he finally heard the clunk of boots at the top.

"Barry?" a gruff voice called.

Travis closed his eyes again and cursed silently. What if the man didn't come down the stairs?

"Fuck you doin?"

Just come down, Travis prayed, knowing it was an odd and awful thing to ask for.

The man didn't call for assistance, but his footsteps were slow and cautious when he started down the stairs. Travis met the eyes of one of the prisoners, and the man mouthed the word *sword.* Travis didn't really need the tip, though. While the prisoner could see it for sure, Travis hadn't had any doubt that the guard would have his sword drawn and at the ready. Nonetheless, Travis gave a quick nod of acknowledgment. He held his own bloody sword up to his shoulder like a club, preparing to swing it as such.

Travis cursed himself for not moving the dead body out of sight. He'd been dazed and distracted, but he knew that was no excuse. If he survived the next two minutes, he would have to focus better. Plan better. Pay attention to the details.

The guard stopped at the bottom of the stairs. Travis could not yet see him, but he could see the man's sword, and he could hear his breathing. Could the guard see his dead comrade? Was he about to yell for help, or run back up the stairs? Travis gripped the handle of his sword, holding his breath.

"Hey, come see what I did," one of the prisoners yelled, yanking on his chains. Travis jumped at the sudden, harsh sound, then silently cursed himself.

"What the hell?" the guard on the steps muttered.

"That's right," the prisoner said. He grinned in the shadows, gesturing toward the dead guard. "See?"

"You fucking—"

As the man lunged forward, holding his sword out, Travis swung. He aimed for the neck again, because he was afraid he wouldn't mortally wound the man if he hit him anywhere else. As the blade sliced into the guard's throat, the man's sword jerked up, reflexively. The dull side of the blade hit Travis's arms, knocking them up, and he stumbled, trying to keep his grip on the sword buried in the guard's throat.

Travis could barely hear the man's gargling cry over the roar of blood in his own ears. He yanked his blade free with a wet sucking sound, and blood immediately sprayed him in a hot torrent. He flinched, then reached forward and grabbed the guard's shirt, jerking him away from the stairs, to the side, and the man stumbled and tumbled to the floor, his own sword clattering on the wooden floor as his blood pumped onto the boards.

Travis bent over and vomited by the guard's feet, but it had been so long since he'd eaten that the only things that came up were bile and the little water he'd had. His stomach cramped painfully, and he gagged, shoving his filthy sleeve against his mouth. Then, realizing that he was covered in blood, he pulled his arm away and retched again. The man was trying to crawl across the floor, trailing a river of red that actually appeared a shiny black in the dim room.

"Kid."

Travis heard the boots the same moment the prisoner's low voice sounded, and he turned, pressing his back against the wall, desperately trying to blink the tears from his burning eyes. His stomach churned, and his throat felt raw, and he wanted the nightmare to be over. He closed his eyes for a moment, and tried to picture his sister's face. For a moment, the image eluded him. Then he heard her voice, whispering in his head: *Whatever it takes.* That's what she had always done, for all of them: Whatever it took. With the soft words, her face finally swam into focus, and he felt a strange sense of relief. He opened his eyes.

The next guard reached the bottom of the steps, said, "What—" and was promptly decapitated. Travis didn't hesitate this time, or pull back at the last second, and the blade severed the man's head completely. The blood spurted upward even as the man's head thunked onto the bottom step and rolled with a sickening thud onto the floor. The man's knees folded and his headless body sank onto the stairs, where it sat for a moment before pitching forward.

You've killed three men, Travis thought. *If that won't guarantee you a place in Hell, nothing will.*

Immediately on the heels of that thought came this: *I'm already in Hell. I'm trying to get us all out.*

Travis put his bloody sword on the ground, grabbed the headless man's arm, and dragged him toward the second guard's body. It wasn't easy. Travis was malnourished and weaker than usual, and shaky from fear and exertion. He got the man away from the bottom of the stairs, however, and kicked the head after the body with a grimace and a stifled gag. He snatched the sword off the floor and glanced toward the stairs, listening for the sound of another approach. For the moment, all was quiet from above.

Travis checked the two most recent corpses for keys to release the chained men, and found none. He grabbed their two swords, and a dagger from the last man's ankle-sheath, and handed the weapons to three of the prisoners. "You might be able to free the chains from the walls," he said. His voice sounded hoarse.

The man on the end held up the canteen. "This last is for you," he said. "Drink."

Travis was too tired and thirsty to argue, even though he thought he should. He stepped forward, took the skin, and swallowed the last of the water. Then he took a deep breath and let it out. He set the empty canteen on the floor and glanced toward the stairs again. Should he wait for someone else? Or take the fight to them while they might still be unsuspecting? It would be easier to take them on, one at a time, as they came down the stairs.

Until they stopped coming. As soon as the men upstairs wised-up to what was going on, they would stop rushing down to meet his blade. They only had to wait at the top. The men, women, and children below would perish quickly enough without food or water. While Travis didn't think the slave-traders wanted that—they would have nobody to sell if all of their prisoners died, after all, and the whole trip would be for naught—he did think that they would choose to save themselves first. His choices, at that point, would be to stay below and die or climb the stairs and die.

No, he would have to go up before they had a chance to lay an ambush for him. Before they knew that they should. Before they knew that Barry and the other two were not going to be coming back up, at least not in the same condition they'd gone down in.

He wanted to give the women and children at least one weapon with which to defend themselves, and thought it would be a mistake. He wanted them to be able to claim innocence, if the guards came down after he was killed, and if they were armed, they would not be shown mercy. If they did not fight, the guards would have no logical reason to kill them, and they would certainly be more valuable alive than dead. Praying he was making the right decision for them, and knowing that they deserved to have someone better looking out for them, he took another deep breath and started toward the stairs.

"Kid."

He hesitated and looked back, painfully aware of the passage of time and how short his window of opportunity was likely to be. "Travis," he said, quietly.

"Travis. Be careful. Don't hesitate, don't let them talk. It's harder if you let them talk."

Travis swallowed. Doing his best to cling to some vestige of bravado, he nodded, and went to the bottom of the stairs. Looking up, he thought the climb seemed impossibly steep. He couldn't tell if his vertigo was from the swaying of the ship or his own unsteady mind. Holding the bloody sword in his right hand, he started up the stairs.

* * *

"You alright?" Luca asked, his eyes sliding to her slightly-swollen lip. He was standing in the galley doorway, with his arms crossed and a hip propped against the door frame. It was a defensive posture, and it was clear that he expected to be reprimanded.

Ella turned the handle of her pan to the side and stepped toward him. He tensed, and she felt a surge of guilt. She put her hands on his upper arms and felt his muscles bunch. He was far too thin, and she was guilty for that, as well. "I'm fine. Are you alright?" she asked. He'd finally cleaned his face, and was left with a blackening eye and a split lip.

"Sure," he answered. "Sorry," he added, but the apology sounded grudging and sullen. Of course he wasn't really sorry, just as she wouldn't be sorry for coming to his defense. Looking into his young face, with its mixture of anger and concern, she was overwhelmed by a surge of love for him. No matter what else went on between them, no matter how angry they might be with each other, she prayed that he would always know that she loved him. He and Travis were her whole life, her only reason for living, and had been for so long that she could scarcely remember when they hadn't been in her world.

"Thank you, Luca," she said, holding his gaze. "For being here with me. For...always being there for me."

He shifted uncomfortably, glancing around to see if anyone was listening. He shrugged, and she let go of his arms. "I owe you a lot more than you owe me," he muttered.

She shook her head. "We're going to be alright, Luca. We're going to have a better life. Can you feel it?"

"Sure," he said. "Sure I can, El." She wasn't sure if he believed it, and she wasn't sure if she did, either. All she knew for sure was that things would never be the same. They would never again huddle together in their room in Baytown, the three of them, to keep warm. They might never see Baytown again. Even if they did, it would be different. Her relationship with Luca was different, and she had already begun to mourn the loss of the innocent love he'd once felt for her.

"You should go find a seat. I'll be serving supper shortly."

Luca frowned. "Have you seen Bart?"

"No. You?" Ella asked, also frowning. She hadn't seen Bart sleeping off his liquor in the bunks, or eating lunch with the other men. While she supposed it would be natural for him to avoid her, and Luca, she couldn't help but wonder where he was. Had Captain Swan (*Colin*, her mind whispered) sent for him? And, if so, what had the outcome of that meeting been?

"No. Lucky for him."

"Luca, you can't fight. You heard Captain Swan. Besides, he didn't do anything, not really."

Luca bent close, and she could see the hurt beneath the anger on his face. "So maybe I can't keep Swan's hands off you," he hissed. "But I can keep everyone else's."

She tried to reach for his arm, but he was already retreating into the dining area, and she stopped. She didn't want to cause a scene in front of the other men, and she wasn't sure what to say, anyhow. While she understood Luca's feelings, and was touched by them, she was also deeply disturbed. She had to do whatever she could to get to her brother, but she didn't want to sacrifice Luca in the process. He was almost as much of a brother to her as Travis, and right now Luca seemed to be unraveling. And, as she'd been when Travis was captured, she was helpless to prevent it.

95

Seven men. Seven. You've killed seven people, Travis.

He stood in a narrow, stuffy corridor, feeling the sway of the ship beneath his feet, drenched in blood, with his arms hanging heavy and achy at his sides. The truth was, he'd never expected to last so long. While he hadn't relished the idea of death, a part of him had expected it to be a release from the pain and fear and responsibility, and he had enough presence of mind to recognize his own cowardice in that.

His mind was having difficulty processing much else. His world had become a violent and incomprehensible place. He knew he had to move and didn't know if he could. It wasn't just because he was exhausted and hurt, but also because his brain seemed incapable of commanding his body. Or, perhaps his body was incapable of obeying his brain. They both amounted to the same immobility.

He was bleeding, he wasn't even sure from how many places. His left arm was trickling blood onto the floor. He had a slice across his abdomen, although he didn't think it was terribly deep. He'd been cut once on his chin. He couldn't distinguish his own blood from that of the men he'd killed; he was covered in the stuff from head to foot. He could feel it sticking his clothes to his body. He could feel it between his toes. He could smell it.

He could taste it.

There was a small clinking sound behind him, and he whirled, sword up, before his brain had even registered the noise. His paralysis was broken, but his mind was still a swirl of grief and horror and fear and confusion, and even as he reacted to the sound, he doubted his own instincts.

He hesitated, with his sword raised and his heart slamming and his nose stinging with the stench of blood.

The man before him—just a boy, really, probably around Travis's age—stood with the chamber pot clutched in both hands, held before himself like a shield, his eyes wide and face slack with surprise. He was thin, and dark-skinned, with a pink scar puckering one cheek. His clothes were dirty and torn and ill-fitting. His wrists were scarred from the chafing of past shackles. The little finger on his left hand was missing.

All of these details, Travis registered in a heartbeat.

"Don't kill me."

Don't hesitate...It's harder if you let them talk.

The sword in Travis's hand trembled. He knew that the boy before him was, himself, a slave. While that didn't necessarily make him trustworthy, it meant that he was not responsible for the imprisonment of Travis and the others. Without the hesitation, Travis would have decapitated the boy. They stood, staring at each other, neither moving, and Travis was overcome with self-doubt. He had no idea what to do. He had killed seven men already. Had all of them deserved it? Had he killed someone innocent in his bloodbath?

"Who are you?" Travis heard himself ask in a low voice, a voice he scarcely recognized.

"Jesiah," the other boy said. "You one o' the prisoners?"

Travis slowly lowered his sword. The moment for action had passed, and he knew that the man in chains had been right: It was harder if you let them talk. Travis would not be able to kill this boy, certainly not in cold blood. He was unarmed, from what Travis could see, and clearly not as well-fed or well-dressed as the slave-traders. Would he be an ally, or a hindrance? That remained to be seen.

Travis opened his mouth to ask how many men were on-deck, and how many were below, but the words didn't leave his mouth. Jesiah's eyes widened, and he said, "Look out."

Travis spun without pausing to consider that it might be a trick. The man that had just entered the corridor was tall, bearded, and swinging his sword. Travis dropped and heard the blade slice the air above his head. There was no time for thought, only instinct, and Travis rolled and came up with his sword buried in the other man's chest. Travis stepped back, his hands empty, as the other man gaped at him, with his own weapon still held up at an angle.

Travis fumbled for the second sword still sheathed at his side, as the mortally-wounded man seemed to realize that he still had time to kill the boy before succumbing to death himself. With a grimace of pain and rage, he lunged with his sword, and Travis stumbled backward, still unable to free his backup weapon with his shaking hands. He tripped over his own feet and fell. His teeth snapped together as he hit the wood. He tried to scramble backward. Looking up at the man's face—pale above the beard, because he'd already lost so much blood—Travis knew that his time was up. The bearded man was going to die, but so was Travis.

Eight men, he thought, grappling with his fear. *It's better than I hoped for*.

The black boy, whom Travis had almost completely forgotten, stepped forward and threw the contents of the chamber pot into the bearded man's face. The man reared back with a roar of disgust—mingled with the pain and anger—and his sword tipped up instead of lancing Travis's heart. Travis pushed himself back, somehow managing to get to his feet. The man was swiping at his face, trying to clear the piss from his eyes in spite of the fact that he was impaled with a sword. Travis had time to draw his second sword, and then he stood there, unsure of what to do. A moment before, he'd been certain of his own impending death. Now, on his feet with a sword in his hands, facing a dying man who was more concerned with the feces in his beard than the armed boy before him, Travis felt that he had, by far, regained the upper-hand.

That would likely not last, however. Any number of men could be attracted to the sounds of their skirmish. The man was not being quiet. Travis stepped forward, squinting his eyes, and yanked the sword from the other man's body, pulling the length of the blade out quickly—although not without effort. His tired, sore arm protested, and the sound of the blade leaving the body made

Travis's stomach churn. The man screeched in agony, his own weapon apparently forgotten, and dropped to his knees.

For a moment, Travis was sure he was going to be sick again. Or, perhaps he would pass out. The world was suddenly swirling around him, and he wondered briefly if it would be so terrible to black out. If he was lucky, they would kill him before he awoke.

He shook his head, as much in denial of that thought as in an effort to clear it. The man on his knees before him had a bloody hand held out in supplication. Blood was bubbling from his lips. His eyes were wide and glassy with pain and fear. All fight had gone from him. He would have killed Travis, given the chance, and Travis had to keep reminding himself of that to keep from screaming apologies for what he'd done.

Travis held a sword in each hand. He dropped one, clutched the other with both hands, and quickly decapitated the man knelt before him. Bile stung the back of his throat, and tears burned his eyes and nose. Even as the man's head thumped to the floor, followed by his still-bleeding body, Travis bent and grabbed the sword he'd dropped and awkwardly shoved it, left-handed, into the sheath at his hip. The one in his right hand had killed eight men since he'd come into possession of it. How many people had died by that blade before, at the hands of the guard it had belonged to? Travis shoved the thought away, before the horror of possibility could convince his hand to drop the weapon.

When he turned toward the slave boy, Jesiah took a step back, his own eyes wide with horror. "You were never here," Travis said. "Go wherever you're supposed to be before they find you. Act normal. Can you do that?"

Jesiah stared at him. "Wh-what ab-bout y-you?" he stammered.

"Take care of yourself. Stay out of the way of the fighting," Travis said. He was surprised that no one had come, yet. He glanced nervously back at the corner the now-dead man had come around. "Where is everyone?" he asked.

"Most is on deck," Jesiah said.

Travis heard the unmistakable sound of boots—more than one set—hurrying toward them. "Go," he said. He bent, grabbed the chamber pot, and shoved it into Jesiah's hands before pushing him back the way he'd come.

"Come with me," Jesiah whispered, urgently, even as he retreated. "We can hide you."

Travis shook his head. "Go," he said again. To his relief, Jesiah turned and ran, disappearing at the end of the corridor into what Travis imagined was probably the hall toward the kitchen. He wasn't sure. His knowledge of ships was limited. He knew the bunks and galley must be on this level, but he hadn't seen them since his climb from the bowels of the vessel.

He turned and braced himself, knowing that the element of surprise was the only thing he had going for him. When the men came around the corner, he would have to kill them before they realized what was going on. It probably wasn't possible. It sounded as though three men were coming, possibly four. Travis raised his sword and took a deep breath.

Chapter Six

The ship slowly drifted to a stop, until the only motion was the gentle swaying. The sails were furled, but the anchor was not lowered. The sky overhead was blue, and clear, and the air was warm and calm. Off to the west, barely visible, a pod of whales was breaching. The sound made its way—impossibly, it seemed—to the ship.

There was land in sight, still most of a day and night away, a short stretch of sand and trees. Tarot.

Ella stood on the deck, looking toward this mysterious island of whose existence she'd never known. The water sparkled and shimmered between it and the ship, making it difficult to judge the distance. She wondered what it would be like to live in such a place, surrounded completely by water and separated from the rest of the world.

Ella sensed the captain's presence and turned her head to look back at him. She didn't know why they were stopped. She was anxious to get to her brother. That had not, and would not, change. It was impossible to ignore the beauty of the day, however, and the sun on her face and arms was comforting. Swan had said that they would be coming into bad weather after their layover at Tarot, and she had to take him at his word. There was no hint of trouble in the sky, though, and the ocean was calm. It was difficult to imagine that changing. She knew the sea could be unpredictable, violent, and cruel. She didn't want to think of what might be waiting ahead.

"We're going to be landing at Tarot tomorrow," the captain said. "This is a chance for the men to...freshen up."

She raised her eyebrows. "Freshen up?" she repeated. "How do—"

Her question was answered before she could finish it, however, as the first crew member—Marty, if she wasn't mistaken—sent up a shout and leaped from the bow. Several men, gathering at the railing, cheered, and before Ella had a chance to react, two more had jumped overboard.

With a mixture of apprehension and excitement, she hurried toward the men and peered over. Below, the three men, still fully-clothed, were treading water and laughing. The sight of all that dark and unexplored water was unnerving, and she felt a stab of fear at the thought of plunging into its cold depths. The fear was outweighed by anticipation, however, and she knew that she had to go in. She'd always loved swimming, and she could practically feel the cold water against her skin already.

As much as she hated the idea of asking for permission—from him, or anyone—Ella was determined to keep the relationship between herself and Swan civil. He'd come to stand beside her, again, and she forced herself to turn toward him. "May I go in?" she asked.

He seemed surprised by the question, and why wouldn't he be? She'd proven that asking was not first nature for her. His dark brows lifted. "Do you want to?" he asked.

She nodded, unable to hide her excitement.

"Well, then," he said, with a small gesture of his hand. There were several splashes and yells as more men abandoned the ship.

Ella grabbed the railing with both hands. She wondered, briefly, how she would be expected to return to the ship. She wasn't sure she was strong enough to climb a rope, in spite of her penchant for hard work. She'd been malnourished for so long, her body was only beginning its slow recovery process—a process that, she knew, might never be completed, because once she got off *Voyage*, her meals would likely never be so regular again.

It didn't matter. If she had to a climb a rope, she would manage, if that was her price for enjoying the ocean water.

She hesitated and turned to look at Captain Swan. He was watching her; he seemed tense, more so than usual. "Are you going in?" she asked.

He shook his head, slowly, once. "I don't leave my ship at sea," he said. His voice was a low rumble, and she felt a shiver pass through her. He leaned forward. For one heart-stopping moment, she thought he was going to kiss her. *Finally*, her traitorous mind whispered. She felt a familiar heat creeping up her throat and fidgeted nervously. "Should you be swimming?" he asked, his voice even lower, and she realized that he was bent close so that no one would overhear.

His face was so close, though...Her gaze drifted to the dark stubble on his chin, and she imagined how rough it would feel against her fingers, against her cheek, against her lips...She swallowed. In her disappointment at realizing he wasn't going to kiss her, it took a moment to understand his question. Why shouldn't she swim?

As the answer dawned on her, she felt her face flame even hotter. "You mean, will I attract sharks?" she muttered, forcing herself to meet his dark, intense gaze in spite of her embarrassment.

His surprise was brief, quickly replaced by the unmistakable sparkle of humor in his eyes. His lips quirked, and a hint of a dimple appeared in his cheek. "Something like that," he murmured.

Her bleeding had been finished since the night before. She knew that her admission could mean so much more than a license to swim; it could mean that there was nothing stopping him from joining her in bed—his bed. "No sharks," she said, and when her eyes slid, of their own accord, to his mouth, she saw his lips part slightly. She licked her own, her heart stampeding in her chest. The world had disappeared. The ship beneath them, the men on deck and in the sea below, the ocean around them, the sky above...

Captain Swan cleared his throat, and she struggled to pull herself together. Embarrassed by what must seem to him a shameful wantonness, she turned back to the rail, determined to plunge into the dark sea to cool the humiliation from her face. She put her foot on the bottom rung, and the captain put a hand on her arm, surprising her.

"You can swim, right?" he asked.

"I guess we'll find out," she said.

Before she could pull herself up, he tightened his grip on her arm. "I'm serious," he said. She looked down at his hand, marveling at the heat the contact was spreading up her arm. He released her quickly, with a muttered, "Sorry."

She turned toward him once again. "If I get into trouble, will you come in to save me?" she asked. It was meant to be a joke, to lighten the mood. She would never expect him to come in after her, particularly since he'd claimed he never left his ship when it was unanchored.

His gaze was anything but light, however. "Yes," he said. It was little more than a breath, and she could almost believe she'd imagined it. "Although I suspect I wouldn't have to," he added, nodding past her. She turned to find Luca coming toward them, with a fading black eye and a scowl—the scowl that seemed to be permanently affixed to his face, now. Ella sensed, rather than saw, Captain Swan drawing away, and she felt a pang of loss that she knew was ridiculous. Instead of dwelling on it, she focused on Luca.

"Are you going in?" she asked.

Luca stopped before her and shrugged sullenly.

She knew she should make an effort, but she suddenly found her irritation flaring. She didn't want to have to cajole him. It was supposed to be fun. If he was going to pout, then it was best he stay away, so as not to spoil her enjoyment.

"Suit yourself," she muttered. She turned and climbed the railing quickly. She saw Captain Swan, from the corner of her eye, watching her.

"Ella," Luca said, sounding alarmed as he stepped forward.

Ignoring him, without giving him a chance to stop her, she jumped.

It was a long drop to the ocean, and although it passed in a flash, she had time to feel the fear and joy and exhilaration and apprehension. She saw the faces of the men below as they watched her descent, and she felt the impact as she burst into the shockingly-cold water. As the ocean swallowed her in its cool embrace, she barely managed to keep from gasping seawater into her lungs. She let herself plunge downward, nervous about what might be waiting in the darkness to meet her.

She felt another body drop into the ocean beside her, and she finally spread her arms and kicked herself toward the surface. In a few strokes, she'd broken into air, and she pulled in a deep breath, shaking her head to clear the saltwater from her eyes. The men were applauding and whistling, and she felt—for the first time—truly accepted by the crew. She grinned, treading water. A moment later, Luca surfaced beside her.

"Bloody hell, El," he gasped. "You could've killed yourself."

At least the sullen scowl was gone, and she was glad for that. He'd followed her in, as she should've known he would. He might be having a difficult time, but he was still Luca. She smiled at him, sorry for the impatience she'd been feeling toward his mood. "We're swimming in the middle of the ocean," she said, raising her eyebrows at him.

Suddenly, unable to help himself, he grinned in return. She knew they were both thinking the same thing: it would be better if Travis were there, to enjoy the experience with them. Nonetheless, she was determined to have fun while she had the chance. She splashed Luca in the face, on impulse, and he laughed and tried to dodge. She stretched back and slid away from him through the water with easy strokes of her arms. Luca laughed again and followed.

Squinting against the bright sky, Ella looked up and saw Captain Swan standing on the railing, holding the angled rope, as she'd seen him several times before. He was silhouetted against the blue sky, with his dark hair riffling in a slight breeze. She thought he was watching her. No, she knew he was.

Will you come in to save me?

Yes.

She felt another shiver that she tried to convince herself was to be blamed on the cold water.

She wasn't feeling so cold anymore, though. She was thinking about what possibilities the coming night might hold. She was imagining how she might be expected to pay for the bargain she'd struck, and wondering why the flutters of anticipation in her stomach held little fear.

*   *   *

Ella had always been a strong swimmer, and in spite of her thinness she outlasted many of the men in the water. She watched as, one by one, they climbed ropes to return to the ship. Soon there were only a few left in the sea, along with Luca and herself. Ella was growing tired. She was reluctant to leave the soothing water, but she didn't want to wait until she was so weak that she had no chance of climbing up. She also didn't want to be the last in the water, because by then she might have become a nuisance to the captain. So long as there were others in the water, she was not holding up their departure.

She was concerned about Luca, too. He'd been treading water easily enough, but he'd never taken to the water the way Ella and Travis had, and she could see his energy flagging. "You should go up," she said. "I'll follow you in a minute."

Luca shook his head, and glittery droplets of water sparkled around his head. "I'm not leaving you down here," he said.

They'd had such a good time, she was loathe to spoil it by starting another argument. She suppressed a sigh. "I want to do a lap around the ship," she said. She wasn't entirely sure it was a good idea. The ship was large, and doing so would expend a lot of valuable energy. It would take several minutes, at least, and she would run the risk of annoying the crew. Everyone had stayed in the water on the northeast side of the ship. She wanted to see everything she could from her eye-level view of the sea.

"It's too dangerous," Luca said.

"I'll be fine," she answered. "You should go up. You're getting tired."

"I'm not," he lied, scowling.

Determined to keep things from spiraling out of control, Ella moved forward through the water separating them, until their legs were brushing against each other as they kept themselves afloat with slow kicks. "Luca," she said.

Before she realized what he was going to do, he leaned forward and kissed her. She was so startled that she pushed at him, and went under, spluttering water as she struggled to regain her buoyancy. Luca was reaching for her arm, and she pulled away, trying to keep from going under again.

"I'm sorry," he said, and while he did look almost as shocked as she was, he also looked hurt. There was nothing she could do about that at the moment. He had no right to kiss her, and she thought she'd done her best to make that clear to him. She probably could have reacted better, but her shock was giving way to anger.

"Are you alright?" a voice called. One of the crew members still in the water was slowly swimming toward them.

Ella didn't want a big deal to be made. She could handle Luca. They would sort through their issues in private, when she was calmer. "We're fine," she said. Then, afraid of sounding rude when the man was only concerned about her, she added, "Thank you." She glared at Luca and lowered her voice. "I'll speak to you, later. Climb on the ship before you drown."

Luca scowled and clenched his jaw. His throat worked for a moment as he struggled with his words. "Stop treating me like you're my fucking mother!" he finally said, his anger and words stunning her as much as his kiss had.

Some of her own anger dissipated in the face of his, because she knew that his came from a place of pain. Before she could think of anything to say, he'd turned and crossed to the rope with a few long strokes of his arms. She watched for a few moments, treading water, as he started climbing, his muscles bunching beneath his clinging clothes. Did she treat him like a child? She supposed she did, sometimes. It was hard for her, even after everything they'd been through, to think of him as a grown man. Even Travis was grown up, really. He was still a boy, still innocent in many ways, but he was not a child.

And Luca certainly wasn't, either, in spite of his sometimes-juvenile behavior.

She tore her gaze away from his climb, blinking tears from her eyes. The men in the water were watching her, trying to pretend they weren't, and she kicked herself forward impulsively. She started swimming, pulling herself through the water. For just an instant, she was tempted to cut out to sea, to swim until she could no longer swim, to flee her life until the ocean finally swallowed her submissive body and accepted that life from her. It was an alarmingly-tempting idea. She didn't want to die. She didn't want to give up, not on Travis, not on Luca...And, not on herself, not really. There had to be something better.

Ignoring her brain's sneaky shift to thoughts of Colin Swan, she swam along the side of the ship, letting the water soothe her. She let her mind drift where it wanted, leaving the stressful musings on Travis and Luca and turning instead to fantasies that were stressful in a different way. As she swam, her tension finally began to melt away. She could feel her muscles straining and protesting, but the weary ache was a pleasant reminder that she was alive and healthy and moving forward.

She'd circled around the back of the ship and a quarter of the way along the other side when she finally rolled onto her back to rest her tired arms for a bit. She squinted at the brightness of the sky, from within the shadow of the ship, and saw the captain above her. He was walking along the railing. His presence surprised her, but the surprise almost immediately made way for a sudden fear that he would fall. She watched him walking with the easy grace of a cat stalking its prey and knew that he wouldn't fall, however. And, even if he did, what would it matter? Surely he could swim, and if he couldn't, the men would save him—or she would. She tried to tell herself she was being ridiculous, and tried not to be alarmed by her surge of protectiveness.

He was the only person she could see aside from Goonie, in the crow's nest, and Goonie wasn't looking in their direction. He was staring off toward Tarot, with his back to her and the captain.

Ella couldn't tell for sure if Swan was looking at her. His face was dark against the bright sky. The tingle spreading through her body said that he was watching her, though, and she was suddenly very conscious of her clinging clothes. She fought the instinct to roll over and begin swimming, knowing it would be stupid to risk overtaxing her tired muscles for the sake of modesty. Besides, now that her period had ended, he might soon be seeing far more than her wet clothes were revealing. She swallowed, kicking slowly, and watched him match her progress along the ship.

She hoped he wasn't annoyed with her for taking so long. Should she apologize, or ask if he was anxious to leave? He could always throw down a rope and demand she return to the deck if he was in a hurry, but he didn't. He simply walked the railing with an enviable and easy grace, matching her speed as she pushed herself through the water, silent and—she thought—watchful. Could it be that he was not anxious to leave, but simply concerned about her safety? She knew that she shouldn't read anything personal into his vigil, because he cared about the safety of his crew and, for the time being, she was a part of that crew. She couldn't afford to believe there was any more to it than that. She would only be setting herself up for heartbreak.

When she was about halfway along the ship, she rolled over and began swimming. She set a pretty fast pace, determined to reach the other side before he could demand that she hurry, but she tired more quickly and had to flip onto her back once more as she reached the head of the ship. She was annoyed with her lack of stamina, and frustrated by her weakness. She looked up. Goonie was almost directly above her, silhouetted against the sun, still not looking down at her. Between Goonie and herself, Captain Swan had kept pace with her, and was now very definitely looking down at her. Although his face was still shadowed, she could finally see some of his features. His expression was grim and watchful.

"I don't relish the idea of getting my clothes wet," he said. His voice was low, traveling down to her in a surprising caress. She felt a shiver that had nothing to do with the cold water beneath her.

"I'm fine," she answered. Her voice was a little shaky, and she frowned. He would probably think it was from weakness, or cold, or fear, and she didn't want him believing any of those. They weren't true. She wasn't sure she wanted him to know the truth, either, however. The truth was more embarrassing.

"You're tired," he said. It wasn't a question.

"I'm out of practice," she mumbled. She wasn't sure he would hear her.

"Would you like a rope?"

"No," she said. She knew that her annoyance was unfair to him. He was only looking out for her, as any good captain would for a crew member. "I'm fine. Just resting for a minute."

"Your stubbornness is quite..." he paused, seeming to search for the right word.

"Endearing?" she quipped.

She saw a flash of teeth in the shadows of his face. "Infuriating," he corrected, but she could hear the smile in his voice. She felt a strange rush of relief to know that he wasn't really angry with her. At least, not yet.

"Well, six of one, half dozen of another," she said, and she actually heard him chuckle. She found herself smiling in return, and knew that nothing was going to stop her from completing her lap around the ship. She was going to finish the last leg in a single burst of energy, because he was right—she was stubborn, often infuriatingly so. Her determination would keep her going even if her arms and legs threatened to fall off and sink to the bottom of the sea.

Once she reached the other side, she had no idea how she was going to climb up the side of the ship. She would cross that bridge when she came upon it, however. She simply had to focus on the remainder of her swim, and then she would focus on her return to the deck.

"Think I can make it around without stopping again?" she asked.

"I have no doubt," he answered, and the rush of pleasure his words sent through her instantly energized her flagging muscles. Grinning to herself, she rolled over and kicked herself into a stroke. She rounded the head of the ship and kept going, pulling herself along, focusing on nothing but the feel of the saltwater caressing her skin. Her arms ached, and so did her back, but she would not stop again. She wasn't just out to prove something to Swan. She was proving it to herself, as well, proving that she could follow through on something she'd set her mind to.

There were three ropes dangling from the side of the ship, and she focused on them, making the end of the furthest her goal. She was breathing heavily by the time she reached it, and her body was screaming in protest. She finally came to a rest, sore and pleased with herself as she began to tread water beside the rope. The thought of climbing it was beyond daunting. She wasn't sure willpower would be enough to get her to the top.

While she was taking a moment to gather her thoughts and what little energy she had left, there was a splash to her left, startling her. She turned toward it, expecting some sort of sea creature to be near the surface of the dark water. Instead, she saw with surprise—and relief—that the end of a rope ladder had been tossed to the gentle waves beside her. She looked up. Captain Swan was holding the top. He was no longer perched on the railing, but was standing on the deck. Ivan was beside him. Above them, Goonie was now looking down at her. She still couldn't see any of the other men, and she assumed they were below, drying off and warming up after their cold dip.

Captain Swan didn't say anything, and she knew that his silence was, in itself, a challenge. He was testing her stubbornness, to see if she would refuse his offer of help even though she probably couldn't climb up on her own. She reached out and pulled the bottom rung toward herself, and she felt a surge of gratitude. He might think she would balk at this offering, but she was instead thankful for it.

Not that her pride didn't prickle just a bit—It did. It was unimportant, however, and she knew there was no sense in wasting time. She pulled the rung under the water and managed to get her foot onto it, slipping underwater only once in the process. She shook the water from her face and reached up to grab hold above her head. She looked up. Swan looked down at her.

He started pulling the ladder, hand over hand, rung by rung, without comment, and in a moment she felt it tighten against the bottom of her foot and then, slowly, she felt herself lifting out of the water. She might be a little underweight, yet, but she surely didn't weigh *that* little, and her clothes were full of water. As her body left the sea, and Captain Swan and the ropes absorbed her full weight, she realized that he was far stronger than he appeared. Inside his dark clothes, his body seemed lean, but she knew she shouldn't be surprised by his strength. She'd seen him haul Bart off of Luca, and throw him against the railing, after all.

As she rose higher, she got closer to the side of the ship, until the railing was directly above her. She reached up and grabbed it with one hand. Her leg already felt shaky beneath her, and she wanted nothing more than to sit down for a few minutes to recover from her swim. A moment later, Swan had grabbed her arm and hauled her up and over the railing, once more surprising her with his strength. She suddenly found herself standing on the deck, blinking, dripping, cold in spite of the bright sun warming the top of her head.

The other crew members were gathered near the door. She'd assumed they were already below, getting warm and dry, and wasn't immediately sure what to make of their watchful presence. She met Luca's eyes, for just a moment. He was in the back of the crowd, and as soon as their gazes connected, he turned and disappeared into the shadowy stairwell. One by one, the other men followed, but not before a few of them gave a smattering of applause that made her blush. She was extremely self-conscious, now, and when Ivan handed her a towel, she clutched it against her wet clothes gratefully.

She became aware that Swan's hand was still resting on her arm as she felt the heat of his touch seeping into her chilled skin. The contrast made her shiver, although she tried to suppress it. She ducked her head and finally glanced shyly up at him, embarrassed to find herself standing so close to him and feeling silly for her embarrassment. When their eyes met, his lips quirked a bit. He seemed to be in a rare good mood. She could only hope it would last.

"You should go get dried off and change before you shiver yourself right through the deck," he said in a low voice. Ivan, the only other man left on deck that she could see, had already walked away, leaving her alone with the captain. She wondered if Goonie was watching them and resisted the urge to look up to see.

She swallowed her nerves as best she could and said, barely above a whisper, "Thank you for pulling me up."

He bent close, wreaking havoc on her heartbeat. "Thank you for not drowning," he returned. He sounded amused, but she found her gaze captured by his, and his eyes were dark, intense. For a moment she couldn't breathe, or remember any of the reasons why it would be dangerous to let herself have feelings for this mysterious man. She thought he was finally going to kiss her, and she felt her lips part in anticipation. His gaze shifted to her mouth, and she saw a muscle in his jaw tighten. He let out a breath through his nose. "You're freezing," he said, taking a step back. She immediately had to fight the urge to follow him. His sudden distance made her feel colder than she had a moment before. "There are dry clothes on the bed."

She blinked in surprise. When had he managed that? He'd been right above her the entire time she'd been in the water.

"I had Ivan bring them up," he said, in response to her confusion.

"Oh," she managed. She cleared her throat. "Thanks."

"Call if you need anything," he said.

She nodded, trying desperately to quell her disappointment at the realization that he was not following her to the cabin, that he was not going to kiss her. Self-doubt swirled through her as she walked toward his cabin, hugging the towel against herself. Was she so unattractive to him? There were times—like just a couple of minutes ago—when she thought that he wanted to touch her, to kiss her. Times when she thought the attraction was mutual. But he always pulled away, and she couldn't help thinking it was because she was reading the signs incorrectly and he really had no desire for her.

He was far more beautiful than she was, and she knew that. He could have any woman in the world, but he was stuck with only one on his ship, and Ella supposed that might be the root of the problem. He wasn't attracted to her, but she was the only female around. He was a man, after all. He was bound to have some sort of reaction to a woman standing with her wet clothes clinging to her breasts even if he didn't want anything to do with that woman in particular.

Ella tried to pretend that she wasn't hurt by her own thoughts, but she couldn't fool herself. If Swan finally did give in to his desire and take what she'd offered him, it would only be because she was available and no one else was. Would she be able to live with that knowledge? Would the pain of the aftermath be worth the experience?

She blinked back tears as she stepped inside his cabin and closed—and locked—the door. Did she want him so badly that she would sacrifice her pride—the one thing that she had always clung so desperately to—and give herself to a man who only wanted to sate his own desire? Her skin was cold inside her clothes, and she remembered the heat of his hand on her arm, cutting through the chill of seawater.

Yes, she thought, looking toward the bed and the neatly-folded clothes there. *God help me, I think I would.*

*   *   *

Captain Swan had avoided her all day, and he felt guilty and ashamed as he let himself in to his cabin as quietly as possible. He'd come painfully close to kissing her on the deck, after her swim, and that scared him. Not kissing her so much as the lack of control that he knew would be lurking behind the action. Once he'd kissed her, he had no doubt that he would scoop her, dripping wet, into his arms and carry her to bed. He would have made love to her, because one taste of her lips would have been far, far more than his self-control could stand.

He knew that, and it scared him. Terrified him, in fact.

So did the overwhelming surge of protectiveness he'd felt upon seeing her down in that dark water. He'd come close to jumping in after her several times, and had barely resisted by telling himself he was being ridiculous. When Luca kissed her, and she pushed away—going underwater for a moment—Swan almost dove in. What would he have done, though? Drowned Luca? Sure, she would appreciate that. She loved the boy, for crying out loud. Swan could only assume she didn't want to be kissed with so many eyes upon them.

Luca had not seemed very pleased with the turn of events, however, and Swan was going to be keeping an extra close eye on that kid. Yes, Ella loved him. She'd offered herself just to save him, and that was no small thing for someone with as much pride as she had. Just because she loved him, and thought she knew him, didn't mean he was trustworthy, though, and Luca had already proven that he had a short temper.

When Ella had gone around the ship, however, was when Swan had really felt his nerves. He almost went in the first time she rolled onto her back, and several times after that. The more apparent her tiredness became, the more protective he felt. Then, as she'd neared the end of her circumnavigation, his worry had mostly turned into pride—pride in her, for accomplishing what she had set out to do in spite of her exhaustion. All he'd wanted to do, then, was wrap his arms around her, kiss her until neither of them could breathe, and carry her to bed.

Instead, he'd avoided her for the remainder of the day, afraid that one more

108

close encounter would mean the final unraveling of his control. Now, as he let himself in to his dark room, he could hear her hushed breathing and knew that she was pretending to be asleep. She was afraid that he was going to take her up on her offer, an offer she'd only made to help Luca. Swan sighed and ran a hand down his face. He was beyond tired. He couldn't remember the last time he'd had more than a couple hours of uneasy sleep.

She was still afraid of him, and that fear should curb his desire more than anything else could. The problem was, when they were standing face to face, her fear wasn't always apparent. In fact, sometimes she seemed downright...eager.

He cursed himself as he lowered his tired body into the chair behind his desk. That wasn't fair, and he knew it. He was projecting his own desire on to her, because if he could convince himself that she wanted him, perhaps that would mean he wasn't quite such an asshole. That argument didn't hold up, though, because even now she was lying awake in bed, afraid that he would push himself onto her.

Once he was settled into his creaky chair, he could practically feel her relax into the bed, and he silently cursed himself again—and her. Her fear was understandable, he supposed, but not justified. He'd done nothing, as far as he could think of, that would make her believe he would brutalize her. He wanted her, yes, and every time he was close enough to touch her, he felt his self-control waver and sometimes almost dissolve. He wanted to kiss her, and wanted to feel her naked body squirming beneath him. The thought made him shift uncomfortably in his chair and grit his teeth.

There was no place for pain or fear in his desires, though. He wanted her clinging to his shoulders, begging for more, wrapping her legs around his waist—

He barely managed to suppress a groan as he dropped his head into his hands. Yes, he wanted her. He wanted her *willing*. He knew that would not happen, though, and he was going to drive himself insane with such thoughts. Maybe a visit to Meena would cure him of his crazy fantasies. Maybe it had simply been too long, and the presence of a woman—any woman—was too much for his body to ignore.

Do you really believe that?

He ignored the question, knowing it led to a path he didn't want to travel down.

*   *   *

Ella and Luca were in one of the dinghies together as more than half of the crew of *Voyage* made their way toward Tarot in the rowboats. Ivan was also in Ella's boat, along with Rashad and Timón and a few other men. Ella couldn't keep herself from glancing over at Swan's boat, as it kept pace with hers. Swan was one of the two men rowing—something he, of course, did not need to do, as captain. The sight of his muscles bunching as he rowed was hypnotizing.

109

She pulled her gaze away and almost immediately shot another surreptitious look in his direction.

She was disappointed that she wasn't in his boat, but he'd done everything he could to avoid her for the past day and night. He'd only come into the cabin late at night when he'd thought she was sleeping, and then he'd settled behind his desk with a sigh and eventually fell into a restless and uncomfortable sleep. She'd wanted so badly to rise from his bed and go to him, to comfort him as he slept uneasily. She felt guilty for lying in his bed while he struggled to catch an hour's uninterrupted sleep in his chair. She wanted him to share the bed with her.

Through the long night, it was her own self-doubt that kept her from waking him and tugging him by the hand toward the bed. Part of her thought that he would follow willingly—especially if he was roused from sleep and looking for comfort, and a release from whatever troubled his sleep. A larger part of her was afraid of rejection, and that part of her said that rejection was inevitable. How could it not be? Just look at him. He was way out of her league, and it would be dangerous for her to forget that even for a moment.

He'd put her in a boat with Luca, Timón, and Rashad as a gesture of kindness, she had no doubt. He thought that she would be the most comfortable with them. He probably didn't know that she and Luca had barely spoken since the incident in the water.

They were bringing crates ashore, and she knew that there would be more trips between the ship and the shore with more boxes. She wasn't sure what was in them, or what to expect on Tarot. The island looked beautiful, with white expanses of beach and thick vegetation painting the backdrop. There were people waiting for them on the beach, almost all of them dark-skinned and barely-clothed. There were two white people that she could see, a man and a woman standing side by side, the man in cutoff shorts and the woman in a dress that billowed around her in the breeze.

Ella couldn't help but wonder if Meena was among the women on the beach, and she tried to ignore the stab of jealousy at the thought of Swan rushing to meet this as-yet-faceless woman.

The next time she glanced over at Swan's boat, she was surprised to catch his eyes. They were almost to the shore, and men from the beach were wading in to the water to take the boats' ropes. Soon all four dinghies were pulled up onto the sand, and the men were climbing out. Rashad offered her a hand, and she accepted his help out because her legs felt a little unsteady after so long at sea. In a few moments, she stood beside Luca in the bright, hot sand, staring up at the lush green trees and marveling at the beauty of such a place.

"Long way from home, huh?" Luca mumbled.

"Yeah," she agreed. She looked over at Swan, and saw with a sinking sensation in her stomach that he was walking toward the most beautiful woman Ella had ever seen. Her skin was as black as Rashad's, and glossy. Her breasts—considerably larger than Ella's—were barely covered with a couple of scraps of material tied around her neck and back. She wore a makeshift skirt, knotted around her waist, that stopped high on her muscled thighs. She was the epitome of sensuality, and Ella suddenly felt ugly and inadequate and knew why Swan had shown no interest in her. Why would he, when he knew he had this woman waiting for him?

Meena was hurrying toward him, with her arms outstretched, and Ella tore her gaze away, unable to stomach their hug and kiss of greeting. She felt ill. She wanted to return to the ship and hide her face in a pillow until it was time to set sail again. Short of that, she wanted to run into the jungle, free from prying eyes, until it was time to leave. Instead, she stood straight and frozen on the beautiful beach, wondering if she was going to make a fool of herself by bursting into ridiculous tears.

Swan and Meena were approaching them; Ella could see them in her peripheral vision.

"Ella," the captain said, and she turned toward them in spite of her urge to run. "This is Meena. Meena, Ella, and Luca."

"Nice to meet you," Meena said with a thick, pleasant accent.

"You too," Luca said, glancing at Ella.

"Make yourself at home," Meena said. "The village is through here. Barnard will show you the way, if you wish it," she added, gesturing toward the white man in the shorts. Then, turning toward Swan, she said something in a language that Ella did not recognize. Swan, who'd been frowning at Ella—no doubt perturbed by her rude silence—turned his attention to Meena with his scowl deepening. He spoke quickly and easily in Meena's language, and Ella had never felt more out of place.

In spite of her happiness to see Swan, which was unmistakable, Meena seemed upset. When she spoke again, Swan put a hand on her arm, glanced at Ella and Luca, and said, "Excuse us, please," before leading Meena toward the path that cut into the trees. Ella stared after them, cursing herself for caring and trying not to imagine Swan pressing Meena into a mattress somewhere.

"We're going to unload these boxes and return some supplies to the ship, then bring the next round. Stay close to Barnard and Timón and Rashad," Ivan said. "There are a lot of dangers in the jungle. Don't go wandering off. Understand?"

"Yes," Luca answered, sullenly. He was the one that Ivan was looking at, but Ella got the distinct impression that the warning was actually meant for her.

She knew that there was no way to go after her brother until Captain Swan was ready to leave. She knew that she should take advantage of their stay, however long or brief it might be, to enjoy a little relaxation on the beach or stroll through the village or something—maybe just eat something that hadn't been cooked in a cramped ship's galley by herself and Timón. She knew that she should be grateful for the chance to sink her toes into sand and steady her legs on dry land.

She suddenly wanted nothing less than to be standing on Tarot, however. She could feel her emotions bubbling within her, and felt powerless against the rising tide. It was ridiculous. Swan had never even kissed her, let alone made any kind of indication that he was interested in a relationship with her. She'd known all along that it would be stupid to project her feelings onto him, but hadn't she gone ahead and done it anyway? It would seem so, because the memory of his hand on Meena's arm, and the way Meena pressed her sleek and shiny body close to his, made Ella's stomach and nose burn.

"I'd like to return to the ship with you," she said, quietly, wondering if Ivan would refuse. Swan might have given orders to keep her on land. He might have even told the crew that she was not to be trusted alone. Maybe he thought she would try to steal the ship or something, an idea that was laughable. She didn't know the first thing about sailing a ship, and would have no way to convince the men to do it.

Ivan didn't immediately refuse her strange request, but he did study her for a moment until she shifted uncomfortably. Luca was staring at her, as well. Could they see the shine in her eyes, the paleness of her face? Could she, perhaps, convince them that she simply wasn't feeling well? Wouldn't they then suggest that it would be better for her to remain on solid ground and rest for a bit?

"What's wrong?" Luca asked.

What do you care? was on the tip of her tongue, and she fought back the words because they were unfair. She was hurt by the way Luca had been acting, but he was still concerned about her. She cleared her throat. "Nothing," she said, unable to quite meet his eyes—or Ivan's. "I just...would like to return to the ship."

She still expected Ivan to refuse, and she was determined not to beg. If she had to, she would sneak away into the jungle to catch some time alone to deal with her irrational jealousy and hurt feelings. "Very well, if you're sure you wouldn't like to look around?" Ivan said, surprising her. "I'm sure the women could get you some different clothes, something to eat and drink..."

"Thanks. I...I'd just like to..." she trailed off, because her throat felt thick. She gestured toward the ship, anchored off shore.

"Are you ill?" Timón asked, peering into her face.

She shook her head. "Just tired," she mumbled, wishing they would take their good intentions and leave her alone.

"Very well," Ivan repeated. He seemed troubled. Was her request, and his agreement, going to get him into trouble with the captain? She hoped not. Besides, she doubted Swan would notice her absence for quite some time. "You can get back into this boat, if you'd like. We'll leave in just a minute."

"Thank you," she muttered. As she started to turn back toward the dinghy, Luca touched her arm.

"Are you sure you're alright?" he asked.

"Sure," she answered. She still couldn't quite meet his gaze.

Luca leaned close so that the others couldn't hear. They were all starting away, anyway. "You're not upset about *him?* Leaving you here?" he asked in something close to a hiss.

Ella jerked her arm away from his hand. "You want me to quit acting like your mother, I want *you* to quit acting like my goddam *boyfriend*," she snapped, her flare of temper momentarily pushing some of her hurt aside. "Thanks so much for your concern, Luca," she added, her voice dripping with sarcasm.

"Fine," he said, stepping back, his own face a mask of anger and—yes, it was there—hurt. They just kept on hurting each other. She didn't know how they'd gotten to such a point. Before sneaking on to *Voyage*, she couldn't remember a time when they'd truly been angry with each other. A few quarrels, maybe, but nothing they hadn't gotten over quickly, and they had certainly never set out to wound each other with barbed words. "Have fun on the ship, feeling sorry for yourself. I'm staying here. There are a lot of beautiful girls here, looks like."

"The fact that you think that would bother me proves that you still don't get it," she answered. She regretted the words when she saw him try to hide a wince. She couldn't take them back, and her pride and anger stopped her apology.

"Oh, I get it," he said. "I was just trying to look out for you," he said, backing away from her. "But, have it your way. I'm sure it will all work out with your captain, when he gets back from fucking his girlfriend."

If he'd still been close enough, Ella would have slapped him. A part of her wanted to charge after him and hit him in the face. She was too stunned to follow him, however. She stared as he turned his back and walked quickly toward the men hauling crates up to the path. She stared, her face burning with anger and humiliation, with her fists clenched at her sides and her stomach churning. She felt unsteady, and she tried to convince herself it was just because she hadn't yet gotten accustomed to being back on land.

Afraid that someone would notice her, pale and quaking, staring after Luca in shock, she turned awkwardly and somehow managed to climb into the rowboat. Nothing had been loaded into yet, and no one was nearby. Ivan was halfway up the beach, speaking to one of the natives, and his eyes met hers for a moment before she looked away.

Did everyone see her pining after Swan? Did everyone see her making a fool of herself? It must be obvious to all of them, by now, that he had no interest in her. The men had probably thought when Swan first moved her into his cabin that she'd become the whore she offered to be. They'd surely come to realize, eventually, that that was not the case. Swan was hardly ever in the cabin when she was, and he never touched her in any sort of intimate way when they were on the deck. It would be clear that there was nothing going on between them.

It must also be clear that he was the one rejecting her. It was true that Luca knew her better than anyone, but the whole crew must be able to see her gazing at their captain like a lovesick schoolgirl. Was that why Ivan had agreed to let her return to the ship? Did he feel sorry for her? Did they all talk about her behind her back, and say how sad it was that she couldn't see when her feelings weren't reciprocated?

They were supposed to believe that she and Luca were in love, but they must have realized by now that that was not true, either. His attempt to kiss her, and their subsequent exchange of words, had surely solidified that. Almost the whole crew had borne witness to that, and they must think she was a sad case, alright. And wasn't she? Didn't she know that she was being stupid and pathetic? Hadn't she known from the start that she was only setting herself up to look like a fool? She'd tried to suppress her attraction to him, and it would have been easier if he'd been mean. Instead, he went out of his way to be accommodating, and she found herself developing real, dangerous feelings. She found herself fantasizing about things that she knew would never come to be. She found herself hoping for things she knew she would never have.

"Are you ready?" Ivan asked, and she blinked up at him, horrified to find that his features were blurred by the tears shimmering in her eyes. She bit her lip and nodded, quickly looking down as several men began loading boxes into the boat. She barely saw the crates, and barely saw the men. It didn't matter who they were or what they were loading. All she wanted was to get into the cabin on the ship and lock the door and have her breakdown in private.

Ivan climbed into the dinghy and sat opposite her. She studiously avoided his gaze, praying he would pretend that he hadn't noticed the tears in her eyes or splotches of color in her cheeks.

"Whatever he did or said to upset you, I'm sure he didn't mean it," he finally said.

"It doesn't matter," she muttered, determined to keep some control over herself until she could be alone.

"He cares about you. He wouldn't want to hurt you," Ivan insisted.

"I don't want to talk about Luca," she snapped. She didn't want to be rude, but she was in no mood to talk, either.

"I wasn't," Ivan said after a moment, and she could think of absolutely nothing to say in return.

You don't know what you're talking about, she thought, and her throat burned with unshed tears.

* * *

Ella woke with a headache, puffy eyes, and a large dose of anger that was directed mostly at herself. She was not the type of person who fell apart because things didn't go her way. She was not the weepy, emotional girl who ran away from her problems to bury her face in a pillow and cry herself to sleep. She was not the type to develop ridiculous crushes in the first place, but that wasn't the real problem. Her reaction to reality was the real problem.

Her eyes felt raw and swollen, and she felt a bit queasy—maybe from the headache, maybe because the ship was moving. She frowned out the window ahead, trying to make sense of the sky with her sleep-muddled brain as she sat up on the bed. The light seemed all wrong. For a few moments, she wondered if the storm clouds Swan had predicted had finally rolled in, but that wasn't right. The sky was still mostly clear.

How could she not have awakened when the crew returned to the ship and set sail? Just how long had she been sleeping? She finally understood why the light seemed strange. It was no longer morning. It was late afternoon. She got up, wincing at the thud in her temples, and went to the door. It was still locked. The captain was probably annoyed with her for leaving the island. She couldn't blame him. She was annoyed with herself. Her mind tried to return to the image of Meena wrapping her sleek, muscled arms around his neck, and she quickly did her best to shut the thought down. She opened the door and stuck her head out cautiously. She didn't really want to come face to face with anyone—especially Swan—in the condition she was in. She needed to get some bearings, however. Luckily, she didn't see any of the men. Leaning out, looking back, she saw Tarot, however, and her heart skipped a beat.

She was disappointed that she'd blown her chance—probably the only one she would ever have—to spend time on such a beautiful and exotic island. More than that, she was alarmed to see how far they'd traveled from the only land in sight. They had not just set sail. They had been at sea for hours.

Suddenly remembering the clock in the cabin, she pulled her head back, closed the door, and locked it. Looking at the clock did not reassure her, even though it confirmed her suspicions about the lateness of the afternoon. For a moment, her irrational jealousy, her emotional instability, and her anger were forgotten in a swirl of confusion as she tried to make sense of things. She sat back on the edge of the bed, scrubbing her hands over her face. She felt like she had awakened to find that she'd slept through weeks rather than hours.

They'd had several boatloads of supplies to load and unload, that's what Ivan had said. That should have taken hours. They should have set sail just a short time ago, at the latest, and instead it looked as though they'd left the island shortly after she had. Had something happened? Had there been some sort of altercation?

She considered her options. She definitely did not want to seek out Captain Swan. Or Luca. Ivan?

No, her safest choice, she thought, would be either Timón or Rashad. She would have to make herself more presentable, see if she could get rid of some of the redness around her eyes. She was hungry, too, in spite of her queasiness. It had apparently been a long time since she'd eaten. Not that long ago, this would have been normal, but she'd gotten dangerously accustomed to regular meals, and her stomach protested its emptiness.

Timón, then, she decided. She could go to the kitchen under the pretense of finding something to eat, and to apologize for missing the midday meal, which he must have prepared hours ago. She shook her head, still struggling to wrap her head around the time-lapse, and decided it was pointless to dwell on it. It was over and done with, the island dwindling behind them, and she needed to concentrate on the future. She needed to get to Timón and see if he had any information on their early departure from Tarot, and then she had to prepare herself for a face-to-face with Captain Swan. She couldn't avoid him forever. She might not even be able to get below without running into him.

He might be angry with her for sneaking back to the ship without permission, but she hoped that Ivan hadn't told him anything about her emotional breakdown. It would be humiliating, and she did not want the captain to know the reasons behind her escape. She would have to be prepared to deal with whatever embarrassment their meeting might bring, however, because she still had weeks to spend in his company. They would have to coexist in peace, and that meant she would have to control her feelings.

She went to the mirror and glared at herself, disgusted by the puffy eyes, the dark smudges beneath, and the lines framing her mouth. She looked like she'd cried herself to sleep, and that was unacceptable. She'd finally begun to earn a little respect from the men of the crew, and she didn't want to throw that all away by wandering around like a weepy little girl.

She scrubbed her face with cold water, gasping at the shock against her heated skin.

Then, she finally let herself think of Luca. She should seek him out, too. She should apologize, but to what end? They just seemed to go around and around in a circle these days, and she wasn't sure how to make it better. She couldn't give him what he wanted. She knew that imagining a future with Swan would be foolish, but her silly crush had taught her something. It had shown her that desire was a spontaneous and uncontrollable thing, and every moment that she spent in Swan's presence was charged—on her end—with a sexual tension that she'd never before experienced.

That was something that she could never have with Luca, no matter how much he pursued her. No matter how much she loved him, or how hard he tried to convince her. Her life would be far less complicated if she *could* see him that way, because she knew that he would make a terrific, loyal, dedicated, protective husband to some lucky girl.

If she'd never known what it was like to catch her breath at the sight of Captain Swan, with his hair blowing across his forehead, she might have considered Luca. She might have settled for comfort and friendship, and that would not have been fair to either of them.

Was there any way to make him understand, though? Was there any way to repair the damage that had been done? Was there any way to save her family?

Chapter Seven

Ella had finally gotten herself as presentable as she was likely going to manage, and was just about to leave the cabin in search of Timón and some food and gossip, when she realized that the ship was slowing. She looked out the windows and was stunned to see that *Voyage* was pulling alongside another ship, one that had stopped to let them draw even.

She felt a flutter of unease in her stomach, picturing in her mind just how far they were from land. While Colin Swan had proven himself pretty generous and merciful for a pirate, she was under no illusions about the real danger associated with piracy in the open seas. She tried to convince herself that there was a more innocent reason for this encounter. Maybe the other ship needed help, or had a warning to pass on. Perhaps the captain was friends with Swan and just wanted to say hello.

The whole time they'd been at sea, she had not seen a single ship—not behind them, to either side of them, or ahead. She had particularly been looking ahead, whenever possible, hoping for a glimpse of the vessel carrying her brother. There had been nothing, and when she'd awoken from her self-pity-induced nap, she'd been too preoccupied by the sight of Tarot falling behind to even bother looking ahead.

There was a possibility that Travis was on that ship, and she had to find out. She hesitated at the door, however, afraid to rush into something that might cause problems. If she could just get sight of the name of the ship, she would know if it was the one carrying her brother. The men who'd kidnapped him had loaded him onto the slave ship *Enterprise*, a name that seemed far too fancy for their intellect. She knew why that was: The ship was not owned by the slave-traders or their captain, but by a rich and powerful man in Bohannon by the name of Martin Bauer. In the day and a half she'd had to figure out how to get to Travis, she'd asked around. She'd found out the ship's name, owner, and destination, and she'd found out that Swan's was the only one headed in the same direction for weeks.

She couldn't tell by sight if it was the same boat. She was usually pretty good at keeping track of details, but it had been almost a month, and she'd been understandably upset at the time. All she could say for certain was that it looked similar, and *could* be the ship. She had to see the name painted on the side, and she couldn't see it from the cabin. She opened the door, cautiously, and poked her head out. She could hear voices, and recognized Swan's, but she couldn't quite make out the words. She couldn't see him, either. As she moved a little further toward the deck, she saw the man he was speaking to, on the other ship. The captain, presumably. He was tall, wiry, with dirty blonde hair and an uneven beard, dressed in khaki trousers and a white shirt. Everywhere Swan was dark, this man was light, and Ella distrusted him on sight.

She glanced up and saw that Goonie was in the crow's nest, but all of his attention was focused on the conversation taking place over the narrow expanse of ocean separating the two rocking ships. She stepped further out, trying to identify the blonde's ship and, also, trying to hear what was being said.

"...have a bit of an...upscale clientele," Swan was saying, and she saw the blonde grin—a smile that did not reach his eyes. Even from such a distance, she could see that his expression was appraising. She felt another slithering of unease in her belly.

"...might be able to come..."

Even with the ships stagnant in the water, the wind was whipping their hair, now, and stealing half of their words. Ella glanced toward the horizon ahead, again, part of her expecting to see giant black clouds bearing down on them, rolling across the sky with frightening speed. There was nothing. Well, almost nothing. She thought there might be just a hint of premature darkness, there, at the edge of the world.

"...great...kind of limited...see what..." She turned her full attention back to Swan. He was speaking to the blonde captain, who was motioning to a few of his men. Swan gestured behind himself with an arm, as well, and Ella moved all the way out of the protection of the cabin to see what Swan was showing the other man.

Her heart skipped painfully in her chest.

It was Luca that her eyes lit upon first, of course, but within the span of a few seconds she came to realize something very important: She cared about all of the members of the crew, the men she'd been working with and cooking for, the men who had—aside from a drunken encounter—been courteous and deferential toward her. She considered Rashad and Timón to be her friends, and she was almost certain they felt the same way.

Luca, Timón, Rashad, Marty, Bart, Skip, Chay, Jody...Eight men, all lined up behind the captain, and that wasn't the disturbing part. Their hands were tied in front of them, wrists bound together with rope, every one of them. They were all staring straight ahead, with matching, angry looks on their faces.

She jerked her gaze away from Luca, with her heart slamming in her chest and her headache forgotten in her swirl of frantic thoughts. She didn't know what was going on, but she knew that it was bad. She almost rushed out onto the deck, demanding that Luca and the others be released, but her confusion held her back. She looked at Swan's profile, trying desperately to think of some good reason he might have for tying them up like that.

She almost wished he would sense her presence, and look over at her. Perhaps he could reassure her, even if it was just with a look.

The blonde captain's crew was suddenly hauling several prisoners of their own out onto the deck, each of them shackled at wrists and ankles. Five men, all of them black. Five men, but three of them were really just children. The youngest was probably around twelve, and the other two a few years older. The two adults were fairly young, themselves, surely no more than thirty.

They were silent and watchful as they were lined—roughly, by the crew—along the deck.

Ella's heart was really pounding, now. She'd gotten some confirmation, at least: it was a slave ship. Was Travis stowed somewhere within that floating mass of wood? She swallowed the lump of fear and emotion that was trying to choke her. She clenched her fists at her sides. She wondered if she'd be able to sneak around the other side of *Voyage*, without being spotted as she made her way toward the stern of the ship. If she could get around the head, she could make her way toward the back of the ship with less fear of being spotted by Swan or the other captain, and maybe she could spot the name of the slave ship. She needed to know if it was the one carrying her brother.

And if it is?

Then I'll figure out a way to get to him, no matter what, she thought, immediately.

If it's not? That was, strangely, a more difficult question to answer. Continuing after her brother would, of course, still be her more important objective. That could not make the lives of those five lined on deck, or the others that were likely below, unimportant. And Timón, Rashad, and the others...Luca...She shook her head. The blonde captain was talking, but she still couldn't make out his words. She knew she had to stop worrying and start acting, so she turned to her right, before she could chicken out, and ran without looking back. She didn't hear any shouts of alarm, or calls of any sort, and in a couple of moments she was concealed from view of the other ship by the hulk of the cabin. She didn't slow, however, and hurried around it and along the other side of *Voyage*, her bare feet slapping quietly against the deck as she ran. She didn't see any crew.

Of course, eight of them were inexplicably tied up. Ivan was with Swan. Goonie was in the crow's nest. There were a few men out on the other side of the deck, presumably standing guard over Luca and the others, but where was everyone else? Below, was the only answer, but did they know what was going on above them?

Ella was full of fear by the time she reached the rear of the ship, having been out of sight of the situation for so long. She couldn't hear or see what was going on, and a million terrible scenarios went through her mind regarding what she might see when she rounded the back. She forced herself to slow, however, and make her way quietly and carefully, sneaking around until she could see the other ship.

She hadn't been able to get close enough to see the front of that slave boat, so she couldn't say whether or not the name was painted there the way it was supposed to be. Where it was supposed to be on the rear side, however, a streak of black paint had been smeared, obscuring it. She silently cursed those damned slave-traders—and herself, as well, for not taking a chance to get eyes on the front side. She crept forward, and saw with a real rush of alarm that they had already braced two planks over the spread of water separating the two ships.

Luca was already on the other side, being pulled down roughly onto the slave ship, and Timón and Bart were right behind him. How was that possible?

119

Ella had hurried the length of the ship, and surely no more than a couple of minutes had passed.

The fear that gripped her was the same as when she'd seen Travis being captured, when she'd been unable to reach him, unable to save him, with no one to turn to for help. She looked at Swan, who was watching her best friend—the only family she had left—being loaded onto a ship that would deliver him to a life of pain and humiliation and servitude. Swan's expression was impassive, and he was standing with his hands clasped behind his back, a picture of nonchalance.

The anger came in a rush, and it drove out her fear. She was angry with herself, for spending the day pining over a man who apparently cared for no one but himself. She was angry with Luca, for allowing himself to be boarded onto a slave ship without a fight. She was angry with the slave-traders, of course, and for the crew of Swan's ship for standing idly by—perhaps they were afraid that they would be bound, too, if they interfered, but she never would have expected them to be so cowardly.

Mostly, though, her sudden flash of white-hot anger was directed at Swan, himself.

If she lived through the next few minutes, she supposed she might have to examine those feelings, because even in her preoccupation she knew that she'd been stupid to expect anything different than a pirate. A little politeness did not a gentleman make, any more than a little lust pointed toward everlasting love.

Before the fear could creep back in, Ella was rushing forward, wishing she had a sword or a knife or a rock, or even a shoe to use as a weapon. She was unarmed and had no tangible plan, no idea how she meant to take on both captains at once, as well as their respective crews. She was alone, with no one she could trust. No matter what had happened between them, the only person that she knew would have her back was Luca, and he was restrained on the other ship.

She had a dozen angry words fighting for release, and hadn't voiced any of them when the blonde captain caught sight of her. His eyebrows went up in surprise, and it seemed that in the next moment, every head turned toward her. Unable to help herself, she met Swan's eyes, still hoping against all rationality that he had some good explanation for his actions. How could there be a good explanation, though? There was nothing that would make it alright for Luca to be traded into slavery.

The surprise in Swan's eyes lasted only a moment, but when his eyebrows crashed down into a dark scowl, she knew something—knew it without doubt, instinctively: He hadn't known she was on the ship. He'd never stepped into his cabin after setting sail, and Ivan, for whatever reason, had never told him that he'd brought her back early.

A quick glance at Ivan showed her that his expression was one of surprise, too, but also guilt and alarm. That was confirmation, but she didn't need it. Swan had thought she was still on Tarot when he'd left. She didn't know why, or where he'd thought she was, or when he'd decided to leave her behind, and her stab of pain was as sudden as her anger—and less welcome.

"How many men you want for *her*?" the blonde captain asked, and now that she was close enough to hear him, the amusement in his voice sent a chill down her spine. Her tongue wrapped itself around her angry words and refused to let them go. All of the eight men were on the other ship, and they were standing beside the black men and boys. Luca was staring at her with wide eyes, and when she looked at him, he shook his head, once.

"She's not part of the deal," Swan said. His expression was once more a mask of near-boredom, and he gestured toward the plank with his hand. "Now, kindly send the lads across. I have a schedule to keep."

"I think we need to renegotiate," Blondie said, and underneath that amusement was something dangerous.

"She's mine," Swan said, and the danger in Blondie's voice was dwarfed by that in Swan's.

Swan's words came as a shock, and they only added to her confusion—and her anger. How dare he lay claim to her, when he'd had no interest in her before? How dare he lay claim as though she belonged to him like a book or a shirt or a boat? How dare he think he could own her, and Luca, and the others? No wonder he didn't eat below with the other men. He didn't think of them as his employees. He thought of them as slaves. Were they paid? She'd never asked. She'd been working for passage to Bohannon, for herself and Luca. Had Swan ever had any intention of letting them leave the ship when they got there?

He thought he left you on the island, she thought, and her confusion swirled. Her headache was back, thudding and thumping, and she knew that she had to do something. She was letting the doubt and fear return, and they would not serve her. She had to hold on to the anger. She found herself moving forward, and she saw Luca shaking his head again, more vigorously.

"If you weren't interested in trading her, you should have kept her on a tighter leash," Blondie said.

Luca was on that ship. There was a possibility, however small, that Travis might be, as well. She knew in that moment that she would probably never see her brother again, though. She was going on board that nameless slave ship, and she knew that she had no chance of actually freeing Luca or Travis or the others. Besides, what if she could? Where could they go? To Swan's ship? To the man who'd traded them away in the first place?

Struggling beneath the headache, confusion, anger, fear, and hopelessness, Ella somehow managed to move surprisingly fast. She made a beeline for the plank, because not trying was not an option. She thought—too late—of the garden tools as she passed the hidden patch of dirt. A weapon would have been helpful, but she didn't have time to pause, open the trapdoor, and grab one. She threw herself into the air, leaping toward the plank, unsure if she would make it or miss it. If she plunged between the vessels, would both captains simply leave her to perish, or would they fight over who should pull her out and punish her?

"Go!" Swan shouted. She knew he was hurrying toward her, but she was already on the plank and she didn't think he would follow her across and risk starting a war with Blondie. She thought, for a second, that he'd shouted 'no,' and in that heartbeat she thought that maybe, just maybe, he would be sorry to see her leave. Or die. By the time she felt the warm wood of the plank beneath her feet, however, she had recognized the word for what it was. She didn't try to understand it. It didn't matter.

The plank shifted and wobbled beneath her, and she was almost sure that she had jarred it badly enough that it would drop off one ship or the other and plunge her into the sea. Then she supposed she would find out the answer to one of her questions. The board held, barely, and as it bounced beneath her, she crossed it quickly. So quickly that she didn't even have time to understand the chaos that had already erupted on Blondie's deck. In a few long steps, she was dropping down into the midst of it, looking frantically for Luca.

Luca was fighting. He wasn't tied. He had a knife. All of them had weapons. All of them were fighting. None of them were tied.

There was no time for her to even begin to sort through her confusion, because someone was knocked into her and she stumbled back against the railing, wincing as the wood bruised her back. Men were shouting. Most of Blondie's men seemed as confused as she was, but they were fighting—with swords against the knives of Swan's crewmen. She shoved herself forward, away from the railing, and threw herself at a man swinging his sword toward Timón's head. She didn't think. She saw the blade arcing through the air, saw that Timón was never going to get out of the way in time, and she slammed into his would-be killer, knocking him sideways and sending him spinning into the melee. His blade missed Timón, but caught one of Blondie's other men in the arm on its way around.

Somehow, through the chaos, she caught Luca's eye again. He was fighting, but he was distracted, and he yelled over the din, "El! Look out!"

She turned and ducked, her heart lodged in her throat as a blade whistled through the air above her hair. In an instant, Bart's knife was buried into the chest of the man who'd tried to kill her, and she blinked, straightening as Bart snatched the man's sword away from him, turned, and used it to slice through the throat of another.

For a moment, Ella was frozen to the suddenly-bloody deck. It had been ten seconds since she'd set foot on the boat.

The blonde captain was right in front of her, and she had no idea how he'd gotten there. She felt a chill pass through her when she found herself staring into icy blue eyes. All around them, men were fighting, men were dying, and Blondie seemed oblivious. It was obvious that he didn't care about any of the slaves. One of the black men had gotten his shackle around a man's throat, and was rapidly choking him to death. Blondie didn't care about that, either. His crew seemed as unimportant to him as the slaves.

All of his attention was focused on Ella, and she knew that murder was not what he had in mind. She took a step back. She had no weapon, but she fisted her hands, trying desperately to keep from panicking. She wanted to run, but she wouldn't—and not just because she had nowhere to go. If he thought he was going to get anything from her without the fight of his life, he was in for a nasty surprise. She braced herself, taking bitter comfort from the solidity of the warm wood beneath her bare feet.

Then she was spinning, and she let out a sound of fear and surprise in spite of herself as her feet flew into the air and she was whirled, legs flailing. Someone had her around the waist, the arm a hard band across her stomach, and she drove her fist over her shoulder reflexively, catching him in the face. She heard a curse in response.

She barely felt the pain in her knuckles as her bare feet slapped to the deck. She was released so abruptly that she, dizzy and disoriented, almost fell. As she staggered, reaching a hand toward the rail behind her, she saw Swan turning away from her, with his sword drawn and raised. Blondie's blade met it in mid-air, and the clang seemed to cut through all the other sounds of battle around her.

She watched the two captains fight for several long moments, with a lump of fear in her throat. She didn't know what she should think about Swan, but she knew that she didn't want to see him killed. No matter what he might have done. She didn't want to care about him, and yet there was no way to rid herself of the emotion.

She forced her eyes away from him in time to see Luca kill a man, and she dodged an elbow a second before it would have caught her in the eye. Looking around, she saw that almost all of Swan's crew was now aboard Blondie's ship, including the men that had been unaccounted for during her race along the far side of *Voyage*. Some of them were bleeding. All of them were fighting. She didn't see any of Swan's men down, although there were at least five of Blondie's crew that appeared to be dead. No, make that seven. Eight.

She had never seen so much blood.

Ella was not stupid, and in the span of thirty seconds, maybe a little more, she'd come to realize that she'd misjudged the situation and made a horrible mistake. She did not know what was going on, only that she didn't understand it the way she'd thought she did. There was no time to sort it out. Men were dying every moment, and she did not want any of her friends to join the casualties.

Suddenly, Luca was by her side. He had a sword and a knife, and he thrust the handle of the sword into her palm. There was no time to argue the point, because she had to use it immediately, and she turned and drove the blade into the stomach of the man rushing for her. Luca was shouting, but she couldn't quite make out the words over the roaring in her ears. More men were flooding onto the deck, swarming up from below, but their topside numbers had already been so quickly decimated that Swan's men still had the upper hand.

Ella had no experience with a sword, but she knew that Luca did not, either. He was much more skilled with a knife, and he was having no problem defending himself with his weapon. Ella had her bloody sword raised, but there was nobody for her to fight. Rashad was in front of her, with his back to her, and then there were others, too. Between her and the slave-traders stood six of Swan's men, including Timón—who clearly had little to no fighting experience.

Ella couldn't keep her eyes from seeking out Swan. How long had the two captains been fighting? She couldn't say for sure. A minute? Two? It seemed like a lifetime.

She was mesmerized by the sight, in spite of herself. They seemed to be evenly matched at first, but it only took a few seconds to recognize the grace and strategy that was present in Swan's technique and lacking in Blondie's. Every time the bearded captain's sword made a move toward Swan, her heart skipped, and every time Swan deflected it, she wished bitterly that he would kill the other man and get himself out of danger.

She wanted to make her way below to see if her brother was among the other slaves, if there were any others. She would have to fight her way through the protective barrier of her own friends to do so, however, and she was unwilling to do that. While they were fighting for their lives, she would do nothing to put them into further jeopardy. She wanted to use the sword in her hand to help them fight, but they were keeping all enemies from her.

The blonde captain's sword sliced a line through the front of Swan's shirt, and Ella surged forward without thinking. Luca grabbed her arm and shoved her roughly back, barely looking at her as he used his knife to ward off an attack. Before Ella's heart even seemed to have resumed beating, she saw Swan finish the fight, saw him drive his blade right through Blondie, saw the bearded captain sink to his knees as Swan withdrew the blade.

When Swan turned, his eyes scanned the fight, and met hers for the briefest of moments. His eyes glittered, and his eyebrows were knotted in a scowl, and his jaw was clenched. Blood was spreading around the gaping flaps of his cut shirt—the second time she'd seen him in a white shirt—but he seemed oblivious. His gaze skimmed down her length, then back up, but he didn't meet her eyes again. Ivan was at his side, and Swan gestured in her direction and said a few short words. Her stomach churned with a mixture of fear and guilt.

Ivan strode toward her. He looked angry, as well, and she wondered if she should climb the railing and throw herself into the ocean before he could get his hands on her.

Ivan wasn't the real threat, though, and she knew that. When he drew near, he said, "Come. Now."

She hesitated, not because she wanted to cause further problems, but because she needed to know if her brother was on board. The look on Ivan's face convinced her that he was about two seconds away from tossing her over his shoulder, and she again considered making a break for it. The fight was already winding down. Swan's men had attacked fast and hard, and unexpectedly, and most of the remaining crew from Blondie's ship was surrendering after the death of their captain.

"Go, Ella," Timón said, looking back at her.

"He's not here, El," Luca said, when she still hesitated. She met his eyes. "It's a different ship."

"How...The name..." She wasn't sure what to believe. Luca didn't know the name of the ship that had taken Travis, anyway. Ella had kept that, and the name of its owner, from him—for reasons she hadn't quite been able to explain to herself.

"I promise, El. Go."

Luca would not lie to her about Travis, not even to save her life, and she knew that. He might love her, but he knew that she loved Travis more than herself. If Luca said that it was a different vessel, then she had to believe him, even without understanding how he could know. There was clearly a lot that she didn't understand about the situation. There was clearly a lot that she'd missed, crying herself to sleep like a weepy child.

"Now," Ivan said, reaching for her arm.

Before he could grab her, Ella forced herself to move, and she stumbled forward on unsteady legs. She found her footing after a moment, but by then Ivan *had* taken her arm—to steady her, rather than pull her—and he helped her onto the crooked plank. As she made her way across, she tried not to think about all the blood pooling on the boards of the nameless slave ship. She tried not to think about how much of it might be her fault. She tried not to think about the blood soaking the front of Swan's shirt, or how deep the cut might be.

She tried not to think about what Swan would do when he returned to the cabin.

* * *

Ella stood on the deck of Swan's ship, outside his cabin, watching his crew take over the other ship when the fighting was finished. She could see that no one from her own ship had been killed, and she had never been more thankful for anything in her life. Some of them were injured, including the captain himself. They could still die. He could still die, and her body was cold at the thought. He could be slowly bleeding to death and not even realize it. Or, infection could set in, killing him long before they could reach Bohannon for a healer.

Ella's thoughts and feelings were so tangled together, she wasn't sure she'd ever be able to sort through them. She had jumped to the wrong conclusion, that was obvious, because Luca and the others had been sent across the plank loosely tied and armed. A show of piracy, perhaps, rather than slave-trading. Swan's crew had boarded Blondie's ship with the express purpose of taking it over, it would seem, and they had done so with much bloodshed. Even without her stupid interference, she supposed there would have been blood spilled, but that did not alleviate her guilt.

And, Swan had saved her. He'd told her that he never left his ship while it was at sea, and she knew that he'd never meant to walk across the planks. He'd done it solely because of her, and she hugged herself tightly, more confused than ever. He'd been surprised to find her on his ship. He'd thought he'd left her behind on Tarot. She was certain of it.

It wasn't until his crew, now split into two separate crews and supplemented by a handful of the freed slaves, began slowly turning both ships around that another piece clicked into place for her. Her stomach churned with self-loathing, and she watched Swan directing the men, knowing that he would never forgive her. Why would he? She wouldn't.

Swan had returned to his own ship, but he stood, watching the other ship until both had been turned back toward the island and the sails all lowered. Even then, he didn't look in her direction. He was speaking to Marty, who was on the other ship. It seemed that Marty would be in charge of that other vessel, and directing the crew back to Tarot, and she wondered briefly why the job hadn't fallen to Ivan.

Luca was part of the crew on the other ship. While he was drawing his rope, he kept shooting glances in her direction, but she couldn't quite meet his eyes. No matter how little she understood, or how confused she was, she knew that the shame coursing through her was justified. When Swan finally turned and strode toward her, she struggled to hold her ground. She wanted to apologize, but the angry glint in his eyes had glued her tongue to the roof of her mouth.

As he came toward her, she looked down at his shirt and blanched at the amount of blood. Her fear that he might be bleeding to death returned in a rush. He would not be interested in her concern, however, and she was unable to speak.

He raised his hand and she flinched. She couldn't help it. She expected him to hit her because she knew she deserved to be hit, but she still flinched. He pointed a finger at her face, and she stared at it for a moment, seeing its slight tremble, before somehow forcing her unsteady gaze up to his.

"Get in the cabin and stay there. If I see or hear you, so help me God, I will throw you in the ocean."

She swallowed. His rage was palpable. She could feel it coming off of him in waves. She couldn't help but think it might be better, for both of them, if he would just hit her, after all. She'd punched him in the face, after all, and he had a darkening bruise below the corner of his eye to prove it.

She tried to find the courage to tell him that he should come into the cabin and let her clean and assess his injuries. Before she could convince her tongue to speak, he jabbed his finger in the direction of his cabin, and said, "Now."

She turned and ran toward the door, with her vision blurred by tears, and ducked into the quiet solitude of his room. She heard him use his key to lock the door behind her. Of course, she could always unlock it from within. She would not, however. She would not force her presence onto him when he so clearly despised the sight of her. She didn't think he would ever get over it, and she felt a crushing sense of grief that she could barely process. She'd never had a chance at a relationship with him, anyway, hadn't she been telling herself that all along?

It was probably for the best that he now hated her. If he was less polite and accommodating for the remainder of their journey, maybe she'd finally be able to let go of her foolish fantasies of him falling in love with her and offering to give her a life she'd scarcely been able to dream of.

But, what if he left her in Tarot for real, this time? Suppose he refused to take her to Bohannon? There would be no sneaking onto his ship, this time. If she was forced from his ship, her only choice would be to wait and hope another ship passed through. By then, it would probably be too late to save her brother, and she sank onto Swan's bed, dropping her face into her hands. Why could she never do anything right? Why did she keep failing the people she cared about? Her relationship with Luca was barely being held together by their shared love for Travis. Would Luca stay with Captain Swan's crew? If he made it to Bohannon, he would try to find Travis, with or without Ella, she knew that. He knew even less than she did, though.

She sighed, fighting back her tears. She'd spent enough time feeling sorry for herself. She wasn't going to cry herself to sleep, again. She wanted to go below and see if she could help tend to the injured men. It wasn't Swan's threat that stopped her. She was pretty sure that, in spite of his anger, he would not throw her overboard. She didn't leave the cabin because she didn't want to further defy him. Without giving him the benefit of the doubt—which he'd earned—she'd jumped in and made a mess of things.

She'd killed a man, and the memory made her hands tremble. She crossed her arms, taking a deep breath. She'd had no choice. He would have killed her.

She wanted to be angry at Swan. Part of her was, because he could have told her what was going on.

How could he? He didn't know you were on the ship. Yes, well, that was another reason to be upset with him, but she could only find disgust for herself and her own actions. She'd sneaked onto the ship. So, he'd thought he'd left her behind. If his intention had been to go on to Bohannon, leaving her stranded on Tarot, as she'd briefly thought, then of course she'd have just cause for being angry. It was obvious now that he was returning to Tarot, however, and that had been his plan all along.

She shook her head, again struggling against tears. She certainly had managed to screw things up. She supposed she should be relieved, because at least now she wouldn't have to keep wondering if he liked her or not. She'd done everything within her power to ensure he would want nothing to do with her.

She paced the cabin, unable to rid herself of her nervous tension. The water was choppier, making the ride feel rougher than normal, but she barely noticed the added churning in her stomach. Seasickness was the least of her problems. She couldn't see the island, and didn't know how far away they still were. They couldn't possibly make it in before dark, though. She wasn't even sure they would make it before dawn. Was she to stay in this little room, alone, the entire time? Would the captain ever make an appearance?

127

Did she want him to? Did she want the contempt in his face to remind her of what she'd done?

She didn't need a reminder, but she had to admit to herself—with another flush of self-loathing—that she did want to see him. If nothing else, she wanted to be assured that he was not bleeding to death. Had he gone below to see to his wounds, to avoid her? Or was he simply letting them bleed and possibly gather infection?

She'd been alone, fighting her urge to leave the cabin, for an hour before there was a knock on the door. She jumped, whirling toward the sound, and hurried across to unlock it. She wanted it to be Captain Swan. It never even occurred to her draw the curtain aside to check. She simply pulled the door open, trying to think of something she could say.

It wasn't Swan, though. It was Timón. Even in her disappointment, she felt relief at the sight of him. Relief that she wasn't looking into the glaring face of a man who hated her, and even more, relief to see Timón alive and well when she'd seen him, not that long ago, moments away from death. He was carrying a tray with her supper on it, and her gratitude—she hadn't eaten since breakfast—was secondary to her guilt. Timón didn't look hostile, but he did seem uncharacteristically aloof, and she felt her stomach sink. It must be true, then, that she'd lost every friend she'd made.

"How are you feeling?" he asked, handing her the tray.

"I'm fine," she muttered, glancing past him. There was no sign of Captain Swan or any other crew members. Behind Timón and beyond the railing, however, she could see the slave-ship, running parallel and just a smidge ahead of them. "Are you alright?" she asked, biting her lip. "Would you like to come inside?"

He hesitated.

"That's alright, I understand," she said. She took a step back. The tray felt heavy and unsteady in her hands. "Thank you. For what it's worth, I'm sorry. I didn't...I thought...I'm sorry," she said, blinking the tears from her eyes.

"You saved my life," Timón said, surprising her. "Twas a stupid thing to do, running onto that ship."

"I know," she said, further surprised by his candor.

He shook his head. "I don't think you get it. Why everyone's upset."

She winced. "I do get it. I didn't understand the situation, and I put everyone at risk."

He shook his head again. "You put yourself at risk. That's why everyone is mad. You think anyone on this ship wants to see you get hurt?"

She stared at him, unable to answer. Finally, afraid she was going to drop the tray, she turned and walked unsteadily toward the desk to set it down. "I'm sure they do at the moment," she muttered.

To her surprise, Timón laughed behind her. When she turned back toward him, some of his usual humor seemed to have returned. "Maybe, a good whipping," he said, smiling.

"You guys went over there to fight, didn't you? The ropes were just...for show."

"I understand how it must have looked. We might have told you, if we'd known you were here. You were supposed to be on the island."

"Ivan knew I was here."

"No one thought to ask," he said with a shrug.

"How many people were...hurt?"

"No one from our ship was killed," he answered, confirming what she'd hoped was true. "The injuries are mostly superficial, a few needed stitches. No broken bones. A miracle, really."

She hesitated. "What about...Captain Swan?"

"I haven't seen his injuries. He insists he's fine. I'm not sure where he is. I think he's with Ivan. Maybe Ivan can convince him to get cleaned up."

"Would you tell the men that...I'm sorry? I know it won't make a difference, but..."

Timón stepped into the room and, before she knew what he was going to do, pulled her into a quick embrace. Those damned tears pricked her eyes again, and she wondered when she'd become such an emotional wreck. He pulled back and looked into her face. "You saved my life," he repeated. "Thank you."

She nodded because she couldn't speak.

* * *

The sun was hanging low and red, and Ella hadn't seen anyone but Timón for hours, when she finally unlocked the door and, with a stomach full of nerves, poked her head out into the windy evening. Timón had reassured her about the health of the men on board, and by telling her that all of the injured crew had been brought onto *Voyage*. The other ship had been completely secured, and not one member of Blondie's staff had been left alive. None of them had surrendered, in the end, even though it had looked as though some would; so none had been taken prisoner.

Captain Swan was standing at the railing, with his back to the door, when she looked outside. Her heart stuttered. He was wearing the same white shirt, which meant that his front was still bloody. Why had he not cleaned himself up and, at the very least, changed into a clean shirt? Was he really so loathe to be in the same room with her? He would rather risk a slow and painful death from infection than set foot into the cabin where she was?

"What could be so important as to risk being thrown overboard?" he asked, without turning. His voice was low, carried on the wind, and the sound sent a shiver down her spine. Not of fear, but something else. Something more disturbing. How could his voice still affect her so, after all that had happened? Even knowing how much he must despise her, and knowing that she herself had thought him capable of horrible things just a few hours ago?

She'd been wrong, though, and she knew that.

"You wouldn't throw me overboard," she said. She knew it was true, now, but she couldn't keep the slight tremor from her voice.

He turned to face her, slowly, and she saw an alarming amount of dried blood staining the front of his shirt. The flaps of material hid the injury, so she had no idea how deep or serious it might be. Surely he'd have done something if he thought it warranted stitches...? He wasn't suicidal.

She raised her eyes to his, with effort, and her breath caught. He looked tired and pale, with lines bracketing his mouth that hadn't been there before, but his eyes were as dark and intense as ever. His gaze held hers, and she was unable to look away. She wished she knew what he was thinking. Part of her wished he would yell, or curse, or something. Tell her to get out of his sight, again.

"No," he said. "I wouldn't."

She chewed her lip for a moment, struggling with the enormity of the apology she knew she owed him. Apologies had never been easy for her, but this one seemed too large to choke out and, conversely, too small to make a difference. She took a deep, shaky breath. "I know," she said.

He tilted his head, the tiniest bit, and the lines around his mouth tightened. "Do you?" he asked.

She swallowed, then nodded.

He moved forward, then, and she had to fight the urge to retreat. She was no longer afraid that he would hurt her—at least, not physically. She wanted to run because her emotions were threatening to drown her. She wanted to touch him, and she wanted to beg him for forgiveness, and those desires were terrifying. He stopped in front of her, searched her face for a moment with those dark eyes, and asked, "What have I ever done that would make you think I would traffic slaves?"

She realized something, then: He was hurt. Oh, he might still be angry, too, but it was pain showing in his eyes, pain and even a little confusion. She'd done that to him. It wasn't being sliced open with a sword that was causing the hurt in his eyes. It was her, and the assumptions she'd made.

"Nothing," she said, because it was true. He'd done nothing to make her believe he would trade human lives. "I made a mistake." The words were hard to say, and seemed grossly inadequate. Her natural instinct was to go on offense, to blame him for keeping her uninformed, but she fought against that urge. For once in her life, she would take the scorn she deserved without mouthing back.

He wasn't saying anything, though. He was just standing there, staring at her. She struggled to find more words.

She cleared her throat. "I...didn't think, and...I put everyone at risk, and...I'm—"

Before she could finish, he held up a hand, silencing her. "Go inside," he said, quietly, and she tried to hide the stab of pain his words caused. She swallowed again, and nodded, turning toward the cabin without objection. She could feel the tears once more trying to force their way from her eyes. She was inside and reaching for the door before she realized that he was following her, and her heart jumped into her throat. Facing him, she stepped back, further into the room, as he closed the door behind himself.

"I would never put my crew at unnecessary risk, and I will not tolerate anyone else doing so," he said. The room seemed impossibly small as she stared into his dark eyes. Her skin felt prickly with awareness of his closeness.

She licked her lips, and his gaze flicked toward the movement. "I know," she said, clutching her hands in front of herself to keep them from shaking. "I'm—"

"You put yourself at risk," he said.

She blinked, caught off guard. "What?"

He stepped forward, and she thought she could feel his body heat warming her front. "You scared the hell out of me," he said. His voice was low, and husky, and she felt it shiver down her spine. She tried to make sense of his words. She tried to think of something to say. "You weren't supposed to be on board."

For a moment, she wondered if he was talking about today, or the entire journey. She tried not to feel the hurt that his words caused, but it was pointless. She was helpless to control her feelings around him, it seemed. "I know. I could see that you were surprised to see me. I thought..."

His chin lifted, and his mouth tightened, and he said, "You thought that *I* thought I'd left you behind? That I left you stranded on an island without warning?" She blushed, because she was ashamed to admit that she had. She bit her lip and nodded. "I'm not sure which is worse," he muttered, running a hand through his dark hair. "That you thought I would trade my crew as slaves, or that I would..." He sighed and shook his head. He took a step back, away from her, and she could feel him retreating—not just physically, but emotionally. He was shutting her out completely. A few minutes ago, she had thought he'd already done that. Until she was standing face to face with him, and until she could see it happening.

She grabbed his arm before she could think about it, and he froze. His muscles were tense beneath her hand. "I didn't think. I saw Luca, and...Look, I can't lose him, too, alright? I can't. I've lost—" She blinked, horrified to feel the tears slipping from her eyes. "I wasn't thinking about anything else," she finally muttered, swiping at her eyes. "I'm sorry I hurt your feelings."

His dark eyebrows went up in surprise. "Hurt my feelings?" he said. He sounded as though he was testing the words, tasting them.

"Please. I felt like...maybe we could be...friends. Please don't let my stupidity ruin that."

"Friends?" he repeated. He was staring at her as though she were completely insane, and she felt her blush deepening. She dropped her hand from his arm. "You flinch every time I move near you," he said, softly.

She swallowed and heard the truth slip out unbidden: "I get scared when you're close to me."

Did she imagine his slight wince? She realized that she'd chosen her words poorly, but before she could clarify, he said, quietly, "Although they share most of the same letters, 'pirates' and 'rapists' are not the same thing." The comment might have struck her as funny, under other circumstances.

"But you're not a pirate, are you?" she murmured, because that fact was only beginning to be clear. He'd brought supplies to trade to the residents of Tarot. That was the act of a businessman, a trader, not a pirate. She realized that she could no longer imagine him plundering anyone, robbing anyone...He'd taken over that ship to save the men and boys being held captive on board, not for his own personal gain.

He was scowling. "That is *not* my point," he said.

She shook her head. "No, I know," she answered, trying to focus her thoughts. She wasn't making herself understood. She was too nervous, edgy, and she was making things worse. "Look, it's not rape if I offer myself to you."

As soon as the words left her mouth, she felt hot embarrassment settle over her. Was she incapable of thinking about her words before spewing them out? That might have been the most humiliating thing she'd ever said, and the fear of rejection was suddenly overwhelming. All along, she'd been struggling with the idea that he wasn't attracted to her. Now, she'd given him the perfect opportunity to say it aloud.

He moved forward suddenly. She didn't flinch, but her breath caught. His face was just inches from hers, and now she knew that the warmth from his body was not imagined. "No?" he breathed, his eyes searching hers. There was something close to desperation in his expression. "Is it rape if I ignore the fear on your face every time I—"

"I'm afraid of rejection," she blurted, her cheeks flaming.

He pulled back a bit, and his surprise was genuine. "All the nights I've spent listening to you breathing, *rejecting* you was not in my thoughts."

"You...you have thought..." She bit her lip. "You thought I was unwilling..." She was having trouble breathing, and having trouble believing that her words were true.

He bent close again. "But in my fantasies, you certainly aren't unwilling," he murmured, and her mouth was suddenly dry. For some reason, she got the impression he was trying to frighten her. If so, it wasn't working. His words were having the opposite effect. He studied her face, with a small frown. "What do you want?" he whispered.

"I want..." *you*. The unwelcome memory of Meena, her skin glistening and tight in the sunlight, pressing her body against his, forced its way into Ella's mind. The painful truth was, Ella had essentially no experience with men, and she could never give him the things that someone like Meena could. Meena was beautiful, sensual, confident...Ella had never even spoken to her, and she knew those things. "I want you to...let me look at your stomach."

"Excuse me?" he said.

"You're hurt. Let me look."

He shook his head. "It doesn't matter."

She looked up at him, and she suddenly knew why he hadn't seen to his injury. He wanted the pain or, at the very least, felt that he deserved it. And the bruise that had begun to darken beneath his eye? She'd caused that, and why had he been in line with her fist? Because he was trying to save her life.

"It does matter," she said. "I need to know if you're alright. Please, this is my fault. All of it. Just let me—"

He grabbed her wrist when she reached for the front of his shirt. His grip was gentle, but unyielding. "Ella," he said, and the sound of her name made her belly tighten unexpectedly. "We went after that ship with the intention of freeing those men. All of them. Carter's crew, they were going to be killed or taken prisoner. There was never going to be any sort of trade or negotiation."

"I know. Now."

"It was my responsibility to...I should've known you were on board. My negligence led to a lot of good men getting hurt, and it almost got you killed."

She shook her head. The heat of his hand was spreading through her wrist, up her arm. "I almost got myself killed," she corrected. "You saved me, and got a black eye for your trouble. And, actually, I don't think he meant to kill me. At least, not right away."

She felt his hand tighten, almost painfully, around her wrist. "The world will not suffer the loss of Captain Carter," he muttered, a muscle in his jaw clenching. "Nevertheless, I've told you before—I am responsible for everyone on this ship. And, now, everyone on *The Runner*."

Ella hesitated. "Is that the name of that ship? I mean, the name was painted over..."

"The paint is temporary. The name shows when they're in port, only." He looked down, realized he was holding her arm, and released her immediately. She felt a stab of disappointment. "What did you plan on doing once you got on Carter's ship?"

"I assumed I would be killed," she admitted, quietly. "But...standing by and watching wasn't an option. It was stupid, I know."

"Stupid, yes," he said. "And...brave...Why were you here? Why...I asked Ivan, he said it never occurred to him to tell me he'd brought you back, because we left so suddenly, but...why did you come back to the ship? You were supposed to be in the village. Meena said she'd have the women get you something to wear, and..." He trailed off, studying her, and she couldn't quite meet his eyes. It was humiliating. To admit to her ridiculous bout of jealousy? Her lack of control over her emotions?

"Please let me make sure you're not getting infected," she said, quietly. "I'll...do whatever you want."

"Will you tell me why you were here?"

She hesitated. "Anything but that," she muttered, cursing her flaming cheeks. He would likely think she was guilty of something horrible, some secret plot to steal his ship or something, but her pride wouldn't let her tell him of her jealousy.

He leaned close, oh so dangerously close, and she chanced a quick glance at his face. "You keep offering to do whatever I want," he said, and his voice was like a caress. "What exactly do you think I want from you, Ella?"

She licked her lips nervously. "Well, you said..." Could her cheeks get any hotter? "You said you'd...thought about..."

"Thought about...kissing you until you can't breathe? Thought about...exploring every inch of your body?"

If he wanted to make her unable to breathe, he'd achieved that, already, without even touching her. She could feel his breath fanning her face, and his mouth was so close, she couldn't take her eyes off his lips. She swallowed, the strength of her desire once again shocking her. She could see the stubble across his chin and upper lip, and imagined trailing kisses across his rough jaw.

He sighed, softly. "And, there's the fear," he murmured.

She forced her eyes up to his, realizing he'd once again misinterpreted her reaction. Yes, she was afraid. Not of him, however. She was frightened by herself, and her own feelings. "I'm not afraid of you," she managed.

"No?" he asked. He smiled, but his eyes were serious. Sad, even. "Well, you don't have to be. You're engaged."

She blinked in confusion, and almost asked who she was engaged to. Then, she remembered. Luca. How many lies she'd entangled herself in. "Luca already thinks we're sleeping together," she heard herself say. Why couldn't she let it go? How many times could he refuse her before she would take the hint?

He'd said he'd fantasized about her, though. Maybe her desire wasn't as unreciprocated as she'd thought.

"What?" he asked, his eyebrows again going up. He pulled back to better see her face. "Well, no wonder he's been so...pissed off. Why didn't you tell him?"

She shrugged. "I figured...it was just a matter of time..." she mumbled, looking down.

"In case I failed to make myself clear, Ella: I have *no* intention of forcing myself on you, now or ever."

"You've made that clear," she said. She thought she might finally be growing accustomed to the sting of rejection. "It would be helpful if you'd stop flirting with me," she heard herself add, before her brain had caught up to her tongue.

"Flirting?" he asked, and when she glanced up at him, his expression seemed trapped somewhere between amusement and horror.

"I get that you don't want me," she said in a rush. "Except every time I start to accept that, you do something to—"

He moved forward again, and this time she was sure he was going to kiss her. His body wasn't touching hers, but she could feel every inch of him nonetheless. His lips were inches from hers, his eyes dark and intense as she stared, helplessly, into them.

"—confuse me," she finally finished, breathlessly. "Like that," she added, dropping her gaze to his mouth. She wanted him to kiss her; she had never wanted anything more in her life.

"*I* confuse *you?*" he murmured. "I've been trying to be a gentleman, Ella, but let's get one thing very clear, yes? At no point have I *ever* said I didn't want you, and at no point did I ever mean to imply that."

The rush of pleasure she felt at his words made her hands tremble with its intensity. Gathering her courage, she whispered, "Then why haven't you even kissed me?" They were difficult words to ask, but she managed to maintain eye contact in spite of her nerves. The fact that he found her attractive—and she didn't doubt that proclamation—made her feel emboldened, somehow.

He pulled a breath through his nose and let it out, slowly. "You love Luca, Ella. It doesn't matter whether or not I think he's the right man for you. You were willing to risk your life for him."

He's not the only reason, she thought. *I didn't know if my brother might be on that ship.* She was rendered mute, however, by his middle sentence. *It doesn't matter whether or not I think he's the right man for you.* What did that mean? She tried not to let her imagination run away with her, again, tried not to envision the crazy life she'd taken to fantasizing about. The crazy life that could never, and would never, be. With him standing so close, it was impossible not to think about it, though. A part of her wanted to believe that all she had to do was reach out, and claim him, and he could be hers. She could have that life.

And what of Travis? And Luca? Swan might be able to help her find Travis. He seemed to know quite a bit about the underworld she now knew he was not a part of. And, he might be willing to help. Hell, who was she kidding? Look what he'd just done for the people of Tarot. Of course he would be willing to help, if he could. He might love Meena, but—

Ella shoved that painful thought away. He might, in fact, love Meena, but he couldn't know all of the residents on Tarot, and saving the men and boys was not just for Meena. Some of them might be her family, but not all. Some of the slaves had not even come from Tarot, according to Timón. Some had been on the slave-ship as long as she'd been on *Voyage.*

"I have no desire to be a regret in your life," he said, and the words slid over her, filling her with a mixture of conflicting emotions. She couldn't even begin to sort them out, except to recognize the now-familiar disappointment.

"And I wouldn't want to be one in yours," she muttered. She took a deep breath and, with a reserve of willpower she'd been unaware of, stepped back. He watched her without comment. "If you can forgive me for my...stupidity today, maybe we could go back to being..."

"Friends?" he suggested in a soft voice.

She offered a small smile. "Right. Friends. We were getting along well."

It was his turn to smile. "We were," he said. "Until you thought I was selling your boyfriend and half of my crew."

"Right. Don't forget, I thought you'd intentionally left me behind on the island, too."

"Well...I thought I had, as well. Just not for the reason you thought. Care to tell me why you sneaked back onto my ship, yet?"

"Sneaking onto your ship is sort of my specialty," she said, amazed to feel herself slipping into an easy banter. With a little bit of breathing room between them, she could think more clearly. Maybe they could be friends, after all. Maybe that would be enough.

He grinned, and his beauty stole her breath for a moment, and she forgot whatever she'd been thinking. "In the spirit of friendship, I'd like to ask you a favor," he said.

"A favor?" she repeated through numb lips.

"Next time you think I'm doing—or am about to do—something abominable, could you ask me about it, first? Before throwing yourself in danger?"

She cleared her throat. "I think I learned my lesson," she said after a moment.

"About putting yourself in danger?" he asked, cocking an eyebrow.

"About misjudging you," she returned. "But I'll promise to come to you, first, if you do something for me."

His expression was suddenly wary. "What may I do for you?" he asked.

"Let me clean out the cut on your stomach. So I know you're alright."

"I think having your hands on me could be a dangerous path," he said.

She fidgeted, hiding her confusion. "I won't—"

"I will clean and bandage it, if that will ease your mind."

She let out a breath. "Yes, thank you."

"It's almost dark. We won't reach Tarot until just before dawn. There's going to be rough waters when we set out. You see the dark line along the horizon?"

She looked toward the windows, and nodded. She'd noted the clouds earlier. They seemed impossibly far off, but she knew that was deceiving. She had no reason to doubt his prediction. She felt a shiver of fear at the possibility of being tossed about in a violent storm, with nothing but a few boards to keep her from being swallowed by the vast, swirling ocean.

Nothing but a few boards...And Captain Swan. She took comfort from his calm confidence. Her life was in his hands, as were the lives of the crewmen, but it had been that way since they'd left Baytown. She knew that he did not take that responsibility lightly. If he didn't think he could make it through the storm, he would keep them on Tarot until the danger passed. He would not put a schedule above the safety of his men. She knew that. She trusted it. She didn't question her trust. She wouldn't make the same mistake again; she thought she'd finally begun to see him clearly.

"We'll be going out to meet it. Tomorrow evening...Probably around nightfall. You should sleep as much as you can tonight, because tomorrow night will probably be difficult for you, being unaccustomed to rough waters."

"I slept most of the day," she admitted.

"Did you?" he asked, looking surprised and, a moment later, concerned. "Were you ill?"

"Not exactly," she muttered. "Just..." She shrugged. How could she explain? "Just feeling sorry for myself, really," she finally said. "Don't worry, I'm over it. But it seems like you need the sleep worse than I do. You're not going to get any tomorrow."

He smiled. It seemed genuine enough, although she couldn't help but wonder about that ever-present sadness lurking beneath. She wanted to know who and what had shaped him into the man he'd become. "Sleep is always elusive," he admitted, with a small gesture of his hand.

"I like the way you talk," she said, immediately embarrassed by her words.

"Yes?" he asked, looking surprised.

"You have a, uh...very nice vocabulary."

His teeth flashed white. "Mrs. Darling would be glad to hear so," he said.

"Mrs. Darling? Was she your teacher?"

"In a manner of speaking," he answered, clearly dismissing the subject. "So, in order to hold up my end of our bargain, I suppose I need to see to this troublesome scratch. I'm almost sorry I didn't make that bastard Carter suffer a bit longer." He sighed. Then, to her astonishment, he quickly stripped off his bloody shirt, and she found herself staring at his bare chest. In spite of the copious blood, he'd been right—the wound didn't appear terribly deep. As much as she hated to admit it to herself, his injury was not the first thing in her mind. The sight of his bare chest, the dark curls disappearing into the low waist of his trousers...

He cleared his throat, and she jerked her gaze upward, her face threatening to burst into flames.

His eyes were sparkling with amusement. "You are determined to test my resolve, aren't you?" he asked.

She shook her head. "Don't be ridiculous," she said, raising her chin, and he actually laughed. "Sit down and I'll get something to clean that."

"Oh, no," he said, laughing again. "The deal was that *I* would see to it."

"Fine. Well...I'll, uh...supervise. To make sure you do a good job."

"Of course," he said, with a slight bow, grinning.

Chapter Eight

When Ella awoke, it was still dark, and the edge of the world visible through the windows had not even begun to lighten. Swan was nowhere in sight when she rose and stretched, wincing at the aches in her body. She'd heard him return to the room in the early evening, and was pretty sure he'd slept a bit in the chair, but she'd drifted off again and hadn't heard him leave.

She thought of his words from the evening before: *Sleep is always elusive.* She should have fought harder to convince him to take the bed, but she'd been afraid of angering him when they were once more on relatively good terms. She knew it was going to be a long day and, if his prediction about the weather held true, an even longer night, and no one was going to be more tired than Captain Swan at the end of it. She made herself a promise that once they'd made it through the storm, she would get him to sleep if she had to knock him unconscious.

She felt remarkably serene. She knew that it might be a difficult day, watching him with Meena and knowing that she herself would never have such a relationship with him. Then, it was bound to be a difficult night, as well, when the storm came. There was no sense worrying about those things ahead of time. She'd slept pretty well, and in spite of her aches and pains, her body was relaxed. She knew that she and Swan had come to an understanding of sorts, and while she couldn't fool herself into believing it was all she wanted, it was better than nothing. To know that he didn't hate her, that he was willing to forgive her idiocy so that they could be friends, was important.

She freshened up and dressed quickly, determined to see if Timón or Rashad needed any help before they all left for Tarot again. She'd been derelict in her responsibilities, which was unacceptable. Now, it was the middle of the night, the time when most of the crew should be sleeping, on any other occasion. When she stepped outside, however, the sails had already been raised and the anchor already lowered. She could see the flickering torches marking the beach of Tarot. To the side of *Voyage*, *The Runner* had also stopped, and Marty was supervising the first rowboat being lowered into the water. It was too late to go to Timón and Rashad, then. They would all soon be on the island.

Ella hadn't seen any of the rescued men or boys since the fight on the slave-ship, but she now saw them—some were on *The Runner*, and some were lined along the railing of *Voyage*, staring toward the dark island and murmuring excitedly amongst themselves. The youngest boy was practically bouncing on the balls of his bare feet. They had only been away from their homes for a day. She tried to imagine what the others, those men from Baytown, had been through, and her thoughts inevitably turned toward her own brother. Was he alright? She had to believe he was, because it was the only way she could keep moving forward. She had to maintain hope.

She looked across the dark water and caught Luca's gaze. She could barely see him, but she didn't need to make out his features. She knew they were both thinking of the same thing, of the same person.

Ella had a feeling that Luca was going to seek her out as soon as they landed, perhaps to apologize. Although she wasn't proud of it, she suddenly found herself wishing she could avoid him. He might say he was sorry for the things he'd said, and she might summon an apology of her own, but their conversation would be strained and would almost certainly devolve into another argument. She wasn't sure she had the energy for another argument, or for more angry and hurtful words from the person she had loved for so long .

She sighed, and sensed Captain Swan's presence at her side. "Something wrong?" he asked, quietly, as he joined her near the rail.

She shook her head, and saw Luca turn away from the sight of the two of them. Was there disgust on his face? Anger? Accusation? Hurt?

She couldn't see them, and it didn't matter. Even if they weren't on his face, he was feeling them.

"Did you sleep at all?" Ella asked, turning her head toward Swan. The moonlight glimmered in his eyes, and she felt a shiver of awareness pass through her when their gazes met.

"A bit. Are you cold?"

"What? Oh. No."

She saw his mouth slide into a smile. He leaned down, so that his breath was warm on her ear, and said, "Are you ready to go?"

She licked her lips. "Go?" she asked.

"Minto and the others will be in the first boat. You may go with them, if you wish."

"Minto?" she asked. Why was she having such a difficult time understanding him?

Swan pointed toward the young, dark-skinned boy eagerly waiting to climb down to the first dinghy. "That's Meena's youngest brother. He's twelve."

"Oh. What will...happen to the men from Baytown?"

"Some of them may wish to stay here. Tarot is a nice place, and relatively safe, except when people like Carter come through. It doesn't happen often, and I guarantee the islanders will be more ready to fight, next time. Some of them might want to go to Bohannon. If they want a ride back to Baytown, they're going to have to be willing to wait several months." He shrugged. "Unless they know how to sail that ship, because it's theirs, now."

"Did Carter own that?"

"He did. Most slave-ships are owned by fat, rich men ensconced in their palatial, gated homes. Most pirate ships are owned by the ships' captains."

"Like yours?" she quipped, and she heard his soft chuckle.

"Precisely," he answered. "But Carter was one of the exceptions. He owned his ship, and now he's dead, so it's fair game."

"You could claim it for your own." It wasn't really a question.

"What do I need with two ships?" he asked. He sighed and ran a hand over his face.

139

She turned to face him in the shadows. "How long do you spend in Bohannon before setting sail back?"

"It depends. I have some responsibilities to see to, some people to...visit, but I rarely spend long on land."

She nodded, filled with a disappointment that she couldn't quite understand.

"Would you like to go in with them?" he asked, gesturing toward the men climbing down to the rowboat.

"Which boat are you going in?"

"The last," he said. She couldn't quite make out his expression.

"Then I'll wait," she said. He could have told her which boat to take, or refused to let her ride with him, but he simply smiled in the moonlight.

*   *   *

There were enough torches and bonfires on the beach to allow Ella and the men, as they made their way from the ships to the shore, a clear view of the reunion between Meena and Minto, and the others. When Minto jumped from his boat, Meena met him low on the beach and swung him up into the air as though he were a small child. Watching from out in the water, Ella felt tears sting her eyes. She would not be able to lift Travis like that, anymore, but it suddenly seemed like hardly any time had passed since she could have.

"Are you alright?" Swan asked, softly, and Ella blinked to rid her eyes of the tears. It was dark, but the moon was bright, and she knew he could see it shimmering in her eyes.

"Sure," she answered. It was on the tip of her tongue, then, to tell him about Travis. Why she held her silence, she couldn't precisely say. Maybe it was because of the other men in the boat. Maybe part of it was her own shame, not only at letting her brother be taken prisoner but also for keeping it a secret for so long. Whatever the reason, she didn't speak, and after a few moments, Swan turned his gaze forward once more, toward Meena and the others. Ella could see a small smile curve his lips as he watched Minto and his sister celebrating on the sand.

When they made the beach, Swan stepped ashore and held a hand down to help Ella out. She accepted his hand, but had no more than settled her toes into the sand before Meena was throwing her arms around him. Ella stepped back, stuffing her own hands into the pockets of her borrowed trousers, feeling displaced and lost, and inexplicably alone. She watched for a moment as Meena hugged Swan, as he put his own arms around her and whispered something in her ear.

When Meena turned her head and pressed her lips against Swan's, Ella finally turned away, unable to punish herself any longer. Luca's boat was just beaching, and she felt a moment's panic. She didn't want to deal with him, either. She took a deep breath, trying to calm herself. She wasn't going to run away, again. That had caused nothing but trouble the last time, and it wasn't in her nature to run and mope, anyhow. No, she was going to have to face reality.

Luca was heading straight toward her, with his jaw set determinedly. She held her ground. Before she could think of anything to say, he wrapped his arms around her. She wasn't surprised so much by the hug—Luca had hugged her hundreds of times in his life—as by its fierceness. For a moment, she couldn't breathe, and it was strangely comforting. Luca smelled and felt familiar, and she had to again blink back her damned tears.

He released her before the constriction of his embrace could cause her brain any real alarm, stepped back, and put his hands on her shoulders. She forced herself to meet his gaze in the flicker of firelight. She tried not to think of all the hurt between them. "I'm sorry," he said. "When I saw you come across the plank..." He shook his head. "I'm sorry," he said, again. "I love you, El. I always have, I always will, no matter what."

She knew she should say something, and her brain refused to form any words. She nodded, afraid she was going to burst into humiliating tears. Finally, she managed to whisper, "I love you, too, Luca."

He smiled, and even in the poor light, she could see the sadness. "I know," he murmured. For a moment, his hands tightened on her shoulders. Then he took a deep breath and released her. "I'll see you after we bring in the rest of the supplies. Alright?"

Ella nodded. She watched Luca return to his rowboat, where his fellow crewmen had already unloaded more than half of the crates they'd hauled in from *The Runner*. Then, stealing herself for the probable pain, she turned back toward Swan and Meena.

Meena was draped along his length, impossibly close, as though she would dissolve right into him. Her hand was flattened over Swan's chest, and her cheek was laid against his shoulder. While her brother raced up the beach, Meena seemed content to hold onto Swan, and Ella couldn't say she blamed her.

Ella met Swan's eyes, and her heart stuttered. She cursed herself. How could he still have such an effect on her when he was entangled in the arms of another woman? A woman he was clearly on intimate terms with? Ella turned her face away, embarrassed by her jealousy, afraid he would recognize it for what it was. She had to remind herself that they were friends.

"Meena, it turns out that Ella had returned to the ship," the captain was saying, as he gently pulled himself out of Meena's arms. Meena lifted her head and looked around, spotting Ella, and after a second her dark face split into a warm smile. She extended a hand.

"Ella, so nice to see you again," she said, with that thick, melodic accent. Ella hesitated, unsure what was expected of her. She glanced at Swan, and he gave her the slightest of nods. There was a tiny frown, barely visible in the night, wrinkling his brow. Ella wondered if she would recognize him without it. She stepped forward, and allowed Meena to grasp her hand in both of her own. "Come. We'll get you better clothes, fresh you up. Find you some place to sleep, if you like. We were worried about you, when we could not find you.

We finally assumed you must be on the ship."

"I didn't mean to cause trouble," Ella mumbled.

"It's a good thing she was," Swan said. "She saved Timón's life."

Ella looked at him, trying to hide her surprise. Meena scowled at him. "You did not let her fight?"

Swan raised his eyebrows and smiled. "She didn't ask my permission."

Ella felt herself blushing.

Meena shook her head, apparently disgusted with the captain. He seemed remarkably unperturbed. Turning back to Ella, squeezing her hand, Meena said, "Well, we cannot say our gratitude to all of you. Your safe return will be celebrated greatly. Are you hungry?"

In spite of the heavy accent, Ella had no trouble understanding her, and likewise found it impossible to dislike her. Ella would have preferred to despise this woman, the woman who could have the man that Ella could not. Meena was warm, and kind, and open, however, and Ella only found herself despising her own foolish thoughts.

Ella tried to gather her wits enough to answer. Was she hungry? She wasn't even sure. When was the last time she'd eaten? The meal that Timón had brought to the cabin the night before, but she hadn't even finished that. She'd been too upset about the battle, and her role in it, and the idea that Captain Swan might never forgive her.

"You should eat," the man himself said.

In spite of her own uncertainty, Ella's temper flared immediately, and she heard herself say, without thought, "I'm not hungry. It's the middle of the night."

She glared at him, saw his jaw clench, and heard Meena laugh. Ella looked at her, startled, and in a moment of self-awareness realized how ridiculous she must look and sound. Meena was not laughing at her, however. She was laughing at Swan, and Ella glanced back at him, expecting to see his trademark scowl. Instead, she was caught off guard to find him smiling, again—a small, bemused smile, directed at Meena. Ella felt another stab of jealousy. Meena still had hold of her hand, and Ella had to fight the instinct to jerk away from her.

"Come," Meena said, tugging gently, and Ella followed her lead. "You, too, Cap," Meena called over her shoulder with another laugh, and Ella glanced back to see that he was, in fact, trailing along behind them. He met her eyes. His smile was gone. His expression was grim again. Ella turned her attention forward, trying not to stumble in the dark sand as she followed Meena. The other woman still had her by the hand, and as they left the fairly well-lit beach for the much-darker trail, Ella found herself hoping Meena could be trusted to keep her bare feet safe from any number of hazards that might be lurking in the sand or foliage.

In the dark depths of jungle, with the only light from the moon above, Ella wondered why they didn't at least have a torch. Her heart was thumping in her chest, and she knew that her palm must have grown sweaty in Meena's grip. It felt like there must be a million eyes watching from the dark growth reaching toward her from either side. Each rustle of wind through the leaves sounded like the shifting weight of a giant beast. She had no idea how far it was to the village. She wanted to pull her hand back, turn, and flee toward the relative safety of the beach. The only thing that stopped her was Swan's presence behind her. She didn't want to look like a complete fool in front of him—again. More than that, however, she took a little comfort from his calmness.

"Not much further," came his low murmur from the darkness behind her, and Ella felt herself let out a breath. He sounded close, and reassuring.

"We are almost there," Meena agreed cheerfully, seemingly oblivious to Ella's irrational fear.

When Ella first felt the light touch on her shoulder, she tensed, biting back a scream. The comforting heat of Swan's hand almost immediately soothed her frayed nerves, however, and she felt herself relax under his gentle touch. She felt a surge of gratitude that she couldn't have put into words. The pad of his thumb trailed a light caress along the nape of her neck, and the shiver that passed through her then was not fear-related. She could feel his body close behind her, could suddenly hear his breathing mingled with her own.

In a few moments, she could see the torchlights, marking the edge of the village, flickering through a break in the growth. She felt a mixture of relief and disappointment, and almost laughed at herself. As they continued forward, and the high fires cast their orange glow over them, Swan's hand slid away from her shoulder. His finger trailed down her back for a few seconds, and then was gone, leaving nothing but a ghostly tingle in its wake. She swallowed as Meena turned toward her, grinning.

"Welcome to Tarot," she said, gesturing toward the village suddenly laid before them. The place was alive with activity, surely an anomaly for such a late hour. Everyone seemed to be up and about, those people who were not at the beach clearly waiting for the return of those who were. When they saw Meena and her two followers step from the shadows of the trail, the villagers converged excitedly. Ella stepped aside, a little alarmed, and Meena finally let go of her.

It was immediately apparent that Captain Swan was the one they were interested in, and he accepted their praises and embraces and arm-shakes with equilibrium and a discomfort that he hid pretty well. None of the villagers seemed to notice, at least. Meena was aware of his unease, and she looked ready to intervene if things got too overwhelming for him. Ella wanted to do something to relieve the onslaught—Yes, they were happy to see him, and grateful for what he'd done, but in their gratitude they were a little overbearing. What could she say, though? She didn't even know how many of them spoke her language. Swan was answering them in their own tongue.

Ella stepped forward. She felt Meena's eyes on her, and didn't care. She might alienate her hostess, and make herself unwelcome on the island, but what did that matter? Was there much chance that she would ever be returning to visit? No. Besides, if Meena cared so much about Swan, she should be doing something, herself.

Ella moved close to Swan's side, drawing the attention of the people closest. Many seemed to be seeing her for the first time. She cleared her throat, and suddenly it appeared that all of them were staring at her. How many pairs of eyes were on her? Two dozen? What was she supposed to do, now? "You have a very pretty island," she said, forcing the words out before her nerves could get the best of her.

A woman, her breasts barely covered by a scrap of cloth, reached out a hand and fingered Ella's hair. "You have beautiful hair," the woman said, her accent so thick that it took Ella's brain a moment to recognize the words.

Another hand reached out to touch her windblown hair as Ella managed a small, "Thank you."

"The men are on their way from the beach," Swan said, his tone suddenly businesslike. "We appreciate your hospitality as we get a bit of rest."

"Yes, yes, I think I hear Minto and Charles coming, now," Meena said, and heads turned toward the trail. "Let's let Cap and Ella get to their huts."

Before she could think, Ella was ushered forward, toward a small building with a thatched roof, and then she was inside, the sounds of the village muffled. The room was well-lit, small but cozy, and Ella stood in the middle of it, feeling once more displaced. She knew that this room had been prepared especially for her. Swan had told Meena about her, but what had he said?

Had they been preparing this hut for her even as they were searching for her?

She felt another surge of guilt at the thought, but was the guilt fair? No one had cared when she went back to the ship. No one had come looking for her, then. No one had thought to miss her. If Swan had really cared about her, wouldn't he have come to find her, to tell her he was leaving but that he would return for her? No, he'd left without ever verifying where she was, what she was doing, or if she was alright.

He'd been busy with Meena, though. And, to be fair, time had been understandably limited when Meena told him of her brother's capture. Ella could understand his desire to leave without hesitation, to catch Carter's ship as soon as possible, but that didn't ease the hurt she felt.

He would have had no reason to expect her to have crawled under the covers in his bed, to cry herself to sleep, though, when he'd left Meena with instructions to look after her on the island. Ella gave her head a small shake, annoyed all over again by her foolish and pointless exercises in self-torture.

"Don't venture out of the village," Swan said, and Ella turned to face him, doing her best to keep her expression neutral. "It's not safe," he added, as though he was expecting an argument.

Ella nodded.

"If you want something to eat, I can send—" Meena stopped when Ella shook her head. Swan scowled but said nothing. "Very well," Meena said, smiling. "As soon as everyone is back from the beach, there's going to be a celebration. Do not feel obligated to attend, if you are wishing to sleep. But the people will be happy to have you, if you will come."

Ella nodded again. She didn't know what to say. She had no desire to be rude in the face of hospitality, but was she up for the prospect of an all-night party? With scads of happy people chattering away at her in a language she didn't know? While Captain Swan spent his time wrapped in Meena's embrace? Meena currently had his arm in both of hers and was leaning into him while she spoke to Ella.

Ella avoided his eyes. Nothing good could come of eye contact at the moment. "Thank you," she finally managed, realizing that some sort of response was required.

"So good to have you, Ella," Meena said. "Make yourself at home and if you need anything, ask anyone."

"Thank you," Ella said again, wishing they would leave.

"We will hope to see you at the celebration," Meena said. Then they left, with Swan never saying a single word after his warning not to venture into the wilderness.

For a moment, Ella stood alone in the house, fighting the crazy urge to run from the hut and directly into the jungle. She sighed and ran a hand over her face. She looked around. She wasn't tired. In spite of her refusal of food, she was a little hungry, but she didn't want to eat. She found herself walking toward the door, and she knew—*knew*—that she was going to regret it, and still she had to see. She had to know. She cracked the door and peeked out, unsure what she would say if someone saw her, if Swan saw her.

She didn't have to worry about that, though. He was apparently meant to stay in the hut across the dirt track that passed for the village's street. It was rutted with wagon tracks, uneven, but fairly wide. On the other side, standing outside the dwelling directly across from hers, Swan and Meena were in front of the opened doorway. They couldn't wait to get inside, evidently.

Meena had her arms wrapped around his neck, and his hands were at her waist, and they were kissing, completely absorbed in each other. As Ella watched, helpless to look away, Swan turned Meena into the doorway, backing her into the hut, and swung the door shut behind himself. Ella could no longer see, but the image was burned into her brain. She felt tears prick her eyes, and cursed herself for opening the door in the first place. Hadn't she known that she would see something that she had no right to see?

She let out a breath and pulled back, gently closing her own door.

* * *

There were books in the house, but they were not in a language she could read, and there was nothing to occupy her mind. It was a relief when, after an hour, a knock sounded at the door. She went to open it with a disturbing eagerness, hoping for someone or something to help her escape the torturous confines of her own mind. She would have left the house long ago, to wander the village or find a familiar face, if she hadn't been afraid of running into

Meena and Swan. She knew it was unlikely. They were surely busy catching up. It had been at least a few months since they'd had a chance to—

Ella yanked the door open and found herself staring into the most familiar face she could have found.

Luca.

A part of her wanted to be angry with him. She wanted to shout at him, take her emotion out on him, because he was there. And, yes, she had some reason to be upset with him. She wanted to yell because anger would be easier to deal with than what was bubbling up inside of her at the sight of him. She was horrified to feel her chin quivering. She saw the concern in his eyes, and it was too much.

"El, what's wrong?" he asked.

Across the road, the door to Swan's house opened. She had just a glimpse of him, with his messy hair and his untucked shirt, and she took a hasty step backward. There was no way she was going to let him see her losing her battle with her silly emotions. She reached for the door, without even thinking. She might have slammed it in Luca's face in her haste, but Luca forced his way through the opening with surprising speed and shoved it shut behind himself.

"Talk to me," he said. "Ellie, please. What's wrong?"

When they were boys, Travis and Luca had called her Ellie. Sometimes, Travis still did, if he was feeling sentimental or if he was overly tired, or ill. She felt her face crumple, and she stepped into Luca's arms because everything suddenly seemed to be crushing down on her. She could feel Luca's arms, strong and hard around her, and she buried her face against his chest, shakily breathing in his familiar scent. He'd changed, in his time on the ship. He was stronger, broader. No matter what they'd said to each other, he was still Luca, though. He was an adult. He loved her in a way that she could not reciprocate. She knew that it was unfair to cling to him like she was. She wasn't strong enough to let him go, though, not in that moment. So she held on to him and cried.

It wasn't just because of Swan, either. Yes, she had developed a crush on him. Yes, it hurt to see him kissing someone else. Yes, it hurt to know that she had virtually no chance of ever finding a love story of her own. Yes, she was upset about Swan.

It was so much more, though. She'd killed a man the day before. She'd almost gotten herself killed and, more importantly, she could have been responsible for the deaths of many of her friends, not to mention Minto and the other prisoners. If her rash actions had been a few seconds earlier, Luca and Timón and the others might not have been ready to fight, or Carter might have managed a preemptive strike.

Most of all, it was Travis. Those slaves reminded her of him, and how frightened he must be. If he was alive.

She didn't want to consider the possibility that he might not be. What use would he or the others be as slaves if they didn't survive the trip, after all? It was impossible not to imagine the worst, though. Since his birth, she had never gone so long without laying eyes on him. There were so many things that could've gone wrong. Starvation. Dehydration. Abuse by the captors or even fights with other prisoners over supplies. Travis was relatively small. He had little fighting experience.

No, she didn't want to consider such thoughts, but she suddenly found herself unable to climb out from beneath them, and she stood in Luca's embrace and cried.

"It's going to be alright," he was saying. "Don't cry. We'll get him back. You'll see."

He said other things, but the words were unimportant, and after a little while he fell silent and they stood together without speaking. She could feel the pounding of his heart beneath her cheek, and she slowly started to pull herself together. She didn't like feeling out of control, and she certainly didn't like having two breakdowns in less than twenty-four hours. As her crying slowed to sniffling and then dried altogether, she realized that she felt strangely better. Crying would not help her brother, or change the world, but it had calmed her. She needed the release, and she needed to cry with someone who understood what she was going through. Someone who shared some of her pain.

Luca was the only person who fit that bill.

Ella pulled back and looked at his face. She knew she must look terrible, with her red, puffy eyes and splotchy cheeks and messy hair, but Luca had seen her in far worse shape before. She searched his face for a moment, taking the time to note the subtle changes that she hadn't recognized before. Like his body growing more muscular, the evidence of his adulthood was written on his face in more than stubble. He was not a little boy anymore. Neither was Travis. Would she ever stop thinking of them that way, though?

Ella leaned forward to kiss him without rational thought. She wasn't motivated by desire, so much as desperation. It would make things far less complicated if she could just return the feelings he had for her. She loved him, after all. They knew each other. She trusted that he would never leave her or cheat on her if she willingly gave herself to him. The only thing missing was...the flare of desire she felt every time she saw Captain Swan. Why couldn't she have that with Luca, instead? She thought, maybe, just maybe, she could learn to want him.

He pulled away, though, before she could kiss him. He looked pained. "El, if I thought you were only crying about Travis, that would be one thing, but...Look, you like him, I know you do. It's obvious. And I acted like an ass because I was jealous and hurt, but...I know that I never had a chance with you. I know it now, even if I wish..." He stopped, shook his head, and said, "More than anyone I ever met, Ellie, you deserve to be happy."

She shook her head. "I'm sorry, Luca. I never meant—"

"Apologies have never suited you, El," he said, smiling sadly. "Does Swan know you like him?"

Like him? she thought, grimacing. What were they, twelve years old? Was she supposed to pass him a note? Ask if he would hold her hand on the way home from school?

She wasn't sure how he could *not* know that she "liked" him, as she'd been practically begging him for...well, something. She'd been throwing herself at him, and he'd been dodging, and it was no wonder. With someone like Meena waiting for him, he could afford to be choosy. "It doesn't matter," she finally answered. She swiped at her tears and took a deep breath. She looked at Luca, wondering again why she couldn't feel some pull of attraction for him. Sure, she'd known him since he was a kid, but she'd basically been a kid herself, and it wasn't as if they were related.

To her, they were, though, and that was the problem. It might not be determined by blood, but Luca was her brother, and she would always think of him as such. He and Travis...

She shook her head again. The breakdown (*your second*, her mind sneered) had cleared her head, and in spite of her foolish attempt to kiss Luca, she still felt better. She had always had a habit of keeping her more personal emotions, well, *personal*. Even as a child. Her father had often told her she was a "hard nut to crack," and she'd had no idea what that meant. He always said it with a smile, and she'd known that he didn't mean it as an insult, but even as an adult she sometimes found herself wondering about what he *had* meant. Had he found it difficult to understand her, because she was so reticent? Or had he meant that it was difficult to break through her walls?

She sighed. The time for walking down Memory Lane was over. Swan had told her that a hunting party would be sent out, first thing in the morning, to get fresh meat for the next leg of their journey. Maybe she could con her way into joining them. Or, she could offer her services to Meena in some way, to repay the hospitality that she didn't really deserve. She needed to get to work, on something, somewhere.

"How do you know?" Luca asked.

Ella frowned. "What?"

"How do you know it doesn't matter, if you haven't told him?"

Her frown deepened. "For one thing, he's across the road with...Meena. I hardly think he wants to see me, or anyone else, at his door."

"And he's had you in his—"

Ella realized something then, and the epiphany wasn't without pain: As much as it hurt for her to see Swan and Meena together, it had to be worse for Luca believing that Ella and Swan had been sleeping together. Ella had repeatedly lost patience with Luca for refusing to accept that there would never be anything romantic between them, and for acting childish. Hadn't she been acting exactly the same way? Childish? She'd lost her temper, she'd cried herself to sleep, she'd run away like a little girl, she'd acted rashly and without giving credit where it was due...She had never seen herself as particularly immature, so why was she behaving so badly? And why was she torturing Luca?

"—bed for—"

"Nothing's happened, Luca."

He stopped, staring at her. After a moment, he said, with doubt, "What?"

"We haven't...He hasn't...done anything."

"But you..." he trailed off, clearly lost for words.

"I offered, Luca. And...his rejection hurt, I won't lie. And I am sorry, for so many things, for...taking you for granted...but as for Swan, it just...really doesn't matter. He's rich, well-educated, well-traveled, good-looking...I'm—"

"Seeing yourself has never been your strong suit," he interrupted. "Don't try to sell him to me. I know he doesn't deserve you. But what matters is what *you* want. And, trust me, El, he wants you. Haven't you seen him look at you? He's lucky he's still alive," he added fiercely, his fists clenching at his sides. "But, if he hasn't taken advantage..." he trailed off. He clearly didn't want to say anything charitable about the captain.

Ella reached up and laid her palm against Luca's cheek. He tensed but didn't pull away. "I'm going to find my brother, Luca. That's all that matters. I don't have time for foolish fantasies."

"Well, you *do* have time," he muttered, swallowing. "You have almost a month."

She stared at him, a little startled as the meaning of his words, and what he was suggesting, began to sink in. She shook her head and lowered her hand. "I appreciate you trying to—"

"Oh, stop, Ella," he said, annoyed. "No, it isn't easy for me to think of...you and him, but—in spite of what you seem to think—I am an adult. I admit I haven't been acting like one, much, around you...Like I said, you deserve to be happy. So stop worrying about me and stop worrying about Travis." He held up a hand when she opened her mouth to object. "For now. You know as well as I do, there's nothing we can do for him right now. His ship never stopped here. I asked around, to see if any other slave ships had been by." At her look of horror, he offered a tight smile. "No one was suspicious of my asking, don't worry. I just made it sound like I was worried they might have lost other boys. But none have been by. They said they only get about one a year. For their sake, I hope that doesn't increase if word spreads about them. They need an army."

He looked past her for a moment, lost in his own thoughts. He was probably thinking about the fight from the day before, the first experience either of them had had with taking a life. "There's a hunting party going out at first light," she said.

"I know. I'm going with them. It was supposed to happen yesterday, shortly after we got here the first time, but then...you know. We left."

Ella nodded. "But if Travis's ship didn't stop here, that means they didn't refresh their supplies. Swan is trading all sorts of things for fresh fruits and meats."

"Right. I'll give him that, he's very concerned with nutrition and health."

"My point is that the odds of surviving such a long trip with poor diet—"

"There are a hundred things that could result in Travis's death," Luca said, and when she flinched, he put his hands on her shoulders and held her gaze. "I love him, too. I worry, too. When we get to Bohannon, I'm going to be right beside you when we go after him and hopefully kill the fuckers who took him. But we're not going to be in Bohannon for weeks. The odds of catching up to them now are about a billion to one, I'd say, unless their ship gets damaged in the storm or something. You can't do anything for him. Neither can I. Not right now. We need to prepare for arriving in Bohannon, but we also need to accept that we're in limbo."

Ella had said as much to herself, hadn't she? It was different, hearing the words come from Luca, though. It proved that he had grown up. It seemed so selfish, to imagine that she could or should do anything for herself, or have any fun, or laugh, while her brother's fate was so uncertain. She worked herself hard, to keep her mind occupied, but thoughts of Travis were never far below. She could sit around and fret, worry ceaselessly, starve herself in her sickening concern, but Luca was right. There was nothing they could do. Nothing. And, in all honesty, her own survival was not guaranteed. If she had to sacrifice herself to save Travis—or Luca—she would.

Maybe a little selfishness now, when she was unable to do anything for Travis, was not the worst thing in the world.

She gave herself a mental shake. Maybe so. Maybe it wasn't so awful to occasionally enjoy herself, like during her swim around the ship. Luca was suggesting something else, though, something that simply wasn't possible. Swan had no interest in her, and even if he did, during the rest of their journey, she would always know that he'd slept with Meena. As much as Ella wanted him, and as much as she believed she might never have another chance to experience the feelings that could exist between them, she had no desire to be anyone's second choice. Her pride would not allow her to be his second choice, when he was far from Meena's embrace and longing for a little...sex.

She suppressed a shudder at the thought, because she knew that it would be nothing more than that for him. She couldn't expect it to be anything more. And she wasn't sure she could allow that to be enough for herself. It was tempting. Even now, knowing that he was across the road with someone else, even feeling the stab of jealousy and irrational sense of betrayal, it was tempting.

"You think too much," Luca commented, eyeing her critically.

She smiled. "You're probably right."

"I am right. They're getting the party started, out there. We should go."

She nodded. "I think I want to freshen up a bit. I'll meet you out front in a few minutes."

Luca started toward the door, then hesitated and turned back. "You do like him, right, El?"

She was taken aback by the direct question as much as by the vulnerability in his young face. She considered lying, and dismissed the idea. She bit her lip and nodded. It was a difficult thing to admit, primarily because she could see that the truth hurt Luca.

"He doesn't deserve you," Luca said, quietly. Then, he sighed. "I think he knows that, too, though." She was again caught off guard. "It'd be easier if I could hate him."

Hadn't she thought the same thing about Meena? Meena and Swan probably deserved each other. They were probably good for each other, and *to* each other. Before Ella could think of a response, Luca was through the doorway, disappearing into the sounds of rejoicing coming from the night.

*   *   *

She'd run into Timón, Marty, Ivan, Rashad, Goonie, and about half of the crew, as well as some of the villagers that she recognized—including Minto. She still hadn't been able to find Luca, though, and her concern was warring with her annoyance. She'd told him she would meet him outside in a few minutes and hadn't seen him since. She'd waited outside her hut for a bit, watching the fires being built—in the middle of the road, down the way a bit—and the people singing and laughing and dancing, and he never showed himself. So, eventually she'd gone searching for him. It had been half an hour. The party seemed to be in full swing. She could smell some sort of cooking meat. Roasting pig, she assumed, wondering how long something like that might take. Her stomach rumbled at the scent.

Then, finally, she saw him, and her brief flash of relief was instantly doused in a cold rush. Of all the people he could be hanging out with, on the whole island, he'd chosen to have a conversation with Meena beside a dark hut. Ella tried to ignore her feeling of betrayal, knowing that there was probably a logical explanation. Meena was, after all, their hostess, and Luca might have official business with her. He might be discussing supplies, or—

But, no, because she saw him say her name. He was talking about her. The coldness seemed to be spreading through her. She repeated to herself not to jump to conclusions. She'd already gotten herself, and everyone else, into a heap of trouble by coming to a rash—and ultimately inaccurate—conclusion. She wasn't going to make the same mistake, she wasn't going to fly off the handle no matter how hard her heart was thudding in her chest.

Luca suddenly turned his head to look right at her, and she was so startled that she almost bolted for cover. Luca raised a hand and motioned for her to join them, which was about the last thing that Ella wanted to do. She glanced around, praying that Swan wouldn't be joining them, too. Luca frowned and motioned again, apparently thinking she was being rude by ignoring the first call.

Meena was looking at her, too, with her big eyes and her open face. From the shadows of the hut, not much of Meena was visible. Just enough to remind Ella of her beauty. Taking a deep breath, repeating to herself that she was an adult and needed to stop acting like a foolish girl, Ella squared her shoulders and walked toward them.

"There you are," Luca said.

Ella's temper flared. "I waited outside for you," she said, unable to keep the accusation from her tone.

Luca winced. "Oh, yeah. Sorry about that. Hey, I've been talking to Meena, and she has something you need to hear."

Ella swallowed her uncharitable response, recognizing its inappropriateness and its unfairness. She looked at Meena, who suddenly grinned. "You dislike me," she said, sounding quite pleased by the idea.

Ella opened her mouth to offer some sort of generic reassurance, but it died in her throat. Luca was right—apologies had never suited her, even when she meant them. And now?

To her surprise, Meena laughed, the musical sound somehow cutting through the noises of celebration from the street. Ella's stomach clenched, and so did her fists. Being laughed at was not something she tolerated well, either, but she reminded herself that Meena had been nothing except a gracious hostess so far. "Do not worry, I'm glad," Meena said, and Ella frowned. Why in the world would she be glad to think that Ella didn't like her?

"Come, let's speak in quiet." Meena reached for her arm, and Ella hesitated, fighting her natural instinct to pull away.

"You need to listen, El," Luca said. "Trust me."

Looking at his face, Ella felt the resistance go out of her, and she nodded. And sighed. She was suddenly tired. Her hunger had been forgotten. "Sure, alright," she agreed, relenting, and she followed Meena's lead toward the hut that she'd been assigned. She felt a mild relief that they weren't going toward Swan's, which she assumed was Meena's. Ella hadn't seen him the crowd, and figured he was still in there, likely recovering from his exercises with Meena.

*　　*　　*

Half an hour later, Ella was standing on the beach, staring out at the moonlit ship, full of conflicting emotions. She was alone on the expanse of sand, but as she watched out over the glimmering water, two men brought their rowboat onto the shore and stepped out to pull it up: Marty and Bart, and after exchanging a quick glance, Marty walked toward her.

"Hey, Ella," he said, looking up and down the beach. "You out here alone? Something wrong?"

She shook her head. "Just thinking," she said, somehow managing a smile.

"You should be careful," he said. "There are some dangerous animals in this jungle. You want to walk back with us?"

She hesitated, then shook her head. "No, I'm going to stay here for a bit."

It was his turn to hesitate, and in the moonlight, she saw him chew his bottom lip in indecision. He glanced over his shoulder toward Bart, who was up the beach, near the mouth of the trail. "We can wait a few minutes, if you want—"

"No, really, go on ahead," she said. "I'll be fine."

Still, he stood there, unsure, and she couldn't really blame him. She appreciated his concern, but needed to be alone. Before he could object further, she spoke again.

"I'll be fine. Really," she said. "I just want to be alone, to...clear my head. It's gotten pretty loud in the village."

Marty smiled. "They do know how to celebrate," he said. He seemed uncomfortable, and she expected him to refuse to leave her alone on the beach. After a moment, however, he said, "Well, if you're sure..."

She forced a smile and nodded. "Thank you. I'm fine, really."

"Well, alright," he said. He sighed, and she imagined he was wondering if he was going to be reprimanded for leaving her alone. Finally, though, he turned and joined Bart. Bart muttered something, glancing back at her, and Marty shrugged and shook his head. Ella turned away from them and waited until they'd disappeared into the jungle. She looked out over the sparkling water. Then she looked at the rowboats, knowing that she could never hope to row one by herself, at least not that far. She could have asked Marty and Bart to take her. She might have been able to convince them to do it, but she would have had to give them some sort of explanation. She could have asked Luca to help her, but he'd already done more than she could rightfully expect from him.

No, if she wanted to get to the ship now, in the darkest, earliest part of the morning, there was only one way.

As intimidating as the ocean was in the bright sunlight, it was exponentially more frightening in the dark of night. As the waves glistened in the moonlight, she couldn't help imagining what sorts of creatures might be lurking beneath them. Squaring her shoulders, she walked out into the lapping waves before she could talk herself out of it. She waded knee-deep, clenching her teeth at the surprising chill, and then looked back, scanning the beach and the edge of the jungle. She expected to find herself alone, and when her eyes skimmed across a figure near the trail, her heart stuttered.

It was too dark to see his face, but she suddenly recognized him. After a moment, Luca raised a hand, then lowered it to his side. He wasn't trying to stop her; he was just making sure she was alright. She knew, then, that he would watch her swim all the way out, and she felt a mixture of guilt and relief at the realization. She took a deep breath, offered a wave of acknowledgment, and turned back toward the sea. She braced herself for the coldness. She looked out at the ship. It was a long way out, further than it looked, she knew. There was a very real possibility that, if she wasn't eaten by something, she would drown. She couldn't even be certain she would be able to climb aboard if she did make it. She assumed a rope would be down. She would have to hope her assumption was correct.

She leaned forward and dove into the cold waves.

* * *

You're an idiot, Swan, he thought, pacing the room with his hands clasped

153

behind his back. He sighed. He finally stopped and turned to sit on the edge of the bed. It was true, he must be an idiot. What other explanation could there be? He'd lain with Meena, what? A hundred times? He'd always felt desire when he was near her. He'd always enjoyed her company. Hell, they'd always enjoyed each other. There had never been anything wrong with that. He'd always known that she was with other men while he was gone, and there was nothing wrong with that, either. He'd never made her any promises, and she'd never expected any. It wasn't about love, between them. They respected each other. They were honest with each other. They cared about each other.

That had always been enough.

Sighing again, he leaned back on the bed and stared up at the ceiling. He was tired—painfully so, and yet he felt a million leagues from sleep. He'd always had trouble sleeping, since he was a child, but it had gotten worse in the past year. He folded his hands beneath his head. Who was he kidding? It had gotten even worse in the past couple of weeks, because of Ella. Oh, it wasn't her fault. She couldn't be blamed for the fact that he couldn't control his stupid thoughts and desires.

In fact, if she knew just how much of his time was spent thinking about her, she'd probably be terrified. He was a bit frightened, himself. He wasn't sure how it had happened, exactly. He'd been telling himself for the past few days that things would be better once he reached Tarot, and Meena. He'd told himself—and he thought he'd actually believed it, although it was difficult to be certain—that Meena would make it better, making love to Meena always took some of his stress away and it would certainly take the edge off the irrational desire that flared every time he thought of Ella sleeping in his bed.

At first, on the beach, wrapped in Meena's embrace, he had felt the familiar pull of attraction. When she'd kissed him, though, for the first time in all the years he'd known her, it had felt...wrong.

Swan shook his head in disgust, closing his eyes. Meena had known something was different, no matter how hard he'd tried to convince her—and himself—that it wasn't. Swan had never before thought of someone else while Meena was kissing him. He'd never imagined someone else's body in his hands while holding Meena in his arms. Meena had never been a substitute for anyone, and that wasn't something she deserved to be.

There had been a few times, over the years, when he'd asked himself if he was in love with Meena. He'd even considered the possibility of settling down on Tarot with her, but the call of the sea had always been stronger than the call of Meena. So, he'd assumed there was something broken inside of him that could not be fixed. If he couldn't love Meena, surely he couldn't love anyone. At least, not like that.

He did care for Meena, but he wasn't in love with her, and she wasn't in love with him. In fact, she was the one who'd put an end to the charade, the one who'd finally acknowledged that his heart and mind weren't really in the room. He'd tried his best to lose himself in her kiss, her touch, her scent, her beauty...It would have been unfair to her, and that's the real reason he'd finally admitted the truth to her.

Even though they had always been honest about what was between them, and what wasn't, he might have expected her to be a little hurt. He might even have expected her to be angry, at the admission that he was thinking of someone else while she was kissing him. What he wasn't quite prepared for was her sudden and genuine excitement, or her happiness when she finally realized what the problem was.

You should go to her, she'd said, and for just a moment, he'd truly considered it, as though it could really be so simple. Reason had finally returned, though, and he'd shaken his head. He claimed it was because, even though they'd come to some semblance of trust, he knew that Ella was still keeping secrets from him. How big or small, he didn't know, and he told himself he didn't need to know. Their relationship, whatever it was—friends, she'd called them—was temporary, and when he got her to Bohannon, he might never see he again.

Meena had seen through to the real reason, of course. It wasn't distrust. It was fear. He'd never considered himself to be cowardly, and he'd never shied away from a fight or an uncomfortable situation. Until now. He'd faced down men intent on killing him—most recently, Carter. No one had ever frightened him as much as Ella did, though, and she wasn't even aware of it.

"You're an idiot," he repeated, aloud this time. He'd told Meena that Ella was engaged to marry Luca, and Meena had suggested that maybe the best way to put an end to that was to tell Ella about his own feelings. The problem was, Swan didn't know what his own feelings were. He did know that it would be vastly unfair to burden Ella with them, though. And, did he want to interfere with her relationship with Luca?

Yes, his mind instantly answered, and he felt his body tense with something—*jealousy?*—unpleasant at the thought of Ella marrying Luca, kissing him, making love to him, bearing his children...Swan groaned, cursing himself. He might not like the idea of Ella and Luca together, but he knew that Luca would do anything to protect Ella. He'd seen the proof with his own eyes, more than once. And Ella had risked her own life, and offered her own body, to protect Luca. They loved each other, and Swan felt a stab of pain, and envy, at that.

Swan had spent the majority of his life alone. He had always had a habit of separating himself from those around him. He had never felt so lonely, however, as he did then, staring at the dark ceiling. There was a dull, hollow ache inside of him, and he didn't think there was any way to fill it. At least, not any honorable way.

Ella had offered herself to him, as a payment for someone else's well-being. And, more recently, she'd suggested that she might actually *want* him to touch her. He couldn't allow himself to believe that, however, because every time he got close to her, she looked as though she expected him to attack her. Every time he returned to his cabin at night, she was awake, pretending to sleep, holding her breath to see if this was the time he would force his way

155

into the bed with her rather than settling in to the chair behind his desk.

He had never forced—and *would* never force—himself on any woman. He'd never been with any woman who wasn't completely willing—Hell, eager, actually, because if she was just willing and not enthusiastic, it sort of took the fun out of it—and he'd never been tempted to accept less. Until now. He'd never thought he would accept reluctant willingness as enough incentive to make a move, and he had to keep reminding himself that it was *not* enough. He hadn't been lying when he'd told her that he did not want to be a regret for her.

It was going to be a long journey, the rest of the way to Bohannon. It was certainly going to be a test of his moral mettle.

He had a feeling there was going to be an even harder test, then, when it came time to let her go. When it came time to watch her and Luca head off into their life together, in an unfamiliar country. Would he be able to do that?

He frowned at the ceiling. Well, of course he would, because he wouldn't have a choice. He certainly couldn't keep her against her will, lock her up in the brig. He sighed again.

The knock on the door startled him, and he swung his legs off the bed and stood quickly, scowling at the door. Something must be wrong. His stomach clenched, and he crossed the room in two strides and pulled the door open.

As though summoned from his thoughts, Ella stood on the other side, dripping and shivering, her hair matted to her head and the moonlight shining off the droplets of water on her face. He stared at her, unable to breathe.

"Hi," she said.

Chapter Nine

Ella was tired, shaky, cold, and nervous. She'd had a long time to think, while she swam. To keep her mind off the possibility of sea creatures stalking her from below, she'd considered even more frightening ideas: That he might be angry or horrified to see her; that Meena had either lied or misjudged his feelings; that she would make a complete fool of herself.

"Bloody hell, Ella. What happened? What's wrong?" he asked, grabbing her by the arm and pulling her into the room. His hand was hot on her cold arm, and she felt herself beginning to shiver in earnest. "Are you hurt?" He was holding her by both arms, now, searching her for signs of injury. It was so dark, she wondered how he thought he would be able to see anything, and he finally seemed to realize that, himself. In a heartbeat, he was gone, and a lantern filled the room with its yellow glow. Before she could even register his absence, he was back. "Talk to me. What happened?"

He sounded frantic, and she realized that her silence was frightening him even worse than her appearance. She'd planned out so many things to say, and now she couldn't manage any of them. They seemed stupid, or silly, or inadequate. Plus, her teeth were chattering.

"Are you hurt?" he repeated, searching her face, and she shook her head.

"F-fine, just c-cold," she managed.

"Get your wet clothes off," he said. "I'll get a towel. I've got dry—" He had begun to turn away again, but she grabbed his arm, stopping him. He hesitated, then looked back at her, his expression wary. His eyes were dark, and she felt a slow heat begin to seep through her, tingling in her limbs and pooling in her stomach. "Ella," he said, and there was uncertainty in his voice.

She knew that if she let herself think, she would give in to the fear, again. Looking at him, she suddenly knew that he was afraid, too, and the realization was strangely emboldening. She stepped forward, praying he wouldn't pull away. He watched her, and for a moment he looked heartbreakingly lost and unsure, and then she pressed her chilly lips against his. She slid her fingers into his hair, felt the heat of his chest warming her wet front, felt his hands touch her arms. She thought he was going to push her away, and she pushed herself closer to him, instead, soaking the front of his clothes with seawater.

His mouth opened, tentatively at first, and she felt a rush of desire tempered only by her uncertainty. She had no experience with kissing. She didn't know what was expected of her. He made a sound in his throat and his hands tightened on her arms. Then, suddenly, he took a step back, breaking all contact between them except the touch of his hands on her arms. Her fingers slipped from his hair, and she blinked, stunned as much by her reaction to the kiss as by its abrupt end.

"Talk to me," he said, his voice hoarse and rough. "How'd you get here?"

"I swam," she answered, suppressing a shudder. She was, miraculously, no longer cold.

He scowled. "Yes. Why?"

She licked her lips, nervously, and saw his gaze immediately flick toward the movement. "I hoped you'd be happy to see me," she admitted.

His eyebrows went up in surprise. "Did you?" he asked, softly. "So you risked your life to come out here because...you thought I might miss you?"

She couldn't tell for sure if he was mocking her, but she nodded, anyway, because it was true—in a way. She'd certainly hoped that he was out here, alone, wishing she was with him. "Why did *you* come out here?" she asked.

"I don't like to leave my ship untended," he said. It was true, but it was also a lie, and they both knew it. It wasn't concern for his ship that had driven him to have Marty and Bart row him off the island.

"You weren't coming to invite me to join you at the bonfire? You weren't upset because you saw Luca coming into my hut?"

He studied her for a moment with his jaw clenched. "Well, you know plenty," he said. He seemed angry, but in another flash of intuition, she knew that was just a cover. He wasn't nearly as confident as he appeared. How could anyone so handsome and intelligent, kind and considerate, be insecure? "Where is Luca, anyway?" That was a deliberate dig, and she refused to rise to the challenge.

"I don't want to talk about him," she said. "I want to talk about us."

"Perhaps you want to get out of your wet clothes before you freeze to death," he suggested, in a tight voice, again starting to turn away. This time, she didn't reach for his arm.

Instead, she said, "Please don't turn away."

He froze, half-turned, looking at her from the corner of his eye.

"I was upset when I saw you go off with Meena. Yesterday morning, I mean. That's why I came out here, to feel sorry for myself," she said, speaking quickly. In the absence of contact, her coldness was rapidly retuning, but she did her best to ignore her chill and discomfort. "I was...jealous. I knew it was stupid. But it's true. I was angry, and hurt, and that's part of the reason why I was so quick to assume the worst of you when I saw you talking to Captain Carter. After that, I thought...you'd never forgive me. I thought you'd hate me, and you had a right to. But you were willing to...be friends, which was more than I deserved. I told myself it was enough."

He turned back toward her, slowly.

"I told myself that you were too good for me, anyway, and that you deserved to love someone like Meena."

"It was never about love with Meena," he said, and his expression proved that he was surprised to hear the words slip from his own mouth.

"I saw the two of you, across the road, kissing, and—"

"I didn't—"

"I know. She told me. But it hurt, seeing it, even though I'd told myself over and over again that it didn't matter, that I couldn't let it matter." She could feel the sting of tears, and she blinked them back. The words were flowing surprisingly easily, now. "I didn't know why you kept rejecting me. I thought it must be because you loved Meena, or someone else, or because you didn't find me attractive, or because you didn't think I was good enough—"

He made a sound, caught between a growl and a moan, in his throat, and took a half-step forward. She put a hand on his chest, and he stopped, staring at her.

"That wasn't it, though, was it?"

He shook his head, slowly.

She drew her fingers into a fist, holding the front of his shirt and looking at her hand to gather her flagging courage. "I want you," she said, quietly, chancing a glance up at his face. "But I do have some pride left, you know. Surprisingly. So...this is the last time. I won't ask again."

He reached up a hand and took her wrist. She let go of his shirt and he lowered her arm to her side, stepping forward. He bent his head, and she caught her breath in anticipation. He searched her eyes for a moment, solemn and silent, before covering her mouth with his. Her inexperience didn't mean she couldn't recognize the desperation in his kiss. He made another sound, and then his arms went around her, pulling her tight against his front. She didn't imagine her cold wetness could be pleasant for him.

His raised his arms, pushing his fingers into her wet hair to hold her head, and she opened her mouth to the assault of his lips, instinctively. Without hesitation, he plunged his tongue into her mouth, and she felt desire, hot and sudden, engulf her. It was her turn to make a sound in her throat, and she tried to press closer to him. She had only a vague idea of what she wanted, but she knew that she wanted it badly, and she clutched at his shirt, holding on for dear life.

His fingers were warming her scalp; her whole body yearned for his touch. He hadn't been with Meena in more than half a year, and according to Meena, he almost certainly hadn't been with anyone else since leaving Tarot for the last time. She said he had very rarely sought out other company on either coast. What if Ella was a disappointment after such high expectation?

She shoved the thought away, angry with herself for giving in to self-doubt, even now.

Just when her head had begun to swim from lack of air, he broke his mouth away from hers and dipped his head to press a kiss beneath her ear. Another shiver passed through her, and she tipped her head back.

"You're freezing," he whispered against the side of her neck.

"Not anymore," she breathed.

The soft sound of his chuckle vibrated through her. "It's not too late, you know," he said, after a moment.

She hesitated. She couldn't see his face. "For what?" she finally asked.

He lifted his head, then, to meet her gaze. "To come to your senses," he answered, softly. He slid his hands from her hair to rest on her shoulders. "I was lying in bed, wondering if I would have the willpower to resist you for the next few weeks. Telling myself I would have to find the strength. And now...here you are, and I have to tell you...there's no way I can pass this test.

Unless you tell me to stop."

"So you *were* missing me?" she murmured, smiling.

He groaned. "Oh, God, Ella. I'm so sorry I made you feel rejected, or hurt...The truth is, I've never wanted anyone the way I want you. Ever. It scares the hell out of me."

"Me, too," she admitted, letting out a breath.

He ran a thumb along her jaw. "I don't want you to be scared of me," he muttered. "Tell me what you want."

"Kiss me," she said, without hesitation.

He did, gentler this time, slower, and she felt her legs weakening beneath her. She could feel his desire, hard against her hip, and she felt a moment's fear—not of him, but of her own inexperience. "You need to get your wet clothes off," he finally said, against her lips.

"Alright," she said, her stomach fluttering in anticipation.

"Do you want to take a bath? To warm up? I can start heating some water—"

She shook her head. She was plenty warm enough. All she wanted was him, all of him. She took a quick step backward and peeled her wet shirt up and over her head, tossing it with a thwack onto the wooden floor. He was staring at her, but she couldn't allow herself time for insecurity. She pulled her trousers down and kicked them aside and stood before him in her undergarments, trying not to shiver as the air whispered across her clammy skin.

He seemed to be having difficulty breathing. "Ella," he finally whispered.

"Colin," she answered. She stepped toward him, and suddenly his arms were around her, his heat searing into her mostly-naked body, and he was kissing her. She felt him spin her toward the bed, and a moment later, she felt the edge of the mattress against the backs of her legs. She sat down, holding the front of his shirt, pulling him down with her. She heard him make a small sound of surprise, and as she leaned back, he caught himself with his arms on either side of her, propped on the bedspread.

He looked down at her, searching her face in the dimness. "You're...beautiful," he whispered.

She felt a wash of pleasure at his words, and pressed her hand against his cheek.

"No. You're perfect," he corrected. Then he frowned. "Maybe a little thin, yet," he added, and when she laughed, his face split into a grin.

"If you had your way, I think I'd weigh three hundred pounds," she joked.

He shifted his weight and ran a hand along the bone of her hip, covered only by the thin, wet material of her underwear. He was right, of course. She was still too thin. Years of malnourishment could not be cured in a month. They both watched his hand move its way up, watched her belly quiver at his light touch. She shifted beneath him, anxious for some sort of release.

He dipped his head and, to her astonishment, closed his mouth over her breast, his hot tongue pressing against the thin material covering her nipple.

160

She threw her head back into the mattress, clutching at his shoulders, shocked by the strength of the sensation tearing through her.

She wanted the barriers between them removed, and she tried to focus before she lost control completely. She grabbed his hair and pulled his head up with regret. When he looked at her, she said, "I want to feel you," and reached for the top button of his shirt. He let her fumble at it for a moment, with trembling fingers, and then he reached up a hand and quickly undid the first two fasteners. Then, levering himself up, he pulled the shirt up and over his head and tossed it to the floor.

He waited, staring down at her, judging her reaction. She reached up and laid a hand over his heart, feeling the thud against her palm and the heat of his skin. The bandage across his abdomen was a cold reminder of how close he'd come to dying just the day before—how close they'd both come, probably. She fingered the edge of the bandage gently.

He was supporting himself on one arm, the only contact between them her light touch and his thigh against hers. She wanted to pull him down, beg him to touch every inch of her. But first, she had to know he would be alright. "Does it hurt?" she asked.

"It's fine," he answered. His voice was low, barely more than a vibration in his chest.

"I don't want to hurt you." She looked up, at the bruise beneath his eye. "Again," she added, and saw his lips curve in a smile. Unable to resist such temptation, she curled her hand around the back of his neck and pulled his head down. As his mouth covered hers, hungrily, he shifted his body, and she again felt the proof of his desire pressing against her. She couldn't deny to herself that it inspired another twinge of trepidation, fear mostly of the unknown, but her curiosity and arousal overrode such things.

His bare chest was on hers, now, and she squirmed beneath him, unable to get enough of the feel of his skin against hers. She wanted the rest of her clothes off. And the rest of his. She shifted again, and he made a sound that was close to a groan. She stilled, afraid she was doing something wrong. After a moment, he sensed her hesitation and lifted his head to look at her again. "What's the matter?" he asked, concern etched on his face as he searched hers.

"I thought maybe you wanted me to hold still," she admitted, her cheeks flaming.

He raised his eyebrows. "God, no," he breathed, and she felt a touch of relief at his sincerity. "Tell me what you want."

"You. I want...to feel you..."

Lowering his gaze, he skimmed his thumb over her nipple, smiling when she hissed in a breath. "Sit up, love," he said.

Trying not to over-think the endearment, she did as instructed, and in a flash he'd freed her small breasts from their thin, wet covering. When he reached for the damp underwear, she lifted her hips a bit to help, and soon they'd joined the rest of her wet clothes on the floor. She was completely naked, and she lay still while his gaze slid over every inch of her. His

161

expression was solemn, his eyes dark. When his eyes finally found their way back to hers, she knew that he thought she was beautiful. She had never felt so before, but in that moment, she believed it. She believed him.

He lowered his head, and this time, his mouth closed over her bare nipple, and all rational thought fled her mind. He shifted so that one knee was between hers, and his hand slid slowly up her thigh. She swallowed. Her hands were in his hair, although she didn't know how they'd gotten there. She wanted to hold his head in place so he would never stop what he was doing with his mouth.

His hand, drawing closer to the junction between her thighs, was distracting, though. She squirmed in anticipation, and when his light caress found her center, she clutched handfuls of his hair, barely registering the fact that she might be hurting him. He didn't object. His thumb found its target, and she twitched, gasping. Something was building within her, something that felt far too large, and she felt another twinge of fear. She wished she knew what to expect.

His mouth moved to her other breast, and her whole body was tingling with overwhelming pleasure.

"Colin," she said, barely able to form his name.

"Yes, Ella," he answered against her nipple. She shivered at the sensation.

"I...need..."

"I know," he said, moving his fingers. Her breathing was unsteady, and she felt the world starting to spin. Then he was gone, and she blinked at the sudden abandonment. Before she could even process his absence, though, he'd stripped the last of his clothing off and was back. She got only a glimpse of his erection, and her mouth was dry with a mixture of apprehension and anticipation. His fingers found their mark again as he covered her mouth with his. She could feel his skin against her whole length, and she shifted, wanting to be closer still. She knew she was in danger of losing herself completely; she wasn't sure she would ever be able to recover from such an overload of sensation. She didn't care. She needed him like she'd never needed anything in her life. She ran her hands over his shoulders, down his arms, around his back. Her nipples were hard against his chest.

She slid her hands over his buttocks, wanting to pull him closer, guide him to where his fingers were teasing her toward a breaking point she barely comprehended. In spite of her hesitancy, the low groan in his throat encouraged her, and she tightened her grip, raising her hips—instinctively—against his hand.

"Please," she said.

He shifted, and a moment later, she felt his erection pressing where his fingers had been a second before. She clutched at his backside, urging him on, practically sobbing at the torture of need.

The pain came suddenly and unexpectedly, and she made a small sound. She tried to bite it back, but it was too late. He'd gone completely still. She blinked, trying to catch her breath and make sense of the conflicting sensations. She wanted to raise her hips to meet his in spite of the pain. She wanted to wrap her legs around him and pull him deeper. The pain was not as large as her desire, but it was not small, either.

Swan swore, softly. His eyes were closed. "I didn't...You should've..." He swore again. She tried to fight down her alarm and insecurity.

"What's wrong?" she whispered, afraid that it was something she'd done.

He took a deep breath and opened his eyes. "Nothing. Hold on. The pain will be gone in a minute. Alright?"

Biting her lip, she nodded. She was relieved to feel that it was already fading, and when he slid deeper, the stretching sensation was strangely pleasant. She spread her legs further apart, without thought. He was moving so slowly, she wanted to beg him to move faster. He pulled back a bit, and she tightened around him, trying to keep hold of him. His breathing was harsh, and she could feel his muscles trembling.

He slid further in, then, and she whimpered.

"Are you alright?" he asked.

She nodded. "Please," she begged. "Colin. Faster, please."

His lips were over hers, his tongue plunging into her mouth as his erection filled her completely. He moved in and out, and she quivered against him as his hips moved faster and faster. She cried out but his mouth swallowed the sound. She felt herself tightening around him, felt her whole body trembling, and then the world was shattering around her, and she held onto him as wave after wave crashed over her.

He buried his face against her shoulder. She could hear, and feel, his ragged breathing. Then, moving quickly, he withdrew from her, leaving her feeling unnaturally hollow. He levered himself up and she looked down as he reached a hand between them. He wrapped his fingers around his erection, and after two quick jerks, his semen spurted in hot strands on her stomach. She could feel the tremors rippling through him, and she grabbed his hair, pulling his head so she could kiss him. They were both panting, and in a moment, her head was spinning from lack of air and she had to break away.

He disappeared, leaving nothing but cool air against her skin, and returned in a heartbeat with a damp washcloth. He gently swiped the semen from her skin, and her stomach quivered. "I'm sorry," he said. He seemed upset. She had just experienced the most amazing feeling of her life, and all she wanted was to curl up against him, to feel his arms around her and his heartbeat against hers.

"Sorry?" she heard herself ask, watching his face.

"I didn't know—I thought you and—" He finally looked up and met her eyes. "Why didn't you tell me?" he asked.

She hesitated. "Tell you what?" she asked. And then, suddenly, she understood. She felt herself blush, and she lowered her gaze to his chin. "I thought it was obvious," she muttered, thinking of all her awkward attempts at flirting.

He let out a breath. "It was. It should've been. I...let my own stupid jealousy..." He shook his head and cursed under his breath. "I'm sorry, Ella. I never meant to hurt you." He put a finger under her chin, gently tilting her face up until her eyes met his. "Please tell me you're alright."

"I'm better than alright. Would it have changed your mind? If you knew?"

He winced. "You gave me something I had no right to take," he muttered, his expression full of self-loathing.

"Then I'm glad you didn't know," she said, fiercely. Then, unable to keep the doubt from her voice, she added, "Are you angry with me?"

"Angry?" he repeated. He slid onto the bed beside her, pulling her into his arms, and she pressed her face against his chest, breathing in his warmth and scent. This was what she wanted—to snuggle against him, and even before he answered, she could feel her tension sliding away. "God, Ella. No, I'm not angry with you. You should be angry with me."

"I'm not," she whispered against his skin, and she felt him shiver.

"It won't hurt the next time," he whispered, kissing her temple. She felt a tingle of pleasure at his words, and the promise they held. She tried not to over-think. To be in his arms was enough.

"What did you mean about being jealous?" she asked after a brief silence.

"I spent so much time obsessing over the idea that you and Luca had...you know...that I never stopped to consider the facts."

"You were jealous of Luca?" she asked.

His arms tightened around her in response, and she could feel him considering his answer.

She hesitated, conflicted. She wanted to tell him, then, that she and Luca had never been romantically involved. How would he react to the knowledge that she'd lied to him? While she'd never technically told him that she was engaged to Luca, she'd let him come to his own conclusions, and she knew the distinction did not make it any less of a lie.

"I think Meena is really nice," she said, slowly, after a moment of silence.

"Yes..." he answered, a bit cautiously, the word suspended somewhere between a question and an answer.

"I guess I'm glad I didn't kill her when I saw her kissing you."

He laughed, and she nestled closer against his chest, breathing in his scent and smiling. He was tracing light circles on the back of her shoulder with his finger, and it was both relaxing and arousing. Her body was still sweaty and tingly, and she was already wondering when she could experience the whole thing again. He'd said it wouldn't hurt the next time, but she would gladly accept the pain to have everything else.

"You're not upset that I...hadn't ever..." she ventured after a bit.

"I've never been happier about anything," he murmured, his lips against her wet hair. He sighed, his warm breath tickling her scalp. "Or guiltier," he added. "No wonder you were afraid. I just thought..."

"I told you I wasn't afraid of you," she said.

"I didn't believe you," he admitted. "I'm sorry."

"Well...I didn't exactly show a lot of trust in you when I thought you were a slave-trader."

"I guess we haven't communicated all that well," he answered.

"No," she agreed. His slow caress was becoming quite distracting. "I'm sorry you thought I was afraid of you."

"I'm sorry I hurt you," he said, his arms again tightening possessively.

"It wasn't so bad," she answered, looking to reassure him.

"I could have made it easier, sweetheart. But I didn't just mean the physical pain. I mean everything yesterday, with Meena and Carter...Hell, everything since you've been on my ship."

"I've loved being on your ship," she admitted, surprised to realize that it was true. "For the most part. I never would've guessed...I've gotten used to the rocking, it felt weird to be on land again. And...the ocean all around...It's, I don't know, terrifying and comforting at the same time." She lifted her chin to look at him, afraid that she was opening herself up for a load of questions she wasn't sure she could answer. A part of her wanted more than anything for him to ask her to stay with him, forever, to sail the world with him. Another part, the part that knew her brother was out there, somewhere, prayed that he wouldn't ask.

He searched her face for a moment, then bent his head to kiss her. His lips were gentle, soft, and she felt the now-familiar pull of desire tug at her belly. She shifted her legs, restlessly. Was it even possible to make love again, so soon? She had no idea. He said he was glad about her inexperience, and she hoped that was true. "I'm glad you sneaked onto my ship," he whispered beneath her ear. Her heart skipped. He said, barely audible, "No matter what the reason."

She felt tears prick her eyes. The words bubbled up in her throat, threatening to choke her. She had offered herself to him, a lifetime ago, to save Luca from a cell. She couldn't burden him with her woes, she couldn't ask for his help, when they'd just shared something so intimate. He had no reason to trust her. She could only expect him to believe the worst. That she'd tricked him into accepting her, just to ply him for a favor...And, when he found out that she and Luca had never been an item...

Luca's words came to her, telling her that she needed to be selfish while she could. Holding Swan in her arms felt selfish. Could she continue to deceive him? She didn't think so. He deserved the truth. She owed him the truth. But maybe not yet. Maybe she could keep him for just a few more hours. Maybe she could hold onto the fantasy for just a little while.

"How long before we can...you know. Again."

He laughed softly against her throat. "Honey, I'm pretty sure I could make love to you until I died of exhaustion."

She hesitated. "But that wouldn't really happen, right?"

He lifted his head to look at her. "No, love," he said, kissing the end of her nose. "You're still going to be sore, though...You should rest. Dawn's only a few hours away."

"Do you want me to beg?"

He looked horrified. "No." Then, after a moment, he smiled. "Besides, I doubt you could."

"I don't do so well with begging," she admitted. "But...I can try, if I need to."

"I assure you, you don't."

"No?" she asked, suddenly smiling.

After a moment, his face split into a grin. "God help us both," he said.

*   *   *

Swan woke just after dawn. His arm was asleep beneath Ella. He felt surprisingly content, in those first few moments. He looked down at her face, peaceful in sleep. He'd slept for almost four hours. He couldn't remember the last time that had happened. The physical exertion had something to do with it, probably, but he knew it was more than that. It was her. He'd slept with her wrapped around him, slept easily and deeply.

The guilt and shame swooped down on him, cracking his contentment. He'd assumed things that he'd had no right to assume, and he'd taken her virginity without even knowing he was doing it. She'd come to him willingly. The knowledge held little comfort, however, because she'd barely had enough information to know what she was consenting to.

He'd been drawn to her from first sight, there was no denying that. The attraction had been mutual. She'd been engaged to Luca, though, and for all Swan knew, she still was. The idea made his stomach churn, and not just from guilt. After the past night, the thought of her in another man's arms was even more painful than it had been before. His feelings of possessiveness frightened him with their intensity. He could stake no claim to her that she was not willing to accept, and he wasn't even sure what *he* wanted. Oh, he wanted her, even now. He didn't think he would ever tire of the feel of her body against his. What else did he want, though? Marriage? They barely knew each other. And, even if she were willing, what did he have to offer her? He had money, but no real home outside the ship. Nor was he sure if he would ever want one. It would be unfair to ask her—or anyone—to commit her life to a stifling, rocking hunk of wood.

He suppressed a sigh. He was considering the merits of marriage to a woman who might still intend to marry another man.

Ella stirred in his arms, and he felt a shiver of desire pass through him. She wasn't even awake, and he was imagining how it would feel to bury himself within her as the morning sunlight streaked across her pale skin. She tipped her head up to look at him, and their eyes met and held.

"Hi," she said, a blush creeping into her cheeks as she smiled.

"Good morning," he answered, and he felt himself grinning like an idiot. Her sleepy smile filled him with a happiness that stole much of the power from his guilt and doubts.

"How long have you been awake?" she asked.

"Just a minute," he said. "How do you feel?"

She ducked her face against his chest. "Happy," she said, and he felt his own emotion swell in response. It was amazing, the effect she had on him. It was scary, yes, but it was something he knew he could become addicted to.

"You look beautiful," he said, kissing her tangle of hair.

She made a sound of disbelief. "I was afraid you'd, you know...be sorry..."

"You're the one with the right to regrets," he answered. "Do you have any?" He held his breath, waiting for her response, knowing she should say yes and praying she would say no.

"Not if you don't," she answered. "Maybe...we can both just...be happy."

He let out a slow breath, and said, "How could I be anything else, with you in my arms?"

It was her turn to stop breathing. He waited, thinking she was going to say something. When she finally did, it wasn't what he'd expected. "Where did you grow up?" she asked, softly.

He hesitated, because he wasn't used to speaking of the life he'd led outside his ship.

After a moment, she lifted her head to look at him. "You don't have to tell me," she said, and it was the worry in her eyes that made him answer.

"Bohannon," he said. He saw the surprise on her face and offered a small smile. "No accent, right? Well, I've spent most of my adult life on this ship, with men from all over...I think we all sound alike, now."

She seemed to consider that. "You told me Bohannon was a dangerous place," she said.

"It is," he answered, harsher than he'd intended. He tightened his arm around her and kissed her forehead. "It can be. It's not all bad, though," he allowed, gentler.

She looked unsure, and he suddenly knew where her hesitancy stemmed from: She wanted to ask him about his life, and she was afraid that he would ask about hers. He considered that realization for a moment. He desperately wanted to ask about her intentions, regarding Luca, regarding Bohannon. He wanted to ask why she'd stowed away on his ship to escape the place of her birth and entire life. He wanted to know everything about her, past and future. Could he accept her desire to keep secrets?

Could he give her himself and live with only part of her in return?

Looking into her face, he knew that he did not want to give her up. He also knew that she was in his arms because she wanted to be, not because she wanted something from him. She would stay in his arms if he refused to answer her questions. And, eventually, if he could make her see that he was willing to do the same, she might tell him her own secrets.

"I spent a few years in an orphanage, until I was nine," he said, quietly. "It wasn't a nice place. It was owned by a couple who had more money than they knew what to do with, and they thought that it was...a way to give a little back. They had no idea what went on there. Not until they came by for a visit, one day, decided to check in on their investments around town. The man—

Henry—he was sick already, by then. I think he was looking out for his wife's future, making sure there would be no unpleasant surprises, financially or legally..." For a moment, he was lost in the fog of angry despair that he'd spent much of his childhood struggling to get out of.

She sensed some of it, and pressed her palm against his jaw. "Your parents—?"

He shook his head. "They didn't die. At least, not then. They might be dead, now. I don't know. They never wanted me, finally left when I was five. Left me at the church with a note pinned to my shirt. I don't think they knew that I could read. Told me to sit and be quiet until the priest came to let me in. It was before dawn. I didn't even have mittens. It was January."

"Colin, I'm sorry," she said. She bent her head and kissed his chest, surprising him. "You must have been scared."

"I read their note," he murmured, stroking her back, taking comfort from her presence and the knowledge that the past was distant. "It said, 'His name is Colin, he's five, we won't come back.' Short, to the point, yes?"

He could feel her lips against his skin, could feel her desire to ease his pain.

"Father O'Malley was nice enough, when he finally showed up. I wouldn't talk to him. I was half-frozen, scared...angry...hurt...Hell, it wasn't like I didn't know they didn't want me, but...Anyway, he took me to Darling House. It had been called The Orphanage until the year before. Creative name, right? But Henry Darling had bought it, put some money into fixing the building up, replacing the ratty beds. It's too bad he didn't replace the staff, too, but how could he know? He didn't live there."

"Is the place still there?" she asked, her tone somewhat cautious.

"It is. It's a lovely place, now," he said, and there was a fierceness in his voice that even he could hear. Mrs. Darling had made sure that no child forced, by circumstance, to live there, would ever suffer abuse or neglect, but Swan himself had made it his business to keep close tabs on the place.

"What happened when you were nine?" she asked.

"The Darlings adopted me," he answered, softly.

"Mrs. Darling," she mused. "You said she was your teacher..."

"I said, in a manner of speaking," he corrected. "And she was. She taught me how to be the person I am. At least, whatever good qualities I might have. The bad is all me."

"There isn't any bad," she murmured against his chest. "When did Henry die?" she asked.

He was silent for a bit, and she let him be, waiting to see if he wanted to answer. He found that he did. "A year after I went to live with them. It was a rough year for him, though. For both of them. He was wasting away, and she had to watch him."

"So did you."

"I was an asshole."

"You were a little boy."

"I was angry. I didn't want to make anything easier for them. They never yelled at me. Never hit me. But I think I thought that it was only a matter of time before they got sick of my attitude and sent me away. Then...the last week or so, Henry was completely bed-ridden. Mrs. Darling kept trying to send me in there—to take him food, whatever she could think of, trying to get me to...say goodbye, I think. I refused. Didn't see him for days. Then, I was creeping by his door and heard him call my name. I almost ignored him. In fact, I walked past before stopping. I was scared. That's no excuse, but it's true. I waited. He didn't call out again. If he had, I probably would've run. Never looked back. Never seen him again. But he didn't. It was silent, and after a minute, I crept back into the doorway. He was looking up at the ceiling. He had trouble breathing, and I remember watching his chest and thinking that it could stop at any second."

Ella's breath was warm against his skin, and her arm was possessive across his stomach. Protective, even. He thought of the way she'd come to his defense in the village, the way she'd seen his discomfort and stepped in even before Meena, who'd known him for years, had.

"He turned his head to look at me, and I started crying. I couldn't help it. I'd done my best to act like I didn't care, but the truth was, he was the first man who'd ever been consistently nice to me. The only one who'd ever seemed like he really cared. The priest had been nice enough, like I said, but after dropping me at the orphanage, I rarely saw him. No, Henry was the closest thing I'd known to what a father was supposed to be. And he was dying, right in front of me, and I'd never been anything but rude to him, surly and antagonistic. So I started crying. He said, 'It's alright, Colin. It's alright to be scared and angry. You're going to have to be strong, too, though. Maggie's going to need you.' I told him I didn't know how to be strong."

Swan sighed. "I never told him I loved him, but he knew. I know that now. I sat next to him for a while. Listened to him talk while he could, then told him about what was going on in school. It was alright, you know? It was alright."

She was silent for long moments. "When my parents died, I...didn't know how to go on. If it wasn't for—" She stopped. Her whole body had tensed. He waited to see if she would finish the thought. "They died when the factory burned. I never got to say goodbye to them, or see them again...It was so sudden."

In spite of the questions rattling around in his head, he only said, "That must have been really hard, honey."

Some of the tension went out of her body after a minute of silence. "How long do we have?" she asked, finally.

Forever, he thought, the word floating into his mind unbidden. He was a little alarmed by it. No, make that a lot alarmed. On the heels of the thought came another: *No. Not forever. A month if I'm lucky. Or maybe just until Luca is back on board.* He didn't want to be thinking such things and couldn't help himself. Now that he'd finally felt her, tasted her, held her...it hadn't lessened his desire to keep her. It had only strengthened it.

"An hour. Hour and a half, maybe," he answered. "Marty and Bart—"

She rolled on top of him quickly, surprising him into silence. In a heartbeat, she was straddling his stomach. Her cheeks were flushed, her tangled hair framing her face, and sweetly-painful desire lanced through him, stealing his breath with its intensity. "I hope that's enough time," she said. She smiled with just a hint of insecurity.

There will never be enough time, he thought. "Speaking of Bartholomew," he muttered. His voice was hoarse, and he wondered if she was aware of the throbbing erection just behind her. It might be more frightening in the dawning light of day. He didn't want to see fear in her face. "Should I leave him on Tarot?"

She blinked, confused. "What? No. Why?"

He raised a hand and tucked her hair behind her ear. She shifted slightly, and he suppressed a groan. Struggling to regulate his breathing, he said, "Don't think I forgot what he did. I've been considering ever since whether or not I could trust him."

"He's a good worker, isn't he? He seems to get along with everyone— except maybe Luca." Something like regret flitted across her face, and Swan was sure she hadn't meant to mention the name.

"I meant, if I could trust him around you," he clarified. He was trying his damnedest to keep his eyes off her breasts, but it was difficult. Thinking was growing increasingly difficult. Hell, so was breathing.

"He's fine," she assured him. "Really. He was just drunk. He apologized, anyway, and has been very...polite, ever since. Besides, could you really leave him behind?"

"If you wanted me to," he assured her. "It's not like tossing him out to sea."

"Like you almost did to me?"

He smiled. "He could get a job pretty easily on another ship, when one stopped by. Or at least a ride. Or, he could make a decent life for himself on the island. It wouldn't be so bad."

She frowned. "I suppose not," she allowed, slowly. "If it was his choice. I won't have you banishing anyone to an island because of me, though."

"Very well," he said. While she was sitting, naked and glorious, astride his midsection, he was pretty sure he would promise her anything in the world. His gaze slid down, past her tempting breasts, and he swallowed. "Could you tell me your plan, here?"

"Plan?" she asked, doubtfully. "I don't know. It seemed like a good idea." She also looked down.

"It was," he said, and after a few seconds, she smiled at him. "Any other good ideas?"

"Actually, I was hoping you'd take over from here," she admitted.

"Were you?" he breathed, his hands going to her hips. Her lips parted, and she nodded. He sat up, and she made a sound of surprise. She would have toppled over backwards if he hadn't circled an arm around her back, and in a matter of seconds she was straddling his thighs and he was kissing her. His erection jutted between them, eager and ready, but he was surprised when she arched toward it, impatiently.

"I want you," she whispered, cupping her hands around his face. "Please."

"You need to be ready."

"I am," she said.

"You're going to be sore from last night."

"I don't care."

"I care."

"Please, Colin. I want you."

"Hold my shoulders," he murmured, and her hands went up obediently. He took a deep breath and shifted her hips up and forward. As he settled her down onto his shaft, she let out a sigh and pressed her face against the hollow of his shoulder. He paused, waiting for her to get acclimated, but she surprised him again by moving her hips. He groaned.

"Is that good?" she asked, hesitantly, without looking up.

"God. Yes," he managed, his hands still on her hips. She moved again, more confident, and he slid his arms around her back, burying his face in her hair. They held onto each other as she started to find her rhythm, and then he was unable to keep himself from thrusting to meet each of her gyrations. He felt himself rushing toward climax and fought it, trying desperately to hold on.

She was breathing heavily, the sound in his ears all he could hear. There was nothing else in the world except for her, all around him.

"Come on, love," he urged, closing his eyes. "Come for me."

He felt her tighten around him, felt her body tense and quiver, felt the spasms wracking her body, and he almost lost himself. It would be so easy to bury himself to the hilt, to clutch her close and spill his seed deep within her, and he never wanted to leave her enveloping warmth.

Grabbing her hips, he lifted her backward, his movements frantic and borne of desperation. He'd barely slipped from within her before his semen, hot and thick, pulsed between them. His heart was pounding against his ribcage. He fell back onto the bed, his head tilted back into the pillow, pulling her down with him, and she lay on his chest, their hearts thumping together.

He'd come far too close to losing control, that time.

"Is it always like this?" she whispered.

"No," he said. "It's never been like this."

That was true. He'd had good sex in his life. With Meena, he'd almost always had great sex. It could never have held a candle to this, however. He'd never been so out of control. He'd never been at someone's mercy so completely. He'd never allowed himself to care so much. He'd never had such a hard time pulling out.

She kissed his chest, again. Right over his heart. He closed his eyes, breathing in her scent. "I wish we could stay here all day," she whispered.

Or longer, he thought. "We have a little bit of time, yet," he said.

* * *

171

"Morning," Marty said. His smile was friendly enough, and if he was thinking anything uncharitable, it certainly didn't show on his face. If he was surprised to see her, he wasn't letting that show, either. She had to imagine that her absence had been noticed, and Luca and Meena, no matter how discreet they might have tried to be, would have had to come up with some sort of story.

"Good morning," she said. She felt awkward, but at least she didn't feel any damning heat filling her cheeks. She seemed to blush so much around Swan. She quickly shoved thoughts of him from her mind, lest they bring on the very redness she was afraid of. She glanced past Marty, toward the island. Bart was below, in the dinghy, waiting for them to join him for the trip back to Tarot.

Ella had cleaned up, combed her hair, and dressed in clean, dry clothes, and she knew that there were no visible signs of what she and Swan had done the night before...and less than an hour ago...Still, she was different, and she also knew that there was no going back. She didn't want to. She didn't regret her choice. On the contrary, she wasn't sure she'd ever been happier, even with the worries and doubts and fears lurking in the back of her mind, trying to sneak their tentacles into her brain. She would never be the same, and Marty's calm demeanor seemed almost surreal.

"Half of the men went out hunting," Marty said. "Breakfast is ready in the village, though. They refuse to eat without Cap." He glanced around, because Swan hadn't made an appearance since Marty's return to the ship. He was still in the cabin, shaving and getting ready. She'd been loath to leave his side, but she knew that her presence had been a distraction. So, she'd taken herself onto the deck to watch for their ride.

Swan had asked her several times if she wanted to eat before they left for the island, and she'd refused. Mostly, because it would take time that could be spent cuddled in his arms. They'd stayed in bed as long as they could. Now, at the mention of breakfast, her stomach rumbled. It had been—what? Eighteen hours since she'd eaten? She wasn't sure. It felt like a lifetime ago.

She saw Marty's gaze shift past her, and she closed her eyes for a moment, cursing her traitorous stomach. Then, she looked back over her shoulder as Swan stopped near her arm. He frowned at her, and she had no doubt that he'd heard her gut's hungry grumble. It was difficult to take his scowl seriously, however, after the intimate and tender night they'd spent together. Seeing him, freshly washed and shaven, in the early sun, made her smile. She wanted to run her fingers through his damp hair.

His frown remained, but his eyes softened, and the corners of his mouth quirked in response.

Marty cleared his throat. "Would you like me to fetch anything to take in with us, sir?"

"No. Thank you," Swan said. Then, to Ella, "Are you ready?"

She nodded. Marty turned and went to wait at the top of the ladder, and

Swan put a hand, lightly, at the small of Ella's back. Even that innocent contact sent a frisson of awareness through her, and she wished they could go back to the cabin and ignore the people awaiting their presence on the island.

* * *

Meena was coming toward them, quick and purposeful, and with a grace that Ella still envied. Aside from helping her from the boat, Swan hadn't touched Ella since leaving *Voyage*, and she found herself fidgeting in the sand, trying to ignore her rising insecurity. She'd had little trouble believing that he found her attractive when they were alone in the cabin, and had even found herself able to accept the possibility that he might want to be with her over Meena. It was different, in the bright sunlight, faced with Meena's undeniable beauty, though.

Meena and Ivan were the only two waiting for them on the beach. If Ivan was surprised to see Ella, he made no mention of it, and gave no sign of it. While Bart and Marty secured the boat on the sand, Ivan waited, his expression impassive.

As Meena approached, Ella felt Swan's eyes on her, and she chanced a nervous glance in his direction. His hair was still damp, in spite of the windy ride into shore, and a slight breeze was riffling his dark shirt. He was so beautiful, she could scarcely breathe. How could someone like that possibly want her?

He leaned down to whisper in her ear. He didn't touch her, but his soft breath against her ear made her suppress a shiver. "I want you," he said, the words meant only for her, and it was as though he'd looked into her mind and found exactly where her insecurities lay. She looked up at him, and managed to smile. His words of reassurance meant more to her than she could say— because he cared enough to say them.

Meena was speaking in her rapid, lyrical language, and looking from Swan to Ella, and back again. Ella didn't know what she was asking, and felt a blush creeping into her cheeks anyway. Swan didn't immediately answer, and Meena's pretty face shifted into a slight frown. She said something else, and Ella looked at Swan, again. He was frowning, too, and looked quite uncomfortable. When he finally answered, his voice was low, so the other men wouldn't overhear, and his response was short.

Ella didn't know what he said, but Meena suddenly hit him in the arm— hard. Her quick words seemed like a condemnation, and Ella felt herself bristle, ready to come to his defense if Meena tried to hit him again. Whatever they were talking about, it clearly involved Ella, and she felt a surge of annoyance at being excluded.

Meena made a sound of irritation. "Idiot," she said.

Swan didn't comment on the insult, and Ella heard herself say, "Hey."

"How could you not know?" Meena hissed, her accent thicker than ever in her annoyance.

173

Swan still remained silent, and Ella finally realized what they were talking about. Her. More specifically, her virginity. Her embarrassment and irritation grew. She was conflicted. Part of her still wanted to defend him, because Meena was chastising him. Another part of her wanted to slap him for sharing such an intimate detail.

"Come, Ella," Meena said, grabbing her by the wrist. Ella resisted, because she had not even begun to sort through her thoughts.

When Swan leaned close to her ear again, Ella felt her pulse flutter in spite of her irritation, and she scowled. "She can help you, love."

Ella's scowl deepened. "Help me," she repeated, putting as much scorn as she could into the words to let him know that she was upset. "I don't appreciate—"

"I'm sorry," he murmured, and she snapped her mouth shut, cutting off her rebuke. "She's the best option you have, though."

Ella looked at Meena, who could surely hear at least part of what he was saying, and Meena looked back, patient and calm. "Option for what?" Ella heard herself ask. She could feel the fight seeping out of her, leaving her tired and even more confused.

"She can tell you...many things that I can't," he said. He looked uncomfortable.

Ella supposed that was true. And, she would like to know what she could do to better please him. If she could swallow her pride and jealousy, she might be able to learn quite a bit from Meena. She had, after all, given him pleasure on countless—

She shoved that thought away before it could really sink its claws in. "Alright," she muttered.

Meena smiled. "Come," she repeated, tugging on Ella's wrist again.

"She needs to eat, first," Swan said.

Ella rolled her eyes and saw his brows lift in response. "I can decide when to eat," she said.

"Are you not hungry?" he challenged, his expression daring her to lie.

She sighed. "Yes, I'm hungry," she admitted, and as if on cue, her stomach rumbled.

"We'll get food, and we'll talk," Meena said. Glaring at Swan, she added, "Alone."

It was his turn to sigh.

* * *

"You seem on edge, Cap," Ivan said. "You worried about the storm?"

Swan glanced at him. "Sure," he answered. "Aren't you?"

"Not so much," Ivan said, leaning back a bit to stretch his legs in front of himself. "I've seen you in action."

Swan frowned. "Storms are always dangerous, and unpredictable," he said.

"Are they?" Ivan asked, his expression impassive.

"What are you talking about?" Swan returned, unable to hide his irritation. He was worried, but not about the storm. He'd always found Meena's lack of inhibitions to be refreshing. Now, however, he found himself praying she wouldn't say something to Ella that would upset her, scare her, anger her...Or, God forbid, hurt her. Ella was tough, but underneath that shell she'd built, she was vulnerable and easily hurt. He'd regretted letting Meena take her out of his sight the moment they were gone, but he couldn't very well run after them. He'd look like a controlling lunatic. Besides, Ella needed, and deserved, a woman to talk to. Meena was the best person he could offer her, provided Meena was able to maintain a little tact.

They'd been gone for over an hour, though. The village was quiet. After the late night celebrations, those not out hunting were laying low after the morning feast. He hoped Ella had eaten. He'd barely been able to taste his own food, worrying about her stomach. He'd made sure that food was sent to Meena's hut for both women, but as he hadn't seen them, or the remains of the meal being removed, he couldn't verify if they'd even touched the stuff.

He ran a hand over his face. He had to pull himself together. What he'd said to Ivan was true: Storms were dangerous and unpredictable, and he needed to focus. They had to get the ship far enough away from land before the system hit, so there wouldn't be risk of being driven back into the rocks. Weathering the storm at sea was challenging, and risky, as always. Staying on the island would be safer for the men, but not the ship. If the ship was smashed against the rocks, they would all be in trouble. There was no way to know for sure how long they would be stranded on Tarot before another trade ship came along, and even then, there would not be room for all of them to buy a ride back to either side of the sea.

"You know what I'm talking about," Ivan said, drawing Swan's attention back to the world around him. Now, Ivan seemed annoyed. "I've known you since you were barely old enough to shave. Now, storms are dangerous, we all know that, but unpredictable? To you? I don't think so."

Swan regarded him in silence for a few moments, a little surprised. Finally, he said, feeling strangely cautious, "I have experience with bad weather."

"Sure," Ivan said. He was about to say something more, but Swan was distracted by the sight of Ella coming out of Meena's house. Her eyes found his instantly, and she fidgeted for a moment in the doorway. He was too far away to see for sure, but he imagined the blush creeping up her throat. He had grown very fond of her tendency to blush. He wanted to get up, cross over to her, and kiss her until neither of them could breathe. He restrained himself. He didn't care what anyone—not even Ivan—thought of him, but Ella? He wouldn't be able to stop all of the rumors, but that didn't mean he had to confirm them for any curious eyes that might be watching, either.

He got to his feet as the two women walked toward them, and he was a bit amused by his own nervousness. Did he *want* to know what Meena had told her?

"I'm going to go stretch my legs," Ivan said, also standing.

175

Swan glanced at him, and knew that their conversation had been cut prematurely short. He wondered—briefly—why he should feel such relief at that. "Yeah, alright," he said. "The hunting parties should get back before too long."

"Hopefully," Ivan agreed, glancing toward the distant clouds just visible through a break in the trees.

Swan barely noticed as his longtime friend wandered away. He couldn't take his eyes off Ella. She'd changed her clothes, and was wearing a handmade dress that, although far more modest than anything Meena had ever worn, still showed an alarming amount of skin. She seemed terribly self-conscious, unused to the form-fitting, not-quite-knee-length garment.

White-hot desire dried his mouth and sent every coherent thought from his brain when she stopped before him, tugging lightly at the bottom of the dress. His body was screaming at him to do something—to grab her, to kiss her, to carry her into the nearest hut or shadow, something, anything to touch an inch of that pale, soft skin...

He cleared his throat, with effort, and dragged his gaze up to hers. Her eyes were bright with her own desire, a reaction to his, and that was almost his undoing.

"Doesn't she look beautiful?" Meena prompted. She sounded amused in spite of her scowl.

He somehow managed to swallow. "Yes," he said. He saw some of the worry ease out of Ella's expression and wished he could take away all of her doubts, forever. "Did you eat?" he heard himself ask, and even he winced at the words. He sounded like her father, for crying out loud.

To his relief, she laughed, even if the sound was a little exasperated. "Yes, I ate," she answered. Then, with exaggerated courtesy, "Thank you for asking."

Swan grinned. "You're going to need to keep your strength up, for tonight," he said. He was surprised to hear the words coming from his own mouth, but rewarded by the darkening of her cheeks. No one was within earshot except for Meena, anyway. He knew that Meena wouldn't be offended, or hurt. He was a bit concerned that Ella might be, though.

"Oh, yes, the storm," she said, her eyes twinkling.

"That, too," he answered.

Ella smiled, and he saw Meena roll her eyes. He didn't care if she thought he was acting like a fool. His spirits were abnormally high, and he knew exactly who was responsible for his good mood. "Meena explained a few things to me," Ella said.

Swan groaned, and Meena laughed. Ella merely smiled, still looking unsure of herself. "Would you like a tour of the island?" he asked, on impulse, eager for a chance to get her alone somewhere.

"Sure," she said, after a moment, again fidgeting with her new dress.

He glanced down. "Do you want some shoes?" he asked, thinking of the dangers of the jungle floor.

"I will bring you some sandals," Meena suggested.

"Oh," Ella said, also looking down at her own feet. "Thanks."

When Meena was out of earshot, Swan leaned toward Ella. He didn't touch her; there might still be prying eyes about. "As much as I like you in this dress, it's killing me that I can't rip it off of you."

"It is?" she asked. Her hesitance raised the protectiveness that he'd always felt around her.

"I wish I could make you see yourself like I see you, love," he murmured. His eyes dropped to her mouth and he saw her lips part. He suppressed another groan.

"I feel, uh...self-conscious in this," she said. "But I like the way you're looking at me," she added, with a tentative smile. She cleared her throat. "I don't have to wear it on the ship, though...do I?"

He pulled his gaze back up to hers. "What?" he asked, surprised and horrified by the thought—for a couple of reasons. The idea that she thought she needed to ask permission about what she could wear was disturbing, as was the idea of his crew members watching her walk around with so much of her perfect skin showing. "Ella," he said. "You can wear whatever you want. I don't...I wouldn't..." He was rarely at such a loss for words. Did she really have such a low opinion of him? The thought stung. He'd done a lot of things he wasn't proud of, and had even threatened her, but her spirit and temper and pride were not deterrents to him. They were, rather, parts of his attraction to her. He would never wish to break her spirit, in any way. What he wanted was the opposite, to fill the chinks in her pride and erase her self-doubt.

She must've seen some of his concern on his face, because she placed a palm against his chest. The contact sent a wave of desire rippling through him, and his hand lifted of its own volition, until it was resting against her hip. He knew he should look around, to check for watchful eyes. He knew that he should be more vigilant about her reputation. He couldn't tear his gaze from hers, though, any more than he could tear his hand from her hip. He could feel his heart thumping beneath her hand, and knew she could feel it, too.

"I didn't mean to hurt your feelings," she said, and he frowned. Was he really so easy to read? He'd never thought so, before. Were his feelings more apparent, now, or was she just more attuned to them than anyone else had ever been? "I know you're not like that, I just...like it when you're happy," she said. And, there was that familiar blush in her cheeks, bringing the familiar heat to other parts of his anatomy.

He bent his head forward and murmured, "I am happy." He was surprised, as much by the admission as by its truthfulness. It was a strange feeling, wanting to smile like an idiot. He wasn't accustomed to it, and it made him nervous, even though it wasn't at all unpleasant. Her hand was warm on his chest, the heat seeping through his shirt, and the curve of her hip was enticing his palm. His hand wanted to roam, to explore already discovered territory and seek out new places.

"Well...you're still scowling," she muttered.

"That's because Meena's coming back," he said, quietly. He straightened, letting his hand fall away, and Ella dropped her own arm. He immediately missed her touch. He cleared his throat. "Thanks, Meen," he said, when the woman came up beside Ella with a pair of sandals. "So, how about that walk?" he asked Ella, trying to keep his eagerness in check.

"Maybe you'd like a chaperone?" Meena suggested.

Swan felt his eyebrows dip into a scowl, again. A moment later, Ella laughed at his expression, and he forced his features to soften. Before he could say anything, Ella answered, "I think we'll do fine. Thank you, Meena."

Chapter Ten

"Someone should say something."

Kyra swiped at her tears. "What could we say? He was just a kid."

Tabitha put her hand on Kyra's shoulder, but the girl took little comfort from the contact. There was still so much blood. And the bodies...There had been a lot of debate about what to do with the bodies. One of the prisoners, a man named Cosy, had suggested loading them into one of the rowboats and setting it on fire. They would be down a boat, but they didn't really need it. There were four, total, and they could probably all squeeze into two if they had to. Their numbers hadn't been cut as badly as they'd feared—as badly as they should've been. Travis had saved them, almost all of them.

She looked down at the young face, smooth in death, and her grief squeezed her stomach. Portia was dead. She'd died protecting the children from the two men who'd made their way below, where the woman and youngest kids had been hiding out, waiting for the fighting to end. The men had been beyond caring about profit, and they certainly had no qualms about killing a woman—or children. They didn't touch the kids, though. Portia managed to hold them off until one of the freed men came to her aid, but her wounds were beyond help.

Three more of the freed men were dead. Several more were hurt, only two badly enough to warrant stitches—a task completed by Tabitha after the fighting had come to an end.

Only one child was dead.

All of the crew members, including the captain, were dead, except for three servants—Jesiah among them. The only other life on board consisted of rats, and a mangy, abused, skittish white dog.

"There's a storm coming," someone said. Kyra looked up. Amir.

It had been days since the fighting began, and since it ended, the ship had been in a bit of chaos. No one was in charge. Tabitha had taken over cooking, with the help of the three remaining crew members, but there had already been a few fights over food and other supplies. The freed men had all fought the slave-traders together, but in the absence of a shared enemy, they'd resorted to an every-man-for-himself mentality. If someone didn't do something, it was only going to get worse. The ship was more or less on the same course it had been on at the time of Travis's move, but no one had taken control of the navigation. No one had taken control of anything. There were arguments, not discussions.

Through it all, Amir had been nothing but calm and watchful. Kyra knew nothing about him, and she didn't know if they could trust him, but she knew that they needed to follow his example of levelheadedness. If there was a storm coming, they were going to have to pull together. Otherwise, they would have gained their freedom only to perish at sea, every one of them.

She looked at the dead boy. So young. So innocent. He'd died, not cowering in a corner, but fighting to protect his sister. Eight years old, and brave enough to defend the girl he loved, the twin sister being used as a shield to protect a cowardly murderer from Travis's sword. Because of Anthony, and Travis, Angel was alive.

Anthony was not, however, and no one had taken the boy's death harder than Travis—except Angel.

"We need to get the bodies off the ship," Travis said. He sounded subdued. He had barely spoken in the past few days. "Before we all get sick," he added. He kept his eyes averted from Anthony's young body, even though Kyra knew that he'd spent an unhealthy amount of time with the corpse. She wasn't sure Travis had slept at all, and if he had, it had been in short and fitful bursts. She couldn't blame him for that. Her own sleep had been riddled with nightmares, and she hadn't even killed anyone. She couldn't imagine what he must be going through.

"It seems so...gross to throw them all in the ocean," Kyra said. "All of them, floating..." she shuddered, her stomach roiling at the image in her mind.

"They'll be eaten quickly enough," Travis said. His tone was flat, and she looked up at him, disturbed by his lack of emotion.

"We could burn them, like Cosy said," Tabitha suggested. She looked around. She, Travis, Kyra, and Amir were the only people in the small storage room, with the bodies of Anthony, Portia, and the three prisoners killed during the fighting. Travis was talking about the corpses of the slave-traders, but something was going to have to be done about these bodies, too. Could they bring themselves to throw them into the sea? Him? Anthony? Would any of them be able to stomach the sight of his tiny body dropping to the water? Or the sight of him going up in flames?

Kyra tried to swallow her rising bile. The thoughts were too horrible, and yet they had to be considered, because decisions had to be made.

"Whatever we do, we need to do it soon," Travis said. "Before the storm hits." He looked at Amir. Kyra was suddenly struck—not for the first time—by just how young and heartbroken Travis looked. He blamed himself for Anthony's death, he blamed himself for all of the deaths, and he'd almost completely shut down under the emotional weight of that burden. "Someone needs to do something," he said, barely above a whisper. "Someone needs to take control."

Amir stared back at him, as calm and unreadable as ever. "That is true," he said. He looked up as Garrett appeared in the doorway.

"There's a fight on the deck," the twelve-year-old boy said. He looked from Amir to Travis and back again.

No one spoke for several moments. Kyra got to her feet, again swiping at the tears tracking her cheeks. Every time she saw Anthony's lifeless body, the grief hit her anew. Travis was right. They had to get rid of them, and soon, before they contaminated the whole ship.

When it became clear that Amir was not going to speak, and that Garrett didn't know what to do but stand in the doorway, waiting for a response, Travis finally said, "Let's go see. We need to clear the deck, anyway."

None of them spoke as they made their way to the deck. Kyra felt bad leaving Anthony's body. She always did. It had been days, and there had been no closure for any of them. They'd been busy, first with the fighting, then with the hauling of bodies to the deck and cleaning the blood from the halls, the bunks, the galley...there seemed to be blood everywhere. No one had given any sort of sermon, said any sort of words to express communal grief. Kyra and Tabitha had done their best to comfort Angel, but everything seemed to be in limbo, and that couldn't be healthy for the little girl grieving the loss of her brother.

Kyra blinked when she stepped into the sunlight. She hadn't spent much time on the deck. She didn't want to see the piled bodies or think about what would become of them. She didn't want to wonder whether or not those men had families somewhere, waiting for their return.

Garrett was right, there was a pretty nasty fight still going on. Two men, both with blood gushing from their lips and noses. There was a small crowd gathered. Some of the other men were shouting for them to stop, the rest were cheering the fight on. There were no weapons involved—yet. The men were pummeling each other mercilessly, and it looked as though they were bent on murder. Each had a sword strapped to his hip, and Kyra wondered why they hadn't drawn. She was glad they hadn't, even if she didn't understand the reasons.

Travis looked at Amir, who was standing in the bright sunlight, his features smooth and impassive.

"Stop it!" Tabitha shouted at the fighting men. They showed no sign of having heard her.

"Aren't you going to do something?" Travis asked. The question was directed toward Amir, who was watching the fight without any apparent distress.

Tabitha started forward, and Kyra grabbed her arm, instinctively, afraid of what would happen if the woman got near the melee. She was too slow to stop Garrett, however, as the boy lurched forward. Travis made a grab for his arm, too, belatedly, but Garrett was already hurrying toward the bleeding men.

"Stop it!" the boy shouted. He sounded desperate, scared, and angry, and Kyra could certainly relate to all of those feelings. The men gathered stepped aside with barely a glance toward the kid, and none of them tried to stop him. Kyra shouted his name and the sound was lost in the wind and ruckus. Garrett grabbed at the arm of one of the fighters.

Kyra turned, to beg Travis to do something, but Travis was gone.

As his opponent fell to the deck—again—one man turned and, with no hesitation, punched Garrett squarely in the face. The boy was thrown backward and tumbled to the deck in a heap of flailing limbs. Kyra and Tabitha both surged forward, then, Kyra forgetting about the danger to herself and the other woman. Her rage bubbled suddenly, and the sight of Garrett, holding his bloody nose, made her hands shake with the emotion.

Things happened so quickly, however, that her feet had stopped before her brain had even caught up.

One man on the deck, sitting, bloody and immobile, another man standing, frozen...each man staring down the blade of a sword, each sword held in one of Travis's hands, and Kyra barely recognized the boy. His depression had given way to a rage of his own, and one that he seemed barely in control of. His face was twisted, and she knew, looking at him, that he was using his anger to drown his guilt and grief. For a moment, she was sure he was going to kill them, both of them, without saying a word.

"You want to hit a kid in the face?" he asked, and there was a tremor in his voice that was not rooted in fear. "You want to hit someone your own size?"

It should have be a ridiculous thing to say, because Travis was considerably smaller than the man he was speaking to, and the man had already been embroiled in a fight with someone who *was* his own size. It should have been ridiculous, but wasn't. It wasn't just because they'd all seen how capable Travis had become at killing, either. It wasn't because they'd seen the path of destruction he'd left, or the evidence of it in the heap of bodies. It was the look on his face, and the speed with which he'd drawn two weapons.

"You want to fight with me?" he asked. Kyra finally realized that she knew the man he was speaking to—it was Cosy. She couldn't identify his opponent, still sitting on the deck, through the sheen of blood and puffy bruises.

Kyra looked at Amir. Travis seemed to trust him, and she had to admit that she felt a bit of that herself. Why did he not take leadership? They would follow him. Surely most of the men would, too. He was watching Travis and the other two men. His face was as impassive as ever, and Kyra was surprised to realize that his hand was on the hilt of the sword strapped to his hip. She had never seen him with the weapon in his hand, and had even wondered a few times why he wore it when he was clearly loath to use it.

"Take it easy, kid," Cosy said. His voice sounded thick, probably with blood. His hands were at his sides, his fingers splayed. He was not making a move for his own weapon; it would be pointless, even if he wanted to. Travis's blade was pointed at his throat, and could pierce his neck before his hand had even begun to tug his own sword.

"Take it easy?" Travis repeated.

Don't kill him, Travis, oh God, don't kill him, Kyra thought. It wasn't concern for Cosy, because her own anger was still boiling within her. It was Travis she was thinking of. He had to find a way back to himself, and killing a man who was supposed to be on their side, a man he'd fought almost to the death to free, would not help him do that. She wanted to call out to him and didn't dare.

"That's right," Cosy said. His tongue prodded his split lip, nervously. "No need to get extreme, I didn't even know who I was hitting."

"Do you see that kid?" Travis asked, gesturing toward Garrett with his head.

Cosy glanced toward Garrett and swallowed. "Sorry, kid, didn't mean nothing by it," he said.

Garrett was slowly getting to his feet, still holding his bleeding nose. His fingers were red.

Garrett was staring, over his bloody hand, at Travis, and Kyra knew that his admiration for Travis had just slid into all-out hero-worship territory. Garrett had already looked up to Travis, of course. He hadn't come to tell her, or Tabitha, or Amir, about the fight. He'd come to Travis, expecting Travis to do something. All of the kids trusted Travis, and why shouldn't they? He'd saved them, all of them except Anthony, and he was practically one of them. The slave-traders had considered him enough of a child to put him with the rest of them, and that miscalculation had cost every one of them their life.

Perhaps the expectations of the children were unfair to Travis, and yet Kyra knew that there had been little choice in the matter. He'd become their hero, for better or worse. Garrett's eyes reflected that.

When Travis moved, suddenly, both men flinched. Travis pulled his blades back, though, rather than thrusting forward, and in an instant his swords were sheathed. Cosy stared at him, nervous and uncertain, clearly expecting a trick. "You want to hit someone? Hit me," Travis said, spreading his arms to his sides. "Go ahead."

Cosy again licked his bloody lips, and glanced around, looking for some sort of help. The men gathered around were unnaturally silent. Most of them looked ashamed, and Kyra was glad. They should have put an end to the fight long before Travis was forced into involving himself. Ever since the takeover of the ship, the freed men had been acting like undisciplined children, taking no responsibility. Most of them had helped haul bodies onto the deck, but what of that? Only a couple had helped scrub away blood, only a couple had offered to help with meals or tending injuries or preparing meals, and none had offered any knowledge of sailing a ship. The dark clouds drawing ever nearer were worrisome, because they had no hope of surviving a violent storm if no one knew anything about the mechanics of the vessel.

"He took my—"

Before Cosy could finish, Travis stepped forward, until they were toe to toe. Cosy flinched, in spite of the fact that Travis had to look up to meet his eyes. "He took your what?" Travis demanded. "You have belongings? Three days ago, you were chained to a wall, fixing to be sold into slavery, starving, with barely a shirt on your back. You see all those dead bodies? Have you looked at them? They died so you could be free to do something with your life. Have you seen Anthony? Did you bother to learn his name? Eight years old—" His voice cracked, and he paused a moment before finishing more steadily: "He has no chance at a life, now. Did we make the right decision? Did I make the right decision? Would he have been better off if I'd stayed in that room?"

"It's not your fault the kid got killed," Cosy said, quietly. "It was those men that took him, that took all of us. They were...They didn't care about his life, or yours, or mine."

Travis blinked back his tears, swiping at his eyes with angry jerks of his hands. "Do you?"

Cosy hesitated. "Calm down," he said, again, but his own anger seemed long gone.

"Do. You. *Care?*" Travis asked. Then, in a calculated gesture, he jabbed Cosy in the chest with a finger. Watching, Kyra had the distinct impression that he was still trying to goad the larger man into hitting him. Travis wanted to be hit. He wanted to be punished. Maybe he thought the physical pain would help drown out the emotional.

She was surprised that Cosy hadn't already hit him, and even more surprised when the man clenched his jaw and tolerated being poked in the chest. "I suggested burning the bodies, so we don't all get sick," he said, quietly.

"Have you looked at the sky?"

Cosy followed Travis's gesture with a nervous glance.

"Do you know anything about sailing a ship? Navigation? Because that storm is going to hit us today, and what do you think the odds are we'll all be alive on the other side of it? What are the odds, if we just ignore it?"

"I'm no sailor," Cosy objected. "I'm a damned chimney sweep."

"I don't give a damn," Travis said. "You know what? I don't care what you did, what you will do, all I care about is what you *are* doing, on this ship. I want to get *off* this ship, alive. I want to go home to my family," he said, and his voice cracked again. "And so do the kids," he added, gesturing in Kyra's direction. She was a little bothered by that—she didn't want him lumping her in with the children, thinking of her as just another little girl who needed to be protected. She shoved such silly feelings away, annoyed with herself.

"We've been keeping the same basic course," someone spoke up, hesitantly, from the crowd. "That won't hold forever, though, without adjustment. Maintenance. Calculations. Especially not when the winds and rain hit."

Travis turned on the man, and Kyra didn't miss the look of relief on Cosy's bloody, bruised face. "What's your name?" Travis asked the other.

"Uh. Nathan Gibbs," the man said.

"Are you a sailor?"

"No, I...am a mathematician, actually," the man answered, shuffling his feet.

"How'd an educated man such as yourself wind up in chains on a slave ship?" someone else asked, with a snigger, but he immediately fell silent when Travis glared at him.

"And sometime astronomer," Gibbs added. "Amateur."

"What's an astronomer?" someone muttered.

"Stargazer," another hushed voice answered.

"Navigator?" Travis asked.

"Possibly," Gibbs answered, hesitant. Then, with more confidence, "Yes."

"If we turned around, could you take us back to Baytown?"

"Well...yes...Probably...Or, close..."

"We can't outrun the storm," the man who'd been fighting with Cosy said, finally pushing himself to his feet with a wince.

Travis sighed and ran a hand over his face. "No," he agreed. "Of course not. But we could gain some—"

"Turning around would be a bad idea."

Everyone, including Kyra, turned toward the sound of Amir's voice. He was leaning against the railing, the picture of nonchalance—except for his eyes, alert, watchful as ever, and Kyra wondered again why it felt natural to trust him. His mystery and reservedness should inspire distrust, shouldn't they? She knew nothing about him, and still knew that he was not quite what he appeared to be. Would he prove to be dangerous? She didn't think so, but how did she know?

How did any of them know anything about each other? They were all strangers. Even Travis was now a killer.

Irritation flitted across Travis's features, followed by a brief hopelessness that he somehow managed to push away before it could really take hold. "Why?" he asked. Then, without waiting for a response, he said again, "I want to go *home.*"

They should have had this conversation sooner, days sooner, before any of them had even known the storm was coming, but they had had other things on their minds and had all been wrapped up in dealing with their own roles in the bloodbath. There was no point dwelling on the lost time. They had to deal with the present.

"We are past the halfway point by almost a week," Amir said. "The storm will cost us a day or more."

"We don't have enough supplies," Travis said. It wasn't a question, and the flatness of his voice hurt Kyra as much as that brief flash of hopelessness he'd so quickly hidden.

"Much of the food is spoiled already," Amir said.

"They didn't care about the food 'cept what they was eating," a new voice said, and this time they all looked at young Jesiah. He cleared his throat. "They was good at catching fish..."

"Not taking care of dry goods, though," Amir said. "We could get by with fish stew, of course. There is enough water. Without fresh fruits or vegetables, or bread, many of us might fall ill before we reach Bohannon, anyway. Especially the children."

"A couple are already sick," Garrett said. He was standing between Kyra and Tabitha, now, with smears of blood drying on his face.

"We can't make bread?" Travis asked.

"Most of the flour, rice, and oatmeal is damp, some is already moldy," Amir said. "Keith and JayJay have been sorting out what's salvageable. As an alternative to starvation, though, it could all be eaten. The option—"

"No," Travis said. "The kids are not eating any more spoiled or moldy food. None of us are."

"We will have to continue to fish," Amir said.

"So we'll fish," Travis said.

"What about islands?" someone asked. "If we could find—"

"We passed one. I heard the captain saying we didn't have time to stop. He didn't even go near it. He was real worried about keeping schedule," Jesiah said.

Travis looked at Gibbs.

Gibbs spread his hands. "Well, sure...there are several inhabited islands in the region...Trying to find them without coordinates, though...I mean, if I had seen the place, I might be able to navigate back to it...It would be a huge gamble, this way, though. Like finding a needle in a haystack."

Travis shook his head. "With supplies short, and kids getting sick, we can't risk anything but going forward. First, we have to deal with the two biggest issues. The bodies, and the storm."

"I still think we should burn the bodies," Cosy said, managing to sound somehow defiant and subdued at the same time. "We can lower one of the boats—"

"It'd sink before the bodies burned," Cosy's nemesis interrupted.

"And put the fire out. A waste of time," someone agreed.

"Nobody has any better ideas," Cosy said, glaring at the other bloody young man.

"We could sink the bodies," the man shot back.

"What's your name?" Travis asked him.

"Franklin, sir," the bruised man said. The address seemed to slip from his split lips without thought behind it, and Kyra saw Travis blink in surprise.

Travis was clearly taken aback, but after a few seconds of recovery, he said, "Franklin. What would we sink them with?"

The other man hesitated, then admitted, "I don't know."

"What about the chains?" Garrett suggested. "The shackles?"

Kyra thought that was a surprisingly good idea, but the same problem occurred to her even as Travis voiced it: "That would probably work, except there wouldn't be enough. With that weight, we'd be able to sink...less than half."

"Why don't we just pitch them overboard?" Jesiah asked. He clearly had no lost love for the men he'd been working with, and Kyra could only imagine how they'd treated the few servants they'd had on board.

At the thought of all of those bodies, floating in the sun, she shuddered. Even so, she thought Jesiah might have a point: there was little time for ceremony. Too much time had been allowed to pass, already, with the corpses bloating in the sun, gathering flies and generating who knew what types of diseases.

"We should take a vote," Travis suggested. He looked around. All eyes were focused on him, and Kyra saw something akin to panic flit across his features. "Anyone want to try burning the bodies?"

Everyone glanced at each other, and a few murmurs rippled through the ranks. Cosy and a few others raised their hands.

"Anyone want to just..." Travis waved a hand. "Dump them in?"

Almost everyone else raised their hands. Travis looked at Kyra, and she slowly raised her own hand, as well. She felt guilty about it. As awful as those men had been, they were still human beings, with lives and families somewhere. *It was them or us*, she told herself. *It still is. We have to get rid of them and figure out how to stay alive.*

"Alright," Travis said. He hadn't voted either way, she noticed. Neither had Amir. "Let's get it over with so we can take care of other things."

They all turned toward the pile of bodies at the back of the ship, and Kyra felt her stomach lurch. They were downwind, of course, but the thought of getting nearer, the thought of touching them, of feeling her fingers sink into their bloated flesh...She imagined she could smell them already, that she could feel the flies crawling onto her hands, that she could see the dead eyes staring up at her with hateful condemnation...

No one was moving, and she couldn't blame them.

Then, finally, someone did move: Travis, and she was unsurprised. He walked toward the corpses, stiff-legged, his jaw and fists clenched. She looked around at the faces of the men, all of whom would still be chained in the dungeon without Travis. The white men were pale and bruised-looking, the black men were ashy gray, and all of them were thin and unhealthy. She thought of the children, below, scared and sallow, and she wanted to bring the dead men back to life to ask them what they'd been thinking. As abominable as slavery might be, it seemed like they would at least want to take care of their prisoners until they'd reached their selling point. What good were a bunch of sickly or dead slaves? Who would want to buy a gaggle of malnourished, cold-sore riddled men?

Travis had his back to her, and she saw him bend and take hold of the ankle of one of the bodies. Her stomach churned, and she forced herself to start forward before her brain could stop her. From the corner of her eye, she saw Garrett starting forward at the same time, and she glanced over at the boy. He looked almost green, and when he tried to offer her a smile, it came across as a grimace.

They reached Travis together, and each bent down to help him move the body. Kyra squinted her eyes, trying to imagine it was something—anything— else. Tabitha and Jesiah were the next to join them. Then—surprising her— Cosy, and the rest of the men followed him, and soon the bodies were being tilted off the deck, and over the rush of wind they could hear the splashes from below as the dead crew one-by-one found their way into the salty sea.

Kyra looked over her shoulder and saw Amir. He was the only one not helping. He was standing by the railing, head bowed, eyes closed, apparently praying. She wondered if he was praying for the dead men, or for the rest of them.

* * *

187

It was a beautiful place, Tarot. Even though she'd been aware of that all along, in a distant sort of way, Ella felt like she was really seeing the island for the first time. The growth was thick around them, but the path was well-worn, and wide enough for her and Swan to walk side by side. He didn't touch her when they started out of the village; he walked with his hands clasped behind his back.

The day was warm, already, and the sky was bright above. Almost unnaturally so. The blueness seemed to hold the hint of a warning, and she wondered if it was just her imagination. Was she inventing signs to point toward the storm she knew was coming?

They walked in silence for a few minutes. The silence was surprisingly comfortable, though. She wanted to touch him, and after a bit, she casually brushed her arm against his. He didn't react, and she felt brief disappointment. She glanced sideways at him. She had thought—hoped—that her desire for him would lessen after spending the night together. The opposite had happened. She wanted him more than ever. Now that she'd felt his touch on her body, she wanted it all the time. Now that she knew the taste of his mouth, she wanted to taste nothing else.

She tried brushing her arm against his, again.

They hadn't seen anyone for several minutes. It seemed as though they were the only two people in the world, or at least on the island. Where were the hunters? She didn't think the captain would have suggested walking on this trail if the hunters were nearby, for reasons of safety, but she supposed they could be anywhere.

"It's pretty, here," she said, finally breaking the silence.

He cleared his throat. "It is. There's a waterfall ahead. That's what I wanted to show you."

"Oh," she said, excited by the prospect. She'd only ever seen one waterfall in her life, with her parents and Travis when he was just learning how to walk. It had been huge, much larger than she imagined the one they were about to see, but the idea of seeing something beautiful and romantic with Swan by her side held a different appeal.

She moved, just slightly, until her arm bumped his.

His fingers snaked into hers, surprising her. She glanced sideways at him, again. He wasn't looking at her, but a small smile tipped the corner of his lips. His hand was warm and calloused, and hers was lost in its embrace. She felt the thrill of contact all the way up her arm, and she swallowed, trying not to remember all the other places his hand had touched her.

"Can you hear the waterfall?" he asked.

"All I hear is my heart," she muttered.

He laughed, tipping his head to look at her. "I like it when you blush," he said.

"I always blush," she grumbled.

He flashed his teeth in a grin that stole her breath. "Not always," he corrected.

"No," she agreed. "Only when you, like, look at me, or talk to me, or touch me...or I think about you, or—"

He stopped walking, and turned so abruptly that her words vanished. She stared at him, her lips parted in surprise, caught off guard by the intensity of his dark gaze as he studied her face. "I like it when you blush," he repeated. "That doesn't mean I want to make you uncomfortable."

"You...don't. I mean, you do, but..." She frowned. "I hear voices," she suddenly said, turning her head. "Are there—"

Before she could finish, he pulled on her hand and, before she even knew what was happening, he was hurrying her off the trail and into the thick foliage. She looked down, praying there weren't any snakes or giant spiders or any other creepy creatures around her bare toes. She couldn't see her feet through the green growth. The trees blocked the sun, and it was suddenly dim and quiet and secluded, and her fear of critters disappeared. Swan's strong hand, wrapped around hers, and his nearness, and their privacy, shoved all other thoughts and concerns from her head. She could scarcely remember what they'd been talking about.

He spun her around and her heart was already racing in anticipation when his mouth covered hers. She grabbed the front of his shirt to steady herself, even though he was holding her arms. Her legs felt unsteady. His kiss was frantic, full of desperate desire, and she wondered about his control and nonchalance while on the trail. Had this been lurking beneath his indifference the whole time?

Without taking his tongue from her mouth, he backed her toward a tree. She was grateful for the additional support when she felt the solid trunk behind her, but the bark was hard and rough, and she winced. Swan took a partial step back, finally breaking their kiss, and while she struggled to catch her breath, he slid his arm between her back and the tree.

"Sorry," he murmured. "Alright?" He was searching her face, mere inches away, and she was almost painfully aware of the length of his body, warm and as solid as the tree behind her. She nodded, unable to speak. Her eyes dropped to his mouth. How could something so simple as a kiss make her lose control of herself so quickly and easily? She had never imagined that another person's lips could drive her to distraction, and had certainly never considered the idea that she would hunger for the taste of a man's tongue.

Her body was flushed with desire. She could smell him, and she could feel his heartbeat beneath her hand and his breath fanning her face. She could also feel his desire, straining against her, and knowing that it was her presence that was causing it—not Meena's, or anyone else's—suffused her with a feeling of power that only fueled her arousal.

"I want you," she heard herself murmur. She watched his throat as he swallowed. He shifted, slightly, and a bit of space appeared between their bodies. She fought her urge to move forward and close the gap he'd created.

He lifted the hand not trapped between her and the tree, and tucked her hair behind her ear. She met his dark gaze. He dipped his head, slowly this time,

189

and when their lips met his passion had been reigned in. His lips were gentle, almost teasing, and his fingers snaked into her hair, massaging her scalp. She fumbled with a button on his shirt. She wanted to feel his skin against her palm. She wanted to feel his skin against every inch of her body. With one arm behind her, and his other hand in her hair, Ella was enveloped in his strength and warmth, and the rest of the world didn't matter.

"Ella," he breathed against her lips. His hand left her hair and covered her fingers, stilling them on the button.

She frowned. "What's wrong?" she asked.

He bent his head forward, until they were temple to temple, and said, his voice low and rough in her ear, "I'm afraid of losing control. I seem unable to tell right from wrong when I've got you in my arms."

She let out a shaky laugh. "I don't mind."

He grinned, and said, his breath tickling her ear, "I would love to take you right now, against this tree. Then, again in the bushes. Then at the waterfall." She shivered against him, and felt his lips—ever so lightly—brush against her ear. "Unfortunately, we're not guaranteed privacy. Anyone could—"

As if on cue, a rustle of leaves made her blink in surprise. Before she knew what was happening, Swan had turned and was standing, with his back to her, his stance tense and protective. Just past his arm, she could see the last person she would have hoped to have stumble upon her with the captain.

Luca. He had a bow and a quiver of arrows slung over one shoulder, and was holding a long, stone-tipped spear in his hand.

He looked stricken and uncomfortable, and even guilty, and she felt a rush of guilt, herself. He cleared his throat. Heat was staining his cheeks, and he swallowed as he met her eyes.

Swan moved, just a bit, blocking her completely and cutting off their eye contact. "Did you need something?" he asked. Ella realized that he was expecting trouble, and she couldn't blame him. Swan was under the impression, still, that she and Luca were in a relationship, and he'd seen what Luca did when Bartholomew touched her.

Ignoring him, Luca stepped to the side so he could see Ella's face again. He clearly wanted to be anywhere else. "Are you alright?" he asked. She recognized the effort it took for him to ask. There was no good answer, for Luca. If she said she was alright, he was faced with the physical proof of her attraction to Swan. If she said she was not alright, he was left with the decision of whether or not to defend her against his boss, his captain, and the man who would determine if they made it to Bohannon.

She put her hand on Swan's arm, felt his muscles bunch. She wanted that arm wrapped around her again, not tensed for a possible fight. When she stepped up beside him, he didn't try to stop her. He looked sideways at her, with his jaw tensed, and he seemed to be waiting for her response as much as Luca was.

"I'm fine, Luca," she said, sorry to have to say the words. Even though Luca had, with Meena, helped to arrange for Ella to be with Swan, she knew that the idea still caused him pain. "Thank you."

He swallowed again, then nodded, shifting his spear to the other hand. "A bunch of the guys are hunting this side of the waterfall," he said. He looked at Swan, then, raising his chin just a bit. "Could be anywhere around here."

It was a warning, although clearly not the type Swan had been expecting, and Ella saw the captain's hesitation. "Duly noted," he finally answered.

Without further word, Luca turned to disappear into the thick tangle of growth he'd come from. "Be careful," Ella said, on impulse. He'd told her to stop acting like his mother, but she couldn't help feeling protective.

Before vanishing from sight, Luca mumbled something. She thought, maybe, he'd said, "You too."

Once he was gone, Swan turned to look down at her. His expression was thoughtful, but his emotions were hidden as he studied her. She knew that their brief interlude had ended, and she felt a wave of disappointment. Her desire had not diminished, but the mood had changed.

"Perhaps we should stick to the trail," he finally said. "To the waterfall."

She let out a breath and nodded. When she started to turn away, he put a hand on her shoulder, stopping her. When she looked back, he put a light finger under her chin and bent his head, slowly, holding her gaze. She didn't breathe. He pressed his lips against hers, softly, and her heart hammered at the promise in the brief, tender kiss. Before she'd really had time to react, he pulled back and held out a hand. Looking down, she watched as she twined her fingers through his.

"We're running out of time," he said, and her stomach fluttered. He meant for the day, but she didn't want to think about the deeper truth in his words. "Let's go see the waterfall."

Not trusting herself to speak, she simply nodded and let him guide her back to the trail.

*　　*　　*

Travis wanted to crawl into a bunk somewhere and sleep until the world had turned back into the one he'd always known. That was not an option, however. They'd had a service, of sorts, for Portia and Anthony, and the deceased freed men. Amir had said a special prayer for the boy, and in the end, he'd been lowered into the water below with more care than they'd afforded to any of the slave-traders.

Angel had watched, silent, tears streaking through the dirt on her dark cheeks. She hadn't spoken since her brother's death. She was ill, too. She and one other child had developed a cough, and Angel had scarcely eaten in the past few days. She was hollow-cheeked and her eyes were dull. She was only eight years old, and already seemed to have no desire to fight for life. In a way, Travis couldn't blame her for that. What potential could she see for a happy life? She had no family left, and she was headed toward uncertainty in a land she'd never seen, dependent completely on a ship full of people who'd just put her brother's dead body into the ocean to be eaten by the sea life.

No, he couldn't blame her for her despondency. He wanted to believe she would be alright, that she would live to get off the ship, he wanted to believe that there could be something beyond their bleak horizon. He wanted to believe that he could ensure that for her, and knew he owed her that and more. He'd failed her and her brother, and his rebellion had cost Anthony his life. If there was any way to save her life, he would do it. She would hate him; that was a given. However, if he had to pour soup down her throat to keep her from dying, he would.

Would it be enough, though? Would anything within his power be enough?

He ran a hand over his face, then stared at the dried blood crusted into the creases of his palm. He swallowed.

"What should I do?" Garrett asked, and Travis jumped, whirling toward the sound. The younger boy watched Travis's hand slide toward his sword, and it was Garrett's turn to swallow. Travis took a deep breath, and let it out slowly, trying to fight back the panic trying to claw through him.

Why are you asking me? he wanted to shout. *Why does everyone keep looking at me? I'm barely older than you are.* Travis knew why Garrett and the other kids were watching him, though, expecting him to lead them—why even Kyra and Tabitha were doing the same. He'd been the only champion they had, for all the good it had done Anthony and Portia. In spite of his guilt, and the knowledge that he'd screwed things up pretty royally, even he could understand why they considered him their leader.

The men, though? Why wasn't someone stepping up to take charge? Why wasn't Amir? Clearly a man of God, and one of few words, he seemed more educated than most of the others, and calmer. Why didn't he take control? Why didn't anyone?

"What do you want to do?" Travis asked, because Garrett was still staring at him. They were in the galley. Tabitha and Rocky—the young man, one of the three spared crew members, who had been helping her prepare meals—were making a stew with half of the small reserve of unspoiled, salted meat.

"What do you mean?" Garrett asked, hesitantly.

Travis was tired, and sore, and dirty, with days-old blood on his clothes and skin. It had only just begun to bother him. Although he didn't like to admit it, he knew that he'd spent too much time already mired in self-pity. Things needed to be done, and he had to stop acting like a child. He needed to clean himself up, stop moping, and do what needed to be done to keep Angel and the other kids safe.

"Could you find Amir, and Gibbs, and...Cosy, and...Jesiah...and have them meet me on deck?"

Garrett's eagerness was almost painful to see. "Sure, alright," he said.

"Thanks. I'll be there in a few minutes."

Garrett turned and hurried out to do as bid, and Travis sighed. He looked back at Tabitha, who was watching him as she stirred the steaming stew. "We won't be able to catch any fresh fish until after the storm," he said.

"We'll get by," Tabitha said. "There is food. Enough to make it to Bohannon, if we have to make do."

Travis nodded. "We'll see what we can plan out, later. After the storm." *If we live through it*, he thought, and he knew that Tabitha was thinking the same thing. "Have you seen Kyra?" he asked.

"She's with the kids."

Travis nodded, again. "Thanks." He headed toward the bunk room, where the kids had been since the fighting had ended and they'd been brought up out of the dungeon.

Kyra was telling them a story, and the children were gathered around, sitting on the floor, with Kyra in the middle—all of the children except Angel, who was on one of the beds, staring up at the ceiling. The dirty white dog was curled on the bed beside her. Half of one of the animal's ears was missing, and his tail had long ago been cut off. His fur was curly, wiry, and crawling with fleas. His eyes rolled toward Travis, and his discomfort was evident, even though the dog made no move to leave Angel's side. She was slowly running her hand over his filthy fur, unperturbed by his thinness, his bugs, or his smell.

Perhaps because of her own thinness and smell and, now, bugs.

They were all limited to their soiled rags of clothing, because there had been next-to-no spare outfits in the men's belongings, and the clothes on their backs had gone into the sea with them. What clothing had been scrounged up had been commandeered by the freed men most in need of them. There were supplies on the ship. Amir had overseen a stock of the food, but no one had, as yet, gone through the crates below. The slave-traders could not have been relying on the slaves alone to make a profit, or they would have taken more care with them. As it was, Travis thought at least half of the men and children might have died before reaching shore.

So, there must be something else of value below, and they would have to go through the crates to find out. After the storm had passed. One thing at a time. The children would need to be cleaned up, and given something warmer to wear. There had to be something, somewhere on ship. And, if that mutt was going to be hanging around the kids, he would need to be thoroughly cleaned as well. And determined to be safe. He didn't seem to pose a threat to Angel, and had shown no aggression toward any of the kids, but who knew? He had clearly been mistreated, and fear could make an animal do terrible things.

Kyra looked up and met Travis's eyes when he walked in. He knew that it might be a mistake to burden her with anything more than she'd already shouldered. She'd taken most of the responsibility for seeing to the children, already. Besides, she was just a sixteen-year-old girl, after all. He didn't know who among the men he could really trust, however, and he knew that he could trust Kyra.

"Alright, how about we finish the story later?" Kyra asked. The kids didn't argue. They were still dirty, malnourished, grieving, and subdued, and it might take a long time before they recaptured the energy they should be imbued with at their ages. "I want you all to stay in these two rooms, alright? I'll be back in a little bit, and Tabby will bring you some food in a little while, too. Alright?"

They nodded, and Kyra rose to join Travis in the doorway.

Travis looked at the children for a few moments, and they looked back at him. Tabitha and Kyra had done their best to clean the kids up, but their clothes were filthy, smelly rags, and they'd been forced to fester inside of them for far too long. He wanted to tell them they would figure out how to change that, tomorrow. He wanted to tell them that, after the storm, things were going to get better. The right words wouldn't come to him, however, and in the end, he only said, "See you guys later," before escorting Kyra out with a surge of guilt swelling within him.

When they reached the deck, Travis's gaze immediately slid toward the blood-stained boards that proved those stacked bodies had been real. Not that he needed that proof. Their blood was still stiff on his clothes, creased into his hands. His stomach was still tender and weepy from the blade of one's sword. And most of all, he could still feel their deaths, bearing down on him like the weight of the ship, could still see their dying faces every time he tried to close his eyes, could still feel the shock up his arm every time he remembered what it was like to plunge his blade into another human.

He cleared his throat. There were men roaming about on the deck, but he headed toward the group he'd asked Garrett to assemble for him. They'd all shown up, even Cosy, with his bruised face and sullen expression. They were all looking at him. When he stopped, Kyra looked at him, too. He ran a hand—shaky from fatigue and emotion—down his face, trying not to think about what might be all over that hand. He was wearing two swords, as he had been for days, and they felt heavy against his legs. He wanted so badly to sleep, to find a safe place inside his own head.

"If we make it through the storm, what are the odds of finding our way to Bohannon, or somewhere near it?" he asked. He looked at Gibbs, and after a moment, so did everyone else.

"If the ship is undamaged, I'd say very high," Gibbs answered. "I've gone over the captain's charts and notes. I feel confident I can set us on course. Assuming the sails and masts are intact."

"I've been thinking about that," Cosy said. He sounded almost defiant, as though he expected to be reprimanded for even speaking. There was a reason Travis had wanted him in the group, however, and it wasn't just as a gesture of goodwill. Cosy was smart, even if his actions didn't always reflect that. Travis knew nothing about him except that he was impulsive and sometimes violent, and yet he knew instinctively that the man's input could be valuable. Even though they had chosen not to follow it, his idea about burning the bodies had been a sound one.

"About the sails?" Gibbs asked, raising his eyebrows.

Cosy scowled. "Right. I mean, about making it through the storm. No one on board has much sailing experience, right? A few have some basic knowledge, but none enough to captain a big ship through bad weather. We should pull up sails. Batten the hatches."

194

"Ride it out," Jesiah piped up. Then he glanced apologetically, sheepishly, at Travis and fell silent.

"Drift," Gibbs mused.

"Who knows how far off course we'd be?" Kyra said. "The storm could last days. We'd be completely lost."

"No, my dear," Gibbs assured her. "With the proper coordinates and a clear view of the sky, one cannot be completely lost."

Travis wasn't so sure about that. "You're certain you can find our way to shore," he said, looking at Gibbs. "And, before we run out of supplies."

Gibbs considered the question carefully. "There is always a possibility the ship will be damaged beyond its ability to sail," he said. "Either option is a gamble. I think our best choice would be to gather up any men with even a modicum of sailing experience, and run through a crash-course of rigging, and sail our way through. The sails will give us a better chance of staying afloat. Balance and ballast, its how the vessel is designed. The wind in the sails will—"

"Tip us over," Cosy interrupted.

"Keep us up," Gibbs finished, frowning. "Hopefully," he added, which was not comforting.

"So, without a captain, we have two options, both of which could kill us all," Travis said. Given a choice between sinking and drowning, or drifting until they started dying off one by one, which would be worse? With a disabled ship, floating in the breeze, there was always hope—slim though it may be—of rescue or repair. But the weakest would die first, and the stronger would eventually begin killing each other in a fight for survival...

Travis shook his head, trying to rid himself of his dark thoughts. It was no use. All of his thoughts were dark, these days.

"Maybe we should vote," Kyra said, glancing sideways at him.

"You mean, everyone?" Cosy asked, hesitantly.

"I mean us," Kyra said.

"And then, what, we just tell the men what we're going to do?" Cosy asked.

"What's the alternative?" Kyra answered. "You don't think there are those among us who would take advantage of an opening? If it looks like the ship's in chaos, without a leader—"

"We *are* without a leader," Cosy retorted.

"Then *we* will be the leader," she said. "This group."

Cosy sighed and scrubbed his hands over his bruised face. "And why would they listen to us?"

"Because we'll be the ones talking," Travis said, and everyone looked at him. "Kyra's right," he continued, feeling a rush of gratitude for her. "What's the alternative? We're all strangers to each other. Are we supposed to trust each other?"

"Fine," Cosy said. "So, we keep each other in check. But...who elected *us*?"

195

"Travis did," Garrett said, and Travis suppressed a groan.

"I think this is a fair representation of the people on this ship," Amir said, speaking for the first time since they'd gathered.

For a few moments, they all looked around at each other. "What about him?" Cosy asked, gesturing toward Jesiah with a thumb.

"He knows this ship better than anyone," Kyra said. "He's been working it—"

"Right, he's one of *them*," Cosy said.

"No, he was a servant," Kyra objected.

"Fine. What about the kid?" Cosy asked, instead.

Garrett bristled, and looked at Travis.

"This is the group," Travis said. "We represent the men, women, children, and crew." The fact that Tabitha was the only other woman, and Jesiah was one of only three remaining crew members, was not lost on any of them. No one, not even Cosy, mentioned the deaths that had brought them to their current population.

Travis fully expected Cosy, or someone else, to ask why Travis should choose the group, why they should respect his choice. He didn't have an answer. In truth, he hadn't put much thought into selecting the people around him. Garrett hadn't even been a part of the group, really. But now that they were assembled, Travis knew that they were the right people to make the decisions, at least until someone better was willing to step up and take responsibility. If the rest of them didn't see that, he wouldn't be able to make them.

He let the silence stretch out for long moments before finally realizing that no one was going to ask the question he was expecting. No one was going to challenge his selections. They were all looking around at each other, sizing each other up, and that was a good sign.

"Our choices, unless someone has a third option, are to find men to try to sail us through, or to pull the sails and let the storm blow us where it will. Either way, we could end up sinking. We don't have time to argue. We need to make our decision. Let's vote," Travis said.

He waited. After a few more glances around, Cosy scowled and said, grudgingly, "I vote we pull our sails and close ourselves up."

"I think we should use what skill we have to sail through the weather, or try," Gibbs said.

That opinion held considerable weight, since they would likely be dependent upon Gibbs to get them to port if they survived.

And then what? Travis wondered. *What the hell are you going to do there? How are you going to get home?*

"I vote we sail," Jesiah said, shooting Cosy a defiant look.

"I vote, drift," Kyra said.

"Drift," Garrett agreed. Travis was a little surprised. Garrett was enthusiastic about everything, and fighting their way through the storm seemed like something that would strike his fancy. It seemed that, even at twelve, he recognized the danger in recklessness.

Amir, the man of few words, said, "Sail."

That surprised Travis even more than Garrett's vote. He would have expected Amir, the pacifist, the man of god, to recommend embracing the peace of faith, of placing their lives in the hands of fate. Travis looked around. All eyes were on him, and his tired mind finally recognized the mistake he'd made in withholding his own vote.

He had become the tiebreaker. He closed his eyes, for a few moments, and took a deep breath. He had a headache, most likely caused by lack of sleep, and he was hungry and sore. He opened his eyes and looked around again. The votes for sailing were Gibbs, Amir, and Jesiah. The votes for drifting were Kyra, Cosy, and Garrett.

Gibbs was the mathematician, the man who knew the skies and coordinates, the man of science and knowledge. Amir, although the most reticent, was clearly one of the most intelligent and levelheaded people on the ship. Jesiah had been on the ship longer than any of them, several cross-ocean voyages, and he knew it far better than the rest of them.

Those were strong votes for sailing.

Who was opposing? A sixteen-year-old girl, a twelve-year-old boy, and a hotheaded chimney sweep.

Travis sighed. The truth was, he didn't know what the right answer was. Perhaps there was no right answer. Perhaps they were all doomed to die no matter what. He was not a sailor. He was not a scientist. He was not religious.

"What's it going to be, son?" Gibbs asked.

"Drift," Travis said. He expected argument, dissent, and got none. Garrett looked relieved, likely because he didn't want to be on the opposite side of anything from Travis. Amir seemed as placid as ever, and Travis suddenly found himself wondering if the man had voted to sail simply to create a tie. Jesiah looked unhappy but made no comment.

"So be it," Gibbs said. "We'd best gather the men and start preparing. We have only a couple of hours."

"You, Jesiah, and Cosy get all the adults on deck," Travis said.

The words fell from his mouth before he could consider them, and he was surprised.

He was more surprised by the fact that the three men turned to do as bid without hesitation.

Travis felt Amir's eyes on him, and met his gaze. "Do you think we're making a mistake?" Travis asked.

After a moment's silence, Amir answered, "Your decision was as good as any."

197

Chapter Eleven

The children had all been fed and were gathered in a single bunk room. It had been agreed that no one would be allowed on deck. There was no sense in posting a lookout. The man could—probably would—be killed, and it would serve no purpose. If the ship was going down, they would know below, with or without a man on deck, and there would be nothing they could do about it one way or another. If the ship began to sink, they might be able to make it into the rowboats, but that seemed unlikely.

And ultimately futile. If the large ship couldn't withstand the rigors of the storm, what hope could they have in a dinghy?

In a pinch, they would try, though. They would have to try. Unless that time came, however, they were going to stay, holed up below, in the dark.

The children were going to be frightened.

So were the adults, of course.

For some reason—probably because he was overly tired, and not thinking clearly at all—Travis found himself wondering about the dog, and whether or not he would be affected by the rough waters. Would he be ill? Would he go to the bathroom in the bunk room? So far, he had not. He seemed to be trained to do his business on the deck. He would not be able to get to the deck, however, until the storm had blown itself out.

Travis sighed, cursing himself for thinking of such trivial things.

He would have a single lantern, ready to be lit, but they didn't dare risk a fire in the wooden belly of the ship, and any unexpected lilt could break a lantern in an instant. He would have one close at hand, and he would remain vigilant, in the room with the children. He wanted to believe that none of the men on board would hurt any of the kids, or Tabitha or Kyra, but he wasn't going to make any such assumption when their safety depended upon it. He would hope that the men were trustworthy but trust none of them, not in the dark.

Kyra was finishing her story from earlier. She, Tabitha, and Angel were on one bed. Travis was sitting on the floor, with his back against another bunk, and Garrett and the other four boys were huddled on that mattress. In addition to Kyra's voice, others could be heard, outside the room. Men talking, getting ready to settle in to ride out the storm. Travis felt no need to join them. All preparations that they could make had been made, every precaution taken.

Already the early effects of the storm could be felt in the rocking of the ship. The vessel creaked around them. The motion and the sounds were strangely comforting, in spite of the danger, and Travis felt his heavy eyelids drooping. He was exhausted, and knew that this was not the time to find his way into the comfort of sleep. The images of death swam up to meet him, filling his mind, but he'd already forced his eyes open.

He thought they were open, anyway. He blinked a few times. The blackness of the room was complete, and he tried to ignore the fear clamoring through him. Something wet touched his hand, and he jumped, his heart slamming in his chest. Even as he reached for his sword, he recognized the feel of fur against his hand as the dog pressed its muzzle against his palm.

Travis let out a shaky breath as the animal crawled up against his leg. Ignoring the smell and threat of bugs, Travis laid a hand on the dog's head. His fur was springy and greasy, and his head was heavy on Travis's leg, and his presence was more comforting than Travis could have imagined.

* * *

"God damn it," Swan muttered, running his hand through his hair.

Ivan looked back at him, apologetically.

"How long's it been?"

"He never came back with the hunting party. I mean, everyone split up, but—"

"He's never been here before."

Ivan spread his hands. "He seemed confident."

"Of course he did," Swan snapped. Then, taking a deep breath, he reigned in his anger. It wasn't Ivan's fault, after all.

"Is it possible he doesn't want to be found?" Ivan suggested.

"It's more than possible," Swan mumbled, watching Ella make her way across the beach with Meena. He sighed. She wasn't going to be happy. "Is everything loaded?"

"Yes, sir," Ivan said. "We're ready to leave as soon as everyone's aboard."

"Thank you." Swan left Ivan and headed toward the women. When Ella caught sight of him walking toward her, she smiled and lowered her lashes. Her shyness was enticing. He had to focus on the situation at hand and quit fantasizing about the things he'd like to do with her. "I need to tell you something," he said, stopping before her.

She looked up, and he saw the worry tighten her mouth, and he was sorry for it. "What's wrong?" she asked.

She could surely tell from his demeanor that something was wrong, but it was more than that. She'd had a hard life. He knew almost nothing of it, and still knew it was true. All he had to do was say that he had something to tell her, and she expected the worst.

"We're ready to leave," he said.

"Yes?" she answered, frowning.

He hesitated, and he saw her look past him, saw her gaze sweep along the beach, saw her doing a mental head count, and knew that no matter what had happened between himself and Ella, she loved Luca. At the faintest hint of trouble, the first thing she did was search him out. She didn't see him, of course, and Swan saw the fear in her eyes when her gaze found its way back to his.

Had his and Luca's roles been reversed, and he'd been the one to stumble across his fiancée in the arms of another man, Swan wasn't sure he'd come out of the woods, either. They couldn't wait for the boy. The weather wouldn't wait for the boy, and it wouldn't wait for them. The islanders were preparing for the storm, and the ship's crew needed to do the same. They needed to get away from the island.

"Where's Luca?" Ella asked.

"I don't know," Swan admitted. "He didn't come back with the hunters."

"We need to go look for him," she answered, immediately.

"There isn't time," he said, hoping she couldn't hear the bitterness in his voice. He was ashamed of his jealousy, but helpless not to feel it.

"Something's wrong," she said. "He wouldn't just not show up."

"Are you sure about that?" Swan asked, harsher than he'd intended, and he hated himself when he saw her wince. He leaned forward. "No one's seen him since we did," he said. He kept his voice low. Only Meena was within earshot, and although she was lingering nearby, she had given them a couple of yards of space. "Don't you think it's possible he's decided to stay here?"

She was pale, her expression stricken, and her voice was shaky when she answered, "He wouldn't do that."

"Ella," he said, making an effort to gentle his tone. "I'm sorry. I know you're hurt. But he's made his decision, and we can't wait for him."

She shook her head. Her hand was at her throat, and she was staring at him with wide eyes. "He wouldn't do that," she repeated.

He sighed and ran a hand through his hair. "He's not here," he pointed out. "We need to leave. Maybe you don't know him as well as you thought."

"Please, I can't leave without him. Please."

"You're welcome to stay here, too."

The words left his mouth and hung between them, and he wished he could call them back. He didn't want her to stay. He didn't want to be the reason for the look of pain on her face. He didn't want to see the tears shimmering in her eyes. He swallowed.

"I can't," she said, barely above a whisper.

"Then we need to go," he answered. He wanted to pull her into his arms, and he started to turn away, to keep from reaching for her.

She grabbed his arm. "Colin, please," she said, and he could scarcely breathe at the sound of pleading in her voice. "I can't lose him, too," she said. "Don't leave us. Please. I'll find him. Just give me a little bit of time. Please don't leave me."

Don't leave us. Don't leave me. They were two different requests that boiled down to the same thing. He could wait for Luca or he could leave Ella behind. He searched her face, struggling with his own emotions.

"And if he wants to stay here?" he heard himself ask.

"If he tells me that, then..." She swallowed. "Then I'll leave him. But...something's wrong. He wouldn't just not show up."

"Fine," he said.

"Thank you," she answered, but when she started to turn, he grabbed her wrist.

"No. You're staying here," he said.

"What?" she asked.

"I won't risk you getting lost. We don't have time for this. Stay on the beach. We'll find him, and if we drag him back here and he tells you he's staying, you'll get in the boat. That's the deal."

She hesitated, and he knew that she didn't trust him. Again. The realization brought anger—and hurt—bubbling up within him. After everything...She'd said she trusted him, after her mistake regarding Carter. She'd shown that she trusted him, with her body. Even in the face of his anger, she'd known he wouldn't throw her overboard as he'd threatened, she'd come to realize that he wouldn't intentionally hurt her. Yes, she trusted him. But not where Luca was concerned. Perhaps she was right, too, because Swan found that he really wanted to leave the boy behind. He wanted Luca to choose to stay.

He released her wrist and joined his hands behind his back to keep them from trembling. "That's the deal. Take it or leave it."

She licked her lips. She swallowed. What would he do if she refused? If she insisted that she was going to tramp off into the wilderness to find Luca? Swan was not at all convinced he would be able to leave her. His uncertainty frightened him. He had a whole crew of men to worry about, men whose lives were in his hands.

For long moments, he thought for sure she *was* going to refuse. Then, surprising him, she finally said, "Very well. Thank you." In spite of the tremor in her voice, her chin was up and her tone was formal, and he felt an absurd— and almost overwhelming—urge to apologize. Perhaps, even, to beg for her forgiveness.

He let his anger push out such silly desires, let it push out his hurt and jealousy, too, and turned to Meena. "We need a search party, Meena, please," he said. "The more people we have, the sooner we can be done with this." Turning away from Ella, he called, "Ivan! Gather the crew."

He didn't look back at Ella; he didn't want to see whatever might be lurking in her eyes.

*   *   *

They returned twenty minutes later. Ella had made a shallow trench in the sand, pacing the beach, and when she saw the men trudging toward her, she broke into an awkward run, almost falling as her bare feet slid in the shifting sand. She didn't see Swan, at first, but two men were half-carrying Luca down the beach. He was hopping on one foot, supported more by the two men than by his own leg, and she could see blood staining the tattered pant leg below his bent knee. His face was pale, drawn, and sweaty, and she could see his pain and exhaustion as she hurried up to him.

"Sorry, El," he said, immediately.

She stopped in front of him, then stumbled awkwardly aside to let the men pass. "What happened?" she asked as the trio continued toward the boats, with the rest of the crew coming up behind them in groups.

"He'll be alright," Timón said, falling into step beside her as she trailed behind Luca and the men helping him. "We'll splint his leg as soon as we get on board."

"His leg's *broken?*" she asked, horrified. "Luca, you're bleeding. Are you alright?"

"Stop worrying, El," he answered over his shoulder. "I'm fine. Really."

"Fine?" she muttered, looking at Timón in disbelief. There were a million thoughts running through her mind. She wanted to take away Luca's pain, and she felt guilty because she'd been the last person to see him before whatever accident had befallen him. She also felt guilty because, mingled with her concern for Luca, she couldn't help thinking about how much more difficult their mission in Bohannon would now be.

She did her best to shove those thoughts away, because there were more immediate concerns. Their time in Bohannon likely *would* be more difficult, but first it was imperative that they both make it there. A broken leg—a broken leg on a ship weeks away from port, no less—was dangerous. Life threatening, even. If the break was not set properly, if infection set in, the results could be devastating.

"He's in pain," she said, fighting back her tears. "Shouldn't we...let him rest? Splint it now, so it doesn't—"

"There's no time, El," Luca said. "It'll be alright. We need to get to the ship."

"No, she's right," a voice said from just behind her, and she turned, startled to find that Swan had somehow come to be so close without alerting her to his presence. She'd become so attuned to him, so aware of him at every move, that for a moment she could only blink at him in surprise. He wasn't looking at her, though. He was focused on Timón, and he gestured toward Luca's back. "It's too dangerous to wait. Too much jostling, too much potential for complications. We need to set the break now."

Swan shaded his eyes with a hand and looked out toward his ship, and beyond, toward the horizon. He sighed. The villagers had already moved Carter's ship around the island, into the cove on the other side. It might be afforded some protection, there. Swan could not take the risk with his own vessel, though.

"I'll be fine, Captain," Luca said, trying to look back over his shoulder again. "Really. We have to hurry, I've wasted too much time already."

"Luca, maybe—" Ella stopped, biting her lip. She was trying desperately to keep the tears stinging her eyes from spilling down her cheeks. Gathering her resolve, she walked around in front of him, and forced herself to meet his eyes. "Maybe it's too dangerous for you to go. Once we're on the ship, if anything happens, there's no way to—"

"No!" Luca said. He looked as though she'd slapped him. "I'm not staying here."

Ella put a hand on his chest, and felt his pounding heart. "You need to think about what's best for you, Luca."

"I'm not staying here," Luca said, in a low voice. The men on either side of him looked uncomfortable.

Ella felt Swan's eyes on her, but when she looked past Luca, toward him, his gaze shifted toward Timón and Ivan. "Spread out blankets," the captain said. "We don't have time to take him back to the village. We have dragon's blood on board for the flesh wounds. We need to set the bone and splint it so it won't be further damaged rowing out. Let's hurry, but it needs to be done right."

The men scattered to prepare, and Ella looked at Luca. He met her eyes, but defiantly.

"Let's set him up against a tree," Swan said. As the men turned Luca toward the edge of the jungle, Swan said, glancing sideways at Ella without quite meeting her eyes, "You should keep your distance. This won't be pleasant for anyone."

"I won't leave him," she said, already fearing the pain she knew was coming for Luca.

"Suit yourself," Swan said, turning to stride away. How did he manage such grace in the slippery sand? She could scarcely take a step without stumbling.

"Thank you," she said, but he ignored her. He was upset, angry, and she tried to remember how easy and romantic it had felt in his arms, earlier. The disparity made her want to sit in the sand and cry. That would accomplish nothing, however. Her hurt feelings, and Swan's anger, were not important in the bigger scheme of things. She followed Luca and crouched beside him when the men lowered him to the ground. "You're going to be alright," she said, putting a hand on his arm. The men stepped away to give them privacy for a moment.

"Sure," he said. "Just go away, El. Go out to the ship. I'll be there when they're done."

"I won't leave you," she said.

"No? Isn't that what you just tried to do?"

She stared at him. "I was trying to think of what's best for you, Luca."

"Really?"

"Yes, really! You think I want to leave you here?"

He shrugged.

"Well, I don't. If I did, I wouldn't have begged Swan to go find you. I knew something was wrong. But if you get an infection—"

"Stop, Ella. Just stop, alright? Why do you always have to imagine the worst? Don't we have enough trouble without thinking of all the ways things *might* go wrong?"

He was right, of course. She'd always done that. She'd always expected the worst. She didn't know how to change that.

Meena and several men were coming with blankets and water and rags, and boards and bandages that would be used to splint Luca's lower leg. Just the sight of the supplies made Ella swallow around her lump of fear. She looked at Luca, and saw the terror that he was trying so hard to hide. She saw the scared little boy beneath the stubble, and it gave her courage. His fear meant that she could not be afraid.

"You should get out of here," he said, sounding breathless, while his eyes begged her to stay.

"Don't be ridiculous," she answered. Her voice sounded steady, and when she took Luca's hand, he clutched her fingers.

"This will help a little with the pain," Meena said, handing Luca a cup to drink from.

"Thank you," Luca said, downing the liquid in a gulp. He winced. "Let's get this over with."

Ella looked up and managed to catch Swan's eye, just for a moment, before the captain looked away again. She sighed and turned her full focus onto Luca as the men prepared to set his broken leg.

* * *

It was difficult to keep time, in the dark, with only the sounds of their own voices to anchor them in their rocking, tossing, pitching world. It seemed as though the ocean was roiling and churning inside Travis's stomach, and the sense of growing vertigo was a strange thing in the absolute darkness. With one hand resting on the dog's dirty head, and his other hand gripping the lantern, he tried to focus on Kyra's story. She sounded calm, much calmer than he felt, and he didn't know how she managed it.

Some of the kids would ask questions, on occasion, and the fact that they were caught up in the tale enough to ask questions about it was also a testament to Kyra's storytelling ability.

Travis leaned his head back against the edge of the mattress, unsure if he was staring into the darkness of the room or his own eyelids. He tried to imagine what it must be like, up on the deck, with the wind and the rain and the towering waves. A part of him, in spite of his exhaustion and fear and nausea, wanted nothing more than to race up the stairs to witness it. There might be other storms on this journey, there almost certainly would be, it was getting into that season, now. He would probably never witness any of them. In his life, he might never have such an opportunity, to stand at the rail of a ship being tossed in a massive storm, buffeted by wind and waves in the middle of the ocean, soaked by salty spray and driving rain as thunder filled the world and lightning split the sky.

The mattress shifted against the back of his head, and he started, realizing he'd begun to drift off. He gave his head a shake, straightening his shoulders.

"Travis?"

He turned his head toward the sound of Garrett's voice near his ear. "Yeah?" he said.

"Carl just threw up on the bed," Garrett answered, keeping his voice low.

"Sorry," a young voice—presumably that of Carl—said. He sounded miserable. Travis knew how he felt. His own stomach was a mess, and if he'd had anything to eat recently, he probably would have thrown it up by now, too.

"That's alright," Travis said, struggling up onto his knees. The dog lifted his head, and Travis reached into his pocket for the matches to light the lantern. Just as his fingers touched the carton, however, the ship pitched, and he tumbled sideways, barely throwing his hand out in time to catch his fall. For a moment he was supported on his arm, but then the ship dipped, and he fell all the way to the floor with a wince. He somehow managed to hold the lantern up. Breaking it, or spilling the oil, could be devastating.

"Travis?" That was Kyra. "What happened?"

"Everything's fine," he said, getting up on his knees and one empty hand.

Then came the unmistakable sound of vomiting, and Travis wondered why he hadn't heard Carl. He must have been closer to sleep than he'd thought. He heard Garrett swear and, a moment later, the smell hit Travis and his stomach tried to revolt. He swallowed, keeping his gorge down by a sheer force of will.

"Who was that?" Garrett asked, and it sounded like he was struggling with his own gag reflex.

"Me," a small voice answered. "Jesse. Sorry, Gar."

"That's alright," Garrett said. "Travis?"

Travis crawled awkwardly to the edge of the bed, feeling his way as the floor tilted unpredictably beneath him. "What's going on?" he asked, even though he could imagine all too well.

"I think I'm gonna be sick," Garrett said.

"No, you're not," Travis said, sharper than he'd intended. "Control it."

"It's all over me," Garrett moaned.

"Think of something else," Travis said. "Boys, take your shirts off. Leave them on the bed and crawl over here."

"I don't feel good," one of them said.

"I know. Come on. Shirts off. Jesse, Carl, wipe your mouths off. Leave your dirty shirts."

"I have puke all over my pants," Garrett said.

"Take them off. I'll get you a blanket."

As the boys struggled out of their dirty clothes, Travis crawled toward the bed Kyra, Tabitha, and Angel were on. At least, he hoped he was going in that direction. He was afraid to stand up, and he was clutching the lamp so tightly, he thought he might break it after all.

"Kyra?" he asked when he thought he should be close.

"Travis?" Her voice was to his left. He must have miscalculated, headed toward the wall. He veered toward her voice and a moment later felt the edge of the bed.

"Take the lantern," he said. He held it up and waited for her questing fingers to find it in the dark. "Here," he said, fumbling the box of matches from his pocket. After a few moments, her fingers found his and closed around the carton. The world tilted and he almost knocked them from her hand. She managed to hold onto the box, and he grabbed the edge of the bed to keep from rolling across the floor again. "Damn it," he said. Then, remembering that Angel was right next to Kyra, somewhere, he muttered, "Sorry. Can you light it just long enough for us to move, then put it out?"

"Yeah, sure," Kyra said.

"Here, give me the lamp," Tabitha said. "You light the match."

While they worked that out, Travis crawled back the way he'd come. Garrett had already helped the other boys, stripped to their waists, onto the floor, and Travis had just reached them when a flare of light filled the room from behind him. He squinted in surprise, and saw startled looks on all of the boys' pale faces. Robbie raised his arm to cough into his elbow; he looked pale and unhealthy, with dark-ringed eyes, but he hadn't thrown up.

"Come on, come this way, it's not safe to have the light lit for long," Travis said. Garrett, in his underwear, hunkered beside Carl with a hand on the smaller boy's shoulder. Jesse started to stand, and Travis grabbed his wrist. "Crawl, Jess. It's safer."

They made their way toward one of the other bunks, and Travis pulled the blankets off and handed them to Garrett, who wrapped one around himself.

"Come on, guys, let's sit on the floor," Travis said, and Garrett held the other blanket up, wrapping it around the boys' shoulders as they huddled together against the edge of the bunk.

"I'm sorry I made a mess," Carl said.

"That's alright, it's not your fault. We'll worry about cleaning later." There were no loose chamber pots, because it was too dangerous to have unsecured objects in the room. "If you're going to be sick, do your best to turn away from the blanket. Jesse? You alright?"

The boy nodded. Travis looked at their frightened, sickly expressions, and ruffled Robbie's hair.

"We're going to be alright. Just close your eyes and try to rest. We'd better put the light out. Everybody just try to stay calm and relaxed, alright? It'll be over soon." The dog crawled over and pressed up against the boys' knees, and Jake scratched his head.

A moment later, the room was plunged once more into darkness, and Travis pulled himself up so that he was sitting next to Carl. His abdomen hurt—he was pretty sure he'd pulled open his healing cut during his tumble, and he thought he could feel fresh blood sticking his shirt to his stomach. Carl laid his head on Travis's arm, and Travis leaned his own head back against the bed.

"It'll be over soon," he repeated.

After a few moments of silence, Kyra's voice filled the darkness as she took up her story, punctuated occasionally by Angel's muffled coughing.

* * *

Luca had insisted he could climb onto the ship, but he looked so weak and pale that Swan had ordered him to be raised up. Then he'd ordered Luca to be taken below, and Ella realized that she had essentially been dismissed, along with the men charged with Luca's assistance, when the captain turned and strode toward the front of the ship without so much as a glance in her direction. She debated for a moment. She knew that, in addition to being angry, he was going to be busy preparing the ship and getting them underway.

She decided that she would see Luca safely into a bunk, help Timón apply dragon's blood and bandages to the surface wounds, and then seek out the captain. If he told her to go away—or, perhaps worse, if he refused to speak to her at all—then she would have to respect his wishes until after the storm. Eventually, however, she was determined to make him listen to her.

And what will you tell him?

She frowned as she followed the men, helping Luca, down the stairs. In truth, she had no idea. There were so many things she *should* tell him. She should tell him that she and Luca were not, and had never been, engaged or in a relationship. She should tell him that her brother had been taken captive. She should tell him that she could feel herself falling in love with him, and that she wanted desperately to believe they could have a future together.

She sighed. She didn't know what she would say.

It was half an hour before she made her way back up the stairs, with a bowl of soup and a hunk of bread for the captain. She had decided that she would, at the very least, tell Swan that she and Luca were not together. As to whether or not she would mention Travis, she still hadn't decided. She wanted to trust him. In many things, in many ways, she did. Her brother's life was too important, however. She couldn't take any chances. While she now knew that Swan was not a pirate—at least not the kind his reputation proclaimed him to be—and she knew that he was decidedly not a slave-trader, she could not be certain that he did not have ties to, or relationships with, some or all of the men in those trades. She might be falling for him, and he might even have feelings for her in return, but she was not about to test his loyalty to her against the unknown.

She stopped when she reached the deck. The wind seemed stronger, and colder. She squinted into it, knowing it wasn't her imagination. The sky was preternaturally dark. The sun was behind swollen and bruised-looking clouds. Almost every member of the crew was on deck, preparing the ship to do battle with the storm. Even Rashad was helping.

"He's in his room, miss," someone said, and she turned to find Goonie with a coil of rope over his shoulder. She was surprised. He was almost always in the crow's nest. A quick glance in that direction showed her that the bucket was empty. With a grim smile, Goonie said, "Too windy. Safety first, you know." It was obvious that he was displeased, and that it was not his choice to be out of his accustomed spot. She wondered if, left on his own to decide, he would really stay up there in the wind and rain...and lightning. She suppressed a shudder. She had imagined on many occasions what the world would look like from his vantage point, but during a storm? She would be terrified.

She gave her head a little shake to clear her thoughts. "Thank you," she said, and he nodded as she headed toward the captain's cabin. Hadn't it become her cabin, too? Had that changed? She let out a breath and squared her shoulders, but when she reached the door, she hesitated. She supposed she should knock.

She raised her fist, then changed her mind. If the door was locked, she'd know she wasn't welcome to just walk in. No matter how angry he might be with her, she was not afraid of him, however, and she wouldn't act like she was. So, she twisted the knob and pushed the door open.

He was sitting at his desk, bent over a ledger, and although there was a brief pause in his writing, he didn't look up. Deciding to be emboldened rather than deterred by his silence, she closed the door and crossed to the desk, where she set his supper on the edge.

"Thank you," he said. She took that as a good sign, even if he still hadn't looked up.

After a few moments of silence, she said, tentatively, "I don't mean to disturb you..."

He set his quill down and rubbed his eyes with the thumb and forefinger of one hand. "You disturb the hell out of me," he muttered. Before she could even begin to sort through her feelings about that, or try to understand what he meant, his tired gaze finally met hers. "I owe you an apology, Ella. Once again. I behaved exceptionally badly, even by the standards I've set since knowing you."

She stared at him. She'd expected anger, not self-loathing. She was unprepared for this. She could think of nothing to say.

He sighed. "I am afraid that there really isn't time to properly express..." He ran a hand over his face. "Once we've passed the worst of the weather—"

"What?" she finally managed.

His expression was wary. "I would like to talk to you, if you're willing," he said. He sounded unsure. "Right now, though, I have to deal with—"

"The storm, I know, I don't want to keep you," she said. "But...I don't...why are you apologizing?"

He regarded her for several moments before leaning back in his chair. "Because of my jealousy, I almost left an injured man lost in an unfamiliar world. I almost left a member of my crew behind. I would have you believe that's not something I do, and yet I realize I have no right to expect you to trust me. In that or anything. Since meeting you, I've acted like an imbecile and an ass, and I have no explanation. At least, not one I'm willing to give. You told me there was something wrong. You told me he wouldn't fail to show without explanation. I didn't want to listen, because I wanted to believe he'd chosen to stay behind. I disregarded your word, and your feelings, for my own, and that is inexcusable."

"But you didn't," she finally managed, through numb lips. "You didn't, you listened, because of you he's on the ship and safe, and..."

"I don't think you understand how close I came to leaving without him."

She swallowed. "But you didn't," she repeated.

"Because you told me that you wouldn't leave without him, and I couldn't bring myself to leave without you," he said.

At that admission, she felt her heart stumble in her chest. "I...I'm not..."

"Ella, I really can't do this now. I'm sorry." His expression verified his words.

"Right," she said, giving herself a mental shake. "Right. Sorry. I'll, uh...Should I come back later?"

"I'd like for you to stay, but you'll be safer below. Just be careful, please? Lanterns are only for emergencies. Try not to walk around. Don't leave anything loose."

She nodded. "You be careful, too," she said.

He regarded her for a few moments. "I'm always careful," he finally answered. "I'll send for you when it's safe."

In spite of everything, she was relieved to know that he wanted to talk to her, that he wanted her to come back to the cabin, that he wasn't cutting her off because of her loyalty to Luca. "Thank you," she said. Then, before she could say anything else, knowing it wasn't the time, she turned to leave.

"Ella."

She hesitated with her hand on the doorknob and looked back.

"Did you eat?"

She was surprised, and wondered why she hadn't expected the question. Some things never changed, it seemed. "No," she answered.

"Good. Don't," he said, and she was even more surprised. He met her eyes, and a small, tired smile curved his lips. "Just this once," he added, and she took comfort from the smallest hint of that familiar twinkle in his eyes.

"Don't worry, I hadn't planned on it. The less potential vomit, the better." At his small snort of laughter, she said, "Not that I was planning on telling you that."

They were both smiling when she left, and for that, she was incredibly grateful.

*   *   *

"It's going to be alright. He's a good captain. Maybe the best." Luca spoke grudgingly. She couldn't see him but knew the expression on his face just the same.

"How are you feeling?" she asked. She couldn't fight the unease churning in her stomach, and knew that it wasn't seasickness. At least, not entirely. The ride had gotten bumpy, the tilting and lurching unpredictable and disorienting, but her mind was barely on the rough waters rocking the boat. Not knowing what was going on above was driving her crazy. The idea that men could be getting hurt or killed without her knowing anything about it was eating away at her. She cared about all the men in the crew.

She couldn't kid herself, though. It was Swan's well-being that she was really concerned about, and all she could think about was his penchant for standing on the railing like a bird on a perch. Her mind insisted on placing him there now, in the driving rain, braced against the wind, his feet on the slippery rail...

"We're going to get Travis back, together, El," Luca said in the darkness.

"I know," she answered. She was distracted. For once, Travis was not her primary concern. She knew he should be. His ship must have traveled into this storm, was perhaps still traveling through it, but her mind kept turning back to Swan.

"Do you? Because you tried to leave me behind. I'm not a horse, you know, who needs to be taken out and shot because I have a broken leg."

She blinked in the dark. "What? That's what you think?"

"What am I supposed to think?"

"You're an idiot, Luca," she snapped, and heard his sharp intake of breath. "I was trying to protect you, not get rid of you. You broke your fucking leg. I thought that earned you the right to relax and rest on land, to recover. You think I wouldn't have come back for you? As soon as I got Travis, we would have figured out somehow to get back to Tarot. Hell, maybe we could have stayed there. It doesn't seem like such a bad place to live, and what in God's name do we have to get back to in Baytown?"

He was silent, and his silence annoyed her. She understood that he was hurt, emotionally and physically, but she was tired and scared and worried and she was sick of going around and around with him.

"You keep telling me I'm not your mother. Well, maybe I'm not even your sister. But you're as much a little brother to me as Travis is. My whole life has been about looking out for both of you. I'm not complaining. I chose it. I wouldn't change it. I love both of you and would die to protect you. I'm sorry you're having a rough time dealing with the fact that some tiny little piece of my life doesn't revolve around you at the moment. You're the one who told me to be selfish, remember? While I had this chance? Well, I am, and you're going to have to stop assuming the worst of me, because I'm tired, Luca. I can't keep doing this back and forth crap."

She got up and started toward the door in the blackness. They were alone in the room, and she knew that there was nothing immediately in front of her, and yet she walked like a blind person with her hands stretched before her and her feet shuffling cautiously.

"Ella?" Luca asked.

"I don't want to hear it," she said, because she knew he was gearing up for another apology. She could only take so many. "Just rest, let your pain medicine work."

"What are you doing?" he asked, clearly alarmed to hear her voice coming from the other side of the room.

"Relax," she answered. "I'll be fine. Just stretching my legs."

"You know I spend my whole life worrying about you, too," he said. "You and Travis."

She hesitated at that, feeling the cool door handle against her palm. "I know," she finally answered, feeling real guilt and regret. "I know you do, Luca. But just rest, alright?"

"If something happens to you, I'll never forgive myself," he said. "Or you."

She swallowed. "I'll be fine. We all will," she said, pulling the door open. She couldn't see the hallway. "Hello?" she called, softly. Timón and the injured men were in the other bunk room, and she didn't think anyone else should be below. Swan had all able hands on deck to fight Mother Nature's plans for *Voyage*. Nevertheless, her heart thudded in her chest as she edged into the black hallway, and she trailed a hand along the unseen wall, squinting her eyes for some glimpse of her surroundings. There was nothing, not a hint of light, and with every small step she imagined someone or something lurking before her, waiting to reach out a hand and—

And, finally, she made it to the stairs, and as the world swayed and tilted, she wondered what she was doing. Captain Swan had told her not to walk around, because it was dangerous. Not only had she wandered from the relative safety of the bunks, she was seriously considering climbing the invisible stairs. That act alone—and never mind what might be waiting at the top—was probably the most dangerous thing she could do. In her mind's eye, she saw herself, halfway up the stairs, her arms pinwheeling as the ship pitched and she lost her balance. How long would she lay at the bottom, with a broken back or a cracked skull, before someone found her? Until morning? Longer? There was no way of knowing, and even entertaining the thought of starting up was insane and irresponsible.

So why was her foot already on the bottom step?

That image of Swan standing on the rail, precariously braced against the storm, that was the thing. She couldn't shake it. How many times had she seen him, perched there? Every time, her heart had stuttered in her chest. In the bright sunlight, in the crisp moonlight, with only the wind of motion combing his hair from his face, without the threat of slippery rain or buffeting winds or crashing waves or striking lightning...

She went up the stairs quickly, in part because she was afraid of falling and in part because she knew that if she paused to think about her actions, reason would make her change her mind. At the door, she could hear the thunder, and the whistle of wind, and the beating rain. She told herself she was only going to look, she was only going to check and make sure he wasn't standing up there like a fool, asking to be ripped into the night and swallowed by the sea.

She studiously ignored the logical questions that her mind tried to pose: How would she know for sure, unless she walked the deck, if he wasn't in sight? What would she do if he *was* up there? How would she explain her disobedience if he spotted her? How could she justify the fact that she might be putting herself in the way? Again?

Why was she willing to put herself in danger just to get a glimpse of him, to reassure herself that he was safe?

The wind almost ripped the door from her hand, but she managed to tighten her fingers around the handle in time, and she stepped a foot out onto the wet deck. Rain and spraying seawater soaked her clothes and wind plastered them to her body. Her hair was thrown across her face, and she swiped at it, peering into the night. In spite of the hidden moon and stars, the outside world was bright compared to below.

Her eyes found Swan almost immediately. He was much closer than she'd expected, not at the head of the ship but halfway, and he was standing on the railing as she'd feared (*known*) he would be. Someone else was beside him, and in a flash of lightning, she recognized Goonie. Even as she watched, frozen in place, Goonie was climbing, and she found herself thinking of how out of place he'd seemed on the deck, out of the heights of his regular perch. She watched him swaying in the wind as he struggled to steady himself, and she couldn't make sense of what she was seeing. Why was he climbing?

Swan was shouting, but his words were lost long before they could reach her. He was pointing, and she realized that Goonie was reaching for something. A rope, spinning and flipping in the wind, dancing out of reach, the hook on the end just eluding his grasp.

Ella tried to tell herself that she needed to get back into the dry darkness; she'd satisfied herself—sort of. Yes, she'd confirmed that he was, in fact, putting himself in danger, but she'd also determined that he was still alive. She needed to get below before she attracted attention or got in the way. Her feet wouldn't move, though. Her attention was riveted on not just Swan, but Goonie, as well.

When the lightning filled the night, she flinched. Her heart stuttered as her whole body went suddenly icy cold. She couldn't breathe, and she stared past Swan, into the darkness, praying her eyes were playing tricks on her. Electricity lit the air again, and again, flashing in quick succession, and she watched—helplessly—as a shimmery black wall bore down on them. She wanted to scream, in fear and in warning, but her tongue was still and useless in her mouth.

Swan was shouting at Goonie, and then she saw the captain turn and, wrapping a rope around his arm, brace himself against the pole.

Get down! she wanted to scream. Part of her recognized the fact that there was no time, though. The wave was descending, and men were throwing themselves against masts and ropes and rails, anything they could find to brace themselves, and the ship was leaning away from the wave, and she suddenly realized that she was going to tumble down the stairs, after all.

As she felt gravity begin to tug her toward that dark hole, she was finally able to make herself move. Pulling the door closed, she stepped back, and dropped to her knees on the second step. She threw an arm through the handrail and held it, and the handle of the door, bracing herself against the stairs and praying that the crew would be alright. That the captain would be alright.

The ship continued to tip, and she was afraid it was going all the way over. She felt like she was suspended above a black, bottomless abyss, and she could feel it pulling her, calling her down. She heard the wave crash over the boat, felt the jarring impact and the rush of water beneath the door. Then the ship was upright once more, and before she could think about it, she'd shoved the door outward and rushed into the storm.

Swan was on the railing, still, and she felt a rush of relief. He was in a half-crouch, and the fact that he'd withstood the power of the wave was a miracle that she didn't stop to question. He was struggling to get his arm free, and she wanted to rush to his side. Then she remembered Goonie, and her gaze swung upward.

He was dangling by one arm, and she knew, even before the flash of lightning, that his arm was broken. He was yelling, and she saw the captain look up at him. The men of the crew were all over the deck, every one of them focused on something important, and none of them were paying attention to Goonie. She saw Ivan rushing toward Swan to help the captain free his arm.

Goonie was twisting in the wind, his mouth open in a cry of pain, and then he was falling, and she didn't think. She rushed forward, because no one else would get there in time, and because Swan was yanking frantically at his rope and yelling and no one seemed able to hear him. Goonie's arm flopped unnaturally as his binding gave way and he fell. He cleared the railing, just barely. He almost certainly would have been killed or paralyzed if he'd landed on it. Instead, he plunged past it, flailing downward, and she had already reached the railing by the time he was swallowed by the dark ocean below.

Her bare feet slid on the flooded deck. Then she was climbing, and she heard Swan's voice: "*Ella! Stop!*"

She didn't look at him. She thought of Travis, and of Luca, and she almost stopped. Almost. Then she saw Goonie, arm twisted and bent, disappearing into the tumultuous waves, and before she was aware of making a decision, the wind was roaring in her ears and the sea was rising to meet her.

"*Rope! Rope!*" the captain was yelling, and his voice was the last thing she heard before the ocean enveloped her in its shockingly-cold embrace.

Water filled her nose and ears, and she plummeted down, until it seemed as though she would be sucked straight to the bottom of the sea. She pushed and pulled at the water until she no longer knew which way was up, and panic began to claw at her chest and burn in her lungs, and then, suddenly, unexpectedly, her head broke the surface and she felt the wind on her face. She sucked in a wet breath, coughed, and was swept under a wave. She kicked and found her way out, pulled in another breath, and looked for Goonie, frantic to find him. She knew that, with a broken arm, he would stand no chance against the anger of the sea. Had he already lost the battle? Was she too late?

Would she now drown, too, and in vain? What a foolish way to end her life.

"Goonie!" she shouted, choking on a mouthful of salty water. She spluttered, but she had gotten her bearings and was working with the waves to stay mostly afloat. She could hear the groaning and creaking of the ship and knew that the waves could crush her against it, that the ship could drive her under its berth and she would have no hope of fighting her way out. She had to stay away from *Voyage*, in spite of the waves trying to push her toward the vessel.

She heard her name, as if from a great distance, carried on and distorted by the wind. She bobbed and rolled and squinted into the rain. A dark wave broke over the back of her head, and she snorted water out of her burning nose, kicking her feet and trying her best not to think of all the creatures that might be below her cold toes.

Swan was on the outside of the ship's rail, leaning forward, holding on with only one hand. He had a coil of rope over his shoulder, but he had not yet thrown it, and she knew why. Hadn't she just thought the same thing, herself? Going near the ship, even at the end of the rope, was probably the most dangerous thing she could do. The wooden vessel would chew her up and spit her out with no more thought than the ocean itself would give her. The fear in her belly was colder than the water around her, and as the lightning streaked through the sky, she flinched, almost going under again.

Swan was pointing, she realized, and shouting something she couldn't quite hear. With her heart in her throat, she turned. At first, she could see nothing but water. Waves, swelling and ebbing, lifting her up and sucking her down. Then the sky lit, and the water fell, just for a moment, and she saw him. Goonie. Still afloat, somehow, and she didn't stop to question how. She started toward him, slowly, the water fighting her motion and tiring her much more quickly than normal. She knew she couldn't afford to rest or give up; they would both die and, although they might be doomed to such a fate anyway, she would not allow that to happen without fighting it to her last breath. So, she shoved all thought from her mind, and focused all of her energy into the feel of her arms slicing through the water, the swish of her kicking feet, and the occasional sight of Goonie's head bobbing between the waves.

It seemed she would never reach him, and then she did. His face was white in the night, barely above water, and she could scarcely imagine the strength it must have taken for him to keep himself afloat with only one arm. Looking at him, she knew that he was less than minutes away from drowning—perhaps only seconds. Pain and exhaustion had all but beaten him.

"You're bloody fucking crazy," he said, and she would not have heard him over the roar of the sea had she not been so close.

"You're going to be fine, I've got you," she said, amazed at the confidence she heard in her own voice. She certainly wasn't feeling it.

"Who's got you?" he asked. His head slipped under water, and although he tried to pull himself back up, his unbroken arm was waving slowly through the water.

With strength she didn't know she had left, Ella grabbed him by the shirt and hauled him to the surface. She went under, in the process, but only briefly. "Put your back to me," she said, edging around behind him and bracing an arm across his upper chest.

"You need to worry about yourself, miss," he said. It was clear that the pain and cold were taking their toll on him; he was going into shock, and she wondered how long it would be before she was the only conscious person left in the water.

"I am," she answered. "I'm worrying about both of us." She looked up at the ship, and the captain, leaning from the rail like a masthead. She and Goonie rode up the swell of a wave, and back down, and she momentarily lost sight of the ship. It was amazing, that something so large could vanish from sight so quickly. So far from any land, caught between continents in a seemingly-endless sea, she and Goonie were nothing more than flotsam and jetsam in the cold, dark, merciless ocean. The ship's disappearance was a temporary illusion, but she knew that it would be easy for her and her companion to slip under one angry swell and vanish from the world of air forever.

* * *

The ship tipped, the floor slanting up and up, and one of the boys was crying, and Travis put his arm around the kid's shoulders without knowing which boy it was. He braced himself, pressed tight against the bed, until it seemed that the bed was becoming the floor and the floor was becoming the wall. His heart pounded and his stomach churned, and in the blackness it was impossible to see what had become of the world.

The beds were secured to the floor, but he heard a squeal of metal on wood, and a sound of alarm—he wasn't sure if it was from Tabitha or Kyra—and knew by the sudden scraping sound that the girls' bunk had somehow come loose. As the ship continued to tip, the slight scraping sound turned into a rumble, and as Angel screamed, Travis yelled, "Get under!" and shoved the nearest boy under the bunk. Then everyone was shouting and crying, and in the darkness, he heard the other bed closing in on him and he threw himself over the blanket, trying to push the boys back.

The rogue bed slammed into him, pinning both legs between itself and the other bunk, and he clenched his jaw to keep from screaming. His head was down, and no other part of his body was hit, and for a moment the world was filled with silence. Even the ship's creaking had subsided.

Then one of the kids screamed—he couldn't tell if it was Angel or one of the boys, and then there was crying. Lots of crying. He could feel tears stinging his own eyes, tears of pain and fear, but he didn't think he made any sound. He could feel hands on his back, from under the bed, but he couldn't move his legs and for a few heart-stopping moments he thought that perhaps they'd been cut right off. Or paralyzed. Once he'd taken a couple of breaths, he realized that neither was true. The pain proved they weren't gone, and he could move his feet. He couldn't see them, but he could feel the movement.

"Travis?" That was Kyra. The beds were now together, with the three females on top and the boys beneath, Travis pinned between.

"We're tipping over!" That was one of the boys.

It seemed as though they were already tipped over, or very close to it, but even as the boy said the words, Travis felt his stomach lurch and felt the dark world begin to right itself. It was an even stranger sensation than before, and it occurred to him that his queasy stomach and pain-muddled brain wouldn't be able to tell when the ship was upright.

"Travis?" Kyra repeated, sounding frantic.

"Yeah," he answered. "Is everyone alright?"

"The ship's straightening," Tabitha said.

"Are we going to drown?" One of the boys. Travis was in no state to identify which voice that was.

"No, honey," Tabitha answered.

"We're almost right side up," Kyra agreed.

"Is the storm over?"

"I don't know," Tabitha said.

"Garrett?" Travis suddenly asked, alarmed by the fact that the boy hadn't spoken.

As the ship righted itself, the pressure of the bed eased a bit, but Travis was in a poor position to lever it away from himself. He twisted, looking behind himself—a stupid gesture, really, since it was just as black behind him as it was before him. The boys were there, though, somewhere. Were they alright? He couldn't see any of them.

"Robbie?" Travis asked.

"Yeah?"

"Jesse?"

"What?"

"Carl?"

"Yeah."

"Jake?"

"Uh-huh?"

"Garrett?"

Nothing.

Travis's heart was galloping, now, as he imagined all sorts of grisly scenarios. Maybe the bed had decapitated him, or cut him right in half, or—

Don't be ridiculous, he thought. *It's not that heavy. The worst it could do is pin him, like you, maybe knock him unconscious.*

Still, the fear lingered. "Kyra, can you light the lantern? Do you still have it?"

"Yeah," she said. Her voice was shaky.

Before she could fumble the box of matches from her pocket, however, a loud knock on the door startled everyone. Travis jumped, then winced, wishing more than ever that he could see.

"Yes?" Tabitha called.

"Everyone alright in there?" Travis recognized the voice and couldn't quite identify it. Gibbs, maybe? "The door's locked."

"We're fine," Tabitha answered.

"The storm's almost past," the man said. "The most dangerous part's over."

216

Travis wondered how the man could know that, unless he'd peeked outside.

"Alright, thanks," Kyra called out, finally managing to light the lantern. The glow was pale beneath the beds, but it was bright compared to the blackness they'd been surrounded by. In the wedge-shaped space between the beds, Kyra's face appeared. "Your legs, Travis," she said. "Are you hurt?"

Ignoring her, for the moment, Travis twisted again, looking for Garrett. The other four boys were huddled back against the wall, under the bed, with the dog, but Garrett wasn't there. He wasn't under the beds at all. He'd shoved the boys back—he had to have, Travis himself had only managed to push one under—but he hadn't followed. "Garrett?" he called, even more afraid now that he knew the boy hadn't been pinned between the bunks. "Kyra. Tabitha. Where is he? Do you see him?"

"There he is," Kyra said after a moment, and the bed shifted slightly against his legs as she scrambled off it. The light bounced, casting strange shadows under the beds. "Garrett? Are you alright? I think he hit his head." Tabitha and Angel were off the bed, now, too, and a few seconds later, Kyra had set the lantern down and was standing by Travis's feet. "I'm going to move the bed. Alright?"

"Yeah," Travis said. He could see his toes moving, now, and that was a relief, to have the motion confirmed by his own eyes. He couldn't see any blood, either. Kyra pulled the bunk back, and it made a small screeching sound. Travis could hear Tabitha talking to Garrett.

Then, finally, Garrett was answering. He was alive, at least, and awake, and Travis let out a breath of relief. "Boys, crawl out, it's alright." He hoped that was true. The ship was upright, and the motion was not as rough, but he couldn't see what was going on outside. As the four boys and dog made their ways out from beneath the bed, Travis moved his legs, testing them to see if anything was broken. Although they hurt, they seemed undamaged—bruised, but not broken, so far as he could tell. He sat up carefully.

"Is everyone alright?" Garrett asked in a subdued voice.

"Did you push them under the bed?" Travis asked, looking over his shoulder toward the sound of Garrett's voice.

"I think so. I tried," Garrett said. "I couldn't see."

"Everyone's fine. How's your head?" Tabitha asked.

"Can you stand?" Kyra asked Travis.

"I think so," Travis said. When he started to climb to his feet, Kyra grabbed his arm to help steady him. His legs supported his weight, which was a good sign. Sore, but sturdy. Travis looked over at Garrett in the flickering lantern light. There was a small trickle of blood on Garrett's forehead, from his hairline, but the boy looked at him and seemed alert. "Anyone else hurt?" Travis asked, looking at the four other boys and Angel in turn. They all shook their heads. He looked at the white dog, and the dog sat there, looking back at him. He didn't seem injured, either.

Another knock on the door made them all jump again. "You need help in there?" Travis recognized that voice. It was Jesiah.

217

"Go ahead and unlock the door," Travis said to Kyra, as he made his way to Garrett to inspect the boy's head. "Everyone seems to be walking around."

When Kyra opened the door, Travis looked over his shoulder to find Amir standing with Jesiah.

"Everyone survived the storm," Amir said after his gaze swept the children and Tabitha. "If you'd like to see the sky, the deck is safe now. The lightning is growing more distant."

"I want to see," Angel said, after a few moments of silence. The sound of her voice—after days of not speaking—was a relief. Travis looked into her dark face, and realized that he wanted to see, also.

*　*　*

"We need to lower the goddamned boat."

"It'll be smashed against the ship, Cap, probably before they ever get into it."

Thunder crashed overhead, and Ivan winced. Nothing could make a person feel more vulnerable than a monstrous storm in the middle of an ocean. The captain didn't seem to notice. He was completely focused on the two people in the water, in spite of the fact that Ella and Goonie were only visible half of the time.

"If we only had to worry about Goonie—" Ivan started, but when his captain and longtime friend glared back at him, through the streaking rain, he stopped.

"We don't," Swan said. "We have to worry about both of them."

He'd already ordered half of the sails up. They were no longer trying to fight through the storm. They were trying to hold as steady as possible, until they could fish the people safely out of the water. They were essentially sitting in the storm, waiting for it to decide to pass along.

"Why'd she go in?" Ivan said, finally unable to hold the question—or his frustration—back any longer. He couldn't fault the captain for putting importance on the lives of the two in the sea. Ivan cared about them, too. He'd known Goonie for years, and had a bit of a soft spot for Ella. Nevertheless, the captain was responsible for the lives of far more than two, and he was putting every man on board in jeopardy for the sake of—

"Goonie's arm is broken," Swan answered, his words almost swallowed in the wind.

Ivan stared at the man's dark profile, stunned. He hadn't really understood why Ella was holding onto Goonie. She was undoubtedly a stronger swimmer than Goonie, who spent as little time in the water as possible, but knowing that he was injured changed things. It was highly unlikely that Goonie would have been able to keep himself afloat for very long with a broken arm. How long could Ella keep them both afloat?

Ivan looked up into the rain. The storm could last for days.

As if reading his mind, the captain said, "It'll blow over by morning."

Ivan didn't ask how Swan could be certain of such a thing. It was what it was. Swan knew weather. He knew the sea. He could predict both, read them the way no one else could. Even so, morning was a long time off. Even if they could keep their heads above the waves, and could avoid being eaten by frenzied sea creatures, the ocean was cold. That would take a toll on them. Particularly Goonie, with his injury.

"If she goes under again, I'm jumping in."

"What the bloody good would that do?" Ivan asked, alarmed by the determination in the captain's words. Swan spoke without raising his voice, and Ivan heard him through the wind anyway.

"You'll be captain in my stead," Swan continued. He wasn't looking back at Ivan. He was staring out at Ella and Goonie. "If you have to make a choice—"

"Cap—"

"You save them first."

"You're not going in. Don't be ridiculous."

"I'm not going to stand here and watch her—them drown," Swan said.

"She's an excellent swimmer, Cap, you saw so yourself. As soon as—"

Swan looked back over his shoulder—not at Ivan, but past him, and the expression on his face sent a shiver of apprehension through Ivan as he started to turn, too. "Down!" Swan shouted, and the men nearest them repeated the call as Ivan caught sight of the huge wave bearing down on the ship. He heard Swan say something else, but couldn't quite make out the words.

The wave was going to drive the ship right toward the bobbing refugees, and likely kill them. If Swan dove in now, he would almost certainly be killed. Even if Goonie and Ella survived, Swan would be far too close to the ship. Without thinking about what he was doing, Ivan grabbed the back of Swan's waistband and dropped into a crouch, bracing himself against the railing, preparing for impact. Swan was shouting, but Ivan had no idea if the man was trying to hold on or trying to let go. The railing was between them, and in spite of the awkward angle, Ivan held on until his fingers and arm ached in protest.

The wall of water crashed over the ship, flooding the deck and carrying several men in a rush across the bow. Ivan was pressed against the railing, with his eyes closed against the sting of saltwater, and the water took his breath for several long moments. He wasn't sure if he was going to drown, or have his arm snapped in half, and when the ship canted and the water fled the deck at every opening, he was a bit surprised to find that neither had happened. His shoulder was screeching in protest, however, and his forearm, braced against the solid rail, ached, and his fingers were clenched so tightly that they had begun to cramp.

Men were shouting, and it took a minute to determine that no one had been swept overboard. "Where are they?" Swan was yelling over the wind. "Where are they? Do you see them?"

"No!" Ivan called back, squinting through the railing. The sea was dark and rough, spitting and churning.

"Let go of me," Swan commanded, glaring over his arm at Ivan.

219

"You'll only get yourself killed if you go in!" Ivan answered, straightening up with a wince.

"Let go!" Swan shouted.

Ivan did; he could scarcely hold on anymore, anyway. To his relief, the captain did not plunge into the sea. Instead, he leaned as far out as his single-armed hold would allow, scanning the tumultuous ocean for any sign of Ella or Goonie. Lightning continued to dance across the sky, flicking the sea with maddeningly-brief streaks of light.

"There, Cap!" someone shouted, and Swan and Ivan both looked where the man was pointing. Swiping the rain-soaked hair from his eyes, squinting, Ivan finally saw them: two heads, bobbing between the swells.

"You're bleeding," Ivan called, gesturing toward Swan's arm.

The captain didn't look. "Make sure the boat is ready to be lowered the moment it's safe. No matter what—"

"You can't go in!"

"Do not tell me what I cannot do," Swan said, glaring back at Ivan with lightning flashing in his eyes.

"You're bleeding!" Ivan repeated, pointing. "Do you want to attract the sharks? Or, God knows what other creatures?" He saw doubt in Swan's dark features. "We'll get them out, Cap. She's a strong swimmer. She can hold—"

Lightning hit the highest mast, and they both flinched at the burst of fiery light. The wood cracked and men ran, slipping on the watery deck, as the top of the mast splintered, tipped, and fell. For almost a minute, it hung on the sail, twisting, the end glowing with spluttering flames. Then the sail gave way with a loud ripping sound, louder than the wind, and the broken beam dropped. It hit the deck top-end-first with a crash, breaking partway through one of the boards. Sparks showered down, but everything was wet, far too wet for even the fire of a lightning strike to take hold.

"Hold our course!" Swan shouted. Above, the sail flapped angrily, jaggedly, against the dark sky. Ripped sails and broken masts were a concern for *after* the storm, however. Men were scrambling to compensate for the damage. "What is that?" the captain asked after a moment, and Ivan turned his attention back toward the churning sea. He squinted through the rain, searching for Ella and Goonie, trying to follow Swan's gaze. "Do you see—?" The captain's question was cut off abruptly, and Ivan shot him a nervous glance.

"Captain?" he asked, uncertain. "What—?"

"Look to Ella and Goonie, then straight beyond," Swan said, and something in his voice sent a shiver down Ivan's spine. He looked, and he spotted the people still miraculously afloat. He shifted his gaze further, and frowned. He opened his mouth, then closed it again, tipping his head.

"What is that?" he asked. He glanced at the captain again, but Swan's gaze was steady on the sea before them. His jaw was clenched, his body tense as he perched on the outer side of the rail. "Is that a whale?" Ivan asked, tentatively. Then, as lightning split the sky and lit the sea, Ivan realized what he was seeing, and the cold shiver slid through him again. "Bloody fuck, is that alive?" he asked.

"Have the men adjust the course twenty degrees. Hold steady, not too near. Make sure the boat is ready to be lowered at my command. Have all the spare rope gathered. Light all the lanterns on deck."

"The lanterns are—"

"Do it," the captain said. "The ship won't burn, not tonight, not from up here."

Ivan supposed that was true enough. The rain and seawater would see to it. "Captain, please—"

"I'm not going in," Swan said. His voice was flat, hard, and Ivan could scarcely imagine what emotions the captain was suppressing. "Go."

Ivan swallowed, nodded, and hurried to carry out his boss's orders. He glanced back only once, and saw Swan silhouetted against the electrified sky, staring out into the black sea.

*   *   *

"Goonie!" Ella called, giving the man a shake as she struggled to tread water. Her arms and legs were achy and tired, and Goonie's feet had stopped moving. His head was lolling forward. At the sound of her voice, it lifted, however. "I know you're in pain, and I know you're cold, but do not fall asleep on me," she said, and she could hear the shakiness of fear in her own words. She did not want to find herself alone in the vast blackness of a dangerous and mysterious sea. Her mind was imagining the creatures that must be lurking below her feet, the creatures suspended in the foreign and unforgiving world that was trying to swallow her.

What might be swimming toward Goonie's dangling feet, reaching toward him, preparing to yank him from her grasp, to leave her alone with her fear...And for how long, before it pulled her down, as well?

"You should let me go, Ella," Goonie said. He sounded tired but, thank God, at least he was conscious. "You need to save all your strength for yourself."

"Keep kicking," she muttered. After a short silence, she said, "You've never called me by my name before."

"No?"

She frowned, because he surely knew it was true. "No," she agreed. "Hardly anyone does. Why?"

He was silent so long she didn't think he was going to answer. She was trying to decide if she should push the issue or not. What did it really matter, now? If they survived, there would be time enough for conversations later. And if not, what difference would it make if the crew used her name?

"Most men say it's bad luck having a woman on board at sea," he finally answered.

Whatever she'd been expecting, that wasn't it. "What? They think I'm bad luck? No one ever said—" She stopped, wondering why she was so hurt by the idea. She'd thought the men had come to accept her, for the most part, as a member of the crew. She tried her best to work hard, to pull her own weight, and although she knew she'd made some stupid mistakes, she'd never set out to intentionally hurt anyone.

"Everyone likes you, miss," Goonie said. "Ella," he added after a moment. "No one wanted to hurt your feelings."

"Oh," was all she could say. It was a stupid thing to care about when there were far more pressing matters, and yet she couldn't help replaying all the bad things that had happened since she'd been on the ship. Maybe they were right. Maybe she was bad luck—if nothing else, her reckless actions had caused their bad luck, and she supposed that amounted to the same.

"And now I did," he muttered, trying to look over his shoulder at her. "Sorry. It's just a superstition, nothing to do with you, personally. That's why the men have tried to keep their distance. That, and...Luca threatens to bash in the face of anyone who looks at you or says a word about you, and the captain..."

Now he had her interest. "The captain what?" she prompted, and he sighed.

"I suppose if I don't die out here, I'll regret talking so much," he said.

"You're not going to die," she answered, with more conviction than she felt. "But I hope you'll tell me anyway."

"He threatened to throw any man overboard who laid a hand on you—this after the incident with Bart, whatever happened. Of course, none of us really believed he would, but...he did ban all alcohol after that, and...he certainly seemed to mean it when he said it...So the fact that we didn't believe he'd throw anyone overboard didn't mean we didn't believe he *might*."

"He banned drinking?" she asked, horrified. "No wonder the men hate me."

"Whoa, Ella," Goonie said, again looking back. "No one hates you. No one. Trust me, it would be easier if they did. And yes, we complained—amongst ourselves, of course—about the lack of drink in the evenings, but there wasn't a man among us who didn't envy Luca for punching Bart in the face. Including Bart himself, I think."

She mulled that over in silence for a bit, watching the lightning dance and praying that no one had been hurt when it had struck the ship's mast. She could still see Swan, at least, and she knew that Luca should be relatively safe in the darkness below, likely unaware—hopefully unaware—of her current situation. She looked at the captain, still hanging from the railing, and she knew he was looking at her. She couldn't see his features, but she could picture them clearly. She wanted to press her palm against his stubbled jaw, and watch his pupils dilate and his nostrils flare as they did when he was about to kiss her.

"I think I see something," Goonie said.

At the same time, Ella saw Swan raise his arm, and saw him point in the direction Goonie was looking. Before she could turn her head, a wave swallowed them, surrounding them with swirling, cold, suffocating wetness, and she kicked and pulled with her free arm, trying to propel herself and Goonie to the surface. She could feel him struggling to help, kicking his feet and waving his good arm, but he was weak and tired and his body was going into shock. It would be up to her to keep them both alive.

Her lungs were burning when their heads finally found air. She sucked in a damp breath, and shook her head to clear her eyes. "Goonie?" she gasped, clutching his chest as she fought to keep them up.

He was coughing and spluttering, but at least he was still conscious. She looked around, momentarily disoriented and unable to locate the ship. For a few heart-stopping seconds, she thought maybe it was gone, sucked to the bottom of the sea, even though her brain tried to tell her it would be impossible for it to sink so quickly. Then she managed to spot the vessel, on the wrong side of her. The ocean had turned her, and Goonie, all the way around.

Swan was still there, but he'd dropped into a crouch, on the outside of the railing, his arm still stiff behind him as he supported himself. He looked like he was a breath away from diving into the angry water below, and her heart jumped into her throat at the thought. She wanted to yell at him, order him to stay where he was, but she didn't have the breath to shout and didn't think he would hear her, anyway. Or listen.

He didn't jump in, though. He pointed, again, and she turned her head to look.

"Goonie, what did you see?" she asked. No answer. "Goonie?"

"Don't know," he murmured, his words slurred. "Over there..." She could hear his confusion, though, because the way he was looking was now the wrong direction.

"We got turned around," she said. "It's this way." She was scanning the dark, shifting water, and she saw the lightning reflected in a flash of yellow. Except...it wasn't lightning, because the sky had fallen temporarily dark, everything was dark, and she could still see just a hint of yellow glow...

"Ella," Goonie said.

"I see," she answered, but she still wasn't sure *what* she was seeing. Her stomach was fluttering nervously, however, and she'd once more become painfully aware of the vast, unknown, unseen stretch of water beneath her dangling legs. A flash of light, and she saw the dark shape arcing out of the water, not another wave as her mind tried to convince her but something else, something *in* the water, like she and Goonie were.

"Is that a whale?" Goonie asked.

At first, she thought it was. The domed back of a whale, rising from below. If that was true, however, she couldn't quite make sense of that half-circle of yellow still shining there above the black water. "No," she answered. "Not a whale."

"What is it?" he asked, and the fear and confusion in his voice fueled her own, although she did her best to tamp them down. "Is it alive?"

"I don't know," she answered. Although the waves did not seem as large as the gigantic towers that had crashed over the ship, she was having more trouble keeping her head above water. Some of it was fatigue, some was Goonie's decreasing ability to help himself, but mostly it was the constant churning of the water, pulling her in opposite directions. She knew that the crew could not safely lower a boat for them, just as she knew that it would be difficult to get a rope to her—difficult, and dangerous, because pulling them closer to the ship could prove catastrophic. If the waves didn't smash them against the ship, knocking them both unconscious, it would be a miracle. It would be impossible for the crew to keep the ship steady, especially now that one of the sails had been damaged.

She didn't know how long the storm would last, but she didn't think she could outlast it. If she didn't get out of the water soon, she would never see another sunrise.

She looked at Swan, crouched on the edge of his ship, somehow managing to appear graceful in an awkward position. His arm—he still had the coil of rope over that shoulder, she saw—was raised, and he was pointing. She wondered if he could see any better from his elevated vantage point, or if the swollen waves blocked his view, too. He gestured toward the yellow glow, and her stomach clenched. She didn't want to go toward that thing, not without knowing what it was.

Don't you? Don't you know what it is? She shied away from the idea her mind was trying to show her. It was impossible.

Water slapped against her face, and her arms and legs felt heavy and sore. Swan gestured again. He cupped his hand to his mouth and yelled something, but the words were lost in the wind and thunder. He tried again, and again his voice was muffled and distorted, and she could practically feel his frustration.

It didn't matter, anyway. She knew what he wanted, what he was telling her to do. He wasn't telling her to stay away from that thing, he was telling her to swim toward it. Whether he could see it more clearly than she could, or not, he could certainly see that it was at least partially above water, and that meant there was a chance she and Goonie could climb on. She suppressed a shudder at the thought, and her mind again whispered words that she did her best to ignore. It was impossible, she had to keep reminding herself of that. She didn't think that thing was a whale, but for all she knew, it could be that, or an upended boat, or even some strange, tiny island, or a—

She shook her head and got water up her nose. She looked once more toward that mysterious shape as it bobbed and dipped between the waves. She could make out a vague, mounded shape, but there was no sign of that flash of yellow. Even when the lightning reached toward the ocean, the shape remained dark.

Swan gestured again. How he must hate being disobeyed, and she did it so often. Amazingly, in spite of everything, she felt herself smile at the thought. Poor Colin. So used to being in charge, and she came along into his life, defying him at every turn...

Well, not every turn, she thought with a blush.

"We're going to swim toward that thing," Ella said. "Just relax on your back and kick your feet, alright? I'll do the rest."

"What?" Goonie asked. He sounded lethargic, and she didn't know what she would do if he lost consciousness. Even as she considered the terrifying possibility, his own fear seemed to break through some of his shock. "Go toward it? Why?"

"Because we're going to drown otherwise," she said, and she started swimming—awkwardly, pulling him with her, fighting the swirling water. Looking ahead, she felt like she was making no progress. After several minutes had passed, her arms felt like they were on fire in the cold water, one from working away at the sea and the other from clutching Goonie so tightly across his chest. She felt like she'd swallowed half of the ocean, as well, and the salty metallic taste in her mouth was almost as unbearable as the pain in her limbs. She couldn't tell if she was getting any closer to that hump in the water or not. Every time it disappeared from sight behind a wave, she imagined it would be gone for good, and every time it reappeared, her tired brain insisted it was further away. She knew this was an illusion; she knew that they were getting closer. Her mind was playing tricks on her, and her muscles were preparing a mutiny.

She stopped to rest, finally, hating herself for it, and she momentarily slipped under water. She pulled her head out with more effort than before, breathing heavily.

"Let me go," Goonie said again. "You don't have to do this."

"Don't be ridiculous," she panted, but she would be lying to herself if she didn't admit that the idea had occurred to her. She hadn't given it much consideration, just a moment, but it had been there, a dark flash in her mind, and she was ashamed of it. It wasn't even for Luca or Travis that the notion occurred to her—no, it was a purely selfish desire for self-preservation, a fear of death, that made her consider leaving him to fend for himself. As soon as she recognized the awful idea, she dismissed it, though. She hadn't thought before jumping in after him, but knowing now that she could die with him in the sea, she would not change her decision. To let him die alone out in the cold darkness was unthinkable.

She looked back toward the ship. It seemed slightly closer than before, and she didn't think that was her mind playing tricks on her. Somehow, in spite of the wind and rain and angry ocean, the crew was doing its best to follow her. One mast and sail had been damaged already; people could be hurt. Every moment the ship was in danger of being further damaged by the storm. Instead of focusing on getting through the weather, however, the men were focusing all of their attention on staying safely close to the two people in the water.

And the captain was clearly doing his best to keep his eyes on them. Ella knew that he cared about Goonie, and would have done whatever he could to save him if Ella had not jumped in after him. Swan's attention made her feel cared about, just the same, no matter how many times her tired brain insisted he wasn't only watching out for her, but Goonie, too.

"They're swimming toward—are you *telling* them to swim toward it?" Ivan asked.

"Yes," the captain answered over the roar of wind. He watched as Ella—with Goonie in tow—started moving again, slowly fighting her way through the unforgiving sea.

"Do you know—"

"Yes," Swan interrupted, and his flare of irritation was a poor mask for his worry.

Ivan was silent for a moment. Swan didn't look at him, but knew the man was weighing the pros and cons of questioning the captain further. Swan wasn't in the mood for questions. He felt like he was barely holding himself in control, and he wasn't even sure what would happen if he lost that battle. He barely noticed the ache in his thighs from his awkward crouch, or the strain in his arm from supporting himself, or the bleeding gash along the other arm.

"Do they know?" Ivan finally asked.

Swan stared out into the night, watching the distance slowly close between Ella and the dragon. He'd asked himself that question over and over, since she'd first started toward it. She'd moved in that direction at Swan's gesture. Did she know what she was swimming toward? Swan wanted to believe that she would trust him, that she would know he would not endanger their lives, but he knew that trust did not come easily to her. What would happen when she reached it? Would she panic?

His stomach clenched in fear at the thought. They were out of options. He could barely see her, bobbing and dipping out there, but he knew she was tired. She was losing her battle with the waves. If she were by herself, she could probably last longer. With Goonie, though? Swan would not underestimate her strength or determination, and he figured that if anyone could do it, she could, but he was afraid she would not make it until dawn.

"Is it alive?" Ivan asked.

"Yes," Swan finally answered.

"God," Ivan said, the sound almost—and not quite—lost in the wind. "Do they know?" he repeated, louder.

"I don't know," Swan said.

* * *

"Ella."

She was surprised by the sound of Goonie's voice. She'd fallen into a sort of trance, herself, all of her attention focused on her achy muscles and the task of pulling her way through the water. The world had narrowed itself down to that simple—yet increasingly difficult—action. She found she could barely speak. Her throat was scratchy from seawater, and she was out of breath. She managed, "Yeah?"

"Can you see it?"

She was silent for several awkward strokes. "Yeah," she finally answered.

Goonie was facing away from the dragon. She supposed that was a blessing for him, because the sight was frightening in the stormy darkness. She couldn't really come up with a good reason for moving toward it—except that she would almost certainly drown otherwise. A part of her believed it was dead, in spite of the glowing eye she'd seen. She'd never seen a dead dragon in person, so for all she knew, their eyes always reflected light. Another part of her knew that she was kidding herself, however, and she did her best to ignore that inner voice because it had nothing helpful to say. It certainly wasn't offering up any alternatives.

"How the hell did it get here?" Goonie asked.

She'd puzzled over that question a bit herself, but had decided it didn't matter. "Flew, I guess," she said.

"I never heard of a dragon trying to fly over the ocean," he answered.

She didn't answer. What did she know of dragons' motivations? What did she care, at this point?

"It's dead?" he asked.

I wish, she thought, having just enough presence of mind to marvel at the realization that climbing onto the floating corpse of a dragon could be considered a *good* choice. She and Goonie slid into a dip between waves, and for what seemed to be long moments, the dragon was suspended above them, a dark shape on a dark wave, and then it disappeared down the other side and Ella and Goonie were lifted up until she was looking down at the animal. And it was looking up at her, there was no mistaking that yellow orb. Would it kill her as soon as she got close? *Could* it kill her? She had no idea if it could breathe fire while half under water, or if it would be able to move enough to rip out her throat, or if it was smart enough to throw a wing or tail over her and drown her.

It would be horribly ironic to be burned to death on the brink of drowning. And yet, she did not want to drown. Considering her options, she realized that if she had to die, drowning would be her last choice of ways to go. She was more afraid of the ocean below her than the dragon floating in it, and she kept swimming.

She didn't know what Goonie had made of her failure to answer. He'd responded to her silence with his own.

The dragon had its wings spread out, on either side of its body, just below the surface. Ella touched the edge of one with her hand in mid-stroke and almost had a heart-attack. Her belly and bladder clenched in terror, and she pulled back so quickly that she slipped all the way underwater—and pulled Goonie down, as well. Even as she broke the surface, she was floundering backward, spluttering, with her heart galloping in her chest. Her tired mind hadn't even made sense, yet, of what she'd touched—all she knew was that her hand had encountered something solid in the midst of all that liquid, and she'd already had far too much time to imagine what creatures might be stalking her from below.

"What?" Goonie asked as she tried to get herself under control. She was not being attacked. Nothing had touched her feet or legs or body, yet, and as Goonie said her name, she finally saw the dragon's wing, hovering below the water, stretching toward her. She finally understood, but her fear was slow to diminish. The very idea that she had touched the wing of a dragon was terrifying.

She looked at the gleaming yellow eye; it seemed impossibly large, floating a couple of feet above the water, and as the waves pushed Ella closer to the animal, she watched it blink, slowly. Ella swallowed her lump of cold fear—and saltwater—and looked back toward the ship for what could be her last glimpse of Captain Swan.

Then she reached out and put her hand against the flat of the wing. It felt like wet leather, slippery but not exactly smooth, beneath the water. Ella ran her fingers over the thin membrane, watching the dragon's eye. Kicking her feet was not enough to keep herself and Goonie afloat, however, and she slipped beneath the lapping waves and was forced to pull her hand back.

"We're going to climb on your back," she told the dragon after she'd spit the ocean from her mouth. Her voice was shaky, and she was breathless. "If that's not alright with you, I guess you can probably kill us. I wouldn't blame you. But you seem to float better than we do." So many words left Ella lightheaded and hoarse, and she knew the time for speaking had passed. She reached out again, and this time took hold of the side of the wing. It shifted a bit, but the dragon did not pull it back, and when Ella used the wing to hold herself up, she found that it supported her as the waves washed against them.

"It didn't answer you," Goonie muttered.

"I think she did," Ella mumbled. She wasn't sure why she thought the dragon was a female, or why she suddenly felt so confident that the animal would remain passive. Ella pulled Goonie beside her. His face glowed, pale and round like the moon, in the darkness. His eyes were dark pools that reflected the dancing lightning. For several long moments, they stared at each other in the night. Their fates had become entwined, and it was almost certain that they would live or die together. She knew nothing about him—whether he had a family, where he was from, how long he'd been with Swan, what dreams he'd had for his life—and it was a strange thing to suddenly be hit by the enormity of their forced dependence upon each other.

The waves were still trying to push them under, and the ocean was still trying to pull them down, and the dragon's wing, however improbable, felt like a solid and tangible lifesaver. If the dragon stayed afloat with the added weight of two humans on her back, Ella and Goonie might live to see another dawn.

"Let's do this," Ella rasped. "Ready?"

"Ready," Goonie said.

"Hold on here," Ella said, guiding Goonie's good arm toward the wing. "I'm going up first."

Goonie did as instructed without comment. Mentally bracing herself for something to go terribly wrong, Ella reached up and took hold of the dragon's back. She was near the animal's shoulder, between the head and wing, and she supposed that it would have made more sense to stay as far from the head as possible. She was going to have to pull herself up and then, somehow, pull Goonie up. She couldn't spare the energy it would take to go around to the other side of the spread wing. From the corner of her eye, she could see the dragon blink again. As Ella gathered her courage and strength, and managed to heave herself out of the water, the dragon dipped in the waves a bit and lifted its head. It made no move to attack, and after a few seconds suspended with just her legs dangling in the ocean, Ella was finally able to scramble all the way up onto the mounded, scaly back.

Her heart was pounding, more from exertion than fear, and she took several slow, deep breaths to recover before reaching down for Goonie. He let go of the wing and reached up with his good arm. In spite of his kicking legs, he immediately began sinking, and she grabbed his outstretched arm just as his face slipped under the water. With her knees locked around the dragon's back, and her muscles straining and screaming in protest, she clamped her hands around Goonie's wrist and pulled. Once he was halfway up, and the water was no longer absorbing his weight, the strain became much worse. She was still pulling, but he was no longer moving upward, and for several horrible seconds she didn't think she was going to be able to do it. She would have to either let him fall back into the water, or be pulled off with him.

Then he managed to get a knee onto the edge of the dragon's wing, and he pushed himself up, and swung his leg over the dragon's back behind Ella, and collapsed against Ella's back. They were both panting. Ella was pretty sure she was crying, although it was difficult to tell the rain from the tears.

The animal was floating a little lower, but Ella's feet were out of the water on each side, and she felt a rush of relief that added to her body's shakiness. She looked toward the ship. Swan was standing again, and as she watched, he ran a hand over his rain-slicked face. She turned her face toward the sky, into the falling rain. The thunder was still grumbling, and the lightning was still flicking, and she couldn't tell if the intervals were longer or if her brain was simply processing them more slowly.

She could feel Goonie shivering against her. She was shivering, too, although not quite so badly. She found herself tiredly wondering how much worse she'd be suffering from the cold if Swan hadn't been force-feeding her for the past weeks, and she almost laughed.

"Sorry," Goonie mumbled.

"Don't worry about it," she answered, barely able to keep her teeth from chattering when she spoke. "Stay close to keep warm. We're going to get through this."

"Yeah," he said.

The dragon rose and fell on the waves, carrying them with her, and Ella leaned forward onto the animal's shoulders. Goonie was close against her back, and she took some comfort from what little heat his body was giving off.

She supposed he must feel the same about her.

Ella knew that the worst thing she could do would be to fall asleep. She needed to stay vigilant. They were far from safe. The ocean was full of predators that could attack the floating dragon or try for the people on her back. There was lightning that could strike them, or near them. There was the real threat of hypothermia. Goonie could completely succumb to shock. The dragon could be driven too close to the ship. There were other dangers that her exhausted mind couldn't even summon. It would be a bad idea to fall asleep, the worst idea.

Shivering cold, with rain pouring over her and the sea reaching for her toes, with every muscle in her body sore and her throat raw and scratchy, draped on a dragon with an injured man behind her, being tossed about in the middle of the ocean, sleep should have been impossible, anyway.

As she tried to list the reasons she should keep vigil, exhaustion took over, and her eyes drifted closed, and Goonie's even breathing carried her into oblivion.

Chapter Twelve

"The sky looks like blood."

Travis looked down at Jesse, disturbed by the young boy's declaration. The horizon was streaked with red, painted with unnatural-looking stripes of color, and it did look a bit like the smeared blood that could still be found in parts of the ship. The deck had mostly been washed clean by the hardest rains, but Travis knew where the blood had been spilled.

It was still raining, but it was a light misting, and the maroon-colored stripes in the east meant daylight was coming. Somehow, they'd all survived the night and the storm, and the ship seemed to be intact. Amir and a few other men had been busily inspecting sails, and they were almost all unfurled. The ship had begun to move in the right direction again, and Travis supposed they might make it to Bohannon, after all.

His leg hurt, in addition to all his other aches and pains, but it wasn't broken, and he was grateful for that. He found, in the approaching dawn, that he was grateful for a few things. The lives of the children and men, and Tabitha and Kyra. His own life, which was surprising since he'd almost given up caring about it at all. The ship's ability to resume sailing. The cool breeze on his face, which was an indication of a change of season coming—and proof that the world was still moving. A new day was, indeed, dawning.

The children were exhausted and would need to sleep, and then eat. Before they could sleep, however, the bunk room needed to be cleaned and the linens changed on at least one bed, because the whole room smelled like vomit. After they were all rested and fed, Travis was going to make sure they were all cleaned up and given something to wear other than the filthy rags they were in.

He went through a mental checklist of all that needed to be done: cleaning, laundry, preparing and then serving breakfast, finding something for the kids to wear, heating water for baths...

"Jesiah," he said, turning toward the other boy. "Could you come with me to clean the bunks? Tabitha, if there's enough oatmeal—Thanks," he said, when she nodded and turned to go below. "Kyra? Do you think you and Garrett could go down into the cargo and find something for the kids to wear, or...something we can make *into* something for them to wear?"

"We're going to be set on course soon," Gibbs called from several yards away. "Everything looks good."

Travis nodded. "Thanks," he said, again glancing toward the lightening sky. It was a new day. And the new day felt better than the last.

* * *

Ella awoke with a start, afraid she was falling, clutching the scaly back of the dragon in fear and disorientation. Her whole body felt bruised and achy, and her brain was fuzzy and uncooperative when she tried to figure out where she was and what was going on. The dark water was lapping gently at the sides of the dragon, and the sky was red.

"Easy, honey," a voice said, and she felt an arm circle around her back.

She blinked, more confused than ever. *Goonie*, she thought, and she almost pulled away. The low voice and gentle embrace were too intimate, inappropriate in spite of the ordeal they'd been through together. She was tensed, ready to tell him off, when several things finally clicked into place—almost in unison. First, she realized that the arm around her couldn't be Goonie's, because his was broken. At the same time, her tired brain recognized the voice, belatedly, and when she turned her head, she saw the ship looming, rocking gently, the crewmen watching from the deck. Beside the dragon was a rowboat. Ivan, Marty, and Goonie were in it, Goonie looking decidedly unhealthy but alive and conscious.

"It's morning," she said, hoarsely, looking down at her hands on the dragon's back.

"Nearly," Swan said behind her, and she finally realized that he had actually climbed onto the animal with her. How could she have slept so soundly, for so long, and not even noticed when they'd pulled Goonie from behind her? She had been pretty sure—even in the relief of finding rest on the dragon—that she would never see another red-streaked morning sky. Captain Swan had not given up on her, though, and even when she was snoring through the storm, he was watching over her. And, now, he'd come to the rescue, and his arm was around her, and even though she wanted to believe she was strong and brave, she felt tears stinging her eyes.

She started to turn toward him, trying to pull her leg up with a wince.

"Easy, love, your muscles are stiff," he murmured in her ear, but he wasn't fighting her movement; his strong arms helped her turn until she was sideways in his embrace. She didn't even care about all the men watching. She looked up at Swan's lined, stubbled face, and felt a surge of guilt for having slept while he was keeping vigil. His eyes were dark and watchful, searching her face. "Are you hurt?" he asked.

She shook her head and tears slipped from her eyes. "Is she alive?" she asked. Her throat was scratchy, and her lips felt dry and cracked. She wasn't sure if he would know what she was talking about, but his eyes slid past her for just a moment, toward the dragon's head.

"Yes," he said. "Ella..." His hands were on the sides of her face, now, and when she met his eyes, her breath caught. She thought he was going to kiss her, and her dry lips parted. She wanted to curl up in his arms and forget about everything else. She knew that Goonie had to get onto the ship and get medical attention, though. Also, the crew had work to do fixing the ship, so they could get sailing again. Swan sighed, his warm breath fanning her face. He bent forward and pressed his lips to her forehead. "We need to get you on board. You're freezing." She hadn't even realized that she was shivering. Her clothes were still wet, and she had no idea when the rain had stopped. His clothes were damp, as well, but his hair was dry, so it must have been a while ago.

"We're going to raise the boat up." He looked back toward the rowboat. Goonie was hugging himself with his good arm, shivering. His lips looked purple, and she didn't think it was a trick of red light.

"Goonie's ar-arm n-needs to b-be set," she said. Her teeth had begun chattering now that she'd become aware of her coldness. Swan's body heat was drawing her like a flame drew a moth, and she knew that it would be easy—far too easy, and dangerous—to give in to her desire to curl into his chest.

"Goonie will be alright," Swan said. "Thanks to you," he murmured with a small smile. "Come on, we're going to get you into the boat. Onto the ship. Into bed," he added. He cleared his throat. "To sleep."

"I've b-been sleeping," she muttered, and she felt a low laugh rumble through his chest. "We can't j-just leave the d-dragon here," she said.

"We won't," the captain promised.

* * *

"How b-badly is the ship damaged?" Ella asked, looking toward the broken mast and the hole in the deck. It seemed that every member of the crew was standing about the deck, except for Luca. Had anyone told him where she was or what had been going on? She hoped not. It would not serve any purpose for him to worry. The other injured men were up, however, standing in the early morning light, along with Timón and Rashad and everyone else. They all looked tired and somber, and she knew that no one had had an easy night.

"We'll be fine," Swan said. His hand was at the small of her back, and the heat was comforting. "Take Goonie below," he told Timón. Two men were helping Goonie along the deck. "Then we need to see about rigging something up for the dragon. We might be able to use the ripped sail."

"For what?" someone asked, as a general look of confusion passed among the faces of the crew.

"To pull it up. We'll hook it to the lifeboat pulleys, and—"

"You're thinking to bring that thing on the *ship*?" Ivan interrupted.

Ella turned so quickly that she stumbled on her unsteady legs. Swan's arm held her up as she glared at Ivan. "That animal saved my life, and Goonie's," she said.

Ivan grimaced, glancing at the captain before answering, "With all due respect, any piece of floating debris would've done the same."

"Floating debris?" Ella asked, angrier than ever. "She's a living animal, not a piece of wood. She didn't have to let us climb on her."

"It's half-dead. How could it have stopped you? It was just as helpless as you, it just floats better."

"Ella didn't seem so helpless," one of the men muttered, and there was a smattering of nervous laughs. She had just enough time to realize that the man, whoever it was, had used her name, and then Swan was gently moving her toward the cabin.

She tried to resist, because she was still angry with Ivan, and wanted to make sure they didn't leave the dragon to drown or be eaten by sea creatures. She was too tired, however, and even the captain's gentle pressure at her back was enough to propel her feet forward. "She could have killed us," she insisted over her shoulder. She knew it was true. As tired and possibly hurt as the animal was, it still could have drowned them with a wing or brained them with her tail or possibly even spit enough fire to light them up.

"Be logical," Ivan said. "Bringing her on board is—"

"Hold your tongue," Swan said, angrily. "This is not a debate. Get the sail and stretch it out along the deck. Or go below and help with Goonie."

Ivan's mouth worked for a few moments as he considered his options. Finally, he cleared his throat and glanced at Ella. "I meant no disrespect," he finally said.

She tried to rein in her temper, knowing that it had been a long night for Ivan, too. Not trusting herself to speak, she nodded in acknowledgment.

"Come on," Swan said. "You need to get changed and warmed up." Goonie had already disappeared, with his escorts, into the stairwell. Ella allowed herself to be turned and steered toward the cabin, and when she stepped into the familiar room, the room in which most of the intimacy between herself and Swan had been forged, she felt the space wrap around her like a comforting embrace. Already, the cold and swirling tug of the ocean had begun to feel like a horrible dream. The air inside was surprisingly warm, and it made her damp clothes feel even colder against her skin, and she started to shiver again.

Swan pushed the door shut behind himself. Before she could even process his movement, he'd pulled her into his arms, hugging her so tightly she could scarcely breathe. She buried her face against his shirt, breathing in the scent that she had come to love so much. One of his hands cupped the back of her head, his fingers threading into her damp hair, and she felt him let out a breath.

"How angry are you?" she asked against his chest.

"Angry?" he answered, and she thought she might hear the faint traces of humor in his voice.

"I know I said I wouldn't do anything stupid, after...well, the other stupid stuff..." she trailed off, frowning.

"Goonie would've drowned without you," he said, quietly. "Everyone knows that."

"We both would've drowned without the dragon," she answered. "Did you know what it was? When you told me to swim toward her?"

She could sense his hesitation. "Yes," he said. "Honey, you need to get changed into some dry clothes. Go to bed, alright? Please?" he added, and she pulled her head back to look up at him. He offered a small smile. His eyes were serious.

She gathered her courage. "Will you stay with me?" she asked, quietly, embarrassed by her neediness.

He looked pained for a moment. "I'll come back soon, sweetheart. Very soon. I promise. I need to see to a few things."

She felt guilty for her selfishness. Of course there were more important things than her own desire to have him near. He had a whole ship to worry about. A broken mast, a damaged deck, a ruined sail, God knew what other issues. "Are you really going to bring the dragon on the ship?" she heard herself ask.

"Yes." He kissed her forehead, again. She wanted to feel his lips on hers, and had to clench her jaw to keep from begging. "I'll see to the dragon, and then I'll come back. Alright?"

He was asking her permission to leave, she realized. She clearly wasn't hiding her emotions well. How fragile and desperate she must seem. "You don't need to worry about me," she said. "You have more important things to do. Worry about the ship. I'll be fine."

"Ella..." Her name was almost a sigh, and his arm tightened around her. "I wouldn't leave if I didn't owe her for your life."

She felt a warm ripple pass through her at his soft words.

"I will be back very soon, Ella, and we'll discuss what is more or less important than you. Alright? Now, please, get warmed up. I'll have some breakfast brought up." She opened her mouth to object and he pressed a finger to her lips, surprising her. She met his dark gaze. "Arguing with me now would be unfair, as I'm in no mood to deny you anything. Please, Ella. Get warm, eat, stay safe until I come back. Please."

She swallowed, completely disarmed by his open vulnerability. "Alright, Colin," she said. His expression tightened, for just a few seconds, before his hands cupped her jaw and his lips covered hers. Her mouth opened, and she felt hot desire blossom in her belly. She wanted to hold onto him, she wanted to drag him to the bed and refuse to let him leave, she wanted to undress him and straddle—she broke the thought off, her cheeks flaming with a mixture of arousal and embarrassment.

He pulled back, searching her face as he tucked her hair behind her ear. "Take what clothes you want from the dresser and get some rest. I'll be back before you know I'm gone."

I doubt that, she thought. After another chaste kiss on her head, he turned, opened the door, and disappeared, pulling it shut. She stood in the middle of the floor, hugging herself, trying to remind herself that she was not being abandoned—trying to remind herself that she was not some wimpy, weepy girl who needed a man's strong arms around her to feel safe. He was going to try his best to save the dragon, and Ella was grateful for that. It almost balanced out her sudden loneliness.

* * *

"This isn't going to work," Ivan muttered. "How are we supposed to get the dragon into it, even if we can get it hooked up?"

Swan glared at him. Even though he knew Ivan had been looking out for the captain's safety, and even though Swan knew—now that he was thinking more clearly—that he would have accomplished nothing by jumping into the water, he was still angry that Ivan had taken that choice from him. If Ella had drowned...Swan gave his head a little shake. She was fine, so was Goonie, and there was no point imagining what might have happened. If Ivan hadn't kept him from jumping in, Swan would have drowned, even if Ella had not.

"We should be repairing the mast," Ivan added, refusing to be cowed by Swan's glare.

"Repairs can wait until the crew has had a chance to rest," Swan answered.

Ivan opened his mouth to object, then clearly changed his mind. "As you wish, Captain," he finally muttered.

"Thank you," Swan said, running a hand down his face. He turned to look out at the dragon. He had no idea how long she could survive out there, or how long she'd already been in the water, but he knew that she was in bad shape. Her head did not float, and she could barely hold it out of the water. Every once in a while, her snout would dip into the water, and her yellow eye would blink slowly, and she would somehow manage to lift her face up again.

Looking down at her, Swan felt a real twist of pain for her, and knew he had to do something to ease her suffering. Ella was right; the dragon could have killed her, and Goonie, when they'd tried to climb on her back. As he watched, the animal's large eye found him, and his breath caught as he stared back at her. Her huge wings rippled beneath the water, and lifted partway up, the tips pointing skyward as waterfalls of seawater cascaded down. He could see the suction of the ocean bowing those powerful wings, could see the animal's body dip lower into the water, and knew what he had to do.

The dragon gave up, collapsing back into the sea, her face sliding beneath the shallow waves before slowly reappearing. She was exhausted. Swan hesitated for almost a minute. If it were just himself he had to worry about, there would be no deliberation. He couldn't do what needed to be done by himself, however. Saving the dragon was going to become very dangerous for some members of his crew, and he needed to give that the careful consideration it deserved.

He held the animal's weary gaze for another few seconds, then turned toward his waiting crew. They had the ripped sail spread out as well as they could along the confines of the deck. It flapped in the breeze. Torn, he hoped it was still tough and useable for what needed to be done. They would normally try patching before breaking out a spare sail, as the large, heavy sails were in limited supply. These were not normal circumstances, however.

"I'm going to ask for volunteers," he said. He wasn't sure what to expect. He didn't want to force any of them to go along with his plan, but if no one volunteered? Or if only a few did? Ordering them to put their lives into what they may see as unnecessary peril was a quick path to mutiny, as well as something he had never considered doing. "I need at least eight men. Maybe ten," he added, although too many could prove to be more dangerous than not enough.

The men exchanged glances in the morning light. Then, to Swan's relief, they began raising their hands. He hadn't even told them what the plan was, yet, but their expressions showed that they knew there was danger involved. Slowly, every man on the deck raised a hand, including Ivan. Swan felt a rush of gratitude for his men.

"Ella was right," Marty said, glancing around to see if everyone else agreed with him. "The dragon let them climb on her back. She saved both their lives. We can't just let her drown out here."

There was a murmur of agreement among the crew, and Swan met Ivan's eyes. Ivan swallowed, then nodded. "Gather up the sail with four men in a row boat," the captain said. He scanned the crowd and picked four of the largest men. "Ivan, you're staying on board to be captain in my stead," Swan said. There was no need to mention he had an ulterior motive for leaving Ivan behind. He didn't need any arguments when it came time to do what needed to be done, and Ivan would almost certainly object. "Five of you are in this boat, with me," Swan continued, gesturing toward the nearest dinghy. He saw the men exchange a few more looks, but no one objected, and in less than two minutes, the first boat was being lowered into the water. As the men in that boat rowed out from the ship, the second boat was lowered, with six men—including the captain—inside it.

Once they were in the water, Swan called to the other boat to stop and wait for him, and soon the two dinghies were side by side. He had the men in each boat hold the edge of the other to keep them steady, and he stepped into the boat with the sail in it. With the added weight of the heavy sail, he hadn't wanted to make the rowboat any more difficult to lower than necessary. He motioned for Marty to join him in the heavily-loaded dinghy, as well, and then there were only four men in one and six, and a folded sail, in the other.

They rowed up on each side of the dragon, and Swan met the yellow eye again when it shifted toward him. Up close, the dragon's size was impressive, and intimidating, particularly knowing how much of it must be submerged. His stomach was doing a nervous little dance, but he knew there was no backing down.

"What's the plan, Cap?" Marty asked when Swan got to his feet in the low-riding boat.

Swan cleared his throat and took a deep breath, shooting a quick glance toward the ship. "I'm going in the water," he said.

This proclamation was greeted by silence from the men. The water lapped against the boats and dragon, and behind the captain, his ship—his home—creaked. Swan looked down. The dragon's wing was stretched in front of the boat, just below the surface of the water. He was not quite close enough to reach out a hand and touch the animal's side, but he could see the scaly skin in clearer detail than he'd been able to in the red light of dawn. Her skin looked paler and slimier at the edge of the water, and he was afraid that the salty sea had done irrevocable damage to her body. They wouldn't know until she was up and out, and if she couldn't fly, he didn't think they would be able to save her. He didn't want to face that possibility. He wasn't sure he would be able to live with himself if he had to sail away and leave her behind, floating her way to certain death.

He didn't want to have to tell Ella that he'd been unable to make good on his promise to save the animal, either.

"You're going to have to help us out, here," he told the dragon, and she looked at him with a slow blink.

"Captain, it might...be better if, uh, you let me go in," Marty spoke up, finally, sounding nervous. "You'd be safer in the boat. If you tell me what your plan is—"

"Thank you, but no," Swan said, effectively cutting off any further argument. He pulled his shoes off, one at a time, and dropped them into the boat. Then he stripped his shirt off and discarded that, as well. Before anyone had a chance to stop him, he stepped onto the edge of the boat and dropped into the ocean. The boat tipped and was pushed away from the dragon as Swan sank into the cold water. By the time he'd kicked himself to the surface, gasping at the cold shock, the men had steadied the boat and were rowing it closer.

In the water, beside the dragon, he couldn't help thinking his plan was foolish and unrealistic. He turned toward his boat, treading water, and told them to open the sail up over the edge of the boat. The men worked to do as bid, spreading their weight out to keep the dinghy balanced. They lowered a corner of the sail into the water, and it floated outward, reaching toward Swan. He took hold of it and pulled backward, kicking his way toward the dragon's head.

The men in the boat doled it out as the captain moved, and the sail spread itself out across the water, making pockets of air and rippling just below the surface in places, reminding him of the dragon's wings. Swan was right beside one large eye, and he couldn't help his shiver of apprehension. In the water, the sight was formidable. On land—or on the ship, with limited space—it would be even more frightening. He knew, however—knew without question—that the dragon meant him no ill-will. She was tired, sick, weak...close to giving up. He found himself wondering what could have driven her to attempt a flight across the ocean. He wasn't even sure the trip could be made under the best circumstances.

"We're going to do this, girl," he murmured, kicking slowly around to the other side of her head. The sail dragged up tight against her shoulder and slid across her skin as he made his way around, and he hoped he wasn't further damaging her wet scales. The sail went under her chin, so it was against her throat and below her shoulders. He couldn't see her front legs. He had to get the sail behind them, however. He had to get the end of the sail to the other boat, first. If he went under, pulling the makeshift sling with him, he would almost certainly not be able to force it back to the surface with the water dragging it down. The ends needed to stay up or the mission would surely fail.

He reached the boat and handed the corner of sail up to the men, instructing them to pull until there was some slack around the dragon and the men on each side had little extra in their boats. Swan swam back to the

238

dragon's front and did his best to keep the material from rubbing as it was pulled along her skin. When the boats had the sail spread pretty evenly between themselves, Swan patted the dragon's snout, took hold of the edge of material, pulled in a deep breath, and slipped beneath the water. The coldness enveloped him, muffling the world, and he dove down along the dragon's front, squinting his eyes to see through the dark water.

He felt his way along the animal's leg, pushing the sail ahead of himself and kicking deeper and deeper until it seemed he would never reach her foot. Finally, he felt his way beneath the dangerous talons. His lungs were beginning to burn, and he was sure he would have to surface for a breath before doing the same thing at her other front leg. Then, suddenly and unexpectedly, the animal moved, and the water swirled, pushing Swan aside as his heart skipped. If he got tangled in the sail or pinned beneath the dragon, he would drown.

Even as he was trying to keep himself from panicking, he realized that the sail had been pulled down. He tugged at it, and it moved—slowly—behind both of the animal's front legs. She'd pulled her other leg up, essentially stepping over the sail beneath the water, and Swan felt a rush of relief and gratitude. His lungs were screaming for oxygen, and he propelled himself toward the surface, sucking in a deep breath when his face found air. He put his hand on the dragon's snout and she looked at him.

"Good girl," he said. "Good girl. Almost there." He turned and swam to the nearest boat, grabbed the edge, and levered himself up. Two of the men grabbed his arms and hauled him in, and he took a few moments to catch his breath. There were now five men in each boat, and the sail was stretched between them, under the dragon's chest. That was the easy part. He looked up toward the ship, and his eyes immediately found Ella's. She wasn't on the deck; she was watching from the window of the cabin. He supposed he should be upset with her for not following his simple request that she get some rest, but he was touched by her concern—concern that was evident in the palm she had flattened against the window beside her pale face. Some of that concern was likely for the dragon, and the other men, but some of it was for Swan, too. He knew that.

He tried not to think of her, shivering and exhausted, asking him to stay with her, tried not to think about how he'd turned and walked out of the room. He had to finish the task at hand.

"Spread your weight out," he called to the men in the other boat. He could see only the tops of a few of their heads on the other side of the dragon's shoulders. He gestured to the men in his own boat to do the same. It would be easy to tip or sink the boats, and the men had to do everything they could to put safety first. Five men standing in a rowboat was dangerous enough. "Spread out and everyone hold the edge of the sail. We're going to move slowly and carefully. Everyone needs to work together and worry about balancing. We're going to start lifting when I count to three. Is everyone ready?"

"Ready, Cap," came a chorus of replies.

"Slowly," Swan repeated. "One, two, lift."

They pulled, and the sail on each side was lifted out of the water inch by inch until it was tight beneath the dragon's chest. Then it stopped, and the men were immobile for a moment, the muscles in their arms bunched as the dinghies began to tip a bit under the force.

"Lift," Swan said, his own muscles straining as they continued to pull upward. The dragon moved, lifting up in the water. They didn't have to bear her weight, not really, they only had to get her high enough that she could get her wings free from the clinging waves. Swan hoped, prayed, that she would be able to help herself from there. "Come on," he muttered under his breath, not even sure if he was talking to the men, the dragon, or himself. Higher, they lifted her, and the strain became greater as more of her bulk rose above the surface of the sea. The men stepped further back as the boats tipped closer and closer to the water. Swan glanced down. Soon, water would spill over the edge of the boat.

The wing joints were out of the water, and as the men strained at the sail, the dragon drew her wings up, partially folding them, and finally managed the pull them from the water with a loud sucking sound. The roar of water pouring back to the sea was loud, but the men all seemed in awe of the giant wings suddenly stretching themselves out over their heads. With her wings out, the dragon's weight pulled the men and the boats further down, as they struggled to pull up, and water began to slop over the side of Swan's boat. He couldn't see if the others were having the same issue.

A loud ripping sound split the air, and he knew the tough sail was beginning to give way along the tear caused by the broken mast. Even if the boats stayed up, the sail might tear through the middle before the dragon was up.

"Come on," Swan said, and the wings flapped, showering them with a spray of water and buffeting them with a wave of air. Just when he was sure they were going to have to let go, and risk losing her back into the water, to prevent the boats from sinking, the weight was eased from their arms and the dragon lifted up until only her feet were beneath the waves. He heard one of the men swear, either in fear or awe, and he felt a mixture of the two, himself.

She gave another flap of her large wings, and several of the men ducked even though they were hit with nothing more substantial than another spray of water. The sail/sling was now hanging loose in the water, and the men in the two boats could see each other clearly as the dragon lifted all the way into the air. There were several inches of water in the bottom of the boat around Swan's bare ankles, but neither boat had been sunk, and that was what mattered. He watched as the dragon rose higher, her shadow spilling over the men in his boat, and he saw that the skin on her belly and legs and tail had, indeed, begun to peel and fall away. If he wasn't mistaken, he thought he glimpsed some sores that may have been caused by fish and other sea animals nibbling at her underside. Now that she was out of the water, they should heal quickly.

Dragons' blood had regenerative powers, which was why it was used to treat many types of wounds in humans.

The dragon turned in a slow circle, and for a second the captain was afraid she was going to take off, attempting to continue her journey to the other side of the sea. In her condition, there was no way she would make it, and they might not come across her again if she wound up floating somewhere else in the gigantic body of water. To his relief, however, she tilted back toward the ship. The men backed away from the rails, watching the animal looming toward them with wariness. The only space large enough, and open enough, for her to land was the roof of the captain's cabin, and as everyone watched, the dragon circled and sank onto that flat roof, folding her wings to her sides. Her head dropped, in exhaustion, onto the wood, and her large eyes closed.

Swan looked at the other dinghy and saw the men grinning and patting each other on the back. He couldn't help smiling, too. Who would have thought they'd be so happy to have helped a dragon onto their ship? There would be time for celebrating later, though. They had to get the rowboats, themselves, and the sail, back onto *Voyage* so the men could eat and rest before beginning the necessary repairs to the ship.

"Let's bail out as much water as we can while we row," he said, as the men all lowered themselves, carefully, onto the benches. By the time they'd reached the side of the ship, most of the water was out of the bottoms of the dinghies, and the sail was trailing behind them like the shed skin of a massive white snake, held only by one of the men in Marty's boat. It was in far worse shape than it had been in, before, but it still needed to be returned to the ship. Leaving it in the ocean would be disrespectful and, worse, dangerous to the animal life and possibly even other ships.

Plus, it could still be salvaged to make patches.

Swan looked up and saw the dragon on the roof of his cabin and, below the animal's large head, Ella's face watching from the window. Then the dinghy was pulled closer to the ship, and he lost sight of both.

*   *   *

Ella sat on the captain's bed, dressed in a shirt that hung to her knees when she was standing. On the bed, her legs were tucked up beneath her, and the shirt covered everything but her toes. Some of her tiredness had disappeared as she'd watched Swan dive into the ocean to drag the sail beneath the dragon. She'd been awed by his beauty, grace, and courage, and terrified for his safety, and had not been able to relax until she saw that he and the men were once more on deck of the ship. After seeing them on board, she'd closed the curtains one at a time.

Then, knowing he would return to the cabin before too long, and knowing that he'd asked her to rest, she'd climbed onto the bed and pulled her legs up. Her breakfast, uneaten, was on the desk. She knew she should eat it before he arrived. It would ease his mind. Her stomach was a mess of queasy knots, though, a confused tangle of anticipation and trepidation. She wasn't hungry, and she wasn't sleepy.

She watched the door open, and her heart skipped when Swan—shirtless and glistening with seawater—filled the space. His shirt was slung over his shoulder, and his shoes hung from two fingers. His presence seemed to suck all of the air from the room, and she stared at him, her lips parted, unable to breathe. He seemed momentarily taken-aback to find her gaze, but his hesitation was brief. He pushed the door shut and flipped the lock, and her stomach fluttered. He dropped his shoes and shirt onto the floor.

His gaze skated over her face, down the length of her folded body, and she saw him swallow. She wanted him to cross to the bed, but he stayed where he was, watching her, silent. What was he thinking? She'd gotten adept at reading his moods, most of the time, but now she wasn't sure.

Finally, he spoke. "I'm going to get out of these wet clothes," he murmured, his voice a low rumble. Faint color stained his cheeks, and she finally realized why she was having trouble identifying his mood. He was actually embarrassed, the self-consciousness so far removed from his usual grace and confidence that she was stunned when she recognized it. Her eyes, of their own accord, slid downward, and she saw the arousal straining at the front of his wet trousers and knew why he was uncomfortable. He hadn't walked in that way. Seeing her had caused the reaction, and she felt a rush of pleasure and answering desire at the knowledge.

"You're blushing," she said, unable to hide her amusement.

He cleared his throat. "Seems only fair, you do it so often," he answered, and she laughed. It felt good to laugh, and she saw some of the tension around his mouth and eyes ease. "Considering what you've been through, I have no intention of—"

"You don't?" she interrupted, not even trying to mask her disappointment.

He raised his eyebrows. "I do fancy myself a bit more of a gentleman than that," he said.

"I'm fine," she responded. He regarded her in silence. Finally, hugging herself, she asked, "What did you mean to happen when you came back in here?" She'd been waiting for him in such anticipation that she hadn't considered any scenarios that didn't end with him in the bed beside her.

"My plans were to crawl into bed with you and hold onto you until I knew for sure you were really safe," he admitted, surprising her. "I didn't plan to have such an...unwelcome response to the sight of you, though."

"Unwelcome?"

"Inappropriate," he amended.

"I want you to come to bed with me," she said.

Something like pain flitted across his features. "I will," he answered. "I promise. Just let me get some dry clothes on and get myself under control, Ella."

"I want you to make love to me," she clarified, and she saw his nostrils flare. "Isn't that what you want?" she asked, with a shy smile. She was not

242

feeling insecure; she knew he wanted her. For him, that was the problem.

"I think you can see that I do," he answered, wryly. Some of his humor seemed to be returning, and she took that as a good sign.

"Thank you for saving the dragon," she said after a few moments of silence.

"Thank you for not drowning," he responded, and the words seemed to surprise him as much as they did her. It was the second time he'd said that to her, but this time, it held even more weight.

"Come to bed," she murmured, reaching a hand toward him.

He moved forward, either unable or unwilling to ignore such a direct plea. When he reached her outstretched hand, however, he sank into a crouch before her and pulled her knuckles to his lips. "Ella," he said, her name a soft breath against her fingers. There was that vulnerability, again, the open emotion that made her want to give him every part of herself. She pressed a hand to his cheek, and he closed his eyes, briefly. "I wanted to be in the water with you," he admitted.

She shook her head. "The only reason I came up...when you told me to stay below..." She hesitated, afraid to remind him that she'd disobeyed more than one of his commands. "Was to make sure you were alright. I kept thinking about you standing on the railing...That's dangerous, you know," she said, frowning.

He grinned, showing a flash of teeth. "So is jumping overboard in a storm," he countered. "Were you really so worried about me?"

"Of course I was," she answered, studying his face, memorizing all the lines of stress that marred his handsome features. "And when I was in the water...I thought you...I mean, you looked like you were about to dive in. I kept praying you would stay on the ship, stay...safe..."

He frowned. "I tried to jump in. You kept going under."

"What do you mean, you tried to jump in?"

"Ivan held onto my belt. He's lucky I didn't kill him."

"Remind me to thank him," she said. "Without him, I might never have been able to kiss you, again."

"Who says you can?" he teased, smiling.

"I'd like to see you stop me," she retorted, arching her eyebrows.

With a laugh, he said, "I don't think I'd be very good at that game."

"Oh, you seem to like playing hard to get," she countered.

"It's not playing hard to get," he said. "It's pretending to be a gentleman."

"I suppose I should pretend to be a lady, then," she said with an exaggerated sigh.

He shuddered, his eyes twinkling with humor. "God forbid," he answered.

She slid her fingers to his lips and met his eyes. "It's a shame you don't want me to kiss you," she said. "Your lips are very tempting."

"Are they?" he breathed.

"Maybe we can work out a deal," she suggested. "What would you want in return?"

He arched a brow. "For you to have the pleasure of kissing me?" He seemed to consider the question. "Hmm. Perhaps for you to eat your breakfast?"

She laughed and clapped a hand to her forehead. "God, you're so obsessed with my diet. I really think you'd find me more attractive if I was fat."

"Not possible."

She hesitated. "What?"

"For me to find you more attractive. Not possible."

She swallowed the sudden lump of emotion in her throat. All the terms of endearment, and reassurances that he wanted her, and the concern for her safety and health...His attentiveness made her feel loved, and even though she knew that it might be an illusion and could almost certainly not last, she didn't want to fight it. She wanted to bask in the feeling and give what she could in return.

She leaned forward, barely aware of the protest from her sore muscles. He didn't move, and she held his hooded gaze as she pressed her lips against his. She threaded her fingers into his damp hair just in case he was thinking of pulling away. His mouth opened for her exploration, but he was otherwise still. His hands were on her leg, immobile. She pushed her tongue into his mouth the way he'd taught her, and she was rewarded by a low sound of desire from his throat.

Her fingers ached to touch the bare expanse of chest just inches away, and she trailed a hand down his neck, to his shoulder, and across his breastbone, running a light finger toward his navel. He broke away from her mouth to hiss in a breath.

Ella shifted to tug the shirt from beneath herself, and she stripped it up and over her head, tossing it past his shoulder toward the floor. She sat, completely naked, feeling remarkably confident. It was a new experience for her, to feel attractive and desirable, and she owed it to him.

"You're sore," he said. He sounded breathless, and it wasn't a question.

"Yes," she admitted. "But not that sore."

"Are you sure?"

"Yes."

He stood and quickly stripped off his wet pants. She scarcely had time to admire the sight of his body before she was laying back on the bed, with him stretched over her. He bent his head, and his mouth found her nipple, suckling gently. She grabbed his hair, gasping. His touch at her hip was light, too, and she wanted to tell him that she wasn't fragile. She was unable to speak, though, as desire exploded within her. The ache between her legs had become almost unbearable, already, and when his gentle fingers found their way between her thighs, she whimpered in expectation.

He lifted his head, searched her face, and slanted his mouth over hers. She arched against his hand. She wanted him to move faster, and frustration warred with her desire. He teased her with his fingers and she struggled to hold onto herself, struggled to fight the building sensation, because she wanted him inside of her.

Finally, afraid she was going to lose control, she pulled her mouth from his. "Please," she begged. "Colin."

She tried to shift her hips away, desperate to keep her release at bay, and the sweet, torturous pressure of his fingers disappeared. "What's wrong?" he asked, and she wanted to ease the worry from his expression. "Ella?"

Her brain was having difficulty forming the words she needed, and her desire had robbed her of patience. He wanted her; there was no hiding his arousal, and there was no sense denying them both what they so desperately craved. On impulse, she put her hands on his chest and pushed him toward the wall. He rolled off of her easily, flopping onto his back, and mixed with the desire in his eyes was a combination of confusion and concern. He seemed to think she was putting an abrupt end to things—something she wasn't sure she could do if she wanted to, and she certainly didn't want to.

She rolled on top of him and pushed herself up until she was straddling his stomach, and she felt his muscles quivering beneath her thighs. She thought she saw alarm in his eyes, now, and she felt a moment's doubt. She was moving on instinct, and she was afraid she might do something wrong.

"Is...this alright?" she asked. Her body was screaming at her to ignore her misgivings and plunge ahead.

"Alright?" he repeated. "Ah, God. Ella. Tell me what you what, honey."

"You," she answered, blushing. She shifted against him and his jaw tightened. His hands went to her hips. She wasn't sure if it was to steady her, or himself. Now that she was up, she was embarrassed and awkward, and unsure how to proceed. His erection was behind her. They'd been in this position, before, and she'd asked him to take over. He'd done so readily, lifting her and settling her into place. "This was a bad idea," she finally mumbled, blushing even darker. "It's better when you're in control." She started to shift sideways, but his hands tightened on her hips, and she stopped, forcing herself to meet his gaze.

"Ella, I've never been in control with you," he said. "Look at me. It's just you and me, here. There are no bad ideas, love. Trust yourself."

She chewed on her lower lip for a moment. "If I hurt you—"

"You won't," he said. She shifted, and he tried to hide a wince. Seeing her slight frown, he said, "This is not a bad pain, Ella." One of his hands slid up onto her thigh, and her breath hitched as her muscles clenched in desire. "It's like that," he murmured, holding her gaze.

She let out a breath. There was only one sure way to end the torture for both of them, and with that realization, her nervousness slipped away. He was right. It was the two of them, together, and he wanted her as much as she wanted him. By giving in to her self-doubt, she was denying both of them the kind of pleasure that most people would likely never be lucky enough to know.

"Can you help me?" she asked.

"Lift your hips," he answered. She did, and he reached a hand between them, shifting a bit until he had himself positioned beneath her, one hand holding his erection in place. "Lower yourself down," he said.

When she felt his tip pressing into her, she knew she wasn't going to last long. The pressure was already building within her.

He moved his hand and held her hips to steady her. "When you're ready, take your time," he said, through gritted teeth, and she realized that she was torturing him even more than she was torturing herself. Leaning forward a bit, she put her hands on his shoulders and sank onto him, sheathing him completely in her hot wetness, and his eyes closed. His hands tightened on her hips, but they weren't restricting her; there was no doubt that he was now holding on to steady himself.

It was a strange experience for her, looking down at him during the moment of penetration, to know that she was responsible for joining them together. She wanted to stay in place and savor the moment, but her body was screaming for release, and telling her to move. She could feel him twitching inside of her. His stomach muscles were quivering. His jaw was clenched, his breathing labored. She knew that he was fighting his own body's instinct to thrust, fighting it with all of his willpower. He was doing his very best to give her control, and she knew in that moment that she'd already fallen hopelessly in love with him. There were no ifs or whens involved, not anymore. She was probably going to have her heart broken, but not now. Now they were together, and when his eyes opened and found hers, she could believe that he might love her, too.

Her body started moving, following its instinct, and the pressure inside of her was building, looming impossibly large, and she could feel herself tightening around him as her body tried to swallow him deeper. He was thrusting to meet her, his chest slick with sweat beneath her hands. She felt herself beginning to convulse, and the world began to shatter around her. As the waves of sensation rippled through her, she could feel his body tensing, inside her and beneath her.

He lifted her hips, suddenly, freeing himself, and she felt a moment's disappointment. She wanted to know what it would feel like to have his seed spilled within her. She was sitting on his thighs, still quivering from her own orgasm, and his swollen erection was in front of her. He moved quickly, setting her back and reaching for himself in a matter of seconds, but she managed to knock his hand aside. She circled her hand around him, and he jerked, gasping. He stared up at her, curling his hands into fists at his sides.

She didn't give herself time to feel doubt. She'd seen him finish himself off, and she slid her hand up and down his shaft, marveling at the silky smoothness against her palm. He pushed his head back into the pillow, breathing raggedly. "Oh, God," he groaned, and she watched in amazement as his hips shifted beneath her and hot semen spurted from his tip, spilling onto her hand and wrist and splattering onto his stomach. He clutched at the bedspread, as spasms rocked through him.

She released him reluctantly, some of her disappointment tempered. Yes, she wanted him to come inside of her, but at least this way she'd been able to see what she could do to him. She'd given him a taste of the pleasure he'd given her, and she was glad for that.

"Ella," he said, and before she could say anything, he'd pulled her forward, onto his chest, and his mouth was beneath hers, claiming hers, and she could feel his spent manhood between them and his racing heart against her breast. Their heavy breathing was mingled as they kissed, struggling to draw air without pulling apart, until she was lightheaded and giddy and he finally turned his face away to let them both breathe.

She laid her cheek against his chest, listening to the thump of his heart and savoring the feel of his arms around her. She closed her eyes, pulling in a deep breath full of his scent. *I love you,* she thought, overwhelmed by the emotion. She couldn't say it. That didn't mean she didn't feel it.

His hand was tracing light circles on her back, as his breathing began to return to normal. "Ella, I—"

"Did I do well?" she asked. It was mostly a joke, but she was alarmed by what she thought he'd been about to say.

A low laugh rumbled through his chest, but then he was silent for a long time. She could sense that he was disturbed by her interruption. She might be wrong about what he'd been about to say, but she didn't think so, and he was almost certainly puzzling through why she'd cut him off. She didn't want to spoil the moment, and she lifted her head, meeting his hooded gaze. Leaning up, she kissed his lips, softly, pressing her palm against his cheek. Their eyes held, and she saw the moment he decided not to push the issue. She wasn't sure if she was grateful or disappointed, or both.

"Far better than I would've done," he said, finally, and she felt most of her tension slip away.

She found herself smiling down at him. "It was fun," she said, and he laughed again. She glanced down. "Am I squishing you?" she asked.

"How could you? You weigh less than my pillow," he joked.

She made a face. "Hardly," she scoffed. "Besides, I don't want to damage my favorite part of you." She raised her eyebrows, grinning again.

It was his turn to make a face. "I feel so cheap," he said, and she laughed, laying her cheek against his chest again.

"I should get cleaned up," he said after a minute. "I'm getting you all...messy..."

She lifted her hand so they could both see the streaks of semen down her wrist.

"Hell," he said, and he sounded genuinely grieved by the sight. "Sorry. Here, let me—"

"I like it," she said. "I was thinking of leaving it there."

His surprised silence was broken by a short laugh. After a brief hesitation, he said, almost cautiously, "I'm glad you're here." There could be so many different meanings hidden in those four words.

Her heart stuttered in her chest, and she blinked back the sting in her eyes. It wasn't a declaration of love, but it was still frightening. Their emotions had gotten so strong and serious so quickly. She could feel his heartbeat against her cheek, and she closed her eyes, thinking about how far she'd come in just a few weeks. Not geographically, although she was certainly further from her home than she'd ever been by a long shot. It was so much more than that, though. She'd been on the verge of starvation when Ivan hauled her out into the sunlight, and now she was well-fed and healthier than she'd been in a long time.

She'd made stupid mistakes since stepping foot onto the ship, but she'd gained confidence and knowledge in the process, and she'd learned how to open herself up—maybe not completely, but far more than she ever had. She was different than she'd been before meeting him, and it was a change that she wouldn't be able to reverse even if she wanted to. The world was different...or, she saw it differently. She saw possibilities she'd never believed in, before.

"So am I," she said, and she knew that, no matter how selfish it was, her temporary happiness had nothing to do with her brother. She'd come onto the ship with no goal in mind except to get to Travis. Now, she had no idea if her brother was alright, and even though she was worried about him, she had found something she hadn't been looking for. Something that had nothing to do with Travis, or Luca, or anyone except Colin Swan and herself.

"Are you cold?" he asked.

"No," she murmured. As her body relaxed, she was growing sleepy, and she fought the drowsiness. He would have to get up before too long to see to the men and the ship's repairs. He needed to rest, first, and she wanted to enjoy his company. She wanted to sleep curled against him and know that he was deep in peaceful slumber in her arms. "Will you stay here and sleep with me?" she asked.

"For as long as I can," he answered, softly, and she couldn't help but hear a double meaning in his words. "Let me clean up and we'll sleep."

"Before you do," she said, lifting her head to look at him. "You think maybe we could make a little more to clean up?"

His eyebrows lifted in surprise, and his eyes darkened. "I thought you were tired?" he murmured, the corner of his mouth quirking in amusement.

"Not that tired," she said. "Besides, I think I was just getting the hang of it. I might need a little more practice."

He chuckled, and the vibration sent shivers through her body. "I might need a little more self-control," he returned, his tone self-deprecating.

She pushed herself up, amazed by her lack of embarrassment when his gaze slid to her bare breasts. The air was cool against her still-sweaty skin, and her nipples protruded, seeming to beg for his attention. She was straddling him, again, his hip bones against the insides of her thighs, his stirring erection against her backside, out of sight. She smiled down at him, her tiredness forgotten as the desire in his eyes fueled her own.

"Do you need time to get ready?" she joked, her belly tightening when his finger traced a light line up her thigh.

He laughed, again, his eyes twinkling. "Surprisingly, no," he said.

* * *

When Ella woke, she was snuggled against Swan's side, with one leg over his, and an arm draped across his chest. They were both naked, and under the blanket. He was on his back, with an arm beneath her head, and with a brief twinge of guilt, she wondered if his hand was numb. She didn't want to move, afraid she would disturb him, but when she cautiously lifted her head, she found him watching her.

He smiled, and her stomach fluttered. She couldn't imagine a better way to wake up. "How long have you been awake?" she asked.

"Not long," he murmured, his fingers drawing figure-eights on her back. "How do you feel?"

"Happy," she answered without thinking, and his smile widened. She stretched with a wince and lifted herself onto an elbow to take the burden from his arm. "Sore," she admitted. She flattened a hand over his heart, relishing its steady thump against her palm. "You?"

"Reluctant to get out of bed," he answered.

"You could just stay here," she suggested.

His expression suddenly serious, he said, "I won't leave again if you ask me to stay."

She was surprised. It certainly hadn't been weighing on her mind, and she didn't like to think it had bothering him this whole time. "I shouldn't have asked you to stay, earlier," she said. "It was selfish and unfair." When he opened his mouth, she shook her head and pressed a finger to his lips. "Please, believe me. I never would've forgiven myself if you'd stayed. And I was only kidding, Colin, I know you have things to see to. I need to find Timón, anyway, and see what I should be doing."

"You should stay here, and rest," he said. "Timón will say the same, if he knows what's good for him."

"I'm sure that scowl would intimidate him, but it won't work on me, Captain Swan," she said. "Although if you ordered me to stay here, I would," she added, hesitantly.

He smiled. "I doubt that," he answered.

"Well, I don't react well to being told what to do..." she admitted.

"I've noticed a hint of stubbornness in you," he teased.

"Gee, glad you don't have any of that," she returned.

He laughed and kissed her forehead. "Would you consider staying here and resting, just for today, if I asked you very, very nicely?"

"How nicely?" she asked, raising her eyebrows.

"Very nicely," he murmured, tucking her hair behind her ear.

"Well, if I stay here, I won't have anything to do all day except think of things to do tonight," she said.

"Hmm," he answered. "Maybe you should go to work, after all."

She laughed and slapped gently at his chest. "I have to check on Luca, and

249

I want to see the dragon, but...I promise I won't do much, today, if it makes you happy."

"That does make me happy."

"Alright, then," she said. "So long as you promise to reward me for good behavior when you come back tonight."

"I might be awfully tired..."

"Well, then, you can just lay here and doze and I'll have my way with you."

He leaned his head back into the pillow and laughed. "I might be able to contribute something," he allowed.

"Maybe if I put on something special? Like...what I'm wearing now?"

"That damned door had better be locked, then."

She grinned. "I'll just leave the curtains open, though, so I can see when you're on your way."

He growled, and she laughed at his scowl. "Maybe I should lock you in the dungeon," he suggested.

"That might solve your problem," she agreed.

"It would cause a mutiny, I'm sure," he said. "Not that I would notice, as I'd be spending all my time in the dungeon," he added with a sudden, breathtaking smile.

"Is it raining?" she asked after a minute.

"Yes. It probably will for the next day or so, but...we shouldn't hit any more bad weather for a little while. We'll have to get the new mast up and try to make up some time. What?" he asked, shifting to see her face better.

"Ivan was right, wasn't he? You can sort of...feel the weather?"

He hesitated. "I've spent a lot of time on the sea," he said. He was hedging a bit, but she decided not to press the issue. There would be time for talking later. They had things they needed to do, and the longer they stayed in bed, the harder it would be to leave its comfort.

So, with regret, she said, "Alright, let's get up before I change my mind. If I go get some lunch, will you have time to eat with me, or should I just bring you something on the deck?" After getting cleaned up, and before going to sleep, they'd shared her bowl of breakfast. Now her stomach rumbled at the thought of food, and she blushed. It was frightening, how dependent she'd become on regular meals.

"You can eat when you go below. I'll grab something in an hour or so. We can have supper together, later."

"Naked?" she suggested.

He laughed. "Depends on what's for supper, I suppose," he said.

*　*　*

"Is she hurt?" Ella asked, looking up at the dragon. The day was gray, and the rain, lighter than the night before but steady, ran between her scales in rivulets.

"Well, she flew, so that's a good sign," Swan said, also looking up at the huge animal. He knew that the cabin was sturdily built enough to bear her weight, even though she appeared impossibly heavy for the wooden frame. "I'm worried about her skin," he said, gesturing toward her legs and underside, where the scales were softened and grayed by the ocean, and where the sealife had nibbled away bits of her tough flesh. "I think she should be able to heal, though...when it stops raining and she's able to dry out..."

"What's she going to eat?"

"Fish, mostly, I suppose," Swan answered. "It's the one thing we can replenish easily."

"Do dragons eat fish?" Ella asked, doubt evident in her tone.

"Probably not her first choice of diet, but she'll eat it if she's hungry enough," he assured her, and Ella turned toward him, squinting against the trickles of rain catching in her eyelashes.

"How do you know so much about dragons?" she asked.

Swan shrugged. His wet hair was plastered to his forehead, and she longed to push it back. She refrained, unsure whether he was open to displays of affection in front of his men. "I've always had a bit of a fascination with them, I suppose. I don't have any firsthand experience, or anything," he added, tipping his head. "You should get out of the rain. We should have the new mast in place in another hour or so, then we'll run the sail and—what?"

It was her turn to shrug. "I didn't really know you could, like, change a whole mast in the middle of the ocean," she said. She was continually awed by his preparedness and resourcefulness, and even without sailing experience, she knew that crew members on other ships would not be so well taken care of.

"The ocean is...unforgiving," he said. "All we can do is plan for the worst and hope we didn't need to. How's Luca?"

The sudden shift in topics caught her by surprise. "He's fine," she said. "He doesn't know what happened. None of the men told him."

"Are you going to?" he asked. His expression was unreadable, and she was bothered by her inability to read what he was thinking. She could understand his moods so well, sometimes, and other times he was closed off completely.

"Later," she answered. "When he's feeling better. There's no sense worrying him now that it's over."

Swan nodded. "I hear Goonie is doing better. They set his arm."

"Yes," she agreed, wondering why she felt so awkward. She supposed it was not knowing what he was thinking, or feeling, or what he wanted. When they were alone in his cabin, it was different. Out in the open, with the crew working busily about the deck, she didn't know what was expected of her. "I'll let you get back to work. Do you need me to do anything?"

"Just get dried off and rest, sweetheart," he said. He seemed surprised by the endearment, and fell silent, regarding her in the rain.

"I'll see you later, then," she finally answered. She didn't want to leave him and didn't know how to stay with him. She would have to retire to his cabin and find some way to be patient. "Hopefully not too much later," she muttered.

He noted her darkening cheeks with a smile that made them darken even more. "No," he said. "As soon as I can."

"Then I'll be waiting," she said, turning toward the cabin before she could give in to the impulse to kiss his rain-slick lips.

"With the door locked," he said, behind her.

"Yes, Cap," she called, without looking back, and she heard his low chuckle.

*   *   *

She did lock the door, even though she knew that no one else would enter without knocking. The curtains were already drawn against the beauty of the setting sun, and the cooling bowls of stew were on the desk. She knew she should probably be ashamed of her wantonness, and her eagerness, but she wasn't. She was anxious to see him, to touch him, to see his eyes darken with desire, and to feel his body pressing hers into the bed. She smiled and hugged herself at the thought, sitting on the bed and drawing her legs up. She was still a little sore, although she hadn't done much of anything for the latter half of the day.

She heard the slight rattle of the door handle only because she was waiting for it. Was he testing her, to make sure she'd locked the door as instructed? She supposed she should be offended, or annoyed, but she couldn't summon anything other than anticipation and a burst of happiness at his arrival. His key turned in the lock, and she waited for the door to open. Instead, he knocked, two short raps on the wood.

"Come in," she called, and the door opened.

His dark hair was plastered to his head from the wind and rain, spiked across his forehead in wet clumps. The lowering sun, behind, made his head glisten. His clothes were wet and clingy, and his cheeks were pinked from the cool wind. He must be the most gorgeous man in the world, and she felt a flicker of self-doubt. How could someone like him possibly want her? The flicker died away at the heat in his gaze when their eyes met. She might not understand how or why, but he did want her, and she knew that was true. She had to learn how to let go of her insecurities.

He looked amazing, but he also looked cold and wet. And tired.

He closed the door and locked it. She had lanterns lit, and they were suddenly the only light in the room. The rest of the world seemed to have disappeared. Her stomach squirmed in anticipation.

"Hi," he said, a small smile quirking his lips.

"Hi," she answered. "Is everything alright?"

"With the ship? Sure. We were already behind schedule, of course, so there's no way we can make the time up completely, but if we don't run into any more problems..."

He trailed off, and she found herself thinking of Goonie, telling her that it was considered bad luck to have a woman on board. Even without necessarily subscribing to the superstition, she couldn't fault the logic, in this case—she had been the cause of much of the trouble on *Voyage*, and she would do everything within her power to avoid causing more for the duration of their trip. She didn't need any more delays keeping her from Travis, and she also didn't want to see any more harm come to the crew or the ship.

"Is everything alright...*not* with the ship?" she asked. Then, before he could answer, "You look tired."

He smiled. "I *was* tired, until I walked in here," he said.

She was relieved, glad to know he was happy to see her, but she sighed, anyway. "Then why are you still over there? You always stand on the other side of the room, where I can't touch you," she said.

"That's because the closer I get to you, the less I can think," he answered. He crossed the room and stopped at the edge of the bed, frowning down at her. "What's wrong?" he asked, reaching out a hand to tuck her hair behind her ear.

She put her feet on the floor, and he took half a step backward to make room for her to stand. His frown had deepened. She raised a hand and brushed at the crease between his brows with her thumb. "I missed you," she admitted, and his expression softened.

"Did you?" he breathed.

She nodded and leaned against him, pressing her face against his chest and putting her arms around him. His shirt was cool and wet against her forehead, and against the front of her shirt, but his heat quickly fought its way through.

"I don't want to get you wet," he said.

"No? I thought you did," she answered, and her face instantly burned with embarrassment. Luckily, she was mostly hidden from view against his damp shirt. She heard, and felt, his quick intake of breath. "I can't believe I said that," she muttered.

"Neither can I," he said, and she could hear the amusement in his voice. His arms wrapped around her, warm and strong and solid, and she reveled for a moment in the sense of security his embrace gave her. "I do like the way your mind works, though."

"Since I met you, my mind's been constantly in the gutter," she said, and he laughed, his arms tightening around her. She grinned against his chest. She wasn't sure there was anything better than making him laugh. Well...there might be something better. She pulled her head back to look at him. His face was dark with stubble; he had smudges beneath his eyes. She promised herself that, this time, she wouldn't fall asleep until he had. "Are you hungry?" she asked. He must be. The stew was probably cold, but there were worse things in the world.

A dimple appeared in his cheek when he smiled.

She tried to scowl and failed. "I meant for supper," she said, and she was rewarded with another chuckle. She sighed. "Come on," she said, tugging on the front of his wet shirt. "Let's get this eating thing over with so we can get onto the fun stuff."

He laughed and put his arm across her shoulders, following her lead toward the desk. "You really are insatiable, aren't you?" he asked.

"Is that bad?" she asked, feigning concern.

He bent his head and kissed the corner of her mouth, sending a mixture of desire and frustration rippling through her. She wanted to grab his hair and bring his mouth back to hers, and the twinkle in his eyes told her he knew exactly how his touch affected her. "Best surprise of my life, actually," he said. He pulled the chair back for her and gestured with a flourish.

"You need to get out of your wet clothes," she told him as she sank into her seat. "Before you catch pneumonia."

"I imagine it would be ungentlemanly to sit down to supper with a lovely lady, such as yourself, in my birthday suit," he said, circling behind the desk.

"I won't tell anyone," she said, grinning, refraining from pointing out, again, that she was certainly no lady. "Do you need help?"

"You're determined to turn me into a scoundrel, aren't you?" he asked, with a scowl that contradicted that peeking dimple in his dark cheek.

"I'll take mine off, if you take yours off," she challenged, and when she saw his eyebrows lift in speculation, she almost called her offer back. She resisted. She wouldn't let embarrassment get the best of her. In fact, she decided she wasn't going to wait for his response. She shifted so she could pull the shirt from under her, and she stripped it up over her head before she could chicken out. She was completely naked on the chair, the air cool against her flushed skin. It was a strange and heady mix of embarrassment, vulnerability, freedom...and power. He'd stopped breathing, and his pupils were dilated, and his hands were in fists at his sides, and her stomach squirmed at the desire she saw in his face. "Your turn," she said, amazed she could speak at all.

He cleared his throat and dragged his eyes up to hers. "You do know you're beautiful, don't you?" he asked.

She flushed with pleasure and embarrassment, and gave her head a little shake. His eyebrows immediately slid into a frown. "I'm glad you think so," she muttered, because there was no denying he found her attractive. The evidence, if she needed any more, was straining at the front of his damp trousers.

"Tell me what you don't like about yourself," he said. His expression was serious, his voice commanding but soft.

"Why?" she asked, hesitantly. She certainly didn't want him to start seeing her the way she saw herself, and pointing out all of her flaws was setting a mood very different than the one she wanted.

"Please," he said.

"Will you take off your clothes?" she asked.

A small smile appeared and vanished. "Deal," he said.

She hesitated again. She hadn't meant to make a deal, and she considered for several moments while he waited, regarding her in silence. "I'm too skinny," she finally said, unsure. She glanced away. She knew that was one thing that had bothered him from the start.

"You are skinny," he agreed, and his musing tone made her pull her gaze back to his. "Not so much as before, though. Besides, that's not a flaw—it's a sign of a hard life and of putting others' needs before your own." His words were reassuring, but she was distracted by his fingers—slowly unbuttoning his shirt as he spoke. He pulled the damp shirt off and tossed it over the back of his unoccupied chair. "Next?" he asked.

The sight of his bare chest had driven most coherent thought from her mind. "Um," she said, and he quirked an eyebrow. "I'm uh...impulsive," she managed.

He frowned. "Reckless, you might even say," he agreed. "Although only when you see someone who needs help." He bent his leg up and pulled off a shoe, tossing it beside the door. Then he followed suit with the other.

She didn't want to rehash the fight with Blondie, and how she'd caused it by jumping in—literally—without verifying the facts, first. "I don't apologize well," she admitted without thinking. The words surprised her, and she felt a squirm of uneasiness. That somehow felt like a more personal admission than the others. It was something she truly disliked about herself, and something she'd tried to work on.

He stripped off one sock, then the other, and tossed them onto the back of his chair with his shirt. "Makes it mean more when you do," he said with a small shrug. "Besides, I don't like it when you're sorry."

She realized that she was supposed to be naming physical traits she didn't like about herself, not character flaws. Why didn't she think she was beautiful? Or, rather, how did she know she wasn't? She chewed on her lip for a moment, looking at the floor. She thought of Meena, and her stomach churned. "My breasts are small," she said in a rush, "My skin is too pale, I always have circles under my eyes, I'm too skinny, my feet are too big, I've got freckles—"

"Come here," he said, and she looked up, startled. He was scowling, all trace of humor gone from his eyes. His look, and the command in his voice, should be intimidating, but when he held out a hand, she reached for it automatically. He tugged her to her feet, and before she knew what he meant to do, he'd scooped her up into his arms and was turning toward the bed. His bare chest was cooler than she'd expected, his skin a bit clammy from the damp shirt he'd removed. His arms were warm and hard.

"But you didn't finish undressing," she objected.

"The deal's off," he said.

"That's not fair," she answered, although she couldn't care much less about the deal they'd struck. She wanted him out of his clothes, not in the interest of fairness, but because she was eager to see and touch his body.

He laid her on the bed without comment, and she looked up at him, trying to figure out what he was thinking. He was bent over her, and as he studied her face, his expression softened, and he lowered his head. She expected to be kissed, and was disappointed when his lips pressed against her nose instead of her mouth. "I like the way the sun brings out your freckles," he said, trailing kisses down to the corner of her mouth. She turned her head, instinctively, and he dodged her kiss. She squirmed impatiently. He ran the pad of a thumb, lightly, beneath her eye. "You don't sleep enough, because you worry too much. You don't get enough sun, because you work too much. I don't know about your feet, but your breasts fit my hands perfectly," he said, demonstrating by cupping one in his palm. "What was the other thing?"

"What?" she gasped as his hand slid over her hip. "I don't know..."

"Oh. Too skinny," he said, and his hand curved under her hip and she could feel his fingers on the inside back of her thigh, just inches from her most sensitive place, and her legs shifted apart automatically. "I think we covered that one," he murmured, and before she could even make sense of the words, he'd dipped his head and pulled a nipple into his mouth and she made a sound that she barely heard over the thudding of her heart.

"I want you," she managed, frustrated by the wet cloth of trousers between them. His hand was cupping her butt, and she wanted desperately for his fingers to move a little further. "You aren't even...undressed," she gasped, tilting her head back against the pillow as his tongue tortured her nipple. She realized her hands were in his hair, and in a moment of resolve, she tugged his head up so he was looking at her. Her breast popped free of his mouth, and she almost laughed at the sight. His expression was still serious, even troubled, though, in spite of the sheen of desire in his eyes. "Take your pants off," she said.

"Tell me something you like about yourself," he countered in a low, gravelly voice.

She frowned. "Trying to strike a new deal? After you backed out of the last one?" she asked, half-jokingly.

He lowered his head until his lips were mere inches from hers, his hot breath fanning her face. "That deal was an exceptionally bad idea on my part," he murmured, his hooded gaze holding hers. "You're beautiful, Ella. I know you don't see it, although I had no idea how low your opinion of yourself was."

She shifted beneath him, desperate to be closer to him, and under his hot scrutiny she actually *felt* beautiful. It was because of the way he saw her, however, not how she saw herself. Could she think of something she liked about herself? She knew she should be able to. She didn't back away from fights that needed to be fought, and that was something. Considering the stupid mistakes she'd made while on the ship, however, she didn't think that was the best quality to mention. She liked her eyes, because they were the only part of her in which she could sometimes see her mother.

Her body was tingly and achy with desire, and her mind was consumed with thoughts of Swan. He was all she could think of, all she wanted to think about.

"I like the way you make me feel," she heard herself say.

"I like the way you feel," he countered with a smirk.

Emboldened by his obvious desire, she slid a hand between them and cupped his crotch. His eyes widened and he hissed in surprise, his body tensing. "I like this," she said, with a smirk of her own.

"Do you," he grated, his eyes narrowing. He bent his head. His breath tickled her ear. "While that definitely belongs to you, I meant something—"

"I don't want to talk about me," she said, the fullness of his erection in her hand making it difficult for her to keep from ripping his pants off his hips. "Please, Colin," she said, turning her face toward him.

He met her lips with an eagerness that matched her own, and she fumbled at the button of his trousers. "I love the taste of your mouth," he murmured against her lips, and her heart skidded at the 'L' word. For a moment, her fingers faltered at his button. She wanted to tell him that she loved him, more than she'd ever wanted to say anything, and she wasn't sure what was stopping her. Fear? She was afraid. Of rejection. Of being hurt. Of hurting him, even more so. Of losing Travis. Of admitting to Swan that she'd been lying, and seeing the disappointment and distrust in his eyes.

He pulled his head back a bit to look at her. She thought he was going to say it. She didn't know how to feel, how to react. If he said he loved her, would that make it easier? Or harder?

"And the taste of everything else," he said, after a moment, and ducked his head to her breast. She felt a rush of relief, and tried not to think about it. She managed to unbutton his fly, finally, and she tugged the wet material apart, pushing it down his hips. While she struggled against the frustrating trousers, he slid a finger into her, making her gasp in surprise and pleasure. "You are eager," he murmured as she automatically spread her legs further.

"You made me this way!" she said, and he chuckled against her nipple. "I didn't know I could feel—ah," she cried when his finger ventured further inside. She tipped her head back, clutching at his bare hips. "Please, I can't get your damn pants off," she managed after a few seconds, and he laughed again at the frustration in her voice.

"Insatiable, love?" he asked, his amusement evident.

She didn't freak out at the endearment. He'd used the word, in that context, many times. "Insatiable?" she asked, glaring at him. "It's been all day! I've been sitting here, behaving myself, bored out of my—"

"Ah, so this is your reward?" he asked, arching a brow.

She narrowed her eyes. Before he knew what she meant to do, she slid her hands into the front of his stubborn trousers, cupping his erection. He jerked in her grasp, gasping, and closed his eyes. "Fuck," he muttered raggedly.

"I've been trying," she quipped.

His laugh was strained. His finger slid into her, again, and twisted, and he smiled at her. So, two could play that game. Oh, how they could torment each other, she thought as she flexed her hand. His jaw tightened, and she caught her breath as a second finger joined his first. "You're a quick study," he muttered.

"Does that mean you like it?" she asked. She was half-joking. She could certainly tell how she was affecting him, but since she had almost no experience, she was still afraid of doing something wrong—something that he wouldn't like or, worse, something that would hurt him. As much as she wanted her own release, a part of her wished he'd stop his ministrations so she could focus on pleasing him.

"Yes," he hissed. "God, Ella," he said, suddenly withdrawing from her hand and shifting his hips away. He was breathing raggedly, and for a moment she was afraid she'd done what she'd feared—that she'd somehow hurt him. He saw her expression, and bent his head, murmuring against her lips, "It'd be a shame to finish early, love." Then he kissed her, and his tongue was slow. His finger was moving quickly, however, and she felt her body tightening and building toward orgasm.

She felt a flare of desperation as she tried to resist the coming wave, afraid he was going to finish her off with his fingers without getting anything for himself. She was lightheaded from lack of air, and his tongue was mimicking the motion of his fingers, and she was powerless to fight the rising tide. She almost pushed him away, but then he was above her, his hand replaced by the head of his erection, and she felt a rush of relief. She clutched at his shoulders, trying to pull him closer, and as he sank into her, she wrapped her legs around his hips, instinctively pulling him all the way in.

He made a sound of surprise and pleasure, and turned his mouth from hers to catch a breath. He was sheathed completely, and for long moments, he stayed still, his muscles quivering with the effort. Then he moved slowly, and she gasped, calling his name, her arms and legs around him.

His hot breath fanned her ear, and then his mouth was under her jaw, and she tipped her head to give him better access. She wanted to beg him to move faster, and couldn't form the words. As though reading her mind, his pace quickened, and he thrust into her, and again, harder and faster, and she felt herself beginning to come undone.

"Come on, sweetheart," he said, hoarsely, against her throat, and the gentle command was enough to push her over the edge. Her body twitched and spasmed, tightening as the world splintered. He made a sound in his throat and started to withdraw. Still convulsing around him, acting purely on instinct, she locked her legs around his hips, desperate to keep him with her. "Ella," he said, and his hands were braced on the bed on either side of her. She knew that she was no match for him in strength, and if he was hell-bent on pulling away, he would.

"Please," she cried, clutching him, and his whole body was tense, hard. He made a noise, half-groan and half-growl, and claimed her mouth quickly, hungrily, and a bit desperately. With a final thrust, she felt him spill his seed inside of her, a strange and wonderful feeling, and the tremors passing through his body made her feel powerful and overwhelmingly happy. He finally turned his head so they could both breathe and, a moment later, he collapsed against her, his skin slick with sweat against hers. He shifted slightly so that he wasn't crushing her beneath him, but he was still sheathed within her, and when he laid his head against her breast, the gesture seemed filled with such vulnerability that she rested her hand on his damp hair. They were both breathing heavily, their chests rising and falling in unison.

She didn't want the moment to end. She wanted to stay, joined with him, forever.

She did wonder if he would be angry, though. He didn't want her to get pregnant; she understood that. They barely knew each other, and she certainly didn't want to get pregnant, either. While the very idea of having Swan's baby was appealing—dangerously, unexpectedly appealing—she knew that it would be selfish and irresponsible. She couldn't even feed herself, how could she be expected to provide for a child? Swan had money, of course, but she would not allow him to be tied to her and a child he didn't want.

She was worrying about ridiculous things, however, and she again forced her mind back into the moment. She ran her fingers, slowly, through the damp, dark curls of his hair, swirling lightly at his temple, as their mingled breathing slowed. She didn't want him to be upset with her. There had been no ulterior motives behind her actions; her body had wanted to claim him, all of him, and her brain had been several steps behind.

His breathing had returned to normal, and the sweat was cooling on their bodies. She wondered if she should break the silence. As she was trying to find the words, trying to decide if she should muster an apology or explanation, he finally stirred, levering his hips to slide—slowly and carefully—out of her. A sense of achy hollowness replaced the fullness, and with it came disappointment. Would he leave? Leave the bed, get dressed, and leave the cabin?

He rolled onto his side, facing her, and she turned her head to look at him, afraid of what she might see. His face was shadowed, his expression difficult to read, but after a moment he shifted and pressed his lips against hers, softly, gently. He tucked her hair behind her ear, and she felt relief. Still afraid he might be readying to push her away, however, she squirmed a little closer, and he put an arm over her. She snuggled her head under his chin, her relief making way for happiness, and she found herself smiling against his chest. No matter what might happen down the road, she would never allow herself to regret this time.

He moved his arm, just long enough to pull a blanket over their cooled bodies, and then he wrapped her in his warm embrace and kissed her temple. He hadn't said anything, and she lay there, heavy-lidded, relaxed, half-asleep, still wondering if she should say something. All the tension had eased from her body, though, and she could feel herself losing the battle to stay awake.

"You didn't get to eat," she murmured sleepily.

"In the morning, love," he answered softly. "Go to sleep."

"You won't leave?" she asked. She couldn't seem to open her eyes.

After a hesitation, he said, "No, Ella. Just sleep, honey."

She was drifting away, and she wanted to make him promise that he would sleep, too. She wanted to stay awake until he fell asleep, to make sure he rested. She'd promised herself she would. His arms were warm and solid, the blanket soft and comforting, their mingled heat and breathing soothing, and she slid into sleep.

When she woke, she was facing the wall, alone in the bed. She blinked, trying to clear the sleep from her mind and eyes, and rolled toward the inside of the cabin. She was afraid he'd changed his mind, and left her alone, after all. He was sitting behind the desk, however, and as she turned over, their eyes met. As she was still trying to decide whether or not this counted as him leaving her, he spoke.

"Morning," he said, quietly. The curtains were still drawn, but the sun was peeking past the edges. The sea felt pretty calm, and she wondered if they were making up time, yet.

"Morning," she answered, stretching. "How'd you get out of bed without waking me?" she asked.

He offered a small smile. "You seemed pretty exhausted."

"Did you sleep?" she asked, trying to fight down her guilt.

"Sure," he answered. Then, almost reluctantly, "Some."

She opened her mouth, then hesitated. "Were you...upset...?" she asked. She propped herself up on her elbow, to better gauge his expression.

He raised an eyebrow. "Upset?" he repeated, seeming to taste the word. He studied her for a few moments, then rose and crossed toward the bed. Despite her worries, she felt her stomach flutter in appreciation at the sight of his bare chest. He was wearing a pair of black trousers, and nothing else. His jaw was stubbled, as it seemed to be a lot, lately, his hair mussed. His eyes were dark and serious.

He sat on the edge of the bed in front of her stomach and laid a hand on her hip. "I didn't mean..." She stopped, biting her lip. "I wasn't—"

"Ella," he said, and the soft sound of her name sent a shiver of awareness through her. "I didn't want to disturb your sleep. That's the only reason I left the bed. I'm sorry if I made you think..." He frowned. "I'm not upset, honey. Last night was...perfect." While she could tell that he was being sincere, and even though his words made her happy, she could see something else, as well—he was determined that it would not happen again. He didn't need to say so. And it was alright, because in the light of morning, she fully realized how irresponsible she'd been. She'd let her body override her common sense, and it didn't matter that he wouldn't let it happen again—*she* wouldn't let it happen, again.

She told herself that the twinge of hurt she felt was ridiculous. Of course, she couldn't blame him for being determined not to get her pregnant; as she'd told herself last night, they barely knew each other and had certainly made no promises to one another.

"You look tired," she said.

He smiled. "You look beautiful," he countered. "Don't worry about me. I do have things to see to, however. Now that you're awake, I really hate to leave, but..." He tucked her tangle of hair behind her ear. "I'll come back as soon as I can."

"I have work to do, anyway," she said. He seemed unhappy with her words, but he didn't object. "You look beautiful, too," she muttered after a moment, blushing. She lowered her face, embarrassed, and he put a finger beneath her chin to gently lift it back up.

"Thank you," he said. "Even if I know it's untrue. Now, do you need anything?"

She shook her head, and bit her lip. "Just you, but I guess I can wait," she said, and she was rewarded with a sudden grin.

He leaned forward, propping himself on one hand behind her back, and kissed her. It was fairly chaste, and full of promise. "I hope I can, too," he said.

"Were you...waiting for me to wake up?" she asked, hesitantly. "To leave, I mean?"

"I might have been watching you sleep," he said, smirking at her. "I promised I wouldn't leave, Ella."

"I know," she answered. She pressed her fingertips against the dark curls on his breastbone. She could feel his heartbeat. "I didn't mean to keep you from...Thank you," she said.

"Eat something?"

She sighed. "Yes," she agreed.

He grinned, and her breath caught. "Feel free to stay here all day, if you'd like, although I doubt you will."

"I think I can manage to be waiting when you come back," she said, smiling, and he laughed.

He bent and kissed her again. "I'll make the day go as quickly as I can," he murmured, and then he was crossing the room to get dressed.

Chapter Thirteen

"Has she eaten anything?" Ella asked.

Swan shook his head. "We tried fish, even a little boar from Tarot, vegetables...She isn't interested. She's barely moved. Ivan said she's flown out over the water a few times, at night, to, uh...relieve herself, but not as much as she should. She's dehydrated," he said, pointing toward the dragon's underside. They could see that her scales were gray and flaky, especially on her lower half. Her wounds did not seem to be healing, either.

The dragon was awake, and regarding them solemnly with one large eye. She'd shown no signs of aggression, just as she'd shown no interest in the food or water given to her. She'd been on the ship for a week. If she didn't improve soon, Swan was afraid he was going to find himself with a dead dragon atop his cabin.

"Is she sick?" Ella asked.

Swan stared into that large, yellow eye, considering the question. "It might sound crazy," he answered, after a bit, "but I think...she's..."

"Sad," Ella supplied.

"Depressed," Swan agreed, looking at Ella in surprise. "Yes. I don't know why she was out here in the middle of the ocean, but whatever the reason...she isn't fighting to live."

Ella shifted, and her arm brushed against his. The contact was brief and deliberate, and unusual. She was usually so careful not to touch him while there were men around. Whenever he was near her, Swan wanted to kiss her, touch her, hold her...He'd respected her unspoken desire to avoid public displays of affection, however, and he'd resisted the urge to ask her why she was so determined to act as though there was nothing between them. It wasn't as if the men didn't know; they were far from stupid.

Was she ashamed of their relationship? She didn't seem to be when they were alone.

Relationship? his mind mocked. *Is that what you have?* The truth was, he didn't know. He knew that they'd made love every night, and he couldn't think of it as anything less than that. It wasn't just sex, and he knew that he was not alone in feeling that way. Their lovemaking had often been slow and gentle, sometimes rough and quick, and had always left him physically relaxed and mentally anxious.

Actually, it was scaring the hell out of him. He found himself searching the deck, all day, for some glimpse of her while she was working. When he hadn't seen her for an hour, he made up an excuse to seek her out or send for her. In fact, he'd gone below more times in the past few days than in the whole previous season, and all because he couldn't stand to be out of her presence for any length of time.

He knew almost nothing about her, still. She wouldn't talk about her childhood, her personal life. She didn't come right out and say she wouldn't talk about it, but she dodged his infrequent questions and changed the subject, and he didn't push. He tried to tell himself it was respect for her privacy, respect for her desire to avoid certain topics. Wasn't he afraid, though? Afraid of what her answers might be? Afraid that she might come right out and say, that when the ship anchored in Bohannon, she would leave? Leave with Luca, perhaps? Or, leave alone. Her reasons for sneaking onto the ship were still unclear, and without knowing the purpose for her dangerous journey, how could Swan possibly hope to guess what her plans might include?

He sighed, and felt her gaze on him. He avoided her eyes for a moment, thinking. Sometimes, she seemed to read him perfectly, to understand him the way no one—*no one*—had ever done before. Particularly while they were making love, they had grown to know every breath the other took, every nuance of feeling, they'd come to know exactly what the other needed and when. At other times, when she was looking at him, he felt as though she could actually read his mind. He wasn't accustomed to such intimacy, and even though it scared him, he found that—to his surprise—he didn't want to run from it. He wanted to embrace it. He wanted to share every part of himself, for the first time in his life. He wanted to share all of himself with someone who was willing to share next to nothing of herself, and he had to figure out what he was going to do about that.

He turned his head to look at her, and was struck as much by her beauty as by the frown marring her forehead. She was worried, and not just about the dragon. She was worried by Swan's mood, and he knew that they could only pretend for so long. They could only ignore the real world for a little while, because the further they sailed, the closer the real world was. He reached out a hand and smoothed her forehead with the pad of his thumb, smiling. Some of the tension eased from her, and he lowered his arm, mindful of her avoidance of public contact.

"I hope she gets better," she said.

Swan turned his attention back to the dragon. Its eyes were closed, its head resting on its feet like a dog's, its tail curled around its body, its wings folded in. He sighed, again. He knew that fish would probably not be her first choice, but if she wanted to eat, she would accept the offerings they'd presented over the past few days. He walked toward the front of the cabin and climbed up so that he was looking at her lethal talons, curled under her chin.

"Hey," he said, and the eye closest to him opened, gleaming in the sun. The most recent fish were laid on the roof of the cabin beside her, slowly spoiling in the sun. They would have to be discarded in a few hours, if she didn't decide to eat. It was a waste of food, a waste of time, effort, and resources to catch the fish, and worst of all, it was an unnecessary expenditure of life. Swan did not take any life lightly, even that of a fish, and he wondered how long, in good conscience, he could continue to make the effort.

The dragon's eye seemed to stare right into him, and she made no move—didn't even tense at his close proximity, or the sound of his voice. She just stared at him, and he knew that he had to do whatever he could to help her heal. She'd saved the lives of Goonie and Ella.

She'd also saved her own life, by flying onto the ship as soon as she was able, and that indicated hope. Maybe a little bit of that fight was still in her, somewhere. Swan reached out a hand, toward her snout.

"Col—Captain Swan, please be careful," Ella said, softly, and he looked down at her, hesitating. She was watching him with a hand at her face, radiating tension. She was afraid for him, even after she'd climbed onto the back of the same dragon.

"Don't worry, l-lass," he said, changing from 'love' to 'lass' with a slight stutter. He saw her lips twitch in the hint of a smile. "She won't hurt me." He glanced toward Ivan, and the small group of crewmen gathered near the railing, before turning his attention back to the animal. "Will you, girl?" he asked, pitching his voice low. She blinked, and when he closed the distance between his hand and her nose, she didn't flinch. Her snout was cool and dry, and he gave her a light pat. "Good girl. Now, you and I both know that you can heal yourself up, good as new." He was pretty sure that was true, anyway. Dragons were famous more for their healing abilities than anything else. "All you have to do is eat and drink, get your strength up a little. You can do that, right?"

She blinked, slowly, and gave a small snort, surprising him. The intelligence in her gaze was unmistakable, just as the sadness was, and he found himself wishing that she could speak to him, to tell him what was wrong.

"You don't like fish?" he asked, and it didn't escape him that he probably looked like an idiot to the men below. "What about some water? You can drink some water, right?" he asked, indicating the bowl beside the fish. An animal of her size would swallow that much liquid in a lick, but she hadn't touched it. "You don't want any?" he asked, his stomach sinking when she simply blinked again. "You're unhappy, huh?" he murmured, sighing. "Were you trying to get somewhere?" A blink. "To someone?" he asked, and she shifted, until he could suddenly see both large eyes. His stomach fluttered at the realization that she could kill him in an instant, and he'd probably never even know it was coming. His fear was quick to pass, however, because he knew that she wouldn't hurt him. Just as he'd trusted that she would allow Ella and Goonie to find sanctuary from the sea on her back, he knew that she meant him no harm.

He glanced down at Ella, who was still nervous.

He leaned closer to the dragon, and lowered his voice even further, so that no one but the animal could hear him over the rush of wind. "We're going to Bohannon. I don't know if you know where that is, or not, but if you were looking for someone, you won't be able to keep looking if you die before we get there." The dragon stared at him, and he wondered if it was her baby, or some other family member. Dragons were very familial, and some humans were ruthless, killing adults for their blood, bone, talons, scales, teeth, milk, and anything else they could think to harvest, but also capturing the young and selling them for huge profits. The baby dragons were sometimes put in carnival shows, sometimes tortured for the entertainment of the depraved, and sometimes even slaughtered and sold as delicacies.

Swan's stomach was churning at the thought, and he prayed that if this dragon's baby had been stolen, it could be found alive and well somewhere.

"There's still hope, right?" he asked, softly. He wondered, though. Was it dead, whoever, whatever, she was looking for? Could she sense it? Was that why she'd given up? He didn't think so, though, because she stirred again at his words. "Still hope," he repeated, looking down at Ella.

*   *   *

Ella wanted desperately to climb up there and put herself between Swan and the dragon. The animal had given no signs of aggression, and Swan was showing no signs of fear, but Ella would not relax until he was down on the deck beside her again.

She couldn't hear what he was saying, but he seemed to have captured the dragon's interest, at least. As Ella watched, Swan glanced down at her, then leaned even closer to the dragon to murmur something. Ella's heart stuttered at how close his face was to the dragon's. She held her breath, waiting.

The dragon blinked, and the eye closest to Ella shifted, and suddenly the dragon was looking at her with one large, slitted pupil. Ella was frozen, stunned by the sudden eye contact, and it wasn't fear that she was feeling, exactly. As the dragon regarded her, she was filled with a sense of awe— amazement at the enormity of the animal, the intelligence in its gaze, and the fact that it was looking at her. Really and truly looking at her, as though it could read her mind.

Then the animal shifted a bit and Swan straightened. The dragon moved so quickly that Ella didn't even have time to register the lurch in her stomach, and the fish bodies were gone as though they'd been magicked away. Ella's heart slammed in her ribcage, and her hands shook, belatedly, even though Swan himself had never flinched. Ella wasn't sure if she wanted to hug him or hit him.

The dragon sucked up the water from the mixing bowl and once more laid her head on her feet.

"Thank you," Swan said. He grabbed the empty bowl and tossed it over Ella's head to Ivan, who caught it easily enough in spite of the look of startlement on his face. "We'll bring you some more in a bit," Swan said, with a quick pat on the dragon's nose.

Ella watched as he dropped gracefully to the deck and straightened. "What did you say to her?" she asked, impressed and glad that he'd convinced the dragon to eat even though her heart was still racing.

He smiled, but his eyes were serious. "I'll tell you later," he said.

She was surprised by his hesitance, her curiosity more than a little piqued. "Alright," she said. "Whatever it was, I'm glad it worked," she said, looking past him toward the dragon. "Although," she added, lowering her voice a little,

"I might kill you the next time you decide to practically crawl inside her mouth."

He laughed, and he seemed inexplicably relieved. She wondered again what he'd said, and why he didn't want to tell her. "She wasn't going to hurt me," he answered.

"Maybe not," Ella allowed. "Still..."

Grinning, he said, "I think we should call her something. How about Destiny?"

"I like it," Ella said. The odds against coming across the dragon, in the vast expanse of ocean, were unimaginable. She'd been there, though, just when Ella and Goonie had needed her the most. "Destiny," Ella murmured.

"I have work to do. I'll see you tonight, Ella."

She felt a shiver of anticipation at the silky promise in his voice, and knew by his dark gaze and flashing dimple that he was well aware of what she was thinking.

* * *

"Hey, Cap, I talk to you?"

Swan turned away from the sparkling sea to look at Ivan. "Of course," he said. "Something wrong?"

They'd been friends a long time, but they hadn't been talking much, lately, not outside of business. Not since the night of the storm, and the dragon. Swan knew that Ivan had almost certainly saved his life, and he was not ungrateful for that. He wasn't angry, anymore. Ivan was not the same, though. He was tense, terse with the crewmen, aloof...And whenever he was near the captain, he was all-business.

Now, he seemed nervous. Edgier than normal, even more so than he'd been lately. His demeanor immediately put Swan on alert.

"Think we can talk private?" Ivan asked.

Frowning, Swan said, "Sure. Come on in my room, I think Ella's below." In fact, he knew she was. Swan was very aware of her presence whenever she stepped foot on deck.

"She is," Ivan agreed, and something in his tone made Swan's neck prickle with apprehension.

He led the way into his cabin and gestured toward the chair in front of his desk. "Have a seat," he offered.

Ivan fidgeted. "Think I'd rather stand," he muttered, glancing around. He'd been in the cabin innumerable times, but Swan suddenly realized that Ivan had not stepped inside once since Ella had moved in. None of the men had. He found himself glancing around, as well, wondering if she had left an imprint on the room. She had no clothes to speak of—her ratty dress was folded away in the bottom drawer of his dresser, along with her shoes. She had no personal belongings, no toiletries. They shared everything, from the bed to the soap, and he didn't think the room looked any different than it always had.

He knew it *was* different, though. It no longer felt like *his* room. It felt like *theirs*, and that was a strange, and new, and not unpleasant, sensation. He looked back at Ivan to find the other man watching him. Swan cleared his throat, and took his seat behind the desk. "What's on your mind, Ivan?" he asked.

"I've known you a long time," Ivan began. Then he hesitated and, after a moment, began pacing slowly.

"Yes," Swan agreed, the knot of apprehension tightening in his stomach.

"You're my boss," Ivan continued. "But...you're my friend, too. Best one I ever had, actually. Longest, too." Although Swan was touched by this statement, it only made his worry increase. "I've never seen you like this."

Swan hesitated. "Like what?" he asked, wondering if he wanted to know the answer.

"Happy," Ivan said.

Swan was surprised. "Happy?" he repeated, frowning. "You've never seen me *happy*?"

"I've seen you...Well, not like this..." He stopped pacing and sighed, running his hand down his face. "I don't want to see you hurt."

"Why don't you just say what you want to say," Swan said. Did he really seem happier? His mood always lightened when he saw Ella, and even his worry about the future couldn't diminish the happiness he felt when they were together. Did he really seem different, though? Had she left more of a visible imprint on him than on the room?

"How much do you know about her?"

Almost nothing, was the immediate thought. "I know what I need to know," Swan said, bristling.

"You know she's still seeing Luca?"

Swan's stomach was churning in earnest, now. He could feel his face heating, and he forced himself to take a slow breath to keep from snapping something he might come to regret. "Luca is injured," he said, speaking carefully.

"They talk, whisper together in the corner, stop whenever someone comes by."

"Your point?"

"Talk about papers? About how she might say she's his fiancée to get into Bohannon? Because he has papers as a workman but she doesn't—"

"You overheard this conversation how, exactly?" Swan asked, trying not to think about the implications if Ivan's words were true.

"I heard them before they knew I was in the room," he answered. "I thought you should know that she—"

"I will not condone you spying on others on my ship," Swan interrupted.

Ivan stared at him, clearly caught off guard by the clipped words. "I've always been your eyes and ears on the ship," he finally said, hesitantly. "You've always depended on me to tell you what—"

"What happens amongst the crew while I'm not around—only if it affects their work, safety, or my ship. I've never asked you to relay to me their personal conversations—Nor have you ever offered to do so. Before now."

Ivan opened his mouth, then closed it again, frowning. His face was darkening in something akin to indignation. "With all due respect, Captain, if you are being blinded by lies, it affects the safety of all of us."

Swan couldn't fool himself into thinking Ivan's accusations about Ella were impossible. He would have to figure out his feelings on that matter later. His instinct to leap to her defense was clouding his judgment. Being accused of putting his personal feelings ahead of his concern for his crew, however, was unacceptable. He could feel slow, hot anger spreading through him.

"Blinded?" he repeated.

"If you don't know why she snuck on the ship—"

"Who says I don't know?" Swan asked, struggling to hold onto his temper.

"What? I...I said, 'if.' If you trust her, that's fine," Ivan said. "You know her better than me. I just mean that you don't see her all the time, and every spare second she has below she spends with the kid. Don't get me wrong, I like Ella. The whole crew does. She's not a bad girl, surely, but she'll do whatever it takes to get what she wants. Sleeping with her is one thing, but—"

Swan put his palms flat on the desk, to keep them from curling into fists, and rose to his feet. "You are dangerously out of line," he said, in a low voice. "Why Ella sneaked onto my ship is not your concern, it's mine. What she says or does with Luca, or anyone else, is her business. I respect her privacy. And you *will* show her respect. There will be no insinuations, no speculations, no assumptions, am I understood?"

Ivan was silent for several moments, as he tried to find a response. He was clearly taken-aback, perhaps even hurt, by Swan's reaction. Ivan was, after all, only trying to look out for the captain and the ship. His tactics were unacceptable, though. "Understood, sir," Ivan finally said. "My apologies."

"I'm not the one you've insulted," Swan answered. His body was practically thrumming with anger. He never could've imagined a scenario in which he would be fighting an urge to punch his friend in the face. "Unfortunately, you can't apologize to her because she will *not* know about what you've said. I can't stop the men from thinking whatever they want, but they'd better be keeping those thoughts to themselves."

Sounding subdued, Ivan said, "The men all like Ella, they wouldn't want to hurt her feelings."

"Good. Is there something else I can help you with?"

"No, sir," Ivan muttered.

Swan pulled in a deep breath, trying to calm his emotion. He thought that if he lifted his hands from the desk, they would shake. "I appreciate your concern," he said, but it sounded false and clipped to his own ears. He paused, then tried again. "I do, Ivan. I've always trusted you to keep me informed. You do see that this is different, though?" After a slight hesitation, Ivan nodded. "Then we're finished."

"Thank you, sir," Ivan said, heading toward the door.

Swan watched him leave, then sank back into his chair. He wanted to pace, to release the pent-up anger and frustration, but he forced himself to settle into his seat. He took a deep breath and let it out slowly. He had to gain control of his emotions. Underneath the anger were other, more complicated, emotions. He'd never asked Ella if she was still planning to marry Luca. Of course, he'd been thinking about it. There had been many times when the question was on the tip of his tongue. He didn't want to admit that he was afraid of the answer, but he knew that was part of it. The other part was a desire to respect her privacy and give her the space she needed to make whatever decisions she had to make. Didn't he think, perhaps, that giving her that space and respect would make her realize that she loved him, that she could have a future with him?

Did he think she'd been using him all along? No. He didn't. She'd never meant to be caught, but once she had been, she'd offered to do anything necessary to save herself and Luca. And, yes, she'd even offered her virginity to a complete stranger—although Swan hadn't realized it at the time. Things had changed, though, and they'd gotten to know each other. Not in details, it was true, he knew next to nothing about her life. He knew what she was capable of, however, and what she was willing to do to protect others. It wasn't just Luca. She'd almost died to save Goonie, and those were not the actions of a person bent on manipulating others for her own gain.

She might not love Swan, he wasn't so naïve that he couldn't accept that. She still didn't fully trust him, either. And, since he knew she would do anything necessary to protect those she loved, he had to admit that it was possible she would lie to him, sleep with him, and maybe even kill him if she had to, to protect Luca. She would never hurt anyone without a damned good reason, though, and Swan didn't think he'd shown himself to be a threat to Luca.

He sighed. She wasn't faking the connection they shared; he had to believe that, because what he felt for her was the most real thing in his life. Was it possible she was still planning to leave the ship with Luca, though? Yes, unfortunately. Swan had to decide if he wanted to ask.

* * *

Ella had decided that she needed to tell Swan the truth. About everything. He might be able to help her get her brother back. That was the most important thing. He might be angry. Hell, he *would* be angry, of course he would, and who could blame him? She'd lied, mostly by omission. He might never be able to forgive her, although he'd already forgiven her for other transgressions. In many ways, the other things she'd done—things that had endangered the lives of him and his crew—were worse, and yet she felt like her continued deception was the worst betrayal. She loved him, and she valued honesty. Would she ever be able to convince him of that once she'd told him the truth?

Not telling him about her brother was one thing. Not telling him about her childhood, that was understandable, as it was a mostly unhappy tale—at least after the deaths of her parents. It was not admitting the truth about her relationship with Luca that was upsetting her, and that she was worried about. Swan didn't ask her about her visits to see Luca in the bunks, but she could tell that he wanted to, and she could tell that it was troubling him. The longer she kept silent, the worse the deception seemed, and it really didn't matter that she'd never actually come out and said that she and Luca were engaged. She'd let Swan believe it, and even now that they'd come to know each other in the most intimates ways imaginable, he didn't know if she planned to disembark and marry Luca when they reached Bohannon.

The days had been mostly cloudy, and rainy, and growing cooler. The deck was sometimes cold enough for her to consider wearing her shoes, and she knew that she would before the end of the journey. She was glad for the colder weather, and the damp air, though, because they served as reminders that time was running short. It was time to bring herself down out of the clouds, out of the fantasy world she'd allowed herself to create, and into reality.

She had to believe that Swan would help her find Travis, even if the captain no longer wanted anything to do with her. He would do it because it was the right thing, and Travis's safety was paramount. After that, she might not have a future with Swan, no matter how much she wanted to believe that what they shared was real and unbreakable. If she didn't tell him the truth, however, she *definitely* didn't have a future with him.

The dragon had been eating and drinking for days, albeit reluctantly. She showed no signs of recovering much spirit, although some of her wounds had already begun to heal after a little nourishment. Whatever Swan had said to her had, at least, convinced her to help herself physically.

Ella hadn't asked him again, because she'd been nervous about his hesitancy, and he had not volunteered the information. In fact, they'd been talking less and less as the days passed, most of their time alone being spent finding new ways to please each other in bed. She always fell asleep before him, no matter how determined she was not to let it happen, but she'd awoken a few times to find him sleeping in her arms. She was relieved to know that he *did* sleep, some.

He frowned when he was sleeping, though, and that was troubling. She wished she knew what worries were weighing on his mind, what troubles of the world haunted him even into slumber, and she wished that she could take them from him.

She'd spent most of the day with Luca, when Timón and Rashad didn't need her help, and she'd told Luca that she was going to come clean with the captain. She would do her best to ensure that, if Swan was angry, it was with her and not Luca. Still, he deserved a heads-up, just in case. Luca had been asking nearly every day why she hadn't asked for the captain's help, though, so his reaction was predictable enough. They'd discussed many plans for tracking down Travis, all of them sketchy at best, and she knew that Luca was afraid he was not going to be able to help. The idea that Swan might have some weight to throw around was comforting, because Luca knew that they were ill-equipped to handle the situation on their own.

Ella thought, as she lay beside Swan, feeling the sweat cooling on her skin, that this might be the night she didn't precede him in sleep. Her body was tired, but her mind was alive with worries and doubts. She couldn't tell him after making love to him. She wouldn't sully what they'd just shared, and she wouldn't take advantage of his post-coital feelings of affection and relaxation. It would be his choice, whether or not he wanted to touch her again, after he learned the truth.

She told herself, again, that it wasn't so bad, her dishonesty. She should've trusted him enough to tell him about Travis, and she should have told him, before sleeping with him for the first time, that she'd never been engaged to Luca. Swan had been under the impression that she had already given herself to her friend, and had he known the truth, she might still be a virgin. She didn't think he would have willingly taken her virginity, and she couldn't bring herself to regret all the nights they'd spent together. He'd been robbed of his choice in the matter, though, and that was unfair.

His breathing was slow and even, as she lay with her head on his arm, thinking about the past, the future...and the present, and how comfortable it was to lay beside him, and how much she wished it could last forever. The nights had been cloudy, drizzly, and cold, but tonight the moon was shining past the shades, filling the cabin with its pale white glow. She'd come to love the small cabin, as well, she realized. It was familiar, and comfortable, and most importantly, it was a space that she and Swan had come to share.

It was strange to think that there was a dragon sleeping just above them, on the roof. A dragon that Swan had saved, at considerable risk to himself and his ship and his crew, because it was the right thing to do.

Ella let out a slow breath, careful not to disturb the man she cared so much about. After a moment, she shifted, carefully, tipping her head to see his face. She'd expected him to be asleep, and was surprised to find him watching her. She should've known better.

"If you tell me what's bothering you, I might be able to help," he said. His voice was a soft rumble in his chest. His expression was somber in the moonlight.

It was on the tip of her tongue to tell him that she loved him, and that he was the only man she had ever loved, and that she would never lie to him for the rest of her life if he could find a way to love her in return. Instead, she heard herself say, "I was just thinking about how little we really know each other."

She lowered her gaze, unable to withstand the intensity of his stare, and waited. It would be the perfect opportunity for him to point out that she knew far more about him than he did about her. She wondered if she was *daring* him to call her out, asking him to confront her about her secrecy.

After a few long moments of silence, Swan asked, "What would you like to know?"

Her guilt almost won out over her curiosity. Almost. "What's the first thing

271

you usually do in Bohannon?"

"See that the cargo is unloaded and delivered, and then I visit Maggie. Make sure no one's been bothering her in my absence."

"Bothering her? Who would bother her?" she asked.

He was silent for so long, she lifted her head to look at him. "I know we never talked about this, but I realized today that I never told you...that...I do have papers for you to get into Bohannon."

"What?" she asked, staring at him, several thoughts swirling in her brain at once. She thought of her conversation with Luca, and wondered if there was some way Swan could have heard it. "What do you mean?"

"Papers. All the workers on the ship have papers to get in. I just wanted you to know that you do, too. In case you were worried about it."

"When...did you do that?"

He frowned. "After Ivan hauled you on deck and I decided to put you to work instead of throwing you overboard."

In spite of herself, she smiled at the memory. "I thought you might just do that," she said, softly. To her relief, after a moment, his lips curved in a small smile, too. "I never really thought about needing papers, at first," she said. "I just planned on sneaking in, you know...but you were looking out for me, huh?"

"As soon as you joined the crew, you became my responsibility." He seemed hesitant to say something else.

"What?" she asked, putting her hand on his chest.

"I don't want you to think...I mean..." He paused again. He was rarely at a loss for words, but he seemed to flounder for a moment. "You will have pay when we arrive, too. For the work you've done, with Timón and Rashad..." He trailed off, watching her to gauge her reaction.

"Oh," she said, after a moment. She hadn't considered that possibility. Any little bit of money would help when she and Luca set out to find Travis. Or, when she set out on her own, if Luca was still disabled.

"I just wanted you to know you...have options," he said, sounding unaccountably nervous.

"I...know..." she answered. She debated, chewing her lip. She'd had no intention of telling him, not now, here, tonight, but he was giving her the perfect opportunity. There was the possibility that he would think she'd decided not to marry Luca just because Swan had offered her immigration papers and money. If she was completely honest, though...

"Martin Bauer," he said.

Her heart skipped. "What?" she asked, as cold prickles began to spread through her body. She had not mentioned the man's name, not even in whispers, not even to Luca, so there was no way she could have been overheard. She stared at Swan, her mind a swirl of confusion.

"He's a man who lives in Bohannon," Swan said. "Actually, he lives above Bohannon. Are you alright?"

"Yes," she managed, swallowing. "What about him?"

272

Frowning, Swan said, "He's the one who sometimes bothers Maggie. What's wrong?"

"Nothing," she said. Part of her was relieved, because the mention of Bauer's name seemed to be a coincidence. The rest of her, however, was trying to process the idea that Swan had an unpleasant history with the man she was going to find. "Why does he bother her?"

"I've cost him a lot of money over the years," he answered, studying her far too closely. "He's the richest man in Bohannon, and I guarantee he didn't earn a penny honestly. He schedules his ships around my schedule, now," he added, with a humorless smile. "Tired of me, uh, running into them out here. Always makes sure they're a few days ahead, now."

"Is he...dangerous?" she asked.

"He's fat and lazy and rich," Swan said, his expression darkening. "And mean. He doesn't do much of his own dirty work, but he has shown up on Maggie's doorstep a few times, making veiled threats. He wouldn't dare lay a finger on her, of course, but...Money can solve a lot of problems, or it can create a lot of problems, depending on what kind of person has it. He's threatened to close down Darling House."

"He can't do that, can he?" she asked, alarmed at the thought of all the children that would be displaced.

A muscle in his jaw twitched, and he shifted, bending his arm under his head. "He could make things difficult, if he did more than threaten. But he underestimates my ability to fight. Not with a sword—I think he's learned that lesson," he added, with a flash of white teeth in a smile that didn't quite reach his eyes. "Anyway, my first stop is to see Maggie and make sure he—or anyone else—hasn't been around making trouble. There's no need to worry. Are you, uh...looking forward to seeing anything in Bohannon?"

The question was posed awkwardly, and Ella knew it wasn't what he really wanted to ask. She considered for a few moments. She hadn't thought about Bohannon, much, past her objective. She hadn't imagined what the scenery would be like, what kind of landmarks or monuments there would be, or how she would find her way around. She had to face the possibility that, when she managed to find Travis, they might be stuck in Bohannon for a long time— maybe the rest of their lives. While they had nothing to go home to, the prospect of starting over, in a strange country, was daunting. Terrifying, actually. She tried to tamp down the fear; the most important thing was finding Travis, and as long as he and Luca were alright, she would do whatever she needed to do.

For the first time in her life, however, there was a part of her that wanted to rebel against the responsibility. A part that wanted to be selfish, and that selfish part of her wanted Colin Swan. Not just for the rest of the journey but forever. And, strangely enough, she though he might accept her if she offered herself to him. She thought he might just want something more with her, too, that she wasn't alone in the feeling.

"I haven't thought much about it," she admitted. She couldn't really think about it now, either—she wasn't even thinking about Travis. All she could think about was Martin Bauer and how much trouble he might cause. What would Swan say if she told him, now, about Bauer's ship taking Travis?

She knew what he'd say. He'd offer to help. He'd tell her she didn't need to worry, that he would help her get her brother back. Suddenly, she knew that without any doubts, and she knew that she couldn't let him do that—not if he already had troubles of his own with Bauer.

"I..." he began, but he stopped, looking unsure.

She had a feeling he was going to offer to show her around Bohannon, and her stomach clenched. If he offered, she might lose all her will to refuse. She needed time to think things through. The fact that she had work papers to get into the country was good information to have, and she had to reevaluate how Swan's relationship with Bauer might affect her plans.

"I like this ship," she said, quietly. "It feels safe." She hadn't meant to say that, and she stilled, afraid of the door she might have opened.

"You've been in danger a few times," he pointed out, after a hesitation.

"Not on your ship," she said, with a small smile. "Only when I was stupid enough to leave it."

He was silent for long moments, and she peeked up at his face, wondering what he was thinking. "What about your run-in with Bartholomew?" he finally asked.

She frowned. "Bart?" she asked, and then she remembered. Bart and Luca had been the ones in danger, then, though. "I could have handled him," she said.

"I'm sure," he agreed, and it was his turn to offer a small smile. "Nevertheless..."

"Goonie said you banned liquor."

"I did."

"Because of me?"

"Because of Bart's bad behavior," he said. Then, while she was trying to find the appropriate words, he said, quietly, "Yes, because of you. I will do everything I can to keep you safe, Ella."

"I know you care about the safety of your crew," she said, trying to keep her tone light and joking.

"I care about your safety," he corrected, and she met his dark gaze. "I love you, Ella. You need to know that."

Her heart stumbled in her chest. Happiness and sudden fear warred within her, and she opened her mouth with no idea of what she would say. She felt tears burning in her eyes, but they were good tears, in spite of all of her doubts. The man lying beside her was perfect, the one person in all of the world that she would want beside her forever, and he loved her. In spite of everything she'd done to cause him trouble, all of her annoying habits, he loved her.

He shifted and pressed a light finger against her lips, stopping whatever words were prepared to tumble from her mouth. "You don't need to say anything, Ella. Whenever you—"

She leaned forward, and he moved his hand out of her way. She kissed him, her heart and throat swollen with emotion. She wanted to tell him that she loved him, too, but the words were stuck in her throat. If she told him that, then she would have to tell him everything, because anything less would be unfair. And if she made a commitment to him, she would have to be willing to accept his help and support, and until she'd had time to consider the ramifications, she simply wasn't prepared to do that.

She kissed him with all the love that was trying to burst out of her, though, and when his hands rose to cup her face, she rolled up and on top of him. She pulled away from his mouth to look down at him, and something in her face made him smile. She braced her hands on either side of his head, straddling his stomach, and leaned down until her mouth was just above his.

"Am I too heavy for you?" she breathed.

"No." His hands had slid to her bare hips, and their heat seared into her.

"Are you tired?" she asked.

"Nope."

She smiled and kissed him, again, doing her best to tamp down her guilt.

* * *

"Jacko," a voice called, and Travis looked over his shoulder as Angel appeared. The dog, sitting beside him at the railing, rose and turned in response to the girl's call. Jesiah had told them that the crew had always called the animal "Dog," or worse, and so the children had come up with a new name. It had been voted upon, but it was Angel who came up with it. It seemed to fit the scruffy white dog, somehow.

Angel had come a long way in the past week. All of the children were clean, and dressed in handmade clothes—Tabitha had sewn them out of bolts of fabric found in the cargo hold, fabric that was clearly intended to be sold, as imported goods, for a hefty profit. For a week, they had been regularly and well fed, from what good stores there were mingled with fresh-caught fish, and they'd spent much time in the sun. The difference was amazing. The pale, emaciated little boys were tanned and healthier-looking, already.

Angel looked better, as well. Her cough had receded, and she was trying to come to terms with the loss of her brother. They could all see her, struggling to cope with the reality of his death, the reality of his *absence*, and the fact that she was eating and wandering around the ship was a good sign. It would take her a long time to heal, longer than they would be on the ship, but watching her begin the process had helped Travis begin to deal with his own guilt and grief, as well.

"Travis!"

He looked toward the sound of his name as Jacko left him to join Angel. It was Gibbs, calling him from the stern, and there were three men with him. *Great*, Travis thought. *Now what?* One of the men was Franklin, and it seemed that every scrap of trouble since taking over the ship had involved him. Suppressing a sigh, Travis made his way toward the gathered men.

"What's going on?" he asked, as he approached.

"We need to adjust the sails," Gibbs said, glaring at Franklin. "Adjust our coordinates," he elaborated, after a moment.

"He wants to adjust every fucking hour, seems like," Franklin objected. "I don't think he knows where the hell we're going. Says we got a course set, then all the sudden, oh, no, gotta make an adjustment again. We're going to float around out here forever."

"Winds change," Gibbs snapped. "Or haven't you noticed? I'm aiming for land the best I can based on the sky, I can't see the fucking continent any better than you can."

"You don't know where we're going to land," Franklin accused.

The other two men fidgeted uneasily, looking back and forth between the two arguers. They must have been asked to adjust the sails, and now they didn't know what to do.

"I will get us to dry land if you stay out of my way," Gibbs said, in a low voice.

"Yeah? Where?" Franklin said, spreading his hands. "We could end up in some godforsaken land with cannibals, or—"

"Land is land, yes?" Travis interrupted, trying not to let his irritation show. Why was he being called into an argument between two adults older than himself? What was he supposed to do, referee? "Do you think you can navigate better?"

"I don't think he should get to make decisions for all of us," Franklin said. He looked and sounded sullen, now.

"Then who? Look, we've been heading in more or less the same direction," Travis said, gesturing toward the horizon. "Make the adjustments he wants, for crying out loud. We're not going to—"

"Travis! Travis!"

He turned at the sound of his name, called frantically across the deck, and saw Jesiah hurrying toward them, waving an arm. This seemed more important than the argument about coordinates, because Jesiah's distress was apparent. Travis started toward him with a knot of apprehension in his stomach, trying to imagine all of the things that could have happened to cause such alarm. "What's the matter?" he asked, as the other boy skidded to a stop before him.

Gibbs and the others had come up behind him, also distracted by Jesiah's call, and at the other end of the deck, Travis could see Amir, Cosy, and Garrett heading in their direction.

"We have a problem," Jesiah said, as though that wasn't obvious by his appearance. He held his hands up. "I didn't know, swear to God I didn't."

Travis's heart was racing, and so was his mind. "Didn't know what? What happened?"

"Come on," Jesiah said, gesturing with his hand. "Come on. You need to see."

Travis was suddenly sure that, whatever it was, he didn't want to see, and yet he followed Jesiah's lead toward the stairs and down into the dimness. "What is it?" he asked Jesiah's back as they descended. "Is someone hurt?"

"No, no..." Jesiah said, setting a quick pace down the stairs. Travis and the others—he didn't look back to see how many of them were coming—followed his lead. "We were still inventorying, like you asked," he said as he hurried along. "Yesterday and today we were going through the crates in the far back, and we got all the way back, and...There was this big box, right? All the way behind all the others but with this little path leading to it, but we were goin' front to back, like Amir showed us, and Kyra was writing everything down, and..."

Travis wanted to curse the kid, tell him to spit it out, just say what it was they'd found. Travis was trying to imagine what it could be, in a crate in the back of the stores, to cause such a commotion. "What was in the box, Jesiah?" he asked, irritated and breathless from the quick pace and the adrenaline coursing through him.

They had finally reached the room, though, and Jesiah led the way in and then quickly stepped aside so that Travis could see Kyra, Tabitha, and Carl standing halfway back. Boxes of different sizes had been opened and pulled aside, making a wide pathway between the crates toward the back. There was a larger, wooden crate back against the wall. The front panel had been removed, and then leaned back against the box, hiding from view whatever was inside.

Feeling frustrated and anxious, Travis strode toward the crate, determined to solve the mystery once and for all so that he knew how he was supposed to react. "Be careful, Travis," Kyra said, as he pulled aside the wooden front.

The dragon blinked at him, its eyes slitted against the light of the lanterns. It was hunched back into the corner of the crate, all bony angles and dull, shadowy scales, and as its eyes locked onto Travis, it let out a hiss that made him take a startled step backward.

A dragon, his eyes insisted, even though his mind was trying to deny the evidence. *A baby dragon.* He wanted to whirl on Jesiah and ask why he couldn't have just said that they'd found a baby dragon, why he'd had to let the shocking sight tell its own story, but he couldn't. He couldn't take his eyes off the animal. It was emaciated, all of its bones jutting in points. In fact, it looked like it should be dead, or would be very soon.

And that wasn't all, because the dragon wasn't alone. Or, at least, it hadn't been. In the crate was another dragon, this one dead, and by the looks of the corpse, Travis could only assume it had starved to death. Several days ago, at least, maybe as much as two weeks earlier. It was impossible to tell; he knew nothing about the decomposition of dragons. He'd heard stories that dragons burned their own after death. That they essentially cremated their loved ones.

This young dragon, however, had had no one to cremate it, because its crate-mate would not be able to spit fire to save its own life. It was far too young. They were likely siblings, the two of them, probably twins. Bile was stinging the back of Travis's throat, and his stomach was a squirming mess of anger, guilt, sorrow, and disgust. All this time, he'd been totally unaware of the young animals slowly starving to death. He looked over the crate. It had a few small holes punched in the top, presumably for air, and one four-inch square opening near the top of the front panel. To insert food, Travis imagined, although he couldn't figure out how the animals were supposed to be given water without the crate being opened.

There were a few fish skeletons in the bottom of the crate, and what looked like some chicken bones, but there was no dish for water. There were no signs of recent food. How long had it been? Travis's stomach churned. He looked at the face of the living dragon; it was hunched, terrified and defensive, surely almost dead but still trying to put on a tough front.

Travis knew the best thing he could do would be to take out his sword and kill the baby swiftly, put it out of its misery at long last. The animal shifted, slightly, and the clink of metal drew Travis's attention to the fact that the young dragon was not only confined to a crate, but chained to the bottom of it, as well. For a moment, Travis thought he might be ill. He reached for his sword, then stopped. Everyone seemed to be waiting for him to do something, and the room was silent except for the harsh breathing of the frightened animal.

It was not the fear and desperation in the baby dragon's eyes that kept Travis from drawing, or at least not entirely. It was the sight of the dead animal, which his eyes kept returning to. Curled on its side, the corpse was decomposing, and Travis could smell it—although the smell was fainter than he'd have expected, being closed up in the box for so long. In fact, the smell was almost musty, and he could only imagine that dragons decomposed differently than people. What really mattered, however, was that the corpse was intact, from head to tail.

Travis would like to think that he would never resort to cannibalism, even to avoid starvation, but he could not predict what he or anyone else would do in that situation. Animals did it all the time, though. This baby animal was starving to death, and its end seemed to be quite near, from the looks of it. It had not put a single bite-mark in its sibling, had not taken advantage of the available body to nourish itself. It would have gotten very little sustenance from the other baby, starved itself, but it would have been something.

Travis dragged his gaze back to the yellow, slanted eyes of the live dragon.

"He's scared!"

Travis turned, startled, toward the sound of Angel's voice. She was beside Travis, and he'd been so preoccupied, he hadn't even heard her approach. A glance over his shoulder showed him that Kyra had crouched down and had an arm around Jacko to keep him from getting close to the dragon. "Be careful, stay back," Travis told Angel.

"What the hell are you waiting for?" Cosy asked. "The thing's dead, anyway."

"He just needs to eat," Angel said.

Travis looked back at Jesiah. "How could this happen—what's the point?"

278

While it was true that the animal hadn't been fed since the ship had been taken over, it was also obvious that the starvation had begun long before that. "Was someone supposed to be—"

"I didn't know they was here," Jesiah said, putting his hands up. "I swear. Maybe Cheddy knew—" He turned to Garrett. "Go get Cheddy," he said.

"We can figure out why, but first we need to put that thing down," Cosy said. Then, catching Travis's look, he added, gentler, "I can do it." He put his hand on his sword.

Angel started forward suddenly, saying, "It's alright," to the coiled, emaciated dragon. Travis turned, reaching for her, as she neared the crate. The dragon, with a hiss, lunged at her, swiping toward her like a cat with talons deadlier than any tiger's claws. Travis yanked the girl back, and those talons missed her by less than an inch. The dragon collapsed into a huddle, panting, glaring up at them with anger, fear, and pain. Its chains were stretched tight as it lay, struggling to breathe, half out of its box.

Jacko was trying to get away from Kyra, to get closer to the animal— probably to protect Angel—and Kyra barely managed to keep hold of the mangy dog.

Travis's heart was slamming in his chest at the close call. He had a handful of Angel's shirt in his hand, and he was afraid to let go, afraid she would move again and be eviscerated right in front of him. She was trembling, too—the dragon's lunge had frightened her, and that was good. Advancing on any hungry, frightened, and cornered animal was a terrible idea, let alone a *dragon*.

A BABY dragon, his mind whispered, as he looked into those yellow eyes. He put his hand on his sword, again, barely aware that he was still holding Angel.

"Don't hurt him," the little girl said, looking up at Travis. Her eyes were shining with tears, and Travis swallowed.

"Get the girl out of here," Tabitha said, although Travis didn't know who she was speaking to. It was Jesiah who stepped forward and reached for Angel.

"No, please," the girl cried, reaching for Travis's arm. "Please, he's just scared and hungry."

"Go with Jesiah," Travis said, feeling like an ass. Tears were streaming down the girl's face as she reached for him, as Jesiah pulled her backward.

"Do you want me—" Cosy began.

"No," Travis snapped. He ran a shaky hand over his face and again looked at the miserable animal before him. It would be merciful. Killing the animal would end its suffering.

If the young dragon had eaten its sibling, or even tried to, Travis thought he would be able to do it. He would draw his sword and take the animal's head off. It would certainly be no harder than killing a man. He looked back and saw that Jesiah, with Angel—and Jacko—was gone. Travis met Kyra's eyes.

"Get some fish, and water," he said, quietly.

"What? Why?" Cosy asked.

"It's a bad idea, son," Gibbs said. "Look what that thing almost did to the girl, and it's half-dead, now. Think of what it could do if it had its strength."

Cheddy had arrived, following Garrett, and his eyes widened at the sight of the dragon. "He's s'posed to be dead," he exclaimed.

"You knew they was here?" Jesiah asked.

"Why didn't you say anything?" Travis asked, as Kyra hurried out, past Cheddy and Garrett.

"The captain ordered them to be killed after one got Hank's hand through the hole when he was feeding them."

"That's what happened to his hand?" Jesiah said. Then, before Cheddy could answer, "That was almost a month ago."

Travis's stomach clenched. A month without food? Or water? How was that possible? Could any creature really survive that long? "Why were they here if they were just going to let them die?"

"Captain hadn't never tried transporting dragons before. Wasn't worth the risk after Hank got hurt. Captain said he could make money selling 'em locally, wouldn't try takin' 'em 'cross the ocean no more."

"So they were going to let them starve?" Gibbs asked.

Cheddy spread his hands. "Nicks said they were dead. Thought they was gonna sell the skins and teeth and stuff."

"It already hurt someone, hear that?" Cosy asked. "If you don't kill it, I will."

"Then you'll have to go through me to do it," Travis said, barely aware he was going to make such a proclamation. He could still hear Angel's pleas in his mind, even though she was out of earshot.

"Kid, you killed most of the men on this ship. This is a dragon. This is not the time for weakness," Cosy said.

"Mercy isn't weakness," Gibbs said, although he spoke grudgingly—he agreed that the animal should be put down.

"Having a dragon on board is good luck," Amir said, speaking for the first time since reaching the dragon.

"Hasn't worked much, so far," Cosy answered.

"Hasn't it?" Amir asked mildly. "Are you dead? Are you still in chains? Are you hungry? Thirsty? Do you think a teenaged boy stood a chance against a whole shipload of unscrupulous men? And yet, here we all are."

Travis didn't know what to say to that, or even how to feel about it. He wasn't sure he believed in omens or luck, and his motives for protecting the dragon had nothing to do with either.

"We're alive because of Travis," Garrett said, glaring at Amir with his chin out.

Rather than taking offense at the scrawny boy's defiance, Amir smiled. "Of course, my boy," he said. "No one is disputing Travis's bravery."

Travis shifted his feet, uncomfortable with being the topic of discussion, and said, "We're not killing this dragon. It might die, anyway," he added, glancing back at the animal as it started crawling backward into its crate. "But...not because I didn't try to save it."

280

"You're crazy," Cosy said, although he made no moves toward his sword. "What if it—"

"I'll take responsibility for it," Travis interrupted. "Me, alone. You think I would endanger the kids on this ship? Or you? Any of you? I want all of us to get to land, safe, alive, and as soon as possible. But this animal was taken away from its family the same as we were. It was mistreated, just like we were. Maybe you think you deserve life more than he does, but I think he's got as much a right to eat, drink, and be free as I do."

"How do you know if he's a he?" Garrett asked, peering in at the animal.

Travis shrugged. He had no idea if it was a boy or a girl, the male pronoun just tasted better than saying 'it.'

"You can tell by the ridges above the forehead," Gibbs said. He stepped forward but stopped when the dragon hissed, and pointed, adding, "And the spikes on the end of the tail, although his are barely showing. He can't be more than...well, it's hard to say for sure, because the starvation has likely stunted him, but...I'd say four months at the most."

"How'd they get them away from their mother?" Garrett asked. He seemed fascinated by the dragon, and Travis knew he'd have to stress the importance to him, and the younger children, of staying away from the animal. Travis had volunteered to take responsibility, and he didn't take that lightly.

"She's probably dead," Gibbs said, apologetically.

Travis saw emotion flit across Garrett's face, quickly hidden, and knew that the boy was remembering the death of his own mother. So was Travis. It was impossible not to. It might be a dragon, but it had more in common with these orphaned boys than the adults seemed to realize.

"Everyone should leave," Travis said, when Kyra came in with two pails— one of water, one of fish. "Everyone staring around glaring at him isn't going to help calm him down."

"Nothing's going to calm him down," Cosy said. "He's a *dragon*. And, he's hungry."

"He's right," Gibbs said. "He's not a pet. He'll rip your throat out if you give him a chance."

"I guess that'd be my problem, then, wouldn't it?" Travis asked, sighing. He was tired. And, the longer they stood around arguing, the longer the baby was going without food. Travis didn't think its life was numbered in days, anymore, but hours or even minutes. He might not even be *able* to eat. Maybe that's why he hadn't eaten his—"Was this one a girl, then?" he asked, looking at Gibbs.

"Yes."

His sister. Maybe he had been too far gone to eat her, and the fish would simply taunt him. There was only one way to find out. Travis took the buckets from Kyra, thanking her, and looked at Cosy. Cosy raised his hands and his eyebrows and, without further objection, turned and left. After a moment, Gibbs followed, then Amir.

Before Travis could say anything, Garrett said, "Can I stay, Travis? Please?

I'll stay back and be real quiet, I promise."

Travis hesitated, and looked at Kyra. "Alright," he said. "But don't talk or move around, alright? You'll only scare him more."

Garrett nodded and walked over to sit on a crate. After a moment, Kyra went and sat beside him, and Travis suppressed a smile. He wouldn't have dared ask her to leave, anyway.

When Travis approached the crate, slowly, the dragon pulled back, hunching into the corner, opening his mouth. Travis stopped where—he hoped, anyway—the dragon couldn't reach him if it lunged again. Travis lowered himself in a crouch, carefully, and took a fish from the bucket in front of him. He tossed it carefully into the front of the crate. The dragon flinched, hissed, and bumped against the back of the box.

"Sorry, buddy," Travis said, pitching his voice low. He held still and watched the animal's nostrils flare. After a few moments, the dragon's head moved forward, just a little, and it shifted, keeping its yellow eyes on Travis. Then, almost before Travis could register the movement, the fish disappeared into the dragon's mouth and was swallowed. "Guess that answers that question," Travis muttered. The dragon was staring at him, still slightly stretched. Travis tossed another fish. The dragon flinched back, again, but only a little, and then he snatched the fish and swallowed.

Travis slid the bucket of water forward, slowly. The dragon drew back and Travis hesitated, unsure if it was going to lunge at him when he got his arm within reach. He met the dragon's eyes, and the animal blinked. Travis could sense its confusion. Its fear and pain were at war with the desire for food and water.

"It's just water, see?" Travis said, softly. "Just gonna push it close enough so you can get a drink."

"Maybe—" Kyra started, but she stopped when the dragon jerked his startled gaze toward her.

"Go ahead," Travis told her, keeping his own eyes on the dragon.

"Maybe you should use a broom or something to push it closer," she said.

"Or put the front back on the crate and then take it away when the bucket's close," Garrett suggested in a stage-whisper.

Neither was a bad idea. Travis pulled another fish from the pail, reached his arm forward, and tossed it right in front of the dragon. The animal sniffed it, looked at Travis, and ate it. "See?" Travis said. "I'm not so bad, right? You want some water?" He pushed the bucket a little closer, and saw the dragon's eyes flick toward the sloshing liquid. "Water, buddy, see? Don't take my arm off." *Or my face,* he thought, moving forward cautiously in an awkward crouch-walk, sliding the bucket in front of himself. "You'll feel better if you get a drink, alright?"

The chain rattled as the dragon shifted, and Travis pushed the water a little closer. He was pretty sure it—and his arm—was now in the animal's range. The dragon shifted again, and Travis hesitated, with his heart thumping nervously. Then he reached his fingers into the bucket, swirling the water, and lifted his hand, letting the liquid drip back into the pail. The dragon inched forward. Travis knew he should back up, but he wanted to make sure the animal could actually reach the bucket.

As the dragon crawled forward, dragging itself along with its eyes on Travis and its mouth opened to pant, Travis did begin to move backward. The chain rattled and scraped along the floor, and finally the dragon reached the bucket. He sniffed it, stuck his snout in, and began swallowing gulps of water.

"Whoa," Travis said, alarmed. "Whoa, buddy, slow down, you'll make yourself sick." *Sick?* his mind scoffed. *He's practically dead.* The dragon had already sucked up half of the water, and Travis reached for the bucket, afraid that the animal's stomach would explode, or something, after being empty for so long. He grabbed the handle of the pail to pull it back, and the dragon reared up, making an awful sound of anger and fear, and swiped at him with those razor-sharp talons.

Travis jerked backward, and fell onto his butt, pulling the bucket over and spilling most of the remaining water on himself and the floor. The dragon missed him—barely—and collapsed in a bony heap, staring up at him, too exhausted to even hiss, anymore. The dragon's front foot was just inches from Travis's own foot, and looking at the dragon, Travis knew—*knew*, without a doubt—that the dragon would have sliced him open if it had really wanted to. The animal was unsure, though, confused, and that confusion had made it hesitate and, ultimately, pull its swipe a little.

Travis swallowed around the lump of emotion in his throat, wrought by the sight of the young animal's weakened state. He asked himself if he was doing the right thing. Would it be better for the animal if Travis simply ended its life with a blade, quickly and mercifully? He didn't want to do it. He wasn't even sure if he could, after looking into those yellow eyes, so full of fear and confusion. Maybe it was what the animal wanted, though. Its sister was dead, its mother was either dead or gone, it was in terrible pain from starvation...

Travis, still sitting on the floor, picked up another fish. "You're gonna be alright, Buddy," he said, barely aware that he'd just capitalized the word into a name. "We'll get you some more water and something besides fish, but for now, you can have one more." Slowly, carefully, Travis turned his legs and leaned toward the crate, laying the fish in front of Buddy.

The dragon sniffed it, but seemed too weak to lift his own head. Travis slid a little closer, and the dragon made a small growling sound in his throat. He was still, though. Travis inched closer. He knew that if he'd underestimated the young animal, or overestimated its weakness, it might kill him. But if he was right, this was an opportunity to show Buddy that Travis didn't mean to hurt him.

The dragon was weak and vulnerable, and in spite of its deadly talons and teeth, it was at Travis's mercy. The look in those yellow eyes told him that the animal was aware of it, too. The fear almost made Travis stop. Almost. But what if the dragon did recover? And built its strength up? If it was still afraid, then, it would be far more dangerous. Travis had to show the animal, now, while it was too weak (*probably*) to attack, that not all humans were bad. That not all humans wanted to hurt him. That not all humans deserved to be killed or maimed.

Travis pushed the fish forward with his fingers, until it touched the dragon's snout. Buddy's nostrils flared. Travis pushed it against his nose a little more, and Buddy lifted his head. Travis stilled, holding his breath. He was far into the danger zone, now. Buddy nibbled on the edge of the fish, watching Travis. No more gobbling, he was too tired for that, and he chewed off small pieces of fish.

"Good boy, Buddy," Travis whispered. "Good boy. See? Fish. We'll see what else we can find, alright? You just need to rest. Good boy." Travis lifted his hand, slowly, slowly, and brushed his fingers against the dragon's snout. It was cool, and wet from the plunge into the water pail. The dragon didn't move. Or breathe. Neither did Travis, he just let his fingers linger, barely touching, surprisingly steady, for long moments.

He pulled his hand back just as slowly as he'd extended it; it would be a shame to be allowed to touch the animal only to have his hand ripped off during the retreat. When Travis was no longer touching him, Buddy began nibbling feebly at the fish, again. Travis set another fish down, and drew back, taking the two pails with him, until he was far enough away to safely stand. Only then did he let out a breath of relief, wincing at the pain in his back from crouching so awkwardly.

He turned toward Kyra and Garrett. They were staring at him with almost identical expressions of disbelief, although Kyra's held a little more fear than Garrett's. Travis almost laughed at their faces, but he suppressed the urge. He smiled, instead, hoping it looked more reassuring than it felt. "He'll make himself sick if he eats or drinks too much, too fast. Four fish are probably too many, but...he also needs enough substance in him to keep him alive through the night."

"You think he will? Live, I mean?" Garrett asked.

"It's hard to say," Travis answered. "He tired himself out trying to attack. But he has fight in him, he proved that. And...his sister has been dead a while, and he's still keeping on, it has to be sheer willpower keeping him alive this long. I'll give him some more water in a couple of hours. If he makes it through the night, he'll start to get his strength back."

"How do you know so much about dragons?" Kyra asked.

Travis's face must have shown his surprise. "Me? I don't know anything about dragons, really. Just what we learned in school. But...I know about hunger."

Travis saw her swallow. Yes, all three of these children knew about hunger, and being without parents, and being taken from their homes and held prisoner, and being hurt and scared and lonely. Travis thought of his sister, and his stomach clenched with a longing to see her that was so powerful it almost dropped him to his knees. He missed Luca, and would give almost anything to see him again, but he loved and missed Ella so much that for a few moments he wasn't sure he could bear the pain of it.

Garrett and Kyra were watching him, though. He was luckier than they were; he knew that, somewhere in the world, there were at least two people who loved him, missed him, and would do anything within their power to get to him. While Travis had learned early on not to underestimate his sister, he didn't think that even she could find a way to cross the ocean to get to him. And, even if she could, how would she know where he was? No, if he was ever going to see her again, he would have to find a way back to her.

You have a ship, he thought. Then, immediately, *It's not mine.* Whose was it, though? The captain was dead, killed by Travis himself. The ship was owned by whatever rich, sadistic man was profiting from the sale of human lives. Travis would rather die than hand the vessel back to the man who would only staff it with another crew willing to steal children to sell. He would rather sink it. But, perhaps there was another option. *You don't know anything about sailing. You'd get yourself killed in the middle of the ocean, and anyone stupid enough to go with you.* That was probably true, and it was the reason why he had to get the children safely to dry land first. After that, though...?

He shoved the thought away. Yes, he wanted to get back to Ella and Luca, more than he'd ever wanted anything in his whole life. Even the pain of losing his parents seemed dull in comparison, because he'd been so young then that he barely remembered them. Ella was the one who'd always been there, from day one, the one person who had never left him, never let him down, never let anything bad happen to him. And, now that he was old enough that he should be able to take care of himself, and give her some help, what did he do? He went and got himself captured by slave-traders, loaded onto a ship, and taken across the ocean. He knew that she would be feeling guilty, because she always blamed herself. It wasn't her fault he was stupid, though.

"We'll leave the crate open," Travis said, and his throat was thick with unshed tears. "I won't lock him back in that box, especially not while his sister is still there. I don't want to risk upsetting him by taking her out, though, not yet. He's too weak to move right now, but I'll have to put a guard outside to make sure none of the kids come in here. Especially Angel. It's too dangerous, if she and that dog came in here alone, who knows what would happen. Tomorrow, if he's looking any better, I'll bring her in to see him."

"Can I stand guard?" Garrett asked, and his eagerness gave Travis pause. "Please? You can trust me, Travis."

It occurred to Travis, not for the first time, that he wasn't so much older than Garrett, himself. Five years might seem like a lot to Garrett, but to Travis, who could vividly remember himself at the age of twelve, it felt like a drop in a bucket. Garrett did not speak to Travis like one boy to another; to Garrett, Travis was not just one of the men on the ship, he was *the* man, the boss, the captain. If the rest of the men on the ship decided to challenge Travis's opinion on anything, Garrett would side with Travis without question—even if it cost him his life. This was a terrifying realization to Travis. He'd never been responsible for the life of any child, let alone six of them—seven, counting

285

Kyra—and he wondered if Ella had felt this fear when she'd found herself responsible for him and Luca.

"You understand that you can't go near the crate, right?" he asked, reluctantly.

Garrett nodded. "I would stay back here, I swear. And not let anyone in. And get you if anything happens."

Travis looked at Kyra. "It's hard to know which men we can trust," she said. She spoke slowly, and Travis thought about Franklin and Gibbs, fighting over the navigation. "I'm not even sure about Jesiah, anymore. He says he didn't know about the dragons, but Cheddy did..."

"It is true, I trust you two more than anyone," Travis said. He saw Garrett practically puff with pride. "Gar, are you sure you want to do this? It's going to be boring down here, all alone."

Garrett nodded enthusiastically. "I do. I can do it, really."

"I'm sure you can," Travis agreed. "Alright. I'm going to come back in a couple of hours with more water. Yell if you need me for anything, alright? I'll make sure Tabitha, Jesiah, and JayJay know to listen for your call. Right now, I need to go see Gibbs and Franklin and try to sort out our sails."

And, Travis thought, it might be time to go through the dead captain's paperwork. Gibbs and Amir had sorted through some of it, taking note of coordinates and other relevant details. No one had made a point of going through the rest of the ledgers and drawers, though. If Travis meant to find out who owned the ship, he would have to find the answer in the cabin.

No one had been living in the captain's quarters. They'd all moved into the bunks below, and Travis again wondered why none of the men had stepped up and claimed leadership and everything that went along with it.

* * *

During the night, Buddy had crawled back into his crate—his prison had become the safest place he knew, which was terribly sad—and he was curled in the corner. Every bone seemed to jut, poking against his tight skin, and Travis marveled again at the dragon's ability to survive for so long.

Garrett had made a pallet of blankets inside the door, but he'd stayed awake all night. He looked exhausted but appropriately proud of himself. He got to his feet when Travis walked around him into the room. Travis had come down three times since the initial feeding, the most recent visit at just after midnight. Now, dawn was breaking outside, and Garrett deserved a chance to get some breakfast and sleep in a bed.

"Anything happen since the last time?" Travis asked, noting that all of the fish had been eaten. The skeletal remains of them were in the bottom of the crate, which meant that Buddy had stopped swallowing them whole. That showed restraint, because he must still be terrible hungry.

"Nope," Garrett said, stretching. "No one came down, either. How's Angel?"

286

"She's alright," Travis answered. "Tabby told her that we didn't kill the dragon." He didn't mention that the little girl had thrown her arms around him, crying, and had thanked him, or how awful her gratitude had made him feel—partly because he hadn't really done it for her, and mostly because he'd been unable to protect her brother the same way he was protecting the dragon. At the same time, he wasn't entirely sure that he *hadn't* made his final decision to help Buddy because of Angel's pleas, because her sob-choked words had certainly echoed through his head ever since. The sight of her, reaching for him as Jesiah pulled her out, had haunted his attempts at sleep. Which had affected him more, in the end? The sight of the dragon, or the memory of Angel pleading for mercy?

Travis didn't know. All he knew was that the decision had been made, and that it was the right one. He wasn't going to back away from his commitment, and he was very glad to find that the dragon had survived the night. Travis had had his doubts. The last time he'd come down, Buddy had been laying on his side, one wing beneath him and the other bent awkwardly. He'd been breathing heavily, still, and he barely opened an eye at the sound of Travis's approach. Travis had wanted to move the dragon into a more comfortable position, or sit beside him to offer comfort, but he had assumed that his presence or touch would inspire more stress, instead.

So, he'd given the dragon food, water, privacy, and quietness, along with a personal bodyguard in the form of Garrett, and the dragon had gotten enough strength to crawl into the box and curl up. A good sign. Dragons might be notoriously good healers, but Travis had no idea if that extended to illnesses and malnutrition, or only applied to injuries. It seemed as though he would be finding out soon enough.

"Brought you some potato peels," Travis said. The few potatoes left on the ship were soft and sprouting, but they had still been determined edible. Tabitha had begun a stew to use the last of them up before they completely went to rot. "And some more fish. Sorry about that. We're all eating a lot of fish, Buddy."

The dragon watched him approach, and Travis knew he had to be more careful than ever. Buddy was stronger than he'd been the day before, and if he decided to attack again, he would be faster. As Travis neared the crate, the dragon tensed, lifting his head. Travis stopped, and tossed a handful of potato peelings into the crate. After a few moments, Buddy dipped his head to sniff them. Finding them suitable, he quickly made them disappear, and Travis tossed a fish in. He was going to have to find a way to clean the bones out of the area, and he really needed to get rid of Buddy's sister before the decomposition got even worse.

Travis lowered himself into a crouch and held a fish out. "Hey, Buddy, you want to be friends?" he asked, knowing he must sound like a lunatic. Garrett was the only person around to hear him, and Travis didn't think Garrett would judge. The dragon stretched his neck a bit to smell the fish, then drew back. Not interested. At least, not yet. "Buddy, do you think I could take your sister out of here?" As an experiment, Travis reached a slow hand toward the corpse.

Buddy hissed and rose quickly. Travis jerked his hand back, startled into an inability to move cautiously. The baby dragon stood, glaring at him, its mouth opened to show daunting teeth. His stance was aggressive, and protective. He didn't lunge, though—a good thing, since Travis was within the length of the chain.

"Alright, not yet, alright," Travis said, backing away. The dragon watched him retreat, and didn't relax until Travis was on his feet and far enough away from the corpse to no longer be a threat to it. Watching Buddy protect his dead sister broke Travis's heart. Even an animal as young as Buddy must understand the difference between dead and alive, and yet his sister was all he had. And he loved her. Travis had never given much thought to whether or not dragons could feel emotions like love, but now, he didn't question it. It was obvious.

"Is it true that they burn other dragons when they die?" Garrett asked when Travis joined him inside the doorway.

"I don't know," Travis said. It had always seemed far-fetched to him. Now, he found it far more plausible. "Probably. A lot of them stay with their families their whole lives." Again, he thought of his own sister, and quickly stomped down the sudden flood of emotions trying to bubble up. He looked at Buddy, and his gaze slid to the corpse. They'd decided against burning their own deceased, but would they be able to burn one small, dead dragon? Was it worth the risk? If they caught the ship on fire, they would all be dead—they could maybe escape into the rowboats, but they would almost certainly die before ever managing to row the rest of the way to Bohannon.

"Can we burn her?" Garrett asked, tentatively, clearly following the same line of thought as Travis.

Travis put an arm around the younger boy's shoulders. "We'll try," he said. Then, looking at Buddy, he said, "We'll figure out a way."

* * *

"When are you going to tell him?"

Ella sighed and ran a hand through her hair. "Luca," she said.

He scowled. "You've been saying for a week that you're going to tell him," he retorted. "He can help. He's got money. If he cares about you—" He stopped at the look on her face, and it was his turn to sigh. "What's the name of the guy that owns the ship?"

She still didn't understand why she'd never shared that information with Luca. At its root, her silence on the matter was an effort to protect him. On the other hand, however, she'd always known that if something happened to her, and she was unable to get to Travis, Luca would be his only hope. How would Luca have any hope of finding him, if he didn't know the name of the ship or the man that owned it?

She didn't want to admit to herself that she'd known all along that she was going into Bohannon alone. Luca's broken leg was an excuse. The fact that she'd used him to get onto the ship was an unwelcome realization, and one that

288

she'd been trying to ignore for a while. There were two people on the ship that she loved more than herself, two men that she would die for without hesitation, and she was going to hurt both of them. She'd already made the decision, and was just beginning to realize it. She could tell herself that there would be time to make it up to them, time to come back and make things right, time to show them that she loved them and had only done it to save her brother and protect them, but the truth was, there was no guarantee there would be time. She might not ever make it back.

And, would they hate her? The thought sent a spear of pain through her. She thought Luca would understand, and forgive her, after some time, because he loved Travis, too.

Colin, she thought, picturing the face she'd come to love so much. Would he ever forgive her? He'd asked her to come to him if she needed help. He'd implored her to trust him. In many things, she did. She would trust him with her life. However, she couldn't trust that he would protect himself. It terrified her to realize that she couldn't choose to put Swan's life in danger, even to protect Travis or Luca.

She had to protect all of them. The fear was churning inside of her, threatening to drown her. Colin, Luca, and Travis all had to live. That's all that mattered. They might be hurt. They might be angry. They might hate her, and they might never forgive her.

She might die.

The three of them would live. The three men—although Travis was only just becoming such—that she loved more than she could put into words. She could barely believe that Swan had become so important to her, so quickly, but she didn't waste time questioning it. She would do what had to be done.

"You're not going to tell him," Luca said, interpreting the play of emotions on her face. "Why the hell not?"

"It's complicated," she answered.

"You care about him, I get it," Luca said, a muscle twitching in his jaw. "But he can take care of himself. Is it more important—"

"I won't put him in danger," she interrupted. "There's more to it than you know. He has people in Bohannon to worry about, people who depend on him. And...you'll have to trust me, Luca."

"Trust you? We were supposed to be in this together, and you're going to leave me behind," he said, his voice and expression challenging her to deny it. He could read her too well.

"I'll come back, with Travis."

The hurt in his face was inescapable. "Would you have left me if I hadn't gotten hurt?"

She hesitated. "Yes," she finally admitted. "Although I didn't know it at first. I hadn't thought that far ahead, Luca. You know how fast everything happened. One day, we were going about our lives, and then..." She shook her head, swallowing. "I had to get on a ship, and go after him, that's all I could think of. All either of us could think of," she corrected. "I never could have done it without you. No crew would've hired me."

"Not even Swan?" Luca asked, making a valiant effort to keep the bitterness from his voice.

She tried to imagine what might have happened, had she shown up at the harbor, asking for a job. What would he have said? What would he have thought of her? There was no use speculating, though, because she couldn't know how things might have played out. She and Luca had put their plan, such as it was, in motion, and now they were where they were. "I never could have done it without you," she repeated, covering his hand with her own. "The next part, I have to do alone. Then we'll be a family, again. I promise."

"Right," Luca said. "You, me, Travis, and Swan?"

She hesitated. "I don't know what will happen. Things might not be the same as they were before. But..."

"What if I tell him?"

She pulled her hand back. "You can't do that."

"Why not? It's for your own good. You're going to get yourself killed." The fear and desperation in his eyes were quickly hidden, though not quickly enough.

"I told you, there are things you don't understand. You'd be putting him, and the people he loves, at risk."

"What do I care about him or his family? I care about *your* safety, even if that means going to him for help." She could tell that the words tasted bitter in his mouth. "Even if it means making you mad at me," he added, defiantly.

"It's not a matter of being angry, Luca," she answered quietly. "If anything happens to him..." She shook her head. "If you want me to beg, Luca, I'll beg. I don't want to lose you. If you tell him, and he puts himself in danger..."

"Let me guess, you'll never forgive me," he muttered. There was just a hint of sarcasm in his voice, beneath the bitter hurt, but he must have seen something in her expression, something she was powerless to hide. His eyes widened, just a bit, and he swallowed. "Seriously?"

"I love you, Luca." They'd been through this before. "But I love him, too. I *love* him. I will protect him, even if I have to lose him."

"And what about Travis?" Luca asked. He was trying to hide his pain, and was unsuccessful. She knew him too well.

"Travis? Everything I've ever done has been about Travis. This whole trip was about him. I won't give up until I find him, and he's safe. You know that. That's why I'm going to—"

"I'll never see you again," he said, and there was no use trying to hide his pain, now. His voice was raw with it, his expression etched in it. "What am I supposed to do, all alone?"

"You won't be alone. Luca. You're not a kid, anymore. You don't need me to take care of you. Look at yourself. You're a member of this crew. You can travel the world, pay your way to anything you want."

"Right, like Swan would keep me on after you leave."

"He will," she said, and she believed it. "He hired you because he saw your potential, and you've been a good worker, up until you got hurt."

"I've been a pain in the ass," he muttered.

"He's good at forgiving that sort of thing," she said, with a small smile. "Trust me, Luca. He won't throw you out on your own. I know him. But, even if he did, you'd be fine. You can get a job. You're smart, strong, a hard worker, friendly. You could do whatever you wanted. I'm going to get Travis and bring him back to you, though."

He regarded her in silence for long moments. "If anyone can do it, you can," he finally said, quietly. "You know, he might not forgive you if you don't tell him the truth."

"I know, believe me," she sighed. "It's a chance I'll have to take."

"And you won't tell me why you think he needs protecting? Why you think he can't take care of himself? He's rich, powerful, and we've both seen him with a sword."

"It's complicated," she repeated.

"Right," Luca said. For a moment, she thought he was going to accuse her of treating him like a child, of always keeping him in the dark, of leaving him out of this important decision. Instead, she heard him say, "I won't tell him."

She tried to temper her relief, alarmed to feel tears of gratitude in her eyes. Even if she managed to come back, and the captain was willing to forgive her, how could a relationship built on lies hope to survive? The fact that she was glad, grateful, that the dishonesty was going to continue, proved that the relationship was certainly doomed.

He'll be safe, though. If he doesn't know, he can't get involved. She looked Luca in the eyes. "Promise me," she said.

Luca hesitated for what seemed like a long time, with a muscle in his jaw clenching. "I promise," he finally answered.

She let out a breath. "Thank you," she said. Luca did not make promises lightly, and she knew she could trust him, above all else, to keep his word. She also knew, however, that even if he broke his vow and went to Swan, Luca didn't know Bauer's name—or the name of his ship. There might not be many slave-traders in Bohannon, or there might be a lot; she didn't know. Swan could probably figure it out, knowing that the ship had left shortly before his own. At the very least, keeping the name to herself would buy time. If Swan came looking for her, it would already be over, one way or the other.

291

Chapter Fourteen

"We've already waited too long. We have to do it, now." Travis was crouched in front of the crate, looking in at Buddy, but he was speaking mostly to the people standing behind him. Amir, Gibbs, Jesiah, Cosy, Garrett, and Kyra, the people he'd chosen to come down with him to figure out a solution to their problem. The same group he always seemed to seek out.

None of the kids had been allowed down to see Buddy, not even Angel, who'd been speaking of little else. Only Garrett had been in the room, as Buddy's near-constant bodyguard, a role that Garrett had grabbed hold of eagerly, giving no one else a chance to volunteer to ease the burden. Travis had not allowed Garrett to feed or water the dragon, because Buddy's temperament had not improved much with time and nourishment. While he grew stronger by the day, he still hunched up and hissed at the sight of Travis's approach, and had lunged at him several times, once missing Travis's hand by less than an inch as he snatched it back.

A part of Travis had begun to believe it may have been a mistake, after all, to spare the animal's life. If it was going to be a danger to the people on the ship, something would have to be done. He was determined that he wouldn't make any rash decisions, however, telling himself—and the others—that it would take time for Buddy to believe that Travis didn't mean him any harm. Regular meals and fresh water had already wrought a remarkable change in the dragon's physicality, and Travis was glad, in spite of his growing unease at the animal's aggression. Even if he ended up having to kill the dragon, he couldn't bring himself to regret sparing its life and giving it a chance, first.

"If we try to get her out of there, he'll rip us apart," Gibbs answered.

Travis sighed and ran a hand over his face. "Yeah," he agreed. They should have taken the corpse out while Buddy was too weak to defend her. How could he have ever hoped to earn the animal's trust after that, though? "She's rotting away, though."

"Maybe that's not such a bad thing," Cosy suggested. "I mean, the smell isn't exactly nice down here, but in another week—"

"In another week we'll be on land," Gibbs interrupted.

"All the better," Cosy said. "We'll turn him loose and not have to—"

"He won't leave her," Garrett said, before Travis could.

"What?" Cosy asked, turning toward the boy with a scowl. "Of course he will. He's a wild animal. God knows how we're supposed to get the chains off him, but as soon as we do—"

"No, he's right," Gibbs said, surprising everyone. "Look at him. He won't leave her. He'll probably stay at the crate until he dies, rather than leave her body. He's already proven he'd rather starve than desecrate her corpse."

"She'll be gone before he starves," Cosy answered, pointing toward the disintegrating body. "There won't be anything but bones..." Finally, something seemed to click, and realization dawned on his face. "Oh," he finally said.

"But the bones won't burn, anyway, will they?"

"The burned bones become thinner, brittle, and turn to dust," Gibbs said. "That's not really the point, though."

"It's the ceremony," Amir said, speaking for the first time since coming downstairs. "A way to honor their loved ones, the same as a funeral or cremation serves us."

"So, should we take the whole crate upstairs?" Kyra asked.

Travis looked back at the box, and the angry dragon huddled within. "We could close him back inside, haul it up..."

"Doesn't even look like it'll fit up the stairway," Cosy said.

"It'll fit," Gibbs said.

"They got it down here somehow," Garrett added, frowning.

"They could've assembled the crate in this room," Cosy retorted, also scowling.

"It'll fit," Gibbs repeated. "It'll be heavy, though, and awkward, especially if he moves around inside. And, we'd have to make sure the front is refastened tightly, because we could be in big trouble if it opens while we're carrying it."

"What are we supposed to do if we manage to get it up on the deck?"

"I'll figure it out," Travis answered. "I can't get it up by myself, though."

"I'll help," Garrett volunteered. Travis smiled and nodded; he didn't have the heart to point out the obvious. Garrett, while willing to work hard, was still a scrawny, twelve-year-old boy.

"Me, too," Kyra offered.

"So, the boy and the girl have volunteered eagerly," Amir said, looking around. His words surprised Travis, if for no other reason than he usually spoke so few. And, he was never voluntarily confrontational, that Travis had seen. "Are the men going to follow suit?"

"I'll help," Jesiah said. He frowned, as though his participation should have been assumed. To Travis, it was; Jesiah had proven himself to be a hard and willing worker.

"Of course, we'll help," Cosy said, shooting Amir a dirty look. "We're only being practical, here. Trying to figure out what your plan is. How safe it is."

Travis opened his mouth, but before he could answer, Amir spoke, again: "I think it would be a good idea for us to trust Travis, at this point. Yes?"

Travis stared at him, honestly stunned. Cosy cleared his throat. Jesiah shuffled his feet. Kyra and Garrett smiled at Travis. And, finally, Gibbs spoke for all of them. "Of course, we do," he said.

*   *   *

Putting the front panel onto the crate had been nerve-wracking, enough— Travis had held it before himself, edging closer, and the dragon had finally begun to retreat, angrily and reluctantly, until it was all the way inside the box. Once Travis had the panel in place, Jesiah and Cosy had hurried forward to nail the sides shut. The whole time, Travis had expected the animal to throw himself against the front, knocking it and Travis over.

That hadn't happened, however, and they'd managed to haul the heavy crate up the stairs, and out onto the deck. Most of the men, and all of the children, were gathered on the deck to watch. Travis directed the crate to be put against the railing, so that it could act as an extension of the crate on one side and help keep Buddy confined to a smaller area. He would be able to move in front of the box, and to one side, but could be more easily corralled back inside.

Everyone was moved back, well out of range of the chain that was still fastened inside the crate, and Travis alone pried the freshly pounded nails out of the wood. He backed away, holding the panel before himself, until the hunched dragon was visible in the shadows. Buddy's yellow eyes glinted, narrowed, as he peered out at Travis, blinking at the sight of bright sunlight. How long had it been since he'd the sun? There was no way of knowing if the dragon had *ever* seen it, but it had been almost two months, at least. Probably half of the animal's life, if not longer.

"Let's give him a little while to get used to the wind," Travis said, leaning the crate's panel against the rail.

"How are we going to get the body out?" Jesiah asked from beside the children.

"How are we going to get the box back downstairs?" Cosy muttered.

"We're not," Travis said. "We'll be on land, soon. He'll stay here until we can turn him loose." He turned toward the kids. "Look at me," he said, and they all turned their gazes to him. "You're not to go anywhere close to this box, or the dragon. Alright? He's not a pet, he's very, very dangerous. And," he added, pointing toward the dog, who was being held on a length of rope by Angel, "Jacko needs to be kept away. He could be hurt, very badly, or even killed, if he gets too close. Do you all understand?"

They nodded, each looking solemn.

Travis couldn't let that be enough, though. "Each of you needs to promise me. This is important. Come on."

"I promise," they said, almost in unison. All of the boys.

"Angel?" Travis said.

"I promise," she answered, grudgingly. She couldn't seem to keep her eyes off the dragon, and Travis knew he was going to have to keep a very close eye on her.

Jacko, at least, seemed calm, which was encouraging. He was sitting by Angel's side, looking at the dragon, with his tongue lolling from the corner of his mouth. He appeared far more relaxed than the dragon, and far less aggressive.

Jesiah handed Travis a bucket of water, and Travis set it on the deck and pushed it toward Buddy with his foot, until it was just within reach of the chain. Buddy glared out at him and opened his mouth. His wings were folded back, his neck stretched forward, and he looked like he wanted to bite Travis's face off. Of course, he couldn't, which likely irritated the animal even more—knowing that he was, still, completely at the mercy of the species that had caused him so much harm and cost his sister her life.

He'd have to wait a while longer for his freedom, though. Travis would unchain him somewhere in the woods outside Bohannon—he could only assume there would be such a place, as he'd never seen the continent. Somewhere away from the city and its population. Could Buddy survive on his own? Travis would make sure the dragon had gathered as much strength and health by that point as possible, and then it would be up to the animal to find its own way. Based on the way it had repeatedly lunged for Travis, its hunting instincts seemed intact.

"Let's all get back to our work," Travis said, turning his back on the dragon. "Just keep this whole area clear. We'll deal with the body after he calms down a little." Buddy calming down was unlikely, Travis knew. He had a plan for getting the dead girl out, though. "We'll come back after supper and...have a funeral," he said, glancing at Angel. He knew that the grief of losing her brother was still raw, even if she was showing signs of improvement, and he wasn't sure she'd be able to handle another funeral— even if it was for a dragon.

"Come on, boys, you can help me," Jesiah said, motioning for the kids to follow him. Carl, Jake, and little Robbie followed him willingly, but Jesse hesitated. He looked at Travis, then Garrett, and his gaze skidded across the other men before returning to Travis.

"Can I help up here?" he asked, tentatively.

Jesse was nine years old, and although Travis knew he would try his hardest to be helpful, he wasn't sure any of the men would volunteer for the responsibility of having a boy underfoot.

"Come, my lad," Amir said, before Travis could answer. "We'll teach you to sail a ship."

Jesse's face lit up. He took one step toward Amir, however, and hesitated again, looking at Travis. "Is it alright?" he asked.

Amir was regarding Travis, as well, and Travis met his eyes for a moment. "Sure," he answered. "Just be careful, alright?"

"Oh, sure," Jesse said, hurrying to Amir.

Travis turned and looked at Garrett and Kyra, standing nearby. "I'm going to keep guard," Garrett said. Then, after a short pause: "Right?"

"That would be great, thank you, Gar," Travis answered. He let out a breath and looked out over the water. He was tired. He wanted to go to sleep for, at the very least, a few hours. He couldn't, though. There were things that needed to be done, preparations for the burning that needed to be seen to. People were depending on him; namely the children. Angel was still standing on the deck, but Tabitha took her hand to lead her below, telling the girl she could help prepare supper.

"Can I talk to you?" Kyra asked, coming up beside Travis.

He looked at her. She seemed nervous. "Sure," he answered, frowning. Garrett was taking a seat against the railing, out of reach of the dragon but close enough to keep anyone else away. There were men around, some working, some milling about aimlessly. "You want to walk this way?" Travis asked, gesturing with his head.

She nodded, and they started walking toward the back of the ship, side by side, until they found themselves alone. There, they stopped and leaned against the railing, looking out at the ocean they'd crossed. It was difficult for him to comprehend how far away from home he was; how far away from the people he loved. It felt like he'd been on the ship for a lifetime, and yet it was nearly impossible to gauge the passage of distance. They were traveling under the power of nothing more than wind, a felt but unseen force, and the flap of the sails and the rush of air and the waves behind the ship were the only signs of how quickly they were moving. With each hour, they were closer to Bohannon, further from Baytown, and the sea was passing beneath them without comment. Above, the sky was gray, heavy with clouds, and even the arc of the sun was difficult to determine.

"It's crazy, isn't it? To think how far away we are? I mean...from everything," Kyra said after a few moments of silence. "Do you think we'll ever get back?"

Travis thought of his sister, and thought, *I have to.* "Do you want to?" he asked, knowing that most of them didn't have much—if anything—to return to.

"I don't know," she answered. "All the times I dreamed of getting out, getting away...starting over...this wasn't the way I imagined it. You know?"

He nodded and turned his head to regard her. "So, what's going on?" he asked.

She glanced at him, then away, sighing as she looked out at the water. "I thought we should talk about what's going to happen when we get...wherever we're going," she finally said.

He was surprised. Mostly by the 'we,' but also by the grown-up pragmatism underneath the wistful sigh. Orphans grew up faster than other kids, he knew, but there was more to it than that. He felt like he and Kyra could understand each other; they thought alike, which was a rare thing for him to find in a girl so close to his own age. In his experience, the teenaged girls fit into two categories: those who were trying to act older than they were, and pretend they had the world already figured out, and those who really *did* seem to him to have the world figured out. The latter group was far too smart for him, even though they were the ones willing to give him the time of day. The former group wanted nothing to do with boys his age, thinking their quickest way to adulthood was flirting with men with twice their years.

Kyra didn't fit into either category. She was somewhere in between, wise beyond her years and willing to face the world head on, but aware of all the things she didn't know and justifiably afraid of them. She would run circles around the fake girls and probably feel a little insecure around the others, but when Travis looked at her, he saw himself. Of all the people on the ship, she was the one who was really in the same place he was. Emotionally, intellectually, developmentally...and in terms of the level of fear and responsibility they were shouldering, because he knew that she felt as much obligation to protect the younger kids as he did. It was a strange thing. They were not adults themselves, not really, still trapped somewhere before the border, and they were surrounded by actual adults—some of whom, at least, were responsible enough to take charge of Angel and the boys. Tabitha, Gibbs, Amir, none of them would let harm come to the children.

And yet it was Travis and Kyra who stood, looking at each other, knowing that they would not trust anyone else with the burden. As their gazes held, a strange sort of duality seemed to shiver through Travis, dividing him. He felt young, like the boy he was, with sweaty palms and a racing heart and a new desire to kiss the pretty girl standing before him. At the same time, he felt as though he'd aged at least a decade in the past two months, and he knew that he could no longer afford to be a giddy, giggling child. He didn't have the luxury of exploring a childish crush or young attraction. Without fully understanding why, he knew that if anything happened between himself and Kyra, it would be serious, and important, and adult. It was a frightening realization, because it made him realize—in a way that even killing all those men could not—that there was no going back.

Maybe in more ways than one.

Ella, his mind whispered. "I have to see my sister again," he said, quietly. "And Luca. One way or another, I...have to get back. I have to let her know I'm alright. I owe her that. I mean, I owe her way more than that, but...she's spent my whole life taking care of me, worrying about me, putting me ahead of herself. She deserves a break from that. She deserves a life of her own. But if I don't get back to her, she won't ever have that. She'll worry about me until she worries herself into the ground. She needs to know I'm alright."

Kyra nodded. "You're not the same as you were when we left, though."

"No," he agreed. "None of us are."

"What should we do with the kids?"

He regarded her, solemnly. "We might run into trouble when we get to shore," he answered. "None of us have papers. I guess we wouldn't need them if they were just going to sell us, but...I can't imagine that's legal in Bohannon any more than it is in Baytown. Which means...they had to have had a plan to smuggle us in, somehow. I asked Jesiah and Cheddy, but they didn't know. So there's no way to know what to expect when we get off the ship. I can't imagine they would cause trouble for the kids once we explain what happened, though. We'll have to find a home for them."

"An orphanage," she murmured, turning to gaze at the water.

"Someplace they'll be safe and taken care of," Travis answered. "I promise, I won't leave until they're settled somewhere safe."

"And then?" she asked, quietly. She wasn't looking at him.

He was silent, watching her profile. The question shouldn't be so difficult to answer, he knew. He would get on the first ship headed toward Baytown, no matter what he had to do to get on board. That's what he should say. That's what he should want. In the past month—hell, in the past few days, if he was being honest—the world had become so much larger than he'd ever imagined. He still couldn't quite understand the shift within himself, but he did recognize a longing to be in control of his own life.

"I don't know," he finally admitted. "I...I can't just...start a new life and...and...send a letter and sit back and hope it got to her..."

"Do you think she'd like to come over to Bohannon, too? Start over..."

Travis considered that question. He was still studying Kyra's profile, still trying to sort out his thoughts and feelings, and she was still avoiding his eyes. It was a testament to what they were leaving behind—or, rather, how little they were leaving behind—that the idea of starting over in an unfamiliar country was as appealing as it was frightening. Did he think Ella would object to leaving what had been their home? No, not really. There might be opportunities in Bohannon that had never been available to them in Baytown. Would Luca mind leaving? Probably not. They were a family, no matter how unconventional, and Travis knew that they would feel the same way he did: that home was where your family was.

Would Bohannon be better, though? In truth, he had no way of knowing. He wanted to believe it would be. "We'd never be able to afford the tickets," he said. "At least...not unless I could find work, and..." He trailed off.

"You have a ship," Kyra said, quietly.

He hesitated, then said, "What?"

She looked at him. "This ship," she said.

"This isn't mine," he answered, suddenly uncomfortable. "Besides, even if it was, I don't know how to sail it." Hadn't he already considered the possibility, though? Even if he was afraid to admit it out loud? "I'd get myself killed, and anyone else on board with me."

"You haven't so far," she said.

"Gibbs and Cosy and—"

"No, Travis. You're the reason we're all here. Maybe you don't know how to sail, but you can learn. What's important is that people trust you, and you can lead them. You can get a crew. Most of these men would probably go back with you."

"How would I pay them?" he asked.

"There's money in the captain's cabin," she answered. "You know there is."

He looked away. "That's stealing," he said. Wouldn't claiming the ship be stealing, too? It might have been different if the captain, killed by Travis's sword, had been the owner, but he wasn't.

"Stealing from a slave-trader?" Kyra asked.

Travis considered that, then shrugged. "Stealing is stealing," he said.

*   *   *

"Are you sure this is going to work?" Cosy asked, nervously.

"Pretty sure," Travis muttered. Everyone else was well out of harm's way, but they were all tensed, worried for him. While he appreciated their concern, it added a little edge to his own nervousness. He was holding the front panel of the crate in his hands, and he turned it and laid it on its side, holding it upright. The crate was a little more than half as wide as it was tall, and the panel, on its edge, was higher than Travis's waist. Maybe not high enough, but the best option he had. He slid it forward slowly, watching for the dragon's reaction. Buddy drew back, hissing. Quickly realizing that Travis meant to push the panel into the box with him, however, the dragon moved forward, instead, swiping angrily at the wood. He almost knocked it out of Travis's grasp.

Buddy was out of the way, so Travis moved quickly, before the dragon had a chance to figure out what was going on. Travis, on the other side of the panel, between it and the railing of the ship, shoved it forward. Buddy reared up, his teeth bared, as he realized—too late—that the barrier had been shoved between himself and the corpse of his sister. He threw himself at the panel, knocking it into Travis and Travis, in turn, against the railing. The panel was slanted against him, and Travis had already dropped himself into a crouch behind it. The panel would provide protection for only a few moments. Once Buddy realized he couldn't get to Travis above or around it, he would either flip it up and go underneath, or tear through it.

Travis grabbed the decaying corpse, ignoring the sickening feel of his fingers sinking into the remains, and pulled, shoving it behind himself. Luckily, the skin was still leathery enough to keep the skeleton together, because he knew there wouldn't be time to grab for a bunch of loose pieces. Cosy, hurrying forward, grabbed the dead dragon with a grappling hook and pulled it away as Buddy slammed into the panel separating himself from Travis.

Travis's head smacked one of the rails, and pain flared. He lost his balance, with one hand pressed against the wooden panel and the other against the railing, in an awkward crouch, and he suddenly couldn't move. Two razor-sharp talons tore through the wood in front of his face, and he tried to push against the panel but couldn't seem to budge it in his unsteady position. He struggled to move his foot further beneath him, putting his other hand against the panel and using the railing behind his back for stability. What would happen if he was shoved through the railing and into the cold ocean rushing below?

Buddy's talons disappeared from the holes in the wood and, a moment later, curved around the side of the panel and slashed a tear through Travis's forearm. He bit back his scream—barely—as fiery pain exploded up his arm. Someone yelled his name and he somehow managed to get his feet up and against the wooden panel. He pushed, with all of the strength in his legs, with his back against the railing and his hands—one slick with blood—on the deck. His arm screamed in pain, and he could feel tears burning his eyes.

"Hey! Dragon! Buddy!" That was Cosy, and suddenly the pressure against the panel was gone. Even as Travis scrambled to the side, he caught sight of Cosy, holding the dead dragon's skeleton up by its tale with a look of disgust on his face. Buddy lunged in that direction, even though he had no hope of reaching his sister, and the crate slid a couple of inches along the deck. Travis had already found his feet and managed to stumble away from the box, leaving the wooden panel canted against the railing.

"Are you alright?" Kyra asked, as she and Tabitha rushed forward to examine Travis's bloody arm.

Buddy had collapsed to the deck—not in exhaustion, but despair. Travis didn't doubt the emotion shining in the young animal's eyes. "Cosy, put her down," he said, sharper than he'd intended. He was grateful for the help, still barely able to comprehend that he was still alive, but he couldn't stomach the sight of the corpse being dangled like that—or by Buddy's emotional reaction to it. Travis half-expected Cosy to toss the corpse to the deck. To his relief, however, Cosy bent and set it down.

"Let me see your arm," Tabitha was saying.

"Later," Travis said. The sun was low and would soon be swallowed by the sea. After mostly-drizzly days, dark with clouds, this evening had fallen calm and dry. The sky was streaked with colors. Rain would've been better, but the weather couldn't be forced to cooperate. "Jesiah, Franklin, get the tub," he called. He was trying desperately to ignore the pain in his arm. It was worse than anything he'd suffered at the end of a sword, and he didn't dare look at his left arm, afraid he would see the bone gleaming whitely through his torn flesh.

"Travis," Kyra said, clearly alarmed by the amount of blood.

"I'm fine. Look at him," Travis said, gesturing toward Buddy with his thumb. "Maybe this was a mistake."

Garrett was helping Jesiah and Franklin drag the heavy metal washtub, removed earlier from the captain's cabin, across the deck. The boy glanced at Travis's arm and gulped. "It's alright, Buddy," he croaked, tearing his gaze away from the injury.

In spite of the pain, Travis bent to grab the dead dragon from the deck, wincing as his own blood splattered the corpse. He picked the body up and laid it in the tub, where they'd already placed a pile of packing straw. Buddy was watching, but he didn't even lift his head, all fight gone from his limp body. Travis's stomach clenched.

"This is your sister, Buddy," Travis said. "You love her. You did everything you could to protect her. She's gone. She's gone," he repeated, his voice cracking. He refused to believe the same was true for himself. His own sister wasn't dead, although she felt impossibly far away. He glanced at Angel and saw her dark face glistening with tears. She was kneeling, hugging Jacko. Kyra was crying, too, and Robbie, and Garrett was struggling to keep his own face composed. "She didn't deserve to die, Buddy, but she doesn't deserve to rot away in a box," Travis said, his own throat thick with emotion. "Gibbs."

The man handed him a can of oil and a pack of matches, and Travis sprinkled just enough oil around the straw to start the fire. He lit a match and dropped it in, flinching as the fire puffed to life with a *whoosh*. The straw caught quickly, and the washtub was filled with flames in moments. The orange heat engulfed the corpse, surrounding it, but it didn't immediately begin to burn. The skin was tough, even in death.

Buddy had lifted his head. His eyes glowed orange instead of yellow as he stared at the flames. After several seconds, he pushed to his feet, opened his mouth, and let out a screech of grief that pierced Travis's heart and even dulled the pain in his arm. The world was consumed in red and orange and yellow. The sky, the fire, the slanted eyes. Travis's blood was just another shade of red.

* * *

"Land," Travis said, unnecessarily. "Where's Bohannon?" he asked, scanning the visible line of continent.

"If I had to guess," Gibbs said, squinting into the brightness. Then he was silent, considering. After a few moments, he pointed. "I'd say, there. Based on the ships. Looks like there's another harbor over there, clearly less trafficked. For Bohannon, we're just a little off-course. We can head for either."

Travis nodded. "We'll head for Bohannon. There might be a reason that one's not used, but it doesn't matter. Almost all trade seems to go through Bohannon. It's where this ship is due."

"We might be wise not to draw too much attention to ourselves, though," Gibbs said, shifting. "The man who owns this ship is not going to be happy when we show up."

"He's not going to be happy about the paperwork we found in the captain's cabin," Travis answered. "We're not going to sneak in with our heads down and hope to be unnoticed. We're coming in under our own power, with our own freedom, and Martin Bauer is going to pay for what his ships have done."

After several seconds of silence, Cosy, standing behind them, cleared his throat, and said, "We'll adjust course."

Travis shook his head. "Let's get closer to land, first," he said, pointing straight ahead toward what appeared to be unpopulated woodland. "We might find a place to release Buddy." His arm was bandaged, but the blood had again soaked through. It wouldn't stop bleeding. Tabitha had tried to sew it up, but the jagged edges of flesh were too torn. The gash wasn't to the bone, as Travis had feared, but if it didn't stop bleeding, he was going to be in real trouble.

* * *

Angel had Jacko on a three-foot length of frayed rope, and was standing well out of reach of Buddy. Garrett and Robbie were standing on either side of her and the dog. Travis could see them talking, but couldn't hear the conversation over the rush of wind. The shore was close; they'd adjusted their sails and were running almost parallel to the land, heading toward the wooded area at an angle.

"Think we'll be able to get him off without actually putting him in a rowboat?" Gibbs was asking.

Travis barely heard him. He was frowning toward the kids, and the dragon.

301

Angel had been obsessed with Buddy, spending almost all her time watching him from a distance, usually with Jacko by her side. Jacko had shown no aggression toward the dragon, and had made no attempts to free himself from his tether, and Travis knew that Garrett took his vigilance very seriously.

Now, though, looking back at Angel and Robbie, the two smallest children, Travis felt a growing knot of apprehension. Buddy was outside of his box, crouched, watching the three kids and the dog with his large yellow eyes. Regular meals had made a world of difference for the dragon, and even from a distance, Travis could see the change in the animal's size in just a couple of days. Travis hadn't known if Buddy would recover from the loss of his sister's body, but he had been reassured that he'd made the right decision. After the burning, Buddy had curled up in the box. He'd resumed eating by morning, however, and his despondency was now gone.

Something was wrong, though. Travis could feel it, and he started walking toward them, trying to identify the reason for his sudden nervousness. Angel was holding Jacko's leash in both hands, to her side. Robbie had something in his hand, too, and as he drew nearer, Travis realized what it was: a fish. His stomach clenched. No one—not Garrett, not even any of the adults—had been allowed to feed Buddy, no one but Travis. Buddy, although no longer starving, exactly, had only recently been at death's door. He had not forgotten his hunger, and he would not forget it any time soon.

Garrett had his hand on Robbie's shoulder; without hearing the words, Travis knew that Garrett was telling the younger boy that he could not feed the dragon. Whether or not Robbie was willing to respect Garrett's authority was not really the issue, because the dragon was well aware of the fish's presence. Buddy was straightening, and Travis found himself running toward the scene.

Garrett had apparently realized that something was wrong, as well, and as Travis hurried toward them, Garrett was already pulling the younger kids back by their shoulders. The dragon had spread its wings until one was pressed against the railing, and as it lifted its head higher, straightening its body, it suddenly looked impossibly large. The children, from Travis's perspective, were dwarfed before the animal.

Travis was almost there. He heard Angel's voice: "Give him the fish!" He saw Garrett reach down, snatch the fish from Robbie's hand, and toss it toward the dragon's feet.

Buddy stepped forward, barely missing the offering with the lethal talons of one foot. He didn't look down. He was no longer interested in dead fish, it seemed.

Garrett pushed the kids behind himself. He ushered them back, but when he tried to retreat, he stumbled over Jacko. The dog managed to get out of the way, skittering around beside Angel, but Garrett was falling. Robbie grabbed Angel's hand, and pulled her back as Travis finally reached them.

It wasn't until Travis was beside Garrett that he really understood what the problem was, what his mind had been struggling to reconcile; Buddy was out of his box. Too far out. A quick glance showed Travis that the shackle was still around the dragon's ankle. As though to prove his inexplicable freedom, Buddy stepped further forward. Travis's heart was slamming in his chest, and not just from running. He'd always known where the limits of the tether were, and although he had sometimes been within reach, he had always taken precautions. Now there was nothing separating him from the dragon, not even a thin panel of wood, and the pain in his arm flared as a reminder of what the dragon was capable of.

"Move, Gar," he said, in a low voice, through numb lips. Without looking away from Buddy, Travis could sense Garrett crawling backward and, after a moment, getting to his feet. "Get the kids inside." Travis said. He didn't know who he was speaking to; he had no idea how many people were within earshot. He knew that someone would get the children to safety.

Buddy watched Garrett for a few heartbeats, then turned his yellow gaze onto Travis. Standing as it was, the dragon was taller than Travis. Their eyes met and held. Buddy opened his mouth, letting out an angry hiss. Travis wasn't sure if the dragon would have gone after one of the kids, or the dog, but there was no mistaking the danger that Travis had stepped into. The dragon's eyes were bright and alert, his teeth bared, his chin raised and read to strike...Those angry eyes said that it was time for payback.

As the animal's hiss died, the only sound was the rush of wind. Travis thought—suppressing a shudder—that he might as well be standing on a ghost ship. He assumed, and hoped, that everyone had gone below to safety, especially the kids, but there was a part of him that wished someone would be willing to step in front of *him*. With all the men, older than he was, on board, why did it always fall to him to stand strong?

He pushed the thought away. It didn't matter, anyway—everything he'd done had been his choice, and his choices had led him to this moment, facing an angry dragon. And, now, he was faced with another choice. If he went for his sword, Buddy would likely kill him before he could draw. If he *could* manage to get a sword from its scabbard, he would certainly not get more than one swing.

Buddy shifted; the rattle of his chain was loud in the quiet. On impulse, Travis put up a hand and found his palm pressed against the animal's dry chest. Buddy stopped, and Travis could swear that the dragon's large eyes showed real surprise. He was more than a little surprised, himself. He had no idea what his plan was—he certainly couldn't hope to keep the animal back with physical strength. Thanks to Travis's dedication to feeding Buddy, the dragon was strong, and the arm stretched between them was weak, wrapped in a bloody bandage.

Under his palm, Travis could feel the dragon's heart pounding. The sensation was eerie, and although he'd never felt a dragon's heartbeat before, Travis suddenly knew, without a doubt, that the rapid pounding inside Buddy's chest was indicative of fear, not anger. The anger was an act, albeit a convincing one.

It had been such a short amount of time since Travis first laid eyes on

303

Buddy, huddled and starved, wasting away in misery beside his dead sister. Travis had been unable to kill the dragon then, and he didn't think he'd be able to do it now, not even to save his own life. The truth was, Buddy had suffered terribly at the hands of men. Of course he was afraid, and willing to lash out, full of hatred and distrust. He didn't know any better. A few meals could not make up for the weeks without, just as a few kind words could not make up for being ripped from his home and left to rot in a crate.

And what had Travis done to earn the animal's trust? He'd fed him. He'd spoken to him. He'd treated his sister's corpse with as much respect as he could. He'd done everything he could to show Buddy that he meant him no harm. Everything, except turn him loose on the ship. Travis had been unable to do that, because he had the safety of the children to worry about. And the safety of the men. And the safety of Buddy, himself, as several of the men would have gladly killed the beast. Did Buddy understand any of that, though? Or did he simply see Travis as another human eager to keep him a prisoner?

Well, he wasn't a prisoner anymore. He still had a heavy length of chain attached to his leg, though. He was probably strong enough to make it to land, but what would happen then? What would happen if he made his way into the woods and the chain snagged? How many trees would he be able to uproot or break before he could go no further? Would he chew off his own leg to get free?

These musings were unproductive, and Travis couldn't believe he was standing on a ship, thousands of miles from the only home he'd ever known, with his hand against a dragon. Before he could rethink his decision, he shoved his free hand into his pocket, closing his fingers around the keys from the former captain's chambers. At the sudden movement, Buddy made a sound and lurched forward, shoving Travis with his body, and Travis stumbled backward and fell, one hand still in his pocket and the other held up in supplication. He hit the deck, hard, wincing as his teeth snapped together and the shock of impact rolled through his body.

Buddy loomed over him, raised a taloned foot, and lashed out. His claws sliced through the air, missing Travis's stomach by inches. Travis couldn't breathe. He looked down at himself with wide eyes, convinced he'd been gutted, and couldn't quite make sense of the lack of pain. His whole body was trembling. He couldn't have gotten to his feet if he'd wanted to; the dragon was leaning over him, growling, and Travis's legs wouldn't have supported him, anyway.

"Easy, Buddy," Travis said, surprised to find he could speak.

The dragon's head tilted, and he stared down at Travis, one taloned foot still raised. Had the dragon tried to kill him? Or, had he missed on purpose? Travis's mind was a jumble, and he couldn't be sure. He'd pulled the keys from his pocket, though, and he held them up. They jingled in his trembling hand. The yellow eyes focused on them.

Travis knew that this was his best, and probably only, chance to go for his sword. He was sitting in an awkward position, but he had the dragon

304

distracted, and he thought he could draw and have the blade up by the time the animal came down on him. The dragon's own weight would work against him if and when he attacked, driving the blade through his heart.

Travis still didn't reach for his sword. Instead, he leaned forward, wincing, squinting his eyes in anticipation of the blow he expected to come. He reached out, almost dropping the keys several times, and when he finally extended the right key toward the shackle's lock, his whole body was hunched and tensed, waiting for an attack that still hadn't come. He unlocked the cuff quickly in spite of his shaking hands, and the chain fell away from the dragon's foot. The ankle was raw and sore-looking, and Travis felt a surge of guilt.

Gathering all of his courage, Travis pulled back and looked up at the dragon. "It's up to you, now, Buddy," he said. "I'm not going to try to kill you, and...I don't think you want to kill me, either." The dragon wrinkled his snout, showing even more of his fangs. "Yeah, yeah, I know," Travis said. "You're mad. I don't blame you. But I didn't do it. You know I didn't do it. I never hurt you. Look, I brought you to land, right? Go. You're free. Fly. Hunt animals. Get away from people."

Travis knew he should feel like an idiot, but while he was staring up at the dragon, it was easy to believe Buddy understood him. For several long moments, Travis thought the animal was going to kill him, anyway, slice him open from throat to crotch, perhaps, or side to side. Then, Buddy pulled down into himself, seeming to shrink, and Travis was again reminded of how young the animal was. Buddy lowered, tensed, and pushed up in a jump that made Travis flinch. With a flap of wings, the dragon lifted into the air, blocking out the sun and casting Travis in an impossibly large shadow.

Travis craned his neck to watch the dragon fly—awkwardly, possibly for the first time—and he was filled with a confusing jumble of emotions. Relief, predominantly, but there was also a bit of residual fear, and more than a little grief. The latter surprised him; he was sad to see the dragon go, even though he'd been sure, just a minute before, that the animal was going to kill him. Buddy let out a single screech as he banked and flew between the masts, out over the water. Travis couldn't interpret the sound, but he wanted to believe it was a goodbye, of sorts. Buddy *could* have killed him, and almost had. Almost. Travis was still alive, and not freshly injured—aside from a sore backside and a bruised elbow from his fall—and Buddy was off the ship, heading for land without looking back.

Travis could feel his heart rate slowly returning to normal. He looked at his hands. They were trembling. He pushed himself forward, to look at the chain. He expected it to be broken away from the wood of the crate, but he was wrong. The links had been twisted and broken in the middle. Half of the chain was still attached to the crate; the other half ended in the shackle that had just been unlocked from Buddy's ankle.

Travis let out a shaky breath, frowning. There was no way Buddy could have broken the chain by simply pulling on it. He would have accomplished nothing except to drag the heavy box around the deck. In order to break the chain in the middle, he would have had to either stand on one end and pull, or use his talons to pry them apart...Travis had no idea what kind of capabilities dragons had regarding their dexterity. He wished he could have seen the chain break, if for no other reason than to satisfy his curiosity.

Finally feeling ready to stand, he got to his feet slowly, carefully, and saw Buddy landing at the edge of the trees. Letting out another breath, finally allowing himself to really feel the relief, he turned and caught sight of Amir. The deck was not deserted, as Travis had imagined. There were five men in sight. Cosy, Gibbs, and two others were grouped loosely together, with swords. Amir was alone, with a bow and arrow. They were held down at his side, but the arrow was notched, and Travis suddenly knew that Amir would have put that arrow through Buddy if he'd thought Travis was in real danger.

Considering how convinced Travis had been, for a little while, that the dragon was going to kill him, he could scarcely understand how Amir had resisted the urge to shoot. On legs that felt a bit rubbery, Travis walked toward Amir. The others were slowly stowing their swords, and as Travis approached, Cosy said, "Damn, kid. That was crazy."

"How'd you know he wasn't going to gut me?" Travis asked Amir. It wasn't an accusation; just an honest question.

"You're the only friend he's ever known," Amir said.

Travis opened his mouth, then closed it. He had no idea what to say to that.

* * *

"We'll be in Bohannon tomorrow."

Ella turned her head to look at Swan. He was staring out over the glittery water. He'd been exceptionally quiet, lately, but so had she. They spent little time talking about anything that wasn't superficial, and she could feel that weighing on his mind. It was weighing on hers, too. She hadn't wanted their last few days together to be wasted in awkwardness and unhappiness. She loved every moment spent in his company, no matter how bittersweet.

"How long before you get to see Maggie?" she asked.

"We'll reach the harbor around midnight, if the wind holds out." He paused, then added, "And it will. We'll anchor off shore and dock just after daybreak. Should be at Maggie's by nightfall."

"I bet she'll be happy to see you," Ella said, smiling. She thought of her brother, and how much she longed to see his face.

"She'd love you," Swan said.

He said 'she'd' rather than 'she'll,' and the distinction was not lost on either of them as they looked out at the sea. "I'd be honored to meet her," she finally said, quietly. "If I—" She stopped, biting her lip. "What would you say if I...said there was something I needed to...take care of by myself?" she asked, hesitantly. She hadn't meant to broach the subject at all. If she'd been strong enough to leave him at the docks without warning, she would have, with the intention of returning to explain as soon as possible. She could feel him slipping away, though, and knew it was her fault. She was making him doubt her feelings.

He sighed and turned toward her, propping a hip against the railing. "Ella," he said. "I'd say...you don't have to take care of anything by yourself."

"If I wanted to take care of it myself..." she muttered, trying desperately not to cry.

He regarded her in silence. Then he sighed, again. "I wish you'd tell me what's wrong," he said, and even though he spoke softly, she could hear the raw frustration in his words. Then, hesitantly, "Does it have to do with Luca?"

He looked like he wanted to call the words back. Before he could say anything else, she put a hand against his chest. She didn't care who might be watching. "I'm not marrying Luca, if that's what you're asking," she said. She'd had no intention of telling him that, either, at least not until she returned with Travis. She couldn't stand the insecurity in his expression, though. Insecurity didn't suit him.

He looked just a little relieved, but he shook his head. He didn't understand, of course. She almost explained, everything. The words were on the tip of her tongue. She almost told him about Bauer, and how the men of his ship had stolen her brother. She didn't know Bauer, but Swan did, and she knew Swan. He would involve himself. To help her. To help Travis. He would put himself at risk without hesitation.

"I can't tell you my reasons for going to Bohannon," she said. "But...Luca and I are just friends. We've never been more than that." She waited for him to pull away. She waited for the anger to darken his face. What she saw, instead, was worse.

He looked hurt. "Why didn't you tell me?" he asked. He hadn't pulled away...yet.

"At first, I...didn't think it would matter. We needed to get to Bohannon, and then I thought...we'd probably never see you again. But then, when I got to know you, I was afraid you'd hate me for lying to you."

"When you got to know me?" he said, quietly. "If you knew me, you'd know I wouldn't—"

"I do, now," she said, quickly, desperately. "I was wrong. It just got harder and harder, the more I started to care about you..." She stopped and took a deep breath. "I'm sorry, Colin," she said. "I never meant to lie to you. I swear I didn't. And I would rather die than hurt you."

"That worries me," he said, softly.

"I can take care of myself, believe—" *me*, she'd been about to say, but she stopped, realizing the absurdity of it. How could he believe anything she said, when she'd just admitted she'd been lying to him? When she was still lying to him, or at least, not being fully honest?

"Trust is a two-way street, Ella," he answered.

She bit her lip. "I know," she muttered, after a moment, dropping her gaze.

"I won't stop you when you try to leave, if that's what you're worried about."

307

She shook her head. "No, I...I know..."

"Not because I won't want to," he added. She forced her gaze back up to his. "I wish you'd let me help you. I wish you'd...stay."

His sincerity and forgiveness were far more than she deserved, and she felt tears prick her eyes. "I can't..." she said.

His jaw clenched for a moment, and then he nodded. "I can't force you," he finally murmured.

"If I...Can I...What if I came back?" she asked, knowing she had no right to ask and doing it anyway.

"Then you can find me at Darling House," he answered. "At least until I set sail, again."

"I..." She stopped, struggling to find the right words.

"I have work to do," he said. He kissed her forehead, quickly, and stepped back. "I'll see you later, Ella." Before she could respond, he turned and strode away.

Chapter Fifteen

Part of her expected to sleep alone that night; if Swan avoided her, the way he had in the early days of sharing the cabin, she wouldn't blame him. She ate dinner alone, and dressed for bed in one of his shirts, like usual, and crawled into bed. She hadn't spoken to him since he'd told her he'd see her later. He'd had plenty of time to realize that he wanted nothing to do with her.

It was late when she heard the door open. She'd left it unlocked. Even though it was habit—per his instructions—to keep it locked, she'd been afraid to do anything to deter him from entering. She lay on her side, with her back to the door, unmoving, listening to the muffled sounds of his entry. She wanted to roll over and let him know she was awake; she was afraid that would chase him away. She waited to see if he would join her, or sink into the chair behind his desk. She heard him lock the door. She heard him stripping off his clothes.

She felt him sit on the edge of the bed. He stayed there, for long moments, with his back to her and his feet on the floor. Then he turned and stretched out behind her, close, and she could feel his breath on the back of her neck. She could smell him, his scent, as always, familiar, comforting, and arousing. His hand was on her hip, and then, slowly, trailing up the side of her ribcage. She rolled toward him. His chest was bare, and warm, and she pressed her palms against his skin, reveling in the desire he so easily inspired within her. He was wearing shorts, and nothing else, and she could feel his desire against her thigh, and she instinctively pressed closer.

His mouth covered hers, hungrily, a bit desperately. She met his tongue with her own, just as eager to taste and feel every inch of him. He rolled over her, pushing her into the mattress with his body, and she slid her hands to his hips, straining to be closer, impossibly close. To become a part of him. He pushed her shirt up between them until his hand found the curve of her breast and his thumb found her hardened nipple. She gasped, clutching at him, pulling her mouth from his to draw a shaky breath. She wasn't wearing anything under the shirt, and she could feel his erection straining against her with only his shorts between them.

She slid her hand into the waistband of his shorts, and it was his turn to gasp as her fingers found his manhood. A small shudder passed through him, and he dropped his face against her neck, his hot breath dampening her throat. She pushed his shorts down his hips, and he shifted to make it easier. When there was nothing between them, she arched against him, pulling at his hips. Her legs were spread beneath him, giving him full access. His hand slid along her thigh, between his body and hers, finding the junction between her legs.

His fingers found that she was ready, and he positioned himself. She expected him to enter quickly, but he surprised her, pushing his way in tantalizingly slowly. He bent his head and swallowed her gasp, kissing her as he filled her completely. She wrapped her legs around him, trying to pull him even deeper, knowing it was impossible. She held onto his sweat-slicked body.

She couldn't beg him to move faster, because he'd claimed her mouth. She was growing lightheaded from lack of air; it was not an unpleasant sensation.

Finally, he pulled his mouth from hers and, as he began moving his hips, he murmured, "I love you."

He was at his most vulnerable, physically, and she knew the enormity of the courage it took for him to say the words that she had never yet reciprocated. "I love you, too," she breathed. She was already building toward her climax, and his pace was quickening. She watched his face—the face she loved so much it hurt—as he brought them both to the brink. Then she plunged her fingers into his damp hair and brought his face down to hers, claiming his mouth as she tightened around him and the world began to splinter.

He didn't pull out, and she was happily surprised to feel him shuddering inside of her, to feel his seed released into her body, and she wanted to keep him inside forever. As his sweaty body relaxed against hers, she could feel their hearts pounding together. He shifted to the side, and she felt a pang of loss as he withdrew from her body. His arm and leg were draped across her, however, and he kissed her shoulder.

"I want you to stay," he whispered. "Whatever it is, we can talk about it."

She swallowed. She thought about what he was asking, and what it would mean. He would help get Travis back. They would set sail back toward Baytown, or wherever Swan's next destination might be. While she might be giving up a life on dry land, she would have the people she loved. And, while on the ship, they would be out of Bauer's reach. All of them. Sure, he might send a ship after them, depending on how angry he might be, but Swan and his men had proven they could take care of another crew. Besides, there might not be any reason for Bauer to be angry. Perhaps Swan would be willing to simply buy Travis...

The very idea made her stomach churn, though, and her chest burn with anger. Bauer would not get money for Travis, because Travis was not a possession to be bought, sold, or stolen. Neither were the countless others that Bauer had taken and traded or sold. He had to be held accountable, and that might take time. It would also make him angry. He might send a ship after Swan's, but he might aim for an easier target: the people and places Swan cared about in Bohannon. Namely, Maggie Darling and her orphanage, Darling House.

Swan had already told her his concerns. Bauer's threats, and Swan's concern for Maggie and the kids during his long absences. How could Ella, in good conscience, add to any animosity between Swan and Bauer?

"I love you," she said, again. Now that she'd said it, it felt imperative that he believe it. She felt tears threatening and managed to hold them back. There would be time for tears later, perhaps, but not yet.

"Then stay," he said. His face was close to hers, his damp hair stuck to his forehead. "Talk to me."

"We can talk about it," she agreed. "In the morning." She kissed his lips, wondering if it would be the last time. "Let's get some sleep," she murmured.

"It's going to be a long day, tomorrow."

He reached down and pulled the blanket over their naked bodies. "Am I too heavy?" he asked. Only his arm and leg were across her, and she shook her head, snuggling closer against his chest beneath the blanket. "Goodnight, Ella," he said, kissing her forehead.

"Goodnight, Colin," she whispered.

* * *

He was normally a light sleeper, when he slept at all, and as Ella eased out of the bed she felt a surge of guilt—not just for what she was doing, but because she knew that the only reason he was sleeping so soundly was because she'd put his mind at ease, with a lie. They would not be discussing their future this morning. She looked down at him, for long moments. She knew what she would say if he woke to find her sneaking out, but he was still breathing easily. Part of her hoped that he *would* wake up, and that he would see through her lies and refuse to let her leave.

She pulled her old, ratty dress over her head. She hadn't worn it in such a long time, the formerly-familiar garment felt strange. The material was thin, and it would dry more quickly. And, wasn't there a part of her that believed taking his clothes would be stealing? She blinked back her tears and somehow managed to fight down the urge to crawl back into the bed. The sun would be up in just a couple of hours. Swan might wake at any moment. She had to go, and as she made her way to the door carefully, wincing at the rustle of clothing, she reminded herself why she was leaving him.

She opened the door slowly and peeked outside. She saw no one. She expected Swan to call out to her at any moment, but the only sound from the bed was his steady breathing. She slipped out onto the deck and pulled the door shut with a tiny click. She stood with her heart pounding in her chest, looking up and down the length of the ship. It seemed deserted. She leaned forward and peered up at the crow's nest. In the pale moonlight, she could see someone up there. It couldn't be Goonie, of course; she didn't know who it was. She could see that he wasn't looking at her, though. He was turned the other way, watching out over the ocean.

There were a lot of other ships around, and Ella hesitated, wondering if any of them could be *Enterprise*. Many of them looked alike in shape, and it was too dark to read any names. She shook her head. Travis's ship should have been several days ahead of Swan's. Ella took a deep breath and let it out, slowly. She looked over her shoulder. The dragon was watching her; the yellow eyes glinted in the moonlight.

Ella wanted to say something to the animal—goodbye, thanks, something—but was afraid that even a whisper would carry to the crow's nest. So, before she could change her mind, she moved quickly toward the back of the ship, her bare feet almost silent on the deck. The night was clear and calm, and warmer than the last few had been, but she knew the water was going to be cold. She hesitated and looked back over her shoulder. Up in the basket, the man's dark shape was still turned away from her.

She was going to have to jump, and she could only hope that he'd think the splash was some sort of fish.

She scaled the railing quickly, took a deep breath, and dropped. There was no time for second thoughts.

Second thoughts? As she fell, she was full of fear—fear of the dark water, fear of the cold, fear of the unknown on land, fear of the hurt she would cause, fear for her brother—and her mind mocked her. She'd passed second thoughts, and third, and fourth. She stretched her toes as the water swallowed her, trying to make as little splash as possible. The water was shockingly cold, colder than the night with Goonie, and as it sucked her under, she had to struggle not to gasp. She disappeared from the world, into the dark, cold cocoon of wetness, the water burning her nose and pressing against her eyelids and chilling her skin with its seemingly-icy folds. Her skirt was driven up around her head, and the wet material swirled as she tried to propel herself toward the surface, tickling at her face, and she fought the panic trying to claw its way through her.

The water was calm, unlike the last time she'd been in the sea at such an hour, and she managed to work her way to air without completely losing her head. Even so, when she felt the easy night breeze against her cold face, it was a challenge to keep from making a sound. Part of her—the part that had known this was foolish, all along—wanted desperately to draw attention to herself, to beg someone to toss her a rope, to yell to the world that she'd changed her mind. She kicked herself into motion before she could give in to those feelings, staying close to the ship as she began swimming toward the faraway shore.

She expected the man from the crow's nest, or someone from another ship, or even the dragon, to send up an alarm at any moment. When she rounded the front of the ship, and started through open water, leaving behind its shielding shadow, she was even more prepared to hear a call ring through the night. She kept going, pulling herself through the cold water, not daring to look over her shoulder to see if anyone was watching her. She wanted to hurry and knew it would be unwise; it was a long swim, and she had to pace herself, in spite of the fear she felt of the dark unknown around and beneath her.

The moon was bright, and she could scarcely believe she'd been lucky enough to escape unnoticed. The more distance she put between herself and the ship, the lonelier she felt, and she knew that she would probably never see Swan again—no matter what her intentions. Her tears were warm on her chilled cheeks, but they mingled with the seawater, as unnoticed by the world as her departure seemed to be.

*   *   *

Swan awoke with a jolt, his heart slamming in his chest. He blinked, momentarily confused. He was normally a light sleeper, and easy to wake, but he felt groggy and disoriented, and knew he must have been sleeping more deeply than usual. The first thing he noticed was that it was not yet dawn. The second, that Ella was gone.

Then he realized why he'd come awake—a knock at the door. As he was still trying to assimilate, the sound came again, and he was already out of the bed and on his way to the door. He wondered if Ella had accidentally locked herself out, but even before he saw that the door was unlocked, his waking mind was filling his stomach with apprehension. He reached for the door, realized at the last moment that he was completely naked, and with a curse turned and snatched his shorts off the floor. He stepped into them quickly, scowling as the sleep finally began to clear from his mind.

He yanked the door open to find Marty standing before him, looking for all the world as though he'd rather be anywhere else. "I'm sorry, sir," he said, immediately.

"What's wrong?" Swan asked. He was trying to fight down his rising fear, trying to tell himself not to overreact until he knew what was going on. If Ella was hurt—He shook his head.

"It's Ella, sir," Marty said, shifting uncomfortably. "She's—"

"Where is she? Is she hurt?" Swan asked, resisting the temptation to shove Marty aside to go searching for her. He cursed himself for falling asleep. He cursed Ella for sneaking out, and immediately regretted the thought. He cursed Marty for taking so long to answer.

"She's not hurt, Captain," Marty said. "She's, uh...She..."

"Spit it out," Swan snapped, barely allowing himself to feel relief at the declaration that she wasn't hurt. Something was clearly wrong.

"She's swimming to shore, sir," Marty said. "I...I didn't see her until she was already in the water, and I...wasn't sure if I should...should..."

"What?" Swan asked, through numb lips.

"She jumped in the water, Captain. She's swimming to shore. She's about halfway already. I didn't know if I should send an alarm, and...by the time I climbed down—"

Swan shoved past Marty, hurrying to the bow of the ship, and his eyes found her immediately as she swam through the shimmering sea. He almost called out to her, before he realized how ridiculous that instinct was. She would probably hear him; the night was still and calm. What did he expect her to do, though? Turn around and come back? He wasn't so stupid that he believed she'd fallen in accidentally, that she was swimming for shore out of self-preservation. She'd taken efforts to sneak out of his bed, out of his room, and off his ship, and she was swimming to shore because that's where she wanted to be.

With the knowledge came pain, surprising him with its intensity. He'd known he'd fallen hopelessly in love with her, of course—and early on. No one had been more surprised by that than he was. He supposed he'd always been a bit of a romantic, but he'd learned at a very early age to be realistic, and he'd never expected to meet anyone like Ella.

No one had ever made him feel wanted the way Ella did, and he'd tried to convince himself that she might actually need him, as well. He'd known all along that he would probably be hurt, and he'd decided to let his vulnerability show, anyway. He'd told her how he felt, and what he wanted. And in the end, she'd agreed to talk things over. He'd believed there was hope, but in the pale moonlight, he realized that he'd not only been fooling himself, he'd been doing the thing he'd promised he *wouldn't* do: putting pressure on her.

Ella was a woman who tended more toward fight than flight; not easily frightened into backing down, he'd learned quickly enough that she had no problem battling and risking herself for someone else. It looked like she was fleeing now, but it was really just another form of fighting. Whatever plans she had, whatever reason she had for traveling to Bohannon, she was not about to let Swan or anyone stand in her way.

She could have told him the truth. No matter how badly it hurt, he wouldn't have stopped her from leaving if it was what she really wanted. The fact that she had decided to jump into the cold, dark, dangerous ocean, and to swim for an exhausting distance, rather than face him in the morning...That's where the real pain came from. Not just that she was leaving him, but that she didn't trust him to let her go.

She'd said she loved him, and he wondered if he'd been a complete idiot to believe that. Had she been telling him what he wanted to hear, to pacify him? To keep him from pressuring her with questions? He shook his head. It wasn't all an act. She might not want to stay with him, but she did care about him. They did share a connection unlike anything he'd felt before.

"Captain?" Marty asked, hesitantly, clearly disturbed by Swan's extended silence. "Should I...should we lower a boat?"

Swan swallowed the lump of emotion in his throat. Every second she was getting further away from him. He wanted desperately to go after her. He wanted to pull her from the cold water and make sure she was safe; that was the first thing. He had no idea what he might do after that. Yell at her for endangering herself, yet again? Accuse her of lying to him? Ask her what he'd done to make her fear him more than the sea? Would he spew hurtful words to dull his own hurt? Or ignore his wounded pride and beg her to stay, when she'd already proven it wasn't what she wanted?

He shook his head. "No," he said, quietly. "Let her go." The words were painful. He wasn't sure if he was talking to himself, or Marty.

"Sir?"

"Keep your eyes on her," Swan added, watching her slice her way toward shore in the glimmering light. "I won't rest easy until she's on land." *Who are you kidding? You won't rest easy...a lot longer than that*, he thought. As soon as the sun came up, he would dock the ship and they would begin unloading their cargo. He could scarcely imagine something so routine. He would be seeing Maggie before the day was out, and as much as he was looking forward to seeing the old woman, as much as he'd missed her, what would he say to

314

her?

He found himself thinking of Luca, and wondering if he knew that Ella was gone. And, if so, where she was heading.

*   *   *

Ella wasn't sure she was going to make it, and by the time she reached the shore, she was shaky with fatigue and barely able to stumble up the pebbly ground. Her body was numb from the cold, but she was shivering, hugging herself as she dripped her way from the sea. She hadn't taken any money from Swan's cabin, even though he'd told her she'd been allotted a salary. She hadn't brought any clothes to change into; what would have been the point? She'd had no way to keep anything dry, and no other clothes that belonged to her, anyway.

She had to keep moving, or she would freeze.

She fought against the overwhelming urge to look back. She wanted to see the ship, one more time. She resisted, mostly because it would lend a finality that she didn't want to acknowledge. She wanted desperately to believe she would see the ship again, after she'd found her brother. The ship and, more importantly, its captain. She kept her eyes forward and made her way, slowly, up the shore. She saw no people, which wasn't surprising; sunrise was at least an hour away.

She had no idea what she would do if she met a police officer, or any other official person, demanding some sort of documentation or explanation. She had no idea where she was, or where she was going. She would have to ask someone for directions, but she couldn't do that until the town had begun to wake a bit. She had to keep warm until then and try to dry out a bit. She didn't want to consider stealing, although she supposed if she happened upon some dry clothes on a line, she might give in to temptation. The cold seemed to be embedded in her bones, making her wonder if she'd ever be warm again. She couldn't keep her teeth from chattering.

The rocks were sharp against her feet as she staggered awkwardly up toward the street.

*   *   *

"Captain Swan. We were worried about you."

"We ran into a few delays," Swan said, shaking the other man's hand. They were standing on the dock. The sun was low, struggling its way out of the horizon. The crew had already begun to unload the cargo. Those with families in Bohannon were anxious to see them; those with no ties in the city were anxious to find a soft bed and a woman to lay in it with. They would be hard-pressed to find any pubs open before noon, but by evening, many of them would be several sheets to the wind in celebration for another successful cross.

For the first time in a very long time, Swan thought he could use a drink or

315

two, himself. He gave himself a mental shake. He had people to see and places to go. He couldn't afford to wallow in a bottle. While it might take the edge off for a night, he would be hung over in the morning and Ella would still be gone.

"Have you heard the news about *Enterprise*?"

"I just stepped off my ship, Mac," Swan said, trying to keep his irritation from showing. In spite of his preoccupation, however, Mac's excitement sparked Swan's curiosity. "That's one of Bauer's. What happened?" The ship should have been several days ahead of Swan's, and he wondered if they'd fared poorly in the storm. He knew what kind of business they ran on Bauer's ships, and while he had no compassion for the men willing to do it, he knew that there would be innocent people on board, as well. He certainly wished them no ill-will.

"There was a revolt," Mac said, rolling up on the balls of his feet.

"Revolt?" Swan repeated, frowning. "By whom?" He found it hard to believe that the crew of one of Bauer's ships—crews made up, mostly, of unscrupulous and unlawful men who wouldn't be hired by other ship owners—would overthrow their captain. What would be the point? Unless some ambitious troublemaker wanted to run the show himself, but *Enterprise* was not owned by its captain.

Mac glanced around, leaned forward, and lowered his voice. "The, uh, prisoners."

Swan felt his eyebrows lift. "The prisoners," he repeated. "You mean, slaves?"

Mac shrugged. "I guess. Some the men got loose, seems like, and killed the whole crew. 'Cludin' the cap'n."

Swan's gaze scanned the dawn-filled harbor and came to rest on the ship in question, anchored off-shore. It seemed deserted, at first. Small movement drew Swan's attention to the crow's nest, however, and he saw a single, dark-skinned man sitting in vigil, staring out over the sea. "Where are they?"

"Who?"

"The prisoners," Swan said. "Are they still on the ship?"

"No, sir. Only one man on board we know of. I tend to think he'd shoot an arrow through anyone who tried to board. The men, well...I'm not sure. They sorta went their separate ways, seems like. Immigration police stopped a few, and the kids—"

"Kids?" Swan repeated, alarmed.

"There was kidnapped kids on board. Officials tried to take them into custody."

"Tried?"

"The oldest kid and a woman raised quite a fuss, the boy threatened to kill anyone who laid a hand on them kids. Seems like he meant it, too. He was the biggest o' six boys an' two girls. The police took 'em all. I don't know where. Seems obvious they wouldn't have no papers, being kidnapped like they said, and all."

"Has Bauer been down here?"

316

"No, sir. His men were waiting for the ship. It was late, you know? So I'm sure Bauer ain't happy."

"When did the ship get here?"

"Yesterday. Few days overdue, so's I understand. Don't know many details. Nobody's been able to unload the ship, yet. Not sure why. That fella out there in the basket seems keen on keepin' everyone away, and so far the officials ain't pressed him. Tryin' to sort the situation out, I reckon. Pro'lly won't let it be for long."

"No," Swan agreed, squinting out at the ship. If what Mac said was true, Swan could only assume that the man guarding the ship was one of the so-called prisoners, freed during the revolt. If he had no papers, he would eventually be subjected to interrogation pending an official decision on his status, if he allowed himself to be taken into custody. He would likely be let go—really, Swan could see no reason why he wouldn't be; victims of kidnapping, human smuggling, and slave trafficking were almost always granted asylum, unless there was doubt as to the validity of their claim. With a whole ship of Bauer's being taken over, Swan didn't imagine believability would be an issue.

After the police had released him, he would have Martin Bauer to contend with, though. While Bauer wouldn't give a rat's ass about his crew, neither would he let their deaths go without seeking some retribution. And, if that dark-skinned man in the crow's nest planned to claim the ship, he'd be in for a fight for which he was likely unprepared.

"Hey. New guy?" Mac asked, nodding past Swan. The captain turned his attention away from Bauer's ship and saw Luca coming along the dock toward him. He was limping on his splint, and his face was drawn in pain, but he was walking, just the same. He was unable to help unload the cargo because of his injury. Swan hadn't seen him since they'd anchored, although he knew from Ivan that Luca was still on board. He hadn't really doubted it. Ella had been swimming alone, and she certainly wouldn't have left Luca, with his broken leg, to drown. Plus, whether foolish or not, Swan believed that she'd been telling the truth about at least a couple of things—not planning on marrying Luca being an important one. "What happened to him?" Mac asked.

"Long story," Swan said. "Check with Ivan, would you, on inventory? I'll be over in a few minutes to help. Let's get this ship unloaded."

"Yes, sir," Mac answered, eyeing Luca with open curiosity before turning to head toward Ivan.

Swan walked back up the dock to meet Luca at the halfway mark. "As soon as the cargo's unloaded, the men will line up outside the cabin to collect their payments."

"She's gone, isn't she?" Luca asked. None of the men had asked about Ella's absence on the deck; Swan assumed they all thought she was either sleeping in, or freshening up. None of them, except Marty, knew she had sneaked off the ship in the dark of night. Even Ivan hadn't asked, although Swan was pretty sure he'd guessed. Swan's mood had likely been easy to read.

Swan was surprised by Luca's question, though, and even more so by the hurt in the young man's expression. "She didn't tell you?" he asked, and he could hear the bitterness in his own voice.

Luca sighed and ran a hand over his pale face. "Shoulda known," he muttered, looking up toward town.

"You know where she's going," Swan guessed, making a conscious effort to keep his emotions from showing. His voice was more controlled, now. He had to get a grip on himself, if for no other reason than a desire to keep from worrying Maggie when he came face to face with her.

Luca's jaw tensed. For long moments, Swan didn't think the kid was going to answer, and he warred with himself over whether or not to press the issue. Finally, however, Luca gave his head a small, single shake.

"You expect me to believe that?" Swan asked. "The two of you planned this together—"

"I couldn't care less what you believe," Luca interrupted, scowling. "I know why she's doing what she's doing, but I don't know where, or I'd be on my way there. When she finishes, she'll come find me."

Whether it was Luca's intention or not, Swan felt a stab of real pain at that. He tried to gather his thoughts. He had never felt so out of control of his own emotions and mind, at least not since he was a child. Since meeting Ella, he'd found himself at the edge of self-control many times over, and for many different reasons. This was different, however. He was angry, of course. He was hurt. His pride was wounded. He was also worried, and even though the angry part of himself argued that her plan—which clearly didn't include him— was none of his concern, anymore, Luca's words only added to his worry.

"Why she's doing what she's doing," Swan repeated, quietly, testing the words. "What's she doing?"

Luca's jaw clenched. "If *she* didn't tell you, *I'm* not going to."

For just a moment, Swan had to fight a powerful urge to punch the kid in the face. He knew it would be wrong, and he knew that it would not really make him feel better. It would just make him feel like an asshole. He subdued the urge, not without effort. "She did tell me she was never set to marry you," he said, crossing his arms to avoid temptation.

Luca winced. It was a small tic, barely noticeable, but infinitely telling. "That's because..." he trailed off, clearly waging an internal battle of his own. Swan waited with very little confidence that Luca would finish the thought. As anxious as the captain was to get his boxes unloaded and get to Maggie's house, it was more important to know what Luca was going to say. Luca let out a breath. Squared his shoulders. Lifted his chin. "That's because she loves you," Luca finally said. "She loves me, too. She's loved me longer," he added, sounding for a few seconds like an injured, insecure child in spite of his defiant posture. "But not the same way," he finished, after a pause. Then, quieter, he repeated, "Not the same way." He shook his head. "I'm like a brother to her."

"But you're in love with her," Swan said, quietly. It wasn't a question.

Luca's love for Ella had been the main reason why their alleged betrothal was easy to believe. Looking back, Swan could see that Ella had never shown any signs of romantic feelings for Luca. He'd known they weren't right for each other, of course. He'd lost his objectivity early on, where Ella was concerned.

"Doesn't matter," Luca said with a shrug, surprising Swan again. "I was stupid. I can't lose her. If she wants me to be her brother, that's what I'll be, because I owe her everything."

"Tell me where she went," Swan said.

"I told you, I don't know."

"Tell me why she came here."

"No."

"No?" Swan repeated, trying to tamp down his temper. Several thoughts and threats went through his head, all of them inappropriate. He could threaten to refuse Luca's work papers. Withhold his pay. Hit him.

"I made a promise," Luca said.

He looked terribly young, and his jumble of emotions was palpable. Most notably, he was terrified to find himself alone in an unfamiliar country with no idea where he should go or what he should do. Swan didn't want to feel compassion for this kid who'd conspired against him with the woman they both loved, but the truth was, Swan had hired Luca in the first place because of the kid, not Ella. Because Luca had reminded Swan of himself at that age, young and hotheaded, desperate to prove himself, determined not to let the world see his fear.

Swan could see it, though, and it fueled his own anger because he couldn't even vent his frustrations on the man before him. "I can help her," Swan said, finally.

"If she wanted your help, she'd have asked for it," Luca said.

Swan opened his mouth, then closed it again before the angry retort could leave his lips. That blow had hit home, as well. Luca seemed to have a knack for finding raw nerves. "I'll see you with your pay when we're unloaded," Swan said, turning away. His body was thrumming with anger, and he was glad for it. It masked some of the other emotions.

"Captain," Luca said, behind him. Swan ignored him, striding away before he could change his mind.

*   *   *

Ella again wasn't sure she was going to make it. She'd asked a woman for directions to Martin Bauer's house, at just after dawn. The woman had eyed her suspiciously, if a bit pityingly, and offered a quick set of directions that seemed easy enough to follow. She'd also offered Ella a dry dress, something that surprised Ella and brought tears of gratitude to her eyes. Nonetheless, she'd declined the offer, with real regret. She had no time to waste by accompanying the woman to her house, for one thing. She had no right to accept the kindness of strangers in her current state of self-loathing. She

319

deserved the misery of trudging the streets in a cold, damp dress.

And, as ugly, and thin, and wet as it was, the dress was hers, and the only thing she had to her name. It might be ridiculous to cling to the vestiges of her pride, but she found herself unable to let go. She supposed that foolish pride was part of what was keeping her walking, too. Determination and willpower had already carried her far past her body's point of protest.

Bauer lived at the top of a hill. Not just any hill, but the hill that overlooked the entire expanse of town, a hill that looked daunting from below and was downright intimidating—not to mention exhausting—up close and personal. Ella felt like she'd been climbing forever. The sun was rising at her back, pushing at her, sapping even more of her strength. She had no idea what would happen when she'd reached Bauer's estate. Would she be let in? Turned away at the gate? Arrested? Beaten? Worse?

Was Travis there? Had he already been sold? She had no idea. She knew that, logically, she should stop somewhere and rest, if for no other reason than to have some strength if she needed to defend herself or someone else. She should also compose herself, if she was to have any hope of being granted access to the house or Bauer himself. A man as rich and powerful as he apparently was would not be easy to reach.

She didn't stop, though. Part of her wasn't sure she'd be able to start again, if she rested. More importantly, though: she'd waited months to get to her brother, and she had to find out where he was and if he was alright. So, she kept hacking away at the hill, and the distance to the gate eventually seemed to shrink.

*   *   *

"Come around the house tomorrow," Swan said. "Maggie would love to see you for supper."

"I'll do that," Ivan agreed. "I could use some pleasant company, for a change."

"I will be there, as well," Swan said. He managed a small smile, even though his heart wasn't in the banter. He felt bad for the strain between them; Ivan was his friend, and had been for a long time, in spite of their disagreements.

"Even so," Ivan said, with a shrug. He studied Swan for a moment. "Are you alright?" he asked. "You seem...Where's Ella?"

"Gone, already," Swan said. "She had things to see to."

Ivan didn't try to hide his surprise. "She didn't say goodbye?" he asked. "The men will be disappointed."

"Give them her apologies," Swan said. Ivan was right. The men had been paid, and more than half of them were still hanging around, as if they didn't really know what to do with themselves. Usually quick to disperse, it seemed they were waiting for a chance to say their goodbyes, an opportunity they were not going to get. Even though Swan knew that the men had come to care for

Ella, he was surprised by the level of fondness their continued presence showed.

"Did she say goodbye to *you*?" Ivan asked, obviously seeing some of Swan's emotions. It took some courage for Ivan to ask, considering the way Swan had reacted the last time they'd discussed Ella.

"Come around the house," Swan repeated, clapping Ivan on the arm. "I have to go." Then, knowing he couldn't shirk the responsibility, he raised his voice and called, "We had a good run, men. Thank you all for your hard work, and for getting all of us, and the cargo, here safely. I'll post the next departure date in a few days. I hope to see you all back here again, but if I don't, just know it was a pleasure, as always, to sail with you. Now, go have fun. You've earned it."

The men milled about for a few beats, murmuring amongst themselves. A few cast curious glances back toward the ship. Then, finally, they started to drift off, heading away from the docks. Swan let out a breath, nodded at Ivan, and turned away. "What about him?" Ivan asked, giving him pause. Swan looked back, reluctantly, and saw Ivan gesture toward the beach. Luca was sitting, on a rock, alone, with a makeshift cane leaning beside him. He was staring out at the water, with his splinted leg stretched before him.

"Fuck him," Swan muttered, before he could check the words. He started away, again. He managed five steps. Then he stopped. "God damn it," he said. His hands clenched into fists, and he couldn't have said who he was the angriest with: Luca, Ella, Ivan, or himself. He looked at Luca, again. Then he looked back at Ivan.

"You want me to take him with me? Get him a room somewhere?" Ivan offered.

"God damn it," Swan said, again. He pulled in a deep breath and held it, before releasing it slowly. "No. No, Ivan, go. You've earned your leave several times over. I'll take care of it."

Ivan hesitated, and apparently decided not to press the issue. "Alright, Cap. See you tomorrow."

Swan waited until he was alone. Then, before he could change his mind, he strode down the beach toward Luca. The younger man heard his approach, and looked back. "Come on," Swan said. "Let's go."

"Go?" Luca repeated, looking surprised and a little suspicious. "Where?"

"Do you have another option, son?"

Swan didn't want to see the things flickering across Luca's face—fear, pain, loneliness—and was helpless to avoid them. "I won't tell you anything," the boy finally muttered, but he no longer seemed defiant or brave or strong.

"No," Swan agreed. "I know that. Let's go."

He expected to have to do some convincing, but Luca got to his feet slowly, with a wince and the help of the stick he had commandeered as a cane. He limped up the beach and, after a few seconds, managed to meet Swan's eyes. "I'm sorry about the stuff I said." He spoke quietly, and Swan felt a grudging sense of respect. That apology could not have been easy. "You should know that she loves you. She really does, man."

Swan swallowed with effort. He cleared his throat. "Come on," he said, again. He touched Luca's shoulder, briefly. "We'll hail a hansom at the corner. It's not far."

*   *   *

Ella was barely aware of the passing wagons; she was far too preoccupied with her own struggle to make it up the hill without collapsing. As she finally began to crest the slope, however, and she could see the wrought-iron fence stretching away to the sides, she realized that the gate was open. The morning sun filled the drive, and she stopped, breathing heavily, as another cart wheeled past her, up the slant, through the gate, the horses clopping toward the front of the mansion. There were people unloading crates, carrying cases into the house through several different doors, and as she watched, two wagons came out and headed down the hill. The drivers glanced at her as they passed, but she ignored them.

There was a lot of activity, and her apprehension suddenly outweighed her exhaustion. She continued on, slowly, more alert than she'd been in an hour. She could hear people shouting. She could see servants, each looking harassed, and she wondered if they were there voluntarily, or if they'd been ripped from their homes, stripped of rights and options, and sold as commodities in a strange country. Thinking of Travis, of course, she forced her feet to move more quickly, and she soon approached the open gate. She stepped aside as another buggy came out.

"Excuse me," she said, when the driver looked at her. "What's going on, here?"

The man looked her over. To his credit, his face remained polite. "Just settin' up for the party, tonight."

"Party?" she asked, her stomach clenching.

"He's still havin' the celebration, in spite o' what happened."

"What happened?" she echoed. It wasn't really a question so much as an attempt to make sense of his words through her haze of worry and exhaustion.

"With the ship. Have a nice day, miss," he said, urging the horses to pick up speed before she could form an intelligible question.

He's still having the celebration, in spite of what happened. With the ship. She tried to tell herself not to panic, prematurely. After all, Bauer had several ships, at least. And even if something had happened with *Enterprise*, that didn't mean Travis wasn't alright. It didn't mean the ship had sunk, or anything so catastrophic. The small part of her brain still capable of logical thought insisted that she calm down and keep trudging on. She had to see her plan, as weak as it was, through. What choice did she have?

The majority of her tired brain, however, was clamoring on about a dozen worst-case scenarios, and she knew that she had to be realistic. She was suddenly sorry that Luca wasn't with her, even though she knew it was

322

irrational. With his injured leg, he never would've made it up the hill, for one thing. For another, there was no reason to wish her pain and fear onto someone else.

Luca was the only other person who knew Travis, and loved him like she did, though. He would understand.

Colin would understand, if you'd told him, she thought, and she was alarmed to feel tears burning her eyes. It was true, she knew. She did want Luca with her; they were family. But, even more, she wanted Swan's arms around her. She wanted his voice in her ear, telling her he loved her, and that everything would be alright. She wanted him to ride up to the house, with his sword drawn, and demand they send Travis out to her. She wanted him to make everything alright.

She shook her head. She was being ridiculous, and she despised herself for her desire to have someone else solve her problems. When had she gotten so weak? She'd never needed a man to take care of her, before, and she didn't need that now, either. He would have, if she'd given him the opportunity. She knew it. She'd made her choices.

She was just tired. She wasn't thinking with her head, she was letting her emotions rule her. She had to get a handle on herself. She meant to go up to the door and ask for a job. Beg, if she had to. Offer whatever it might take. She knew it was dangerous. There was no guarantee that she would ever get out, if she was let in. She couldn't very well walk up and ask about her brother, though. Her only way to get into the house, to get information, was to offer herself as a maid or whatever she could think of.

She would offer anything, and her stomach churned and burned at the thought. She'd offered herself to Swan in exchange for passage, before she'd gotten to know him. She'd been afraid of him, in spite of her unexpected attraction to him. She'd come to know the kind of man he was, though. Without ever having met Bauer, she had a good idea what kind of man *he* was, too. Would she be able to go through with it? Now that she knew what it was like to love someone...

She shook her head, again. That was a very last resort solution, and there was no sense worrying about it when it might not become an issue. Especially in her current state of dishevelment. It was in the back of her mind, though. If she managed to get Travis to safety, she wanted to go back to Swan. She wanted to apologize, more than she ever had in her life. She wanted to throw her pride to the wind and beg him to give her another chance. Could she return to him, however, if she'd allowed another man...If she allowed Bauer...She swallowed the bile stinging her throat and blinked back her tears. She told herself again that that was a last resort. They were setting up for a party. Maybe they needed extra help.

She knew it was unlikely that anyone, especially someone as wealthy as Bauer, would want to hire a filthy, bedraggled waif such as herself. She would try, though. She somehow managed to square her aching shoulders and in a minute she'd passed through the open gate with a pounding heart. People looked at her, but no one shouted at her to stop, and no one hollered for the police to be fetched, and she walked up to the front door with her chin held high.

The front door was open, as well. Inside, she could see men and women moving furniture around, carrying crates, and polishing everything in sight. She saw no sign of her brother, of course; she hadn't expected to. That didn't mean he wasn't in the house, but even that seemed like a long shot.

She raised her hand to knock on the open door, and hesitated when a man turned and caught sight of her. Judging by his attire, she would guess he was the butler. He frowned, and walked toward her, and she braced herself for him to order her away from the house and off the property.

"May I help you?" he asked. His accent was thick; she couldn't identify it, but knew it hadn't originated in Bohannon. His demeanor was somewhere between caution and politeness, although she thought she could see a bit of something closer to alarm lurking beneath his facade.

"I, uh...I came to see...Mr. Bauer," she said, painfully aware of her atrocious appearance and foreign accent.

"In regards to...?"

"I need...I'm looking for a job," she answered.

His eyebrows went up, and his mouth tightened. "And you came here?" he asked, and she felt her stomach sink a bit. "I suggest you go back down the hill, miss." He reached for the door, apparently meaning to close it in her face.

She held out a hand. "Wait. I can't," she said. There was no hiding the desperation in her voice, but she supposed that might be helpful; it was likely the only thing that made him pause. He did pause, with his hand on the door, and regarded her. "Please," she said. "I...I need a job, and I can't go anywhere else. I...I don't have...I'm not...I sneaked onto a ship," she finally said.

He raised his eyebrows again. He pressed his lips together, then leaned forward and said, in a low voice, "Listen, lass, you don't want to be here. Go see Margaret—"

"Benji!" a voice boomed through the large room behind the butler. He flinched, and closed his eyes, briefly. "Where the hell are you? What—" The other man stopped in the middle of the room when he caught sight of Ella standing in the doorway. "What in tarnation is going on, here?" he asked. Looking at him, Ella knew it was Martin Bauer. His wide, ruddy face, and wider midsection, spoke of years without manual labor. A lifetime, perhaps. His eyes were cold and appraising, and as he looked her up and down, his lip curled in disgust. Ella fought the urge to cross her arms, protectively, in front of herself.

"Are you Mr. Bauer, sir?" she asked, hoping the contempt couldn't be heard in her voice. "I heard you might be able to help me, sir. I need a job, and...I'm willing to do anything..."

"Benji. See to Natalie."

"Yes, sir," the butler said, turning to pass his boss as Bauer came to the door.

"Who told you to come here?" Bauer asked. There was nothing welcoming or friendly about him, and she again wondered what her chances would be of making it out of the house once she'd gotten in. If she got in.

"I don't, uh, know who they were, sir," she said. "The people by the docks, they all said you were the, uh...most powerful man in town and if anyone could help me, you could." A lie, of course, and a gamble, because she doubted anyone would direct her toward this man for assistance. The question was, did he know how others felt about him, or was his ego so large that it blinded him to reality?

"How'd you get here?"

She was honestly confused by the question; her body and mind were exhausted. "I...walked, sir." She'd never said 'sir' so many times in her life, and the word tasted bitter in her mouth.

"Don't be cheeky, now," he said, and the glint in his eye was enough to tell her that he could be a very dangerous man to anger.

"I...I don't mean to be. I'm not thinking clearly, perhaps, I...It's been a long night and day, and..."

"How did you come to be in Bohannon?"

"I snuck on a ship, sir. I hid with the cargo."

"What ship?"

She hesitated. Now, she knew she could be in trouble. She tried to think clearly. The problem was, she only knew the names of two ships, and she couldn't make one up because she assumed that Bauer would know the competition. She couldn't say she'd been on *Enterprise*, for more than one reason. She didn't even know if the ship had arrived, yet, or in what condition. More importantly, she did not believe for a second that Bauer would react kindly to a stowaway on a ship that he owned. If she said she didn't know the name of the ship she'd been on, he might assume it had been one of his, anyway.

"I think it was called...*Voyager*," she said.

Bauer's eyes widened, then narrowed. "You mean *Voyage*? Do you know who the captain of that ship is?"

"No, sir," she said with a churning stomach.

He glared at her for a moment, then smirked. After a moment, his eyes slid down the length of her body. She suppressed the urge to flee. "You're not as skinny as most beggars," he mused.

She swallowed the angry objection that sprang to her lips; it would not benefit her to proclaim that she wasn't a beggar. *You have Captain Swan to thank for that*, she thought, but didn't say. She didn't want to think about Swan, and his obsession with feeding her. "I had access to the stores," she mumbled, fidgeting.

"We might be able to work something out," he said, still smirking. "You say you're willing to do anything. Well, we're setting up for a party, and I find myself short-staffed. My new workers didn't show up. I assume you don't mind working for room and board. Just as a start, of course."

You fucking asshole, she thought. Yes, she could see that he thought he was untouchable, above reproach, rich and powerful enough that everyone should and would be at his mercy. He saw a dirty, homeless girl before him, someone willing to step into his greedy clutches, someone he could abuse and hold hostage. She saw it all, glimmering in his mean little eyes, and she knew how he expected the story to unfold.

She had a different story in mind, however, and she had no intention of letting him in on the plot secrets. "Of course not," she managed. "I'd appreciate any generosity you could offer."

His smile widened. "What's your name?"

She considered lying, mostly because she didn't want to give any part of herself to this slimy creature. She was not an actress, however, and had no confidence that she would be able to keep up the charade of a fake name. "Ella," she finally allowed.

"Well, Ella, come inside."

Ignoring every instinct telling her to leave, she stepped past him into the house. *You're never going to get out of here,* her mind whispered, and she hugged herself to suppress a shudder.

Chapter Sixteen

Swan opened the front door and immediately heard voices coming from the living room. He motioned Luca inside and closed the door. He could hear children, and he wondered if Maggie was having some of the orphans over for a visit. He didn't see any of the servants, but he hadn't knocked, either. He walked toward the sounds with Luca limping along slowly behind him.

Maggie was sitting in her favorite chair, across from what had once been her husband's favorite chair. Henry's usually sat empty; Swan had never had the heart to sit in it, himself, and anyone who knew its history refrained out of respect. It wasn't empty now, though. Sitting in it was a teenaged boy. He was leaning forward, with his elbows on his knees, watching. His eyes were bright and alert, and sparkled with amusement, but they were ringed by dark circles and his face was lined with what could only be weariness.

It was a little boy that he was watching, and so was Maggie. Swan took a quick head count. Aside from the boy in the chair, there were two girls—one a teenager, herself, and one younger than ten—and an adolescent boy sitting on the sofa. Four younger boys stood grouped in the middle of the floor, and the smallest was gesticulating wildly, to the amusement of all in the room.

There was a scruffy white dog curled beside the couch. Swan wasn't necessarily surprised by the fact that he didn't recognize any of the children; he was gone for long periods of time, and orphans were constantly coming and going. He was, however, surprised by the dog's presence. So far as he knew, pets had never been allowed in the orphanage; it would be difficult to place a child *and* a pet, and although it might be fun and therapeutic for the children to love and care for an animal in the short term, forcing a child to leave a pet they'd grown attached to could prove detrimental when that child had already lost so much.

Maggie had never had a pet in this house, either, so far as Swan knew. He might have liked one as a child, but he'd certainly never asked.

"With great big wings," the little boy was saying, and with his arms spread to mimic flying, he tilted to the side and made a whistling sound.

It was the oldest boy, the one in the chair, who caught sight of Swan, first. His expression became instantly guarded, cautious, all trace of amusement gone, and he rose to his feet, slowly. The dog, suddenly alerted by the boy's tension, looked around and rose, too. After a moment, everyone turned to find the object of the boy's attention.

Interesting, Swan thought. In spite of his own emotional turmoil, he found himself intrigued, and knew that he wanted to hear the story of this group with their strange, yet obvious, dynamic. Maggie had caught sight of him, however, and was getting to her feet. There was no mistaking the happiness in *her* expression, and he smiled, walking toward her, as surprised as always by just how much he'd missed her.

"Maggie," he said, reaching out to hug her. She seemed smaller, frailer, than the last time. He thought that every time he returned, and every time it made his stomach clench. He didn't see her as much as she'd like; as much as he'd like. He loved her, though. She was his family. To lose her would be devastating, and he thought—not for the first time—that he was being selfish by spending so much time at sea. He was never comfortable on land, though. After a few days, the itch to be at sea always returned, no matter how much he loved her.

"Colin," she said, hugging him tightly. "I didn't expect you until tonight."

Swan opened his mouth to tell her how good it was to see her. Before he could utter the words, a voice behind him said, "Travis?"

Everyone turned, including Swan. He looked at Luca, then at the other teenaged boy. They were staring at each other with matching expressions of disbelief. "Luca?" the boy—Travis, presumably—finally said. "What... How...?"

"Travis." Luca started forward, limping, barely seeming to notice the pain in his leg. "Trav, Trav, Trav—" He dropped his cane on the floor with a clatter that made the dog jump, and a moment later, he and Travis were hugging—hard.

A cold lump had settled into Swan's stomach, and was beginning to spread outward.

"How did you get here?" Travis asked, and his voice was thick with emotion. He pulled back to look at Luca's face, and both boys had tears shining in their eyes. Neither seemed embarrassed by their emotion. In that instant, Swan was pretty sure they'd forgotten that anyone else was in the room.

"We came after you," Luca said, squeezing Travis's shoulder and leaning back slightly to look him over. "Are you alright? What happened to you?"

"You came after me, *how*?" Travis asked, frowning. "And..." The sudden fear in his face was undeniable.

As clearly as if he'd spoken it aloud, Swan could hear the rest of Travis's question hanging in the air: *Where's Ella?* And, although he couldn't claim to really understand what was going on, the captain was pretty sure he understood far more than he had a few minutes earlier. Pieces had begun to snap into place with a frightening speed. "Whose ship were you on?" Swan asked, even though he already knew the answer.

Travis's frown deepened as he looked at Swan. "Martin Bauer," he said. "His crew took all of us. Mrs. Darling said you would help me."

"Help you with what, exactly?" Swan asked. He felt like he should either sit down, or turn and run straight to Bauer's estate. Was Ella there? Looking at Luca, he asked, "Did she know whose ship took him?"

"He's going to pay for what he's done," Travis said, and there was a cold surety in the boy's voice, drawing Swan's attention. "With or without your help. The police brought us here because none of us have parents back home. They can't in good conscience ship us back to nothing, apparently. So they brought us here, and don't get me wrong, I'm grateful. I didn't know how I was going to make sure the kids had a safe place to stay. But now that they do, I have a job to do. With or without your help," he repeated.

"Travis," Luca said, and then he stopped, seemingly at a loss for words.

"Let's all take a breath for a moment and figure this out," Maggie said.

Swan looked at Luca. After a moment, Luca said, reluctantly, "She wouldn't tell me his name, but she knew it."

"My sister went to Bauer?" Travis asked, alarmed. The kid was quick, Swan would give him that. Alert, intelligent, and determined, and Swan would bet money that the kid had shed some blood recently. Likely some of his own, as well as others'. He had the look about him, and the note in his voice. Swan didn't think the kid had properly begun to process whatever had happened on the ship, even though Travis might believe he had.

"Calm down," Swan said, even though he felt far from calm, himself. If it was true that Ella had gone to Bauer's house to look for this boy (*her brother*, his mind whispered), they had to get to her as quickly as possible. Bauer was a dangerous man, and the very thought of Ella being anywhere near him—

"Calm down? Look, with all due respect, I don't know you. I was told you would help me, but I don't need to be—"

"Travis," Luca said, sharply. "Stop it."

Travis's mouth snapped shut. He looked genuinely startled, and for long moments, silence filled the room. Travis and Luca were staring at each other. They had not expected to come face-to-face with each other so suddenly, and neither knew exactly what the other had gone through to get there. Their love and respect for each other had not changed, but they had; both of them were different people than they'd been when they left Baytown, and they were going to have to figure out what that meant for their relationship.

Now was not the time, however. There were more important things at stake. "Travis," Swan said, drawing the boy's attention from Luca. "Listen to me. You've seen terrible things. You probably feel like you've done terrible things. And maybe you feel like you're drowning, and if you stop for just a second, you'll go under. But hear me well, son. You're not in the water anymore. I will get your sister here. I give you my word. We cannot afford to rush out of here without a plan. Let's go sit down and work out some details."

Travis hesitated, then looked at Luca. "Can I trust him?" he asked.

"Yes," Luca said, without hesitation, surprising Swan. "He's right. We need to get Ella, but...we need a plan. In case she made it to him."

"Why don't I take the children to get settled in," Maggie said. "Come along, loves. You can bring the dog, for now."

"Thank you, Maggie," Swan said, bending to kiss her on the cheek. "We'll be in the library."

"The ship was late," Maggie said, gesturing toward Travis with her chin. "The arrival party was postponed until the ship was spotted yesterday, coming down the shore."

"We made a detour," Travis said, glancing at the other kids.

Swan shook his head. "You mean there's a party tonight?" he asked

Maggie. His thoughts and emotions were a jumbled mess. His advice to Travis had been good; they needed to take time to clear their heads and devise a plan, because he was feeling decidedly reckless, himself. If he were by himself, he would likely grab a horse and rush up the hill to Bauer's to find Ella—whether she wanted him to, or not. He couldn't afford such impulsiveness. There were other people to worry about.

"Be careful," the teenaged girl was saying, laying a hand on Travis's sleeve.

"I'll see you guys soon, as soon as I find my sister," he answered. He looked over at the huddled, now-somber children. "Be good, alright? Everything will be alright. You're safe now. Gar, come here."

The oldest of the other boys walked forward and said, "I can come with you. I can help. You know I can fight..."

"Garrett," Travis said, setting a hand on his shoulder. "I do know you can fight. And I know you're the best man to watch after the kids while I'm gone. There's no one I'd trust more, alright?"

Garrett swallowed and raised his chin. "Alright," he said. "Don't worry about us."

"Come along, children," Maggie said, putting an arm around the small girl's shoulders.

"Jacko," the girl called, looking back. The dog hesitated, looked at Travis. Travis pointed, and the dog—reluctantly, it seemed—followed after the girl.

Garrett ushered the boys along.

"Kyra," Travis said. "If I don't..." He stopped, took a breath, and stepped close to her, lowering his voice so the other children couldn't hear. "The men will be at the edge of the woods north of the dock tomorrow afternoon. If I don't come back, tell them they can take the ship and head back. The kids will be safer here."

She hesitated. She clearly wanted to object. After several beats of silence, however, she nodded, leaned forward, and kissed him quickly on the lips. "I know you'll come back," she said. "But if you can't, I'll tell them."

* * *

Travis was sitting at the table with his head in his hands. He looked like he was on the verge of collapsing. "Son, you need to rest," Swan said.

"I'm fine," Travis answered. "I'll rest when my family is safe and together."

Like sister, like brother, Swan thought. "You won't do anyone any good like this. We have a few hours before we need to get ready. Trust me, you'll feel a lot better. You don't need to go to one of the bedrooms if you don't want, you can use the sofa here in the library. You need to rest, though."

"He's right," Luca said. "He won't leave without you, Travis. I promise."

Travis sighed and scrubbed his hands over his face. "Alright. But wake me if anything changes."

"I'm going to go check in with Maggie," Swan said, as Travis headed

330

toward the couch. Luca caught the captain in the doorway, however.

"Can I talk to you?"

"Alright."

"Travis doesn't know what went on between you and Ella, and that's probably good. But I know that you love her, and this plan of yours—"

"You didn't object when we came up with it."

"Because Travis needs to believe it. But I don't. She'll never forgive you if anything happens to Travis. Never."

"Forgive me?" Swan asked, his temper flaring. "*She* left *me*, Luca. She lied to me."

"You still hope to get her back, don't pretend you don't. You'll forgive her because what she did, she did for her brother. And because…when you love someone, you forgive them for anything…"

"I promised I would get her back to you and her brother. That's what I intend to do." Swan started away, walking more briskly than Luca could manage with his cane.

"Could she be pregnant?"

Swan stopped. After a moment, he turned, and his fist itched to punch Luca in the face. "That is *not*—"

"She lived in a room with you for more than a month. Think about it. You should fucking know."

Swan opened his mouth, then closed it again. His hands had begun to shake, so he clenched them into tighter fists at his sides. His head was spinning. "Did she say…"

Luca scowled. "Of course not. Do you really think she would've jumped into the cold ocean if she'd realized?"

Swan pulled in a deep breath through his nose and shook his head. Ella would risk her life without hesitation, as she'd proven repeatedly. She did not risk the lives of others, at least not intentionally, and Swan knew without a doubt that she would not risk the safety of her unborn child, not if she knew about it.

He tried to tell himself that Luca's question didn't prove anything, but the truth was, Luca was right. She had missed her last period. Swan had slept with her every night. It had never occurred to him; he'd been too preoccupied. It was disturbing that Luca had somehow figured it out. "Maybe she's just…"

Luca shook his head. "I've lived with her since she *got* her first period," he said, his cheeks flaming. He didn't want to have this conversation any more than Swan did, and that sapped the last of the captain's anger. "She's never late. And she always has really bad…you know…"

Swan nodded. He'd seen the pain the first time around. *Pregnant?* The idea brought a strange flutter to his stomach. There was no way to know for sure, of course. Not without asking Ella, and unless she'd come to the conclusion since he'd last seen her, the question would likely be as startling to her as it was to him.

"Right," Luca said, sounding angry. In this case, Swan didn't blame him.

"So. If you expect me to let you and Travis go—"

"We've gone over this," Swan said. "No matter how good your intentions or how strong your will, you would slow us down and be a liability."

"Go without him."

Swan hesitated, surprised. "What?"

"Leave while he's sleeping. He doesn't know the way, yet, and I can probably delay him until the time you scheduled to leave by telling him you're running errands or something."

"You promised him you wouldn't let me leave without him. Do you make promises so lightly, then?"

"I'd rather die than break a promise to Travis or Ella. But I'll break any promise I need to if it's to save their lives. Go get her and bring her back and I'll worry about whether or not Travis can forgive me."

"No," Swan said. "Look, the plan isn't...going to go exactly as he thinks, alright? He'll be safe. I give my word. And, if Ella's there, she and Travis will leave together."

"The three of you."

Swan shrugged. "If possible," he allowed. He hadn't planned on letting Luca in on any of it, but faced with Luca's concern for the only two people he loved, Swan knew that the boy deserved, and needed, to know that Swan was not going to endanger their lives.

Luca studied him for long moments in silence. "Get them together and you won't need to worry about them. They'll take care of each other."

"Ella has a tendency to put herself in harm's way," Swan pointed out with a humorless smile.

"She loves you," Luca repeated. He spoke grudgingly, and there was real pain in the tightening around his mouth. "Given a choice, she'll protect her brother, though. If it's your life or his."

"I'm counting on that," Swan muttered.

*   *   *

"Mr. Bauer must like you," Natalie said. "He never hires beggars."

"I wasn't begging," Ella answered, before she could stop herself. "I just...needed a job..."

"And you came here?" Ric scoffed.

"She didn't know no better," Betty told him, scowling.

"I don't...have any papers," Ella said, feeling like an idiot. These people thought she was an idiot for voluntarily coming to work where they did, and what did that tell her? That she'd made a colossal mistake? There was no sign of her brother or, so far as she could tell, any new additions to the serving staff. All of the workers had been in Bauer's employ for years, it seemed. Not that any of them seemed pleased about it. Did they really have nowhere else to go, and nothing else they could do?

And do you? her mind mocked, reminding her exactly how alone she was.

"None of us do. The difference is, we didn't have a choice." That was Natalie. She seemed to be the least friendly of the staff, or at least the most openly-hostile toward Ella, but Ella supposed she couldn't really blame her. Not if what Ella suspected to be true actually *was* true.

"We don't have time to argue about things that cannot be undone," Betty said. "Mr. Bauer will not tolerate things being less than perfect when the guests arrive."

"Then he should've let us set up days ago," Natalie muttered.

"Hush, girl," Ric said, frowning at her.

"Where's...Mrs. Bauer?" Ella asked.

"She's at her mother's. She always leaves when there's to be a party," Ric answered.

"She doesn't like parties?" Ella asked. She was barely paying attention to her own words.

"Mr. Bauer doesn't like her to be seen by many people," Betty said. "Come on, now. There's work to do."

"But...why?" Ella asked.

"Bruises," Natalie said.

Betty pushed her toward the door. "Go clean the fireplace."

"I've done it."

"Do it again. Make yourself look busy."

"First thing to learn here, lass, is keep your eyes and ears open, and your mouth shut," Ric said, quietly.

Ella swallowed. "What, um...what's the party for?"

"None of your never mind," Ric answered.

"The boss thought one of his ships was lost, but...it turns out there was just a delay," Betty said. She and Ric exchanged a look that made Ella uneasy.

"A sight more than a delay," Ric muttered. "Why he wants to have this—"

"You know bloody well why," Betty said. "To show the loss of money means nothing, and...that he cannot be hurt..."

"Loss of money?" Ella asked, crossing her arms in an attempt to hide her trembling. "But you said the ship arrived...?"

"Aye, it did," Ric answered. "In a manner of speaking."

"What was, uh...on the ship?" she asked.

Ric scowled. "Why the interest in the boss's business?" he asked. "You're going to get us all in trouble if we don't get you to work."

"Sorry," Ella muttered. She had a dozen questions that needed to be answered, but she couldn't come right out with any of them. They might be afraid of their boss. They might even hate him. Those things might not necessarily be in her favor, though. Their fear might make them run straight to him with tales of her duplicity, in order to secure themselves into Bauer's good graces.

"Go back to the kitchen, Ric. We'll be along as soon as I get Ella outfitted."

After dividing his scowl between Ella and Betty for a few seconds longer, Ric offered a curt nod and turned to leave. "I guess no one wants me to be here," Ella muttered.

"And why did you come here?" Betty asked, crossing her own arms and regarding Ella shrewdly. "You don't look like you've been starved recently. You don't look like you stowed away in a cargo hold for two months."

"I had...access to the food stores," Ella answered, fighting the urge to fidget.

"Put this on," Betty said, snatching up a skimpy maid's uniform. "And clean yourself up. You have five minutes."

"Yes, ma'am," Ella muttered.

*   *   *

"Well, well, the little beggar cleans up alright."

The voice sent a shiver down Ella's spine, and she resisted the urge to flinch away from Bauer's approach. She felt very exposed in the small, revealing outfit, in spite of the fact that all of the women in the house were similarly dressed. Betty had given her shoes, and Ella's feet felt swollen and raw inside. Somehow, she managed to paste a smile to her face before turning around. "I really appreciate this opportunity, Mr. Bauer," she said.

His gaze slid down the length of her body, slowly. "Don't make me regret my decision," he said. "Tonight is an important night."

She swallowed. "Right. The, uh, party. It must be a big celebration."

His eyes were cold. "Celebration? I lost a ship, Ella. Do you know how much money ships cost? More importantly, I lost my cargo. Much more valuable than the ship. Rest assured, those responsible will pay, in due time. I will recover my losses if I have to squeeze gold from their flesh. But for tonight, the world will see that Martin Bauer is far more powerful than a few dollars."

"What happened to your ship?" she asked, through numb lips. By 'cargo,' did he mean the people on board? The people he'd meant to sell? Her brother?

"I'm not in the habit of discussing business matters with my servants," he answered. His eyes glinted dangerously, and she realized that he *wanted* to discuss it. His ego insisted that he boast about his power and wealth, and his ability to take a hit—financially speaking—while his anger made his tongue itch to lambast those responsible for stealing something from him.

"Please, forgive me, sir, I didn't mean to step out—"

He waved a hand, silencing her. "Nothing that can't be fixed. Tonight, however, my house will be brimming with the most important people in Bohannon, and further. Everything will be perfect. Am I understood?"

"Yes, sir."

"You will not speak unless spoken to. You will not touch anyone, or refuse to be touched by anyone. If someone asks you a question, your response, as appropriate, will either be 'yes, sir or ma'am,' or 'I'll check for you.' The word 'no' is not in your vocabulary. Clear?"

"Yes, sir," she managed. *You will not refuse to be touched by anyone. The word 'no' is not in your vocabulary.* She wanted to ask more questions, because she needed to know what happened on her brother's ship. Serving at a rich man's party had not been in her plans, especially when she felt like she was close to collapsing, already. There had been no opportunity to sleep, and likely wouldn't be before the celebration. And, no matter how tired she was, she doubted she'd be able to sleep under Bauer's roof, anyhow, without knowing where Travis was.

"Good girl. Come see me after the party. We'll...discuss things more thoroughly, then."

I'll bet, you pig, she thought. "Yes, sir."

"Get back to work. Betty will make sure you're on track."

*   *   *

"The guests will begin arriving in half an hour," Ric said. "Look, everything's set up. Just...look busy, alright? You'll be serving drinks. Be in the kitchen no later than five minutes before the hour. Paulo will show you what will be served. Don't drop anything. Don't spill anything. If someone asks for a drink you don't recognize or remember, tell them you'll see to it and go ask Paulo. For the next twenty minutes, keep moving. Dusting is usually your best bet. Dust, make sure everything is shiny."

"Alright," Ella said. She wanted to crawl into a corner for at least a few minutes and rest her eyes and achy muscles. The idea of carrying a tray of drinks was daunting. She couldn't rest, however. When Ric left her alone, she took the duster and wandered toward the back of the house, dusting shelves and statues and wainscoting as she went. She'd had no opportunity to find out more about the ship, at least not without drawing unwelcome attention and wrath onto herself. She didn't know where the rest of the staff was; she didn't see anyone, or hear any voices. The house, decked out in impressive glory for the coming celebration, seemed unnaturally deserted. It gave her the creeps, due in part to her raw nerves and exhausted body.

There was no dust; she waved the duster across surfaces that had already been thoroughly cleaned, and made her way toward Bauer's office with a pounding heart. She wasn't sure where he was, but she didn't think he'd left the house. She passed the fireplace, with the giant portrait secured above, and the painted faces of Martin Bauer—looking severe and imposing—and his wife—looking beautiful and meek—watched her on her way. She could feel their eyes, and even though her tired mind insisted that she was being ridiculous, she felt like the house around her was haunted with unseen forces.

As she neared her new—and temporary—boss's office, she heard the faint hint of voices, ghost-like and indecipherable. She dusted along the dustless frames of various works of undoubtedly expensive art, wondering vaguely if Bauer himself had had any hand in choosing the paintings. They were a show of money, of course, but they were also beautiful and rich with color, and Martin Bauer did not seem like the kind of man who'd appreciate them for anything other than their price tags. Did Mrs. Bauer select the art? When she wasn't being beaten or scuttled off to her mother's? Was she as much a prisoner of her husband as the men and women he'd indentured? If she chose to stay with her mother, refused to come home, would he go to fetch her, drag her home, and beat her until she couldn't breathe?

Ella shook her head. Such musings were pointless and unsubstantiated. She'd never even seen the man's wife, except in portrait, and Ella couldn't afford to worry about her or anyone else at the moment. The only life she was worried about was Travis's, so she edged right up to the office door, barely breathing, holding the duster like a shield. Would it be an adequate excuse if he burst out of the room and found her hovering there? She didn't know. It didn't matter. She had to get information, and he was speaking—which meant he wasn't alone. The door was closed, of course, but as she leaned close, she found she could hear the two male voices clearly enough.

"...gotten anyone onto her, yet?"

"No. That black motherfucker thinks he's in control, but he's going to be surprised. I let him bide his time, but tomorrow, he's going to be dragged off of there, preferably alive so I can teach him what happens—"

"Is he the one that started it?"

"The fuck should I know?" Bauer snapped, and she could hear the anger in his voice. Even without seeing him, she knew that he was annoyed with being interrupted, and she wondered if the man in there with him—whoever he was—was aware of that. "He's not talking, is he? Someone's going to pay, though, and if he wants to sit up there with his bow and arrows and pretend like he's someone, well, then..."

"Is it true, they're all dead?"

"Yes."

"How..." the man trailed off, either in deference to some expression, or because he remembered Bauer's response from a few moments earlier.

"A couple of the men were heard talking to a guy at the docks, before they disappeared like cowards. Seems like one of the slaves got loose and overpowered a guard, then freed the other men, and they started a revolt. God damn it. Do you have any idea how much money those fuckers were worth?"

The man didn't answer, at least not aloud. Ella felt cold and shaky. Her mind was struggling to make sense of the scenario that Bauer had laid out. The prisoners had started a revolt against Bauer's men?

Is it true, they're all dead?

She shook her head, suddenly unable to breathe.

She tried to think of some other explanation for those words. She tried and failed. If the prisoners started a fight against the armed and ruthless men of Bauer's employ, they couldn't have stood much of a chance at all. If they were all killed, that meant that Travis...She felt the hallway begin to tilt around her, and she put a palm against the wall. She'd come all this way for nothing. She'd hurt Luca, she'd hurt Colin, and she'd hurt herself, and she'd still failed to save her brother.

She wanted to believe her brother was alive. She wanted to hold onto hope and faith, but her tired mind could think of no way that Travis could have survived when no one else had. She wanted to be strong and keep fighting, but she could feel the very last of her hope slipping away.

The blood was roaring in her ears, and beneath the pain, she felt her anger building. She clutched at it, eagerly, desperate for anything to dull the onslaught of grief. She wanted to rush into the office and rip Bauer apart. It didn't matter that he hadn't even been on the ship; it was *his* ship, and *his* crew, working on his orders, stealing and selling people for *his* profit. So he could have the biggest house on the largest estate on the highest hill in one of the most important international port-towns. So he could have the power and freedom to beat his wife, and then cart her off to her mother's when it was time to rub shoulders with the illustrious and influential people of Bohannon.

There was at least one other man in the room with him. In her current state, Ella thought she could kill him, too, whoever he was, and any others that might be lurking silently within. What would happen then, though? She would never make it out of the house. The servants might be happy to be rid of Bauer, but the guests would be arriving any minute, and she knew she would be caught. They would either hang her or drag her off to a cell.

The world had crumbled around her. Hanging might be preferable to a cell, where she'd have ample time to reflect on the ways she'd failed her family and feel the loss of her brother. She shoved her hand against her mouth to hold back a sudden sob. She wanted to see Luca, and he deserved to know what had happened. If she rushed into Bauer's office and actually managed to kill the man, without first getting herself killed, Luca might never know the truth.

She wanted to see Swan. Suddenly, more than anything in the world, she wanted Colin, wanted to crawl into his arms and sob against his chest. She would give anything to bring Travis back. However, barring that, she desired nothing more than Swan's presence and love and comfort. Things she couldn't have and didn't deserve.

If she thought things through, however, she might be able to see him again. And Luca. If she *could* think things through. If she could think at all.

Travis is dead, she thought. Her nose and throat were burning, but she fought her tears, glancing back along the hallway. She couldn't get caught standing outside Bauer's office. She turned and hurried away, praying she wouldn't run into anyone until she'd had a chance to gather her thoughts and compose herself. She was going to have to serve the party and pretend like her world hadn't come to a grinding halt. She would have to find a way to smile at the rich assholes while she fetched their drinks, and she would have to find the strength to be in the same room with Bauer without attacking him.

Then, when all of the guests were gone and the house was quiet and only the staff was left to clean up the mess, she would go to Bauer's room—either invited, or otherwise—and she would kill him. She would run him through with a sword, or she would slit his throat, or she would skewer him with a fork, or tear his face off with her bare hands, if she had to. If she could, she would get out of the house without anyone knowing he was dead. If she could, she would find Darling House, to catch a glimpse of Colin. If she could, she would leave him a note, explaining how sorry she was and how much she loved him and why he would never see her again.

Then she would find Luca.

"What are you doing? You should be on your way to the kitchen."

Betty's voice startled Ella, and she whirled, holding the duster before her like a sword. "I...I...needed to..."

"Go. Freshen up. You'd better be presentable and on time."

Ella nodded, handed Betty the duster, and rushed toward the servants' quarters.

Chapter Seventeen

Ella scanned the crowd, wondering how many of the gathered guests knew what kind of man Bauer was. At least some of them must, and what did that make *them*? Some of the men in the room were probably associates of his, willing to buy and sell children, and it was unnerving to realize that she couldn't tell the difference by looking at them. In their fancy tuxedos, with their wives gussied up in ball gowns that cost more money than Ella had ever seen in her lifetime, they all seemed so respectable.

Everyone was talking and laughing, some were eating, and a few couples were already dancing. None of them knew or cared that her life had been shattered into a million little pieces. No one noticed how hard she was struggling to keep herself together, or how close she was to grabbing a kitchen knife and running across the crowded room to plunge it into Bauer's throat. She didn't think she would actually manage to kill him, if she tried, not with so many people around. She would probably get herself killed, instead. She didn't want to admit how tempting the idea was.

As more people came through the front door, Ella's gaze automatically skimmed over them. Walking through the door was Travis.

Her heart seemed to skid to a halt in her chest before breaking into a gallop.

Her brother's name bubbled up to her lips, and it was all she could do to keep from shouting it out. She didn't understand how he'd come to be there; she didn't understand how he was still alive. Relief and happiness warred with her confusion, for a moment, but it was fear that beat everything else down. Yes, she was happy to see her brother, so happy that her eyes and throat burned and her hands trembled. He couldn't be in Bauer's house, though. It wasn't safe. Maybe Bauer's men hadn't managed to kill all of the kidnapped people, as she'd believed, but that didn't mean they hadn't tried.

No matter how things had unfolded on *Enterprise*, she knew what kind of man Bauer was, and her plan was not simply about avenging her brother. Bauer needed to be stopped, and who would stop him? The men and women laughing and drinking, dancing and eating? No. They'd had their chance, and had clearly chosen to join him rather than oppose.

Travis looked across the room. Their eyes met for only a second, and then his gaze moved on. Her heart continued to pound erratically. She had no idea what was going on. He'd seen her, and recognized her; she knew he had. He'd shown none of the appropriate surprise, however, and as she stood, rooted beside the door to the kitchen, she tried to imagine what chain of events could possibly have led to his presence in Bauer's house.

Had he been sold into slavery, after all, in spite of the rumors of the fatal uprising on the ship? Perhaps someone, intent on commandeering the trade profit for themselves, had lied in an effort to rip off Bauer. If so, she couldn't imagine the deceit would go undiscovered for long. In the meantime, however, she needed to determine what sort of situation Travis was in before she went ahead with her plan. It might turn out that he still needed to be rescued before she could go after Bauer. She couldn't risk her own life without knowing he would be safe after all was said and done, not now that she knew he was alive.

Travis was wandering into the room, looking tall and nonchalant, but she didn't have time to ponder the changes in him. She couldn't be caught staring at him. For whatever reason, he was studiously ignoring her, and she knew that was the smart thing to do even though she could barely stand to tear her eyes away from him.

As the next person stepped into the room behind Travis, Ella's gaze automatically shifted, and she found herself staring into a familiar set of eyes. Her breath caught. She stared across the crowded room, completely captured by that dark, intense gaze. She had tried to reconcile herself to the fact that she would likely never see him again, no matter how much she wanted to, and the sight of his handsome face, the face she loved so much, brought a lump of tears to her throat.

No, no, you can't be here, she thought, knowing it wasn't safe for Swan in Bauer's home. Swan had made their animosity clear to her. Somehow, she managed to pull her gaze from his. Her hands were shaky and sweaty. She could scarcely breathe. She looked past Swan, half-expecting to see Luca limping in behind him.

Apparently, only two of the three people she loved had stepped into the lion's den.

Her eyes slid toward Swan, again. She couldn't help it. She was both relieved and disappointed to find that he was no longer looking at her. He was standing straight, with just his head bowed forward, his hands clasped behind his back, talking to Travis. She could only see Swan's profile, and didn't know what he was saying. She could see Travis's face, however. He was listening to Swan, calmly, his face giving nothing away. His gaze flicked toward Ella, then away.

She didn't understand. Did Swan know who Travis was? How had they come to be together? Travis was not dressed like a slave, she realized. He was in a nice suit, and he was standing with his chin raised and shoulders squared. It seemed clear that Swan and Travis had come to the party together, and the idea filled her with relief. Yes, there was confusion, and fear, but she knew one thing for sure: Swan would keep Travis safe. No matter what reason they had for being there, she knew her captain, and she knew that he would protect Travis.

And who will protect Colin?

He can take care of himself, she thought, uneasily. She knew it was true, and yet the knowledge did not alleviate her fear. She'd left him behind to keep him from further conflict with Bauer, to protect him.

"Ella," Natalie said, startling her. Ella jumped, almost knocking the tray from the other woman's hands. "What are you doing?" Natalie hissed, glancing around. Ella looked around, too, and spotted Martin Bauer near the stairs. He was speaking with a group of men, but he'd seen her standing by the kitchen, doing nothing, and she felt her stomach clench in response to the coldness in his eyes. He gestured once, with his chin, and she knew that she would not get another warning. She was supposed to be working, and they both knew that it didn't matter that she'd come to his door asking for a job. She was no different than the other men and women working in the house; for all intents and purposes, she belonged to Bauer.

She couldn't let Swan interfere with that. Or Travis. She was in the position she was in to protect Swan and, now that she knew he was alive, Travis.

"You'd better get to work," Natalie said, moving past Ella and into the room.

"Right. Sorry," Ella answered. She turned toward the kitchen, unable to slow her racing heart. She was suddenly more mindful of her outfit, and how revealing (and demeaning) it was. While Swan had certainly seen every inch of her body, the idea of serving people drinks, in such skimpy attire, in his presence, was humiliating. And the idea of her brother seeing her in such a state...

She shook her head as she entered the kitchen, trying to clear her head. She couldn't let her wounded pride distract her. She'd put the clothes on, after all, and she had no one but herself to blame for her presence at Bauer's party. She stopped inside the kitchen, trying to catch her breath. The other servants were all looking at her, and she knew she must look like she'd seen a ghost. In many ways, she felt like she had.

Travis is alive, she thought, hugging herself. She couldn't afford to hide in the kitchen, though. Bauer would be looking for her, having noted her lack of serving, and she had to give the impression that she was working as diligently as everyone else.

"Everything alright?" one of the cooks asked, scowling at her.

"Sure," she answered. "I just need to get—"

The door burst open behind her, and she stepped aside, startled, looking back as Natalie hurried into the room with an empty tray. "Oh my God," she said, keeping her voice—full of nervous excitement—low. "You'll never guess who's here."

A knot of apprehension settled into Ella's stomach, even as someone asked, "Who?"

"Captain Swan!" Natalie hissed, glancing over her shoulder to make sure the door had closed behind her.

"What? No, he wouldn't..." A round of murmuring passed through the room.

"Has he seen him, yet?" someone asked.

Natalie shook her head. "Swan's wandering through the room, shaking hands, talking to people like he's got every right to be here. When the boss sees him..."

Ella's stomach was more unsettled than ever, and she tried to keep her face from showing her growing alarm. "What's going on?" she asked, in a mostly-steady voice.

"The boss *hates* Cap'n Swan," Leon said. "Think the feelin's mutual, matter o' fact."

"Oh," Ella said. "So why do you think he would come here?" She tried to tell herself that he hadn't come to look for her; part of her wanted nothing more, than to know that he loved her enough to track her down. She'd left him for his own safety, though, and the idea that he'd somehow followed her was unacceptable. Luca couldn't have told him where she was, even if he'd been willing to break his promise. If Swan had figured out who Travis was, however, and which ship he'd been on, then it wouldn't take much of a leap to determine where Ella would be.

She wanted to deny it, but she knew, in her heart, that Swan was only in Bauer's house because of her.

"Who knows? Maybe he means to make a scene."

Oh, God, I hope not, Ella thought.

"You need to get back out there," Natalie said, grabbing a full tray and shoving it into Ella's hands. The drinks sloshed and slid but didn't spill. "Don't think he'll take it easy on you because it's your first night."

Thinking of the look in Bauer's eyes as he'd appraised her, Ella suppressed a shudder and shook her head. "No, of course not," she mumbled. "I'm sorry."

The apology tasted bitter in her mouth, and she turned to leave the kitchen, praying Swan would take Travis and leave. As soon as she stepped into the party, however, she knew that things had changed. Her eyes sought out Colin and Travis, automatically. They were standing near the food, seemingly oblivious to the difference in the room. The laughter had faded out, and the conversations had become hushed, as a sort of nervousness seemed to have settled over the crowd. Swan was speaking to an older gentleman, and the captain was the picture of relaxation. Beside him, Travis looked almost bored.

Swan's gaze found hers, and she saw that his smile did not reach his dark eyes. The man he was speaking to did not appear to have noticed. Swan turned his attention back to the conversation, laughing at something the older man said. Ella's gaze cut across the room to Bauer, and knew instantly why the room had become so subdued. Bauer was aware of Swan's presence in his home, at his party, and his smile could not hide his anger.

Bauer was keeping an eye on Swan, although he was being subtle about it. Ella wondered how long that would last. Had Colin come just to antagonize Bauer? What could he have planned?

She forced herself to move into the room, offering drinks to guests. Most of them already had drinks, and her presence was nothing more than an opportunity for the men to ogle her. Her stomach rolled and churned as men looked her up and down. She kept walking, praying Travis and Colin were not watching.

"Mind if I take one of these?"

The voice, so familiar, so low, and so close, made her turn so suddenly that she almost dropped the tray. Swan, standing beside her, his expression unreadable, raised a hand as though to steady it. She quickly grabbed the side with her other hand, however, and he dropped his arm back to his side. He was so close that she could smell him, and if her hands weren't full, she'd be able to reach out and press her fingers against his chest.

With her mind racing, she tried to think of a way to get him to leave. She didn't want to hurt him more than she already had, but if she needed to, in order to get him safely out of Bauer's house, she would. She resisted the urge to glance over her shoulder to see if Bauer was watching. "Of course, sir," she managed, holding the tray in front of herself like a shield.

"Thank you," he said, plucking a drink off the tray. His gaze was so intense, she was powerless to look away. She could feel him practically vibrating with tension, and she wondered if anyone else could sense it. He looked relaxed. His stance was cocked, nonchalant, his drink held loosely near his hip. Even his face seemed composed, unaffected, except for the tiny tic in his cheek.

His eyes, however...She swallowed, trying to convince herself that the anger burning in his eyes was not important. "You need to get out of here," she heard herself say. Her voice was low, but she didn't know the words were going to leave her mouth until they hung between them. A few people were throwing them glances—because of the scandal of Swan's presence, she knew, and not because of anything to do with herself. No one was close enough to hear her, and she suddenly knew why that was, too: no one wanted to be too close to him and risk incurring Bauer's wrath.

Swan seemed completely unaware of, or unconcerned by, this.

At her words, his eyes narrowed, and the muscle in his jaw jumped; otherwise, his expression remained impassive. She had just a moment to marvel at his self-control, and then she looked past him, toward Travis. Her brother. Alive. Dressed up, and talking to strangers in fancy suits as though it were the most natural thing in the world. As she looked at him, he glanced sideways toward her, then laughed at something a woman was saying to him. No matter how they felt about Swan's presence, the guests seemed perfectly willing to talk to her brother.

"Please take him—"

Before she could finish, Swan leaned his head forward, and she struggled to keep from stepping back. As angry as he seemed, she wasn't afraid of him, not really, but his presence was intimidating—not least because she so desperately wanted to throw the tray to the ground and beg him to take her into his arms.

"Don't mistake my patience for indifference," he murmured, and his sudden sincerity was too much. She had to drive him away, and fast, before his presence pushed Bauer over the edge. Before it pushed *her* over the edge.

"Don't mistake my tolerance for—" She stopped, though. She couldn't do it. He'd already pulled back, looking for just a moment as though she'd slapped him. She wanted to call her words back, the ones said and the ones unsaid, but they hung in the air between them. *Please leave,* she thought. And then,

343

selfishly, *I'm sorry. Please don't go.* Before she knew what she was going to say, the words tumbled from her mouth: "Please, you don't understand." Her voice cracked, and her tray trembled, and she knew she had to get away from him while she still could.

"How about you trust me for *once*," he growled. "Just *one* goddamned time."

She was stunned—not so much by his anger, because she expected him to be angry with her. No, what shocked her most was his words. She *did* trust him, in a way she'd never trusted anyone before. She felt tears burn her eyes and desperately tried to blink them back. She hated having to hurt him.

As he looked at her, for just a heartbeat, she saw his control slip, and she saw the raw emotion he was so carefully keeping in check.

He told you he loved you. He offered you everything, and this is how you repay him?

Then his expression hardened, and his gaze slid past her. Before she could say anything—and what would she say? Beg him for forgiveness? Apologize and try to explain that she was only trying to protect him, and Travis, and all the others that had been stolen, or would be stolen if Bauer wasn't stopped? Tell him she loved him, that it hadn't been a lie?—she heard a voice just behind her, and a chill crept down her spine.

"Well, well, Mr. Swan," Martin Bauer said. "What a surprise. When did you get back on dry land?"

Swan forced a smile and raised his glass in a mock salute. "Bauer," he said. "Surprised you went through with this. After the loss of your crew, and ship."

"Oh, I'll get my ship back," Bauer answered. "In fact, I've heard it's in the harbor as we speak."

"Glad to see you're not all torn up about the loss of your men," Swan said.

Ella stood, frozen, trying to come up with a plan. Her mind was blank. She looked at Travis. He was standing in a group of people, watching the confrontation. He might have come with Swan, but he'd somehow become a part of the spectators. She didn't have time to wonder at that—his easy insinuation, or the reason for it—because Bauer dropped a hand onto her shoulder, startling her so badly that she again almost dropped the tray. Swan grabbed the edge of it and pulled it from her hands before she could object. Holding it by the edge, somehow managing to keep the drinks from spilling, he turned and handed it to Natalie as she tried to sneak past on her way to the kitchen. She looked startled, but she took the drinks and scurried on her way.

The pressure of Bauer's hand, as he squeezed the tender muscle in her shoulder, was painful. "Sorry about her," Bauer said. "She's new." Then, to Ella, "Get lost."

"What do you think happened with your ship?" Swan asked.

Bauer released her shoulder and gave her a nudge toward the kitchen. She started to walk away, thinking that she had to get to the kitchen and find something she could use as a weapon if a fight started. She couldn't imagine Bauer instigating a physical confrontation; he was fat and lazy and slow compared to Swan, and he wouldn't risk looking like a fool in front of all his guests. He probably wouldn't set his security onto the captain, either. It was more likely that he would wait until he could hurt Swan without witnesses. Just in case she was wrong, she had to be ready.

"Which ship?" Bauer asked, and she could hear the smile in his voice. Then, "Oh, *Enterprise*? Sorry, unlike you, I have so many, it's difficult to keep track. It was a terrible misfortune. Tragic loss. Don't worry, though. I'll make up the lost profits in no time."

"Not with that ship."

"No, of course not, it will have to be thoroughly checked out before it can make another run across the ocean. And I'll have to find a new captain, of course."

"It already has a captain," Swan said.

A murmur passed through the hushed crowd, and Ella paused with her hand on the kitchen door.

"Now, now, is that why you're here?" Bauer asked, his tone deceptively light. "You know that's not how it works. You might have killed my captain, but he didn't own my ship. Or anything that I'm aware of. Perhaps you could look up his wife, if he had one, claim her instead?"

An uneasy ripple of laughter shivered through the room. Ella frowned. Swan hadn't killed the captain of Bauer's ship. The only captain he'd killed was Carter, and that was weeks ago. Did Bauer really believe he'd had something to do with the uprising? She couldn't sort through her confusion. She waited with her back to the room for Swan's response.

"I didn't kill your captain," Swan said. "And, I'm not claiming your ship."

A cold sense of dread had begun to seep through her, and she swallowed, suddenly terrified. Swan hadn't been on that ship...However, Travis had. She wanted to shake her head in denial. Travis couldn't kill anyone. He was just a boy.

She knew that wasn't true, though. Even before she'd left Baytown, she'd known that he was growing up. He was almost an adult. Hadn't she been startled to realize the same about Luca? She'd spent so much time worrying about them, and looking after them, that she'd missed the fact that they were becoming men. Something had changed since then, though. Travis had changed. She didn't want to imagine what horrors he'd suffered, in order to propel him further into adulthood. She could tell by his posture, and his controlled expression, that he was no longer the boy he'd been.

"Of course you're not," Bauer said, with a nasty laugh.

"I am."

The voice rang loud and clear through the room. Ella closed her eyes. She felt like her heart and stomach had changed places. Her hand was shaking, and she dropped it to her side. Instead of going into the kitchen, she turned, slowly, and saw that all eyes—except Swan's—were on Travis. The people gathered near him had begun to retreat, putting space between him and themselves.

Swan was watching Bauer, and he must be seeing the same look of confusion, mixed with contempt, that Ella was seeing. Bauer hadn't yet decided that Travis should be in danger; he was still trying to puzzle the situation out.

"Who the hell are you?" Bauer asked, frowning.

Travis strode into the middle of the room with his chin up, and said, distinctly, "My name is Travis Fisher." In spite of her fear, she felt a surge of pride in her brother. "I come from Baytown, where your men captured me, locked me up, and took me from my home and family."

If the room was quiet before, at Travis's proclamation, near-silence descended. The only sound was the ticking of the grandfather clock. Even the kitchen behind her was silent. "You must be mistaken, my boy," Bauer said after several moments.

"Along with me, and the men and women, there were seven children, between the ages of twelve and six. Kidnapped and taken from the only country they knew. Starved. Left in their own filth like unloved animals. One of the boys, Anthony, died. He was eight." For the first time, Travis's composure slipped just a bit, and Ella wanted to run across the room and take him in her arms. He got control of himself quickly, though. "You might think that because you're rich, and people are afraid of you, you can do whatever you want. And, you might hire men who are no better than you are to do your dirty work for you."

Bauer's silence through this speech was surprising to Ella. She knew he would find his tongue soon. She wasn't sure what route he would take, however. Would he deny the allegations and attempt to discredit Travis—a boy whom nobody else in the room knew? Would he have Travis arrested for murder? Have him hanged? Her stomach churned. Challenge him to a duel? As fat and slow as Bauer was, Travis was a boy. So far as she knew, he'd never even held a sword.

"I don't know who you think you are, son," Bauer finally said. "It's clear that—"

"My name is Travis Fisher," Travis repeated.

"—Swan must have put you up to this. You shouldn't involve yourself in adult matters."

"I've claimed your ship as mine," Travis said into the stunned room. "I killed your captain and his crew."

Ella felt like she'd been punched in the stomach. She stared at her brother, unable to believe his words and unable to deny the truth in his young face. She wanted to shake her head. She suddenly knew that her plan didn't matter. In that moment, she wanted Bauer to die, still, for what her brother and the others had been through. But it didn't matter. Killing him didn't matter, getting revenge didn't matter. What mattered was getting her brother, and Swan, and herself, out safely. She and Travis could go back to Baytown. As angry as he was with her, and as hurt, she was confident that Swan would take them home if she asked. The pain it would cause her, to spend months on his ship without being able to touch him, talk to him, and show him that she loved him, was

346

unimportant. She could do it. She and Travis, and Luca, could go home, and they could start over.

What about Swan, and Maggie?

They would go to the police. It was a far more sensible option than trying to kill Bauer herself. No matter how rich and powerful he was, he would have to answer to authorities when faced with the proof of his illegal dealings...right? He'd brought men, women, and children into the country without paperwork, children that were kidnapped from their homes—even if those homes were orphanages—and adults that could testify to their detainment and illegal deportation.

Yes. She had to get Travis and Swan out, and go to the police.

"Are you confessing to murder?" Bauer asked, in a low voice that carried through the still room.

"No. Your men kidnapped us, chained us, abused and neglected and starved us. Our uprising was self-defense, and justified."

"I will be investigating the allegations, of course, that my employees were engaged in illegal activities," Bauer said, glancing around the room. "We'll get to the bottom of this. As for the ship, even if what you say is true, killing the captain doesn't make the ship yours. As I told Swan—"

"I'm not asking," Travis said. "I didn't come to argue about a ship. Or to let you hide behind lies, trying to make yourself look innocent. The ship is mine. I've come to challenge you to a duel."

Ella's heart stopped. She took a step forward, and Swan shot her a look that stopped her in her tracks. She swallowed. He'd asked her to trust him; she *did* trust him. She couldn't stand by and let her brother get killed, though, not when she'd just learned that he was still alive. Still, she hesitated, rooted to the spot, undecided.

"Don't be ridiculous," Bauer said, but he sounded uneasy as he again glanced around the room. Murmurs and whispers were rippling through the room. Travis was silent, waiting. Swan was standing, watching Travis and Bauer appraising each other, with his hands clasped behind his back. He still appeared relaxed, in spite of the look he'd shot Ella. Realizing that Travis was not backing away from his challenge, Bauer frowned, squared his shoulders, and said, "That's a very serious thing to say, boy. I don't think you understand the ramifications. How old are you?"

"I turned eighteen today," Travis answered, to another round of mutters. Ella felt another jolt at that. She'd completely lost track of the days, and the realization that it was her brother's birthday was another shock to her exhausted mind.

"And you think you're prepared to die like a man?"

"I was prepared to die when I made the decision to leave the dungeon of your ship. I was prepared to die when I made the decision to try and save those kids, even if I had no hope of succeeding. I was prepared to die when I faced your men, one by one, with a bloody sword." As horrifying as the words were for Ella to hear, she stood, like the rest of the room, enthralled by Travis's

347

speech. "I was prepared to die a dozen times over, but I didn't. Because I was meant to come here, and tell everyone what kind of man you are, and to tell you that you aren't going to steal any more children or rob any more men and women of their lives and freedom."

"Enough!" Bauer said, with an angry wave of his hand. "I've tried to be patient. I've told you I don't know what you're talking about. This is your last chance to leave before I have you arrested."

"Are you going to refuse the challenge of a duel?" someone asked from the crowd.

Bauer hesitated. "I'm trying to show mercy," he finally answered, seeming to realize that he was losing support from the room.

"Since when?" someone scoffed, and Ella glanced around, surprised by the rising animosity in the crowd.

"Very well," Bauer said, his expression hardening. "I accept your challenge, boy. May God have mercy on you. Tomorrow—"

"No," Travis answered. "Now."

"Now!" Bauer blurted. "I have guests. A gentleman—"

"He made the challenge," came another voice from the crowd. "He sets the rules."

"Fine!" Bauer said. His face was splotchy with anger, and Ella knew that he was already imagining all the ways he could make Travis suffer. "Outside."

Travis nodded, once, in agreement. He seemed calm, far calmer than Bauer.

A man stepped forward from the group, and almost every pair of eyes turned toward him. "Someone needs to vouch for this boy's age," he said, speaking clearly.

Ella lifted her chin. "He's my brother," she said, and she heard a collective gasp from the room. She wanted to offer to fight for him. She wanted to claim the burden for herself. When Travis looked at her, however, she realized that she could not protect him from this. In the months since she'd seen him, he'd lived a life she knew nothing about. In ways she could scarcely comprehend, he'd grown up. He had his reasons for challenging Bauer. She had to let him make his own decisions, no matter how badly she wanted to help him. She had to trust him.

And, she had to trust Swan. He'd brought Travis to this house, to challenge Bauer, for a reason, too. They must have some sort of plan. Swan would not have simply brought the boy into the lion's den to be eaten. He must know something Ella did not. She had to trust both of them.

"Were you his legal guardian?" the man asked. Ella didn't know who he was, but he must be somebody important. She ignored the surprised, murderous look that Bauer was giving her. She ignored the stares of the guests and servants. She nodded. "And you'll verify his eligibility to participate?"

She looked at Swan, and met his eyes. His expression, still, was unreadable, his dark gaze hooded. This was her last chance to refuse, or to accept the challenge on her brother's behalf. She could offer to fight. She could deny consent. Or she could trust.

"Yes," she heard herself say.

Was that relief on Swan's face? It was hidden so quickly, it was difficult to say for certain. "Very well," the man was saying, but Swan had already turned his back on Ella, toward the room.

"Governor," he said, addressing the important-sounding man. "I volunteer to fight in the boy's place."

The surprise on Bauer's face was nothing compared to that on Travis's. He had not expected Swan's offer, and he wasn't happy about it.

"What's going on here?" Bauer asked, but the crowd ignored him, for the moment.

"He has no apparent need for a stand-in," the governor responded, looking a bit uneasy, himself. He looked at Travis. "And, his sister has testified to his legal age. This is your sister, right?"

Travis met Ella's eyes. "Yes," he said. He took a deep breath, and let it out, slowly. He was working to keep his composure, now.

"While this boy may be of legal age today, he is not of sound body. He has an infected wound across his arm, incurred during his struggle for life on this man's ship. He has other healing wounds, less severe. And, while I would argue that his mind is sound enough to know what he is risking, his emotional state is damaged by the loss of the young boy he mentioned, a boy he feels he failed to protect."

The mention of an infected wound made Ella's stomach clench with renewed fear. And the shock and grief suddenly at war in Travis's expression made it difficult for her to breathe. She again suppressed the urge to rush to her brother's side, with effort.

Turning toward Travis, the governor said, "Do you want this man to fight in your place?"

No, Ella thought, immediately, barely managing to keep from blurting the word out. *No, no, anybody else. Let me fight*, she thought. Swan wasn't looking at her. She couldn't see his face, but she could hear his voice, in her head: *Trust me.* Swan had planned this, she realized. He'd always meant to let Bauer accept Travis's challenge, and then step into the boy's place. He'd never planned on letting Travis fight. He couldn't stop him, though, not without help.

"That's not fair," Bauer said. Then, seeming to realize how childish that sounded, he raised his chin and continued, "This was obviously a trick to get me to consent to a fight with Swan. Even my own maid seems to have conspired—"

"Are you saying you wouldn't have agreed to a duel, had I challenged you myself?" Swan asked.

Bauer stopped, his ruddy face working as he tried to think of something to say that would not make him look like a coward. He almost certainly would *not* have agreed to the fight, in spite of the goading from the crowd, because he was far more afraid of Swan than he was of Travis. That much was written on his face, although Bauer seemed unaware of the fact.

Travis had not yet objected to the turn of events, although his expression made it clear that he wanted to. His hands were clenched by his sides. The anger on his face made Ella afraid that he would rush Bauer himself, and ignore propriety. He stood, unmoving, and she prayed he would remain that way. His sleeves were buttoned at his wrists, and she tried not to imagine how his arm might be infected beneath.

"You'd fight a boy, but not a man?" someone jibed.

"Maybe not a man—maybe it's just Swan he's afraid of," someone else suggested, and several people sniggered.

"This man is a thief and a murderer," Bauer said, gesturing toward Swan.

"He stepped up to fight for the boy," the governor pointed out, quietly. He was regarding Bauer with a calm expression and a dangerous glint in his eyes. Ella had no idea what type of dealings they might be involved in together, what sort of relationship had brought the governor to the Bauer home, but she knew that the governor was not an idiot. He might be involved in the business of slaves, himself—she had no idea. He clearly did not mean to be dragged through the mud with Bauer, one way or another. He'd drawn a line between himself and the other man, and Ella knew that Bauer could see it.

"He's a pirate," Bauer said, trying one more time. He really was terrified of fighting Swan. She wondered if his fear would win out over his pride. "He has no honor. I have no desire to stoop to his level—"

"You could never be on his level!" Ella heard herself exclaim, before she knew she was going to speak. Her fear was almost gone, squashed beneath her rising anger. "He has more honor in his little finger than you have in your whole body. A thief, a murderer, a liar, a cheat, a criminal—a person who sells children? That's *you*."

"Shut up, you fucking whore," Bauer spat. From the corner of her eye, she saw Travis start forward. In an instant, before she even realized what was happening, Swan drew back a fist and punched Bauer in the face. Travis stopped, watching as Bauer stumbled backward and fell with a resounding thud. Sitting on the floor, Bauer clapped his hands over his bleeding nose, staring up with shocked, watery, hate-filled eyes.

"Now, now," the governor chided mildly.

"I want him arrested for assault!" Bauer cried, his voice muffled.

"Challenge him to a duel," someone mocked, and a titter of laughter followed.

Swan was standing, his feet spread, his hands by his sides, glaring down at Bauer. "Are you going to fight, or not?"

"Give me my fucking sword," Bauer shouted, struggling to push himself to his feet. He spat blood on the floor and winced. His lips were red. Blood dripped from his chin. He was breathing heavily through his mouth.

"And bring one for Captain Swan," the governor added, as several servants rushed off to fetch their boss's blade.

"No," Travis said. "Bring one for *me*." Most of the room didn't seem to hear him, but Ella did. And, it would appear, so did Swan. He'd casually begun

350

to move toward Travis, while keeping his attention focused on Bauer.

"What about the ship?" someone called. "Does the boy still get the ship?"

"Of course not!" Bauer said.

"Spoils of war go to the victor," Swan said.

"What war?" Bauer scoffed.

"The one you initiated by taking them against their will—"

In a low voice, Bauer interrupted, "How many times do I have to—"

"Did I forget to mention we have proof?" Swan asked, his voice mild. He was nearly by Travis's side.

Bauer stopped talking and glared at him, swallowing. "Impossible," he said.

Swan motioned Travis forward. Travis seemed to have forgotten himself, in his anger at having been robbed of a duel, and he gave himself a little shake before stepping toward Swan. He pulled what appeared to be several sheets of folded parchment from inside his suit jacket.

"I can understand your doubt," Travis said, holding Bauer's decidedly-worried gaze. "You must be confused, knowing what an inconsiderate, uneducated slob your captain was, by the idea that he might have kept records. My guess is that he knows you'd sell your own family for a buck, yeah? That you'd sooner have his throat slit than call on the police at the merest hint of a missing coin. You like making people afraid of you, don't you? I mean, I've never met you before today, but that seems obvious. You'd like the idea that your crews are too terrified to rip you off. This time? Your captain's fear is going to be your downfall. I'll bet a quick search of your other ships, and their records, will be the same."

Bauer swallowed several times. "Whatever those papers say, they have nothing to do with me."

"May I see those?" the governor asked, reaching for the parchment. Travis hesitated, holding them tightly, and looked at Swan. Swan nodded, and Travis reluctantly handed the papers over. The governor scanned them, flipping through pages with a deepening frown, before looking up at Bauer. "They do seem damning," he murmured.

"Every person listed on those ledgers can testify, except the six that died. 'Small black boy' is Anthony. 'Teenaged white boy' is me. Oh, and I forgot to mention, we didn't kill every member of the crew." Travis turned and motioned toward a young man barely older than Travis himself, and he and two others stepped forward, fidgeting awkwardly in their dress clothes. "Do you recognize them? Probably not. They were just the cleaning crew. They know a lot about your business, though, and what we went through to get free. Jesiah, Cheddy, and JayJay."

Servants were handing swords to Bauer and Swan. Bauer looked so angry, Ella was afraid he wasn't going to wait for the duel, and rush Travis, instead, running him through. In a handful of seconds, Bauer's life seemed to be crumbling, and a desperate man who suddenly saw that he might be losing everything could be dangerously unpredictable.

"Well, if you're alive tomorrow, it looks like you'll have some explaining to do," Swan said.

Ella found herself wondering why they were goading Bauer *before* the fight. They'd tricked him into accepting a duel with Swan; then, once the deal was struck, they showed him that the duel didn't really matter, because he was going to lose everything, anyway. Swan was making Bauer angrier by the second, and by the time they got to the yard, the only thing Bauer would have left was the desire to make Swan suffer as much as possible.

"It's a shame you won't be around to see me beat these despicable allegations," Bauer said with a flash of bloody teeth that barely resembled a smile.

"Let's get started," Swan said, sounding bored. "It's getting late, and I have things to do."

"The only thing you have to do is die," Bauer retorted, raising his sword, and the statement was uttered so ridiculously that the crowd laughed. Ella looked around. How quickly the people had shifted, and in that moment, she hated them. If she were to draw a line between Swan and Bauer, now, she had no doubt which side these rich people would step to. Ten minutes ago, however? They were not siding with righteousness, or morality; they were siding with power, and looking out for their own self-interests. They did not want to go down with a sinking ship. What about afterward, though? Would their loyalty to Swan hold, or would they—including the governor, about whom she knew nothing—turn on him? And if so, what would happen to Maggie and the orphans?

Ella shoved that thought away. Swan wouldn't do anything to endanger the old woman, or the children. And if something happened to him, Ella would make sure Maggie was safe if she had to sleep on the doorstep herself.

No, no, he's going to be fine, Ella thought. *He has to be. You have to be alright, Colin.*

"No," Travis repeated, louder. "No, I didn't agree to step down. I'm going to honor my challenge."

"Son, if you're truly injured, as the captain says," the governor began, but Travis interrupted him.

"I'm fine. I came here to fight. I deserve to fight him."

"Lift up your sleeve, boy," the governor said.

"He said he's fine," Bauer inserted. "If the boy wants to duel—"

"Yeah, you'd like that," someone called.

"Lift your sleeve," the governor commanded, more forcefully.

Travis glanced toward Ella. "I respectfully refuse," he said, speaking through clenched teeth.

"Travis," Swan said, motioning the boy closer. Travis glared at him. Swan leaned forward to whisper something into his ear. Travis's eyes widened and cut toward Ella, again. Before she could begin to imagine what Swan had said, Travis pulled back and, to her utter shock, punched Swan squarely in the face. The crowd seemed to gasp in unison. Swan took a single step back as blood

352

ran from his nose and lip.

Ella was hurrying forward, trying to get to them, desperate to get between them. She wasn't even sure which one of them she was hoping to protect. Swan could lay Travis out easily, she knew, but he was making no move to do so. He was simply standing, holding Travis's angry gaze with his own dark, steady eyes.

"Fine," Travis said, finally. His fists were clenched by his sides. Ella slowed to a stop, glancing toward Bauer, who'd moved dangerously close to Swan while the captain was focused on Travis.

She realized that Swan was leading the way outside, and her heart leaped into her throat. How could he turn his back on Bauer? The eyes of the crowd would not be enough to keep the man honest, not when Bauer knew that the eyes had already begun to condemn him. He walked several paces behind Swan, with his sword clutched in his hand tightly enough to turn his knuckles white. Travis walked behind Bauer, and Ella was painfully aware that her brother was unarmed. Bauer could just as easily turn and attack him.

The men and women, including the governor, merged behind the three, following them toward the door, and Ella could no longer see Travis, Bauer, or Swan. Panic surged within her, and she started forward, desperate to get to them. Someone grabbed her arm, and she looked back, startled. It was Natalie.

"What the hell is going on?" the other woman hissed. Her fingers were digging into Ella's arm hard enough to hurt. "You know Captain Swan? And...and...your brother..."

Ella jerked her arm away. "I don't have time for this," she said. "If you want to stay here, that's your business." She was already hurrying to the back of the crowd, but it was too late; Swan and Bauer were out of the house and she still couldn't see them. She pushed into the throng of people, not caring about the dirty looks or angry exclamations, trying to fight her way through. She was cursing herself for letting them out of her sight, for getting separated from the people she loved when their lives were on the line.

Then, finally, she saw Travis, at the edge of the crowd, and she felt a brief flare of relief. She craned her neck, trying to see around the bodies, and couldn't get her eyes on Swan or Bauer. With a churning stomach, she struggled her way toward her brother. Travis was scanning the crowd, and after a moment his eyes met hers and he surged toward her. As soon as they reached each other, Ella threw her arms around him. He felt different. Taller. Stronger. It hadn't been that long since she'd seen him, and she wondered how much of the change was in her mind.

"I thought you were dead," she said, and the crack in her voice was unmistakable.

"I'm fine," he answered, hugging her. "Shh, Ellie, it's gonna be alright."

She closed her eyes. For a moment, they were both silent, and she knew they were both thinking of all the times she'd said that to him over the years. "Whatever it takes," she murmured, and for just a second, his arms tightened around her. "Where's Colin?" she asked, stepping back and swiping at her tears.

"Getting ready to fight. This isn't how it was supposed to go," Travis answered. "I'm supposed to be fighting."

Ella grabbed her brother's hand. "Come on," she said, tugging him into the crowd. "I have to—Where—Hurry. Move, move," she said, shoving her way through the throng, pulling her brother with her. When she finally broke into the clearing, her eyes met Swan's. Had he been looking for her? As their gazes caught and held, his jaw clenched. He was on the far side of a rough circle of grass the bystanders had formed. Bauer was nearer to her, yelling at one of his frazzled servants.

It would be dark, soon. The sun was low, casting the yard in long shadows and painting the sky in streaks of purple and red and orange. If they didn't begin the fight soon, it might be too dark to continue. Would they set up lanterns and go on, anyway? She knew next to nothing about the rules or guidelines relating to duels. Where she came from, men settled their disputes with fists or, sometimes, whatever they could lay their hands on. Brawls, she'd seen. Duels, she had not, unless Swan's fight with Carter counted. She was not excited about seeing Swan involved in one, now or ever again. The idea of watching him being hurt...

She shook her head and, steeling herself for the rejection she expected to come, she gathered her courage and pulled Travis onto the grass. People looked at her as she cut across the circle, and she ignored them. She was aware of her inappropriate attire, and not just because the evening air was chilly against her exposed skin. She could feel the eyes on her, could feel the people appraising and judging her, and didn't care. She only cared about Swan's opinion, and she couldn't read his expression in the dimness as she crossed to him.

Before she could say anything, Swan looked past her at Travis, and said, "I know you're angry, son. I'm sorry."

"This should be my responsibility," Travis said. He didn't mention whatever secret had passed between them, or apologize for hitting Swan in the face. The captain had wiped the blood from his nose, but the dark redness was beaded on his split lip.

Swan was shaking his head, but Ella had already turned to face her brother. "Travis, stop," she said, and he looked at her, startled. Ella grabbed his other hand, so she was holding both of his in hers. "I can't lose you again. Listen to me. I would give anything to keep him from getting hurt, and...I don't want to...watch him fight," she said, swallowing around the lump in her throat. "But I trust him. He's going to be fine. He...he has to be," she added, struggling against her threatening tears. Travis studied her for a moment, then looked past her at Swan. "Just give me a minute," she told her brother. "Please?" she added.

Travis nodded. She expected him to object, or to complain, but she was surprised. His quiet resignation was further proof of his maturity. He stepped back and turned away, heading toward the edge of the crowd. Ella took a deep breath. Across the small clearing, Bauer was surrounded by servants, now, trying to ready him for battle. Behind her, Swan was alone, although she suspected that was by choice. Surely at least some of the men would have jumped at the opportunity to align themselves with him, now, before the fight. From the corner of her eye, she saw Travis step up beside the governor at the edge of the crowd, saw the governor nod and murmur something to him.

Ella turned to face Swan. He was holding his suit jacket out, dangling from the tips of his fingers. She hesitated, surprised. His face was stubbly and shadowy, his hair blowing a bit in the breeze. She wanted so badly to step into his embrace, to feel his comforting warmth and smell his familiar scent and, most importantly, to feel his arms wrap around her in return. She started to reach for the jacket, but her hand was shaking.

Swan stepped forward and, with an easy flick, wrapped the jacket around her. She slipped her arms into the sleeves, immediately grateful for the warmth against her chilled skin. He was standing close, so close that she could easily lean her head forward and lay her forehead against his chest. She resisted the temptation. "Thank you," she said. She wanted to believe that it was encouraging, that he hadn't stepped away, yet. And, he didn't seem angry, anymore. Maybe he was just putting his emotions aside to prepare for the duel.

She hugged the jacket around herself to keep from touching him. There were a million things she wanted to say, but this wasn't the time. He had to stay focused. The only thing that mattered was him winning the fight. She had to believe there would be time for apologies and explanations later. There was only one thing she had to make sure he knew.

"I love you," she said, trying desperately to ignore the fear of rejection that was making her voice tremble. "I know I screwed everything up. I know you probably hate me. I hope you'll give me a chance to apologize, later, even if you don't want to accept it. Thank you for protecting Travis, but...please be careful. Please."

"Come on!" Bauer shouted from across the yard. "Let's get this fucking thing over with."

Swan ignored him. He was studying her, and she wished she knew what he was thinking. She thought he was going to say something. Instead, after a moment, he nodded and stepped back. Still hugging his jacket around herself, Ella turned and made her way over to her brother, praying the fight would end quickly—with Bauer's death or submission.

Travis put his arm around her shoulders and she leaned into him, overwhelmed with gratitude for his presence. "I love you, Ellie," he murmured, kissing her hair, and she felt tears burn her eyes.

"I love you, too," she answered. "I missed you so much. I thought...I would never see you again..."

"I can't believe you're here," he said. "In Bohannon, I mean. I can't believe you followed...Well, yes, I can," he amended with a small laugh. "You'll have to tell me all about it, later."

"I'm sure you have far more to tell," she said, watching Swan and Bauer advance toward each other.

"If Captain Swan wins this—"

"When," she interrupted. "He will win. He has to."

"When he wins this, should I challenge him to another?"

She turned her attention away from Swan, startled. "What? Why?"

Travis searched her face for a moment. "Just wondering," he finally answered.

"What did he tell you?"

"We can talk about that, later," he answered, quietly.

Unable to keep her gaze from Swan, she looked back in time to see him and Bauer circling each other, blades raised. "I love him," she answered. "I left him to protect him, from...this. From everything. I planned on going back after I found you, but then I overheard them talking about the uprising on the ship, and they said everyone was dead, and...I thought..." She stopped, shaking her head. "All I could think about was making someone pay for what happened to you, and Bauer was the one behind it all. It was stupid to come here. I should've gone back to Colin. I never should've left him in the first place," she amended. "I hurt him."

Travis was silent. They watched as Bauer made the first strike, swinging with his sword. Swan deflected it easily. He didn't return the blow, though. After a moment, Bauer tried again, and Swan once more knocked his blade aside. It was strange for Ella, watching the two men. She was still frightened for Swan, but she was also awed—again—by his beauty. Bauer was outmatched in every way; strength, height, grace, leanness...courage. Honor. Patience.

The crowd shifted and mumbled, uneasy or unhappy with the lack of immediate bloodshed. Bauer and Swan continued to circle each other, and Bauer swung wildly. Each deflected blow left him exposed, and Swan could have killed him several times. Instead, he remained calm and watchful, expending only the minimal amount of energy necessary to keep Bauer's blade from reaching him.

"What's he doing?" the governor asked. "Why isn't he fighting?"

"He's tiring him out," Travis answered.

Ella shook her head, finally understanding. "No," she said, with a surge of love for Swan. "He's not trying to kill him. He's trying to—"

"Ruin him," Travis finished, realization dawning in his expression.

Ella glanced at her brother, then looked back at Swan, nodding.

"How's he going to keep him from coming after him, later? Or his family?" the governor asked.

Before she could answer, Travis turned to the man, and answered, "Isn't that your job?"

The governor opened his mouth—likely to point out that he was not the police—and then closed it again. Ella ignored him. She was focused on the battle in the yard. Bauer was growing angrier by the minute. His face in the dimming sunlight was sweaty and flushed. His swings and jabs were more erratic, and he was sending up a near-constant string of curses and insults.

The crowd was growing impatient, and Ella felt another flare of disgust for them.

"Fight back!" Bauer suddenly shouted, jabbing. Swan stepped aside and circled.

"Yes! Fight back!" several people called.

"I'm going to kill you," Bauer said, swinging his blade. Swan's met it in air and knocked it aside. Bauer swung the other way, grunting, "I'm going to kill your friends." Clang. "Your family." Clang. "Your whore. You know, she offered herself—"

There was a collective gasp as Bauer's sword was knocked from his hand. Bauer stood, stunned, unarmed. Then, suddenly realizing he'd hit a nerve, he flashed a mean grin.

"Was that part of the plan?" he asked. "Or did she just decide on her own to find out—"

"Pick up your sword," Swan said.

"—what a real man's like?"

Don't believe him, Ella thought, hugging herself. *Don't let him upset you.* Then, her nasty inner voice said, *Why wouldn't he believe him? He knows you offered yourself to him, for passage across the ocean.*

That's different, she thought. Was it, though? Would Swan see it that way?

"Pick up your sword," Swan repeated.

Bauer walked toward it with a nonchalance that Ella knew he wasn't really feeling. He bent, reached for the sword, and grabbed a handful of dirt, instead, flinging it toward Swan's face. Swan sidestepped, squinting his eyes as some of the grit peppered his face, but when Bauer snatched his sword and rushed him, Swan was ready. Bauer growled in frustration, clutched his sword in both hands, and swung wildly. Rather than waste energy trying to deflect the blows, Swan retreated, backing and circling, just out of reach of Bauer's blade.

In spite of herself, Ella smiled. She would have felt bad for Martin Bauer, had she not known the type of person he was.

"It's getting dark," Travis said.

The sun had slipped behind the trees, and the yard was cast in purple light. Dusk would be the worst time for visibility; Ella knew that Swan had excellent eyesight, though. "He'll be alright," she said.

"You'll never be good enough for your whore, now," Bauer was saying. Like a dog with a bone, he wasn't going to let it go, not once he'd realized it might be a chink in Swan's armor. "One taste of me—" He stumbled backward, barely deflecting the first blow that Swan had initiated. Bauer's surprise was quickly replaced by more of the same smug arrogance, however.

"He's getting tired," Travis said.

Ella knew he didn't mean Swan. Bauer was the one sweating and breathing heavily. He was the one whose swings were growing heavier as his arms tired. She couldn't breathe easily, though. Not yet. Because Bauer would do anything. If his lies about her failed to get the desired reaction, he would try a different approach.

"You're probably going to spend some time in jail," Captain Swan said, moving in a slow, wide circle, forcing Bauer to turn. "With the testimonies of the prisoners from just one ship, but we will find more. I imagine some of your own staff might have some interesting stories. I sent a man to your mother-in-law's house, by the way. Just to check on your wife. I hear she always begins to feel a little ill on the evenings you throw these wonderful parties." The clang of steel, again and again, couldn't quite drown out Swan's words, and he never paused in his speech as he parried. "And since Travis has legally claimed your ship—"

"That's not legal!" Bauer spat, swinging.

"Since Travis has legally claimed your ship," Swan repeated. "Your profits for the year will be...shall we say...cut a bit. Although that's the least of your worries, really. I mean, think about it. Every international port authority is going to be alerted to your illegal dealings. And while many of them have known for some time, it's going to be different, now. If you're lucky, they'll still let your holdings trade in their countries, although I'm sure you'll be subjected to regular searches, at the very least. I don't imagine it will be easy for you to hire crews, either, as I plan to make it very clear that I will be watching vigilantly for any sign of one of your ships on the open sea. Still, you can probably manage to scrape by, with a couple of ships, maybe, and a basic trading operation. You know, bolts of cloth, handmade jewelry, maybe some dry goods if you find a market...All of this is hypothetical, of course, and dependent on you being out of jail while you're still young enough to run a business at all."

Bauer was silent except for his labored breathing, devoting all of his energy to his angry, desperate blows. Ella thought his face was purple, although it was difficult to see in the rapidly darkening evening. She wished things would hurry along, because the stress was going to kill her. She had her arms crossed in front of herself, holding Swan's jacket tightly.

"Will he go to jail?" Travis asked the governor.

"There will be an investigation. The ledgers seem to be damning, but we'll have to prove that Bauer's money paid for the capture, relocation, and eventual sale of slaves. And that he knew about it. With witnesses and testifying victims, though...I'd say there's a very good chance he'll be convicted. He's made enough enemies with his *legal* dealings that he won't find many allies if he falls."

Ella was barely listening. She no longer cared about what might happen to Bauer after the fight. Thoughts of revenge had given way for prayers for Colin's safety. She wanted to take him and Travis and leave. She knew it was selfish. Her mind was heavy with exhaustion, though, her body achy with fatigue, and she wanted a rest. She wanted to forget about the real world, even if it was only for a couple of hours. Travis had his arm around her shoulders, and she had to keep reminding herself not to lean on him.

"You've been threatening Maggie again, too," Swan was saying. "Now, I

358

don't find it so interesting that you only hassle her while I'm gone, because everyone here has seen your cowardice firsthand. I'm not so surprised that you like to bully and threaten old women and orphans. What I cannot quite understand, however, is how you expect to get away with such things. I mean, personally, I'd put money on Maggie if *she* challenged you to a duel, but you've underestimated her in so many ways, it's almost funny. All these years, you've been making money off others' pain, you've been blackmailing and extorting, threatening and bullying, making enemies even of the people you think are your allies. During that time, Maggie has helped this town and everyone in it, one way or another. And she's never made a single enemy. Except you, of course. Who do you think the town is going to side with?"

"Shut up and fight!" Bauer yelled, swinging. The crowd seemed to agree with him, at least on that sentiment. They were more than ready for blood to be spilled—Ella was pretty sure they were, by now, hoping it would be Bauer's blood. The litany of charges against him could come as no surprise—they all knew what he was like, at least in part. Hearing Swan lay the crimes out loud was having an effect, nonetheless. As Swan had no doubt anticipated.

"You'll have to sell the house. Even your vast fortune won't cover all of the damages when the men and women you abducted are finished suing you. My attorney will begin interviewing them tomorrow."

"You call me a coward! You're afraid to fight like a man! Fight me!"

"You don't want that, Bauer," Travis muttered. Ella glanced at him. He had a small, grim smile on his face.

"Kill him already!" someone shouted.

Swan smiled. "I'm not going to kill you," he told Bauer. "I want to see you answer for the things you've done."

"You're just angry I fucked your girlfriend!" Bauer yelled.

Ella felt Travis's arm tighten around her. People glanced toward her in the dim light, and she pulled the jacket closer. She knew it wasn't true. Bauer hadn't assaulted her—not yet. She had no doubt that he would have, given time. She wanted to step forward and deny his claims, but her pride didn't matter. She would do nothing to risk distracting Swan from the fight.

"You realize you sound like an idiot?" Swan asked, driving Bauer backward with several quick, hard blows against his blade. "I'm glad your wife isn't here to hear your filthy, disrespectful lies."

"It's going to be alright, El," Travis murmured in her ear. "Look, see those guys over there?" She followed his point and saw the men he'd introduced, earlier, as members of the ship's crew. She nodded. "I'm going to go down there for a minute. I'll be right back, alright? I want them out of here before the fight's over. I don't want them taken in for questioning until I can go with them."

She nodded, again. She didn't want him out of her reach, and she wasn't sure she could stand on her own much longer, but she straightened and watched him make his way along the edge of the crowd. Suddenly, several shouts rang out, and she heard Swan yell her name. Before she could turn, pain

359

exploded above her ear and she stumbled sideways. She felt someone grab her arm—the governor, she thought—as people began yelling, and a moment later, her knees hit the ground. She barely felt the impact, as she blinked, trying to clear her mind. Someone screamed.

Hands were holding onto both of her arms, now. She couldn't focus. Her head was on fire, her vision blurred, her body weak. She couldn't lift her chin. Her body felt limp and uncooperative, and the voices seemed to fade around her.

Chapter Eighteen

She opened her eyes. She didn't recognize the room around her. There was a dull ache in the side of her head, not unbearable. "Colin?" she said, blinking to bring the room in focus. Movement drew her attention to the left, and she saw Travis and Luca, both sitting in chairs. Travis was leaned forward.

"He's not here," her brother said. "Relax. You're alright."

Disappointment almost immediately gave way to fear, and she struggled to sit up. Travis put a hand on her shoulder, to keep her down, frowning. "Where is he? Is he hurt? What happened?"

"He's fine," Travis said. "He's downstairs, somewhere. He's fine."

"What happened?" she repeated, raising a hand to the bandage on the side of her head. "I don't...Where are we?"

"Mrs. Darling's house," Travis answered. "Calm down, Ella. Really. Everything's fine."

"Where's Bauer?" she asked. "Is he dead?"

"No," Travis said, after a hesitation.

"No?" Ella repeated, unable to shake her unease. "But...Colin won...right?"

"He cut off Bauer's hand," Luca said, speaking for the first time. He raised his arm and made a slow chopping motion halfway between his wrist and elbow. "Wish I'd been there to see it," he added, leaning forward to prop his elbows on his knees. "How are you feeling, El? Does your head hurt?"

"Did someone hit me? I don't remember..."

"Bauer threw a rock at you," Travis said, and his anger was palpable. "He threw one at Swan, and Swan dodged, and before anyone knew what he meant to do, he turned and whipped the other one at you. I'm sorry, El. I should've been beside you."

"I would've killed him," Luca said.

"*I* would've killed him," Travis repeated. Then, after a pause, "Swan was right, though. He needs to suffer for what he's done. And he's going to suffer, now. I have to say, I don't know how he found the restraint to take off his arm instead of running him through the gut."

"He's downstairs?" she asked, uncertainly. She knew she shouldn't feel hurt by his absence. She had, after all, left him. Lied to him. Hurt him.

Travis turned his head to look at Luca, and she was too confused and preoccupied to understand the look they exchanged. She was struck again by how much they'd both changed, in just a couple of months. She loved them so much that it made her chest ache, and she was incredibly glad to have them together, safe and relatively sound. Then she remembered Travis's infected wound, and frowned.

"How's your arm? Have you been treated? Colin will find you a healer."

"He already did," Travis said, studying her face. "Don't worry about me. El, you...really do love him, don't you?"

"I do," she said. "I ruined everything, though."

"I need to ask you something," Travis said. His expression clearly said that he didn't want to. He hesitated.

"She doesn't know," Luca said.

Ella looked from one to the other. "I don't know what?" she asked.

"I hear Travis slugged Swan in the face," Luca said, with a grim smile. "I would've done it myself, except...I've seen firsthand what it's like when you two are together. Travis, he has some doubts. Understandably, of course."

In her fear and uncertainty, and pain and confusion, she'd somehow managed to forget all about Travis punching Colin in the face. Now, she focused on her brother. "What did he say to you?" she asked.

"He told me...that I needed to stay by you, because you're pregnant," Travis said, reluctantly.

It took a moment for the words to make sense. Then, a strange, cold tingle began to spread through her. She shook her head, opened her mouth to deny it, and found herself shocked speechless. She'd lost track of the passage of time, and had forgotten her brother's birthday. That wasn't all she'd forgotten, apparently. She struggled to think back. She was a couple of weeks late, and she was never late. How could she not have realized? Menstruation would've interrupted her relationship with Colin, but she'd never even noticed the lack.

"If he asks you to marry him, because of the baby..." Travis said. Beside him, Luca leaned back in his chair.

Ella shook her head. She still couldn't speak. She put her palm over her stomach. The coldness was receding, replaced by warmth. Was she really pregnant? With Colin's baby? She remembered jumping from the ship, and the shock of cold water, with horror. She could've drowned, and she wouldn't have just been killing herself, but Colin's child, as well. Or the cold could have harmed the baby. What if she'd already miscarried, and they just didn't know it yet? She would never be able to forgive herself. Endangering herself was one thing. If she'd known she was carrying his child, though...

No wonder he didn't want to be in the same room as her. No wonder he hadn't answered her, when she'd told him she loved him.

"We can do whatever you want, now, El," Travis said. "I have a ship. Swan doesn't think the crew will show up tomorrow where they're supposed to meet me, but they will. At least half of them. And Luca has experience. We can go anywhere. I don't have money, but we can get by on fish until we can—"

"Travis," she said, putting a hand on his arm. "Just...stop a minute, honey. I...Give me a minute," she said. She swallowed again.

"I know you love him. I can see that," Travis said. "But if he asks you to marry him, now, you'll never know if it was just because of the baby." His tone was apologetic, yet determined.

Ella met Luca's eyes. His expression was unreadable. "That's not the problem," she said, softly. Luca offered a small smile, and she looked back at her brother. "He doesn't lie, Travis. He loves me, for me. Or, at least, he did. I'm the one who can't be trusted, not him. If I go crawling back, now, he'll never know that I really love him, or if I'm just doing it because of

362

the...baby..." The word was strange in her mouth. *Baby.* She was afraid to hope, afraid that she'd already done too much to endanger the child. She could feel herself beginning to believe, though, and with the belief came happiness. Yes, there was apprehension. It was secondary, though.

Travis sighed. "I asked Swan why he forced me out of the duel. Told him *he* should've been the one protecting you, if he loved you so much."

She licked her lips, nervously. "What did he say?"

"He told me I'd done enough killing." He paused, and as their eyes met, she saw his face begin to crumple. He'd worked so hard to be strong, and brave, for so long. Watching the pain fill his eyes, she felt tears fill her own. She reached for him, and he leaned forward, pressing his face against the bedspread beside her. She held his head, wishing she could erase all of his horrors.

"Shh," she said. "It's alright, now," she said. "You're safe. We'll get through this. I love you guys." Luca leaned forward, too, and put an arm across Travis's back. Travis cried into the blanket, one arm over his sister, the other bent beside his head. She stroked his hair. She looked toward the door at the hint of movement, hope surging within her. It wasn't Colin, though. It was a small, elderly woman. Maggie, she assumed. The old woman smiled but didn't enter. She clearly didn't want to interrupt.

Ella motioned for her to enter. "How are you feeling, dear?" Maggie asked, quietly. Travis didn't lift his head.

"I'm alright," Ella answered. It was true, she thought. The pain in her head was barely significant. Her muscles were still a little achy, but she had no dominant pain anywhere. No cramping in her stomach. That was a good sign, she hoped. "Thank you for...having us in your home," she added, wanting desperately to ask about Colin and afraid of offending the woman. What did Maggie know of their relationship? Would she be happy to learn that Colin was going to be a father? Or would she see Ella as nothing more than a money-hungry whore?

"Of course, dear," Maggie said, and her smile was genuine. Open. "May I get you anything? Are you hungry?"

Ella couldn't remember the last time she'd eaten. She'd had nothing at Bauer's; she'd had no appetite, anyway. She hadn't eaten since leaving Swan's ship, and even then, she found it difficult to remember her last meal. One more way she'd been endangering the child she hadn't known she was carrying. She cringed inwardly at the thought. Swan was right. She was reckless. Irresponsible. Impulsive.

She was hungry. She wanted to see Colin. She knew she had to put the baby's needs first, though. No matter what, she could no longer put herself in danger without also putting Colin's child in danger. "Yes," she answered, telling herself she had to work on being patient. She was going to do things the right way, from now on. "Thank you."

"Robert," Maggie said, over her shoulder.

To Ella's surprise, a man in a suit appeared in the doorway with a tray. A bowl of soup, three glasses of milk, and three sandwiches were arranged on the tray. Travis had finally straightened, and his tears had stopped. His face was a little splotchy. He held Ella's hand in one of his, and with the other, wiped at his damp cheeks. He showed no embarrassment, for his show of emotion, and Ella was proud of him for it. He couldn't hide from his feelings, or let them fester. They all had emotions they needed to face and work through.

"Here, boys," Maggie said, handing a plate with a sandwich, and a glass, to Luca, who thanked her. Travis helped Ella sit up, fluffing the pillow behind her back, before taking his own sandwich and milk. Then, Robert carefully set the tray across Ella's lap. The smell of the soup made her stomach rumble. "Don't overdo it," Maggie warned. Robert nodded in acknowledgment of Ella's thanks, then slipped from the room. "Don't eat too fast, or too much," Maggie said. "You might get a little queasy, from the head injury."

"How are the kids doing?" Travis asked, as Ella sipped hot soup from her spoon.

"They're settling in well," Maggie said. "The other children love Jacko, of course."

At Ella's glance, Travis said, "Jacko's a dog. He was on board. Wait until you hear what else we had on board."

"Can't compare to what we had," Luca said, smiling at Ella. "Your sister and Swan rescued a dragon."

Travis was surprised. "We had a dragon," he said. "A baby."

It was Ella's turn to be surprised, and she saw the same on Luca's face. Before she could say anything, Maggie spoke. "Many believe dragons to be good luck. Perhaps that's why you are all together, now."

Ella and the two boys looked around at each other. They resumed eating without comment, each thinking their own thoughts. Ella had never been prone to superstition, but knowing that most of the sailors thought it was bad luck to have a woman on board, she wondered if they believed the dragon's presence had contradicted her own.

"I'll let you eat and get some rest," Maggie said. "Don't hesitate to call if you need anything. The staff is at your disposal, feel free to make yourself at home."

"Thank you," Ella said, feeling fresh tears of gratitude prick her eyes.

"There's another guest room across the hall, if you boys want to get some sleep. There are two beds. Just ask if you need hot water." At their repeated thanks, Maggie left the three of them alone.

"I'm going to take her up on the offer of a bed," Luca said, setting his empty glass on his empty plate on the chair as he stood. "Travis?"

"Yes, Travis. You look exhausted," Ella said.

Travis smiled. "The bags under your eyes are pretty dark, too, sis."

She laughed, amazed to find that she could. After a moment, she said, "You are taking care of your injuries, though?"

"Yes, ma'am," he said, and she laughed again, relieved that they were all, miraculously, alright. A broken leg, an infected wound, and a concussion, but they were alive, and together. "I love you, Ellie. And you, Luc," he said, looking up at the older boy standing beside him.

"And I love both of you, too," Luca said. He met Ella's eyes, and he smiled in spite of the hint of sadness in his expression. "Come on, Trav. Let's go and let her eat and rest."

Travis got to his feet and put his dishes beside Luca's. "We'll be across the hall if you need anything. El...Thanks for coming after me. Both of you," he added, looking at Luca. "I thought I was going to die on that ship, and never see you guys again. But even when I thought I was alone, I wasn't. You both have always been there for me. Always," he stressed, holding Ella's gaze. "I'm who I am because of you, Ella. I was scared. I didn't want to fight. I didn't want to die. But I knew that if you were there, you would protect me and the kids, no matter what. You're the reason I fought back. You were there with me, El. Always."

Tears were streaming down her face. "I wish our parents could see the man you've become," she said, quietly. "They'd be proud, just like I am."

Travis smiled, bent, and kissed her cheek. "I'll see you later," he promised. He walked across the room, and out into the hallway. Luca hesitated beside the bed.

"Your parents and grandma would be proud of you, too," Ella told him. "I'm sorry I hurt you. But I do love you, Luca. I hope you believe that."

"I know," he answered. He regarded her in silence for a moment. "He's in the library, El."

"What?"

"Down the stairs, to the right, down the hallway, at the end. Be happy, Ella. No one deserves it more than you."

"Thank you," she said, swallowing. After Luca was gone, as well, she turned her attention to her meal. Her stomach was rumbling, still. She was filled with nervousness, though, and she wanted to shove the food aside and rush downstairs and beg for forgiveness. She forced herself to eat, and think. She had to be reasonable. She also had to be careful. If she rushed anywhere, she would probably get dizzy, pass out, and hurt herself or the baby. She couldn't take that risk.

She ate slowly, and every last bite, and drank the last drop of her milk. Then she swung her legs from the bed, cautiously, and stood, slowly and carefully. Her legs were a little rubbery, so she stood, supporting herself against the bed, waiting to see if she would feel any lightheadedness. Her temple thudded dully beneath the bandage, but the room didn't spin around her, which was a good sign.

Someone had changed her into a pair of soft, flannel pajamas. She wasn't even embarrassed by the thought, grateful to be out of the awful maid's uniform.

She found a chamber pot beside the bed, and made her way cautiously across to the door. Robert was standing in the hallway, beside the door, with his back to the wall. She was surprised to see him. He turned at the sound of her approach. "Miss?" he asked. "May I assist you?"

"I'm just going to shut the door and...freshen up a bit," she said.

"Very well, miss," he said. "Would you like hot water?"

"Um...no, thank you. Not just now."

"Would you like me to remove your dishes?"

"Oh," she said. It was bizarre, knowing that she'd been a servant just a couple of hours earlier. "Um, sure. Alright. Thank you." She watched while he gathered the plates, glasses, and bowl onto the tray and took them from the room. She looked at the grandfather clock in the hallway. Her room was well-lit by lanterns, the drapes drawn against the darkness outside. The clock said it was after ten. It seemed impossible. Twenty-four hours ago, she was laying in Colin's bed, waiting for him. In the span of one day, a lifetime seemed to have passed. So much had changed.

She closed the door. She used the chamber pot, then examined herself in the mirror above the wash basin. The water was cold, but clean, and she scrubbed her wet hands over her face, carefully avoiding the bandage taped above her ear. She wanted to take that off, and examine the damage, but she didn't. The bandage was there for a reason, and she would leave it there until she was told to remove it. She knew that she'd been seen by a healer, while she was unconscious. She didn't need to be told; Swan would have seen to it.

Her hair was a dirty tangle. She combed wet fingers through it on one side, but there was nothing she could do about the side with the bandage taped in the way. It didn't matter. Colin had seen her looking better, but he'd seen her looking worse, too. Her appearance was not important. Her words were. She knew what she wanted to say, what she needed to say. After that, it was out of her control. She would have to accept whatever he said to her.

The hallway was empty when she stepped outside.

No matter how angry he was with her, she knew that Swan would come to her if she asked for someone to fetch him. Since she was the one who'd left, however, it was only fair that she go to him. She made her way down the hallway to the stairs. She wasn't dizzy or lightheaded, but she moved carefully, nonetheless, with a hand over her stomach and the other against the wall. She wasn't going to take any chances.

She held the railing as she went down the stairs. She didn't see anyone. At the bottom, she paused. To her left, from what she assumed was the den, or living room, she could hear quiet voices. One was Maggie. The other voice belonged to a man, but it wasn't Colin's. Ella thought it was Robert. She turned right, saw the hallway that must stretch back to the library, and headed for it.

Her steps quickened as she neared the door at the end. She couldn't help it. She wanted to move slowly and cautiously, but anticipation was getting the best of her. She wanted to see him. Even if he sent her away, she wanted to see him. The door was ajar, and she hesitated, wondering if she should knock. She couldn't see far into the room. She could see shelves of books, lining the far wall from floor to ceiling. She edged a little further, pushing the door inward an inch or so. Then, gathering her courage, she pushed it open and stepped inside. She wasn't even certain he would be there, or if he was alone.

There was a large fireplace in the far right wall, and more books than she'd ever seen in her life. There was a large, soft-looking sofa facing the fireplace and, at a right angle to the couch, the most comfortable-looking chair she'd ever seen. In fact, she didn't think she'd ever loved a room, on immediate sight, more. A person could happily get lost for hours, or even days, in such a place.

Colin was sitting in the chair, with his legs stretched before himself, crossed at the ankles. He wasn't reading. His arms were crossed. His chin was lowered to his chest, but something alerted him to her presence. His eyes opened and his head lifted. She saw his surprise give way to a frown, even as he uncrossed his arms and unfolded himself from the chair.

Ella closed the door behind herself, before she could chicken out. All of the words she'd so carefully planned out in her head had fled at the sight of his stubbled face and shadowy gaze. His dark hair was slightly mussed; she wanted to run her hands through it, smooth it against his scalp.

"Are you alright?" he asked. His voice was low, deep. He was moving toward her, and she stood, unable to move, unable to speak. She nodded. She tried to swallow and found her mouth dry. "Ella. Come. Sit," he commanded softly. "You're too pale." He held out a hand but didn't touch her when she finally managed to move forward on her own. She was disappointed, and glad, at the same time. If he touched her, she was pretty sure she would throw herself into his arms, whether he wanted her to or not. Instead, she managed to maintain a modicum of restraint, and she made it to the couch, lowering herself into the cushions.

"I was really careful coming down the stairs, and...I ate all my food," she managed, afraid he would think she'd once again endangered herself and the baby.

She stared up at him in the firelight, and saw the ghost of a smile touch his lips. "I'm glad to hear it," he murmured. He studied her for a few moments. "Are you alright?" he asked, again, looking down at her. She nodded, again. "You shouldn't be out of bed, Ella," he said.

"I had to see you," she muttered.

He lowered himself into the chair and leaned back. He looked relaxed, except for his expression. "All you had to do was ask," he said, softly. "I was giving you time with your brother and Luca. I would've come to check on you."

"I know that. I just...Are you hurt?" she asked. She could see that his lip was swollen a bit from Travis's punch.

"No."

Her heart was pounding. She knew what she wanted to say and couldn't form the right words in her mouth. The sight of him, as always, was enough to rob her of her breath. "I didn't know I might be pregnant. Colin, I...I swear I didn't."

"I know."

367

She was surprised. "You do?" she asked, uncertainly.

"Your life is the only one you seem determined to endanger," he said. His gaze was steady, dark, and intense. He didn't seem angry, but she couldn't be certain. She couldn't even sort out her own emotions, at the moment.

She fidgeted nervously. "I know I messed everything up," she finally said. Her throat was thick with unshed tears. "I know you think I left because I didn't trust you. But that's not it."

"I don't think that."

"What? You...said..."

He winced. "I'm sorry. I never should've said what I said to you. I...let my emotions get the best of me, when I saw you in that goddamned outfit."

"He never touched me, Colin. I swear."

"I didn't suppose he had," he muttered. "Or I would've cut off more than his arm."

"I thought you might believe him..."

"No."

"Oh."

"I doubt he'd have made it to his party if he'd tried anything with you," Colin said, and that little ghost of a smile was back, briefly.

"I was going to kill him tonight," she heard herself admit. "I thought...I thought Travis was dead. I overheard him talking, and...I must've misunderstood...He said they were all dead, and...I almost went in that room right then but...I knew I probably wouldn't get out of the house if I did, so I decided...I mean, I wasn't really in a great state of mind to decide anything, but I thought I'd wait until after the party when everyone was asleep and then kill him and then maybe I might make it out and be able to see you again. I meant to do everything I could to come back, but...Travis...Travis—and Luca, they've been my whole life for...for my whole life, it seems like. The only reason I managed to get up every morning and ignore the cold and hunger and depression."

"I understand why you did what you did."

She blinked and felt her tears spill over her cheeks. "You do?" she asked, afraid to hope.

He was silent for long moments. "I watched you leave, Ella. I watched you all the way to shore, terrified that something would happen to you and I wouldn't be able to help. And then I had to watch you walk away. You never looked back." The raw emotion in his voice tore at her, and she couldn't think of any way to take away the pain she'd caused him.

It seemed to her that she'd offered more apologies while in Bauer's house than she had in her entire life before that point, and she hadn't meant one of them. "I'm sorry," she said, now, and she'd never meant the words more. "I couldn't. I wouldn't have had the strength to leave you. I didn't...know you saw me. I'm so sorry, Colin."

"Don't cry, Ella. It's alright. Your brother's safe. So is Luca. All of you are safe here."

His kind expression made her tears fall faster. "Why are you being nice to me?" she muttered. "I don't deserve it."

"Don't cry," he repeated, leaning forward. "Please."

Before she could chicken out, she stood and crossed the short distance between them. He looked up at her, clearly startled, tensed and ready to stand. "I'll do whatever you want. Whatever you say," she said. She no longer gave a damn about her pride.

"The fuck you will," he blurted, looking alarmed. "Bloody hell, Ella, do you think I want you to be...*obedient*? *Submissive*?"

"I know I don't deserve another chance. You've forgiven me so many times already."

"I haven't forgiven you anything, because there's been nothing to forgive. Sit down. Please. Are you feeling dizzy?"

Gathering the rest of her courage, she turned and sat, sideways, on his lap, drawing her knees up. She wouldn't blame him if he shoved her to the floor, but she knew he wouldn't. She was surprised, and grateful, when his arms circled her, pulling her against his chest. She laid her cheek against his shoulder, knowing she was taking advantage of his kindness.

"Ella. Please. You're upset. You should really be in bed. There will be time for talking tomorrow. You'll all be safe here for as long as you want to stay. I promise you."

"I love you," she said.

He didn't immediately answer, and her stomach clenched. His arms tightened around her, though. "I was hurt and confused when you left, Ella. And scared. For you, but also at the prospect of going back to life without you. Then the anger came, although it was really just a mask for the pain. I assumed you'd left the way you did because you thought I'd keep you from leaving. Or, because you thought I'd be either unable or unwilling to help. Luca wouldn't tell me why you'd come here. But you'd left him, too, and the only reason I could think that you'd have done that was to protect him. It wasn't until I met Travis that most of the pieces clicked into place. When I found out how he'd gotten here, and figured out where you'd gone...I was even angrier, on the one hand, because I'd talked to you about Bauer, told you what kind of man he was, and all the time you listened without letting on that you knew the name, or that you meant to find him. But I knew that was the problem...I'd told you that he'd threatened me, and Maggie, and the orphanage. I can be a little slow, sometimes, but I finally figured it out.

"I was still angry, though. At myself, at Bauer, at you. I was scared, because I didn't know if you were alright, and I couldn't rush in and rescue you because Travis deserved justice and Bauer deserved punishment. The moment I walked in that door and saw you standing there..." His arms tightened again, almost painfully so. She wished he'd never let her go. "The first feeling was relief. But you were dressed like...that...and you looked like you were ready to fall over from exhaustion, and all you'd had to do was *ask*, Ella, and I would've done anything to get your brother back for you. Instead, you put yourself in danger. And you let him rob you of your pride." He sighed. She didn't speak, afraid that he was readying himself to say goodbye, to tell her that it was over, once and for all. That she'd pushed his limits too far, too many times. "I shouldn't have spoken to you the way I did. That was all the pain, and fear, and anger...and relief at finding you alive and unhurt...all coming to a head. I'm sorry."

"I trusted you," she said.

"Part of me had that figured out already by then. But I saw you, ready to jump in to protect your brother. You didn't. I had a plan, but you didn't know that. You trusted me with your brother's safety, and I can't imagine how difficult that was. Then...when that rock...For a minute, I thought you were dead, or dying...Your head was bleeding..."

"I was so scared while you were fighting him," she said.

"You left me to protect me. I get that," he said. "And I thought you'd gotten yourself killed. I've had time to think about a lot of things, Ella. At Bauer's, you finally decided to have faith, trust me to be able to take care of myself. Just like when I saw you, I knew that I'd let my emotions get in the way of what I knew—that you can take care of yourself. That you're the strongest person I've ever met. That knowledge won't keep me from worrying about you. Because I know you'll always do anything and everything to protect your family. I know it because I'll do the same."

She let out a breath. "You love me," she finally mumbled.

"Yes."

"Then...you aren't going to leave me?"

"No, Ella," he said, kissing the top of her head. "How could I? If there's one thing I learned for sure today, it's that I don't know how to live without you."

"I thought..."

"I was afraid to touch you," he admitted. "The second I walked into Bauer's house, I wanted to pick you up and...take you somewhere...and try to sort out all the frustrations of the day. Then, when you were unconscious, you were limp in my arms, and I couldn't get that memory out of my head, until I saw you standing in the doorway, alive, awake, beautiful...I wanted to..." He sighed. He shifted, slightly, and she felt his growing erection against her hip. She felt a thrill of desire in response. "Sorry," he murmured against her unbandaged temple. "So many times today, I thought I'd never feel you in my arms like this."

She lifted her head and saw his lips part. She swallowed. "I didn't think you'd want to," she said.

"Ella, I'm going to be yours until the day I die. I couldn't change that if I wanted to, which I certainly do not."

"I forgot what it was like to be happy. I mean, I must've been, once. And I've been happy with the boys, we have fun, you know. In spite of everything. We've always had each other. I've been happy with them. But not *really* happy. You know? I never did anything for myself. I never wanted to, until I met you.

You made me want...a life...and I couldn't believe that you might want the same thing. And I've made so many mistakes, and you're still here. And I figured something out, too. Travis and Luca, they don't need me. Not like they used to. I think...I think you need me more than they do."

He smiled. "Does that mean you won't leave me again?"

"Not ever," she vowed.

He bent and kissed her lips. His pressure was light, but her mouth opened eagerly, and he groaned deep in his throat. He pulled his mouth away and kissed her chin. "Do you really think you're pregnant?" he whispered.

"Yes," she answered after brief consideration. It was still a strange and new idea, but as she sat in his arms, the thought filled her with warm happiness. "I haven't had time to...process it," she said. "How do you...feel about it?"

"I can't think of anything better in the world," he said.

"I love you," she told him, unable to keep from grinning. She felt impossibly happy, and she vowed to herself that she wouldn't let anything interfere with that again.

"Would you marry me, then? I'd get down on one knee, but I'd have to disrupt you, first, and I'd much rather keep you where you are."

She laughed. "Maybe you'd rather move to the couch...?" she suggested.

"Maybe when you don't have a concussion," he said, raising his eyebrows.

She laughed, again. "I don't know if I can wait that long."

He smiled. "Is that a yes?"

"Oh," she said, feigning surprise. "You mean about the marriage thing? I guess so."

He laughed, softly. "We can look for a house whenever you're feeling up to it. Tomorrow, next week, next month, whenever. Maggie will be happy to keep us until then."

"What?"

"Anything you want."

She'd finally realized that she might actually deserve to be happy, and she'd finally decided what she wanted. Her life had been mostly miserable, and Travis and Luca had been her only reasons for going on. Swan had been unhappy, too, though. He'd told her that the only place he'd found a modicum of peace in his life was on the open sea. He was restless on land. Even his love for Maggie couldn't keep him on the continent for long. Even his guilt about leaving her for months at a time couldn't dissuade him from setting sail.

He was offering to buy a house and settle into it with Ella and their child. To make a home on the land that he'd spent so much time avoiding. To give up the respite he'd worked so hard to create for himself. In time, he might come to resent her for it. That didn't matter, though, because she wasn't about to let it happen.

"I don't want a house," she said.

He frowned. "I have money, Ella. That means *you* have money. You don't have to worry about things like that anymore. Anything that you—"

"This room is my second favorite place in the world," she said, glancing

371

toward the crackling fire. "I could spend hours in here. Days, even. Do you know where my favorite place is?" Before he could answer, she said, "The cabin of your ship. It feels like the first real home I ever had. I feel a little guilty saying that, because the boys and I had a home, sort of, and a life together. But your room is where I found myself, and that's home, to me. I know you feel the same. You love your ship. You love the ocean. So do I. I just didn't know it before I met you."

"I love you more," he murmured.

"You'll have both."

"The sea is a dangerous place, Ella. Especially in the winter. And you're pregnant."

"Well, good. I won't be able to do anything stupid. I'll be too busy sitting around eating and getting fat."

He laughed, hugging her. "You'll be eating for two."

She groaned. "Oh, God, I can't even imagine how much food you'll force onto me, now."

"Maybe we can spend our winters here," he suggested after a silence. "It's true that the ship has been my home...and the only place I really feel comfortable...but things are different, now. Wherever you are, that's my home."

"We can figure it out, together," she said. "Tomorrow. You need some sleep."

"*I* need sleep?" he said, snorting.

She narrowed her eyes. "You do, and that's the only reason I'm not having my way with you right now."

He uttered a surprised laugh. His arousal was still against her hip. "You know I love you?"

She let out a breath. "Yes. Although I'm still not quite sure why," she added, smiling.

"Let's go to bed," he said. "Only if you promise to behave yourself, though. I'm not particularly aroused by head injuries."

It was her turn to laugh. "I'll try my best," she said, grinning.

* * *

"Good morning," Maggie said, looking up with a smile when Ella and Colin walked in, with their arms around each other.

"Hi," Ella said, blushing. Swan's arm tightened around her reassuringly. They hadn't made love the night before, to Ella's disappointment: It seemed that he was serious about the whole head-injury thing. They had slept together, though, in his bed. Ella had no idea how Maggie was going to feel about that.

Luca and Travis, and a girl that Ella didn't know, were eating breakfast at the table. Travis stood when his sister walked in. "Ella, this is Kyra," he said. "Kyra, my sister, Ella. And...Captain Swan, who you didn't really have a chance to meet yesterday," he added, sitting back down.

"Nice to meet you," Ella said, feeling a little flustered. Colin held a chair for her and she sank into it gratefully.

"You, too," Kyra said, smiling shyly across the table at her. "Travis talked about you a lot."

"How are you feeling?" Maggie asked, setting a plate of pancakes in front of Ella as Colin took a seat beside her.

"Oh. Um, good, thanks," Ella said.

"I'm going to go meet the guys," Travis said. "In a couple of hours. I think...it's only fair to let them know I won't be able to offer them anything. Is there some way to get them papers? So they can find legal work, here?"

"Are you sure they'll show up, man? They might have split," Luca said.

"They'll show up," Travis answered. "At least...ten of them..." he added after a brief consideration. He looked at Kyra. "You think?"

She nodded. "You know they'll sail with you without any money, Travis."

"But I can't just leave," Travis said with a quick glance at his sister. "I mean, when we got here, I didn't know...there'd be anything for me..."

Swan got to his feet and looked down at Ella. "Do you mind if I speak to your brother alone?" he asked.

"You're not going to make him hit you again, are you?" she asked, frowning.

Swan laughed. "I hope not," he said. He bent and kissed her on the forehead, then stood behind her chair. "Travis? Could I have a minute?"

Travis hesitated, then nodded. "Alright," he said, also standing once more.

"You'd better keep your hands in your pockets," Ella told him.

Travis snorted. "Do you fight all his battles for him?" he asked with a small smile.

"We made a deal. He fights mine and I fight his," she said.

"I don't remember agreeing to that," Swan said behind her, but she could hear the amusement in his voice. She grinned at her brother, and after a moment, everyone laughed. Even Luca, who seemed relatively peaceful. At least, until Swan said, "Luca. Care to join us?"

Luca shot Ella a surprised look. She shrugged. She didn't know what Swan wanted to discuss, but she wasn't worried about it. "Sure," Luca said. He and Travis followed Swan out of the room.

Maggie lowered herself into a chair and smiled at Ella. "I've never seen Colin so happy," she said, and Ella blushed again.

"He makes me happy, too," she answered, smiling in return.

* * *

"Travis. Luca. I'd like to ask your permission to have your sister's hand in marriage. I've asked her, and she's said yes. You're her family, though, and I hope to have your blessings."

"She loves you," Travis said. "I never thought Ella would...I've never seen her like this. You make her happy, so...I mean, it's not like I could stop her if I wanted to," he added with a small smile. "But...If you hurt her..."

"I won't."

"Alright, then," Travis said.

Swan looked at Luca, who'd so far been silent. Swan had lumped them together as her brothers, because that was how Ella thought of them. He knew that Luca might take offense, considering the feelings the older boy had for his surrogate sister. Instead, after a few beats, Luca said, "She deserves to be happy, and Travis is right. She's happy with you."

"I appreciate that," he told them, and he meant it. "Now, I'd like to discuss business with you. I've got a proposition for you. Travis, I'd like to rent your ship."

After a long hesitation, Travis said, hesitantly, "Rent it? What do you mean?"

"With your ship and mine, I can transport twice the cargo, essentially making two trips at once. That way we can spend the spring here until after the baby is born. I'd pay for the license, inspection, taxes, cleaning, everything that goes into preparing your ship. And the cargo, of course. I'll pay the crew's wages. I'll split the profits with you after the loads are delivered."

"What about my men?" Travis asked.

"If they show up and want to sail, that's your choice. You're the captain. I do ask that you let me select at least a few experienced sailors of my own to join them. And, we'll sail together. Keeping your ship in sight will be in my best interests, financially."

"And put Ella's mind at ease," Travis suggested with a small smile.

"We would have to leave in about a week," Swan said. "The trip to Baytown shouldn't be too bad, but the return trip will be cold, and rough weather will slow us down."

"Are you leaving Ella here?" Luca asked.

"No," Swan answered. "I couldn't if I wanted to, which I don't. Luca, you're welcome to return to my crew, or join Travis's. You have experience and could help him, in spite of your injury. That's up to the two of you. Travis, your ship will have to be thoroughly cleaned and inspected before we can set sail. If you'll allow me, I'll see to that tomorrow."

"Alright," Travis said, sounding a little bemused. "Will the men get work papers, if they sail?"

"I will see to their documentation whether they want to sail or not. I'm going to be speaking to the governor this evening about the legal proceedings against Bauer, just to make sure things stay on track. Assuming he doesn't die of infection," he added, his tone suggesting he would not be heartbroken by such a development. "And, speaking of infections, I know the healer has seen to you, but you will both need a clean bill of health to set sail. I will be hiring a healer for each ship, though. With your sister's condition, I'm not taking any unnecessary chances."

"I need to make sure the kids are going to be taken care of."

"I promise you, they'll be well cared for in Darling House."

"I know, but...I need to be sure. I need to talk to them. Especially Angel..."

"Of course. Think about it and let me know when you decide so I can arrange for the shipment, alright?"

"Yeah. Thanks, Captain Swan," Travis said, extending a hand to shake.

As he took it, Swan said, "Call me Colin. We're going to be family, after all." He shook Luca's hand, as well.

"I'm almost sorry I hit you," Travis said, and Luca snorted.

Swan smiled. "I'm not. You must've learned to fight from your sister." At that, Luca laughed outright.

"I learned everything from my sister," Travis said. "One more thing, Captain—I mean, Colin. There's a boy, Garrett. He's twelve, almost thirteen. I'd like him to be in my crew."

Swan hesitated. "The ocean is a dangerous place for kids," he said. "As I know you know."

"I trust him, and...the truth is, we all know that people aren't going to be lining up to adopt him. He's got as much experience on a ship as I do, at this point. But he's the hardest worker I know, and...I'll take responsibility for him." He raised his chin as though expecting Swan to point out that he was a child himself. Legally an adult for a day, perhaps, but still a child.

"He has no family?"

"No, sir. None of them do."

"Alright," Swan said. "Gather whatever crew you have this afternoon, including the kid. Who's on the ship, now?"

"Amir. I think he plans on staying here, though. Once we've returned to the ship."

"Alright, son. Get your men together, and we'll take stock and work out our arrangement."

* * *

"Mrs. Darling asked if I wanted to stay here. She says she gets lonely in the evening when most of the staff goes home. But, really, I think she knows that not many people are going to want to take a sixteen-year-old home with them. Unless it's to be a servant, or...something else..."

"What did you tell her?"

"That I'd be happy to stay here. I mean, at least a few months. Maybe the next time you set sail..."

"After this trip, we're going to stick around here for a while. Until after my sister has her baby, at least. When I'm ready to take a crew out without Swan babysitting me, then...I'd like you to come, too. Right now, it's too dangerous. I'm not sure I should take Garrett, but...it feels right..."

"You're going to be great, Travis," Kyra said. "I'll miss you."

After a moment, he leaned forward and kissed her lips, shyly. "I'll miss you, too. I'll see you at dinner, alright? I'm going to get Garrett and go meet the men. If they show up," he added, in spite of the confidence he'd shown when

Luca had asked if they would.

"They'll be there. You're their captain, Travis," she said with a smile.

Epilogue

"You nervous?"

"Excited," Ella answered, grinning at her husband. "Well, a little nervous about Travis."

"I went over every inch of that ship. And Ivan's going to be on board to help him with the crew, although I don't think Travis will need the help. I didn't expect the men to show up, even when he said they would. It's a rare thing to find a group of men willing to follow the command of a teenager. I was wrong to underestimate him. It seems your brother is a born leader."

"I know, you've taken care of everything," she said, leaning her head on his arm. "Can we get on the ship, yet?"

He laughed. "Anxious, are we, Mrs. Swan?"

"Yes," she said, and he laughed again. "I feel like we're going home. By the time we get back, I'm sure I'll be happy to settle in and enjoy living on land for a while. But for right now, I can't wait to get you back in our little room."

He kissed her temple. "I love you, Ella."

"Did you ask the men if they were alright with me coming back on board?"

"I told you they'd be happy. They love you."

"But, did you ask them? Goonie said a lot of them think it's bad luck."

"They're aware that you're going to be around forever," Swan said with a chuckle. "And, look. Every man showed up to sail. They like you better than they like me."

"Maybe you should scowl less," she joked. A chorus of shouts drew their attention before he could respond, and they turned to find several people on the docks pointing toward the sky. "What—Colin, is that...Destiny?" Ella asked, shielding her eyes against the sun to see the looming shape.

"That's her, but...she's not alone."

They watched the two dragons soar along the edge of the woods before banking toward the water. The two dragons split apart over the sea, and in less than a minute, Destiny had settled onto the roof of Colin's cabin. A few seconds later, the smaller dragon dropped onto the roof of Travis's cabin on the other ship.

Travis was walking toward Ella, and called, "That's Buddy. Is that Destiny?" They'd exchanged stories about the dragons, but no one had guessed that the mother and son might belong to each other.

Ella looked at Swan. "That must be why she was trying to cross the ocean. And they found each other!"

"It looks like they want a ride back home," Swan said, looking at Travis. "Are you alright with having the dragon on your ship?"

"Sure," Travis said. Jacko was panting by his side. The orphanage had agreed to let Angel keep the dog, at least for a while, because they knew what the girl—what all of the kids from the ship—had been through. Angel had surprised them all, however, by telling Travis that Jacko wanted to go with

377

him. It was true; they could all see that the dog thought he belonged to Travis. Travis would not have taken him if Angel had not been the one to suggest it, though. "Garrett," Travis called, and the younger boy jogged over eagerly. "Buddy's going to be riding back with us, it looks like. I'm going to put you in charge of him, but don't get too close. Alright?"

"Sure!" Garrett said. He couldn't contain his pride and excitement at being chosen to accompany Travis on the ship. He idolized Travis.

In the past week, Ella had seen Travis beginning to look at Colin the way Garrett looked at Travis, and it made her heart feel impossibly full. Luca was going to be on Travis's ship—which Travis had renamed *Justice*. Luca, Travis, and Colin had overseen all the preparations leading up to the trip together. And, at the small wedding ceremony, Ivan stood beside Colin, and Travis and Luca walked her down the aisle. There were only a few people in attendance— Maggie, Travis and Luca, a handful of men from Swan's crew, and the other children from Travis's ship.

Tabitha had been hired onto Travis's crew as cook. Jesiah was the only member of the original crew to return, but Cosy, Gibbs, and the others had been added to a roster overseen by Ivan, and everyone had gotten a thorough lesson in sailing from Swan himself.

A healer had been added to the staff of each ship. Amir, once relieved of his guard-duty, said goodbye and went in search of family he claimed to have in the area. Travis was going to miss him, even though he knew next to nothing about the man.

"I'm going to send a crew for a few more supplies," Swan said, drawing Travis's attention. "We need to ensure we have extra for the dragons, now. Just in case we're delayed. If you'd like, you can begin boarding your crew. It shouldn't take more than an hour for the extra inventory."

"Oh. Alright. Sure, thanks," Travis said. He looked at Garrett. "Come on, Gar, let's get ready to sail."

"An hour?" Ella groaned when she and Swan were alone.

He laughed and kissed her—chastely—on the mouth. "I wonder how many days the crew will go without seeing me before they worry?" he mused.

She giggled, feeling giddy. "I need you more than they do."

"I hope you don't get sick this time."

"I don't think I will."

"Why not?"

"I've got your child growing inside of me. He would never get seasick."

"I'm glad you sneaked onto my ship, Ella."

"I'm glad you didn't throw me overboard," she smiled.

"Maybe we can sneak on now, together. Let me send Ivan after supplies for the dragon, and we might be able to steal a few minutes."

"Yes!" she agreed, rubbing her hands together. "Let's do that."

He chuckled. "You're insatiable, love."

"Is it wrong to enjoy my husband's body?" she asked innocently, batting her eyelashes.

Grinning, he said, "I live to give you enjoyment, Ella. Give me five minutes to find Ivan and I'm yours forever."

"Three minutes," she countered, leaning up to kiss him, showing him just how serious she was.

Thanks
for
reading!